HERO AND PROPHET

VICTOR HUGO, a major leader of the French Romantic Movement, was one of the most influential figures in nineteenth-century literature. By the age of thirty, he had established himself as a master in every domain of literature—drama, fiction, and lyric poetry. Hugo's private life was as unconventional and exuberant as his literary creations. At twenty, he married after a long idealistic courtship; but later in life was infamous for his scandalous escapades. In 1851, he was exiled for his passionate opposition to Napoleon III. Hugo's rich, emotional novels, *Notre Dame de Paris* and *Les Misérables,* have made him one of the most widely read authors of all time.

About the Editor:

Paul Bénichou, Professor of French Literature at Harvard University, has published numerous scholarly works on French and Spanish literature, philology, and folklore. For this edition of *Les Misérables,* Professor Bénichou has written an informative introduction and abridged Hugo's mammoth novel to encourage the general reader to attempt the complete work. This abridgement retains Hugo's plot structure and the characterizations of his major figures.

Les Misérables
Victor Hugo

Translated by Charles E. Wilbour

*Abridged, Edited,
and with an Introduction
by Paul Bénichou*

WSP

WASHINGTON SQUARE PRESS
PUBLISHED BY POCKET BOOKS
New York   London   Toronto   Sydney   Tokyo   Singapore

A Washington Square Press Publication of
POCKET BOOKS, a division of Simon & Schuster Inc.
1230 Avenue of the Americas, New York, NY 10020

Copyright © 1964 by Simon & Schuster Inc.

All rights reserved, including the right to reproduce
this book or portions thereof in any form whatsoever.
For information address Pocket Books, 1230 Avenue
of the Americas, New York, NY 10020

ISBN: 0-671-50439-8

First Pocket Books printing November 1964

29   28

WASHINGTON SQUARE PRESS and WSP colophon are
registered trademarks of Simon & Schuster Inc.

Printed in the U.S.A.

Contents

St. Denis

Jean Valjean

Introduction

THE prospectus circulated by Lacroix, the Belgian publisher of *Les Misérables*, shortly before the publication of the novel, presents it to its future readers as a work which is above all contemporary in spirit: "*Notre-Dame de Paris* was the resurrection of the Middle Ages; *Les Misérables* is the life of the nineteenth century." In 1862, after the novels of Balzac and Stendhal, a novel of contemporary life must not have seemed much of a novelty to French readers. Yet what the publisher was announcing really was an innovation: a modern novel using the imaginative and symbolic techniques of *Notre-Dame de Paris*, something which neither Balzac nor Stendhal had attempted. Hugo had been planning such a book for a long time. His correspondence and manuscripts reveal that even before writing *Notre-Dame de Paris* he already had in mind the subjects and even some of the characters of *Les Misérables*.

The Romantic penchant for modern subjects had appeared very early in France. Even before the Revolution of 1830, Hugo himself had written *Le dernier jour d'un condamné*, in which humanitarian reflections on the penal code accompany a realistic account of the moments which precede an execution. The presentation of certain scenes and social classes, which generally had been excluded from literature because of their scandalousness or vulgarity, is again linked with the humanitarian theme in *Claude Gueux* (1834). We have here two of the principal materials with which Hugo will construct, on an infinitely vaster scale, *Les Misérables*.

Like all the French Romantics, Hugo, from the outset of his literary career, believed that the poet had a social mission as educator of the people and interpreter of the intentions of the Divinity. His first poems proclaim this mission. Between 1830 and 1843 he believed he could perform his social duty by appealing to the masses through the theater, but the humanitarian symbolism in his plays seems pale in comparison with their exuberant historical color. The revolution which he brought about by these plays seemed primarily literary: he employed the vast panorama of European history in all its arresting color as a means of destroying the Greco-Latin traditions of the French Classical theater. One hardly has time to pay attention to the teachings which these plays are supposed to contain, and of whose existence Victor Hugo laboriously reminds us in his prefaces. After the failure of *Les Burgraves* in 1843, Hugo abandoned the theater. He had, no doubt, convinced himself that the poet's sacred mission should be carried out by more direct means and by the use of more modern literary themes. In 1845 he began the composition of his great novel.

The Elaboration and Publication of the Novel. As we have seen, Hugo had been thinking about *Les Misérables* for more than fifteen years. He had first contracted with a publisher for a two-volume work in 1832. But since that date, distracted by other occupations, he had allowed himself to be outdistanced in a path which he had been one of the first to discover: the 1840's brought forth a host of social novels that treat the plight of the common people in the light of democratic ideas. This was the epoch of George Sand's *Compagnon du Tour de France,* and of *Les Mystères de Paris,* by Eugène Sue. It is possible that the enormous success of the latter novel encouraged Hugo to write his own. We know that between 1845 and 1848 he devoted himself exclusively to its composition. However, the novel which he wrote at that time, but did not complete, is somewhat different from the one we read today. It is entitled *Les Misères;* the names of several of the characters are different from those which appear in *Les Misérables;* it is more sparing in details and episodes and in historical and philosophical digressions. But these are differences of degree rather than of kind. The text of *Les Misères* was published in 1927 by Gustave Simon. It is a first version of *Les Misérables,* less elaborate, but still very close to the definitive work in its general spirit, in its architecture, in most of its text, and, most important, in its leading ideas and symbolic implications. We know that when Hugo's contract was renewed in 1847, his publishers had great difficulty in getting him to eliminate an immense chapter of religious philosophy which he was planning to write, "Le Manuscrit de l'Evêque." [1]

Hugo interrupted his writing on January 21, 1848. The revo-

---

[1] It is probable that this chapter was never written. It has not been found among Hugo's papers.

lution, which followed almost immediately, and the subsequent political events, in which he played an active role, prevented him from continuing the novel. *Les Misères* was abandoned at the point in Part Four where Jean Valjean learns of the love of Marius and Cosette by means of the reflection of a blotting pad in a mirror. In spite of a resolution to continue the book in August 1851, Victor Hugo did not return to it until April 1860, during his exile at Guernsey, more than thirteen years after he had abandoned it. He worked from his old manuscript, augmenting and revising the text and adding a conclusion to Part Four and an entire Part Five. He finished the book on May 19, 1862. Meanwhile, the first three parts had already appeared in April and May; the last two parts were published in June.

The novel, published in ten volumes in Belgium and France simultaneously, met with a prodigious success. Hugo had sold the rights to his manuscript for a period of twelve years to the publisher, Lacroix, for 300,000 francs (the equivalent of about 60,000 dollars in 1862). In only six years Lacroix's net profit from this transaction rose to 517,000 francs. Translations appeared in many languages all over the globe, notably in the United States, where *Les Misérables* fascinated the public even in the midst of the Civil War. Such a success is all the more remarkable when one considers that the novel appeared after a long delay, at a time when the Romantic spirit was already a thing of the past. In 1862, the age of Flaubert, of the Goncourt brothers, of positivistic and pessimistic novels, *Les Misérables* was a relic of a former time. It is therefore not surprising that the young literary generation should have given the book a cool reception. But the great enthusiasm of the public proves that, in spite of the fluctuations of popular taste and literary doctrines, the Romanticism of Hugo remained meaningful for the French society throughout the nineteenth century.

Symbol and Reality. Baudelaire, who belonged to the now generation, showed an admirable grasp of Hugo's intentions when he wrote: "It is obvious that in *Les Misérables* the author wished to create living abstractions, ideal figures, each one of which, representing one of the principal types necessary for the development of his thesis, was elevated to an epic height. It is a novel constructed like a poem, where each character is only *exceptional* because of the hyperbolic manner in which he represents a generality." [1] In thus defining *Les Misérables* as a work whose essence is symbolic, constructed by means of type-characters in order to develop a thesis, Baudelaire was only following Hugo's own declarations, so often reiterated, concerning his plays. It is certainly true that *Les Misérables* is the most finished example of a technique which the Romantics preferred to all others: the development of an idea by means of a story.

Les Misérables, however, is not purely a work of the imagination. Hugo had always been fascinated by facts and documents. It is known that he borrowed more than one important episode in *Les Misérables* from reality. The story of Mgr. Myriel receiving Jean Valjean reproduces with amazing fidelity the real experiences of a Bishop of Digne, Mgr. Miollis, and of a convict, Pierre Maurin. The episode where Monsieur Bamatabois shoves a handful of snow down the back of the unfortunate Fantine only transposes a scene which Hugo himself witnessed in Paris and which he related in *Choses vues* under the date January 9, 1841. The rescue of a sailor aboard the "Orion" imitates a real event that took place at Toulon. Hugo learned of the incident from the written account of it which a friend of his, a naval officer, sent to him. Victor Hugo inquired into the black-glass industry in order to write the chapters that describe Monsieur Madeleine's success, and into the history of Christian doctrine in order to discuss the writings of Mgr. Myriel. He even visited the prisons at Brest and Toulon. The book is also filled with recollections of his personal life: the young Marius is none other than Victor Hugo at the age of twenty, torn between his bourgeois and royalist environment and the past glory of his father, one of Napoleon's generals; the spiritual evolution of Marius is that of Hugo himself between 1825 and 1830; the poverty of the young man is that which Hugo had known some years before. Critics have found, in innumerable details of the book, allusions to real people and to incidents in the life of Victor Hugo.

Les Misérables is first of all the product of a varied experience of the world, containing the perceptions of an entire life.

And this image of reality is also a realistic image. The

symbol, as Hugo uses it, does not idealize things; rather, it expresses their spiritual meaning without disguising them. It is true that the characters are exaggerated and simplified in order to intensify their meaning and emotional impact, but who would deny that even the most symbolic among them—Jean Valjean, Fantine, Mgr. Myriel, Javert, Thénardier —come to life as individuals? In these creations, life and symbolic value are not in contradiction; they intensify each other.

The Action. This enormous novel, whose contours may appear vague at first glance, is in reality built on the most solid of frameworks. Hugo conceived the chronology with painstaking care; in planning both the main structural elements and the details, he paid close attention to their logical coherence and connecting links as well as to the harmony of the total effect. The First Part of the novel, which takes place between 1815 and 1823, contains Jean Valjean's visit to Mgr. Myriel at Digne, the beginning of his rehabilitation, his metamorphosis into an honorable citizen at Montreuil-sur-mer, and, finally, his voluntary sacrifice when he reveals his identity to the court at Arras and is arrested by Javert. A parallel line of action includes the ordeal of Fantine, his feminine analogue, and the promise he makes to the dead Fantine to care for her daughter, Cosette. The initial appearances of Mgr. Myriel, Jean Valjean, Fantine, and Javert are opportunities for flashbacks which describe the previous lives of these characters.

The Second Part takes place between 1823 and 1824 and continues the events of the First: It describes the escape of Jean Valjean, his trip to Montfermeil where he takes away Cosette, his flight from the police, and his refuge in the convent of the Petit Picpus. Here again, the appearance of a character, in this case Thénardier, gives rise to a retrospective view of his life.

The Third Part goes back in time to tell the story of a new character, Marius, and his relatives. The lives of his father and grandfather are presented, but from the year 1827 the book relates the story of Marius, of his father's death, and of his conversion to revolutionary ideas, up to the year 1828, when Marius leaves the family home. Since Jean Valjean and Cosette leave the Petit Picpus about the same time, the novelist was enabled to bring the two young people together and thus give a new impulse to the action of his novel. He had abandoned Jean Valjean and Cosette during the years they spent at the convent, which is not very surprising since nothing important happened to them at that time. What is, perhaps, more surprising is that the meeting of Marius and Cosette in the Luxembourg Gardens does not occur until several years after Marius sets out from his grandfather's house and Cosette leaves the convent.

In passing over the period from 1829 to 1831, Hugo omitted years of capital importance which saw the fall of the Bourbon dynasty. It is a paradox that the Revolution of 1830 should be missing from this social novel, which only refers to it by allusions to some of its consequences. But, since Victor Hugo's design required that he describe a defeated insurrection, the three triumphant days of July 1830 were far from suiting his purpose; at the time he wrote *Les Misérables*, from 1845 to 1848, and again from 1860 to 1862, the struggle for the democratic ideal in France had taken on the character of a martyred cause, and it was this perspective that he carried over into his novel. Marius and Cosette, therefore, become acquainted in the summer of 1831.

With this meeting, which takes place in the middle of the Third Part—that is, at the midpoint of the novel—begins a new line of action running to the end of the work and employing all the characters whom the author caused to gravitate toward each other during the first half of the book. From this point, the action, which contains no more flashbacks, becomes denser, more precipitate: the end of the Third Part, the Fourth Part, and practically all of the Fifth take place in a single year, from the summer of 1831 to the summer of 1832. This year contains the love and the separations of Marius and Cosette in the Luxembourg Gardens and in the house on the rue Plumet, the shock Jean Valjean receives when he learns of the idyl, and the drama of the barricade and of the rescue of Marius by Jean Valjean. At the end of the Fifth Part the action slows down again, and a whole year, up to the summer of 1833, is necessary to include the convalescence of Marius, the marriage of the young people, and the renunciation and death of Jean Valjean.

Throughout the second half of the novel, Thénardier and the dregs of the Parisian population, along with secondary characters newly introduced into the novel—Gavroche, Eponine, and Monsieur Mabeuf—give rise to several episodes which are all closely related to the central action. And from beginning to end, through all the interruptions and the innumerable subsidiary adventures, the novel develops the magnificent story of Jean Valjean, escaped convict, hero, and saint.

The Education of the People and the Symbols. Those who dislike *Les Misérables* point to its melodramatic tone, the naïve artifices of its technique, the eternally repeated coincidences which invariably bring together the same characters in all sorts of places over a period of ten years. These defects can also be found in the works of Balzac. They can, perhaps, be largely explained by the fact that the use of the novel as a vantage point for viewing society was still an innovation in the generation of Hugo, and writers were still searching for an appropriate technique. But there is something else: The same defects in the works of Hugo and Balzac have neither the same accent nor the same origin. With Hugo everything follows from his intention to use the novel as a means of educating the masses. It is this intention, either missing or unimportant in the work of Balzac, which is Hugo's justification for his simplified and touching image of life, his moral and philosophical commentary, his device of bringing together the same symbolic figures at various stages of the action. "Yes," he writes to Lamartine on June 24, 1862, after the publication of the novel, "as much as it is permitted man to will, I come to destroy human fate, I condemn slavery, I drive away poverty, I teach ignorance, I treat sickness, I light up the night, I hate hatred. That is what I am, and that is why I wrote *Les Misérables*. To my mind, *Les Misérables* is nothing other than a book having fraternity for a base and progress for a summit." Thus, Hugo intended his book to be something more than a simple story: he wanted it to spread the great verities which were to form the religion of modern man. He intended to write a work in which everything would be striking and profoundly meaningful to the reader, a sort of life-giving legend or epic of our time, born with it and linking the present to the future. It is in this spirit that one should read the book.

There is a carefully calculated and intimate bond between the structure of the novel and the lesson Hugo wished to convey. What is this lesson? The precepts of ordinary morality, no doubt: the common happiness as a goal, rectitude, charity, self-sacrifice as means, theft denounced, chastity exalted. But Hugo's morality goes beyond mere conformity: it is an emancipating force; it calls for a new society superior to our own. This morality is perhaps the one commonly accepted by the nineteenth century, but only to the extent that it called for democracy and the regeneration of society. The characters and the action of the novel are organized in relation to this fundamental position. Javert, who incarnates the very essence of moral conformity—the blind defense of established social norms—is indispensable to the novel. It is, however, remarkable that, among the several incarnations of social orthodoxy in *Les Misérables*, it should be a policeman who is the most elevated and, all things considered, the noblest; Bamatabois, the rentier, and the Public Prosecutor at Arras are odious; only Javert, who in his own way is more dreadful than any of them, possesses the aura of disinterestedness and a kind of purity that force our respect. The revolutionary tone of the novel followed from the decision to portray in this fashion the established order. Hugo did not believe he could present a dignified image of it in the person of a proprietor or magistrate,[1] no doubt because he found these types too grossly interested in its conservation to be idealized; he portrayed it instead in a policeman, an abstract, pure, but obviously intolerable symbol of conservatism. And finally, Javert, who represents a morality based on the letter of the law and traditional social values, is doomed: the logic of the story condemns him to take his own life from the moment he discovers that Conscience is above the Law he represents.

This Conscience above the Law was for Victor Hugo, as he wrote in several places, God himself. The man of conscience, the central character of *Les Misérables*, is a former convict precisely to show that the purifying action of Conscience upsets the legal order. And in the person of the saintly bishop who, on a plane far above the religious hierarchy and Roman Catholic law, incarnates the spirit of the Gospel, it is God himself who attracts the convict. The most important act of the reformed convict is to go to the aid of the prostitute, to rescue her, to confound the Law through charity. Thus, the

---

[1] Monsieur Gillenormand clearly does not play this role. He humorously represents the old monarchical France and has only sarcasm for the current regime.

quartet of the Policeman, the Bishop, the Convict and the Prostitute strikingly act out the fundamental idea of *Les Misérables:* the appeal to a spiritual force in order to regenerate the social order. This force animates the entire novel, infusing it with a spirit which is as much supernatural as human. Hugo at least, let us make no mistake about it, understood his novel in this way.

The purification of Jean Valjean proceeds by stages, by successive and progressively more elevated spiritual crises. The first of these takes place immediately after his departure from Digne; the second—the "tempest in a brain"—when he decides to reveal his identity and sacrifice himself in order to save an innocent man; the third when, even after his discovery of Cosette's love, he goes to the barricade to protect Marius, the cause of his misfortune; the last when, after Cosette's marriage, he decides to renounce her. All these crises are described dramatically and at length. If Hugo elaborates upon them, it is not simply for love of eloquence: these interior episodes are certainly not digressions, they form instead the very heart of his novel. The same is true of the meditation which leads Javert to suicide. Even those characters whose symbolic value is less important, those figures destined for happiness, are examples of a youthful humanity on the road to truth. Their characters, too, develop only through a series of initiations which are an integral part of the novel's action. Marius discovers who his father was; he becomes a Bonapartist; he then gets to know the Friends of the A B C and becomes a convert to democracy; but only at the end of the book, when he finally understands and venerates Jean Valjean, is his spiritual emancipation complete. Cosette's road is less difficult, but it requires that the influence of Marius tear her away from the temptation of frivolity, and that she suddenly find in herself the immensity of love which, according to Hugo, is also God.

Opposite the symbols of good are the symbols of evil. Evil exists in this novel, and those who represent it, from the tormentors of Fantine to the criminals of the Patron-Minette, swarm throughout the book. Thénardier is at the head of this evil host, as tenacious in his rancor and evil-doing as Satan himself and, all things considered, just as impotent and ridiculous as Satan. This proliferation of crime which fills *Les*

Misérables might have been a justification for the ideas of Javert, if the true remedy did not lie elsewhere, in the improvement of social conditions rather than in repression. In fact, the movement toward Progress, a central theme of the novel according to Hugo's repeated declarations, exists not only on the level of the individual conscience, but also on the level of social conflict. What opposes Javert is not only an inner voice, but also the revolutionary action of the Friends of the A B C and the fighters on the barricade. On the one hand we have the bishop, whose charity brings back to life a dead soul; on the other there is Enjolras on his barricade, proclaiming the future brotherhood of mankind: messengers both of them, according to Hugo, of the invisible God.

Les Misérables *and the Universe.* This novel, which is, as we have seen, a system of symbols, can, paradoxically, give the impression of being a chaos. This is because Victor Hugo, even while believing he was penetrating to the hidden meaning of things, still retained a vivid consciousness of their disorder, which he carried over into his novel. In *Les Misérables* he scattered, among the symbols of Conscience and Progress, symbols of Chance. The characters who incarnate Chance are among the most poignant in this work, perhaps because the meaning of their fate is obscure and uncertain. There is Eponine, degraded and noble, sending to his death the man for whom she has a hopeless love, and dying in the attempt to rescue him. There is Gavroche, the unloved child, an atom of the city of Paris, who dies heroically at the age of twelve. There is Monsieur Mabeuf, the harmless old bibliophile, whom despair obscurely pushes toward his death on the barricade, and whom the fighters absurdly mistake for a surviving hero of the Revolution of '89. Poor creatures all of them, living on the fringes of Hugo's symbolic and providential world, a world over which their very existence casts a doubt. They contribute to the harmony of the novel only by the fraternal pity they evoke.

The most essential moments of the action, those whose symbolic meaning should alone remain with us, stay imprinted on our minds mainly in the form of images. The bishop's dining room, the courtroom at Arras, Gorbeau's hovel, the Field of the Lark, the garden on the rue Plumet, the sewers of Paris, the bank of the Seine at the Invalides Bridge, are all places just as unforgettable as the inn in *Don Quixote* or the pavilion at Coulommiers in *La Princesse de Clèves*. They prove that *Les Misérables* is a real novel, that is, an account of a series of fortuitous and particular events which, first of all, impress us by their intensity, even before they teach us anything. The lesson only comes afterward and would escape us were it not fixed in us by this first vivid impression.

Les Misérables is rich in digressions. These are not, however, the chapters of philosophical reflection which are woven into the fabric of the action, but rather the documentary and historical dissertations that interrupt it. Whether or not Hugo intended the effect, they counteract the tendency of the novel to become too systematic. They make it possible for sections of symbolic drama to alternate with panoramic passages or pages in which the author takes the reader aside for a chat. They make us remember that the novel is a representation of our world as much as an explanation of it.

Readers in our time should no longer be disconcerted by what is disorderly, ungainly, and arbitrary in this novel. Perhaps Hugo himself felt that his design for a symbolic and didactic novel might lead him to produce an excessively naïve work. He therefore instinctively embellished and overloaded the plot, adding an infinity of small convolutions and continually opening new vistas to the reader. This explains why, during his revision of *Les Misérables,* he constantly enlarged the text and multiplied the episodes; it was as if Hugo had wished that his novel, which was to reflect the design of the universe, were at the same time the universe itself.

PAUL BÉNICHOU
Harvard University

Editor's Note: The aim of the present abridged edition is to allow the general American reader an easier access to a work which, by virtue of its great length, might otherwise discourage him.

We have tried to retain the essential characteristics of the novel, with respect not only to plot and characters, but also to the philosophical intentions of the author. Our hope is that this abridgment will encourage the reader to experience the complete work.

Selected Bibliography

Editions of Les Misérables

THE original ten-volume edition of *Les Misérables* was published simultaneously in Brussels by Lacroix, and in Paris by Pagnerre, in 1862. Among the editions that have appeared since the death of Victor Hugo, the most noteworthy are:

"Imprimerie Nationale" edition. *Les Misérables.* 4 vols. Paris, 1908-1909. (This edition includes a description and the variants of the manuscript, the dates of the composition of the various parts, and the text of the passages Hugo omitted from the definitive version, which were later found among his papers; in addition, it gives a detailed historical account of the composition and publication of the novel.)

ALLEM, MAURICE (ed.). *Les Misérables.* 1 vol. Paris: Gallimard. (Bibliothèque de la Pléiade), 1951.

GUYARD, M.-F. (ed.). *Les Misérables.* 2 vols. Paris: Garnier, 1957. (These last two editions both give the variants of the manuscript and contain interesting introductions.)

The text of 1845-1848 has been published under the title:

Les Misères. Edited by GUSTAVE SIMON. 2 vols. Paris: Baudinière, 1927. (Since the text of 1845-1848 remained uncompleted, the editor added a conclusion from an abridged version of the definitive text.)

The best-known English translations are those of Sir Lascelles Wraxall, London, and Charles E. Wilbour, New York, both of which appeared in 1862. They have frequently been reprinted.

Studies of Les Misérables

In addition to the introductions to the principal editions, one can profitably consult:

BENOÎT-LÉVY, EDMOND. *Les Misérables de Victor Hugo.* Paris: Malfère, 1929. (This is a well-documented study of the novel.)

Another work, by Swinburne, is worthy of mention:

SWINBURNE, ALGERNON CHARLES. A *Study of Victor Hugo's*
"Les Misérables." Edited with an Introduction by EDMUND
GOSSE. London: Privately printed, 1914.

General Works on Victor Hugo

The bibliography on Victor Hugo is immense. We can list
here only a very few texts:

MAUROIS, ANDRÉ. *Olympio; the Life of Victor Hugo.* Translated by GERARD HOPKINS. New York: Harper & Row, 1956.

GRANT, ELLIOTT MANSFIELD. *The Career of Victor Hugo.*
Cambridge: Harvard University Press, 1945.

BARRÈRE, JEAN-BERTRAND. *Hugo; l'homme et l'oeuvre.*
Paris: Boivin, 1952. (This is a good up-to-date study of the
life and work of Victor Hugo.)

Preface

So long as there shall exist, by reason of law and custom, a social condemnation, which, in the face of civilization, artificially creates hells on earth, and complicates a destiny that is divine, with human fatality; so long as the three problems of the age—the degradation of man by poverty, the ruin of woman by starvation, and the dwarfing of childhood by physical and spiritual night—are not solved; so long as, in certain regions, social asphyxia shall be possible; in other words, and from a yet more extended point of view, so long as ignorance and misery remain on earth, books like this cannot be useless.

Hauteville House, 1862

Fantine

An Upright Man

In 1815, Monsieur Charles François-Bienvenu Myriel was Bishop of D——. He was a man of seventy-five, and had occupied the bishopric of D—— since 1806.

When Monsieur Myriel came to D—— he was accompanied by an old lady, Mademoiselle Baptistine, who was his sister, ten years younger than himself.

Their only domestic was a woman of about the same age as Mademoiselle Baptistine, who was called Madame Magloire, and who, after having been the servant of Monsieur le curé, now took the double title of *femme de chambre* of Mademoiselle and housekeeper of Monseigneur.

Monsieur Myriel, upon his arrival, was installed in his episcopal palace with the honors ordained by the imperial decrees, which class the bishop next in rank to the field marshal. The mayor and the president made him the first visit, and he, on his part, paid like honor to the general and the prefect.

The installation being completed, the town was curious to see its bishop at work.

The bishop's palace at D—— was contiguous to the hospital; the palace was a spacious and beautiful edifice, built of stone near the beginning of the last century.

The hospital was a low, narrow, one-story building with a small garden.

Three days after the bishop's advent he visited the hospital; when the visit was ended, he invited the director to oblige him by coming to the palace.

"Monsieur," he said to the director of the hospital, "how many patients have you?"

"Twenty-six, monseigneur."

"That is as I counted them," said the bishop.

The bishop ran his eyes over the hall, seemingly taking measure and making calculations.

"It will hold twenty beds," said he to himself, then raising his voice, he said:

"Listen, Monsieur Director, to what I have to say. There is evidently a mistake here. There are twenty-six of you in five or six small rooms; there are only three of us, and space for sixty. There is a mistake, I tell you. You have my house and I have yours. Restore mine to me; you are at home."

Next day the twenty-six poor invalids were installed in the bishop's palace, and the bishop was in the hospital.

In a short time donations of money began to come in; those who had and those who had not, knocked at the bishop's door; some came to receive alms and others to bestow them, and in less than a year he had become the treasurer of all the benevolent, and the dispenser to all the needy. Large sums passed through his hands; nevertheless he changed in no wise his mode of life, nor added the least luxury to his simple fare.

On the contrary, as there is always more misery among the lower classes than there is humanity in the higher, everything was given away, so to speak, before it was received, like water on thirsty soil; it was well that money came to him, for he never kept any, and besides he robbed himself. It being the custom that all bishops should put their baptismal names at the head of their orders and pastoral letters, the poor people of the district had chosen by a sort of affectionate instinct, from among the names of the bishop, that which was expressive to them, and they always called him Monseigneur Bienvenu.

In 1815 he attained his seventy-sixth year, but he did not appear to be more than sixty. He was not tall; he was somewhat fleshy, and frequently took long walks that he might not become more so; he had a firm step, and was but little bowed, a circumstance from which we do not claim to draw any conclusion—Gregory XVI, at eighty years, was erect and smiling, which did not prevent him from being a bad bishop. Monseigneur Bienvenu had what people call "a fine head," but so benevolent that you forgot that it was fine.

When he talked with that infantile gaiety that was one of his graces, all felt at ease in his presence, and from his whole person joy seemed to radiate. His ruddy and fresh complexion, and his white teeth, all of which were well preserved, and

which he showed when he laughed, gave him that open and
easy air which makes us say of a man: he is a good fellow;
and of an old man: he is a good man. At the first view, and
to one who saw him for the first time, he was nothing more
than a goodman. But if one spent a few hours with him, and
saw him in a thoughtful mood, little by little the goodman
became transfigured, and became ineffably imposing; his large
and serious forehead, rendered noble by his white hair, became noble also by meditation; majesty was developed from
this goodness, yet the radiance of goodness remained, and
one felt something of the emotion that he would experience
in seeing a smiling angel slowly spread his wings without
ceasing to smile. Respect, unutterable respect, penetrated you
by degrees, and made its way to your heart, and you felt that
you had before you one of those strong, tried, and indulgent
souls, where the thought is so great that it cannot be other
than gentle.

As we have seen, prayer, celebration of the religious offices,
alms, consoling the afflicted, the cultivation of a little piece of
ground, fraternity, frugality, self-sacrifice, confidence, study,
and work, filled up each day of his life. Filled up is exactly
the word, and in fact, the bishop's day was full to the brim
with good thoughts, good words, and good actions. Nevertheless it was not complete if cold or rainy weather prevented
his passing an hour or two in the evening, when the two
women had retired, in his garden before going to sleep. It
seemed as if it were a sort of rite with him, to prepare himself for sleep by meditating in presence of the great spectacle
of the starry firmament. Sometimes at a late hour of the night,
if the two women were awake, they would hear him slowly
promenading the walks. He was there alone with himself,
collected, tranquil, adoring, comparing the serenity of his
heart with the serenity of the skies, moved in the darkness
by the visible splendors of the constellations, and the invisible splendor of God, opening his soul to the thoughts
which fall from the Unknown. In such moments, offering up
his heart at the hour when the flowers of night inhale their
perfume, lighted like a lamp in the center of the starry night,
expanding his soul in ecstasy in the midst of the universal
radiance of creation, he could not himself perhaps have told
what was passing in his own mind; he felt something depart
from him, and something descend upon him, mysterious in-

terchanges of the depths of the soul with the depths of the universe.

He would sit upon a wooden bench leaning against a broken trellis and look at the stars through the irregular outlines of his fruit trees. This quarter of an acre of ground, so poorly cultivated, so cumbered with shed and ruins, was dear to him, and satisfied him.

What was more needed by this old man who divided the leisure hours of his life, where he had so little leisure, between gardening in the daytime, and contemplation at night? Was not this narrow enclosure, with the sky for a background, enough to enable him to adore God in his most beautiful as well as in his most sublime works? Indeed, is not that all, and what more can be desired? A little garden to walk, and immensity to reflect upon. At his feet something to cultivate and gather; above his head something to study and meditate upon: a few flowers on the earth, and all the stars in the sky.

The Fall

I

An hour before sunset, on the evening of a day in the beginning of October, 1815, a man traveling afoot entered the little town of D——. The few persons who at this time were at their windows or their doors, regarded this traveler with a sort of distrust. It would have been hard to find a passer-by more wretched in appearance. He was a man of middle height, stout and hardy, in the strength of maturity; he might have been forty-six or seven. A slouched leather cap half hid his face, bronzed by the sun and wind, and dripping with sweat. His shaggy breast was seen through the coarse yellow shirt which at the neck was fastened by a small silver anchor; he wore a cravat twisted like a rope, coarse blue trousers, worn and shabby, white on one knee, and with holes in the other, and an old ragged gray blouse, patched on one side with a piece of green cloth sewed with twine; upon his back was a well-filled knapsack, strongly buckled and quite new. In his hand he carried an enormous knotted stick; his stockingless feet were in hobnailed shoes; his hair was cropped and his beard long.

The sweat, the heat, his long walk, and the dust, added an indescribable meanness to his tattered appearance.

His hair was shorn, but bristly, for it had begun to grow a little, and seemingly had not been cut for some time.

When he reached the corner of the rue Poichevert he turned to the left and went toward the mayor's office. He went in, and a quarter of an hour afterward he came out.

There was then in D—— a good inn called *La Croix de Colbas.*

The traveler turned his steps toward this inn, which was the best in the place, and went at once into the kitchen, which opened out of the street. All the ranges were fuming, and a great fire was burning briskly in the chimney place. Mine host, who was at the same time head cook, was going from the fireplace to the saucepans, very busy superintending an excellent dinner for some wagoners who were laughing and talking noisily in the next room. Whoever has traveled knows that nobody lives better than wagoners. A fat marmot, flanked by white partridges and goose, was turning on a long spit before the fire; upon the ranges were cooking two large carps from Lake Lauzet, and a trout from Lake Alloz.

The host, hearing the door open, and a newcomer enter, said, without raising his eyes from his ranges:

"What will monsieur have?"

"Something to eat and lodging."

"Nothing more easy," said mine host, but on turning his head and taking an observation of the traveler, he added: "For pay."

The man drew from his pocket a large leather purse, and answered:

"I have money."

"Then," said mine host, "I am at your service."

The man put his purse back into his pocket, took off his knapsack and put it down hard by the door, and holding his stick in his hand, sat down on a low stool by the fire. D—— being in the mountains, the evenings of October are cold there.

However, as the host passed backward and forward, he kept a careful eye on the traveler.

"Is dinner almost ready?" said the man.

"Directly," said mine host.

While the newcomer was warming himself with his back turned, the worthy innkeeper, Jacquin Labarre, took a pencil from his pocket, and then tore off the corner of an old paper which he pulled from a little table near the window. On the margin he wrote a line or two, folded it, and handed the scrap of paper to a child, who appeared to serve him as lackey and scullion at the same time. The innkeeper whispered a word to the boy and he ran off in the direction of the mayor's office.

The traveler saw nothing of this.

He asked a second time: "Is dinner ready?"

"Yes, in a few moments," said the host.

The boy came back with the paper. The host unfolded it hurriedly, as one who is expecting an answer. He seemed to read with attention, then throwing his head on one side, thought for a moment. Then he took a step toward the traveler, who seemed drowned in troublous thought.

"Monsieur," said he, "I cannot receive you. I have no room."

"Well," responded the man, "a corner in the garret, a truss of straw. We will see about that after dinner."

"I cannot give you any dinner."

This declaration, made in a measured but firm tone, appeared serious to the traveler. He got up.

"Ah, bah! But I am dying with hunger."

"I have nothing," said the host.

The man burst into a laugh, and turned toward the fireplace and the ranges.

"Nothing! And all that?"

"All that is engaged."

The man sat down again and said, without raising his voice: "I am at an inn. I am hungry, and I shall stay."

The host bent down his ear, and said in a voice which made him tremble:

"Go away!"

At these words the traveler, who was bent over, poking some embers in the fire with the ironshod end of his stick, turned suddenly around, and opened his mouth as if to reply, when the host, looking steadily at him, added in the same low tone: "Stop, no more of that. It is my custom to be polite to all. Go!"

The man bowed his head, picked up his knapsack, and went out.

He took the principal street; he walked at random, slinking near the houses like a sad and humiliated man; he did not once turn around. If he had turned, he would have seen the innkeeper of the *Croix de Colbas*, standing in his doorway with all his guests, and the passers-by gathered about him, speaking excitedly, and pointing him out, and from the looks of fear and distrust which were exchanged, he would have guessed that before long his arrival would be the talk of the whole town.

He saw nothing of all this: people overwhelmed with trouble do not look behind; they know only too well that misfortune follows them.

He walked along in this way some time, going by chance down streets unknown to him, and forgetting fatigue, as is the case in sorrow. Suddenly he felt a pang of hunger; night was at hand.

Some children who had followed him from the *Croix de Colbas* threw stones at him. He turned angrily and threatened them with his stick, and they scattered like a flock of birds.

He passed the prison; an iron chain hung from the door attached to a bell. He rang.

The grating opened.

"Monsieur Turnkey," said he, taking off his cap respectfully, "will you open and let me stay here tonight?"

A voice answered:

"A prison is not a tavern; get yourself arrested and we will open."

The grating closed.

Night came on apace; the cold Alpine winds were blowing.

He began to tramp again, taking his way out of the town, hoping to find some tree or haystack beneath which he could shelter himself. He walked on for some time, his head bowed down. When he thought he was far away from all human habitation, he raised his eyes, and looked about him inquiringly. He was in a field; before him was a low hillock covered with stubble, which after the harvest looks like a shaved head. The sky was very dark; it was not simply the darkness of night, but there were very low clouds, which seemed to rest upon the hills, and covered the whole heavens. A little of the twilight, however, lingered in the zenith, and as the moon was about to rise these clouds formed in midheaven a vault of whitish light, from which a glimmer fell upon the earth.

The earth was then lighter than the sky, which produces a peculiarly sinister effect, and the hill, poor and mean in contour, loomed out dim and pale upon the gloomy horizon; the whole prospect was hideous, mean, lugubrious, and insignificant. There was nothing in the field nor upon the hill but one ugly tree, a few steps from the traveler, which seemed to be twisting and contorting itself.

He retraced his steps; the gates of D—— were closed. He passed through a breach and entered the town.

It was about eight o'clock in the evening. As he did not know the streets, he walked at hazard.

So he came to the prefecture, then to the seminary; on passing by the cathedral square, he shook his fist at the church.

At the corner of this square stands a printing office. Exhausted with fatigue, and hoping for nothing better, he lay down on a stone bench in front of this printing office.

Just then an old woman came out of the church. She saw the man lying there in the dark and said:

"What are you doing there, my friend?"

He replied harshly, and with anger in his tone:

"You see, my good woman, I am going to sleep."

The good woman, who really merited the name, was Madame la Marquise de R——.

"Upon the bench?" said she. "You cannot pass the night so. You must be cold and hungry. They should give you lodging for charity."

"I have knocked at every door."

"Well, what then?"

"Everybody has driven me away."

The good woman touched the man's arm and pointed out to him, on the other side of the square, a little low house beside the bishop's palace.

"You have knocked at every door?" she asked.

"Yes."

"Have you knocked at that one there?"

"No."

"Knock there."

THAT evening, after his walk in the town, the Bishop of D——
remained quite late in his room. He was busy with his great
work on Duty, which unfortunately is left incomplete. He
carefully dissected all that the Fathers and Doctors have said
on this serious topic.

At eight o'clock he was still at work, writing with some inconvenience on little slips of paper, with a large book open
on his knees, when Madame Magloire, as usual, came in to
take the silver from the panel near the bed. A moment after,
the bishop, knowing that the table was laid, and that his sister
was perhaps waiting, closed his book and went into the dining
room.

This dining room was an oblong apartment, with a fireplace, and with a door upon the street, as we have said, and
a window opening into the garden.

Madame Magloire had just finished placing the plates.

While she was arranging the table, she was talking with
Mademoiselle Baptistine.

The lamp was on the table, which was near the fireplace,
where a good fire was burning.

One can readily fancy these two women, both past their
sixtieth year: Madame Magloire, small, fat, and quick in her
movements; Mademoiselle Baptistine, sweet, thin, fragile, a
little taller than her brother, wearing a silk puce-colored
dress, in the style of 1806, which she had bought at that time
in Paris, and which still lasted her. To borrow a common mode
of expression, which has the merit of saying in a single word
what a page would hardly express, Madame Magloire had
the air of a peasant, and Mademoiselle Baptistine that of a
lady.

Just as the bishop entered, Madame Magloire was speaking with some warmth. She was talking to mademoiselle upon
a familiar subject, and one to which the bishop was quite accustomed. It was a discussion on the means of fastening the
front door.

It seems that while Madame Magloire was out making
provision for supper, she had heard the news in sundry places.
There was talk that an ill-favored runaway, a suspicious vaga-

bond, had arrived and was lurking somewhere in the town, and that some unpleasant adventures might befall those who should come home late that night. Then Mademoiselle Baptistine, endeavoring to satisfy Madame Magloire without displeasing her brother, ventured to say timidly:

"Brother, do you hear what Madame Magloire says?"

"I heard something of it indistinctly," said the bishop. Then turning his chair half around, putting his hands on his knees, and raising toward the old servant his cordial and good-humored face, which the firelight shone upon, he said: "Well, well! What is the matter? Are we in any great danger?"

Then Madame Magloire began her story again, unconsciously exaggerating it a little. It appeared that a barefooted gypsy man, a sort of dangerous beggar, was in the town. He had gone for lodging to Jacquin Labarre, who had refused to receive him; he had been seen to enter the town by the Boulevard Gassendi, and to roam through the street at dusk. A man with a knapsack and a rope, and a terrible-looking face.

"Indeed!" said the bishop.

This readiness to question her encouraged Madame Magloire; it seemed to indicate that the bishop was really well-nigh alarmed. She continued triumphantly: "Yes, monseigneur; it is true. There will something happen tonight in the town; everybody says so. And I say, monseigneur, and mademoiselle says also—"

"Me?" interrupted the sister. "I say nothing. Whatever my brother does is well done."

Madame Magloire went on as if she had not heard this protestation:

"We say that this house is not safe at all, and if monseigneur will permit me, I will go and tell Paulin Musebois, the locksmith, to come and put the old bolts in the door again; they are there, and it will take but a minute. I say we must have bolts, were it only for tonight, for I say that a door which opens by a latch on the outside to the first comer, nothing could be more horrible, and then monseigneur has the habit of always saying 'Come in,' even at midnight. But, my goodness! There is no need even to ask leave—"

At this moment there was a violent knock on the door.

"Come in!" said the bishop.

THE door opened.

It opened quickly, quite wide, as if pushed by someone boldly and with energy.

A man entered.

That man, we know already; it was the traveler we have seen wandering about in search of a lodging.

He came in, took one step, and paused, leaving the door open behind him. He had his knapsack on his back, his stick in his hand, and a rough, hard, tired, and fierce look in his eyes, as seen by the firelight. He was hideous. It was an apparition of ill omen.

Madame Magloire had not even the strength to scream. She stood trembling with her mouth open.

Mademoiselle Baptistine turned, saw the man enter, and started up half alarmed; then, slowly turning back again toward the fire, she looked at her brother, and her face resumed its usual calmness and serenity.

The bishop looked upon the man with a tranquil eye.

As he was opening his mouth to speak, doubtless to ask the stranger what he wanted, the man, leaning with both hands on his club, glanced from one to another in turn, and without waiting for the bishop to speak, said in a loud voice:

"See here! My name is Jean Valjean. I am a convict; I have been nineteen years in the galleys. Four days ago I was set free, and started for Pontarlier, which is my destination; during those four days I have walked from Toulon. Today I have walked twelve leagues. When I reached this place this evening I went to an inn, and they sent me away on account of my yellow passport, which I had shown at the mayor's office, as was necessary. I went to the prison, and the turnkey would not let me in. I went into the fields to sleep beneath the stars: there were no stars; I thought it would rain, and there was no good God to stop the drops, so I came back to the town to get the shelter of some doorway. There in the square I lay down upon a stone; a good woman showed me your house, and said: 'Knock there!' I have knocked. What is this place? Are you an inn? I have money: my savings, one hundred and nine francs and fifteen sous which I have earned in the galleys by my work for nineteen years. I will pay. What do I care? I have money. I am very tired—twelve leagues on foot, and I am so hungry. Can I stay?"

"Madame Magloire," said the bishop, "put on another plate."

The man took three steps, and came near the lamp which stood on the table. "Stop," he exclaimed, as if he had not been understood, "not that, did you understand me? I am a galley slave—a convict—I am just from the galleys. There is my passport, yellow as you see. That is enough to have me kicked out wherever I go. There you have it! Everybody has thrust me out; will you receive me? Is this an inn? Can you give me something to eat, and a place to sleep? Have you a stable?"

"Madame Magloire," said the bishop, "put some sheets on the bed in the alcove."

Madame Magloire went out to fulfill her orders.

The bishop turned to the man.

"Monsieur, sit down and warm yourself; we are going to take supper presently, and your bed will be made ready while you sup."

At last the man quite understood; his face, the expression of which till then had been gloomy and hard, now expressed stupefaction, doubt, and joy, and became absolutely wonderful. He began to stutter like a madman.

"True? What! You will keep me? You won't drive me away? A convict! You call me monsieur and don't say 'Get out, dog!' as everybody else does. You are really willing that I should stay? You are good people! Besides I have money; I will pay well. I beg your pardon, Monsieur Innkeeper, what is your name? I will pay all you say. You are a fine man. You are an innkeeper, an't you?"

"I am a priest who lives here," said the bishop.

"A priest," said the man. "Oh, noble priest! Then you do not ask any money? You are the curé, an't you? The curé of this big church? Yes, that's it. How stupid I am; I didn't notice your cap."

While speaking, he had deposited his knapsack and stick in the corner, replaced his passport in his pocket, and sat down. Mademoiselle Baptistine looked at him pleasantly. He continued:

"You are humane, Monsieur Curé; you don't despise me. A

good priest is a good thing. Then you don't want me to pay you?"

"No," said the bishop, "keep your money."

The bishop sighed deeply.

The man continued: "As you are an *abbé*, I must tell you, we have an almoner in the galleys. And then one day I saw a bishop; monseigneur, they called him. It was the Bishop of Majore from Marseilles. He is the curé who is over the curés. You see—beg pardon, how I bungle saying it, but for me, it is so far off! You know what we are. He said mass in the center of the place on an altar; he had a pointed gold thing on his head, that shone in the sun; it was noon. We were drawn up in line on three sides, with cannons and matches lighted before us. We could not see him well. He spoke to us, but he was not near enough; we did not understand him. That is what a bishop is."

While he was talking, the bishop shut the door, which he had left wide open.

Madame Magloire brought in a plate and set it on the table.

"Madame Magloire," said the bishop, "put this plate as near the fire as you can." Then turning toward his guest, he added: "The night wind is raw in the Alps; you must be cold, monsieur."

Every time he said this word monsieur, with his gently solemn, and heartily hospitable voice, the man's countenance lighted up. "Monsieur" to a convict is a glass of water to a man dying of thirst at sea. Ignominy thirsts for respect.

"The lamp," said the bishop, "gives a very poor light."

Madame Magloire understood him, and going to his bedchamber, took from the mantel the two silver candlesticks, lighted the candles, and placed them on the table.

"Monsieur Curé," said the man, "you are good; you don't despise me. You take me into your house; you light your candles for me, and I haven't hid from you where I come from, and how miserable I am."

The bishop, who was sitting near him, touched his hand gently and said: "You need not tell me who you are. This is not my house; it is the house of Christ. It does not ask any comer whether he has a name, but whether he has an affliction. You are suffering; you are hungry and thirsty; be welcome. And do not thank me; do not tell me that I take you into my house. This is the home of no man, except him who needs an asylum. I tell you, who are a traveler, that you are more at home here than I; whatever is here is yours. What need have I to know your name? Besides, before you told me, I knew it."

The man opened his eyes in astonishment.

"Really? You knew my name?"

"Yes," answered the bishop, "your name is My Brother."

"Stop, stop, Monsieur Curé," exclaimed the man. "I was famished when I came in, but you are so kind that now I don't know what I am; that is all gone."

The bishop looked at him again and said:

"You have seen much suffering?"

"Oh, the red blouse, the ball and chain, the plank to sleep on, the heat, the cold, the galley's crew, the lash, the double chain for nothing, the dungeon for a word—even when sick in bed, the chain. The dogs, the dogs are happier! Nineteen years! And I am forty-six, and now a yellow passport. That is all."

"Yes," answered the bishop, "you have left a place of suffering. But listen, there will be more joy in heaven over the tears of a repentant sinner than over the white robes of a hundred good men. If you are leaving that sorrowful place with hate and anger against men, you are worthy of compassion; if you leave it with good will, gentleness, and peace, you are better than any of us."

Meantime Madame Magloire had served up supper; it consisted of soup made of water, oil, bread, and salt, a little pork, a scrap of mutton, a few figs, a green cheese, and a large loaf of rye bread. She had, without asking, added to the usual dinner of the bishop a bottle of fine old Mauves wine.

The bishop's countenance was lighted up with this expression of pleasure, peculiar to hospitable natures. "To supper!" he said briskly, as was his habit when he had a guest. He seated the man at his right. Mademoiselle Baptistine, perfectly quiet and natural, took her place at his left.

The bishop said the blessing, and then served the soup himself, according to his usual custom. The man fell to, eating greedily.

Suddenly the bishop said: "It seems to me something is lacking on the table."

The fact was, that Madame Magloire had set out only the three plates which were necessary. Now it was the custom of the house, when the bishop had anyone to supper, to set all six of the silver plates on the table, an innocent display. This graceful appearance of luxury was a sort of childlikeness which was full of charm in this gentle but austere household, which elevated poverty to dignity.

Madame Magloire understood the remark; without a word she went out, and a moment afterward the three plates for which the bishop had asked were shining on the cloth, symmetrically arranged before each of the three guests.

IV

AFTER having said good night to his sister, Monseigneur Bienvenu took one of the silver candlesticks from the table, handed the other to his guest, and said to him:

"Monsieur, I will show you to your room."

The man followed him.

As may have been understood from what has been said before, the house was so arranged that one could reach the alcove in the oratory only by passing through the bishop's sleeping chamber. Just as they were passing through this room Madame Magloire was putting up the silver in the cupboard at the head of the bed. It was the last thing she did every night before going to bed.

The bishop left his guest in the alcove, before a clean white bed. The man set down the candlestick upon a small table.

"Come," said the bishop, "a good night's rest to you; tomorrow morning, before you go, you shall have a cup of warm milk from our cows."

"Thank you, Monsieur l'Abbé," said the man.

Scarcely had he pronounced these words of peace, when suddenly he made a singular motion which would have chilled the two good women of the house with horror, had they witnessed it. He turned abruptly toward the old man, crossed his arms, and casting a wild look upon his host, exclaimed in a harsh voice:

"Ah, now, indeed! You lodge me in your house, as near you as that!"

He checked himself, and added, with a laugh, in which there was something horrible:

"Have you reflected upon it? Who tells you that I am not a murderer?"

The bishop responded:

"God will take care of that."

Then with gravity, moving his lips like one praying or talking to himself, he raised two fingers of his right hand and blessed the man, who, however, did not bow, and without turning his head or looking behind him, went into his chamber.

A few moments afterward all in the little house slept.

V

TOWARD the middle of the night, Jean Valjean awoke.

Jean Valjean was born of a poor peasant family of Brie. In his childhood he had not been taught to read; when he was grown up, he chose the occupation of a pruner at Faverolles.

Jean Valjean was of a thoughtful disposition, but not sad, which is characteristic of affectionate natures. Upon the whole, however, there was something torpid and insignificant, in the appearance at least, of Jean Valjean. He had lost his parents when very young. His mother died of malpractice in a milk fever; his father, a pruner before him, was killed by a fall from a tree. Jean Valjean now had but one relative left, his sister, a widow with seven children, girls and boys. This sister had brought up Jean Valjean, and, as long as her husband lived, she had taken care of her younger brother. Her husband died, leaving the eldest of these children eight, the youngest one year old. Jean Valjean had just reached his twenty-fifth year; he took the father's place, and, in his turn, supported the sister who reared him. This he did naturally, as a duty, and even with a sort of moroseness on his part. His youth was spent in rough and ill-recompensed labor; he never was known to have a sweetheart; he had not time to be in love.

At night he came in weary and ate his soup without saying a word. While he was eating, his sister, Mère Jeanne, frequently took from his porringer the best of his meal: a bit of meat, a slice of pork, the heart of the cabbage, to give to one of her children. He went on eating, his head bent down nearly into the soup, his long hair falling over his dish, hiding his eyes; he did not seem to notice anything that was done.

He earned in the pruning season eighteen sous a day; after that he hired out as a reaper, workman, teamster, or laborer. He did whatever he could find to do. His sister worked also, but what could she do with seven little children? It was a sad group, which misery was grasping and closing upon, little by little. There was a very severe winter; Jean had no work; the family had no bread; literally, no bread, and seven children.

One Sunday night, Maubert Isabeau, the baker on the Place de l'Eglise, in Faverolles, was just going to bed when he heard a violent blow against the barred window of his shop. He got down in time to see an arm thrust through the aperture made by the blow of a fist on the glass. The arm seized a loaf of bread and took it out. Isabeau rushed out; the thief used his legs valiantly; Isabeau pursued him and caught him. The thief had thrown away the bread, but his arm was still bleeding. It was Jean Valjean.

All that happened in 1795. Jean Valjean was brought before the tribunals of the time for "burglary at night, in an inhabited house." He was found guilty; the terms of the code were explicit; in our civilization there are fearful hours—such are those when the criminal law pronounces shipwreck upon a man. What a mournful moment is that in which society withdraws itself and gives up a thinking being forever. Jean Valjean was sentenced to five years in the galleys.

He was taken to Toulon, at which place he arrived after a journey of twenty-seven days, on a cart, the chain still about his neck. At Toulon he was dressed in a red blouse, all his past life was effaced, even to his name. He was no longer Jean Valjean; he was Number 24,601. What became of the sister? What became of the seven children? Who troubled himself about that? What becomes of the handful of leaves of the young tree when it is sawn at the trunk?

Near the end of the fourth year, his chance of liberty came to Jean Valjean. His comrades helped him as they always do in that dreary place, and he escaped. He wandered two days through the fields. During the evening of the second day he was retaken; he had neither eaten nor slept for thirty-six hours. The maritime tribunal extended his sentence three years for this attempt, which made eight. In the sixth year his turn of escape came again; he tried it, but failed again. He did not answer at roll call, and the alarm cannon was fired. At night the people of the vicinity discovered him hidden beneath the keel of a vessel on the stocks; he resisted the galley guard which seized him. Escape and resistance. This the provisions of the special code punished by an addition of five years, two with the double chain. Thirteen years. The tenth year his turn came round again; he made another attempt with no better success. Three years for this new attempt. Sixteen years. And finally, I think it was in the thirteenth year, he made yet another, and was retaken after an absence of only four hours. Three years for these four hours. Nineteen years. In October, 1815, he was set at large; he had entered in 1796 for having broken a pane of glass, and taken a loaf of bread.

Jean Valjean entered the galleys sobbing and shuddering: he went out hardened; he entered in despair: he went out sullen.

What had been the life of this soul?

VI

Let us endeavor to tell.

It is an imperative necessity that society should look into these things: they are its own work.

He was, as we have said, ignorant, but he was not imbecile. The natural light was enkindled in him. Misfortune, which has also its illumination, added to the few rays that he had in his mind. Under the whip, under the chain, in the cell, in fatigue, under the burning sun of the galleys, upon the convict's bed of plank, he turned to his own conscience, and he reflected.

He constituted himself a tribunal.

He began by arraigning himself.

He recognized that he was not an innocent man, unjustly punished. He acknowledged that he had committed an extreme and a blamable action; that the loaf perhaps would not have been refused him, had he asked for it; that at all events it would have been better to wait, either for pity, or for work; that he should, therefore, have had patience; that that would have been better even for those poor little ones; that it was an act of folly in him, a poor, worthless man, to seize society in all its strength forcibly by the collar, and imagine that he could escape from misery by theft; that that was, at all events, a bad door for getting out of misery by which one entered into infamy; in short, that he had done wrong.

Then he asked himself:

If he were the only one who had done wrong in the course of his fatal history. If, in the first place, it were not a grievous thing that he, a workman, should have been in want of work; that he, an industrious man, should have lacked bread. If, moreover, the fault having been committed and avowed, the punishment had not been savage and excessive. If there were not a greater abuse, on the part of the law, in the penalty, than there had been, on the part of the guilty, in the crime. If the excess of penalty were not the effacement of the crime; and if the result were not to reverse the situation, to replace the wrong of the delinquent by the wrong of the repression, to make a victim of the guilty, and a creditor of the debtor, and actually to put the right on the side of him who had violated it.

He questioned himself if human society could have the right alike to crush its members, in the one case by its unreasonable carelessness, and in the other by its pitiless care.

If it were not outrageous that society should treat with such rigid precision those of its members who were most poorly endowed in the distribution of wealth that chance had made, and who were, therefore, most worthy of indulgence.

These questions asked and decided, he condemned society and sentenced it.

He sentenced it to his hatred.

He made it responsible for the doom which he had undergone, and promised himself that he, perhaps, would not hesitate someday to call it to an account.

And then, human society had done him nothing but injury; never had he seen anything of her but this wrathful face which she calls justice, and which she shows to those whom she strikes down. No man had ever touched him but to bruise him. All his contact with men had been by blows. Never, since his infancy, since his mother, since his sister, never had he been greeted with a friendly word or a kind regard. Through suffering on suffering he came little by little to the conviction that life was a war, and that in that war he was the vanquished. He had no weapon but his hate. He resolved to

sharpen it in the galleys and to take it with him when he
went out.

There was at Toulon a school for the prisoners conducted
by some not very skillful friars, where the most essential
branches were taught to such of these poor men as were willing. He was one of the willing ones. He went to school at
forty and learned to read, write, and cipher. He felt that to
increase his knowledge was to strengthen his hatred. Under
certain circumstances, instruction and enlightenment may
serve as rallying points for evil.

It is sad to tell, but after having tried society, which had
caused his misfortunes, he tried Providence which created
society, and condemned it also.

Thus, during those nineteen years of torture and slavery,
did this soul rise and fall at the same time. Light entered on
the one side, and darkness on the other.

Jean Valjean was not, we have seen, of an evil nature. His
heart was still right when he arrived at the galleys. While
there he condemned society, and felt that he became wicked;
he condemned Providence, and felt that he became impious.

We must not omit one circumstance, which is, that in physical strength he far surpassed all the other inmates of the
prison. At hard work, at twisting a cable, or turning a wind-
lass, Jean Valjean was equal to four men. At one time, while
the balcony of the City Hall of Toulon was undergoing repairs, one of Puget's admirable caryatids, which support the
balcony, slipped from its place, and was about to fall, when
Jean Valjean, who happened to be there, held it up on his
shoulder till the workmen came.

His suppleness surpassed his strength. Certain convicts,
always planning escape, have developed a veritable science of
strength and skill combined—the science of the muscles. A
mysterious system of statics is practiced throughout daily by
prisoners, who are eternally envying the birds and flies. To
scale a wall, and to find a foothold where you could hardly
see a projection was play for Jean Valjean. Given an angle
in a wall, with the tension of his back and his knees, with elbows and hands braced against the rough face of the stone,
he would ascend, as if by magic, to a third story. Sometimes
he climbed up in this manner to the roof of the galleys.

He talked but little, and never laughed. Some extreme emotion was required to draw from him, once or twice a year, that lugubrious sound of the convict, which is like the echo of a demon's laugh. To those who saw him, he seemed to be absorbed in continually looking upon something terrible.

He was absorbed, in fact.

Through the diseased perceptions of an incomplete nature and a smothered intelligence, he vaguely felt that a monstrous weight was over him. In that pallid and sullen shadow in which he crawled, whenever he turned his head and endeavored to raise his eyes, he saw, with mingled rage and terror, forming, massing, and mounting up out of view above him with horrid escarpments, a kind of frightful accumulation of things, of laws, of prejudices, of men, and of acts, the outlines of which escaped him, the weight of which appalled him, and which was no other than that prodigious pyramid that we call civilization.

If a millet seed under a millstone had thoughts, doubtless it would think what Jean Valjean thought.

All these things, realities full of specters, phantasmagoria full of realities, had at last produced within him a condition which was almost inexpressible.

Sometimes in the midst of his work in the galleys he would stop, and begin to think. His reason, more mature, and, at the same time, perturbed more than formerly, would revolt. All that had happened to him would appear absurd; all that surrounded him would appear impossible. He would say to himself: "It is a dream." He would look at the jailer standing a few steps from him; the jailer would seem to be a phantom; all at once this phantom would give him a blow with a stick.

For him the external world had scarcely an existence. It would be almost true to say that for Jean Valjean there was no sun, no beautiful summer days, no radiant sky, no fresh April dawn. Some dim window light was all that shone in his soul. The beginning as well as the end of all his thoughts was hatred of human law, that hatred which, if it be not checked in its growth by some providential event, becomes, in a certain time, hatred of society, then hatred of the human race, and then hatred of creation, and reveals itself by a vague and incessant desire to injure some living being, it matters not who. So, the passport was right which described Jean Valjean as "a very dangerous man."

From year to year this soul had withered more and more, slowly, but fatally. With this withered heart, he had a dry eye. When he left the galleys, he had not shed a tear for nineteen years.

VII

As the cathedral clock struck two, Jean Valjean awoke.

He had slept something more than four hours. His fatigue had passed away. He was not accustomed to give many hours to repose.

He opened his eyes, and looked for a moment into the obscurity about him; then he closed them to go to sleep again.

When many diverse sensations have disturbed the day, when the mind is preoccupied, we can fall asleep once, but not a second time. Sleep comes at first much more readily than it comes again. Such was the case with Jean Valjean. He could not get to sleep again, and so he began to think.

He was in one of those moods in which the ideas we have in our minds are perturbed. Many thoughts came to him, but there was one which continually presented itself, and which drove away all others. What that thought was, we shall tell directly. He had noticed the six silver plates and the large ladle that Madame Magloire had put on the table.

Those six silver plates took possession of him. There they were, within a few steps. At the very moment that he passed through the middle room to reach the one he was now in, the old servant was placing them in a little cupboard at the head of the bed. He had marked that cupboard well, on the right, coming from the dining room. They were solid, and old silver. With the big ladle, they would bring at least two hundred francs.

His mind wavered a whole hour, and a long one, in fluctuation and in struggle. The clock struck three. He opened his eyes, rose up hastily in bed, reached out his arm and felt his haversack, which he had put into the corner of the alcove; then he thrust out his legs and placed his feet on the ground, and found himself, he knew not how, seated on his bed.

He continued in this situation, and would perhaps have remained there until daybreak, if the clock had not struck the quarter or the half-hour. The clock seemed to say to him: "Come along!"

He rose to his feet, hesitated for a moment longer, and listened; all was still in the house; he walked straight and cautiously toward the window, which he could discern. The night was not very dark; there was a full moon, across which large clouds were driving before the wind. This produced alternations of light and shade, outdoors eclipses and illuminations, and indoors a kind of glimmer. On reaching the window, Jean Valjean examined it. It had no bars, opened into the garden, and was fastened, according to the fashion of the country, with a little wedge only. He opened it, but as the cold, keen air rushed into the room, he closed it again immediately. He looked into the garden with that absorbed look which studies rather than sees. The garden was enclosed with a white wall, quite low, and readily scaled. Beyond, against the sky, he distinguished the tops of trees at equal distances apart, which showed that this wall separated the garden from an avenue or a lane planted with trees.

When he had taken this observation, he turned like a man whose mind is made up, went to his alcove, took his haversack, opened it, fumbled in it, took out something which he laid upon the bed, put his shoes into one of his pockets, tied up his bundle, swung it upon his shoulders, put on his cap and pulled the vizor down over his eyes, felt for his stick, and went and put it in the corner of the window, then returned to the bed, and resolutely took up the object which he had laid on it. It looked like a short iron bar, pointed at one end like a spear.

It would have been hard to distinguish in the darkness for what use this piece of iron had been made. Could it be a lever? Could it be a club?

In the daytime, it would have been seen to be nothing but a miner's drill. At that time, the convicts were sometimes employed in quarrying stone on the high hills that surround Toulon, and they often had miners' tools in their possession. Miners' drills are of solid iron, terminating at the lower end in a point, by means of which they are sunk into the rock.

He took the drill in his right hand, and holding his breath, with stealthy steps, he moved toward the door of the next room, which was the bishop's, as we know. On reaching the door, he found it unlatched. The bishop had not closed it.

VIII

Jean Valjean listened. Not a sound.

He pushed the door.

He pushed it lightly with the end of his finger, with the stealthy and timorous carefulness of a cat. The door yielded to the pressure with a silent, imperceptible movement, which made the opening a little wider.

He waited a moment, and then pushed the door again more boldly. This time a rusty hinge suddenly sent out into the darkness a harsh and prolonged creak.

He stood still, petrified like the pillar of salt, not daring to stir. Some minutes passed. The door was wide open; he ventured a look into the room. Nothing had moved. He listened. Nothing was stirring in the house. The noise of the rusty hinge had wakened nobody.

This first danger was over, but still he felt within him a frightful tumult. Nevertheless he did not flinch. Not even when he thought he was lost had he flinched. His only thought was to make an end of it quickly. He took one step and was in the room.

A deep calm filled the chamber. Jean Valjean advanced, carefully avoiding the furniture. At the further end of the room he could hear the equal and quiet breathing of the sleeping bishop.

Suddenly he stopped; he was near the bed, he had reached it sooner than he thought.

Nature sometimes joins her effects and her appearances to our acts with a sort of serious and intelligent appropriateness, as if she would compel us to reflect. For nearly a half hour a great cloud had darkened the sky. At the moment when Jean Valjean paused before the bed the cloud broke as if purposely, and a ray of moonlight, crossing the high window, suddenly lighted up the bishop's pale face. He slept tranquilly. He was almost entirely dressed, though in bed, on account of the cold nights of the lower Alps, with a dark woolen garment which covered his arms to the wrists. His head had fallen on the pillow in the unstudied attitude of slumber; over the side of the bed hung his hand, ornamented with the pastoral ring, and which had done so many good deeds, so many pious acts. His entire countenance was lit up with a vague expression of content, hope, and happiness. It was more than a smile and almost a radiance. On his forehead rested the indescribable reflection of an unseen light. The souls of the upright in sleep have vision of a mysterious heaven.

A reflection from this heaven shone upon the bishop.

But it was also a luminous transparency, for this heaven was within him; this heaven was his conscience.

At the instant when the moonbeam overlay, so to speak, this inward radiance, the sleeping bishop appeared as if in a halo. But it was very mild, and veiled in an ineffable twilight. The moon in the sky, nature drowsing, the garden without a pulse, the quiet house, the hour, the moment, the silence, added something strangely solemn and unutterable to the venerable repose of this man, and enveloped his white locks and his closed eyes with a serene and majestic glory, this face where all was hope and confidence—this old man's head and infant's slumber.

There was something of divinity almost in this man, thus unconsciously august.

Jean Valjean was in the shadow with the iron drill in his hand, erect, motionless, terrified, at this radiant figure. He had never seen anything comparable to it. This confidence filled him with fear. The moral world has no greater spectacle than this: a troubled and restless conscience on the verge of committing an evil deed, contemplating the sleep of a good man.

In a few moments he raised his left hand slowly to his forehead and took off his hat; then, letting his hand fall with the same slowness, Jean Valjean resumed his contemplations, his cap in his left hand, his club in his right, and his hair bristling on his fierce-looking head.

Under this frightful gaze the bishop still slept in profoundest peace.

The crucifix above the mantelpiece was dimly visible in the moonlight, apparently extending its arms toward both, with a benediction for one and a pardon for the other.

Suddenly Jean Valjean put on his cap, then passed quickly, without looking at the bishop, along the bed, straight to the cupboard which he perceived near its head; he raised the drill to force the lock; the key was in it; he opened it; the first thing he saw was the basket of silver; he took it, crossed the room with hasty stride, careless of noise, reached the door, entered the oratory, took his stick, stepped out, put the silver in his knapsack, threw away the basket, ran across the garden, leaped over the wall like a tiger, and fled.

IX

THE next day at sunrise, Monseigneur Bienvenu was walking in the garden. Madame Magloire ran toward him quite beside herself.

"Monseigneur, the man has gone! The silver is stolen!"

While she was uttering this exclamation her eyes fell on an angle of the garden where she saw traces of an escalade. A capstone of the wall had been thrown down.

"See, there is where he got out; he jumped into Cochefilet Lane. The abominable fellow! He has stolen our silver!"

The bishop was silent for a moment; then raising his serious eyes, he said mildly to Madame Magloire:

"Now first, did this silver belong to us?"

Madame Magloire did not answer; after a moment the bishop continued:

"Madame Magloire, I have for a long time wrongfully withheld this silver; it belonged to the poor. Who was this man? A poor man evidently."

"Alas! Alas!" returned Madame Magloire. "It is not on my account or mademoiselle's; it is all the same to us. But it is on yours, monseigneur. What is monsieur going to eat from now?"

The bishop looked at her with amazement:

"How so! Have we no tin plates?"

Madame Magloire shrugged her shoulders.

"Tin smells."

"Well, then, iron plates."

Madame Magloire made an expressive gesture.

"Iron tastes."

"Well," said the bishop, "then wooden plates."

In a few minutes he was breakfasting at the same table at which Jean Valjean sat the night before. While breakfasting, Monseigneur Bienvenu pleasantly remarked to his sister who said nothing, and Madame Magloire who was grumbling to herself, that there was really no need even of a wooden spoon or fork to dip a piece of bread into a cup of milk.

Just as the brother and sister were rising from the table, there was a knock at the door.

"Come in," said the bishop.

The door opened. A strange, fierce group appeared on the threshold. Three men were holding a fourth by the collar. The three men were gendarmes; the fourth Jean Valjean.

A brigadier of gendarmes, who appeared to head the group, was near the door. He advanced toward the bishop, giving a military salute.

"Monseigneur—" said he.

At this word Jean Valjean, who was sullen and seemed entirely cast down, raised his head with a stupefied air.

"Monseigneur!" he murmured. "Then it is not the curé!"

"Silence!" said a gendarme. "It is monseigneur, the bishop."

In the meantime Monseigneur Bienvenu had approached as quickly as his great age permitted.

"Ah, there you are!" said he, looking toward Jean Valjean. "I am glad to see you. But I gave you the candlesticks also, which are silver like the rest, and would bring two hundred francs. Why did you not take them along with your plates?"

Jean Valjean opened his eyes and looked at the bishop with an expression which no human tongue could describe.

"Monseigneur," said the brigadier, "then what this man said was true? We met him. He was going like a man who was running away, and we arrested him in order to see. He had this silver."

"And he told you," interrupted the bishop, with a smile, "that it had been given him by a good old priest with whom he had passed the night. I see it all. And you brought him back here? It is all a mistake."

"If that is so," said the brigadier, "we can let him go."

"Certainly," replied the bishop.

The gendarmes released Jean Valjean, who shrank back.

"Is it true that they let me go?" he said in a voice almost inarticulate, as if he were speaking in his sleep.

"Yes! You can go. Do you not understand?" said a gendarme.

"My friend," said the bishop, "before you go away, here are your candlesticks; take them."

He went to the mantelpiece, took the two candlesticks, and brought them to Jean Valjean. The two women beheld the action without a word, or gesture, or look, that might disturb the bishop.

Jean Valjean was trembling in every limb. He took the two candlesticks mechanically, and with a wild appearance.

"Now," said the bishop, "go in peace."

Then turning to the gendarmes, he said:

"Messieurs, you can retire." The gendarmes withdrew. Jean Valjean felt like a man who is just about to faint.

The bishop approached him, and said, in a low voice:

"Forget not, never forget that you have promised me to use this silver to become an honest man."

Jean Valjean, who had no recollection of this promise, stood confounded. The bishop had laid much stress upon these words as he uttered them. He continued, solemnly:

"Jean Valjean, my brother, you belong no longer to evil, but to good. It is your soul that I am buying for you. I withdraw it from dark thoughts and from the spirit of perdition, and I give it to God!"

X

JEAN VALJEAN went out of the city as if he were escaping. He made all haste to get into the open country, taking the first lanes and bypaths that offered, without noticing that he was every moment retracing his steps. He wandered thus all the morning. He had eaten nothing, but he felt no hunger. He was the prey of a multitude of new sensations. He felt somewhat angry, he knew not against whom. He could not have told whether he were touched or humiliated. He saw, with disquietude, shaken within him that species of frightful calm which the injustice of his fate had given him. He asked himself what should replace it. Although the season was well advanced, there were yet here and there a few late flowers in the hedges, the odor of which, as it met him in his walk, recalled the memories of his childhood. These memories were almost insupportable, it was so long since they had occurred to him.

Unspeakable thoughts thus gathered in his mind the whole day.

As the sun was sinking toward the horizon, lengthening the shadow on the ground of the smallest pebble, Jean Valjean was seated behind a thicket in a large reddish plain, an absolute desert. There was no horizon but the Alps. Not even the steeple of a village church. Jean Valjean might have been three leagues from D——. A bypath which crossed the plain passed a few steps from the thicket.

In the midst of this meditation he heard a joyous sound.

He turned his head, and saw coming along the path a little Savoyard, a dozen years old, singing, with his hurdy-gurdy at his side, and his marmot box on his back.

One of those pleasant and gay youngsters who go from place to place, with their knees sticking through their trousers.

Always singing, the boy stopped from time to time, and played at tossing up some pieces of money that he had in his hand, probably his whole fortune. Among them there was one forty-sous piece.

The boy stopped by the side of the thicket without seeing Jean Valjean, and tossed up his handful of sous; until this time he had skillfully caught the whole of them upon the back of his hand.

This time the forty-sous piece escaped him, and rolled toward the thicket, near Jean Valjean.

Jean Valjean put his foot upon it.

The boy, however, had followed the piece with his eye, and had seen where it went.

He was not frightened, and walked straight to the man.

It was an entirely solitary place. Far as the eye could reach there was no one on the plain or in the path. Nothing could be heard but the faint cries of a flock of birds of passage, that were flying across the sky at an immense height. The child turned his back to the sun, which made his hair like threads of gold, and flushed the savage face of Jean Valjean with a lurid glow.

"Monsieur," said the little Savoyard, with that childish confidence which is made up of ignorance and innocence, "my piece?"

"What is your name?" said Jean Valjean.

"Petit Gervais, monsieur."

"Get out," said Jean Valjean.

"Monsieur," continued the boy, "give me my piece."

Jean Valjean dropped his head and did not answer.

The child began again:

"My piece, monsieur!"

Jean Valjean's eye remained fixed on the ground.

"My piece!" exclaimed the boy. "My white piece! My silver!"

Jean Valjean did not appear to understand. The boy took him by the collar of his blouse and shook him. And at the same time he made an effort to move the big, ironsoled shoe which was placed upon his treasure.

"I want my piece! My forty-sous piece!"

The child began to cry. Jean Valjean raised his head. He still kept his seat. His look was troubled. He looked upon the boy with an air of wonder, then reached out his hand toward his stick, and exclaimed in a terrible voice: "Who is there? Ah! you here yet!" And rising hastily to his feet, without releasing the piece of money, he added: "You'd better take care of yourself!"

The boy looked at him in terror, then began to tremble from head to foot, and after a few seconds of stupor, took to flight and ran with all his might without daring to turn his head or to utter a cry.

At a little distance, however, he stopped for want of breath, and Jean Valjean in his reverie heard him sobbing.

In a few minutes the boy was gone.

The sun had gone down.

The shadows were deepening around Jean Valjean. He had not eaten during the day; probably he had some fever.

He had remained standing, and had not changed his attitude since the child fled. His breathing was at long and unequal intervals. His eyes were fixed on a spot ten or twelve steps before him, and seemed to be studying with profound attention the form of an old piece of blue crockery that was lying in the grass. All at once he shivered; he began to feel the cold night air.

He pulled his cap down over his forehead, sought mechanically to fold and button his blouse around him, stepped forward and stooped to pick up his stick.

At that instant he perceived the forty-sous piece which his foot had half buried in the ground, and which glistened among the pebbles. It was like an electric shock. "What is that?" said he, between his teeth. He drew back a step or two, then stopped without the power to withdraw his gaze from this point which his foot had covered the instant before, as if the thing that glistened there in the obscurity had been an open eye fixed upon him.

After a few minutes, he sprang convulsively toward the piece of money, seized it, and, rising, looked away over the plain, straining his eyes toward all points of the horizon, standing and trembling like a frightened deer which is seeking a place of refuge.

He saw nothing. Night was falling, the plain was cold and bare, thick purple mists were rising in the glimmering twilight.

He said: "Oh!" and began to walk rapidly in the direction in which the child had gone. After some thirty steps, he stopped, looked about, and saw nothing.

Then he called with his might: "Petit Gervais! Petit Gervais!"

And then he listened.

There was no answer.

The country was desolate and gloomy. On all sides was space. There was nothing about him but a shadow in which his gaze was lost, and a silence in which his voice was lost.

A biting norther was blowing, which gave a kind of dismal life to everything about him. The bushes shook their little thin arms with an incredible fury. One would have said that they were threatening and pursuing somebody.

He began to walk again, then quickened his pace to a run, and from time to time stopped and called out in that solitude, in a most desolate and terrible voice:

"Petit Gervais! Petit Gervais!"

Surely, if the child had heard him, he would have been frightened, and would have hid himself. But doubtless the boy was already far away.

Jean Valjean began to run again in the direction which he had first taken.

He went on in this wise for a considerable distance, looking around, calling and shouting, but met nobody else. Two or three times he left the path to look at what seemed to be somebody lying down or crouching; it was only low bushes or rocks. Finally, at a place where three paths met, he stopped. The moon had risen. He strained his eyes in the distance, and called out once more: "Petit Gervais! Petit Gervais! Petit Gervais!" His cries died away into the mist, without even awakening an echo. Again he murmured: "Petit Gervais!" but with a feeble, and almost inarticulate voice. That was his last effort; his knees suddenly bent under him, as if an invisible power overwhelmed him at a blow, with the weight of his bad conscience; he fell exhausted upon a great stone, his hands clenched in his hair, and his face on his knees, and exclaimed: "What a wretch I am!"

Then his heart swelled, and he burst into tears. It was the first time he had wept in nineteen years.

Jean Valjean wept long. He shed hot tears, he wept bitterly, with more weakness than a woman, with more terror than a child.

While he wept, the light grew brighter and brighter in his mind—an extraordinary light, a light at once transporting and terrible. His past life, his first offense, his long expiation, his brutal exterior, his hardened interior, his release made glad by so many schemes of vengeance, what had happened to him at the bishop's, his last action, this theft of forty sous from a child, a crime meaner and the more monstrous that it came after the bishop's pardon, all this returned and appeared to him, clearly, but in a light that he had never seen before. He beheld his life, and it seemed to him horrible; his soul, and it seemed to him frightful. There was, however, a softened light upon that life and upon that soul. It seemed to him that he was looking upon Satan by the light of paradise.

How long did he weep thus? What did he do after weeping? Where did he go? Nobody ever knew. It is known simply that, on that very night, the stage driver who drove at that time on the Grenoble route, and arrived at D—— about three o'clock in the morning, saw, as he passed through the bishop's street, a man in the attitude of prayer, kneel upon the pavement in the shadow, before the door of Monseigneur Bienvenu.

To Entrust Is Sometimes
to Abandon

I

THERE was, during the first quarter of the present century, at Montfermeil, near Paris, a sort of chophouse; it is not there now. It was kept by a man and his wife, named Thénardier, and was situated in the Lane Boulanger. Above the door, nailed against the wall, was a board, upon which something was painted that looked like a man carrying on his back another man wearing the heavy epaulettes of a general, gilt and with large silver stars; red blotches typified blood; the remainder of the picture was smoke, and probably represented a battle. Beneath was this inscription: To THE SERGEANT OF WATERLOO.

Nothing is commoner than a cart or wagon before the door of an inn; nevertheless the vehicle, or more properly speaking, the fragment of a vehicle which obstructed the street in front of the Sergeant of Waterloo one evening in the spring of 1818, certainly would have attracted by its bulk the attention of any painter who might have been passing.

It was the forecarriage of one of those drays for carrying heavy articles, used in wooded countries for transporting joists and trunks of trees. Why was this vehicle in this place in the street, one may ask? First to obstruct the lane, and then to complete its work of rust. There is in the old social order a host of institutions which we find like this across our path in the full light of day, and which present no other reasons for being there.

The middle of the chain was hanging quite near the ground, under the axle, and upon the bend, as on a swinging rope, two little girls were seated that evening in exquisite grouping, the smaller, eighteen months old, in the lap of the larger, who was two-and-a-half years old.

A handkerchief carefully knotted kept them from falling. A mother, looking upon this frightful chain, had said: "Ah! There is a plaything for my children!"

The mother, a woman whose appearance was rather forbidding, but touching at this moment, was seated on the sill of the inn, swinging the two children by a long string, while she brooded them with her eyes for fear of accident with that animal but heavenly expression peculiar to maternity. At each vibration the hideous links uttered a creaking noise like an angry cry; the little ones were in ecstasies, the setting sun mingled in the joy, and nothing could be more charming than this caprice of chance which made of a titan's chain a swing for cherubim.

Suddenly the mother heard a voice say quite near her ear: "You have two pretty children there, madame."

A woman was before her at a little distance; she also had a child, which she bore in her arms.

She was carrying in addition a large carpetbag, which seemed heavy.

This woman's child was one of the divinest beings that can be imagined: a little girl of two or three years. She might have entered the lists with the other little ones for coquetry of attire; she wore a headdress of fine linen; ribbons at her shoulders and Valenciennes lace on her cap. The folds of her skirt were raised enough to show her plump fine white leg; she was charmingly rosy and healthful. The pretty little creature gave one a desire to bite her cherry cheeks. We can say nothing of her eyes except that they must have been very large, and were fringed with superb lashes. She was asleep.

She was sleeping in the absolutely confiding slumber peculiar to her age. A mother's arms are made of tenderness, and sweet sleep blesses the child who lies therein.

As to the mother, she seemed poor and sad; she had the appearance of a workingwoman who is seeking to return to the life of a peasant. She was young—and pretty? It was possible, but in that garb beauty could not be displayed. Her hair, one blond mesh of which had fallen, seemed very thick, but it was severely fastened up beneath an ugly, close, narrow nun's headdress, tied under the chin. Laughing shows fine teeth when one has them, but she did not laugh. Her eyes seemed not to have been tearless for a long time. She was pale, and looked very weary, and somewhat sick. She gazed upon her child, sleeping in her arms, with that peculiar look which only a mother possesses who nurses her own child. Her form was clumsily masked by a large blue handkerchief folded across her bosom. Her hands were tanned and spotted with freckles, the forefinger hardened and pricked with the needle; she wore a coarse brown delaine mantle, a calico dress, and large heavy shoes.

It was one of those beings which are brought forth from the heart of the people. Sprung from the most unfathomable depths of social darkness, she bore on her brow the mark of the anonymous and unknown. She was born at M—— sur m——. Who were her parents? None could tell; she had never known either father or mother. She was called Fantine—why so? Because she had never been known by any other name. She could have no family name, for she had no family; she could have no baptismal name, for then there was no church. She was named after the pleasure of the first passer-by who found her, a mere infant, straying barefoot in the streets. She received a name as she received the water from the clouds on her head when it rained. She was called Little Fantine. Nobody knew anything more of her. Such was the manner in which this human being had come into life. At the age of ten, Fantine left the city and went to service among the farmers of the suburbs. At fifteen, she came to Paris, to "seek her fortune." Fantine was beautiful and remained pure as long as she could. She was a pretty blonde with fine teeth. She had gold and pearls for her dowry; but the gold was on her head and the pearls in her mouth.

She worked to live; then, also to live, for the heart too has its hunger, she loved.

To him, it was an amour; to her a passion. The streets of the Latin Quarter, which swarm with students and grisettes, saw the beginning of this dream. In short, the eclogue took place, and the poor girl had a child.

The father of her child gone—alas, such partings are irrevocable—she found herself absolutely isolated, with the habit of labor lost, and the taste for pleasure acquired. She had committed a fault, but, in the depths of her nature, we know dwelt modesty and virtue. She had a vague feeling that she was on the eve of falling into distress, of slipping into the street. She must have courage; she had it, and bore up bravely. The idea occurred to her of returning to her native village M——— sur m———; there perhaps someone would know her, and give her work. Yes, but she must hide her fault. And she had a confused glimpse of the possible necessity of a separation still more painful than the first. Her heart ached, but she took her resolution. It will be seen that Fantine possessed the stern courage of life. At twenty-two years of age, on a fine spring morning, she left Paris, carrying her child on her back. He who had seen the two passing must have pitied them. The woman had nothing in the world but this child, and this child had nothing in the world but this woman. Fantine had nursed her child—that had weakened her chest somewhat—and she coughed slightly.

Toward noon, after having, for the sake of rest, traveled from time to time at a cost of three or four cents a league, in what they called then the Petites Voitures of the environs of Paris, Fantine reached Montfermeil, and stood in the Lane Boulanger.

As she was passing by the Thénardier chophouse, the two little children sitting in delight on their monstrous swing had a sort of dazzling effect upon her, and she paused before this joyous vision.

There are charms. These two little girls were one for this mother.

She beheld them with emotion. The presence of angels is a herald of paradise. She thought she saw about this inn the mysterious HERE of Providence. These children were evidently happy; she gazed upon them, she admired them, so much affected that at the moment when the mother was taking breath between the verses of her song, she could not help saying what we have been reading.

"You have two pretty children there, madame."

The most ferocious animals are disarmed by caresses to their young.

The mother raised her head and thanked her, and made the stranger sit down on the stone step, she herself being on the doorsill; the two women began to talk together.

"My name is Madame Thénardier," said the mother of the two girls. "We keep this inn."

This Madame Thénardier was a red-haired, browny, angular woman, of the soldier's-wife type in all its horror, and, singularly enough, she had a lolling air which she had gained from novel-reading. She was a masculine lackadaisicalness. Old romances impressed on the imaginations of mistresses of chop-houses have such effects. She was still young, scarcely thirty years old. If this woman, who was seated stooping, had been upright, perhaps her towering form and her broad shoulders, those of a movable colossus, fit for a market woman, would have dismayed the traveler, disturbed her confidence, and prevented what we have to relate. A person seated instead of standing—fate hangs on such a thread as that.

The traveler told her story, a little modified.

She said she was a workingwoman, and her husband was dead. Not being able to procure work in Paris she was going in search of it elsewhere, in her own province; that she had left Paris that morning on foot; that carrying her child she had become tired, and meeting the Villemomble stage had got in; that from Villemomble she had come on foot to Montfermeil; that the child had walked a little, but not much, she was so young; that she was compelled to carry her, and the jewel had fallen asleep.

And at these words she gave her daughter a passionate kiss, which wakened her. The child opened its large blue eyes, like its mother's, and saw—what? Nothing, everything, with that serious and sometimes severe air of little children, which is one of the mysteries of their shining innocence before our shadowy virtues. One would say that they felt themselves to be angels, and knew us to be human. Then the child began to laugh, and, although the mother restrained her, slipped to the ground, with the indomitable energy of a little one that wants to run about. All at once she perceived the two others in their swing, stopped short, and put out her tongue in token of admiration.

Mother Thénardier untied the children and took them from the swing saying:

"Play together, all three of you."

At that age acquaintance is easy, and in a moment the little Thénardiers were playing with the newcomer, making holes in the ground to their intense delight.

This newcomer was very sprightly: the goodness of the mother is written in the gaiety of the child; she had taken a splinter of wood, which she used as a spade, and was stoutly digging a hole fit for a fly. The gravedigger's work is charming when done by a child.

The two women continued to chat.

"What do your call your brat?"

"Cosette."

"How old is she?"

"She is going on three years."

"The age of my oldest."

The three girls were grouped in an attitude of deep anxiety and bliss; a great event had occurred: a large worm had come out of the ground; they were afraid of it, and yet in ecstasies over it.

Their bright foreheads touched each other—three heads in one halo of glory.

"Children," exclaimed the Thénardier mother. "How soon they know one another. See them! One would swear they were three sisters."

These words were the spark which the other mother was probably awaiting. She seized the hand of Madame Thénardier and said:

"Will you keep my child for me?"

"I must think over it," said Thénardier.

"I will give six francs a month."

Here a man's voice was heard from within:

"Not less than seven francs, and six months paid in advance."

"Six times seven are forty-two," said Thénardier.

"I will give it," said the mother.

"And fifteen francs extra for the first expenses," added the man.

"That's fifty-seven francs," said Madame Thénardier.

"I will give it," said the mother. "I have eighty francs. That will leave me enough to go into the country if I walk. I will earn some money there, and as soon as I have I will come for my little love."

The man's voice returned:

"Has the child a wardrobe?"

"That is my husband," said Thénardier.

"Certainly she has, the poor darling. I knew it was your husband. And a fine wardrobe it is too, an extravagant wardrobe, everything in dozens, and silk dresses like a lady. They are there in my carpetbag."

"You must leave that here," put in the man's voice.

"Of course I shall give it to you," said the mother. "It would be strange if I should leave my child naked."

The face of the master appeared.

"It is all right," said he.

The bargain was concluded. The mother passed the night at the inn, gave her money and left her child, fastened again her carpetbag, diminished by her child's wardrobe, and very light now, and set off next morning, expecting soon to return. These partings are arranged tranquilly, but they are full of despair.

A neighbor of the Thénardiers met this mother on her way, and came in, saying:

"I have just met a woman in the street, who was crying as if her heart would break."

When Cosette's mother had gone, the man said to his wife:

"That will do me for my note of 110 francs which falls due tomorrow; I was 50 francs short. Do you know I should have had a sheriff and a protest? You have proved a good mouse-trap with your little ones."

"Without knowing it," said the woman.

The captured mouse was a very puny one, but the cat exulted even over a lean mouse.

What were the Thénardiers?

They belonged to that bastard class formed of low people who have risen, and intelligent people who have fallen, which lies between the classes called middle and lower, and which unites some of the faults of the latter with nearly all the vices of the former, without possessing the generous impulses of the workman, or the respectability of the bourgeois.

They were of those dwarfish natures, which, if perchance heated by some sullen fire, easily become monstrous. The woman was at heart a brute; the man a blackguard: both in the highest degree capable of that hideous species of progress which can be made toward evil. There are souls which, crab-like, crawl continually toward darkness, going back in life rather than advancing in it, using what experience they have to increase their deformity, growing worse without ceasing, and becoming steeped more and more thoroughly in an intensifying wickedness. Such souls were this man and this woman.

To be wicked does not insure prosperity—for the inn did not succeed well.

Thanks to Fantine's fifty-seven francs, Thénardier had been able to avoid a protest and to honor his signature. The next month they were still in need of money, and the woman carried Cosette's wardrobe to Paris and pawned it for sixty francs. When this sum was spent, the Thénardiers began to look upon the little girl as a child which they sheltered for charity, and treated her as such. Her clothes being gone, they dressed her in the castoff garments of the little Thénardiers, that is in rags. They fed her on the orts and ends, a little better than the dog, and a little worse than the cat. The dog and cat were her messmates. Cosette ate with them under the table in a wooden dish like theirs.

Her mother, as we shall see hereafter, who had found a place at M—— sur m——, wrote, or rather had someone write for her, every month, inquiring news of her child. The Thénardiers replied invariably:

"Cosette is doing wonderfully well."

There are certain natures which cannot have love on one side without hatred on the other. This Thénardier mother passionately loved her own little ones—this made her detest the young stranger. Cosette could not stir that she did not draw down upon herself a hailstorm of undeserved and severe chastisements. A weak, soft little one who knew nothing of this world, or of God, continually ill-treated, scolded, punished, beaten, she saw beside her two other young things like herself, who lived in a halo of glory!

The woman was unkind to Cosette; Eponine and Azelma were unkind also. Children at that age are only copies of the mother; the size is reduced, that is all.

A year passed and then another.

People used to say in the village:

"What good people these Thénardiers are! They are not rich, and yet they bring up a poor child that has been left with them."

They thought Cosette was forgotten by her mother.

From year to year the child grew, and her misery also.

So long as Cosette was very small, she was the scapegoat of the two other children; as soon as she began to grow a little, that is to say, before she was five years old, she became the servant of the house.

Cosette was made to run errands, sweep the rooms, the yard, the street, wash the dishes, and even carry burdens. The Thénardiers felt doubly authorized to treat her thus, as the mother, who still remained at M—— sur m——, began to be remiss in her payments. Some months remained due.

Had this mother returned to Montfermeil, at the end of these three years, she would not have known her child, Cosette, so fresh and pretty when she came to that house, now thin and wan. She had a peculiar restless air. "Sly!" said the Thénardiers.

Injustice had made her sullen, and misery had made her ugly. Her fine eyes only remained to her, and they were painful to look at, for, large as they were, they seemed to increase the sadness.

It was a harrowing sight to see in the wintertime the poor child, not yet six years old, shivering under the tatters of what was once a calico dress, sweeping the street before daylight with an enormous broom in her little red hands and tears in her large eyes.

In the place she was called the Lark. People like figurative names and were pleased thus to name this little being, not larger than a bird, trembling, frightened, and shivering, awake every morning first of all in the house and the village, always in the street or in the fields before dawn.

Only the poor lark never sang.

The Descent

I

WHAT had become of this mother, in the meanwhile, who, according to the people of Montfermeil, seemed to have abandoned her child? Where was she? What was she doing?

After leaving her little Cosette with the Thénardiers, she went on her way and arrived at M—— sur m——.

This, it will be remembered, was in 1818.

Fantine had left the province some twelve years before, and M—— sur m—— had greatly changed in appearance. While Fantine had been slowly sinking deeper and deeper into misery, her native village had been prosperous.

Within about two years there had been accomplished there one of those industrial changes which are the great events of small communities.

From time immemorial the special occupation of the inhabitants of M—— sur m—— had been the imitation of English jets and German black-glass trinkets. The business had always been dull in consequence of the high price of the raw material, which reacted upon the manufacture. At the time of Fantine's return to M—— sur m—— an entire transformation had been effected in the production of these "black goods." Toward the end of the year 1815, an unknown man had established himself in the city, and had conceived the idea of substituting gum-lac for resin in the manufacture, and for bracelets, in particular, he made the clasps by simply bending the ends of the metal together instead of soldering them.

This very slight change had worked a revolution.

In less than three years the inventor of this process had become rich, which was well, and had made all around him rich, which was better. He was a stranger in the Department. Nothing was known of his birth, and but little of his early history.

The story went that he came to the city with very little money, a few hundred francs at most.

From this slender capital, under the inspiration of an ingenious idea, made fruitful by order and care, he had drawn a fortune for himself, and a fortune for the whole region.

On his arrival at M—— sur m—— he had the dress, the manners, and the language of a laborer only.

It seems that the very day on which he thus obscurely entered the little city of M—— sur m——, just at dusk on a December evening, with his bundle on his back, and a thorn stick in his hand, a great fire had broken out in the townhouse. This man rushed into the fire, and saved, at the peril of his life, two children, who proved to be those of the captain of the *gendarmerie*, and in the hurry and gratitude of the moment no one thought to ask him for his passport. He was known from that time by the name of Father Madeleine.

II

HE was a man of about fifty, who always appeared to be preoccupied in mind, and who was good-natured; this was all that could be said about him.

Thanks to the rapid progress of this manufacture, to which he had given such wonderful life, M—— sur m—— had become a considerable center of business. Immense purchases were made there every year for the Spanish markets, where there is a large demand for jet work, and M—— sur m——, in this branch of trade, almost competed with London and Berlin. The profits of Father Madeleine were so great that by the end of the second year he was able to build a large factory, in which there were two immense workshops, one for men and the other for women; whoever was needy could go there and be sure of finding work and wages. Before the arrival of Father Madeleine, the whole region was languishing; now it was all alive with the healthy strength of labor. An active circulation kindled everything and penetrated everywhere. Idleness and misery were unknown. There was no pocket so obscure that it did not contain some money and no dwelling so poor that it was not the abode of some joy.

Father Madeleine employed everybody; he had only one condition: "Be an honest man!" "Be an honest woman!"

As we have said, in the midst of this activity, of which he was the cause and the pivot, Father Madeleine had made his fortune, but, very strangely for a mere man of business, that did not appear to be his principal care. It seemed that he thought much for others, and little for himself. In 1820, it was known that he had six hundred and thirty thousand francs standing to his credit in the banking house of Laffitte, but before setting aside this six hundred and thirty thousand francs for himself, he had expended more than a million for the city and for the poor.

The hospital was poorly endowed, and he made provision for ten additional beds. M—— sur m—— is divided into the upper city and the lower city. The lower city, where he lived, had only one schoolhouse, a miserable hovel which was fast going to ruin; he built two, one for girls, and the other for boys, and paid the two teachers, from his own pocket, double the amount of their meager salary from the government, and one day, he said to a neighbor who expressed surprise at this: "The two highest functionaries of the state are the nurse and the schoolmaster." He built, at his own expense, a house of refuge, an institution then almost unknown in France, and provided a fund for old and infirm laborers. About his factory, as a center, a new quarter of the city had rapidly grown up, containing many indigent families, and he established a pharmacy that was free to all.

At length, in 1819, it was reported in the city one morning, that upon the recommendation of the prefect, and in consideration of the services he had rendered to the country, Father Madeleine had been appointed by the king, Mayor of M—— sur m——.

M—— sur m—— was filled with the rumor, and the report proved to be well founded, for a few days afterward, the nomination appeared in the *Moniteur*. The next day Father Madeleine declined.

In 1820, five years after his arrival at M—— sur m——, the services that he had rendered to the region were so brilliant, and the wish of the whole population was so unanimous, that the king again appointed him mayor of the city. He refused again; but the prefect resisted his determination, the principal citizens came and urged him to accept, and the people in the streets begged him to do so; all insisted so strongly that at last he yielded. It was remarked that what appeared most of all to bring him to this determination was the almost angry exclamation of an old woman belonging to the poorer class, who cried out to him from her doorstone, with some temper:

"A good mayor is a good thing. Are you afraid of the good you can do?"

III

LITTLE by little in the lapse of time all opposition had ceased. At first there had been, as always happens with those who rise by their own efforts, slanders and calumnies against Monsieur Madeleine; soon this was reduced to satire, then it was only wit, then it vanished entirely; respect became complete, unanimous, cordial, and there came a moment, about 1821, when the words Monsieur the Mayor were pronounced at M—— sur m—— with almost the same accent as the words Monseigneur the Bishop at D—— in 1815. People came from thirty miles around to consult Monsieur Madeleine. He settled differences, he prevented lawsuits, he reconciled enemies. Everybody, of his own will, chose him for judge. He seemed to have the book of the natural law by heart. A contagion of veneration had, in the course of six or seven years, step by step, spread over the whole country.

One man alone, in the city and its neighborhood, held himself entirely clear from this contagion, and, whatever Father Madeleine did, he remained indifferent, as if a sort of instinct, unchangeable and imperturbable, kept him awake and on the watch.

Often, when Monsieur Madeleine passed along the street, calm, affectionate, followed by the benedictions of all, it happened that a tall man, wearing a flat hat and an iron gray coat, and armed with a stout cane, would turn around abruptly behind him, and follow him with his eyes until he disappeared, crossing his arms, slowly shaking his head, and pushing his upper with his under lip up to his nose, a sort of significant grimace which might be rendered by: "But what is that man? I am sure I have seen him somewhere. At all events, I at least am not his dupe."

This personage, grave with an almost threatening gravity, was one of those who, even in a hurried interview, command the attention of the observer.

His name was Javert, and he was one of the police.

He exercised at M—— sur m—— the unpleasant, but useful, function of inspector. He was not there at the date of Madeleine's arrival.

Certain police officers have a peculiar physiognomy in which can be traced an air of meanness mingled with an air of authority. Javert had this physiognomy, without meanness.

He was born in a prison. His mother was a fortuneteller whose husband was in the galleys. He grew up to think himself without the pale of society, and despaired of ever entering it. He noticed that society closes its doors, without pity, on two classes of men: those who attack it and those who guard it; he could choose between these two classes only; at the same time he felt that he had an indescribable basis of rectitude, order, and honesty, associated with an irrepressible hatred for that gypsy race to which he belonged. He entered the police. He succeeded. At forty he was an inspector.

In his youth he had been stationed in the galleys at the South.

The face of Javert consisted of a snub nose, with two deep nostrils, which were bordered by large bushy whiskers that covered both his cheeks. One felt ill at ease the first time he saw those two forests and those two caverns. When Javert laughed, which was rarely and terribly, his thin lips parted, and showed, not only his teeth, but his gums, and around his nose there was a wrinkle as broad and wild as the muzzle of a fallow deer. Javert, when serious, was a bulldog; when he laughed, he was a tiger. For the rest, a small head, large jaws, hair hiding the forehead and falling over the eyebrows, between the eyes a permanent central frown, a gloomy look, a mouth pinched and frightful, and an air of fierce command.

This man was a compound of two sentiments, very simple and very good in themselves, but he almost made them evil by his exaggeration of them: respect for authority and hatred of rebellion; in his eyes, theft, murder, all crimes, were only forms of rebellion. In his strong and implicit faith he included all who held any function in the state, from the prime minister to the constable. He had nothing but disdain, aversion, and disgust for all who had once overstepped the bounds of the law. He was absolute, and admitted no exceptions. On the one hand he said: "A public officer cannot be deceived; a magistrate never does wrong!" And on the other he said: "They are irremediably lost; no good can come out of them." He shared fully the opinion of those extremists who attribute to human laws an indescribable power of making, or, if you will, of determining, demons, and who place a Styx at the bottom of society. He was stoical, serious, austere: a dreamer of stern dreams; humble and haughty, like all fanatics. His stare was cold and as piercing as a gimlet. His whole life was contained in these two words: waking and watching. He marked out a straight path through the most tortuous thing in the world; his conscience was bound up in his utility, his religion in his duties, and he was a spy as others are priests. Woe to him who should fall into his hands! He would have arrested his father if escaping from the galleys, and denounced his mother for violating her ticket of leave. And he would have done it with that sort of interior satisfaction that springs from virtue. His life was a life of privations, isolation, self-denial, and chastity: never any amusement. It was implacable duty, absorbed in the police as the Spartans were absorbed in Sparta, a pitiless detective, a fierce honesty, a marblehearted informer, Brutus united with Vidocq.

Such was this formidable man.

Javert was like an eye always fixed on Monsieur Madeleine, an eye full of suspicion and conjecture. Monsieur Madeleine finally noticed it, but seemed to consider it of no consequence. He asked no question of Javert, he neither sought him nor shunned him, he endured this unpleasant and annoying stare without appearing to pay any attention to it. He treated Javert as he did everybody else, at ease and with kindness.

Javert was evidently somewhat disconcerted by the completely natural air and the tranquillity of Monsieur Madeleine.

One day, however, his strange manner appeared to make an impression upon Monsieur Madeleine. The occasion was this:

IV

MONSIEUR MADELEINE was walking one morning along one of the unpaved alleys of M—— sur m——; he heard a shouting and saw a crowd at a little distance. He went to the spot. An old man, named Father Fauchelevent, had fallen under his cart, his horse being thrown down.

The horse had his thighs broken, and could not stir. The old man was caught between the wheels. Unluckily he had fallen so that the whole weight rested upon his breast. The cart was heavily loaded. Father Fauchelevent was uttering doleful groans. They had tried to pull him out, but in vain. An unlucky effort, inexpert help, a false push, might crush him. It was impossible to extricate him otherwise than by raising the wagon from beneath. Javert, who came up at the moment of the accident, had sent for a jack.

Monsieur Madeleine came. The crowd fell back with respect.

"Help," cried out Fauchelevent. "Who is a good fellow to save an old man?"

Monsieur Madeleine turned toward the bystanders.

"Has anybody a jack?"

"They have gone for one," replied a peasant.

"How soon will it be here?"

"We sent to the nearest place, to Flachot Place, where there is a blacksmith, but it will take a good quarter of an hour at least."

"A quarter of an hour!" exclaimed Madeleine.

It had rained the night before, the road was soft, tho cart was sinking deeper every moment, and pressing more and more on the breast of the old carman. It was evident that in less than five minutes his ribs would be crushed.

"We cannot wait a quarter of an hour," said Madeleine to the peasants who were looking on.

"We must!"

"But it will be too late! Don't you see that the wagon is sinking all the while?"

"It can't be helped."

"Listen," resumed Madeleine, "there is room enough still under the wagon for a man to crawl in, and lift it with his back. In half a minute we will have the poor man out. Is there nobody here who has strength and courage? Five louis d'ors for him!"

Nobody stirred in the crowd.

"Ten louis," said Madeleine.

The bystanders dropped their eyes. One of them muttered:

"He'd have to be devilish stout. And then he would risk getting crushed."

"Come," said Madeleine, "twenty louis."

The same silence.

"It is not willingness which they lack," said a voice.

Monsieur Madeleine turned and saw Javert. He had not noticed him when he came.

Javert continued:

"It is strength. He must be a terrible man who can raise a wagon like that on his back."

Then, looking fixedly at Monsieur Madeleine, he went on, emphasizing every word that he uttered:

"Monsieur Madeleine, I have known but one man capable of doing what you call for."

Madeleine shuddered.

Javert added, with an air of indifference, but without taking his eyes from Madeleine:

"He was a convict."

"Ah!" said Madeleine.

"In the galleys at Toulon."

Madeleine became pale.

"Oh! How it crushes me!" cried the old man.

Madeleine raised his head, met the falcon eye of Javert still fixed upon him, looked at the immovable peasants, and smiled sadly. Then, without saying a word, he fell on his knees, and even before the crowd had time to utter a cry, he was under the cart.

There was an awful moment of suspense and of silence.

Madeleine, lying almost flat under the fearful weight, was twice seen to try in vain to bring his elbows and knees nearer together. They cried out to him: "Father Madeleine! Come out from there!" Old Fauchelevent himself said: "Monsieur Madeleine! Go away! I must die, you see that; leave me! You will be crushed too." Madeleine made no answer.

The bystanders held their breath. The wheels were still sinking and it had now become almost impossible for Madeleine to extricate himself.

All at once the enormous mass started, the cart rose slowly, the wheels came half out of the ruts. A smothered voice was heard, crying: "Quick! Help!" It was Madeleine, who had just made a final effort.

They all rushed to the work. The devotion of one man had

given strength and courage to all. The cart was lifted by twenty arms. Old Fauchelevent was safe.

Madeleine arose. He was very pale, though dripping with sweat. His clothes were torn and covered with mud. All wept. The old man kissed his knees and called him the good God. He himself wore on his face an indescribable expression of joyous and celestial suffering, and he looked with tranquil eye upon Javert, who was still watching him.

Fauchelevent got well, but he had a stiff knee. Monsieur Madeleine, through the recommendations of the sisters and the curé, got the old man a place as gardener at a convent in the Quartier Saint Antoine at Paris.

V

SUCH was the situation of the country when Fantine returned. No one remembered her. Luckily the door of Monsieur Madeleine's factory was like the face of a friend. She presented herself there, and was admitted into the workshop for women. The business was entirely new to Fantine; she could not be very expert in it, and consequently did not receive much for her day's work, but that little was enough; the problem was solved; she was earning her living.

When Fantine realized how she was living, she had a moment of joy. To live honestly by her own labor, what a heavenly boon! The taste for labor returned to her, in truth. She bought a mirror, delighted herself with the sight of her youth, her fine hair, and her fine teeth, forgot many things, thought of nothing save Cosette and the possibilities of the future, and was almost happy. She hired a small room and furnished it on the credit of her future labor: a remnant of her habits of disorder.

Not being able to say that she was married, she took good care, as we have already intimated, not to speak of her little girl.

At first, as we have seen, she paid the Thénardiers punctually. As she only knew how to sign her name she was obliged to write through a public letter writer.

She wrote often; that was noticed. They began to whisper in the women's workshop that Fantine "wrote letters," and that "she had airs."

So Fantine was watched.

Beyond this, more than one was jealous of her fair hair and of her white teeth.

It was ascertained that she wrote, at least twice a month, and always to the same address, and that she prepaid the postage. They succeeded in learning the address: _Monsieur Thénardier, Innkeeper, Montfermeil._ The public letter writer, a simple old fellow, who could not fill his stomach with red wine without emptying his pocket of his secrets, was made to reveal this at a drinking house. In short, it became known that Fantine had a child. "She must be that sort of a woman." And there was one old gossip who went to Montfermeil, talked with the Thénardiers, and said on her return: "For my thirty-five francs, I have found out all about it. I have seen the child!"

All this took time; Fantine had been more than a year at the factory, when one morning the overseer of the workshop handed her, on behalf of the mayor, fifty francs, saying that she was no longer wanted in the shop, and enjoining her, on behalf of the mayor, to leave the city.

Fantine was thunderstruck. She could not leave the city; she was in debt for her lodging and her furniture. Fifty francs were not enough to clear off that debt. She faltered out some suppliant words. The overseer gave her to understand that she must leave the shop instantly. Fantine was moreover only a moderate worker. Overwhelmed with shame even more than with despair, she left the shop, and returned to her room. Her fault then was now known to all!

She felt no strength to say a word. She was advised to see the mayor; she dared not. The mayor gave her fifty francs, because he was kind, and sent her away, because he was just. She bowed to that decree.

VI

MONSIEUR MADELEINE had known nothing of all this. The best men are often compelled to delegate their authority. It was in the exercise of this full power, and with the conviction that she was doing right, that the overseer had framed the indictment, tried, condemned, and executed Fantine.

Fantine offered herself as a servant in the neighborhood;

she went from one house to another. Nobody wanted her. She could not leave the city. The secondhand dealer to whom she was in debt for her furniture—and such furniture!—had said to her: "If you go away, I will have you arrested as a thief." The landlord, whom she owed for rent, had said to her: "You are young and pretty, you can pay." She divided the fifty francs between the landlord and the dealer, returned to the latter three-quarters of his goods, kept only what was necessary, and found herself without work, without position, having nothing but her bed, and owing still about a hundred francs.

She began to make coarse shirts for the soldiers of the garrison, and earned twelve sous a day. Her daughter cost her ten. It was at this time that she began to get behindhand with the Thénardiers.

However, an old woman, who lit her candle for her when she came home at night, taught her the art of living in misery. Behind living on a little lies the art of living on nothing. They are two rooms: the first is obscure; the second is utterly dark.

Fantine learned how to do entirely without fire in winter, how to give up a bird that eats a farthing's worth of millet every other day, how to make a coverlid of her petticoat, and a petticoat of her coverlid, how to save her candle in taking her meals by the light of an opposite window. Few know how much certain feeble beings, who have grown old in privation and honesty, can extract from a sou. This finally becomes a talent. Fantine acquired this sublime talent and took heart a little.

The old woman, who had given her what might be called lessons in indigent life, was a pious woman, Marguerite by name, a devotee of genuine devotion, poor, and charitable to the poor, and also to the rich, knowing how to write just enough to sign MARGERITTE, and believing in God, which is science.

There are many of these virtues in low places; someday they will be on high. This life has a morrow.

At first, Fantine was so much ashamed that she did not dare to go out.

When she was in the street, she imagined that people turned behind her and pointed at her; everybody looked at her and no one greeted her; the sharp and cold disdain of the passers-by penetrated her, body and soul, like a north wind.

She must indeed become accustomed to disrespect as she had to poverty. Little by little she learned her part. After two or three months she shook off her shame and went out as if there were nothing in the way. "It is all one to me," said she.

She went and came, holding her head up and wearing a bitter smile, and felt that she was becoming shameless.

Excessive work fatigued Fantine, and the slight dry cough that she had increased. She sometimes said to her neighbor, Marguerite: "Just feel how hot my hands are."

In the morning, however, when with an old broken comb she combed her fine hair which flowed down in silky waves, she enjoyed a moment of happiness.

VII

SHE had been discharged toward the end of winter; summer passed away, but winter returned. Short days, less work. In winter there is no heat, no light, no noon, evening touches morning, there is fog, and mist, the window is frosted, and you cannot see clearly. The sky is but the mouth of a cave. The whole day is the cave. The sun has the appearance of a pauper. Frightful season! Winter changes into stone the water of heaven and the heart of man. Her creditors harassed her.

Fantine earned too little. Her debts had increased. The Thénardiers, being poorly paid, were constantly writing letters to her, the contents of which disheartened her, while the postage was ruining her. One day they wrote to her that her little Cosette was entirely destitute of clothing for the cold weather, that she needed a woolen skirt, and that her mother must send at least ten francs for that. She received the letter and crushed it in her hand for a whole day. In the evening she went into a barber's shop at the corner of the street, and pulled out her comb. Her beautiful fair hair fell below her waist.

"What beautiful hair!" exclaimed the barber.

"How much will you give me for it?" said she.

"Ten francs."

"Cut it off."

She bought a knit skirt and sent it to the Thénardiers.

This skirt made the Thénardiers furious. It was the money

that they wanted. They gave the skirt to Eponine. The poor
lark still shivered.

Fantine thought: "My child is no longer cold; I have clothed
her with my hair." She put on a little round cap which concealed her shorn head, and with that she was still pretty.

A gloomy work was going on in Fantine's heart.

When she saw that she could no longer dress her hair, she
began to look with hatred on all around her. She had long
shared in the universal veneration for Father Madeleine;
nevertheless by dint of repeating to herself that it was he who
had turned her away, and that he was the cause of her misfortunes, she came to hate him also, and especially. When she
passed the factory at the hours in which the laborers were at
the door, she forced herself to laugh and sing.

An old workingwoman who saw her once singing and
laughing in this way said: "There is a girl who will come
to a bad end."

She took a lover, the first comer, a man whom she did not
love, through bravado, and with rage in her heart. He was a
wretch, a kind of mendicant musician, a lazy ragamuffin, who
beat her, and who left her, as she had taken him, with disgust.

She worshiped her child.

The lower she sank, the more all became gloomy around
her, the more the sweet little angel shone out in the bottom of
her heart. She would say: "When I am rich, I shall have my
Cosette with me," and she laughed. The cough did not leave
her, and she had night sweats.

One day she received from the Thénardiers a letter in these
words: "Cosette is sick of an epidemic disease. A miliary fever
they call it. The drugs necessary are dear. It is ruining us, and
we can no longer pay for them. Unless you send us forty francs
within a week the little one will die."

She burst out laughing, and said to her old neighbor:

"Oh! They are nice! Forty francs! Think of that! That is
two Napoleons! Where do they think I can get them? Are
they fools, these boors?"

She went, however, to the staircase, near a dormer window,
and read the letter again.

Then she went downstairs and outdoors, running and jump-
ing, still laughing.

As she passed through the square, she saw many people

gathered about an odd-looking carriage on the top of which stood a man in red clothes, declaiming. He was a juggler and a traveling dentist, and was offering to the public complete sets of teeth, opiates, powders, and elixirs.

Fantine joined the crowd and began to laugh with the rest at this harangue, in which were mingled slang for the rabble and jargon for the better sort. The puller of teeth saw this beautiful girl laughing, and suddenly called out: "You have pretty teeth, you girl who are laughing there. If you will sell me your two incisors, I will give you a gold Napoleon for each of them."

"What is that? What are my incisors?" asked Fantine.

"The incisors," resumed the professor of dentistry, "are the front teeth, the two upper ones."

"How horrible!" cried Fantine.

"Two Napoleons!" grumbled a toothless old hag who stood by. "How lucky she is!"

Fantine fled away and stopped her ears not to hear the shrill voice of the man who called after her: "Consider, my beauty! Two Napoleons! How much good they will do you! If you have the courage for it, come this evening to the inn of the *Tillac d' Argent*; you will find me there."

Fantine returned home; she was raving, and told the story to her good neighbor Marguerite.

"And what was it he offered you?" asked Marguerite.

"Two Napoleons."

"That is forty francs."

"Yes," said Fantine, "that makes forty francs."

She became thoughtful and went about her work. In a quarter of an hour she left her sewing and went to the stairs to read again the Thénardiers' letter.

On her return she said to Marguerite, who was at work near her:

"What does this mean, a miliary fever? Do you know?"

"Yes," answered the old woman, "it is a disease."

"Does it attack children?"

"Children especially."

"Do people die of it?"

"Very often," said Marguerite.

Fantine withdrew and went once more to read over the letter on the stairs.

In the evening she went out, and took the direction of the rue de Paris where the inns are.

The next morning, when Marguerite went into Fantine's chamber before daybreak, for they always worked together, and so made one candle do for the two, she found Fantine seated upon her couch, pale and icy. She had not been in bed. Her cap had fallen upon her knees. The candle had burned all night, and was almost consumed.

Marguerite stopped upon the threshold, petrified by this wild disorder, and exclaimed: "Good Lord! The candle is all burned out. Something has happened."

Then she looked at Fantine, who sadly turned her shorn head.

Fantine had grown ten years older since evening.

"Bless us!" said Marguerite. "What is the matter with you, Fantine?"

"Nothing," said Fantine. "Quite the contrary. My child will not die with that frightful sickness for lack of aid. I am satisfied."

So saying, she showed the old woman two Napoleons that glistened on the table.

"Oh! Good God!" said Marguerite. "Why there is a fortune! Where did you get these louis d'or?"

"I got them," answered Fantine.

At the same time she smiled. The candle lit up her face. It was a sickening smile, for the corners of her mouth were stained with blood, and a dark cavity revealed itself there.

The two teeth were gone.

She sent the forty francs to Montfermeil.

And this was a ruse of the Thénardiers to get money. Cosette was not sick.

Fantine threw her looking glass out of the window. Long before, she had left her little room on the second story for an attic room with no other fastening than a latch, one of those garret rooms the ceiling of which makes an angle with the floor and hits your head at every moment. The poor cannot go to the end of their chamber or to the end of their destiny, but by bending continually more and more. Her creditors were more pitiless than ever. The secondhand dealer, who had taken back nearly all his furniture, was constantly saying to her: "When will you pay me, wench?"

Good God! What did they want her to do? She felt herself

hunted down, and something of the wild beast began to develop within her. About the same time, Thénardier wrote to her that really he had waited with too much generosity, and that he must have a hundred francs immediately, or else little Cosette, just convalescing after her severe sickness, would be turned outdoors into the cold and upon the highway, and that she would become what she could, and would perish if she must. "A hundred francs," thought Fantine. "But where is there a place where one can earn a hundred sous a day?"

"Come!" said she, "I will sell what is left."

The unfortunate creature became a woman of the town.

VIII

WHAT is this history of Fantine? It is society buying a slave.

From whom? From misery.

From hunger, from cold, from loneliness, from abandonment, from privation. Melancholy barter. A soul for a bit of bread. Misery makes the offer, society accepts.

The holy law of Jesus Christ governs our civilization, but it does not yet permeate it; it is said that slavery has disappeared from European civilization. This is a mistake. It still exists, but it weighs now only upon woman, and it is called prostitution.

It weighs upon woman, that is to say, upon grace, upon feebleness, upon beauty, upon maternity. This is not one of the least of man's shames.

At the stage of this mournful drama at which we have now arrived, Fantine has nothing left of what she had formerly been. She has become marble in becoming corrupted. Whoever touches her feels a chill. She goes her ways, she endures you, and she knows you not; she wears a dishonored and severe face. Life and social order have spoken their last word to her. All that can happen to her has happened. She has endured all, borne all, experienced all, suffered all, lost all, wept for all. She is resigned, with that resignation that resembles indifference as death resembles sleep. She shuns nothing now. She fears nothing now. Every cloud falls upon her, and all the ocean sweeps over her! What matters it to her! The sponge is already drenched.

She believed so at least, but it is a mistake to imagine that man can exhaust his destiny, or can reach the bottom of anything whatever.

Alas! What are all these destinies thus driven pell-mell? Whither go they? Why are they so?

He who knows that, sees all the shadow.

He is alone. His name is God.

IX

THERE is in all small cities, and there was at M—— sur m—— in particular, a set of young men who nibble their fifteen hundred livres of income in the country with the same air with which their fellows devour two hundred thousand francs a year at Paris. They are beings of the great neuter species: geldings, parasites, nobodies, who have a little land, a little folly, and a little wit, who would be clowns in a drawing room, and think themselves gentlemen in a barroom, who talk about "my fields, my woods, my peasants," hiss the actresses at the theater to prove that they are persons of taste, quarrel with the officers of the garrison to show that they are gallant, hunt, smoke, gape, drink, take snuff, play billiards, stare at passengers getting out of the coach, live at the café, dine at the inn, have a dog who eats the bones under the table, and a mistress who sets the dishes upon it, hold fast to a sou, overdo the fashions, admire tragedy, despise women, wear out their old boots, copy London as reflected from Paris, and Paris as reflected from Pont-à-Mousson, grow stupid as they grow old, do no work, do no good, and not much harm.

Eight or ten months after what has been related in the preceding pages, in the early part of January, 1823, one evening when it had been snowing, one of these dandies, one of these idlers, a "well-intentioned" man, very warmly wrapped in one of those large cloaks which completed the fashionable costume in cold weather, was amusing himself with tormenting a creature who was walking back and forth before the window of the officers' café, in a ball dress, with her neck and shoulders bare, and flowers upon her head. The dandy was smoking, for that was decidedly the fashion.

Every time that the woman passed before him, he threw out at her, with a puff of smoke from his cigar, some remark which he thought was witty and pleasant as: "How ugly you

arel" "Are you trying to hide?" "You have lost your teeth!"
etc., etc. This gentleman's name was Monsieur Bamatabois.
The woman, a rueful, bedizened specter, who was walking
backward and forward upon the snow, did not answer him,
did not even look at him, but continued her walk in silence
and with a dismal regularity that brought her under his
sarcasm every five minutes, like the condemned soldier who
at stated periods returns under the rods. This failure to secure
attention doubtless piqued the loafer, who, taking advantage
of the moment when she turned, came up behind her with a
stealthy step, and stifling his laughter stooped down, seized
a handful of snow from the sidewalk, and threw it hastily into
her back between her naked shoulders. The girl roared with
rage, turned, bounded like a panther, and rushed upon the
man, burying her nails in his face, and using the most frightful
words that ever fell from the off-scouring of a guardhouse.
These insults were thrown out in a voice roughened by brandy,
from a hideous mouth which lacked the two front teeth. It
was Fantine.

At the noise which this made, the officers came out of the
café, a crowd gathered, and a large circle was formed,
laughing, jeering and applauding, around this center of
attraction composed of two beings who could hardly be
recognized as a man and a woman, the man defending himself,
his hat knocked off, the woman kicking and striking, her head
bare, shrieking, toothless, and without hair, livid with wrath,
and horrible.

Suddenly a tall man advanced quickly from the crowd,
seized the woman by her muddy satin waist, and said: "Follow
me!"

The woman raised her head; her furious voice died out at
once. Her eyes were glassy, from livid she had become pale,
and she shuddered with a shudder of terror. She recognized
Javert.

The dandy profited by this to steal away.

X

JAVERT dismissed the bystanders, broke up the circle, and
walked off rapidly toward the Bureau of Police, which is at the
end of the square, dragging the poor creature after him. She

made no resistance, but followed mechanically. Neither spoke a word. The flock of spectators, in a paroxysm of joy, followed with their jokes. The deepest misery, an opportunity for obscenity.

When they reached the Bureau of Police, which was a low hall warmed by a stove, and guarded by a sentinel, with a grated window looking on the street, Javert opened the door, entered with Fantine, and closed the door behind him.

On entering, Fantine crouched down in a corner, motionless and silent, like a frightened dog.

The sergeant of the guard placed a lighted candle on the table. Javert sat down, drew from his pocket a sheet of stamped paper, and began to write.

Javert was impassible; his grave face betrayed no emotion. He was, however, engaged in serious and earnest consideration. It was one of those moments in which he exercised without restraint, but with all the scruples of a strict conscience, his formidable discretionary power. At this moment he felt that his policeman's stool was a bench of justice. He was conducting a trial. He was trying and condemning. He called all the ideas of which his mind was capable around the grand thing that he was doing. The more he examined the conduct of this girl, the more he revolted at it. It was clear that he had seen a crime committed. He had seen, there in the street, society represented by a property holder and an elector, insulted and attacked by a creature who was an outlaw and an outcast. A prostitute had assaulted a citizen. He, Javert, had seen that himself. He wrote in silence.

When he had finished, he signed his name, folded the paper, and handed it to the sergeant of the guard, saying: "Take three men, and carry this girl to jail." Then turning to Fantine: "You are in for six months."

The hapless woman shuddered.

"Six months! Six months in prison!" cried she. "Six months to earn seven sous a day! But what will become of Cosette! My daughter! My daughter! Why, I still owe more than a hundred francs to the Thénardiers, Monsieur Inspector, do you know that?"

She dragged herself along on the floor, dirtied by the muddy boots of all these men, without rising, clasping her hands, and moving rapidly on her knees.

"Monsieur Javert," said she, "I beg your pity. I assure you

that I was not in the wrong. If you had seen the beginning, you would have seen. I swear to you by the good God that I was not in the wrong. That gentleman, whom I do not know, threw snow in my back. Have they the right to throw snow into our backs when we are going along quietly like that without doing any harm to anybody? That made me wild. I am not very well, you see! And then he had already been saying things to me for some time. 'You are homely!' 'You have no teeth!' I know too well that I have lost my teeth. I did not do anything; I thought: 'He is a gentleman who is amusing himself.' I was not immodest with him, I did not speak to him. It was then that he threw the snow at me. Monsieur Javert, my good Monsieur Inspector! Just think that I have a hundred francs to pay, or else they will turn away my little one. Oh! My God! I cannot have her with me. What I do is so vile! Do you see, she is a little one that they will put out on the highway, to do what she can, in the very heart of winter; you must feel pity for such a thing, good Monsieur Javert. If she were older, she could earn her living, but she cannot at such an age. Have pity on me, Monsieur Javert."

She talked thus, bent double, shaken with sobs, blinded by tears, her neck bare, clenching her hands, coughing with a dry and short cough, stammering very feebly with an agonized voice. Great grief is a divine and terrible radiance which transfigures the wretched. At that moment Fantine had again become beautiful. At certain instants she stopped and tenderly kissed the policeman's coat. She would have softened a heart of granite, but you cannot soften a heart of wood.

"Come," said Javert, "I have heard you. Haven't you got through? March off at once! You have your six months! The Eternal Father in person could do nothing for you."

At those solemn words: "The Eternal Father in person could do nothing for you," she understood that her sentence was fixed. She sank down murmuring:

"Mercy!"

Javert turned his back.

The soldiers seized her by the arms.

A few minutes before a man had entered without being noticed. He had closed the door, and stood with his back against it, and heard the despairing supplication of Fantine.

When the soldiers put their hands upon the wretched being,

who would not rise, he stepped forward out of the shadow and said:

"One moment, if you please!"

Javert raised his eyes and recognized Monsieur Madeleine. He took off his hat, and bowing with a sort of angry awkwardness:

"Pardon, Monsieur Mayor—"

This word, Monsieur Mayor, had a strange effect upon Fantine. She sprang to her feet at once, like a specter rising from the ground, pushed back the soldiers with her arms, walked straight to Monsieur Madeleine before they could stop her, and gazing at him fixedly, with a wild look, she exclaimed:

"Ah! It is you then who are Monsieur Mayor!"

Then she burst out laughing and spit in his face.

Monsieur Madeleine wiped his face and said:

"Inspector Javert, set this woman at liberty."

Javert felt as though he were on the point of losing his senses. He was stupefied with amazement; thought and speech alike failed him; the sum of possible astonishment had been overpassed. He remained speechless.

The mayor's words were not less strange a blow to Fantine. She raised her bare arm and clung to the damper of the stove as if she were staggered. Meanwhile she looked all around and began to talk in a low voice, as if speaking to herself:

"At liberty! They let me go! I am not to go to prison for six months! Who was it said that? It is not possible that anybody said that. I misunderstood. That cannot be this monster of a mayor! Oh, Monsieur Javert, it is you who said that they must let me go, is it not? Go and inquire, speak to my landlord; I pay my rent, and he will surely tell you that I am honest. Oh dear, I beg your pardon, I have touched—I did not know it—the damper of the stove, and it smokes."

Then addressing herself to the soldiers:

"Say now, did you see how I spit in his face? Oh! You old scoundrel of a mayor, you come here to frighten me, but I am not afraid of you. I am afraid of Monsieur Javert. I am afraid of my good Monsieur Javert!"

As she said this she turned again toward the inspector:

"Now, you see, Monsieur Inspector, you must be just. I know that you are just, Monsieur Inspector; in fact, it is very simple, a man who jocosely throws a little snow into a woman's back, that makes them laugh, the officers, they must divert themselves with something, and we poor things are only for their amusement. And then, you, you come, you are obliged to keep order, you arrest the woman who has done wrong, but on reflection, as you are good, you tell them to set me at liberty, that is for my little one, because six months in prison, that would prevent my supporting my child. Only never come back again, wretch! Oh! I will never come back again, Monsieur Javert! They may do anything they like with me now, I will not stir. Only, today, you see, I cried out because that hurt me. I did not in the least expect that snow from that gentleman, and then, I have told you, I am not very well, I cough, I have something in my chest like a ball which burns me, and the doctor tells me: 'Be careful.' Stop, feel, give me your hand, don't be afraid, here it is."

Suddenly she hastily adjusted the disorder of her garments, smoothed down the folds of her dress, which, in dragging herself about, had been raised almost as high as her knees, and walked toward the door, saying in an undertone to the soldiers, with a friendly nod of the head:

"Boys, Monsieur the Inspector said that you must release me; I am going."

She put her hand upon the latch. One more step and she would be in the street.

Javert until that moment had remained standing, motionless, his eyes fixed on the ground, looking, in the midst of the scene, like a statue which was waiting to be placed in position.

The sound of the latch roused him. He raised his head with an expression of sovereign authority, an expression always the more frightful in proportion as power is vested in beings of lower grade, ferocious in the wild beast, atrocious in the undeveloped man.

"Sergeant," exclaimed he, "don't you see that this vagabond is going off? Who told you to let her go?"

"I," said Madeleine.

At the words of Javert, Fantine had trembled and dropped the latch, as a thief who is caught drops what he has stolen. When Madeleine spoke, she turned, and from that moment, without saying a word, without even daring to breathe freely, she looked by turns from Madeleine to Javert and from Javert to Madeleine, as the one or the other was speaking.

When Monsieur Madeleine pronounced that "I" which we have just heard, the inspector of police, Javert, turned toward the mayor, pale, cold, with blue lips, a desperate look, his whole body agitated with an imperceptible tremor, and, an unheard-of thing, said to him, with a downcast look, but a firm voice:

"Monsieur Mayor, that cannot be done."

"Why?" said Monsieur Madeleine.

"This wretched woman has insulted a citizen."

"Inspector Javert," replied Monsieur Madeleine, in a conciliating and calm tone, "listen. You are an honest man, and I have no objection to explaining myself to you. The truth is this. I was passing through the square when you arrested this woman; there was a crowd still there; I learned the circumstances; I know all about it; it is the citizen who was in the wrong, and who, by a faithful police, would have been arrested."

Javert went on:

"This wretch has just insulted Monsieur the Mayor."

"That concerns me," said Monsieur Madeleine. "The insult to me rests with myself, perhaps. I can do what I please about it."

"I beg Monsieur the Mayor's pardon. The insult rests not with him, it rests with justice."

"Inspector Javert," replied Monsieur Madeleine, "the highest justice is conscience. I have heard this woman. I know what I am doing."

"And for my part, Monsieur Mayor, I do not know what I am seeing."

"Then content yourself with obeying."

"I obey my duty. My duty requires that this woman spend six months in prison."

Monsieur Madeleine answered mildly:

"Listen to this. She shall not a day."

"Monsieur Mayor, permit—"

"Not another word."

"However—"

"Retire," said Monsieur Madeleine.

Javert received the blow, standing in front, and with open breast like a Russian soldier. He bowed to the ground before the mayor, and went out.

Fantine stood by the door and looked at him with stupor as he passed before her.

Meanwhile she also was the subject of a strange revolution. She listened with dismay, she looked around with alarm, and at each word that Monsieur Madeleine uttered, she felt the fearful darkness of her hatred melt within and flow away, while there was born in her heart an indescribable and unspeakable warmth of joy, of confidence, and of love.

When Javert was gone, Monsieur Madeleine turned toward her, and said to her, speaking slowly and with difficulty, like a man who is struggling that he may not weep:

"I have heard you. I knew nothing of what you have said. I believe that it is true. I did not even know that you had left my workshop. Why did you not apply to me? But now, I will pay your debts, I will have your child come to you, or you shall go to her. You shall live here, at Paris, or where you will. I take charge of your child and you. You shall do no more work, if you do not wish to. I will give you all the money that you need. You shall again become honest in again becoming happy. More than that, listen. I declare to you from this moment, if all is as you say, and I do not doubt it, that you have never ceased to be virtuous and holy before God. Oh, poor woman!"

This was more than poor Fantine could bear. To have Cosette! To leave this infamous life! To live free, rich, happy, honest, with Cosette! To see suddenly spring up in the midst of her misery all these realities of paradise! She looked as if she were stupefied at the man who was speaking to her, and could only pour out two or three sobs: "Oh! Oh! Oh!" Her limbs gave way, she threw herself on her knees before Monsieur Madeleine, and, before he could prevent it, he felt that she had seized his hand and carried it to her lips.

Then she fainted.

Javert

I

MONSIEUR MADELEINE had Fantine taken to the infirmary, which was in his own house. He confided her to the sisters, who put her to bed. A violent fever came on, and she passed a part of the night in delirious ravings. Finally, she fell asleep.

Toward noon the following day, Fantine awoke. She heard a breathing near her bed, drew aside the curtain, and saw Monsieur Madeleine standing gazing at something above his head. His look was full of compassionate and supplicating agony. She followed its direction, and saw that it was fixed upon a crucifix nailed against the wall.

From that moment Monsieur Madeleine was transfigured in the eyes of Fantine; he seemed to her clothed upon with light. He was absorbed in a kind of prayer. She gazed at him for a long while without daring to interrupt him; at last she said timidly:

"What are you doing?"

Monsieur Madeleine had been in that place for an hour waiting for Fantine to awake. He took her hand, felt her pulse, and said:

"How do you feel?"

"Very well. I have slept," she said. "I think I am getting better—this will be nothing."

Then he said, answering the question she had first asked him, as if she had just asked it:

"I was praying to the martyr who is on high."

And in his thought he added: "For the martyr who is here below."

Monsieur Madeleine had passed the night and morning in informing himself about Fantine. He knew all now, he had learned, even in all its poignant details, the history of Fantine.

He went on:

"You have suffered greatly, poor mother. Oh! Do not lament, you have now the portion of the elect. It is in this way that mortals become angels. It is not their fault; they do not know how to set about it otherwise. This hell from which you have come out is the first step toward Heaven. We must begin by that."

He sighed deeply; but she smiled with this sublime smile from which two teeth were gone.

Monsieur Madeleine wrote immediately to the Thénardiers. Fantine owed them a hundred and twenty francs. He sent them three hundred francs, telling them to pay themselves out of it, and bring the child at once to M—— sur m——, where her mother, who was sick, wanted her.

This astonished Thénardier.

"The Devil!" he said to his wife. "We won't let go of the child. It may be that this lark will become a milch cow. I guess some silly fellow has been smitten by the mother."

He replied by a bill of five hundred and some odd francs carefully drawn up. In this bill figured two incontestable items for upward of three hundred francs, one of a physician and the other of an apothecary who had attended and supplied Eponine and Azelma during two long illnesses. Cosette, as we have said, had not been ill. This was only a slight substitution of names. Thénardier wrote at the bottom of the bill: "Received on account three hundred francs."

Monsieur Madeleine immediately sent three hundred francs more, and wrote: "Make haste to bring Cosette."

"Christy!" said Thénardier. "We won't let go of the girl."

Meanwhile Fantine had not recovered. She still remained in the infirmary.

Monsieur Madeleine came to see her twice a day, and at each visit she asked him:

"Shall I see my Cosette soon?"

He answered:

"Perhaps tomorrow. I expect her every moment."

And the mother's pale face would brighten.

"Ah!" she would say. "How happy I shall be."

We have just said she did not recover; on the contrary, her condition seemed to become worse from week to week. The doctor sounded her lungs and shook his head.

Monsieur Madeleine said to him:

"Well?"

"Has she not a child she is anxious to see?" said the doctor.

"Yes."

"Well then, make haste to bring her."

Monsieur Madeleine gave a shudder.

Fantine asked him: "What did the doctor say?"

Monsieur Madeleine tried to smile.

"He told us to bring your child at once. That will restore your health."

II

ONE morning Monsieur Madeleine was in his office arranging for some pressing business of the mayoralty, when he was informed that Javert, the inspector of police, wished to speak with him.

"Let him come in," said he.

Javert entered.

He respectfully saluted the mayor, who had his back toward him. The mayor did not look up, but continued to make notes on the papers.

Javert advanced a few steps, and paused without breaking silence. His whole person expressed abasement and firmness, an indescribably courageous dejection.

At last the mayor laid down his pen and turned partly around:

"Well, what is it? What is the matter, Javert?"

Javert remained silent a moment as if collecting himself, then raised his voice with a sad solemnity which did not, however, exclude simplicity: "There has been a criminal act committed, Monsieur Mayor."

"What act?"

"An inferior agent of the government has been wanting in respect to a magistrate, in the gravest manner. I come, as is my duty, to bring the fact to your knowledge."

"Who is this agent?" asked Monsieur Madeleine.

"I," said Javert.

"You?"

"I."

"And who is the magistrate who has to complain of this agent?"

"You, Monsieur Mayor."

Monsieur Madeleine straightened himself in his chair. Javert continued, with serious looks and eyes still cast down.

"Monsieur Mayor, I come to ask you to be so kind as to make charges and procure my dismissal."

Monsieur Madeleine, amazed, opened his mouth. Javert interrupted him:

"You will say that I might tender my resignation, but that is not enough. To resign is honorable; I have done wrong. I ought to be punished. I must be dismissed."

"Ah, indeed! Why?"

"You will understand, Monsieur Mayor," Javert sighed deeply, and continued sadly and coldly:

"Monsieur Mayor, six weeks ago, after that scene about that girl, I was enraged and I denounced you."

"Denounced me?"

"To the Prefecture of Police at Paris."

Monsieur Madeleine, who did not laugh much oftener than Javert, began to laugh:

"As a mayor having encroached upon the police?"

"As a former convict."

The mayor became livid.

Javert, who had not raised his eyes, continued:

"I believed it. For a long while I had had suspicions. A resemblance, information you obtained at Faverolles, your immense strength, the affair of old Fauchelevent—and in fact I don't know what other stupidities; but at last I took you for a man named Jean Valjean."

"Named what? How did you call that name?"

"Jean Valjean. He was a convict I saw twenty years ago, when I was adjutant of the galley guard at Toulon. After leaving the galleys this Valjean, it appears, robbed a bishop's palace, then he committed another robbery with weapons in his hands, on a highway, on a little Savoyard. For eight years his whereabouts have been unknown, and search has been made for him. I fancied—in short, I have done this thing. Anger determined me, and I denounced you to the prefect."

Monsieur Madeleine, who had taken up the file of papers again, a few moments before, said with a tone of perfect indifference: "And what answer did you get?"

"That I was crazy."

"Well!"

"Well, they were right."

"It is fortunate that you think so!"

"It must be so, for the real Jean Valjean has been found."

The paper that Monsieur Madeleine held fell from his hand; he raised his head, looked steadily at Javert, and said in an inexpressible tone:

"Ah!"

Javert continued:

"I will tell you how it is, Monsieur Mayor. There was, it appears, in the country, near Ailly-le-Haut Clocher, a simple sort of fellow who was called Father Champmathieu. He was very poor. Nobody paid any attention to him. Such folks live, one hardly knows how. Finally, this last fall, Father Champmathieu was arrested for stealing cider apples from ———, but that is of no consequence. There was a theft, a wall scaled, branches of trees broken. Our Champmathieu was arrested; he had even then a branch of an apple tree in his hand. The rogue was caged. So far, it was nothing more than a penitentiary matter. But here comes in the hand of Providence. The jail being in a bad condition, the police justice thought it best to take him to Arras, where the prison of the department is. In this prison at Arras there was a former convict named Brevet, who is there for some trifle, and who, for his good conduct, has been made turnkey. No sooner was Champmathieu set down, than Brevet cried out: 'Ha, ha! I know that man. He is a *fagot*.[1] Look up here, my good man. You are Jean Valjean.' 'Jean Valjean, who is Jean Valjean?' Champmathieu plays off the astonished. 'Don't play ignorance,' said Brevet. 'You are Jean Valjean; you were in the galleys at Toulon. It is twenty years ago. We were there together.' Champmathieu denied it all. Faith! You understand; they fathomed it. The case was worked up and this was what they found. This Champmathieu thirty years ago was a pruner in diverse places, particularly in Faverolles. There we lose trace of him. You follow me, do you not? Search has been made at Faverolles; the family of Jean Valjean are no longer there. Nobody knows where they are. You know in such classes these disappearances of families often occur. You search, but can find nothing. Such people, when they are not mud, are dust. And then as the commencement of this story dates back thirty years, there is nobody now at Faverolles who knew Jean Valjean. But search has been made at Toulon. Besides Brevet there are only two convicts who have seen Jean Valjean. They are

———
[1] Former convict.

convicts for life; their names are Coohepaille and Chenildieu. These men were brought from the galleys and confronted with the pretended Champmathieu. They did not hesitate. To them as well as to Brevet it was Jean Valjean. Same age, fifty-four years old, same height, same appearance, in fact the same man; it is he. At this time it was that I sent my denunciation to the Prefecture at Paris. They replied that I was out of my mind, and that Jean Valjean was at Arras in the hands of justice. You may imagine how that astonished me, I who believed that I had here the same Jean Valjean. I wrote to the justice; he sent for me and brought Champmathieu before me."

"Well," interrupted Monsieur Madeleine.

Javert replied, with an incorruptible and sad face:

"Monsieur Mayor, truth is truth. I am sorry for it, but that man is Jean Valjean. I recognized him also."

Monsieur Madeleine said in a very low voice:

"Are you sure?"

Javert began to laugh with the suppressed laugh which indicates profound conviction.

"H'm, sure! But this man pretends not to understand; he says: 'I am Champmathieu: I have no more to say.' He puts on an appearance of astonishment; he plays the brute. Oh, the rascal is cunning! But it is all the same, there is the evidence. Four persons have recognized him, and the old villain will be condemned. It has been taken to the assizes at Arras. I am going to testify. I have been summoned."

Monsieur Madeleine had turned again to his desk, and was quietly looking over his papers, reading and writing alternately, like a man pressed with business. He turned again toward Javert:

"That will do, Javert. Indeed all these details interest me very little. We are wasting time, and we have urgent business. But did you not tell me you were going to Arras in eight or ten days on this matter?"

"Sooner than that, Monsieur Mayor."

"What day then?"

"I think I told monsieur that the case would be tried tomorrow, and that I should leave by the diligence tonight."

Monsieur Madeleine made an imperceptible motion.

"And how long will the matter last?"

"One day at longest. Sentence will be pronounced at latest tomorrow evening. But I shall not wait for the sentence, which is certain; as soon as my testimony is given I shall return here."

"Very well," said Monsieur Madeleine.

And he dismissed him with a wave of his hand.

Javert did not go.

"Your pardon, monsieur," said he.

"What more is there?" asked Monsieur Madeleine.

"Monsieur Mayor, there is one thing more to which I desire to call your attention."

"What is it?"

"It is that I ought to be dismissed."

Monsieur Madeleine arose.

"Javert, you are a man of honor and I esteem you. You exaggerate your fault. Besides, this is an offense which concerns me. You are worthy of promotion rather than disgrace. I desire you to keep your place."

Javert looked at Monsieur Madeleine with his calm eyes, in whose depths it seemed that one beheld his conscience, unenlightened, but stern and pure, and said in a tranquil voice:

"Monsieur Mayor, I cannot agree to that. I ought to treat myself as I would treat anybody else. When I put down malefactors, when I rigorously brought up offenders, I often said to myself: 'You, if you ever trip, if ever I catch you doing wrong, look out!' I have tripped, I have caught myself doing wrong. So much the worse! I must be sent away, broken, dismissed; that is right. I have hands: I can till the ground. It is all the same to me. Monsieur Mayor, the good of the service demands an example. I simply ask the dismissal of Inspector Javert."

All this was said in a tone of proud humility, a desperate and resolute tone, which gave an indescribably whimsical grandeur to this oddly honest man.

"We will see," said Monsieur Madeleine.

And he held out his hand to him.

Javert started back, and said fiercely:

"Pardon, Monsieur Mayor, that should not be. A mayor does not give his hand to a spy."

He added between his teeth:

"Spy, yes; from the moment I abused the power of my position, I have been nothing better than a spy!"

Then he bowed profoundly, and went toward the door.

There he turned around, his eyes yet downcast.

"Monsieur Mayor, I will continue in the service until I am relieved."

He went out. Monsieur Madeleine sat musing, listening to his firm and resolute step as it died away along the corridor.

The Champmathieu Affair

I

THE reader has doubtless divined that Monsieur Madeleine is none other than Jean Valjean.

We have already looked into the depths of that conscience; the time has come to look into them again. We do so not without emotion, nor without trembling. There exists nothing more terrific than this kind of contemplation. The mind's eye can nowhere find anything more dazzling or more dark than in man; it can fix itself upon nothing which is more awful, more complex, more mysterious or more infinite. There is one spectacle grander than the sea, that is the sky; there is one spectacle grander than the sky, that is the interior of the soul.

From the first words that Javert pronounced on entering his office, at the moment when that name which he had so deeply buried was so strangely uttered, he was seized with stupor, and as if intoxicated by the sinister grotesqueness of his destiny, through that stupor he felt the shudder which precedes great shocks; he bent like an oak at the approach of a storm, like a soldier at the approach of an assault. He felt clouds full of thunderings and lightnings gathering upon his head. Even while listening to Javert, his first thought was to go, to run, to denounce himself, to drag this Champmathieu out of prison, and to put himself in his place; it was painful and sharp as an incision into the living flesh, but passed away, and he said to himself: "Let us see! Let us see!" He repressed this first generous impulse and recoiled before such heroism.

Doubtless it would have been fine if, after the holy words of the bishop, after so many years of repentance and self-denial, in the midst of a penitence admirably commenced, even in the presence of so terrible a conjecture, he had not faltered an instant, and had continued to march on with even pace toward that yawning pit at the bottom of which was heaven— this would have been fine, but this was not the case. We must render an account of what took place in that soul, and we can relate only what was there. What first gained control was the instinct of self-preservation; he collected his ideas hastily, stifled his emotions, took into consideration the presence of Javert, the great danger, postponed any decision with the firmness of terror, banished from his mind all consideration of the course he should pursue, and resumed his calmness as a gladiator retakes his buckler.

For the rest of the day he was in this state, a tempest within, a perfect calm without. He went according to his habit to the sick bed of Fantine, and prolonged his visit, by an instinct of kindness, saying to himself that he ought to do so and recommend her earnestly to the sisters, in case it should happen that he would have to be absent. He felt vaguely that it would perhaps be necessary for him to go to Arras, and without having in the least decided upon this journey, he said to himself that, entirely free from suspicion as he was, there would be no difficulty in being a witness of what might pass, and he engaged a tilbury, in order to be prepared for any emergency.

He dined with a good appetite.

Returning to his room he collected his thoughts.

He examined the situation and found it an unheard-of one, so unheard-of that in the midst of his reverie, by some strange impulse of almost inexplicable anxiety, he rose from his chair, and bolted his door. He feared lest something might yet enter. He barricaded himself against all possibilities.

A moment afterward he blew out his light. It annoyed him.

It seemed to him that somebody could see him.

Who? Somebody?

Alas! What he wanted to keep outdoors had entered; what he wanted to render blind was looking upon him. His conscience.

His conscience, that is to say, God.

At the first moment, however, he deluded himself; he had a feeling of safety and solitude; the bolt drawn, he believed himself invisible. Then he took possession of himself; he placed his elbows on the table, rested his head on his hand, and set himself to meditating in the darkness.

His brain had lost the power of retaining its ideas; they passed away like waves, and he grasped his forehead with both hands to stop them.

Out of this tumult, which overwhelmed his will and his reason, and from which he sought to draw a certainty and a resolution, nothing came clearly forth but anguish.

His brain was burning. He went to the window and threw it wide open. Not a star was in the sky. He returned and sat down by the table.

The first hour thus rolled away.

Little by little, however, vague outlines began to take form and to fix themselves in his meditation; he could perceive, with the precision of reality, not the whole of the situation, but a few details.

It seemed to him that he had just awakened from some wondrous slumber, and that he found himself gliding over a precipice in the middle of the night, standing, shivering, recoiling in vain, upon the very edge of an abyss. He perceived distinctly in the gloom an unknown man, a stranger, whom fate had mistaken for him, and was pushing into the gulf in his place. It was necessary, in order that the gulf should be closed, that someone should fall in, he or the other.

He had only to let it alone.

All this was so violent and so strange that he suddenly felt that kind of indescribable movement that no man experiences more than two or three times in his life, a sort of convulsion of the conscience that stirs up all that is dubious in the heart, which is composed of irony, of joy, and of despair, and which might be called a burst of interior laughter.

He hastily relighted his candle.

"Well, what!" said he. "What am I afraid of? Why do I ponder over these things? I am now safe; all is finished. Ah, yes, but, what is there unfortunate in all this! People who should see me, upon my honor, would think that a catastrophe had befallen me! After all, if there is any harm done to anybody, it is in nowise my fault. Providence has done it all. This is what He wishes apparently. Have I the right to disarrange what He arranges? What is it that I ask for now? Why do I interfere? It does not concern me. How! I am not satisfied! But what would I have then? The aim to which I have aspired for so many years, my nightly dream, the object of my prayers to heaven, security—I have gained it. It is God's will. I must do nothing contrary to the will of God. And why is it God's will? That I may carry on what I have begun, that I may do good, that I may be one day a grand and encouraging example, that it may be said that there was finally some little happiness resulting from this suffering which I have undergone and this virtue to which I have returned! It is decided, let the matter alone! Let us not interfere with God."

Thus he spoke in the depths of his conscience, hanging over what might be called his own abyss. He rose from his chair, and began to walk the room. "Come," said he, "let us think of it no more. The resolution is formed!" But he felt no joy.

Quite the contrary.

One can no more prevent the mind from returning to an idea than the sea from returning to a shore. In the case of the sailor, this is called the tide; in the case of the guilty, it is called remorse. God upheaves the soul as well as the ocean.

After the lapse of a few moments, he could do no otherwise; he resumed this somber dialogue, in which it was himself who spoke and himself who listened, saying what he wished to keep silent, listening to what he did not wish to hear, yielding to that mysterious power which said to him: "Think!" as it said two thousand years ago to another condemned: "March!"

He asked himself then where he was. He questioned himself upon this "resolution formed." He confessed to himself that all that he had been arranging in his mind was monstrous, that "to let the matter alone, not to interfere with God," was simply horrible, to let this mistake of destiny and of men be accomplished, not to prevent it, to lend himself to it by his silence; to do nothing, finally, was to do all! It was the last degree of hypocritical meanness! It was a base, cowardly, lying, abject, hideous crime!

For the first time within eight years, the unhappy man had just tasted the bitter flavor of a wicked thought and a wicked action.

He spit it out with disgust.

He continued to question himself. He sternly asked himself what he had understood by this: "My object is attained." He declared that his life, in truth, did have an object. But what object? To conceal his name? To deceive the police? Was it for so petty a thing that he had done all that he had done? Had he no other object, which was the great one, which was the true one? To save, not his body, but his soul. To become honest and good again. To be an upright man! Was it not that above all, that alone, which he had always wished, and which the bishop had enjoined upon him? To close the door on his past? But he was not closing it, great God! He was reopening it by committing an infamous act! For he became a robber again, and the most odious of robbers! He robbed another of his existence, his life, his peace, his place in the world; he became an assassin! He murdered, he murdered in a moral sense a wretched man, he inflicted upon him that frightful life in death, that living burial, which is called the galleys; on the contrary, to deliver himself up, to save this man stricken by so ghastly a mistake, to reassume his name, to become again from duty the convict Jean Valjean—that was really to achieve his resurrection, and to close forever the hell from whence he had emerged! To fall back into it in appearance was to emerge in reality! He must do that! All he had done was nothing, if he did not do that! All his life was useless, all his suffering was lost. He had only to ask the question: "What is the use?" He felt that the bishop was there, that the bishop was present all the more that he was dead, that the bishop was looking fixedly at him, that henceforth Mayor Madeleine with all his virtues would be abominable to him, and the galley slave, Jean Valjean, would be admirable and pure in his sight. That men saw his mask, but the bishop saw his face. That men saw his life, but the bishop saw his conscience. He must then go to Arras, deliver the wrong Jean Valjean, denounce the right one. Alas! That was the greatest of sacrifices, the most poignant of victories, the final step to be taken, but he must do it. Mournful destiny! He could only enter into sanctity in the eyes of God, by returning into infamy in the eyes of men!

"Well," said he, "let us take this course! Let us do our duty! Let us save this man!"

He pronounced these words in a loud voice, without perceiving that he was speaking aloud.

He took his books, verified them, and put them in order. He threw into the fire a package of notes which he held against needy small traders. He wrote a letter, which he sealed, and upon the envelope of which might have been read, if there had been anyone in the room at the time: *Monsieur Laffitte, Banker, rue d'Artois, Paris.*

The letter to Monsieur Laffitte finished, he put it in his pocket as well as a pocketbook, and began to walk again.

The current of his thought had not changed. He still saw his duty clearly written in luminous letters which flared out before his eyes, and moved with his gaze: "Go! Avow thy name! Denounce thyself!"

He felt that he had reached the second decisive movement of his conscience, and his destiny; that the bishop had marked the first phase of his new life, and that this Champmathieu marked the second. After a great crisis, a great trial.

His blood rushed violently to his temples. He walked back and forth constantly. Midnight was struck first from the parish church, then from the city hall. He counted the twelve strokes of the two clocks, and he compared the sound of the two bells. It reminded him that, a few days before, he had seen at a junkshop an old bell for sale, upon which was this name: ANTOINE ALBIN DE ROMAINVILLE.

He was cold. He kindled a fire. He did not think to close the window.

Meanwhile he had fallen into his stupor again. It required not a little effort to recall his mind to what he was thinking of before the clock struck. He succeeded at last.

"Ah! Yes," said he, "I had formed the resolution to denounce myself."

And then all at once he thought of Fantine.

"Stop!" said he. "This poor woman!"

Here was a new crisis.

Fantine, abruptly appearing in his reverie, was like a ray of unexpected light. It seemed to him that everything around him was changing its aspect; he exclaimed:

"Ah! Yes, indeed! So far I have only thought of myself! I have only looked to my own convenience! It is whether I shall keep silent or denounce myself, conceal my body or save my soul, be a despicable and respected magistrate, or an infamous and venerable galley slave: it is myself, always myself, only myself. But, good God! All this is egotism. Different forms of egotism, but still egotism! Suppose I should think a little of others? The highest duty is to think of others. Let us see, let us examine! In ten years I shall have made ten millions; I scatter it over the country, I keep nothing for myself; what is it to me? What I am doing is not for myself. The prosperity of all goes on increasing, industry is quickened and excited, manufactories and workshops are multiplied, families, a hundred families, a thousand families, are happy; the country becomes populous; villages spring up where there were only farms, farms spring up where there was nothing; poverty disappears, and with poverty disappear debauchery, prostitution, theft, murder, all vices, all crimes! And this poor mother brings up her child! And the whole country is rich and honest! Ah, yes! How foolish, how absurd I was! What was I speaking of in denouncing myself? This demands reflection, surely, and nothing must be precipitated. What! Because it would have pleased me to do the grand and the generous! That is melodramatic after all! Because I only thought of myself, of myself alone, what! To save from a punishment perhaps a little too severe, but in reality just, nobody knows who, a thief, a scoundrel at any rate. Must an entire country be let go to ruin! Must a poor hapless woman perish in the hospital! Must a poor little girl perish on the street! Like dogs! Ah! That would be abominable! And the mother not even see her child again! And the child hardly have known her mother! And all for this old whelp of an apple thief, who, beyond all doubt, deserves the galleys for something else, if not for this. Fine scruples these, which save an old vagabond who has, after all, only a few years to live, and who will hardly be more unhappy in the galleys than in his hovel, and which sacrifice a whole population, mothers, wives, children! Take it at the very worst. Suppose there were a misdeed for me in this, and that my conscience should some day reproach me; the acceptance for the good of others of these reproaches which weigh only upon me, of this misdeed which affects only my own soul, why, that is devotion, that is virtue."

He arose and resumed his walk. This time it seemed to him that he was satisfied.

Diamonds are found only in the dark places of the earth; truths are found only in the depths of thought. It seemed to him that after having descended into these depths, after having groped long in the blackest of this darkness, he had at last found one of these diamonds, one of these truths, and that he held it in his hand, and it blinded him to look at it.

"Yes," thought he, "that is it! I am in the true road. I have the solution. I must end by holding fast to something. My choice is made. Let the matter alone! No more vacillation, no more shrinking. This is in the interest of all, not in my own. I am Madeleine, I remain Madeleine. Woe to him who is Jean Valjean! He and I are no longer the same. I do not recognize that man, I no longer know what he is; if it is found that anybody is Jean Valjean at this hour, let him take care of himself. That does not concern me. That is a fatal name which is floating about in the darkness; if it stops and settles upon any man, so much the worse for that man."

He looked at himself in the little mirror that hung over his mantelpiece and said:

"Yes! To come to a resolution has solaced me! I am quite another man now!"

He took a few steps more, then he stopped short.

"Come!" said he. "I must not hesitate before any of the consequences of the resolution I have formed. There are yet some threads which knit me to this Jean Valjean. They must be broken! There are, in this very room, objects which would accuse me, mute things which would be witnesses; it is done, all these must disappear."

He felt in his pocket, drew out his purse, opened it, and took out a little key.

He put this key into a lock, the hole of which was hardly visible, lost as it was in the darkest shading of the figures on the paper which covered the wall. A secret door opened, a kind of falsepress built between the corner of the wall and the casing of the chimney. There was nothing in this closet but a few refuse trifles, a blue smock frock, an old pair of trousers, an old haversack, and a great thorn stick, ironbound at both ends. Those who had seen Jean Valjean at the time he passed through D——, in October, 1815, would have recognized easily all the fragments of this miserable outfit.

He cast a furtive look toward the door, as if he were afraid it would open in spite of the bolt that held it; then with a quick and hasty movement, and at a single armful, without even a glance at these things which he had kept so religiously and with so much danger during so many years, he took the whole, rags, stick, haversack, and threw them all into the fire.

In a few seconds, the room and the wall opposite were lit up with a great red flickering glare. It was all burning; the thorn stick cracked and threw out sparks into the middle of the room.

The haversack, as it was consumed with the horrid rags which it contained, left something uncovered which glistened in the ashes. By bending toward it, one could have easily recognized a piece of silver. It was doubtless the forty-sous piece stolen from the little Savoyard.

But he did not look at the fire; he continued his walk to and fro, always at the same pace.

Suddenly his eyes fell upon the two silver candlesticks on the mantel, which were glistening dimly in the reflection.

"Stop!" thought he. "All Jean Valjean is contained in them too. They also must be destroyed."

He took the two candlesticks.

There was fire enough to melt them quickly into an unrecognizable ingot.

He bent over the fire and warmed himself a moment. It felt really comfortable to him. "The pleasant warmth!" said he.

He stirred the embers with one of the candlesticks.

A minute more, and they would have been in the fire.

At that moment, it seemed to him that he heard a voice crying within him: "Jean Valjean! Jean Valjean!"

His hair stood on end; he was like a man who hears some terrible thing.

"Yes! That is it; finish!" said the voice. "Complete what you are doing! Destroy these candlesticks! Annihilate this memorial! Forget the bishop! Forget all! Ruin this Champmathieu, yes! Very well. Applaud yourself! So it is arranged, it is determined, it is done. Behold a man, a graybeard who knows not what he is accused of, who has done nothing, it may be, an innocent man, whose misfortune is caused by your name, upon whom your name weighs like a crime, who will be taken instead of you, will be condemned, will end his days in abjection and in horror! Very well. Be an honored man yourself. Remain, Monsieur Mayor, remain honorable and honored, enrich the city, feed the poor, bring up the orphans, live happy, virtuous, and admired, and all this time while you are here in joy and in the light, there shall be a man wearing your red blouse, bearing your name in ignominy, and dragging your chain in the galleys! Yes! This is a fine arrangement! Oh, wretch!"

The sweat rolled off his forehead. He looked upon the candlesticks with haggard eyes. Meanwhile the voice which spoke within him had not ended. It continued:

"Jean Valjean! There shall be about you many voices which will make great noise, which will speak very loud, and which will bless you, and one only which nobody shall hear, and which will curse you in the darkness. Well, listen, wretch! All these blessings shall fall before they reach Heaven; only the curse shall mount into the presence of God!"

This voice, at first quite feeble, and which was raised from the most obscure depths of his conscience, had become by degrees loud and formidable, and he heard it now at his ear. It seemed to him that it had emerged from himself, and that it was speaking now from without. He thought he heard the last words so distinctly that he looked about the room with a kind of terror.

"Is there anybody here?" asked he, aloud and in a startled voice.

Then he continued with a laugh, which was like the laugh of an idiot:

"What a fool I am! There cannot be anybody here."

There was One; but He who was there was not of such as the human eye can see.

He put the candlesticks on the mantel.

He now recoiled with equal terror from each of the resolutions which he had formed in turn. Each of the two ideas which counseled him appeared to him as fatal as the other. What a fatality! What a chance that this Champmathieu should be mistaken for him! To be hurled down headlong by the very means which Providence seemed at first to have employed to give him full security.

There was a moment during which he contemplated the future. Denounce himself, great God! Give himself up! He saw with infinite despair all that he must leave, all that he must resume. He must then bid farewell to this existence, so good, so pure, so radiant, to this respect of all, to honor, to liberty! Great God! Instead of that, the galley crew, the iron collar, the red blouse, the chain at his foot, fatigue, the dungeon, the plank bed, all these horrors, which he knew so well! At his age, after having been what he was! Oh, what wretchedness! Can destiny then be malignant like an intelligent being, and become monstrous like the human heart?

And do what he might, he always fell back upon this sharp dilemma which was at the bottom of his thought. To remain in paradise and there become a demon! To re-enter into hell and there become an angel!

What shall be done, great God! What shall be done?

The torment from which he had emerged with so much difficulty broke loose anew within him. His ideas again began to become confused. They took that indescribable, stupefied, and mechanical shape, which is peculiar to despair. The name of Romainville returned constantly to his mind, with two lines of a song he had formerly heard. He thought that Romainville is a little wood near Paris, where young lovers go to gather lilacs in the month of April.

He staggered without as well as within. He walked like a little child that is just allowed to go alone.

He could see nothing distinctly. The vague forms of all the reasonings thrown out by his mind trembled and were dissipated one after another in smoke. But this much he felt, that by whichever resolve he might abide, necessarily, and without possibility of escape, something of himself would surely die; that he was entering into a sepulcher on the right hand, as well as on the left; that he was suffering a death agony, the death agony of his happiness, or the death agony of his virtue.

Alas! All his irresolutions were again upon him. He was no further advanced than when he began.

So struggled beneath its anguish this unhappy soul. Eighteen hundred years before this unfortunate man, the mysterious Being, in whom are aggregated all the sanctities and all the sufferings of humanity, He also, while the olive trees were shivering in the fierce breath of the Infinite, had long put away from his hand the fearful chalice that appeared before him, dripping with shadow and running over with darkness, in the star-filled depths.

II

THE clock struck three. For five hours he had been walking thus almost without interruption, when he dropped into his chair.

He fell asleep and dreamed.

This dream, like most dreams, had no further relation to the condition of affairs than its mournful and poignant character, but it made an impression upon him. This nightmare struck him so forcibly that he afterward wrote it down. It is one of the papers in his own handwriting, which he has left behind him. We think it our duty to copy it here literally.

Whatever this dream may be, the story of that night would be incomplete if we should omit it. It is the gloomy adventure of a sick soul.

It is as follows: Upon the envelope we find this line written: "The dream that I had that night."

I was in a field. A great sad field where there was no grass. It did not seem that it was day, nor that it was night.

I was walking with my brother, the brother of my childhood; this brother of whom I must say that I never think, and whom I scarcely remember.

We were talking, and we met others walking. We were speaking of a neighbor we had formerly who, since she had lived in the street, always worked with her window open. Even while we talked, we felt cold on account of that open window.

There were no trees in the field.

We saw a man passing near us. He was entirely naked, ashen-colored, mounted upon a horse which was of the color of earth. The man had no hair; we saw his skull and the veins in his skull. In his hand he held a stick which was limber like a twig of grapevine, and heavy as iron. This horseman passed by and said nothing.

My brother said to me: "Let us take the deserted road."

There was a deserted road where we saw not a bush, nor even a sprig of moss. All was of the color of earth, even the sky. A few steps further, and no one answered me when I spoke. I perceived that my brother was no longer with me.

I entered a village which I saw. I thought that it must be Romainville (why Romainville?).[1]

The first street by which I entered was deserted. I passed into a second street. At the corner of the two streets was a man standing against the wall; I said to this man: "What place is this? Where am I?" The man made no answer. I saw the door of a house open; I went in.

The first room was deserted. I entered the second. Behind the door of this room was a man standing against the wall. I asked this man: "Whose house is this? Where am I?" The man made no answer. The house had a garden.

I went out of the house and into the garden. The garden was deserted. Behind the first tree I found a man standing. I said to this man: "What is this garden? Where am I?" The man made no answer.

I wandered about the village, and I perceived that it was a city. All the streets were deserted, all the doors were open. No living being was passing along the streets, or stirring in the rooms, or walking in the gardens. But behind every angle of a wall, behind every door, behind everything, there was a man standing who kept silence. But one could ever be seen at a time. These men looked at me as I passed by.

I went out of the city and began to walk in the fields.

After a little while, I turned and I saw a great multitude coming after me. I recognized all the men that I had seen in the city. Their heads were strange. They did not seem to hasten, and still they walked faster than I. They made no sound in walking. In an instant this multitude came up and surrounded me. The faces of these men were the color of earth.

Then the first one whom I had seen and questioned on entering the city, said to me: "Where are you going? Do you not know that you have been dead for a long time?"

---

[1] This parenthesis is in the hand of Jean Valjean.

I opened my mouth to answer, and I perceived that no one was near me.

He awoke. He was chilly. A wind as cold as the morning wind made the sashes of the still open window swing on their hinges. The fire had gone out. The candle was low in the socket. The night was yet dark.

He arose and went to the window. There were still no stars in the sky.

From his window he could look into the courtyard and into the street. A harsh, rattling noise that suddenly resounded from the ground made him look down.

He saw below him two red stars, whose rays danced back and forth grotesquely in the shadow.

His mind was still half buried in the mist of his reverie: "Yes!" thought he. "There are none in the sky. They are on the earth now."

This confusion, however, faded away; a second noise like the first awakened him completely; he looked, and he saw that these two stars were the lamps of a carriage. By the light which they emitted, he could distinguish the form of a carriage. It was a tilbury drawn by a small white horse. The noise which he had heard was the sound of the horse's hoofs upon the pavement.

"What carriage is that?" said he to himself. "Who is it that comes so early?"

At that moment there was a low rap at the door of his room.

He shuddered from head to foot and cried in a terrible voice:

"Who is there?"

Someone answered:

"I, Monsieur Mayor."

He recognized the voice of the old woman, his portress.

"Well," said he, "what is it?"

"Monsieur Mayor, it is just five o'clock."

"What is that to me?"

"Monsieur Mayor, it is the chaise."

"What chaise?"

"The tilbury."

"What tilbury?"

"Did not Monsieur the Mayor order a tilbury?"

"Oh, yes!" he said.

Could the old woman have seen him at that moment she would have been frightened.

There was a long silence. He examined the flame of the candle with a stupid air, and took some of the melted wax from around the wick and rolled it in his fingers. The old woman was waiting. She ventured, however, to speak again:

"Monsieur Mayor, what shall I say?"

"Say that it is right, and I am coming down."

III

IT was nearly eight o'clock in the evening when the cariole drove into the yard of the Hôtel de la Poste at Arras. The man whom we have followed thus far, got out, left the hotel, and began to walk in the city.

He was not acquainted in Arras, the streets were dark, and he went haphazard. Nevertheless he seemed to refrain obstinately from asking his way. He crossed the little river Crinchon, and found himself in a labyrinth of narrow streets, where he was soon lost. A citizen came along with a lantern. After some hesitation, he determined to speak to this man, but not until he had looked before and behind, as if he were afraid that somebody might overhear the question he was about to ask.

"Monsieur," said he, "the courthouse, if you please?"

"If monsieur wishes to see a trial, he is rather late. Ordinarily the sessions close at six o'clock."

However, when they reached the great square, the citizen showed him four long lighted windows on the front of a vast dark building.

"Faith, monsieur, you are in time, you are fortunate. Do you see those four windows? That is the court of assizes. There is a light there. Then they have not finished. The case must have been prolonged and they are having an evening session."

He followed the citizen's instructions, and in a few minutes found himself in a hall where there were many people, and scattered groups of lawyers in their robes whispering here and there.

This hall, which, though spacious, was lighted by a single

lamp, was an ancient hall of the episcopal palace, and served as a waiting room. A double folding door, which was now closed, separated it from the large room in which the court of assizes was in session.

He approached several groups and listened to their talk. The calendar of the term being very heavy, the judge had set down two short, simple cases for that day. They had begun with an infanticide, and now were on the convict, the second offender, the "old stager." This man had stolen some apples, but that did not appear to be very well proved; what was proved was that he had been in the galleys at Toulon. This was what ruined his case. The examination of the man had been finished, and the testimony of the witnesses had been taken, but there yet remained the argument of the counsel, and the summing up of his prosecuting attorney; it would hardly be finished before midnight. The man would probably be condemned; the prosecuting attorney was very good, and never failed with his prisoners; he was a fellow of talent, who wrote poetry.

An officer stood near the door which opened into the court-room. He asked this officer:

"Monsieur, will the door be opened soon?"

"It will not be opened," said the officer.

"Why not?"

"Because the hall is full."

"What! There are no more seats?"

"Not a single one. The door is closed. No one can enter."

The officer added, after a silence: "There are indeed two or three places still behind Monsieur the Judge, but Monsieur the Judge admits none but public functionaries to them."

So saying, the officer turned his back.

He retired with his head bowed down, crossed the ante-chamber, and walked slowly down the staircase, seeming to hesitate at every step. It is probable that he was holding counsel with himself. The violent combat that had been going on within him since the previous evening was not finished, and, every moment, he fell upon some new turn. When he reached the turn of the stairway, he leaned against the railing and folded his arms. Suddenly he opened his coat, drew out his pocketbook, took out a pencil, tore out a sheet, and wrote rapidly upon that sheet, by the glimmering light, this line: "Monsieur Madeleine, Mayor of M—— sur m——";

then he went up the stairs again rapidly, passed through the crowd, walked straight to the officer, handed him the paper, and said to him with authority: "Carry that to Monsieur the Judge."

The officer took the paper, cast his eye upon it, and obeyed.

IV

WITHOUT himself suspecting it, the Mayor of M—— sur m—— had a certain celebrity. For seven years the reputation of his virtue had been extending throughout Bas-Boulonnais; it had finally crossed the boundaries of the little county, and had spread into the two or three neighboring departments.

The Judge of the Royal Court of Douai, who was holding this term of the assizes at Arras, was familiar, as well as everybody else, with this name so profoundly and so universally honored. When the officer, quietly opening the door which led from the counsel chamber to the courtroom, bent behind the judge's chair and handed him the paper, on which was written the line we have just read, adding: "This gentleman desires to witness the trial," the judge made a hasty movement of deference, seized a pen, wrote a few words at the bottom of the paper, and handed it back to the officer, saying to him: "Let him enter."

The unhappy man, whose history we are relating, had remained near the door of the hall, in the same place and the same attitude as when the officer left him. He heard, through his thoughts, someone saying to him: "Will monsieur do me the honor to follow me?" It was the same officer who had turned his back upon him the minute before, and who now bowed to the earth before him. The officer at the same time handed him the paper. He unfolded it, and, as he happened to be near the lamp, he could read:

"The Judge of the Court of Assizes presents his respects to Monsieur Madeleine."

He crushed the paper in his hands, as if those few words had left some strange and bitter taste behind.

He followed the officer.

In a few minutes he found himself alone in a kind of paneled cabinet, of a severe appearance, lighted by two wax candles placed upon a table covered with green cloth. The last words of the officer who had left him still rang in his ear: "Monsieur, you are now in the counsel chamber; you have but to turn the brass knob of that door and you will find yourself in the courtroom, behind the judge's chair." These words were associated in his thoughts with a vague remembrance of the narrow corridors and dark stairways through which he had just passed.

At one moment he made, with a kind of authority united to rebellion, that indescribable gesture which means and which so well says: "Well! Who is there to compel me?" Then he turned quickly, saw before him the door by which he had entered, went to it, opened it, and went out. He was no longer in that room; he was outside, in a corridor, a long, narrow corridor, cut up with steps and side doors, making all sorts of angles, lighted here and there by lamps hung on the wall similar to nurse lamps for the sick; it was the corridor by which he had come. He drew breath and listened; no sound behind him, no sound before him; he ran as if he were pursued.

When he had doubled several of the turns of this passage, he listened again. There was still the same silence and the same shadow about him. He was out of breath, he tottered, he leaned against the wall. The stone was cold; the sweat was icy upon his forehead; he roused himself with a shudder.

Then and there, alone, standing in that obscurity, trembling with cold and, perhaps, with something else, he reflected.

He had reflected all night, he had reflected all day; he now heard but one voice within him, which said: "Alas!"

A quarter of an hour thus rolled away. Finally, he bowed his head, sighed with anguish, let his arms fall, and retraced his steps. He walked slowly and as if overwhelmed. It seemed as if he had been caught in his flight and brought back.

He entered the counsel chamber again. The first thing that he saw was the handle of the door. That handle, round and of polished brass, shone out before him like an ominous star. He looked at it as a lamb might look at the eye of a tiger.

His eyes could not move from it.

From time to time, he took another step toward the door.

Had he listened, he would have heard, as a kind of confused murmur, the noise of the neighboring hall; but he did not listen and he did not hear.

Suddenly, without himself knowing how, he found himself near the door; he seized the knob convulsively; the door opened.

He was in the courtroom.

V

He took a step, closed the door behind him, mechanically, and remained standing, noting what he saw.

It was a large hall, dimly lighted, and noisy and silent by turns, where all the machinery of a criminal trial was exhibited, with its petty yet solemn gravity, before the multitude.

At one end of the hall, that at which he found himself, heedless judges, in threadbare robes, were biting their fingernails, or closing their eyelids; at the other end was a ragged rabble; there were lawyers in all sorts of attitudes; soldiers with honest and hard faces; old, stained wainscoting, a dirty ceiling, tables covered with serge, which was more nearly yellow than green; doors blackened by finger marks; tavern lamps, giving more smoke than light, on nails in the paneling; candles, in brass candlesticks, on the tables; everywhere obscurity, unsightliness, and gloom, and from all this there arose an austere and august impression; for men felt therein the presence of that great human thing which is called law, and that great divine thing which is called justice.

No man in this multitude paid any attention to him. All eyes converged on a single point, a wooden bench placed against a little door, along the wall at the left hand of the judge. Upon this bench, which was lighted by several candles, was a man between two gendarmes.

This was the man.

He did not look for him, he saw him. His eyes went toward him naturally, as if they had known in advance where he was.

He thought he saw himself, older, doubtless, not precisely the same in features, but alike in attitude and appearance, with that bristling hair, with those wild and restless eyeballs, with that blouse—just as he was on the day he entered D——, full of hatred, and concealing in his soul that hideous hoard of frightful thoughts which he had spent nineteen years in gathering upon the floor of the galleys.

He said to himself, with a shudder: "Great God! Shall I again come to this?"

This being appeared at least sixty years old. There was something indescribably rough, stupid, and terrified in his appearance.

At the sound of the door, people had stood aside to make room. The judge had turned his head, and supposing the person who entered to be the mayor of M—— sur m——, greeted him with a bow. The prosecuting attorney, who had seen Madeleine at M—— sur m——, whither he had been called more than once by the duties of his office, recognized him and bowed likewise. He scarcely perceived them. He gazed about him, a prey to a sort of hallucination.

Judges, clerk, gendarmes, a throng of heads, cruelly curious—he had seen all these once before, twenty-seven years ago. He had fallen again upon these fearful things; they were before him, they moved, they had being; it was no longer an effort of his memory, a mirage of his fancy, but real gendarmes and real judges, a real throng, and real men of flesh and bone. It was done; he saw reappearing and living again around him, with all the frightfulness of reality, the monstrous visions of the past.

All this was yawning before him.

Stricken with horror, he closed his eyes, and exclaimed from the depths of his soul: "Never!"

And by a tragic sport of destiny, which was agitating all his ideas and rendering him almost insane, it was another self before him. This man on trial was called by all around him, Jean Valjean!

He had before his eyes an unheard-of vision, a sort of representation of the most horrible moment of his life, played by his shadow.

All, everything was there—the same paraphernalia, the same hour of the night—almost the same faces, judge and assistant judges, soldiers, and spectators. But above the head of the judge was a crucifix, a thing which did not appear in courtrooms at the time of his sentence. When he was tried, God was not there.

A chair was behind him; he sank into it, terrified at the idea that he might be observed. When seated, he took advantage of a pile of papers on the judges' desk to hide his face from the whole room. He could now see without being seen. He entered fully into the spirit of the reality; by degrees he recovered his composure, and arrived at that degree of calmness at which it is possible to listen.

Monsieur Bamatabois was one of the jurors.

He looked for Javert, but did not see him. The witnesses' seat was hidden from him by the clerk's table. And then, as we have just said, the hall was very dimly lighted.

At the moment of his entrance, the counsel for the prisoner was finishing his plea. The attention of all was excited to the highest degree; the trial had been in progress for three hours. During these three hours, the spectators had seen a man, an unknown, wretched being, thoroughly stupid or thoroughly artful, gradually bending beneath the weight of a terrible probability. He made gestures and signs which signified denial, or he gazed at the ceiling. He spoke with difficulty and answered with embarrassment, but from head to foot his whole person denied the charge. He seemed like an idiot in the presence of all these intellects ranged in battle around him, and like a stranger in the midst of this society by whom he had been seized. Nevertheless, a most threatening future awaited him; probabilities increased every moment, and every spectator was looking with more anxiety than himself for the calamitous sentence which seemed to be hanging over his head with ever increasing surety. One contingency even gave a glimpse of the possibility, beyond the galleys, of a capital penalty should his identity be established, and the Petit Gervais affair result in his conviction. Who was this man? What was the nature of his apathy? Was it imbecility or artifice? Did he know too much or nothing at all? These were questions upon which the spectators took sides, and which seemed to affect the jury. There was something fearful and something mysterious in the trial; the drama was not merely gloomy, but it was obscure.

The counsel for the defense had made a very good plea in that provincial language which long constituted the eloquence of the bar, and which was formerly employed by all lawyers, at Paris as well as at Romorantin or Montbrison, but which, having now become classic, is used by few except the official orators of the bar, to whom it is suited by its solemn rotundity and majestic periods, a language in which husband and wife

are called "spouses," Paris, "the center of arts and civilization,"
the king, "the monarch," a bishop, "a holy pontiff," the prosecuting attorney, "the eloquent interpreter of the vengeance of
the law," arguments, "the accents which we have just heard,"
the time of Louis XIV, "the illustrious age," a theater, "the
temple of Melpomene," the reigning family, "the august blood
of our kings," a concert, "a musical solemnity," the general in
command, "the illustrious warrior who," etc., students of the-
ology, "those tender Levites," mistakes imputed to newspapers,
"the imposture which distills its venom into the columns of
these organs," etc., etc. The counsel for the defense had begun
by expatiating on the theft of the apples—a thing ill suited to
a lofty style, but Benign Bossuet himself was once compelled
to make allusion to a hen in the midst of a funeral oration, and
acquitted himself with dignity. The counsel established that
the theft of the apples was not in fact proved. His client, whom
in his character of counsel he persisted in calling Champmathieu, had not been seen to scale the wall or break off the
branch. He had been arrested in possession of this branch
(which the counsel preferred to call "bough"); but he said
that he had found it on the ground. Where was the proof to
the contrary? Undoubtedly this branch had been broken and
carried off after the scaling of the wall, then thrown away by
the alarmed marauder; undoubtedly, there had been a thief.
But what evidence was there that this thief was Champmathieu? One single thing. That he was formerly a convict. The
counsel would not deny that this fact unfortunately appeared
to be fully proved, but even supposing him to be the convict
Jean Valjean, did this prove that he had stolen the apples?
That was a presumption at most, not a proof. The accused, it
was true, and the counsel "in good faith" must admit it, had
adopted "a mistaken system of defense." He had persisted in
denying everything, both the theft and the fact that he had
been a convict. An avowal on the latter point would have
been better certainly, and would have secured to him the indulgence of the judges; the counsel had advised him to this
course, but the defendant had obstinately refused, expecting
probably to escape punishment entirely, by admitting nothing.
It was a mistake, but must not the poverty of his intellect be
taken into consideration? The man was evidently imbecile.
Long suffering in the galleys, long suffering out of the galleys,
had brutalized him, etc., etc.; if he made a bad defense, was

this a reason for convicting him? As to the Petit Gervais affair, the counsel had nothing to say; it was not in the case. He concluded by entreating the jury and court, if the identity of Jean Valjean appeared evident to them, to apply to him the police penalties prescribed for the breaking of ban, and not the fearful punishment decreed to the convict found guilty of a second offense.

The prosecuting attorney replied to the counsel for the defense. He was violent and flowery, like most prosecuting attorneys.

He complimented the counsel for his "frankness," of which he shrewdly took advantage. He attacked the accused through all the concessions which his counsel had made. The counsel seemed to admit that the accused was Jean Valjean. He accepted the admission. This man then was Jean Valjean. This fact was conceded to the prosecution, and could be no longer contested. Who was Jean Valjean? Description of Jean Valjean: "a monster vomited," etc. The auditory and the jury "shuddered." This description finished, the prosecuting attorney resumed with an oratorical burst, designed to excite the enthusiasm of the *Journal de la Préfecture* to the highest pitch next morning. "And it is such a man," etc. etc. A vagabond, a mendicant, without means of existence, etc., etc. Accustomed through his existence to criminal acts, and profiting little by his past life in the galleys, as is proved by the crime committed upon Petit Gervais, etc., etc. It is such a man who, found on the highway in the very act of theft, a few paces from a wall that had been scaled, still holding in his hand the subject of his crime, denies the act in which he is caught, denies the theft, denies the escalade, denies everything, denies even his name, denies even his identity! Besides a hundred other proofs, to which we will not return, he is identified by four witnesses —Javert—the incorruptible inspector of police. Javert—and three of his former companions in disgrace, the convicts Brevet, Chenildieu, and Cochepaille. What has he to oppose this overwhelming unanimity? His denial. What depravity! You will do justice, gentlemen of the jury, etc., etc. While the prosecuting attorney was speaking the accused listened openmouthed, with a sort of astonishment, not unmingled with admiration. He was evidently surprised that a man could speak so well. From time to time, at the most "forcible" parts of the argument, at those moments when eloquence, unable to con-

tain itself, overflows in a stream of withering epithets, and surrounds the prisoner like a tempest, he slowly moved his head
from right to left, and from left to right—a sort of sad, mute
protest, with which he contented himself from the beginning
of the argument. Two or three times the spectators nearest him
heard him say in a low tone: "This all comes from not asking
for Monsieur Baloup!" The prosecuting attorney pointed out
to the jury this air of stupidity, which was evidently put on,
and which denoted, not imbecility, but address, artifice, and
the habit of deceiving justice; and which showed in its full
light the "deep-rooted perversity" of the man. He concluded
by reserving entirely the Petit Gervais affair, and demanding a
sentence to the full extent of the law.

This was, for this offense, as will be remembered, hard labor
for life.

The counsel for the prisoner rose, commenced by compli-
menting "monsieur, the prosecuting attorney, on his admirable
argument," then replied as best he could, but in a weaker
tone; the ground was evidently giving way under him.

VI

THIS time had come for closing the case. The judge commanded the accused to rise, and put the usual question: "Have
you anything to add to your defense?"

The man, standing, and twirling in his hands a hideous cap
which he had, seemed not to hear.

The judge repeated the question.

This time the man heard, and appeared to comprehend. He
started like one awaking from sleep, cast his eyes around him,
looked at the spectators, the gendarmes, his counsel, the jurors,
and the court, placed his huge fists on the bar before him,
looked around, and suddenly fixing his eyes upon the prosecuting attorney, began to speak. It was like an eruption. It seemed
from the manner in which the words escaped his lips, incoher-
ent, impetuous, jostling each other pell-mell, as if they were all
eager to find vent at the same time. He said:

"I have this to say: That I have been a wheelwright at Paris;
that it was at Monsieur Baloup's too. It is a hard life to be a
wheelwright, you always work outdoors, in yards, under sheds
when you have good bosses, never in shops, because you must

have room, you see. In the winter, it is so cold that you thresh your arms to warm them, but the bosses won't allow that; they say it is a waste of time. It is tough work to handle iron when there is ice on the pavements. It wears a man out quick. You get old when you are young at this trade. A man is used up by forty. I was fifty-three; I was sick a good deal. And then the workmen are so bad! When a poor fellow isn't young, they always call you old bird, and old beast! I earned only thirty sous a day, they paid me as little as they could—the bosses took advantage of my age. Then I had my daughter, who was a washerwoman at the river. She earned a little for herself; between us two, we got on; she had hard work too. All day long up to the waist in a tub, in rain, in snow, with wind that cuts your face when it freezes, it is all the same, the washing must be done; there are folks who haven't much linen and are waiting for it; if you don't wash you lose your customers. The planks are not well matched, and the water falls on you everywhere. You get your clothes wet through and through; that strikes in. She would come home at seven o'clock at night, and go to bed right away. She was so tired. Her husband used to beat her. She is dead. She wasn't very happy. She was a good girl; she never went to balls, and was very quiet. I remember one Shrove Tuesday she went to bed at eight o'clock. Look here, I am telling the truth. You have only to ask if 'tisn't so. Ask! How stupid I am! Paris is a gulf. Who is there that knows Father Champmathieu? But there is Monsieur Baloup. Go and see Monsieur Baloup. I don't know what more you want of me."

The man ceased speaking, but did not sit down. He had uttered these sentences in a loud, rapid, hoarse, harsh, and guttural tone, with a sort of angry and savage simplicity. Once, he stopped to bow to somebody in the crowd. The sort of affirmations which he seemed to fling out haphazard came from him like hiccoughs, and he added to each the gesture of a man chopping wood. When he had finished, the auditory burst into laughter. He looked at them, and seeing them laughing and not knowing why, began to laugh himself.

That was sinister.

The judge, a considerate and kindly man, raised his voice. He reminded the "gentlemen of the jury" that Monsieur Baloup, the former master wheelwright by whom the prisoner said he had been employed, had been summoned, but had not appeared. He had become bankrupt, and could not be found. Then, turning to the accused, he adjured him to listen to what he was about to say, and added: "You are in a position which demands reflection. The gravest presumptions are weighing against you, and may lead to fatal results. Prisoner, on your own behalf, I question you a second time, explain yourself clearly on these two points. First, did you or did you not climb the wall of the Pierron close, break off the branch and steal the apples, that is to say, commit the crime of theft, with the addition of breaking into an enclosure? Secondly, are you or are you not the discharged convict, Jean Valjean?"

The prisoner shook his head with a knowing look, like a man who understands perfectly, and knows what he is going to say. He opened his mouth, turned toward the presiding judge, and said:

"In the first place—"

Then he looked at his cap, looked up at the ceiling, and was silent.

"Prisoner," resumed the prosecuting attorney, in an austere tone, "give attention. You have replied to nothing that has been asked you. Your agitation condemns you."

The accused had at last resumed his seat; he rose abruptly when the prosecuting attorney had ended, and exclaimed:

"You are a very bad man, you, I mean. This is what I wanted to say. I couldn't think of it first off. I never stole anything. I am a man who don't get something to eat every day. I was coming from Ailly, walking alone after a shower, which had made the ground all yellow with mud, so that the ponds were running over, and you only saw little sprigs of grass sticking out of the sand along the road, and I found a broken branch on the ground with apples on it, and I picked it up not knowing what trouble it would give me. It is three months that I have been in prison, being knocked about. More'n that, I can't tell. You talk against me and tell me 'answer!' The gendarme, who is a good fellow, nudges my elbow, and whispers, 'answer now.' I can't explain myself; I never studied; I am a poor man. You are all wrong not to see that I didn't steal. I picked up off the ground things that was there. You talk about Jean Valjean—I don't know any such people. I have worked for Monsieur Baloup, Boulevard de l'Hôpital. My name is Champmathieu. You must be very sharp to tell me where I was born. I don't know myself. Everybody can't have houses to be born in; that would be too handy. I think my father and mother were strollers, but I don't know. When I was a child they called me Little One; now, they call me Old Man. They're my Christian names. Take them as you like. I have been in Auvergne, I have been at Faverolles. Bless me! Can't a man have been in Auvergne and Faverolles without having been at the galleys? I tell you I never stole, and that I am Father Champmathieu. I have been at Monsieur Baloup's: I lived in his house. I am tired of your everlasting nonsense. What is everybody after me for like a mad dog?"

The prosecuting attorney was still standing; he addressed the judge:

"Sir, in the presence of the confused but very adroit denegations of the accused, who endeavors to pass for an idiot, but who will not succeed in it—we will prevent him—we request that it may please you and the court to call again within the bar the convicts, Brevet, Cochepaille, and Chenildieu, and the police inspector Javert, and to submit them to a final interrogation, concerning the identity of the accused with the convict Jean Valjean."

"I must remind the prosecuting attorney," said the presiding judge, "that police inspector Javert, recalled by his duties to the chief town of a neighboring district, left the hall, and the city also, as soon as his testimony was taken. We granted him this permission, with the consent of the prosecuting attorney and the counsel of the accused."

"True," replied the prosecuting attorney; "in the absence of Monsieur Javert I think it a duty to recall to the gentlemen of the jury what he said here a few hours ago. Javert is an estimable man, who does honor to inferior but important functions, by his rigorous and strict probity. These are the terms in which he testified: 'I do not need even moral presumptions and material proofs to contradict the denials of the accused. I recognize him perfectly. This man's name is not Champmathieu; he is a convict, Jean Valjean, very hard, and much feared. I often saw him when I was adjutant of the galley guard at Toulon. I repeat it; I recognize him perfectly.'"

This declaration, in terms so precise, appeared to produce a strong impression upon the public and jury. The prosecuting attorney concluded by insisting that, in the absence of Javert, the three witnesses, Brevet, Chenildieu, and Cochepaille, should be heard anew and solemnly interrogated.

The judge gave an order to an officer, and a moment afterward the door of the witness room opened, and the officer, accompanied by a gendarme ready to lend assistance, led in the convict Brevet. The audience was in breathless suspense, and all hearts palpitated as if they contained but a single soul.

The old convict Brevet was clad in the black and gray jacket of the central prisons. Brevet was about sixty years old; he had the face of a man of business, and the air of a rogue. They sometimes go together. He had become something like a turnkey in the prison, to which he had been brought by new misdeeds. He was one of those men of whom their superiors are wont to say: "He tries to make himself useful." The chaplain bore good testimony to his religious habits. It must not be forgotten that this happened under the Restoration.

"Brevet," said the judge, "you have suffered infamous punishment, and cannot take an oath."

Brevet cast down his eyes.

"Nevertheless," continued the judge, "even in the man whom the law has degraded there may remain, if divine justice permit, a sentiment of honor and equity. The moment is a solemn one, and there is still time to retract if you think yourself mistaken. Prisoner, rise. Brevet, look well upon the prisoner; collect your remembrances, and say, on your soul and conscience, whether you still recognize this man as your former comrade in the galleys, Jean Valjean."

Brevet looked at the prisoner, then turned again to the court.

"Yes, your honor, I was the first to recognize him, and still do so. This man is Jean Valjean, who came to Toulon in 1796, and left in 1815. I left a year after. He looks like a brute now, but he must have grown stupid with age; at the galleys he was sullen. I recognize him now, positively."

"Sit down," said the judge. "Prisoner, remain standing."

Chenildieu was brought in, a convict for life, as was shown by his red cloak and green cap. He was undergoing his punishment in the galleys of Toulon, whence he had been brought for this occasion. He was a little man, about fifty years old, active, wrinkled, lean, yellow, brazen, restless, with a sort of sickly feebleness in his limbs and whole person, and immense force in his eye. His companions in the galleys had nicknamed him Je-nie-Dieu.

The judge addressed nearly the same words to him as to Brevet. When he reminded him that his infamy had deprived

him of the right to take an oath, Chenildieu raised his head
and looked the spectators in the face. The judge requested him
to collect his thoughts, and asked him, as he had Brevet,
whether he still recognized the prisoner.

Chenildieu burst out laughing.

"Gad! Do I recognize him! We were five years on the same
chain. You're sulky with me, are you, old boy?"

"Sit down," said the judge.

The officer brought in Cochepaille; this other convict for
life, brought from the galleys and dressed in red like Chenildieu, was a peasant from Lourdes, and a semibear of the
Pyrenees. He had tended flocks in the mountains, and from
shepherd had glided into brigandage. Cochepaille was not less
uncouth than the accused, and appeared still more stupid. He
was one of those unfortunate men whom nature turns out as
wild beasts, and society finishes up into galley slaves.

The judge attempted to move him by a few serious and pathetic words, and asked him, as he had the others, whether he
still recognized without hesitation or difficulty the man standing before him.

"It is Jean Valjean," said Cochepaille. "The same they called
Jean-the-Jack, he was so strong."

Each of the affirmations of these three men, evidently sincere and in good faith, had excited in the audience a murmur
of evil augury for the accused—a murmur which increased in
force and continuance every time a new declaration was
added to the preceding one. The prisoner himself listened to
them with that astonished countenance which, according to
the prosecution, was his principal means of defense. At the
first, the gendarmes by his side heard him mutter between his
teeth: "Ah, well! There is one of them!" After the second, he
said in a louder tone, with an air almost of satisfaction:
"Good!" At the third, he exclaimed: "Famous!"

The judge addressed him:

"Prisoner, you have listened. What have you to say?"

He replied:

"I say—famous!"

A buzz ran through the crowd and almost invaded the jury.
It was evident that the man was lost.

"Officers," said the judge, "enforce order. I am about to sum
up the case."

At this moment there was a movement near the judge. A voice was heard exclaiming:

"Brevet, Chenildieu, Cochepaille, look this way!"

So lamentable and terrible was this voice that those who heard it felt their blood run cold. All eyes turned toward the spot whence it came. A man, who had been sitting among the privileged spectators behind the court, had risen, pushed open the low door which separated the tribunal from the bar, and was standing in the center of the hall. The judge, the prosecuting attorney, Monsieur Bamatabois, twenty persons recognized him, and exclaimed at once:

"Monsieur Madeleine!"

VII

It was he, indeed. The clerk's lamp lighted up his face. He held his hat in hand; there was no disorder in his dress; his overcoat was carefully buttoned. He was very pale, and trembled slightly. His hair, already gray when he came to Arras, was now perfectly white. It had become so during the hour that he had been there. All eyes were strained toward him.

The sensation was indescribable. There was a moment of hesitation in the auditory. The voice had been so thrilling, the man standing there appeared so calm, that at first nobody could comprehend it. They asked who had cried out. They could not believe that this tranquil man had uttered that fearful cry.

This indecision lasted but few seconds. Before even the judge and prosecuting attorney could say a word, before the gendarmes and officers could make a sign, the man, whom all up to this moment had called Monsieur Madeleine, had advanced toward the witnesses, Cochepaille, Brevet, and Chenildieu.

"Do you not recognize me?" said he.

All three stood confounded, and indicated by a shake of the head that they did not know him. Cochepaille, intimidated, gave the military salute. Monsieur Madeleine turned toward the jurors and court, and said in a mild voice:

"Gentlemen of the jury, release the accused. Your honor, order my arrest. He is not the man whom you seek; it is I. I am Jean Valjean."

Not a breath stirred. To the first commotion of astonishment had succeeded a sepulchral silence. That species of religious awe was felt in the hall which thrills the multitude at the accomplishment of a grand action.

Nevertheless, the face of the judge was marked with sympathy and sadness; he exchanged glances with the prosecuting attorney, and a few whispered words with the assistant judges. He turned to the spectators and asked in a tone which was understood by all:

"Is there a physician here?"

The prosecuting attorney continued:

"Gentlemen of the jury, the strange and unexpected incident which disturbs the audience, inspires us, as well as yourselves, with a feeling we have no need to express. You all know, at least by reputation, the honorable Monsieur Madeleine, Mayor of M—— sur m——. If there be a physician in the audience, we unite with his honor the judge in entreating him to be kind enough to lend his assistance to Monsieur Madeleine and conduct him to his residence."

Monsieur Madeleine did not permit the prosecuting attorney to finish, but interrupted him with a tone full of gentleness and authority. These are the words he uttered: we give them literally, as they were written down immediately after the trial, by one of the witnesses of the scene—as they still ring in the ears of those who heard them, now nearly forty years ago.

"I thank you, Monsieur Prosecuting Attorney, but I am not mad. You shall see. You were on the point of committing a great mistake; release that man. I am accomplishing a duty; I am the unhappy convict. I am the only one who sees clearly here, and I tell you the truth. What I do at this moment, God beholds from on high, and that is sufficient. You can take me, since I am here. Nevertheless, I have done my best. I have disguised myself under another name, I have become rich, I have become a mayor, I have desired to enter again among honest men. It seems that this cannot be. In short, there are many things which I cannot tell. I shall not relate to you the story of my life: some day you will know it. I did rob Monseigneur the Bishop—that is true; I did rob Petit Gervais—that is true. They were right in telling you that Jean Valjean was a wicked wretch. But all the blame may not belong to him. Listen, your honors; a man so abased as I has no remonstrance to make with Providence, nor advice to give to society; but, mark you, the infamy from which I have sought to rise is pernicious to men. The galleys make the galley slave. Receive this in kindness, if you will. Before the galleys, I was a poor peasant, unintelligent, a species of idiot; the galley changed me. I was stupid, I became wicked; I was a log, I became a firebrand. Later, I was saved by indulgence and kindness, as I had been lost by severity. But, pardon, you cannot comprehend what I say. You will find in my house, among the ashes of the fireplace, the forty-sous piece of which, seven years ago, I robbed Petit Gervais. I have nothing more to add. Take me. Great God! The prosecuting attorney shakes his head. You say 'Monsieur Madeleine has gone mad'; you do not believe me. This is hard to be borne. Do not condemn that man, at least. What! These men do not know me! Would that Javert were here. He would recognize me!"

Nothing could express the kindly yet terrible melancholy of the tone which accompanied these words.

He turned to the three convicts:

"Well! I recognize you, Brevet, do you remember—"

He paused, hesitated a moment, and said:

"Do you remember those checkered, knit suspenders that you had in the galleys?"

Brevet started as if struck with surprise, and gazed wildly at him from head to foot. He continued:

"Chenildieu, surnamed by yourself Je-nie-Dieu, the whole of your left shoulder has been burned deeply, from laying it one day on a chafing dish full of embers, to efface the three letters T. F. P., which yet are still to be seen there. Answer me, is this true?"

"It is true!" said Chenildieu.

He turned to Cochepaille:

"Cochepaille, you have on your left arm, near where you have been bled, a date put in blue letters with burnt powder. It is the date of the landing of the emperor at Cannes, March 1st, 1815. Lift up your sleeve."

Cochepaille lifted up his sleeve; all eyes around him were turned to his naked arm. A gendarme brought a lamp; the date was there.

The unhappy man turned toward the audience and the court with a smile, the thought of which still rends the hearts of those who witnessed it. It was the smile of triumph; it was also the smile of despair.

"You see clearly," said he, "that I am Jean Valjean."

There were no longer either judges, or accusers, or gendarmes in the hall; there were only fixed eyes and beating hearts. Nobody remembered longer the part which he had to play; the prosecuting attorney forgot that he was there to prosecute, the judge that he was there to preside, the counsel for the defense that he was there to defend. Strange to say no question was put, no authority intervened. It is the peculiarity of sublime spectacles that they take possession of every soul, and make of every witness a spectator. Nobody, perhaps, was positively conscious of what he experienced, and, undoubtedly, nobody said to himself that he there beheld the effulgence of a great light, yet all felt dazzled at heart.

It was evident that Jean Valjean was before their eyes. That fact shone forth. The appearance of this man had been enough fully to clear up the case, so obscure a moment before. Without need of any further explanation, the multitude, as by a sort of electric revelation, comprehended instantly, and at a single glance, this simple and magnificent story of a man giving himself up that another might not be condemned in his place. The details, the hesitation, the slight reluctance possible were lost in this immense, luminous fact.

It was an impression which quickly passed over, but for the moment it was irresistible.

"I will not disturb the proceedings further," continued Jean Valjean. "I am going, since I am not arrested. I have many things to do. Monsieur the Prosecuting Attorney knows where I am going, and will have me arrested when he chooses."

He walked toward the outer door. Not a voice was raised, not an arm stretched out to prevent him. All stood aside. There was at this moment an indescribable divinity within him which makes the multitudes fall back and make way before a man. He passed through the throng with slow steps. It was never known who opened the door, but it is certain that the door was open when he came to it. On reaching it he turned and said:

"Monsieur the Prosecuting Attorney, I remain at your disposal."

He then addressed himself to the auditory.

"You all, all who are here, think me worthy of pity, do you not? Great God! When I think of what I have been on the point of doing, I think myself worthy of envy. Still, would that all this had not happened!"

He went out, and the door closed as it had opened, for those who do deeds sovereignly great are always sure of being served by somebody in the multitude.

Less than an hour afterward, the verdict of the jury discharged from all accusation the said Champmathieu, and Champmathieu, set at liberty forthwith, went his way stupefied, thinking all men mad, and understanding nothing of this vision.

Counterstroke

I

DAY began to dawn. Fantine had had a feverish and sleepless night, yet full of happy visions; she fell asleep at daybreak. The sister who had watched with her took advantage of this slumber to go and prepare a new potion of quinine. The good sister had been for a few moments in the laboratory of the infirmary, bending over her vials and drugs, looking at them very closely on account of the mist which the dawn casts over all objects, when suddenly she turned her head, and uttered a faint cry. Monsieur Madeleine stood before her. He had just come in silently.

"You, Monsieur the Mayor!" she exclaimed.

"How is the poor woman?" he answered in a low voice.

"Better just now. But we have been very anxious indeed."

She explained that Fantine had been very ill the night before, but was now better, because she believed that the mayor had gone to Montfermeil for her child. The sister dared not question the mayor, but she saw clearly from his manner that he had not come from that place.

"That is well," said he. "You did right not to deceive her."

"Yes," returned the sister, "but now, Monsieur the Mayor, when she sees you without her child, what shall we tell her?"

He reflected for a moment, then said:

"God will inspire us."

"But, we cannot tell her a lie," murmured the sister, in a smothered tone.

The broad daylight streamed into the room, and lighted up the face of Monsieur Madeleine.

The sister happened to raise her eyes.

"Oh! God! Monsieur!" she exclaimed. "What has befallen you? Your hair is all white!"

"White?" said he.

She had no mirror; she rummaged in a case of instruments, and found a little glass which the physician of the infirmary used to discover whether the breath had left the body of a patient. Monsieur Madeleine took the glass, looked at his hair in it, and said: "Indeed!"

He spoke the word with indifference, as if thinking of something else.

The sister felt chilled by an unknown something, of which she caught a glimpse in all this.

He made a few remarks about a door that shut with difficulty, the noise of which might awaken the sick woman; then entered the chamber of Fantine, approached her bed, and opened the curtains. She was sleeping. Her breath came from her chest with that tragic sound which is peculiar to these diseases, and which rends the heart of unhappy mothers, watching the slumbers of their fated children. But this labored respiration scarcely disturbed an ineffable serenity, which overshadowed her countenance, and transfigured her in her sleep. Her pallor had become whiteness, and her cheeks were glowing. Her long, fair eyelashes, the only beauty left to her of her maidenhood and youth, quivered as they lay closed upon her cheek. Her whole person trembled as if with the fluttering of wings which were felt, but could not be seen, and which seemed about to unfold and bear her away. To see her thus, no one could have believed that her life was despaired of. She looked more as if about to soar away than to die.

The stem, when the hand is stretched out to pluck the flower, quivers, and seems at once to shrink back, and present itself. The human body has something of this trepidation at the moment when the mysterious fingers of death are about to gather the soul.

Monsieur Madeleine remained for some time motionless near the bed, looking by turns at the patient and the crucifix, as he had done two months before, on the day when he came for the first time to see her in this asylum. They were still there, both in the same attitude, she sleeping, he praying; only now, after these two months had rolled away, her hair was gray and his was white.

The sister had not entered with him. He stood by the bed,

with his fingers on his lips, as if there were someone in the room to silence. She opened her eyes, saw him, and said tranquilly, with a smile:

"And Cosette?"

II

SHE did not start with surprise or joy; she was joy itself. The simple question: "And Cosette?" was asked with such deep faith, with so much certainty, with so complete an absence of disquiet or doubt, that he could find no word in reply. She continued:

"I knew that you were there; I was asleep, but I saw you. I have seen you for a long time; I have followed you with my eyes the whole night. You were in a halo of glory, and all manner of celestial forms were hovering around you!"

He raised his eyes toward the crucifix.

"But tell me, where is Cosette?" she resumed. "Why not put her on my bed that I might see her the instant I woke?"

He answered something mechanically, which he could never afterward recall.

Happily, the physician had come and had been apprised of this. He came to the aid of Monsieur Madeleine.

"My child," said he, "be calm, your daughter is here."

The eyes of Fantine beamed with joy, and lighted up her whole countenance. She clasped her hands with an expression full of the most violent and most gentle entreaty:

"Oh!" she exclaimed. "Bring her to me!"

Touching illusion of the mother; Cosette was still to her a little child to be carried in the arms.

"Not yet," continued the physician, "not at this moment. You have some fever still. The sight of your child will agitate you, and make you worse. We must cure you first."

Monsieur Madeleine was sitting in a chair by the side of the bed. She turned toward him, and made visible efforts to appear calm and "very good," as she said, in that weakness of disease which resembles childhood, so that, seeing her so peaceful, there should be no objection to bringing her Cosette. Nevertheless, although restraining herself, she could not help addressing a thousand questions to Monsieur Madeleine.

"Did you have a pleasant journey, Monsieur the Mayor? Oh!

how good you have been to go for her! Tell me only how she is. Did she bear the journey well? Ah! She will not know me. In all this time, she has forgotten me, poor kitten! Children have no memory. They are like birds. Today they see one thing, and tomorrow another, and remember nothing. Tell me only, were her clothes clean? Did those Thénardiers keep her neat? How did they feed her? Oh! How I want to see her! Monsieur the Mayor, did you think her pretty? Is not my daughter beautiful? You must have been very cold in the diligence? Could they not bring her here for one little moment? They might take her away immediately. Say! You are master here, are you willing?"

He took her hand. "Cosette is beautiful," said he. "Cosette is well; you shall see her soon, but be quiet. You talk too fast; and then you throw your arms out of bed, which makes you cough."

In fact, coughing fits interrupted Fantine at almost every word.

Monsieur Madeleine still held her hand and looked at her with anxiety. It was evident that he had come to tell her things before which his mind now hesitated. The physician had made his visit and retired. The sister alone remained with them.

But in the midst of the silence, Fantine cried out:

"I hear her! Oh, darling! I hear her!"

There was a child playing in the court—the child of the portress or some workwoman. It was one of those chances which are always met with, and which seem to make part of the mysterious representation of tragic events. The child, which was a little girl, was running up and down to keep herself warm, singing and laughing in a loud voice. Alas! With what are not the plays of children mingled! Fantine had heard this little girl singing.

"Oh!" said she. "It is my Cosette! I know her voice!"

The child departed as she had come, and the voice died away. Fantine listened for some time. A shadow came over her face, and Monsieur Madeleine heard her whisper: "How wicked it is of that doctor not to let me see my child! That man has a bad face!"

But yet her happy train of thought returned. With her head on the pillow she continued to talk to herself. "How happy we shall be! We will have a little garden in the first place; Monsieur Madeleine has promised it to me. My child will play in the garden. She must know her letters now. I will teach her to spell. She will chase the butterflies in the grass, and I will watch her. Then there will be her first communion. Ah! When will her first communion be?"

She began to count on her fingers.

"One, two, three, four. She is seven years old. In five years. She will have a white veil and openwork stockings, and will look like a little lady. Oh, my good sister, you do not know how foolish I am; here I am thinking of my child's first communion!"

And she began to laugh.

He had let go the hand of Fantine. He listened to the words as one listens to the wind that blows, his eyes on the ground, and his mind plunged into unfathomable reflections. Suddenly she ceased speaking, and raised her head mechanically. Fantine had become appalling.

She did not speak; she did not breathe; she half-raised herself in the bed, the covering fell from her emaciated shoulders; her countenance, radiant a moment before, became livid, and her eyes, dilated with terror, seemed to fasten on something before her at the other end of the room.

"Good God!" exclaimed he. "What is the matter, Fantine?"

She did not answer; she did not take her eyes from the object which she seemed to see, but touched his arm with one hand, and with the other made a sign to him to look behind him.

He turned, and saw Javert.

III

LET us see what had happened.

The half-hour after midnight was striking when Monsieur Madeleine left the hall of the Arras assizes. He had returned to his inn just in time to take the mail coach, in which he had retained his seat. A little before six in the morning he had reached M—— sur m——, where his first care had been to post a letter to Monsieur Laffitte, then go to the infirmary and visit Fantine.

Immediately upon the discharge of Champmathieu the prosecuting attorney closeted himself with the judge. The subject of their conference was: "Of the necessity of the arrest of the person of Monsieur the Mayor of M— sur m———."

The order of arrest was therefore granted. The prosecuting attorney sent it to M——— sur m——— by a courier, at full speed, to police inspector Javert.

It will be remembered that Javert had returned to M——— sur m——— immediately after giving his testimony.

Javert was just rising when the courier brought him the warrant and order of arrest.

The courier was himself a policeman, and an intelligent man, who, in three words, acquainted Javert with what had happened at Arras.

The order of arrest, signed by the prosecuting attorney, was couched in these terms:

"Inspector Javert will seize the body of Sieur Madeleine, Mayor of M——— sur m———, who has this day been identified in court as the discharged convict Jean Valjean."

Javert came unostentatiously, had taken a corporal and four soldiers from the station house nearby, had left the soldiers in the court, had been shown to Fantine's chamber by the portress, without suspicion, accustomed as she was to see armed men asking for the mayor.

On reaching the room of Fantine, Javert turned the key, pushed open the door with the gentleness of a sick nurse, or a police spy, and entered.

Properly speaking, he did not enter. He remained standing in the half-opened door, his hat on his head, and his left hand in his overcoat, which was buttoned to the chin. In the bend of his elbow might be seen the leaden head of his enormous cane, which disappeared behind him.

He remained thus for nearly a minute, unperceived. Suddenly, Fantine raised her eyes, saw him, and caused Monsieur Madeleine to turn round.

At the moment when the glance of Madeleine encountered that of Javert, Javert, without stirring, without moving, without approaching, became terrible. No human feeling can ever be so appalling as joy.

It was the face of a demon who had again found his victim.

The certainty that he had caught Jean Valjean at last, brought forth upon his countenance all that was in his soul. The deformity of triumph spread over his narrow forehead. It was the fullest development of horror that a gratified face can show.

Javert was at this moment in heaven. Without clearly defining his own feelings, yet notwithstanding with a confused intuition of his necessity and his success, he, Javert, personified justice, light, and truth, in their celestial function as destroyers of evil. He was surrounded and supported by infinite depths of authority, reason, precedent, legal conscience, the vengeance of the law, all the stars in the firmament; he protected order, he hurled forth the thunder of the law, he avenged society, he lent aid to the absolute; he stood erect in a halo of glory; there was in his victory a reminder of defiance and of combat; standing haughty, resplendent, he displayed in full glory the superhuman beastliness of a ferocious archangel; the fearful shadow of the deed which he was accomplishing made visible in his clenched fist the uncertain flashes of the social sword; happy and indignant, he had set his heel on crime, vice, rebellion, perdition, and hell; he was radiant, exterminating, smiling; there was an incontestable grandeur in this monstrous St. Michael.

Javert, though hideous, was not ignoble.

Probity, sincerity, candor, conviction, the idea of duty, are things which, mistaken, may become hideous, but which, even though hideous, remain great; their majesty, peculiar to the human conscience, continues in all their horror; they are virtues with a single vice—error. The pitiless, sincere joy of a fanatic in an act of atrocity preserves an indescribably mournful radiance which inspires us with veneration. Without suspecting it, Javert, in his fear-inspiring happiness, was pitiable, like every ignorant man who wins a triumph. Nothing could be more painful and terrible than this face, which revealed what we may call all the evil of good.

IV

FANTINE had not seen Javert since the day the mayor had wrested her from him. Her sick brain accounted for nothing, only she was sure that he had come for her. She could not endure this hideous face, she felt as if she were dying, she hid her face with both hands, and shrieked in anguish:

"Monsieur Madeleine, save me!"

Jean Valjean, we shall call him by no other name henceforth, had risen. He said to Fantine in his gentlest and calmest tone:

"Be composed; it is not for you that he comes."

He then turned to Javert and said:

"I know what you want."

Javert answered:

"Hurry along."

While speaking thus, he did not stir a step, but cast upon Jean Valjean a look like a noose, with which he was accustomed to draw the wretched to him by force.

It was the same look which Fantine had felt penetrate to the very marrow of her bones, two months before.

At the exclamation of Javert, Fantine had opened her eyes again. But the mayor was there, what could she fear?

Javert advanced to the middle of the chamber, exclaiming:

"Hey, there; are you coming?"

The unhappy woman looked around her. There was no one but the nun and the mayor. To whom could this contemptuous familiarity be addressed? To herself alone. She shuddered.

Then she saw a mysterious thing, so mysterious that its like had never appeared to her in the darkest delirium of fever.

She saw the spy Javert seize Monsieur the Mayor by the collar; she saw Monsieur the Mayor bow his head. The world seemed vanishing before her sight.

Javert, in fact, had taken Jean Valjean by the collar.

Javert burst into a horrid laugh, displaying all his teeth.

"There is no Monsieur the Mayor here any longer!" said he.

Jean Valjean did not attempt to disturb the hand which grasped the collar of his coat. He said:

"Javert—"

Javert interrupted him: "Call me Monsieur the Inspector!"

"Monsieur," continued Jean Valjean, "I would like to speak a word with you in private."

"Aloud, speak aloud," said Javert, "people speak aloud to me."

Jean Valjean went on, lowering his voice.

"It is a request that I have to make of you—"

"I tell you to speak aloud."

"But this should not be heard by anyone but yourself."

"What is that to me? I will not listen."

Jean Valjean turned to him and said rapidly and in a very low tone:

"Give me three days! Three days to go for the child of this unhappy woman! I will pay whatever is necessary. You shall accompany me if you like."

"Are you laughing at me!" cried Javert. "Hey! I did not think you so stupid! You ask for three days to get away, and tell me that you are going for this girl's child! Ha, ha, that's good! That is good!"

Fantine shivered.

"My child!" she exclaimed. "Going for my child! Then she is not here! Sister, tell me, where is Cosette? I want my child! Monsieur Madeleine, Monsieur the Mayor!"

Javert stamped his foot.

"There is the other now! Hold your tongue, hussy! Miserable country, where galley slaves are magistrates and women of the town are nursed like countesses! Ha, but all this will be changed; it was time!"

He gazed steadily at Fantine, and added, grasping anew the cravat, shirt, and coat collar of Jean Valjean:

"I tell you that there is no Monsieur Madeleine, and that there is no Monsieur the Mayor. There is a robber, there is a brigand, there is a convict called Jean Valjean, and I have got him! That is what there is!"

Fantine started upright, supporting herself by her rigid arms and hands; she looked at Jean Valjean, then at Javert, and then at the nun; she opened her mouth as if to speak; a rattle came from her throat, her teeth struck together, she stretched out her arms in anguish, convulsively opening her hands, and groping about her like one who is drowning, she sank suddenly back upon the pillow.

Her head struck the head of the bed and fell forward on her breast, the mouth gaping, the eyes open and glazed.

She was dead.

Jean Valjean put his hand on that of Javert, which held him, and opened it as he would have opened the hand of a child; then he said:

"You have killed this woman."

"Have done with this!" cried Javert, furious. "I am not here to listen to sermons; save all that; the guard is below; come right along, or the handcuffs!"

There stood in a corner of the room an old iron bedstead in

a dilapidated condition, which the sisters used as a camp bed when they watched. Jean Valjean went to the bed, wrenched out the rickety head bar—a thing easy for muscles like his—in the twinkling of an eye, and with the bar in his clenched fist, looked at Javert. Javert recoiled toward the door.

Jean Valjean, his iron bar in hand, walked slowly toward the bed of Fantine. On reaching it, he turned and said to Javert in a voice that could scarcely be heard:

"I advise you not to disturb me now."

Nothing is more certain than that Javert trembled.

He had an idea of calling the guard, but Jean Valjean might profit by his absence to escape. He remained, therefore, grasped the bottom of his cane, and leaned against the framework of the door without taking his eyes from Jean Valjean.

Jean Valjean rested his elbow upon the post, and his head upon his hand, and gazed at Fantine, stretched motionless before him. He remained thus, mute and absorbed, evidently lost to everything of this life. His countenance and attitude bespoke nothing but inexpressible pity.

After a few moments' reverie, he bent down to Fantine, and addressed her in a whisper.

What did he say? What could this condemned man say to this dead woman? What were these words? They were heard by none on earth. Did the dead woman hear them? There are touching illusions which perhaps are sublime realities. One thing is beyond doubt: the sister, the only witness of what passed, has often related that, at the moment when Jean Valjean whispered in the ear of Fantine, she distinctly saw an ineffable smile beam on those pale lips and in those dim eyes, full of the wonder of the tomb.

Jean Valjean took Fantine's head in his hands and arranged it on the pillow, as a mother would have done for her child, then fastened the string of her nightdress, and replaced her hair beneath her cap. This done, he closed her eyes.

The face of Fantine, at this instant, seemed strangely illumined.

Death is the entrance into the great light.

Fantine's hand hung over the side of the bed. Jean Valjean knelt before this hand, raised it gently, and kissed it.

Then he rose, and, turning to Javert, said:

"Now, I am at your disposal."

Fantine was buried in the common grave of the cemetery,

which is for everybody and for all, and in which the poor are lost. Happily, God knows where to find the soul. Fantine was laid away in the darkness with bodies which had no name; she suffered the promiscuity of dust. She was thrown into the public pit. Her tomb was like her bed.

Cosette

Waterloo

DURING the night of the 18th of June, on the battlefield of Waterloo, the dead were despoiled. Wellington was rigid; he ordered whoever should be taken in the act to be put to death; but rapine is persevering. The marauders were robbing in one corner of the battlefield while they were shooting them in another.

The moon was an evil genius on this plain.

Toward midnight a man was prowling, or rather crawling, along the sunken road of Ohain. He was dressed in a blouse which was in part a capote, was restless and daring, looking behind and before as he went. Who was this man? Night, probably, knew more of his doings than day! He had no knapsack, but evidently large pockets under his capote. From time to time he stopped, examined the plain around him as if to see if he were observed, stooped down suddenly, stirred on the ground something silent and motionless, then rose up and skulked away. His gliding movement, his attitudes, his rapid and mysterious gestures, made him seem like those twilight specters which haunt ruins and which the old Norman legends call the Goers.

Certain nocturnal water birds make such motions in marshes.

The night was serene. Not a cloud was in the zenith. What mattered it that the earth was red, the moon retained her whiteness. Such is the indifference of heaven. In the meadows, branches of trees broken by grape, but not fallen, and held by the bark, swung gently in the night wind. A breath, almost a respiration, moved the brushwood. There was a quivering in the grass which seemed like the departure of souls.

The night prowler which we have just introduced to the reader ferreted through this immense grave. He looked about. He passed an indescribably hideous review of the dead. He walked with his feet in blood.

Suddenly he stopped.

A few steps before him, in the sunken road, at a point where the mound of corpses ended, from under this mass of men and horses appeared an open hand, lighted by the moon.

This hand had something upon a finger which sparkled; it was a gold ring.

The man stooped down, remained a moment, and when he rose again there was no ring upon that hand.

He did not rise up precisely; he remained in a sinister and startled attitude, turning his back to the pile of dead, scrutinizing the horizon, on his knees, all the front of his body being supported on his two forefingers, his head raised just enough to peep above the edge of the hollow road. The four paws of the jackal are adapted to certain actions.

Then, deciding upon his course, he arose.

At this moment he experienced a shock. He felt that he was held from behind.

He turned; it was the open hand, which had closed, seizing the lappet of his capote.

An honest man would have been frightened. This man began to laugh.

"Oh," said he, "it's only the dead man. I like a ghost better than a gendarme."

However, the hand relaxed and let go its hold. Strength is soon exhausted in the tomb.

"Ah ha!" returned the prowler. "Is this dead man alive? Let us see."

He bent over again, rummaged among the heap, removed whatever impeded him, seized the hand, laid hold of the arm, disengaged the head, drew out the body, and some moments after dragged into the shadow of the hollow road an inanimate man, at least one who was senseless. It was a cuirassier, an officer, an officer, also, of some rank; a great gold epaulet protruded from beneath his cuirass, but he had no casque. A furious saber cut had disfigured his face, where nothing but blood was to be seen. It did not seem, however, that he had any limbs broken; and by some happy chance, if the word is possible here, the bodies were arched above him in such a way as to prevent his being crushed. His eyes were closed.

He had on his cuirass the silver cross of the Legion of Honor.

The prowler tore off this cross, which disappeared in one of the gulfs which he had under his capote.

After which he felt the officer's fob, found a watch there,

and took it. Then he rummaged in his vest and found a purse, which he pocketed.

When he had reached this phase of the succor he was lending the dying man, the officer opened his eyes.

"Thanks," said he feebly.

The rough movements of the man handling him, the coolness of the night, and breathing the fresh air freely, had roused him from his lethargy.

The prowler answered not. He raised his head. The sound of a footstep could be heard on the plain; probably it was some patrol who was approaching.

The officer murmured, for there were still signs of suffering in his voice:

"Who has gained the battle?"

"The English," answered the prowler.

The officer replied:

"Search my pockets. You will there find a purse and a watch. Take them."

This had already been done.

The prowler made a pretense of executing the command, and said:

"There is nothing there."

"I have been robbed," replied the officer; "I am sorry. They would have been yours."

The step of the patrol became more and more distinct.

"Somebody is coming," said the prowler, making a movement as if he would go.

The officer, raising himself up painfully upon one arm, held him back.

"You have saved my life. Who are you?"

The prowler answered quick and low:

"I belong, like yourself, to the French army. I must go. If I am taken I shall be shot. I have saved your life. Help yourself now."

"What is your grade?"

"Sergeant."

"What is your name?"

"Thénardier."

"I shall not forget that name," said the officer. "And you, remember mine. My name is Pontmercy."

The Ship "Orion"

I

We shall be pardoned for passing rapidly over the painful details. We shall merely reproduce an item published in the *Journal de Paris*, some few months after the remarkable events that occurred at M—— sur m——:

An old convict, named Jean Valjean, has recently been brought before the Var Assizes, under circumstances calculated to attract attention. This villain had succeeded in eluding the vigilance of the police; he had changed his name, and had even been adroit enough to procure the appointment of mayor in one of our small towns in the North. He had established in this town a very considerable business, but was, at length, unmasked and arrested, thanks to the indefatigable zeal of the public authorities. He kept, as his mistress, a prostitute, who died of the shock at the moment of his arrest. This wretch, who is endowed with herculean strength, managed to escape, but, three or four days afterward, the police retook him, in Paris, just as he was getting into one of the small vehicles that ply between the capital and the village of Montfermeil (Seine-et-Oise). It is said that he had availed himself of the interval of these three or four days of freedom, to withdraw a considerable sum deposited by him with one of our principal bankers. The amount is estimated at six or seven hundred thousand francs. According to the minutes of the case, he has concealed it in some place known to himself alone, and it has been impossible to seize it; however that may be, the said Jean Valjean has been brought before the assizes of the Department of the Var under indictment for an assault and robbery on the high road committed *vi et armis* some eight years ago on the person of one of those honest lads who, as the patriarch of Ferney has written in immortal verse,

... De Savoie arrivent tous les ans,
Et dont la main légèrement essuie
Ces longs canaux engorgés par la suie.[1]

This bandit attempted no defense. It was proved by the able and eloquent representative of the crown that the robbery was shared in by others, and that Jean Valjean formed one of a band of robbers in the South. Consequently, Jean Valjean, being found guilty, was condemned to death. The criminal refused to appeal to the higher courts, and the king, in his inexhaustible clemency, deigned to commute his sentence to that of hard labor in prison for life. Jean Valjean was immediately forwarded to the galleys at Toulon.

Jean Valjean changed his number at the galleys. He became 9430.

II

VERY shortly after the time when the authorities took it into their heads that the liberated convict Jean Valjean had, during his escape of a few days' duration, been prowling about Montfermeil, it was remarked, in that village, that a certain old road laborer named Boulatruelle had "a fancy" for the woods. People in the neighborhood claimed to know that Boulatruelle had been in the galleys; he was under police surveillance, and, as he could find no work anywhere, the government employed him at half wages as a mender on the crossroad from Gagny to Lagny.

What had been observed was this:

For some time past, Boulatruelle had left off his work at stone breaking and keeping the road in order, very early, and had gone into the woods with his pick. He would be met toward evening in the remotest glades and the wildest thickets, having the appearance of a person looking for something and, sometimes, digging holes. The worst puzzled of all were the schoolmaster and the tavern keeper, Thénardier, who was

---

[1] ... Who come from Savoy every year,
And whose hand deftly wipes out
Those long channels choked up with soot.

everybody's friend, and who had not disdained to strike up an intimacy with even Boulatruelle.

"He has been in the galleys," said Thénardier. "Good Lord! Nobody knows who is there or who may be there!"

So they made up a party and plied the old roadsman with drink. Boulatruelle drank enormously, but said little. He combined with admirable art and in masterly proportions the thirst of a guzzler with the discretion of a judge. However, by dint of returning to the charge and by putting together and twisting the obscure expressions that he did let fall, Thénardier and the schoolmaster made out, as they thought, the following:

One morning about daybreak as he was going to his work, Boulatruelle had been surprised at seeing under a bush in a corner of the woods, a pickax and spade, as one would say, hidden there. However, he supposed that they were the pick and spade of old Six-Fours, the water carrier, and thought no more about it. But, on the evening of the same day, he had seen, without being seen himself, for he was hidden behind a large tree, "a person who did not belong at all to that region," and whom he, Boulatruelle, "knew very well"—or, as Thénardier translated it, "an old comrade at the galleys"—turn off from the high road toward the thickest part of the woods. Boulatruelle obstinately refused to tell the stranger's name. This person carried a package, something square, like a large box or a small trunk. Two or three hours later, Boulatruelle saw this person come forth again from the woods, this time carrying now not the little trunk but a pick and a spade. The pick and the spade were a ray of light to Boulatruelle; he hastened to the bushes, in the morning, and found neither one nor the other. He thence concluded that this person, on entering the woods, had dug a hole with his pick, had buried the chest, and had, then, filled up the hole with his spade. Now as the chest was too small to contain a corpse, it must contain money; hence his continued searches. Boulatruelle had explored, sounded, and ransacked the whole forest, and had rummaged every spot where the earth seemed to have been freshly disturbed. But all in vain.

He had turned up nothing. Nobody thought any more about it, at Montfermeil.

TOWARD the end of October, in that same year, 1823, the inhabitants of Toulon saw coming back into their port, in consequence of heavy weather, and in order to repair some damages, the ship "Orion," which was at a later period employed at Brest as a vessel of instruction, and which then formed a part of the Mediterranean squadron.

The presence of a vessel of war in port has about it a certain influence which attracts and engages the multitude. It is because it is something grand, and the multitude like what is imposing.

Every day, then, from morning till night, the quays, the wharves, and the piers of the port of Toulon were covered with a throng of saunterers and idlers, whose occupation consisted in gazing at the "Orion."

She was moored near the Arsenal. She was in commission, and they were repairing her. The hull had not been injured on the starboard side, but a few planks had been taken off here and there, according to custom, to admit the air to the framework.

One morning, the throng which was gazing at her witnessed an accident.

The crew was engaged in furling sail. The topman, whose duty it was to take in the starboard upper corner of the main topsail, lost his balance. He was seen tottering; the dense throng assembled on the wharf of the Arsenal uttered a cry, the man's head overbalanced his body, and he whirled over the yard, his arms outstretched toward the deep; as he went over, he grasped the manropes, first with one hand, and then with the other, and hung suspended in that manner. The sea lay far below him at a giddy depth. The shock of his fall had given to the manropes a violent swinging motion, and the poor fellow hung dangling to and fro at the end of this line, like a stone in a sling.

To go to his aid was to run a frightful risk. None of the crew, who were all fishermen of the coast recently taken into service, dared attempt it. In the meantime, the poor topman was becoming exhausted; his agony could not be seen in his countenance, but his increasing weakness could be detected in the movements of all his limbs. His arms twisted about in horrible contortions. Every attempt he made to reascend only increased the oscillations of the manropes. He did not cry out, for fear of losing his strength. All were now looking forward to the moment when he should let go of the rope, and, at instants, all turned their heads away that they might not see him fall. There are moments when a rope's end, a pole, the branch of a tree, is life itself, and it is a frightful thing to see a living being lose his hold upon it, and fall like a ripe fruit.

Suddenly, a man was discovered clambering up the rigging with the agility of a wildcat. This man was clad in red—it was a convict; he wore a green cap—it was a convict for life. As he reached the roundtop, a gust of wind blew off his cap and revealed a head entirely white—it was not a young man.

In fact, one of the convicts employed on board in some prison task had, at the first alarm, run to the officer of the watch, and, amid the confusion and hesitation of the crew, while all the sailors trembled and shrank back, had asked permission to save the topman's life at the risk of his own. A sign of assent being given, with one blow of a hammer he broke the chain riveted to the iron ring at his ankle, then took a rope in his hand, and flung himself into the shrouds. Nobody, at the moment, noticed with what ease the chain was broken. It was only some time afterward that anybody remembered it.

In a twinkling he was upon the yard. He paused a few seconds, and seemed to measure it with his glance. Those seconds, during which the wind swayed the sailor to and fro at the end of the rope, seemed ages to the lookers-on. At length, the convict raised his eyes to heaven, and took a step forward. The crowd drew a long breath. He was seen to run along the yard. On reaching its extreme tip, he fastened one end of the rope he had with him, and let the other hang at full length. Thereupon, he began to let himself down by his hands along this rope, and then there was an inexpressible sensation of terror; instead of one man, two were seen dangling at that giddy height.

You would have said it was a spider seizing a fly, only, in this case, the spider was bringing life, and not death. Ten thousand eyes were fixed upon the group. Not a cry, not a word was uttered; the same emotion contracted every brow. Every man held his breath, as if afraid to add the least whisper to the wind which was swaying the two unfortunate men.

However, the convict had, at length, managed to make his way down to the seaman. It was time; one minute more, and the man, exhausted and despairing, would have fallen into the deep. The convict firmly secured him to the rope to which he clung with one hand while he worked with the other. Finally, he was seen reascending to the yard, and hauling the sailor after him; he supported him there, for an instant, to let him recover his strength, and then, lifting him in his arms, carried him, as he walked along the yard, to the cross-trees, and from there to the roundtop, where he left him in the hands of his messmates.

Then the throng applauded; old galley sergeants wept, women hugged each other on the wharves, and, on all sides, voices were heard exclaiming, with a sort of tenderly subdued enthusiasm: "This man must be pardoned!"

He, however, had made it a point of duty to descend again immediately, and go back to his work. In order to arrive more quickly, he slid down the rigging, and started to run along a lower yard. All eyes were following him. There was a certain moment when everyone felt alarmed; whether it was that he felt fatigued, or because his head swam, people thought they saw him hesitate and stagger. Suddenly, the throng uttered a thrilling outcry: the convict had fallen into the sea.

The fall was perilous. The frigate "Algesiras" was moored close to the "Orion," and the poor convict had plunged between the two ships. It was feared that he would be drawn under one or the other. Four men sprang, at once, into a boat. The people cheered them on, and anxiety again took possession of all minds. The man had not again risen to the surface. He had disappeared in the sea, without making even a ripple, as though he had fallen into a cask of oil. They sounded and dragged the place. It was in vain. The search was continued until night, but not even the body was found.

The next morning, the *Toulon Journal* published the following lines: "November 17, 1823. Yesterday, a convict at work on board the 'Orion,' on his return from rescuing a sailor, fell into the sea, and was drowned. His body was not recovered. It is presumed that it has been caught under the piles at the pierhead of the Arsenal. This man was registered by the number 9430, and his name was Jean Valjean."

Fulfillment of the Promise
to the Departed

I

MONTFERMEIL is situated between Livry and Chelles, upon the southern slope of the high plateau which separates the Ourcq from the Marne. At present, it is a considerable town, adorned all the year round with stuccoed villas, and, on Sundays, with citizens in full blossom. In 1823, it was a peaceful and charming spot, and not upon the road to any place; the inhabitants cheaply enjoyed that rural life which is so luxuriant and so easy of enjoyment. But water was scarce there on account of the height of the plateau.

They had to go a considerable distance for it. The end of the village toward Gagny drew its water from the magnificent ponds in the forest on that side; the other end, which surrounds the church and which is toward Chelles, found drinking water only at a little spring on the side of the hill, near the road to Chelles, about fifteen minutes' walk from Montfermeil.

It was therefore a serious matter for each household to obtain its supply of water. The great houses, the aristocracy, the Thénardier tavern included, paid a penny a bucketful to an old man who made it his business, and whose income from the Montfermeil waterworks was about eight sous per day; but this man worked only till seven o'clock in summer and five in the winter, and when night had come on, and the first-floor shutters were closed, whoever had no drinking water went after it, or went without it.

This was the terror of the poor being whom the reader has not perhaps forgotten—little Cosette. It will be remembered that Cosette was useful to the Thénardiers in two ways: they got pay from the mother and work from the child. Thus when the mother ceased entirely to pay, we have seen why, in the preceding chapters, the Thénardiers kept Cosette. She saved them a servant. In that capacity she ran for water when it was wanted. So the child, always horrified at the idea of going to the spring at night, took good care that water should never be wanted at the house.

Christmas in the year 1823 was particularly brilliant at Montfermeil. The early part of the winter had been mild; so far there had been neither frost nor snow. Some jugglers from Paris had obtained permission from the mayor to set up their stalls in the main street of the village, and a company of peddlers had, under the same license, put up their booths in the square before the church and even in the Lane Boulanger, upon which, as the reader perhaps remembers, the Thénardier chophouse was situated. This filled up the taverns and pothouses, and gave to this little quiet place a noisy and joyous appearance.

On that Christmas evening, several men, wagoners and peddlers, were seated at table and drinking around four or five candles in the low hall of the Thénardier tavern. This room resembled all barrooms; tables, pewter mugs, bottles, drinkers, smokers; little light, and much noise. Thénardier, the wife, was looking to the supper, which was cooking before a bright blazing fire; the husband, Thénardier, was drinking with his guests and talking politics.

Cosette was at her usual place, seated on the crosspiece of the kitchen table, near the fireplace; she was clad in rags; her bare feet were in wooden shoes, and by the light of the fire she was knitting woolen stockings for the little Thénardiers. A young kitten was playing under the chairs. In a neighboring room the fresh voices of two children were heard laughing and prattling; it was Eponine and Azelma.

In the chimney corner, a cowhide hung upon a nail.

At intervals, the cry of a very young child, which was somewhere in the house, was heard above the noise of the barroom. This was a little boy which the woman had had some winters before—"I don't know why," she said, "it was the cold weather,"—and which was a little more than three years old. The mother had nursed him, but did not love him. When the hungry clamor of the brat became too much to hear: "Your boy is squalling," said Thénardier, "why don't you go and see what he wants?" "Bah!" answered the mother; "I am sick of him." And the poor little fellow continued to cry in the darkness.

FOUR new guests had just come in.

Cosette was musing sadly; for, though she was only eight years old, she had already suffered so much that she mused with the mournful air of an old woman.

She had a black eye from a blow of the Thénardiess' fist, which made the Thénardiess say from time to time: "How ugly she is with her patch on her eye."

Cosette was then thinking that it was evening, late in the evening, that the bowls and pitchers in the rooms of the travelers who had arrived must be filled immediately, and that there was no more water in the cistern.

All at once, one of the peddlers who lodged in the tavern came in, and said in a harsh voice:

"You have not watered my horse."

"Yes, we have, sure," said the Thénardiess.

"I tell you no, ma'am," replied the peddler.

Cosette came out from under the table.

"Oh, yes, monsieur!" said she. "The horse did drink; he drank in the bucket, the bucketful, and 'twas me that carried it to him, and I talked to him."

This was not true. Cosette lied.

"Here is a girl as big as my fist, who can tell a lie as big as a house," exclaimed the peddler. "I tell you that he has not had any water, little wench! He has a way of blowing when he has not had any water, that I know well enough."

Cosette persisted, and added in a voice stifled with anguish, and which could hardly be heard:

"But he did drink a good deal."

"Come," continued the peddler, in a passion, "that is enough; give my horse some water, and say no more about it."

Cosette went back under the table.

"Well, of course that is right," said the Thénardiess; "if the beast has not had any water, she must have some."

Then looking about her:

"Well, what has become of that girl?"

She stooped down and discovered Cosette crouched at the other end of the table, almost under the feet of the drinkers.

"Aren't you coming?" cried the Thénardiess.

Cosette came out of the kind of hole where she had hidden. The Thénardiess continued:

"Mademoiselle Dog-without-a-name, go and carry some drink to this horse."

"But, ma'am," said Cosette feebly, "there is no water."

The Thénardiess threw the street door wide open.

"Well, go after some!"

Cosette hung her head, and went for an empty bucket that was by the chimney corner.

The bucket was larger than she, and the child could have sat down in it comfortably.

The Thénardiess went back to her range, and tasted what was in the kettle with a wooden spoon, grumbling the while.

"There is some at the spring. She is the worst girl that ever was. I think 'twould have been better if I'd left out the onions."

Cosette remained motionless, bucket in hand, the open door before her. She seemed to be waiting for somebody to come to her aid.

"Get along!" cried the Thénardiess.

Cosette went out. The door closed.

III

THE row of booths extended along the street from the church, the reader will remember, as far as the Thénardier tavern. These booths, on account of the approaching passage of the citizens on their way to the midnight mass, were all illuminated with candles, burning in paper lanterns, which, as the schoolmaster of Montfermeil, who was at that moment seated at one of Thénardier's tables, said, produced a magical effect. In retaliation, not a star was to be seen in the sky.

The last of these stalls, set up exactly opposite Thénardier's door, was a toyshop, all glittering with trinkets, glass beads, and things magnificent in tin. In the first rank, and in front, the merchant had placed, upon a bed of white napkins, a great doll nearly two feet high dressed in a robe of pink crepe with golden wheat ears on its head, and which had real hair and enamel eyes. The whole day, this marvel had been displayed to the bewilderment of the passers under ten years of age, but there had not been found in Montfermeil a mother rich enough, or prodigal enough, to give it to her child. Eponine and Azelma had passed hours in contemplating it, and Cosette herself, furtively, it is true, had dared to look at it.

At the moment when Cosette went out, bucket in hand, all gloomy and overwhelmed as she was, she could not help raising her eyes toward this wonderful doll, toward "the lady," as she called it. The poor child stopped petrified. She had not seen this doll so near before.

This whole booth seemed a palace to her; this doll was not a doll, it was a vision. It was joy, splendor, riches, happiness, and it appeared in a sort of chimerical radiance to this unfortunate little being, buried so deeply in a cold and dismal misery. The longer she looked, the more she was dazzled. She thought she saw paradise. There were other dolls behind the large one that appeared to her to be fairies and genii. The merchant walking to and fro in the back part of his stall suggested the Eternal Father.

In this adoration, she forgot everything, even the errand on which she had been sent. Suddenly, the harsh voice of the Thénardiess called her back to the reality: "How, jade, haven't you gone yet? Hold on; I am coming for you! I'd like to know what she's doing there? Little monster, be off!"

The Thénardiess had glanced into the street, and perceived Cosette in ecstasy.

Cosette fled with her bucket, running as fast as she could.

IV

As the Thénardier tavern was in that part of the village which is near the church, Cosette had to go to the spring in the woods toward Chelles to draw water.

She looked no more at the displays in the booths, so long as she was in the Lane Boulanger, and in the vicinity of the church, the illuminated stalls lighted the way, but soon the last gleam from the last stall disappeared. The poor child found herself in darkness. She became buried in it. Only, as she became the prey of a certain sensation, she shook the handle of the bucket as much as she could on her way. That made a noise, which kept her company.

Cosette thus passed through the labyrinth of crooked and deserted streets, which terminates the village of Montfermeil toward Chelles. As long as she had houses, or even walls, on the sides of the road, she went on boldly enough. From time to time, she saw the light of a candle through the cracks of a shutter; it was light and life to her; there were people there; that kept up her courage. However, as she advanced, her speed slackened as if mechanically. When she had passed the corner of the last house, Cosette stopped. To go beyond the last booth had been difficult; to go further than the last house became impossible. She put the bucket on the ground, buried her hands in her hair, and began to scratch her head slowly, a motion peculiar to terrified and hesitating children. It was Montfermeil no longer, it was the open country; dark and deserted space was before her. She looked with despair into this darkness where nobody was, where there were beasts, where there were perhaps ghosts. She looked intensely, and she heard the animals walking in the grass, and she distinctly saw the ghosts moving in the trees. Then she seized her bucket again; fear gave her boldness. "Pshaw," said she, "I will tell her there isn't any more water!" And she resolutely went back into Montfermeil.

She had scarcely gone a hundred steps when she stopped again, and began to scratch her head. Now, it was the Thénardiess that appeared to her, the hideous Thénardiess, with her hyena mouth, and wrath flashing from her eyes. The child cast a pitiful glance before her and behind her. What could she do? What would become of her? Where should she go? Before her, the specter of the Thénardiess; behind her, all the phantoms of night and of the forest. It was at the Thénardiess that she recoiled. She took the road to the spring again, and began to run. She ran out of the village; she ran into the woods, seeing nothing, hearing nothing. She did not stop running until out of breath, and even then she staggered on. She went right on, desperate.

Even while running, she wanted to cry.

The nocturnal tremulousness of the forest wrapped her about completely.

She thought no more; she saw nothing more. The immensity of night confronted this little creature. On one side, the infinite shadow; on the other, an atom.

The spring was a small natural basin, made by the water in

the loamy soil, about two feet deep, surrounded with moss, and with that long figured grass called Henry Fourth's collars, and paved with a few large stones. A brook escaped from it with a gentle, tranquil murmur.

Cosette did not take time to breathe. It was very dark, but she was accustomed to come to this fountain. She felt with her left hand in the darkness for a young oak which bent over the spring and usually served her as a support, found a branch, swung herself from it, bent down and plunged the bucket in the water. She was for a moment so excited that her strength was tripled. She drew out the bucket almost full and set it on the grass.

This done, she perceived that her strength was exhausted. She was anxious to start at once; but the effort of filling the bucket had been so great that it was impossible for her to take a step. She was compelled to sit down. She fell upon the grass and remained in a crouching posture.

She closed her eyes, then she opened them, without knowing why, without the power of doing otherwise. At her side, the water shaken in the bucket made circles that resembled serpents of white fire.

Above her head, the sky was covered with vast black clouds which were like sheets of smoke. The tragic mask of night seemed to bend vaguely over this child.

Jupiter was setting in the depths of the horizon.

The child looked with a startled eye upon that great star which she did not know and which made her afraid. The planet, in fact, was at that moment very near the horizon and was crossing a dense bed of mist which gave it a horrid redness. The mist, gloomily empurpled, magnified the star. One would have called it a luminous wound.

A cold wind blew from the plain. The woods were dark, without any rustling of leaves, without any of those vague and fresh coruscations of summer. Great branches drew themselves up fearfully. Mean and shapeless bushes whistled in the glades. The tall grass wriggled under the north wind like eels. The brambles twisted about like long arms seeking to seize their prey in their claws. Some dry weeds, driven by the wind, passed rapidly by, and appeared to flee with dismay before something that was following. The prospect was dismal.

Darkness makes the brain giddy. Man needs light; whoever plunges into the opposite of day feels his heart chilled. When the eye sees blackness, the mind sees trouble. In an eclipse, in night, in the sooty darkness, there is anxiety even to the strongest. Nobody walks alone at night in the forest without trembling. You feel something hideous, as if the soul were amalgamating with the shadow. This penetration of the darkness is inexpressibly dismal for a child.

Forests are apocalypses; and the beating of the wings of a little soul makes an agonizing sound under their monstrous vault.

Without being conscious of what she was experiencing, Cosette felt that she was seized by this black enormity of nature. It was not merely terror that held her, but something more terrible even than terror. She shuddered. Words fail to express the peculiar strangeness of that shudder which chilled her through and through. Her eye had become wild. She felt that perhaps she would be compelled to return there at the same hour the next night.

Then, by a sort of instinct, to get out of this singular state, which she did not understand, but which terrified her, she began to count aloud, one, two, three, four, up to ten, and when she had finished, she began again. This restored her to a real perception of things about her. Her hands, which she had wet in drawing the water, felt cold. She arose. Her fear had returned, a natural and insurmountable fear. She had only one thought, to fly, to fly with all her might, across woods, across fields, to houses, to windows, to lighted candles. Her eyes fell upon the bucket that was before her. Such was the dread with which the Thénardiess inspired her, that she did not dare to go without the bucket of water. She grasped the handle with both hands. She could hardly lift the bucket.

She went a dozen steps in this manner, but the bucket was full, it was heavy, she was compelled to rest it on the ground. She breathed an instant, then grasped the handle again, and walked on, this time a little longer. But she had to stop again. After resting a few seconds, she started on. She walked bending forward, her head down, like an old woman: the weight of the bucket strained and stiffened her thin arms. The iron handle was numbing and freezing her little wet hands; from time to time she had to stop, and every time she stopped, the cold water that splashed from the bucket fell upon her naked knees. This took place in the depth of a wood, at night, in the winter, far from all human sight; it was a child of eight years; there was none but God at that moment who saw this sad thing.

And undoubtedly her mother, alas!

For there are things which open the eyes of the dead in their grave.

She breathed with a kind of mournful rattle; sobs choked her, but she did not dare to weep, so fearful was she of the Thénardiess, even at a distance. She always imagined that the Thénardiess was near.

However, she could not make much headway in this manner, and was getting along very slowly. She tried hard to shorten her resting spells, and to walk as far as possible between them. She remembered with anguish that it would take her more than an hour to return to Montfermeil thus, and that the Thénardiess would beat her. This anguish added to her dismay at being alone in the woods at night. She was worn out with fatigue, and was not yet out of the forest. Arriving near an old chestnut tree which she knew, she made a last halt, longer than the others, to get well rested; then she gathered all her strength, took up the bucket again, and began to walk on courageously. Meanwhile the poor little despairing thing could not help crying: "Oh! My God! My God!"

At that moment she felt all at once that the weight of the bucket was gone. A hand, which seemed enormous to her, had just caught the handle, and was carrying it easily. She raised her head. A large dark form, straight and erect, was walking beside her in the gloom. It was a man who had come up behind her, and whom she had not heard. This man, without saying a word, had grasped the handle of the bucket she was carrying.

There are instincts for all the crises of life.

The child was not afraid.

V

THE man spoke to her. His voice was serious, and was almost a whisper.

"My child, that is very heavy for you which you are carrying there."

Cosette raised her head and answered:

"Yes, monsieur."

"Give it to me," the man continued. "I will carry it for you."

Cosette let go of the bucket. The man walked along with her.

"It is very heavy, indeed," said he to himself. Then he added:

"Little girl, how old are you?"

"Eight years, monsieur."

"And have you come far in this way?"

"From the spring in the woods."

"And are you going far?"

"A good quarter of an hour from here."

The man remained a moment without speaking, then he said abruptly:

"You have no mother then?"

"I don't know," answered the child.

Before the man had had time to say a word, she added:

"I don't believe I have. All the rest have one. For my part, I have none."

And after a silence, she added:

"I believe I never had any."

The man stopped, put the bucket on the ground, stooped down, and placed his hands upon the child's shoulders, making an effort to look at her and see her face in the darkness.

The thin and puny face of Cosette was vaguely outlined in the livid light of the sky.

"What is your name?" said the man.

"Cosette."

It seemed as if the man had an electric shock. He looked at her again, then letting go of her shoulders, took up the bucket, and walked on.

A moment after, he asked:

"Little girl, where do you live?"

"At Montfermeil, if you know it."

"It is there that we are going?"

"Yes, monsieur."

He made another pause. Then he began:

"Who is it that has sent you out into the woods after water at this time of night?"

"Madame Thénardier."

The man resumed with a tone of voice which he tried to

render indifferent, but in which there was nevertheless a singular tremor:

"What does she do, your Madame Thénardier?"

"She is my mistress," said the child. "She keeps the tavern."

"The tavern," said the man. "Well, I am going there to lodge tonight. Show me the way."

"We are going there," said the child.

The man walked very fast. Cosette followed him without difficulty. She felt fatigue no more. From time to time, she raised her eyes toward this man with a sort of tranquillity and inexpressible confidence. She had never been taught to turn toward Providence and to pray. However, she felt in her bosom something that resembled hope and joy, and which rose toward heaven.

A few minutes passed. The man spoke:

"Is there no servant at Madame Thénardier's?"

"No, monsieur."

"Are you alone?"

"Yes, monsieur."

There was another interval of silence. Cosette raised her voice:

"That is, there are two little girls."

"What little girls?"

"Ponine and Zelma."

The child simplified in this way the romantic names dear to the mother.

"What are Ponine and Zelma?"

"They are Madame Thénardier's young ladies, you might say her daughters."

"And what do they do?"

"Oh!" said the child. "They have beautiful dolls, things which there's gold in; they are full of business. They play, they amuse themselves."

"All day long?"

"Yes, monsieur."

"And you?"

"Me! I work."

"All day long?"

The child raised her large eyes in which there was a tear, which could not be seen in the darkness, and answered softly:

"Yes, monsieur."

She continued after an interval of silence:

"Sometimes, when I have finished my work and they are willing, I amuse myself also."

"How do you amuse yourself?"

"The best I can. They let me alone. But I have not many playthings. Ponine and Zelma are not willing for me to play with their dolls. I have only a little lead sword, not longer than that."

The child showed her little finger.

"And which does not cut?"

"Yes, monsieur," said the child, "it cuts lettuce and flies' heads."

They reached the village; Cosette guided the stranger through the streets. The man questioned her no more, and now maintained a mournful silence. When they had passed the church, the man, seeing all these booths in the street, asked Cosette:

"Is it fair time here?"

"No, monsieur, it is Christmas."

As they drew near the tavern, Cosette timidly touched his arm.

"Monsieur?"

"What, my child?"

"Here we are close by the house."

"Well?"

"Will you let me take the bucket now?"

"What for?"

"Because, if madame sees that anybody brought it for me, she will beat me."

The man gave her the bucket. A moment after they were at the big door of the chophouse.

VI

COSETTE could not help casting one look toward the grand doll still displayed in the toy shop; then she rapped. The door opened. The Thénardiess appeared with a candle in her hand.

"Oh! It is you, you little beggar! Lud-a-massy! You have taken your time! She has been playing, the wench!"

"Madame," said Cosette, trembling, "there is a gentleman who is coming to lodge."

The Thénardiess very quickly replaced her fierce air by her amiable grimace, a change at sight peculiar to innkeepers, and looked for the newcomer with eager eyes.

"Is it monsieur?" said she.

"Yes, madame," answered the man, touching his hat.

Rich travelers are not so polite. This gesture and the sight of the stranger's costume and baggage which the Thénardiess passed in review at a glance made the amiable grimace disappear and the fierce air reappear. She added dryly:

"Enter, goodman."

The "goodman" entered. The Thénardiess cast a second glance at him, examined particularly his long coat which was absolutely threadbare, and his hat which was somewhat broken, and with a nod, a wink, and a turn of her nose, consulted her husband, who was still drinking with the wagoners. The husband answered by that imperceptible shake of the forefinger which, supported by a protrusion of the lips, signifies in such a case: "Complete destitution." Upon this the Thénardiess exclaimed:

"Ah! My brave man, I am very sorry, but I have no room."

"Put me where you will," said the man. "In the garret, in the stable. I will pay as if I had a room."

"Forty sous."

"Forty sous. Well."

"In advance."

"Forty sous," whispered a wagoner to the Thénardiess, "but it is only twenty sous."

"It is forty sous for him," replied the Thénardiess in the same tone. "I don't lodge poor people for less."

"That is true," added her husband softly, "it ruins a house to have this sort of people."

Meanwhile the man, after leaving his stick and bundle on a bench, had seated himself at a table on which Cosette had been quick to place a bottle of wine and a glass. The peddler, who had asked for the bucket of water, had gone himself to carry it to his horse. Cosette had resumed her place under the kitchen table and her knitting.

The man, who hardly touched his lips to the wine he had turned out, was contemplating the child with a strange attention.

Cosette was ugly. Happy, she might, perhaps, have been

pretty. Cosette was thin and pale; she was nearly eight years old, but one would hardly have thought her six. Her large eyes, sunk in a sort of shadow, were almost put out by continual weeping. The corners of her mouth had that curve of habitual anguish, which is seen in the condemned and in the hopelessly sick. Her hands were covered with chilblains. The light of the fire, which was shining upon her, made her bones stand out and rendered her thinness fearfully visible. As she was always shivering, she had acquired the habit of drawing her knees together. Her whole dress was nothing but a rag, which would have excited pity in the summer, and which excited horror in the winter. She had on nothing but cotton, and that full of holes, not a rag of woolen. Her skin showed here and there, and black and blue spots could be distinguished, which indicated that places where the Thénardiess had touched her. Her naked legs were red and rough. The hollows under her collar bones would make one weep. The whole person of this child, her gait, her attitude, the sound of her voice, the intervals between one word and another, her looks, her silence, her least motion, expressed and uttered a single idea: fear.

Fear was spread all over her; she was, so to say, covered with it; fear drew back her elbows against her sides, drew her heels under her skirt, made her take the least possible room, prevented her from breathing more than was absolutely necessary, and had become what might be called her bodily habit, without possible variation, except of increase. There was in the depth of her eye an expression of astonishment mingled with terror.

This fear was such that on coming in, all wet as she was, Cosette had not dared go and dry herself by the fire, but had gone silently to her work.

The expression of the countenance of this child of eight years was habitually so sad and sometimes so tragical that it seemed, at certain moments, as if she were in the way of becoming an idiot or a demon.

Never, as we have said, had she known what it is to pray, never had she set foot within a church. "How can I spare the time?" said the Thénardiess.

The man in the yellow coat did not take his eyes from Cosette.

"Oh! You want supper?" asked the Thénardiess of the traveler.

He did not answer. He seemed to be thinking deeply.

"What is that man?" said she between her teeth. "It is some frightful pauper. He hasn't a penny for his supper. Is he going to pay me for his lodging only? It is very lucky, anyway, that he didn't think to steal the money that was on the floor."

A door now opened, and Eponine and Azelma came in.

They were really two pretty little girls, rather city girls than peasants, very charming, one with her well-polished auburn tresses, the other with her long black braids falling down her back, and both so lively, neat, plump, fresh, and healthy, that it was a pleasure to see them. They were warmly clad, but with such maternal art, that the thickness of the stuff detracted nothing from the coquetry of the fit. Winter was provided against without effacing spring. These two little girls shed light around them. Moreover, they were regnant. In their toilet, in their gaiety, in the noise they made, there was sovereignty. When they entered, the Thénardiess said to them in a scolding tone, which was full of adoration: "Ah! You are here then, you children!"

They went and sat down by the fire. They had a doll which they turned backward and forward upon their knees with many pretty prattlings. From time to time, Cosette raised her eyes from her knitting, and looked sadly at them as they were playing.

Eponine and Azelma did not notice Cosette. To them she was like the dog. These three little girls could not count twenty-four years among them all, and they already represented all human society; on one side envy, on the other disdain.

The doll of the Thénardier sisters was very much faded, and very old and broken, and it appeared nonetheless wonderful to Cosette, who had never in her life had a doll, "a real doll," to use an expression that all children will understand.

All at once, the Thénardiess, who was continually going and coming about the room, noticed that Cosette's attention was distracted, and that instead of working she was busied with the little girls who were playing.

"Ah! I've caught you!" cried she. "That is the way you work! I'll make you work with a cowhide, I will."

The stranger, without leaving his chair, turned toward the Thénardiess.

"Madame," said he, smiling diffidently. "Pshaw! Let her play!"

On the part of any traveler who had eaten a slice of mutton, and drunk two bottles of wine at his supper, and who had not had the appearance of a horrid pauper, such a wish would have been a command. But that a man who wore that hat should allow himself to have a desire, and that a man who wore that coat should permit himself to have a wish, was what the Thénardiess thought ought not to be tolerated. She replied sharply:

"She must work, for she eats. I don't support her to do nothing."

"What is it she is making?" said the stranger, in that gentle voice which contrasted so strangely with his beggar's clothes and his porter's shoulders.

The Thénardiess deigned to answer.

"Stockings, if you please. Stockings for my little girls who have none, worth speaking of, and will soon be going bare-footed."

The man looked at Cosette's poor red feet, and continued:

"When will she finish that pair of stockings?"

"It will take her at least three or four good days, the lazy thing."

"And how much might this pair of stockings be worth, when it is finished?"

The Thénardiess cast a disdained glance at him.

"At least thirty sous."

"Would you take five francs for them?" said the man.

"Goodness!" exclaimed a wagoner who was listening, with a horse laugh. "Five francs? It's a humbug! Five bullets!"

Thénardier now thought it time to speak.

"Yes, monsieur, if it is your fancy, you can have that pair of stockings for five francs. We can't refuse anything to travelers."

"You must pay for them now," said the Thénardiess, in her short and peremptory way.

"I will buy that pair of stockings," answered the man, "and," added he, drawing a five-franc piece from his pocket and laying it on the table, "I will pay for them."

Then he turned toward Cosette.

"Now your work belongs to me. Play, my child."

The wagoner was so affected by the five-franc piece that he left his glass and went to look at it.

"It's so, that's a fact!" cried he, as he looked at it. "A regular hindwheel! And no counterfeit!"

Thénardier approached, and silently put the piece in his pocket.

The Thénardiess had nothing to reply. She bit her lips, and her face assumed an expression of hatred.

Meanwhile Cosette trembled. She ventured to ask:

"Madame, is it true? Can I play?"

"Play!" said the Thénardiess in a terrible voice.

"Thank you, madame," said Cosette. And, while her mouth thanked the Thénardiess, all her little soul was thanking the traveler.

Thénardier returned to his drink. His wife whispered in his ear:

"What can that yellow man be?"

"I have seen," answered Thénardier, in a commanding tone, "millionaires with coats like that."

Cosette had left her knitting, but she had not moved from her place. Cosette always stirred as little as was possible. She had taken from a little box behind her a few old rags, and her little lead sword.

Eponine and Azelma paid no attention to what was going on. They had just performed a very important operation; they had caught the kitten. They had thrown the doll on the floor, and Eponine, the elder, was dressing the kitten, in spite of her miaulings and contortions, with a lot of clothes and red and blue rags.

Meanwhile, the drinkers were singing an obscene song, at which they laughed enough to shake the room. Thénardier encouraged and accompanied them.

As birds make a nest of anything, children make a doll of no matter what. While Eponine and Azelma were dressing up the cat, Cosette, for her part, had dressed up the sword. That done, she had laid it upon her arm, and was singing it softly to sleep.

The Thénardiess, on her part, approached the yellow man. "My husband is right," thought she; "it may be Monsieur Laffitte. Some rich men are so odd."

She came and rested her elbow on the table at which he was sitting.

"Monsieur——" said she.

At this word monsieur, the man turned. The Thénardiess had called him before only "brave man" or "goodman."

"You see, monsieur," she pursued, putting on her sweetest look, which was still more unendurable than her ferocious manner, "I am very willing the child should play; I am not opposed to it; it is well for once, because you are generous. But, you see, she is poor; she must work."

"The child is not yours, then?" asked the man.

"Oh dear! No, monsieur! It is a little pauper that we have taken in through charity. A sort of imbecile child. She must have water on her brain. Her head is big, as you see. We do all we can for her, but we are not rich. We write in vain to her country; for six months we have had no answer. We think that her mother must be dead."

"Ah!" said the man, and he fell back into his reverie.

"This mother was no great thing," added the Thénardiess. "She abandoned her child."

During all this conversation, Cosette, as if an instinct had warned her that they were talking about her, had not taken her eyes from the Thénardiess. She listened. She heard a few words here and there.

Meanwhile the drinkers, all three-quarters drunk, were repeating their foul chorus with redoubled gaiety. It was highly spiced with jests, in which the names of the Virgin and the child Jesus were often heard. The Thénardiess had gone to take her part in the hilarity. Cosette, under the table, was looking into the fire, which was reflected from her fixed eye; she was again rocking the sort of rag baby that she had made, and as she rocked it, she sang in a low voice: "My mother is dead! My mother is dead! My mother is dead!"

At the repeated entreaties of the hostess, the yellow man, "the millionaire," finally consented to sup.

"What will monsieur have?"

"Some bread and cheese," said the man.

"Decidedly, it is a beggar," thought the Thénardiess.

The revelers continued to sing their songs, and the child, under the table, also sang hers.

All at once, Cosette stopped. She had just turned and seen the little Thénardiers' doll, which they had forsaken for the cat and left on the floor, a few steps from the kitchen table.

Then she let the bundled-up sword, that only half satisfied

her, fall, and ran her eyes slowly around the room. The Thénardiess was whispering to her husband and counting some money, Eponine and Azelma were playing with the cat, the travelers were eating or drinking or singing, nobody was looking at her. She had not a moment to lose. She crept out from under the table on her hands and knees, made sure once more that nobody was watching her, then darted quickly to the doll, and seized it. An instant afterward she was at her place, seated, motionless, only turned in such a way as to keep the doll that she held in her arms in the shadow. The happiness of playing with a doll was so rare to her that it had all the violence of rapture.

Nobody had seen her, except the traveler, who was slowly eating his meager supper.

This joy lasted for nearly a quarter of an hour.

But in spite of Cosette's precautions, she did not perceive that one of the doll's feet stuck out, and that the fire of the fireplace lighted it up very vividly. This rosy and luminous foot which protruded from the shadow suddenly caught Azelma's eye, and she said to Eponine: "Oh! Sister!"

The two little girls stopped, stupefied; Cosette had dared to take the doll.

Eponine got up, and without letting go of the cat, went to her mother and began to pull at her skirt.

"Let me alone," said the mother; "what do you want?"

"Mother," said the child, "look there."

And she pointed at Cosette.

Cosette, wholly absorbed in the ecstasy of her possession, saw and heard nothing else.

The face of the Thénardiess assumed the peculiar expression which is composed of the terrible mingled with the commonplace and which has given this class of women the name of furies.

This time wounded pride exasperated her anger still more. Cosette had leaped over all barriers. Cosette had laid her hands upon the doll of "those young ladies." A czarina who had seen a moujik trying on the grand cordon of her imperial son would have had the same expression.

She cried with a voice harsh with indignation:

"Cosette!"

Cosette shuddered as if the earth had quaked beneath her. She turned around.

"Cosette!" repeated the Thénardiess.

Cosette took the doll and placed it gently on the floor with a kind of veneration mingled with despair. Then, without taking away her eyes, she joined her hands, and, what is frightful to tell in a child of that age, she wrung them; then, what none of the emotions of the day had drawn from her, neither the run in the wood, nor the weight of the bucket of water, nor even the stern words she had heard from the Thénardiess, she burst into tears. She sobbed.

Meanwhile the traveler arose.

"What is the matter?" said he to the Thénardiess.

"Don't you see?" said the Thénardiess, pointing with her finger to the corpus delicti lying at Cosette's feet.

"Well, what is that?" said the man.

"That beggar," answered the Thénardiess, "has dared to touch the children's doll."

"All this noise about that?" said the man. "Well, what if she did play with that doll?"

"She has touched it with her dirty hands!" continued the Thénardiess, "With her horrid hands!"

Here Cosette redoubled her sobs.

"Be still!" cried the Thénardiess.

The man walked straight to the street door, opened it, and went out.

As soon as he had gone, the Thénardiess profited by his absence to give Cosette under the table a severe kick, which made the child shriek.

The door opened again, and the man reappeared, holding in his hands the fabulous doll of which we have spoken, and which had been the admiration of all the youngsters of the village since morning; he stood it up before Cosette, saying:

"Here, this is for you."

It is probable that during the time he had been there—more than an hour—in the midst of his reverie, he had caught confused glimpses of this toyshop, lighted up with lamps and candles so splendidly that it shone through the barroom window like an illumination.

Cosette raised her eyes; she saw the man approach her with that doll as she would have seen the sun approach; she heard those astounding words: "This is for you." She looked at him, she looked at the doll, then she drew back slowly, and went and hid as far as she could under the table in the corner of the room.

She wept no more, she cried no more, she had the appearance of no longer daring to breathe.

The Thénardiess, Eponine, and Azelma were so many statues. Even the drinkers stopped. There was a solemn silence in the whole barroom.

The Thénardiess, petrified and mute, recommenced her conjectures anew: "What is this old fellow? Is he a pauper? Is he a millionaire? Perhaps he's both, that is a robber."

The face of the husband Thénardier presented that expressive wrinkle which marks the human countenance whenever the dominant instinct appears in it with all its brutal power. The innkeeper contemplated by turns the doll and the traveler; he seemed to be scenting this man as he would have scented a bag of money. This only lasted for a moment. He approached his wife and whispered to her:

"That machine cost at least thirty francs. No nonsense. Down on your knees before the man!"

Coarse natures have this in common with artless natures, that they have no transitions.

"Well, Cosette," said the Thénardiess in a voice which was meant to be sweet, and which was entirely composed of the sour honey of vicious women, "an't you going to take your doll?"

Cosette ventured to come out of her hole.

"My little Cosette," said Thénardier with a caressing air, "monsieur gives you a doll. Take it. It is yours."

Cosette looked upon the wonderful doll with a sort of terror. Her face was still flooded with tears, but her eyes began to fill, like the sky in the breaking of the dawn, with strange radiations of joy. What she experienced at that moment was almost like what she would have felt if someone had said to her suddenly: "Little girl, you are Queen of France."

It seemed to her that if she touched that doll, thunder would spring forth from it.

Which was true to some extent, for she thought that the Thénardiess would scold and beat her.

However, the attraction overcame her. She finally approached and timidly murmured, turning toward the Thénardiess:

"Can I, madame?"

No expression can describe her look, at once full of despair, dismay, and transport.

"Good Lord!" said the Thénardiess. "It is yours. Since monsieur gives it to you."

"Is it true, is it true, monsieur?" said Cosette. "Is the lady for me?"

The stranger appeared to have his eyes full of tears. He seemed to be at that stage of emotion in which one does not speak for fear of weeping. He nodded assent to Cosette, and put the hand of "the lady" in her little hand.

Cosette withdrew her hand hastily, as if that of "the lady" burned her, and looked down at the floor. We are compelled to add, that at that instant she thrust out her tongue enormously. All at once she turned, and seized the doll eagerly.

"I will call her Catharine," said she.

It was a strange moment when Cosette's rags met and pressed against the ribbons and the fresh pink muslins of the doll.

"Madame," said she, "may I put her in a chair?"

"Yes, my child," answered the Thénardiess.

It was Eponine and Azelma now who looked upon Cosette with envy.

Cosette placed Catharine on a chair, then sat down on the floor before her, and remained motionless, without saying a word, in the attitude of contemplation.

"Why don't you play, Cosette?" said the stranger.

"Oh! I am playing," answered the child.

This stranger, this unknown man, who seemed like a visit from Providence to Cosette, was at that moment the being which the Thénardiess hated more than all else in the world. However, she was compelled to restrain herself. Her emotions were more than she could endure, accustomed as she was to dissimulation, by endeavoring to copy her husband in all her actions. She sent her daughters to bed immediately, then asked the yellow man's "permission" to send Cosette to bed—"who is very tired to-day," added she, with a motherly air. Cosette went to bed, holding Catharine in her arms.

Several hours passed away. The midnight mass was said, the revel was finished, the drinkers had gone, the house was closed, the room was deserted, the fire had gone out, the stranger still remained in the same place and in the same posture. From time to time he changed the elbow on which he rested. That was all. But he had not spoken a word since Cosette was gone.

Thénardier moved, coughed, spit, blew his nose, and creaked his chair. The man did not stir. "Is he asleep?" thought Thénardier. The man was not asleep, but nothing could arouse him.

Finally, Thénardier took off his cap, approached softly, and ventured to say:

"Is monsieur not going to repose?"

"Yes," said the stranger, "you are right. Where is your stable?"

"Monsieur," said Thénardier, with a smile, "I will conduct monsieur."

He took the candle, the man took his bundle and his staff, and Thénardier led him into a room on the first floor, which was very showy, furnished all in mahogany, with a high-post bedstead and red calico curtains.

"What is this?" said the traveler.

"It is properly our bridal chamber," said the innkeeper. "We occupy another like this, my spouse and I; this is not open more than three or four times in a year."

"I should have liked the stable as well," said the man, bluntly.

Thénardier did not appear to hear this not very civil answer.

He lighted two entirely new wax candles, which were displayed upon the mantel; a good fire was blazing in the fireplace.

When the traveler turned again the host had disappeared. Thénardier had discreetly taken himself out of the way without daring to say good night, not desiring to treat with a disrespectful cordiality a man whom he proposed to skin royally in the morning.

VII

ON the following morning, at least two hours before day, Thénardier, seated at a table in the barroom, a candle by his side, with pen in hand, was making out the bill of the traveler in the yellow coat.

His wife was standing, half bent over him, following him

with her eyes. Not a word passed between them. It was, on one side, a profound meditation, on the other that religious admiration with which we observe a marvel of the human mind spring up and expand. A noise was heard in the house; it was the lark, sweeping the stairs.

After a good quarter of an hour and some erasures, Thénardier produced his masterpiece.

Then he went out.

He was scarcely out of the room when the traveler came in.

Thénardier reappeared immediately behind him, and remained motionless in the half-open door, visible only to his wife.

The yellow man carried his staff and bundle in his hand.

"Up so soon!" said the Thénardiess. "Is monsieur going to leave us already?"

The traveler appeared preoccupied and absent-minded.

He answered:

"Yes, madame, I am going away."

"Monsieur, then, had no business at Montfermeil?" replied she.

"No, I am passing through, that is all. Madame," added he, "what do I owe?"

The Thénardiess, without answering, handed him the folded bill.

The man unfolded the paper and looked at it, but his thoughts were evidently elsewhere.

"Madame," replied he, "do you do a good business in Montfermeil?"

"So-so, monsieur," answered the Thénardiess, stupefied at seeing no other explosion.

She continued in a mournful and lamenting strain:

"Oh! Monsieur, the times are very hard, and then we have so few rich people around here! It is a very little place, you see. If we only had rich travelers now and then, like monsieur! We have so many expenses! Why, that little girl eats us out of house and home."

The man replied in a voice which he endeavored to render indifferent, and in which there was a slight tremulousness.

"Suppose you were relieved of her?"

"Who? Cosette?"

"Yes."

The red and violent face of the woman became illumined with a hideous expression.

"Ah, monsieur! My good monsieur! Take her, keep her, take her away, carry her off, sugar her, stuff her, drink her, eat her, and be blessed by the holy Virgin and all the saints in paradise!"

"Agreed."

"Really! You will take her away?"

"I will."

"Immediately?"

"Immediately. Call the child."

"Cosette!" cried the Thénardiess.

"In the meantime," continued the man, "I will pay my bill. How much is it?"

He cast a glance at the bill, and could not repress a movement of surprise.

"Twenty-three francs?"

At this moment Thénardier advanced into the middle of the room and said:

"Monsieur owes twenty-six sous."

"Twenty-six sous!" exclaimed the woman.

"Twenty sous for the room," continued Thénardier coldly, "and six for supper. As to the little girl, I must have some talk with monsieur about that. Leave us, wife."

The Thénardiess was dazzled by one of those unexpected flashes which emanate from talent. She felt that the great actor had entered upon the scene, answered not a word, and went out.

As soon as they were alone, Thénardier offered the traveler a chair. The traveler sat down, but Thénardier remained standing, and his face assumed a singular expression of good nature and simplicity.

"Monsieur," said he, "listen, I must say that I adore this child."

The stranger looked at him steadily.

"What child?"

Thénardier continued:

"How strangely we become attached! This child I adore."

"Who is that?" asked the stranger.

"Oh, our little Cosette! And you wish to take her away from us? Indeed, I speak frankly, as true as you are an honorable man, I cannot consent to it. I should miss her. I have had her since she was very small. It is true, she costs us money, it is true she has her faults, it is true we are not rich, it is true I paid four hundred francs for medicines at one time when she was sick. But we must do something for God. She has neither father nor mother; I have brought her up. I have bread enough for her and for myself. In fact, I must keep this child. You understand, we have affections; I am a good beast, myself; I do not reason; I love this little girl; my wife is hasty, but she loves her also. You see, she is like our own child. I feel the need of her prattle in the house."

The stranger was looking steadily at him all the while. He continued:

"Pardon me, excuse me, monsieur, but one does not give his child like that to a traveler. Isn't it true that I am right? After that, I don't say—you are rich and have the appearance of a very fine man—if it is for her advantage—but I must know about it. You understand? On the supposition that I should let her go and sacrifice my own feelings, I should want to know where she is going. I would not want to lose sight of her, I should want to know who she was with, that I might come and see her now and then, and that she might know that her good foster father was still watching over her. Finally, there are things which are not possible. I do not know even your name. If you should take her away, I should say, alas for the little Lark, where has she gone? I must, at least, see some poor rag of paper, a bit of a passport, something."

The stranger, without removing from him this gaze which went, so to speak, to the bottom of his conscience, answered in a severe and firm tone.

"Monsieur Thénardier, people do not take a passport to come five leagues from Paris. If I take Cosette, I take her, that is all. You will not know my name, you will not know my abode, you will not know where she goes, and my intention is that she shall never see you again in her life. Do you agree to that? Yes or no?"

As demons and genii recognize by certain signs the presence of a superior God, Thénardier comprehended that he was to deal with one who was very powerful. It came like an intuition; he understood it with his clear and quick sagacity; although during the evening he had been drinking with the wagoners, smoking, and singing bawdy songs, still he was observing the stranger all the while. He had surprised the searching glances of the old man constantly returning to the child. Why this interest? What was this man? Why, with so much money in his purse, this miserable dress? These were questions which he put to himself without being able to answer them, and they irritated him. He had been thinking it over all night. This could not be Cosette's father. Was it a grandfather? Then why did he not make himself known at once? When a man has a right, he shows it. This man evidently had no right to Cosette. Then who was he? Thénardier was lost in conjectures. He caught glimpses of everything, but saw nothing. However it might be, when he commenced the conversation with this man, sure that there was a secret in all this, sure that the man had an interest in remaining unknown, he felt himself strong; at the stranger's clear and firm answer, when he saw that this mysterious personage was mysterious and nothing more, he felt weak. He was expecting nothing of the kind. His conjectures were put to flight. He rallied his ideas. He weighed all in a second. Thénardier was one of those men who comprehend a situation at a glance. He decided that this was the moment to advance straightforward and swiftly. He did what great captains do at that decisive instant which they alone can recognize; he unmasked his battery at once.

"Monsieur," said he, "I must have fifteen hundred francs."

The stranger took from his side pocket an old black leather pocketbook, opened it, and drew forth three bank bills which he placed upon the table. He then rested his large thumb on these bills, and said to the tavern keeper.

"Bring Cosette."

An instant after, Cosette entered the barroom.

The stranger took the bundle he had brought and untied it. This bundle contained a little woolen frock, an apron, a coarse cotton undergarment, a petticoat, a scarf, woolen stockings, and shoes—a complete dress for a girl of seven years. It was all in black.

"My child," said the man, "take this and go and dress yourself quick."

The day was breaking when those of the inhabitants of Montfermeil who were beginning to open their doors saw pass on the road to Paris a poorly clad goodman leading a little girl dressed in mourning who had a pink doll in her arms. They were going toward Livry.

It was the stranger and Cosette.

No one recognized the man; as Cosette was not now in tatters, few recognized her.

Cosette was going away. With whom? She was ignorant. Where? She knew not. All she understood was, that she was leaving behind the Thénardier chophouse. Nobody had thought of bidding her good-by, nor had she of bidding good-by to anybody. She went out from that house, hated and hating.

Poor gentle being, whose heart had only been crushed hitherto.

Cosette walked seriously along, opening her large eyes, and looking at the sky. From time to time she looked at the goodman. She felt somewhat as if she were near God.

On the evening of the same day, Jean Valjean entered Paris again at nightfall, with the child, by the Barrière de Monceaux. There he took a cabriolet, which carried him as far as the esplanade of the Observatory. There he got out, paid the driver, took Cosette by the hand, and both in the darkness of the night, through the deserted streets in the vicinity of l'Ourcine and La Glacière, walked toward the Boulevard de l'Hôpital.

The day had been strange and full of emotion for Cosette; they had eaten behind hedges bread and cheese bought at isolated chophouses; they had often changed carriages, and had traveled short distances on foot. She did not complain, but she was tired, and Jean Valjean perceived it by her pulling more heavily at his hand while walking. He took her in his arms; Cosette, without letting go of Catharine, laid her head on Jean Valjean's shoulder, and went to sleep.

The Old Gorbeau House

I

FORTY years ago, the solitary pedestrian who ventured into the unknown regions of La Salpêtrière and went up along the boulevard as far as the Barrière d'Italie, reached certain points where it might be said that Paris disappeared. It was no longer a solitude, for there were people passing; it was not the country, for there were houses and streets; it was not a

city, the streets had ruts in them, like the highways, and grass
grew along their borders; it was not a village, the houses were
too lofty. What was it then? It was an inhabited place where
there was nobody, it was a desert place where there was
somebody; it was a boulevard of the great city, a street of
Paris, wilder, at night, than a forest, and gloomier, by day,
than a graveyard.

It was the old quarter of the Horse Market.

Our pedestrian, if he trusted himself beyond the four
tumbling walls of this Horse Market, if willing to go even further than the rue du Petit Banquier, leaving on his right a
courtyard shut in by lofty walls, then a meadow studded with
stacks of tanbark that looked like the gigantic beaver dams,
then an enclosure half filled with lumber and piles of logs,
sawdust and shavings, from the top of which a huge dog was
baying, then a long, low, ruined wall with a small dark-colored
and decrepit gate in it, covered with moss, which was full
of flowers in springtime, then, in the loneliest spot, a frightful
broken-down structure on which could be read in large letters:
POST NO BILLS; this bold promenader, we say, would reach
the corner of the rue des Vignes-Saint-Marcel, a latitude not
much explored. There, near a manufactory and between two
garden walls, could be seen at the time of which we speak
an old ruined dwelling that, at first sight, seemed as small as
a cottage, yet was, in reality, as vast as a cathedral. It stood
with its gable end toward the highway, and hence its apparent
diminutiveness. Nearly the whole house was hidden. Only
the door and one window could be seen.

This old dwelling had but one story.

The door was merely a collection of worm-eaten boards
rudely tacked together with crosspieces that looked like pieces
of firewood clumsily split out. It opened directly on a steep
staircase with high steps covered with mud, plaster, and dust,
and of the same breadth as the door, and which seemed from
the street to rise perpendicularly like a ladder, and disappear
in the shadow between two walls.

The window was broad and of considerable height, with
large panes in the sashes and provided with Venetian shutters;
only the panes had received a variety of wounds which were
at once concealed and made manifest by ingenious strips and
bandages of paper, and the shutters were so broken and dis-
jointed that they menaced the passers-by more than they

shielded the occupants of the dwelling. This door with its dirty look and this window with its decent though dilapidated appearance, seen thus in one and the same building, produced the effect of two ragged beggars bound in the same direction and walking side by side, with different mien under the same rags, one having always been a pauper while the other had been a gentleman.

The staircase led up to a very spacious interior, which looked like a barn converted into a house. This structure had for its main channel of communication a long hall, on which there opened, on either side, apartments of different dimensions scarcely habitable, rather resembling booths than rooms. These chambers looked out upon the shapeless grounds of the neighborhood. Altogether, it was dark and dull and dreary, even melancholy and sepulchral, and it was penetrated, either by the dim, cold rays of the sun or by icy drafts, according to the situation of the cracks, in the roof, or in the door. One interesting and picturesque peculiarity of this kind of tenement is the monstrous size of the spiders.

The letter carriers called the house No. 50-52; but it was known, in the quarter, as Gorbeau House.

II

BEFORE this Gorbeau tenement Jean Valjean stopped. Like the birds of prey, he had chosen this lonely place to make his nest.

He fumbled in his waistcoat and took from it a sort of night key, opened the door, entered, then carefully closed it again and ascended the stairway, still carrying Cosette.

At the top of the stairway he drew from his pocket another key, with which he opened another door. The chamber which he entered and closed again immediately was a sort of garret, rather spacious, furnished only with a mattress spread on the floor, a table, and a few chairs. A stove containing a fire, the coals of which were visible, stood in one corner. The street lamp of the boulevards shed a dim light through this poor interior. At the further extremity there was a little room containing a cot bed. On this Jean Valjean laid the child without waking her.

He struck a light with a flint and steel and lit a candle,

which, with his tinderbox, stood ready, beforehand, on the
table, and, as he had done on the preceding evening, he began
to gaze upon Cosette with a look of ecstasy, in which the expression of goodness and tenderness went almost to the verge
of insanity. The little girl, with that tranquil confidence which
belongs only to extreme strength or extreme weakness, had
fallen asleep without knowing with whom she was, and continued to slumber without knowing where she was.

Jean Valjean bent down and kissed the child's hand.

Nine months before, he had kissed the hand of the mother,
who also had just fallen asleep.

The same mournful, pious, agonizing feeling now filled his
heart.

He knelt down by the bedside of Cosette.

It was broad daylight, and yet the child slept on. A pale ray
from the December sun struggled through the garret window and traced upon the ceiling long streaks of light and
shade. Suddenly a carrier's wagon, heavily laden, trundled
over the cobblestones of the boulevard, and shook the old
building like the rumbling of a tempest, jarring it from cellar
to rooftree.

"Yes, madame!" cried Cosette, starting up out of sleep.
"Here I am! Here I am!"

And she threw herself from the bed, her eyelids still half
closed with the weight of slumber, stretching out her hand
toward the corner of the wall.

"Oh! What shall I do? Where is my broom?" said she.

By this time her eyes were fully open, and she saw the
smiling face of Jean Valjean.

"Oh! Yes—so it is!" said the child. "Good morning, monsieur."

Children at once accept joy and happiness with quick
familiarity, being themselves naturally all happiness and joy.

Cosette noticed Catharine at the foot of the bed, laid hold
of her at once, and, playing the while, asked Jean Valjean a
thousand questions: Where was she? Was Paris a big place?
Was Madame Thénardier really very far away? Wouldn't she
come back again, etc., etc. All at once she exclaimed, "How
pretty it is here!"

It was a frightful hovel, but she felt free.

"Must I sweep?" she continued at length.

"Play!" replied Jean Valjean.

And thus the day passed by. Cosette, without troubling herself with trying to understand anything about it, was inexpressibly happy with her doll and her good friend.

III

THE dawn of the next day found Jean Valjean again near the bed of Cosette. He waited there, motionless, to see her wake. Something new was entering his soul.

Jean Valjean had never loved anything. For twenty-five years he had been alone in the world. He had never been a father, lover, husband, or friend. At the galleys, he was cross, sullen, abstinent, ignorant, and intractable. The heart of the old convict was full of freshness. His sister and her children had left in his memory only a vague and distant impression, which had finally almost entirely vanished. He had made every exertion to find them again, and, not succeeding, had forgotten them. Human nature is thus constituted. The other tender emotions of his youth, if any such he had, were lost in an abyss.

When he saw Cosette, when he had taken her, carried her away and rescued her, he felt his heart moved. All that he had of feeling and affection was aroused and vehemently attracted toward this child. He would approach the bed where she slept, and would tremble there with delight; he felt inward yearnings, like a mother, and knew not what they were, for it is something very incomprehensible and very sweet, this grand and strange emotion of a heart in its first love.

Poor old heart, so young!

But, as he was fifty-five and Cosette was but eight years old, all that he might have felt of love in his entire life melted into a sort of ineffable radiance.

This was the second white vision he had seen. The bishop had caused the dawn of virtue on his horizon; Cosette evoked the dawn of love.

The first few days rolled by amid this bewilderment.

On her part, Cosette, too, unconsciously underwent a change, poor little creature! She was so small when her mother left her, that she could not recollect her now. As all children do, like the young shoots of the vine that cling to everything, she had tried to love. She had not been able to succeed. Everybody had repelled her—the Thénardiers, their children, other children. She had loved the dog; it died, and after that no person and no thing would have anything to do with her. Mournful thing to tell, at the age of eight her heart was cold. This was not her fault; it was not the faculty of love that she lacked; alas, it was the possibility. And so, from the very first day, all that thought and felt in her began to love this kind old friend. She now felt sensations utterly unknown to her before—a sensation of budding and of growth.

Her kind friend no longer impressed her as old and poor. In her eyes Jean Valjean was handsome, just as the garret had seemed pretty.

Nature had placed a wide chasm—fifty years' interval of age—between Jean Valjean and Cosette. This chasm fate filled up. Fate abruptly brought together, and wedded with its resistless power, these two shattered lives, dissimilar in years, but similar in sorrow. The one, indeed, was the complement of the other. The instinct of Cosette sought for a father, as the instinct of Jean Valjean sought for a child. To meet, was to find one another. In that mysterious moment, when their hands touched, they were welded together. When their two souls saw each other, they recognized that they were mutually needed, and they closely embraced.

Taking the words in their most comprehensive and most absolute sense, it might be said that, separated from everything by the walls of the tomb, Jean Valjean was the husband bereaved, as Cosette was the orphan. This position made Jean Valjean become, in a celestial sense, the father of Cosette.

And, in truth, the mysterious impression produced upon Cosette, in the depths of the woods at Chelles, by the hand of Jean Valjean grasping her own in the darkness, was not an illusion but a reality. The coming of this man and his participation in the destiny of this child had been the advent of God.

In the meanwhile, Jean Valjean had chosen well his hiding place. He was there in a state of security that seemed to be complete.

The apartment with the side chamber which he occupied with Cosette was the one whose window looked out upon the boulevard. This window being the only one in the house, there was no neighbor's prying eye to fear either from that side or opposite.

The lower floor of No. 50-52 was a sort of dilapidated shed; it served as a sort of stable for market gardeners, and had no communication with the upper floor. The upper floor contained, as we have said, several rooms and a few lofts, only one of which was occupied—by an old woman, who was maid of all work to Jean Valjean. All the rest was uninhabited.

It was this old woman, honored with the title of landlady, but, in reality, entrusted with the functions of portress, who had rented him these lodgings on Christmas Day. He had passed himself off to her as a gentleman of means, ruined by the Spanish Bonds, who was going to live there with his granddaughter. He had paid her for six months in advance, and engaged the old dame to furnish the chamber and the little bedroom, as we have described them. This old woman it was who had kindled the fire in the stove and made everything ready for them, on the evening of their arrival.

Weeks rolled by. These two beings led in that wretched shelter a happy life.

From the earliest dawn, Cosette laughed, prattled, and sang. Children have their morning song, like birds.

Sometimes it happened that Jean Valjean would take her little red hand, all chapped and frostbitten as it was, and kiss it. The poor child, accustomed only to blows, had no idea what this meant, and would draw back ashamed.

At times, she grew serious and looked musingly at her little black dress. Cosette was no longer in rags; she was in mourning. She was issuing from utter poverty and was entering upon life.

Jean Valjean had begun to teach her to read. Sometimes, while teaching the child to spell, he would remember that it was with the intention of accomplishing evil that he had learned to read, in the galleys. This intention had now been changed into teaching a child to read. Then the old convict would smile with the pensive smile of angels.

He felt in this a preordination from on high, a volition of someone more than man, and he would lose himself in reverie. Good thoughts as well as bad have their abysses.

To teach Cosette to read, and to watch her playing, was nearly all Jean Valjean's life. And then, he would talk to her about her mother, and teach her to pray.

She called him "Father," and knew him by no other name.

This is but personal opinion; but in order to express our idea thoroughly, at the point Jean Valjean had reached, when he began to love Cosette, it is not clear to us that he did not require this fresh supply of goodness to enable him to persevere in the right path. He had seen the wickedness of men and the misery of society under new aspects—aspects incomplete and, unfortunately, showing forth only one side of the truth—the lot of woman summed up in Fantine, public authority personified in Javert; he had been sent back to the galleys this time for doing good; new waves of bitterness had overwhelmed him; disgust and weariness had once more resumed their sway; the recollection of the bishop, even, was perhaps eclipsed, sure to reappear afterward, luminous and triumphant; yet, in fact, this blessed remembrance was growing feebler. Who knows that Jean Valjean was not on the point of becoming discouraged and falling back to evil ways? Love came, and he again grew strong. Alas, he was no less feeble than Cosette. He protected her, and she gave strength to him. Thanks to him, she could walk upright in life; thanks to her, he could persist in virtuous deeds. He was the support of this child, and this child was his prop and staff. Oh, divine and unfathomable mystery of the compensations of Destiny!

IV

THERE was, in the neighborhood of Saint Médard, a mendicant who sat crouching over the edge of a condemned public well nearby, and to whom Jean Valjean often gave alms. He never passed this man without giving him a few pennies. Sometimes he spoke to him. Those who were envious of this poor creature said he was in the pay of the police. He was an old church beadle of seventy-five, who was always mumbling prayers.

One evening, as Jean Valjean was passing that way, unaccompanied by Cosette, he noticed the beggar sitting in his usual place, under the streetlamp which had just been lighted. The man, according to custom, seemed to be praying and was bent over. Jean Valjean walked up to him, and put a piece of money in his hand, as usual. The beggar suddenly raised his eyes, gazed intently at Jean Valjean, and then quickly dropped his head. This movement was like a flash; Jean Valjean shuddered; it seemed to him that he had just seen, by the light of the streetlamp, not the calm, sanctimonious face of the aged beadle, but a terrible and well-known countenance. He experienced the sensation one would feel on finding himself suddenly face to face, in the gloom, with a tiger. He recoiled, horror-stricken and petrified, daring neither to breathe nor to speak, to stay nor to fly, but gazing upon the beggar who had once more bent down his head, with its tattered covering, and seemed to be no longer conscious of his presence. At this singular moment, an instinct, perhaps the mysterious instinct of self-preservation, prevented Jean Valjean from uttering a word. The beggar had the same form, the same rags, the same general appearance as on every other day. "Pshaw!" said Jean Valjean to himself. "I am mad! I am dreaming! It cannot be!" And he went home, anxious and ill at ease.

He scarcely dared to admit, even to himself, that the countenance he thought he had seen was the face of Javert.

That night, upon reflection, he regretted that he had not questioned the man so as to compel him to raise his head a second time. On the morrow, at nightfall, he went thither, again. The beggar was in his place. "Good day! Good day!" said Jean Valjean, with firmness, as he gave him the accustomed alms. The beggar raised his head and answered in a whining voice: "Thanks, kind sir, thanks!" It was, indeed, only the old beadle.

Jean Valjean now felt fully reassured. He even began to laugh. "What the deuce was I about to fancy that I saw Javert," thought he. "Is my sight growing poor already?" And he thought no more about it.

Some days after, it might be eight o'clock in the evening, he was in his room, giving Cosette her spelling lesson, which the child was repeating in a loud voice, when he heard the door of the building open and close again. That seemed odd to him. The old woman, the only occupant of the house besides himself and Cosette, always went to bed at dark to save candles. Jean Valjean made a sign to Cosette to be silent. He heard someone coming up the stairs. Possibly, it might be the old woman, who had felt unwell and had been to the druggist's. Jean Valjean listened. The footstep was heavy, and sounded like a man's; but the old woman wore heavy shoes, and there is nothing so much like the step of a man as the step of an old woman. However, Jean Valjean blew out his candle.

He sent Cosette to bed, telling her in a suppressed voice to lie down very quietly—and, as he kissed her forehead, the footsteps stopped. Jean Valjean remained silent and motionless, his back turned toward the door, still seated on his chair from which he had not moved, and holding his breath in the darkness. After a considerable interval, not hearing anything more, he turned round without making any noise, and as he raised his eyes toward the door of his room, he saw a light through the keyhole. This ray of light was an evil star in the black background of the door and the wall. There was, evidently, somebody outside with a candle who was listening.

A few minutes elapsed, and the light disappeared. But he heard no sound of footsteps, which seemed to indicate that whoever was listening at the door had taken off his shoes.

Jean Valjean threw himself on his bed without undressing, but could not shut his eyes that night.

At daybreak, as he was sinking into slumber from fatigue, he was aroused, again, by the creaking of the door of some room at the end of the hall, and then he heard the same footstep which had ascended the stairs, on the preceding night. The step approached. He started from his bed and placed his eye to the keyhole, which was quite a large one, hoping to get a glimpse of the person, whoever it might be, who had made his way into the building in the nighttime and had listened at his door. It was a man, indeed, who passed by Jean Valjean's room, this time without stopping. The hall was still too dark for him to make out his features, but, when the man reached the stairs, a ray of light from without made his figure stand out like a profile, and Jean Valjean had a full view of his back. The man was tall, wore a long frock coat, and had a cudgel under his arm. It was the redoubtable form of Javert.

Jean Valjean might have tried to get another look at him through his window that opened on the boulevard, but he would have had to raise the sash, and that he dared not do.

It was evident that the man had entered by means of a key, as if at home. Who, then, had given him the key? And what was the meaning of this?

At seven in the morning, he made a roll of a hundred francs he had in a drawer and put it into his pocket. Do what he would to manage this so that the clinking of the silver should not be heard, a five-franc piece escaped his grasp and rolled jingling away over the floor.

At dusk, he went to the street door and looked carefully up and down the boulevard. No one was to be seen. The boulevard seemed to be utterly deserted. It is true that there might have been someone hidden behind a tree.

He went upstairs again.

"Come," said he to Cosette.

He took her by the hand and they both went out.

A Dark Chase Needs
a Silent Hound

I

JEAN VALJEAN had immediately left the boulevard and began to thread the streets, making as many turns as he could, returning sometimes upon his track to make sure that he was not followed.

The moon was full. Jean Valjean was not sorry for that. The moon, still near the horizon, cut large prisms of light and shade in the streets. Jean Valjean could glide along the houses and the walls on the dark side and observe the light side. He did not, perhaps, sufficiently realize that the obscure side escaped him. However, in all the deserted little streets in the neighborhood of the rue de Poliveau, he felt sure that no one was behind him.

Jean Valjean described many and varied labyrinths in the Quartier Mouffetard, which was asleep already as if it were still under the discipline of the middle age and the yoke of the curfew; he produced different combinations, in wise strategy, with the rue Censier and the rue Copeau, the rue du Battoir Saint Victor and rue du Puits l'Ermite.

As eleven o'clock struck in the tower of Saint Etienne du Mont, he crossed the rue de Pontoise in front of the bureau of the Commissary of Police, which is at No. 14. Some moments afterward, the instinct of which we have already spoken made him turn his head. At this moment he saw distinctly—thanks to the commissary's lamp which revealed them—three men following him quite near, pass one after another under this lamp on the dark side of the street. One of these men entered the passage leading to the commissary's house. The one in advance appeared to him decidedly suspicious.

"Come, child!" said he to Cosette, and he made haste to get out of the rue de Pontoise.

He made a circuit, went round the arcade des Patriarches, which was closed on account of the lateness of the hour, walked rapidly through the rue de l'Epée-de-Bois and the rue de l'Arbalète, and plunged into the rue des Postes.

There was a square there, where the Collège Rollin now is, and from which branches off the rue Neuve-Sainte-Geneviève.

The moon lighted up this square brightly. Jean Valjean concealed himself in a doorway, calculating that if these men were still following him, he could not fail to get a good view of them when they crossed this lighted space.

In fact, three minutes had not elapsed when the men appeared. There were now four of them; all were tall, dressed in long brown coats, with round hats, and great clubs in their hands. They were not less fearfully forbidding by their size and their large fists than by their stealthy tread in the darkness. One would have taken them for four specters in citizens' dress.

They stopped in the center of the square and formed a group like people consulting. They appeared undecided. The man who seemed to be the leader turned and energetically pointed in the direction in which Jean Valjean was; one of the others seemed to insist with some obstinacy on the contrary direction. At the instant when the leader turned, the moon shone full in his face. Jean Valjean recognized Javert perfectly.

II

UNCERTAINTY was at an end for Jean Valjean; happily, it still continued with these men. He took advantage of their hesitation; it was time lost for them, gained for him. He came out from the doorway in which he was concealed, and made his way into the rue des Postes toward the region of the Jardin des Plantes. Cosette began to be tired; he took her in his arms, and carried her. There was nobody in the streets, and the lamps had not been lighted on account of the moon.

He doubled his pace.

He passed through the rue de la Clef, then by the Fontaine de Saint Victor along the Jardin des Plantes by the lower streets, and reached the quay. There he looked around. The quay was deserted. The streets were deserted. Nobody behind him. He took a breath.

He arrived at the Bridge of Austerlitz.

A large cart was passing the Seine at the same time, and like him was going toward the right bank. This could be made of use. He could go the whole length of the bridge in the shade of this cart.

From the point where he was, he could see the whole length of the Bridge of Austerlitz.

Four shadows, at that moment, entered upon the bridge. These shadows were coming from the Jardin des Plantes toward the right bank.

These four shadows were the four men.

Jean Valjean felt a shudder like that of the deer when he sees the hounds again upon his track.

One hope was left him: by plunging into the little street before him, if he could succeed in reaching the woodyards, the marshes, the fields, the open grounds, he could escape.

It seemed to him that he might trust himself to this silent little street. He entered it.

III

SOME three hundred paces on, he reached a point where the street forked. It divided into two streets, the one turning off obliquely to the left, the other to the right. Jean Valjean had before him the two branches of a Y. Which should he choose?

He did not hesitate, but took the right.

Why?

Because the left branch led toward the *faubourg*—that is to say, toward the inhabited region, and the right branch toward the country—that is, toward the uninhabited region.

He turned, from time to time, and looked back. He took care to keep always on the dark side of the street. The street was straight behind him. The two or three first times he turned, he saw nothing; the silence was complete, and he kept on his way somewhat reassured. Suddenly, on turning again, he thought he saw in the portion of the street through which he had just passed, far in the obscurity, something which stirred.

He plunged forward rather than walked, hoping to find some side street by which to escape, and once more to elude his pursuers.

He came to a wall.

This wall, however, did not prevent him from going further; it was a wall forming the side of a cross alley, in which the street Jean Valjean was then in came to an end.

Here again he must decide; should he take the right or the left?

He looked to the right. The alley ran out to a space between some buildings that were mere sheds or barns, then terminated abruptly. The end of this blind alley was plain to be seen—a great white wall.

He looked to the left. The alley on this side was open and, about two hundred paces further on, ran into a street of which it was an affluent. In this direction lay safety.

The instant Jean Valjean decided to turn to the left, to try to reach the street which he saw at the end of the alley, he perceived, at the corner of the alley and the street toward which he was just about going, a sort of black, motionless statue.

It was a man, who had just been posted there, evidently, and who was waiting for him, guarding the passage.

Jean Valjean was startled.

Such was the quarter in the last century. The Petit Picpus had what we have just called a Y of streets, formed by the rue du Chemin Vert Saint Antoine dividing into two branches and taking on the left the name Petite rue Picpus and on the right the name of the rue Polonceau. The two branches of the Y were joined at the top as by a bar. This bar was called the rue Droit Mur. The rue Polonceau ended there; the Petite rue Picpus passed beyond, rising toward the Marché Lenoir.

He who, coming from the Seine, reached the extremity of the rue Polonceau, had on his left the rue Droit Mur turning sharply at a right angle, before him the side wall of that street, and on his right a truncated prolongation of the rue Droit Mur, without thoroughfare, called the Cul-de-sac Genrot.

Jean Valjean was in this place.

As we have said, on perceiving the black form standing sentry at the corner of the rue Droit Mur and the Petite rue Picpus, he was startled. There was no doubt. He was watched by this shadow.

What should he do?

There was now no time to turn back. What he had seen moving in the obscurity some distance behind him, the moment before, was undoubtedly Javert and his squad. Javert probably had already reached the commencement of tho street of which Jean Valjean was at the end. Javert, to all appearances, was acquainted with this little trap, and had taken his precautions by sending one of his men to guard the exit. These conjectures, so like certainties, whirled about wildly in Jean Valjean's troubled brain, as a handful of dust flies before a sudden blast. He scrutinized the Cul-de-sac Genrot; there were high walls. He scrutinized the Petite rue Picpus; there was a sentinel. He saw the dark form repeated in black upon the white pavement flooded with the moonlight. To advance was to fall upon that man. To go back was to throw himself into Javert's hands. Jean Valjean felt as if caught by a chain that was slowly winding up. He looked up into the sky in despair.

IV

At this moment a muffled and regular sound began to make itself heard at some distance. Jean Valjean ventured to thrust his head a little way around the corner of the street. Seven or eight soldiers, formed in platoon, had just turned into the rue Polonceau. He saw the gleam of their bayonets. They were coming toward him.

The soldiers, at whose head he distinguished the tall form of Javert, advanced slowly and with precaution. They stopped frequently. It was plain they were exploring all the recesses of the walls and all the entrances of doors and alleys.

It was—and here conjecture could not be deceived—some patrol which Javert had met and which he had put in requisition.

Javert's two assistants marched in the ranks.

At the rate at which they were marching, and the stops they were making, it would take them about a quarter of an hour to arrive at the spot where Jean Valjean was. It was a frightful moment. A few minutes separated Jean Valjean from that awful precipice which was opening before him for the third time. And the galleys now were no longer simply the galleys, they were Cosette lost forever; that is to say, a life in death.

There was now only one thing possible.

Jean Valjean had this peculiarity, that he might be said to carry two knapsacks; in one he had the thoughts of a saint, in the other the formidable talents of a convict. He helped himself from one or the other as occasion required.

Among other resources, thanks to his numerous escapes from the galleys at Toulon, he had, it will be remembered, become master of that incredible art of raising himself, in the right angle of a wall, if need be to the height of a sixth story; an art without ladders or props, by mere muscular strength, supporting himself by the back of his neck, his shoulders, his hips, and his knees, hardly making use of the few projections of the stone, which rendered so terrible and so celebrated the corner of the yard of the Conciergerie of Paris by which, some twenty years ago, the convict Battemolle made his escape.

Jean Valjean measured with his eyes the wall above which he saw a lime tree. It was about eighteen feet high.

The wall was capped by a flat stone without any projection.

The difficulty was Cosette. Cosette did not know how to scale a wall. Abandon her? Jean Valjean did not think of it. To carry her was impossible. The whole strength of a man is necessary to accomplish these strange ascents. The least burden would make him lose his center of gravity and he would fall.

He needed a cord. Jean Valjean had none. Where could he find a cord, at midnight, in the rue Polonceau? Truly at that instant, if Jean Valjean had had a kingdom, he would have given it for a rope.

All extreme situations have their flashes which sometimes make us blind, sometimes illuminate us.

The despairing gaze of Jean Valjean encountered the lamp-post in the Cul-de-sac Genrot.

At this epoch there were no gaslights in the streets of Paris. At nightfall they lighted the streetlamps, which were placed at intervals, and were raised and lowered by means of a rope traversing the street from end to end, running through the grooves of posts. The reel on which this rope was wound was enclosed below the lantern in a little iron box, the key of which was kept by the lamplighter, and the rope itself was protected by a casing of metal.

Jean Valjean, with the energy of a final struggle, crossed the street at a bound, entered the cul-de-sac, sprang the bolt of the little box with the point of his knife, and an instant after was back at the side of Cosette. He had a rope. These desperate inventors of expedients, in their struggles with fatality, move electrically in case of need.

We have explained that the streetlamps had not been lighted that night. The lamp in the Cul-de-sac Genrot was then, as a matter of course, extinguished like the rest, and one might pass by without even noticing that it was not in its place.

Meanwhile the hour, the place, the darkness, the preoccupation of Jean Valjean, his singular actions, his going to and fro, all this began to disturb Cosette. Any other child would have uttered loud cries long before. She contented herself with pulling Jean Valjean by the skirt of his coat. The sound of the approaching patrol was constantly becoming more and more distinct.

"Father," said she, in a whisper, "I am afraid. Who is it that is coming?"

"Hush!" answered the unhappy man. "It is the Thénardiess."

Cosette shuddered. He added:

"Don't say a word; I'll take care of her. If you cry, if you make any noise, the Thénardiess will hear you. She is coming to catch you."

Then, without any haste, but without doing anything a second time, with a firm and rapid decision, so much the more remarkable at such a moment when the patrol and Javert might come upon him at any instant, he took off his cravat, passed it around Cosette's body under the arms, taking care that it should not hurt the child, attached this cravat to an end of the rope by means of the knot which seamen call a swallow knot, took the other end of the rope in his teeth, took off his shoes and stockings and threw them over the wall, and began to raise himself in the angle of the wall and the gable with as much solidity and certainty as if he had the rounds of a ladder under his heels and his elbows. Half a minute had not passed before he was on his knees on the wall.

Cosette watched him, stupefied, without saying a word. Jean Valjean's charge and the name of the Thénardiess had made her dumb.

All at once, she heard Jean Valjean's voice calling to her in a low whisper:

"Put your back against the wall."

She obeyed.

"Don't speak, and don't be afraid," added Jean Valjean.

And she felt herself lifted from the ground.

Before she had time to think where she was she was at the top of the wall.

Jean Valjean seized her, put her on his back, took her two little hands in his left hand, lay down flat and crawled along the top of the wall. As he had supposed, there was a building there, the roof of which sloped very nearly to the ground, with a gentle inclination.

A fortunate circumstance, for the wall was much higher on this side than on the street. Jean Valjean saw the ground beneath him at a great depth.

He had just reached the inclined plane of the roof, and had not yet left the crest of the wall, when a violent uproar proclaimed the arrival of the patrol. He heard the thundering voice of Javert:

"Search the cul-de-sac! The rue Droit Mur is guarded, the Petite rue Picpus also. I'll answer for it if he is in the cul-de-sac."

The soldiers rushed into the Cul-de-sac Genrot.

Jean Valjean slid down the roof, keeping hold of Cosette, reached the lime tree, and jumped to the ground. Whether from terror, or from courage, Cosette had not uttered a whisper. Her hands were a little scraped.

V

JEAN VALJEAN found himself in a sort of garden, very large and of a singular appearance, one of those gloomy gardens which seem made to be seen in the winter and at night. This garden was oblong, with a row of large poplars at the further end, some tall forest trees in the corners, and a clear space in the center, where stood a very large isolated tree, then a few fruit trees, contorted and shaggy, like big bushes, some vegetable beds, a melon patch the glass covers of which shone in the moonlight, and an old well. There were here and there stone benches which seemed black with moss. The walks were bordered with sorry little shrubs perfectly straight. The grass covered half of them, and a green moss covered the rest.

Nothing can be imagined more wild and more solitary than this garden. There was no one there, which was very natural on account of the hour, but it did not seem as if the place were made for anybody to walk in, even in broad noon.

Jean Valjean's first care had been to find his shoes, and put them on; then he entered the shed with Cosette. A man trying to escape never thinks himself sufficiently concealed. The child, thinking constantly of the Thénardiess, shared his instinct, and cowered down as closely as she could.

Cosette trembled, and pressed closely to his side. They heard the tumultuous clamor of the patrol ransacking the cul-de-sac and the street, the clatter of their muskets against the stones, the calls of Javert to the watchmen he had stationed, and his imprecations mingled with words which they could not distinguish.

At the end of a quarter of an hour it seemed as though this stormy rumbling began to recede. Jean Valjean did not breathe.

He had placed his hand gently upon Cosette's mouth.

But the solitude about him was so strangely calm that that frightful din, so furious and so near, did not even cast over it a shadow of disturbance. It seemed as if these walls were built of the deaf stones spoken of in the Scriptures.

Suddenly, in the midst of this deep calm, a new sound arose, a celestial, divine, ineffable sound, as ravishing as the other was horrible. It was a hymn which came forth from the darkness, a bewildering mingling of prayer and harmony in the obscure and fearful silence of the night; voices of women, but voices with the pure accents of virgins, and artless accents of children; those voices which are not of earth, and which resemble those that the newborn still hear, and the dying hear already. This song came from the gloomy building which overlooked the garden. At the moment when the uproar of the demons receded, one would have said, it was a choir of angels approaching in the darkness.

Cosette and Jean Valjean fell on their knees.

They knew not what it was; they knew not where they were, but they both felt, the man and the child, the penitent and the innocent, that they ought to be on their knees.

These voices had this strange effect; they did not prevent the building from appearing deserted. It was like a supernatural song in an uninhabited dwelling.

While these voices were singing Jean Valjean was entirely absorbed in them. He no longer saw the night, he saw a blue sky. He seemed to feel the spreading of these wings which we all have within us.

The chant ceased. Perhaps it had lasted a long time. Jean Valjean could not have told. Hours of ecstasy are never more than a moment.

All had again relapsed into silence. There was nothing more in the street, nothing more in the garden. That which threatened, that which reassured, all had vanished. The wind rattled the dry grass on the top of the wall, which made a low, soft, and mournful noise.

VI

THE child had laid her head upon a stone and gone to sleep.

He sat down near her and looked at her. Little by little, as he beheld her, he grew calm, and regained possession of his clearness of mind.

He plainly perceived this truth, the basis of his life henceforth, that so long as she should be alive, so long as he should have her with him, he should need nothing except for her, and fear nothing save on her account. He did not even realize that he was very cold, having taken off his coat to cover her.

Meanwhile, through the reverie into which he had fallen, he had heard for some time a singular noise. It sounded like a little bell that someone was shaking. This noise was in the garden. It was heard distinctly, though feebly. It resembled the dimly heard tinkling of cowbells in the pastures at night.

This noise made Jean Valjean turn.

He looked, and saw that there was someone in the garden. Something which resembled a man was walking among the glass cases of the melon patch, rising up, stooping down, stopping, with a regular motion, as if he were drawing or stretching something upon the ground. This being appeared to limp.

Jean Valjean shuddered. He said to himself that perhaps Javert and his spies had not gone away, that they had doubtless left somebody on the watch in the street; that, if this man should discover him in the garden, he would cry thief, and would deliver him up. He took the sleeping Cosette gently in his arms and carried her into the furthest corner of the shed behind a heap of old furniture that was out of use. Cosette did not stir.

From there he watched the strange motions of tho man in the melon patch. It seemed very singular, but the sound of the bell followed every movement of the man. When the man approached, the sound approached; when he moved away, the sound moved away; if he made some sudden motion, a trill accompanied the motion; when he stopped, the noise ceased. It seemed evident that the bell was fastened to this man, but then what could that mean? What was this man to whom a bell was hung as to a ram or a cow?

While he was revolving these questions, he touched Cosette's hands. They were icy.

"Oh! God!" said he.

He called to her in a low voice:

"Cosette!"

She did not open her eyes.

He shook her smartly.

She did not wake.

"Could she be dead?" said he, and he sprang up, shuddering from head to foot.

Cosette was pallid; she had fallen prostrate on the ground at his feet, making no sign.

He listened for her breathing; she was breathing, but with a respiration that appeared feeble and about to stop.

How should he get her warm again? How rouse her? All else was banished from his thoughts. He rushed desperately out of the ruin.

It was absolutely necessary that in less than a quarter of an hour Cosette should be in bed and before a fire.

VII

HE walked straight to the man whom he saw in the garden. He had taken in his hand the roll of money which was in his vest pocket.

This man had his head down, and did not see him coming. With a few strides, Jean Valjean was at his side.

Jean Valjean approached him, exclaiming:

"A hundred francs!"

The man started and raised his eyes.

"A hundred francs for you," continued Jean Valjean, "if you will give me refuge tonight."

The moon shone full in Jean Valjean's bewildered face.

"What, it is you, Father Madeleine!" said the man.

This name, thus pronounced, at this dark hour, in this unknown place, by this unknown man, made Jean Valjean start back.

He was ready for anything but that. The speaker was an old man, bent and lame, dressed much like a peasant, who had on his left knee a leather kneecap from which hung a bell. His face was in the shade, and could not be distinguished.

Meanwhile the goodman had taken off his cap, and was exclaiming, tremulously:

"Ah! My God! How did you come here, Father Madeleine? How did you get in, O Lord? Did you fall from the sky?"

"Who are you? And what is this house?" asked Jean Valjean.

"Oh! Indeed, that is good now," exclaimed the old man. "I am the one you got the place for here, and this house is the one you got me the place in. What! You don't remember me?"

"No," said Jean Valjean. "And how does it happen that you know me?"

"You saved my life," said the man.

He turned, a ray of the moon lighted up his side face, and Jean Valjean recognized old Fauchelevent.

"Ah!" said Jean Valjean. "It is you? Yes, I remember you."

"That is very fortunate!" said the old man, in a reproachful tone.

"And what are you doing here?" added Jean Valjean.

"Oh! I am covering my melons."

Old Fauchelevent had in his hand, indeed, at the moment when Jean Valjean accosted him, the end of a piece of awning which he was stretching out over the melon patch. He had already spread out several in this way during the hour he had been in the garden. It was this work which made him go though the peculiar motions observed by Jean Valjean from the shed.

He continued:

"I said to myself: the moon is bright, there is going to be a frost. Suppose I put their jackets on my melons? And," added he, looking at Jean Valjean, with a loud laugh, "you would have done well to do as much for yourself. But how did you come here?"

Jean Valjean, finding that he was known by this man, at least under his name of Madeleine, went no further with his precautions. He multiplied questions. Oddly enough their parts seemed reversed. It was he, the intruder, who put questions.

"And what is this bell you have on your knee?"

"That!" answered Fauchelevent. "That is so that they may keep away from me."

"Keep away from you?"

Old Fauchelevent winked in an indescribable manner.

"Ah! Bless me! There's nothing but women in this house, plenty of young girls. It seems that I am dangerous to meet. The bell warns them. When I come they go away."

"What is this house?"

"Why, you know very well."

"No, I don't."

"Why, you got me this place here as gardener."

"Answer me as if I didn't know."

"Well, it is the Convent of the Petit Picpus, then."

Jean Valjean remembered. Chance, that is to say Providence, had thrown him precisely into this convent of the Quartier Saint Antoine, to which old Fauchelevent, crippled by his fall from his cart, had been admitted, upon his recommendation, two years before. He repeated as if he were talking to himself:

"The Convent of the Petit Picpus!"

"But now, really," resumed Fauchelevent, "how the deuce did you manage to get in, you, Father Madeleine? It is no use for you to be a saint; you are a man, and no men come in here."

"But you are here."

"There is none but me."

"But," resumed Jean Valjean, "I must stay here."

"Oh! My God," exclaimed Fauchelevent.

Jean Valjean approached the old man, and said to him in a grave voice:

"Father Fauchelevent, I saved your life."

"I was first to remember it," answered Fauchelevent.

"Well, you can now do for me what I once did for you."

Fauchelevent grasped in his old wrinkled and trembling hands the robust hands of Jean Valjean, and it was some seconds before he could speak; at last he exclaimed:

"Oh! That would be a blessing of God if I could do something for you, in return for that! I save your life! Monsieur Mayor, the old man is at your disposal."

A wonderful joy had, as it were, transfigured the old gardener. A radiance seemed to shine forth from his face.

"What do you want me to do?" he added.

"I will explain. You have a room?"

"I have a solitary shanty, over there, behind the ruins of the old convent, in a corner that nobody ever sees. There are three rooms."

The shanty was in fact so well concealed behind the ruins, and so well arranged, that no one should see it—that Jean Valjean had not seen it.

"Good," said Jean Valjean. "Now I ask of you two things."

"What are they, Monsieur Madeleine?"

"First, that you will not tell anybody what you know about me. Second, that you will not attempt to learn anything more."

"As you please. I know that you can do nothing dishonorable, and that you have always been a man of God. And then, besides, it was you that put me here. It is your place, I am yours."

"Very well. But now come with me. We will go for the child."

"Ah!" said Fauchelevent. "There is a child!"

He said not a word more, but followed Jean Valjean as a dog follows his master.

In half an hour Cosette, again become rosy before a good fire, was asleep in the old gardener's bed. Jean Valjean had put on his cravat and coat; his hat, which he had thrown over the wall, had been found and brought in. While Jean Valjean was putting on his coat, Fauchelevent had taken off his kneecap with the bell attached, which now, hanging on a nail near a shutter, decorated the wall. The two men were warming themselves, with their elbows on a table, on which Fauchelevent had set a piece of cheese, some brown bread, a bottle of wine, and two glasses, and the old man said to Jean Valjean, putting his hand on his knee:

"Ah! Father Madeleine! You didn't know me at first? You save people's lives and then you forget them? Oh! That's bad; they remember you. You are ungrateful!"

The Convent

I

BEFORE closing his eyes, Jean Valjean had said: "Henceforth I must remain here." These words were chasing one another through Fauchelevent's head the whole night.

To tell the truth, neither of them had slept.

Jean Valjean, feeling that he was discovered and Javert was upon his track, knew full well that he and Cosette were lost should they return into the city. Since the new blast which had burst upon him had thrown him into this cloister, Jean Valjean had but one thought, to remain there. Now, for one in his unfortunate position, this convent was at once the safest and the most dangerous place, the most dangerous, for, no man being allowed to enter, if he should be discovered, it was a flagrant crime, and Jean Valjean would take but one step from the convent to prison; the safest, for if he succeeded in getting permission to remain, who would come there to look for him? To live in an impossible place; that would be safety.

For his part, Fauchelevent was racking his brains. He began by deciding that he was utterly bewildered. How did Monsieur Madeleine come there, with such walls! The walls of a cloister are not so easily crossed. How did he happen to be with a child? A man does not scale a steep wall with a child in his arms. Who was this child? Where did they both come from? Since Fauchelevent had been in the convent, he had not heard a word from M—— sur m——, and he knew nothing of what had taken place. From some words that escaped from Jean Valjean, however, the gardener thought he might conclude that Monsieur Madeleine had probably failed on account of the hard times, and that he was pursued by his creditors, or it might be that he was compromised in some political affair and was concealing himself. Being in concealment, Monsieur Madeleine had taken the convent for an asylum, and it was natural that he should wish to remain there. Fauchelevent was groping amid conjectures, but saw nothing clearly except this: "Monsieur Madeleine has saved my life." This single certainty was sufficient, and determined him. He said aside to himself: "It is my turn now." He added in his conscience: "Monsieur Madeleine did not deliberate so long when the question was about squeezing himself under the wagon to draw me out." He decided that he would save Monsieur Madeleine.

But to have him remain in the convent, what a problem was that! Before that almost chimerical attempt, Fauchelevent did not recoil; this poor Picardy peasant, with no other ladder than his devotion, his good will, a little of that old country cunning, engaged for once in the service of a generous intention, undertook to scale the impossibilities of the cloister and the craggy escarpments of the rules of St. Benedict. Fauchelevent was an old man who had been selfish throughout his life, and who, near the end of his days, crippled, infirm, having no interest longer in the world, found it sweet to be grateful, and seeing a virtuous action to be done, threw himself into it like a man who, at the moment of death, finding at hand a glass of some good wine which he had never tasted, should drink it greedily. We might add that the air which he had been breathing now for several years in this convent had destroyed his personality, and had at last rendered some good action necessary to him.

He formed his resolution then: to devote himself to Monsieur Madeleine.

II

FATHER FAUCHELEVENT rapped softly at a door, and a gentle voice answered: "Come in."

This door was that of the parlor allotted to the gardener, for use when it was necessary to communicate with him. This parlor was near the hall of the chapter. The prioress, seated in the only chair in the parlor, was waiting for Fauchelevent.

The gardener made a timid bow, and stopped at the threshold of the cell. The prioress, who was saying her rosary, raised her eyes and said:

"Ah! It is you, Father Fauvent."

This abbreviation had been adopted in the convent.

Fauchelevent again began his bow.

"Father Fauvent, I have called you."

"I am here, reverend mother."

"I wish to speak to you."

"And I, for my part," said Fauchelevent, with a boldness at which he was alarmed himself, "I have something to say to the most reverend mother."

The prioress looked at him.

"Ah, you have a communication to make to me."

"A petition!"

"Well, what is it?"

Goodman Fauchelevent, ex-notary, belonged to that class of peasants who are never disconcerted. A certain combination of ignorance and skill is very effective; you do not suspect it, and you accede to it. Within little more than two years that he had lived in the convent, Fauchelevent had achieved a success in the community. In this enigmatic and taciturn cloister, nothing was hidden from him; this sphinx blabbed all her secrets in his ear. Fauchelevent, knowing everything, concealed everything. That was his art. The whole convent thought him stupid—a great merit in religion. The mothers prized Fauchelevent. He was a rare mute. He inspired confidence. The congregation thought much of him, old, lame, seeing nothing, probably a little deaf—how many good qualities! It would have been difficult to replace him.

The goodman, with the assurance of one who feels that he is appreciated, began before the reverend prioress a rustic harangue, quite diffuse and very profound. He spoke at length of his age, his infirmities, of the weight of years henceforth doubly heavy upon him, of the growing demands of his work, of the size of the garden, of the nights to be spent, like last night for example, when he had to put awnings over the melons on account of the moon; and finally ended with this: that he had a brother (the prioress gave a start), a brother not young (second start of the prioress, but a reassured start); that if it was desired, this brother could come and live with him and help him; that he was an excellent gardener; that the community would get good services from him, better than his own; that, otherwise, if his brother were not admitted, as he, the oldest, felt that he was broken down, and unequal to the labor, he would be obliged to leave, though with much regret, and that his brother had a little girl that he would bring with him, who would be reared under God in the house, and who, perhaps— who knows?—would someday become a nun.

When he had finished, the prioress stopped the sliding of her rosary through her fingers, and said:

"Can you, between now and night, procure a strong iron bar?"

"For what work?"

"To be used as a lever?"

"Yes, reverend mother," answered Fauchelevent.

The prioress, without adding a word, arose, and went into the next room, which was the hall of the chapter, where the vocal mothers were probably assembled: Fauchelevent remained alone.

III

ABOUT a quarter of an hour elapsed. The prioress returned and resumed her seat.

Both seemed preoccupied. We report as well as we can the dialogue that followed.

"Father Fauvent?"

"Reverend mother?"

"You are familiar with the chapel?"

"I have a little box there to go to mass, and the offices."

"And you have been in the choir about your work?"

"Two or three times."

"A stone is to be raised."

"Heavy?"

"The slab of the pavement at the side of the altar."

"The stone that covers the vault?"

"Yes."

"That is a piece of work where it would be well to have two men."

"The stone is arranged to turn on a pivot."

"Very well, reverend mother, I will open the vault."

"And the four mother choristers will assist you."

"And when the vault is opened?"

"It must be shut again."

"Is that all?"

"No."

"Give me your orders, most reverend mother."

"Something must be let down."

There was silence. The prioress, after a quivering of the underlip which resembled hesitation, spoke:

"Father Fauvent?"

"Reverend mother?"

"You know that a mother died this morning."

"No."

"Father Fauvent, we must do what the dead wish. To be buried in the vault under the altar of the chapel, not to go into profane ground, to remain in death where she prayed in life; this was the last request of Mother Crucifixion. She has asked it, that is to say, commanded it."

"But it is forbidden."

"Forbidden by men, enjoined by God."

"If it should come to be known?"

"We have confidence in you."

"But, reverend mother, if the agent of the Health Commission—"

"St. Benedict II, in the matter of burial, resisted Constantine Pogonatus."

"However, the Commissary of Police—"

"Chonodemaire, one of the seven German kings who entered Gaul in the reign of Constantius, expressly recognized the right of conventuals to be inhumed in religion, that is to say, under the altar."

"But the Inspector of the Prefecture—"

"The world is nothing before the cross. Martin, eleventh

general of the Carthusians, gave to his order this device: *Stat crux dum volvitur orbis.*"

"Amen," said Fauchelevent, imperturbable in this method of extricating himself whenever he heard any Latin.

"Can we count upon you?"

"I shall obey."

"It is well."

"Reverend mother, I shall need a lever at least six feet long."

"Where will you get it?"

"Where there are gratings there are always iron bars. I have my heap of old iron at the back of the garden."

"Father Fauvent, be at the high altar with the iron bar at eleven o'clock. The office commences at midnight. It must all be finished a good quarter of an hour before."

"I will do everything to prove my zeal for the community. Reverend mother, is this all?"

"No."

"What more is there, then?"

"There is still the empty coffin."

This brought them to a stand. Fauchelevent pondered. The prioress pondered.

"Father Fauvent, what shall be done with the coffin?"

"It will be put in the ground."

"Empty?"

"Reverend mother, I will put some earth into the coffin. That will have the effect of a body."

"You are right. Earth is the same thing as man. So you will prepare the empty coffin?"

"I will attend to that."

The face of the prioress, till then dark and anxious, became again serene. She made him the sign of a superior dismissing an inferior. Fauchelevent moved toward the door. As he was going out, the prioress gently raised her voice.

"Father Fauvent, I am satisfied with you; tomorrow after the burial, bring your brother to me, and tell him to bring his daughter."

IV

THE same evening, Jean Valjean, thanks to a small door which is seen from the street, and which opens onto the garden, went out with Cosette while Fauchelevent distracted the attention of the doorman. Then he went back in almost immediately and was officially shown into the parlor by the doorman, who did not notice anything.

The prioress, rosary in hand, was awaiting them. A mother, with her veil down, stood near her. A modest taper lighted, or one might almost say, pretended to light up the parlor.

The prioress scrutinized Jean Valjean. Nothing scans so carefully as a downcast eye.

She looked at Cosette attentively, and then said, aside to the mother:

"She will be homely."

The two mothers talked together very low for a few minutes in a corner of the parlor, and then the prioress turned and said:

"Father Fauvent, you will have another kneecap and bell. We need two, now."

So, next morning, two little bells were heard tinkling in the garden, and the nuns could not keep from lifting a corner of their veils. They saw two men digging side by side, in the lower part of the garden under the trees—Fauvent and another. Immense event! The silence was broken, so far as to say:

"It's an assistant gardener!"

The mothers added:

"He is Father Fauvent's brother."

In fact, Jean Valjean was regularly installed; he had the leather kneecap and the bell; henceforth he had his commission. His name was Ultimus Fauchelevent.

The prioress, having uttered this prediction, immediately been the remark of the prioress: "She will be homely."

The prioress having uttered this prediction, immediately took Cosette into her friendship and gave her a place in the school building as a charity pupil.

V

Cosette, in becoming a pupil at the convent, had to assume the dress of the schoolgirls. Jean Valjean succeeded in having the garments which she laid aside given to him. It was the same mourning suit he had carried for her to put on when she left the Thénardiers. It was not much worn. Jean Valjean rolled up these garments, as well as the woolen stockings and shoes, with much camphor and other aromatic substances of which there is such an abundance in convents, and packed them in a small valise which he managed to procure. He put this valise in a chair near his bed, and always kept the key of it in his pocket.

"Father," Cosette one day asked him, "what is that box there that smells so good?"

A very pleasant life began again for him.

He worked every day in the garden, and was very useful there. He had formerly been a pruner, and now found it quite in his way to be a gardener. He knew all kinds of receipts and secrets of fieldwork. These he turned to account. Nearly all the orchard trees were wild stock; he grafted them and made them bear excellent fruit.

Cosette was allowed to come every day, and pass an hour with him. As the sisters were melancholy, and he was kind, the child compared him with them, and worshiped him. Every day, at the hour appointed, she would hurry to the little building. When she entered the old place, she filled it with paradise. Jean Valjean basked in her presence and felt his own happiness increase by reason of the happiness he conferred on Cosette. The delight we inspire in others has this enchanting peculiarity that, far from being diminished like every other reflection, it returns to us more radiant than ever. At the hours of recreation, Jean Valjean from a distance watched her playing and romping, and he could distinguish her laughter from the laughter of the rest.

For, now, Cosette laughed.

Even Cosette's countenance had, in a measure, changed. The gloomy cast had disappeared. Laughter is sunshine; it chases winter from the human face.

When the recreation was over and Cosette went in, Jean Valjean watched the windows of her schoolroom, and, at night, would rise from his bed to take a look at the windows of the room in which she slept.

God has his own ways. The convent contributed, like Cosette, to confirm and complete, in Jean Valjean, the work of the bishop. It cannot be denied that one of virtue's phases ends in pride. Therein is a bridge built by the Evil One. Jean Valjean was, perhaps, without knowing it, near that very phase of virtue, and that very bridge, when Providence flung him into the Convent of the Petit Picpus. So long as he compared himself only with the bishop, he found himself unworthy and remained humble; but, for some time past, he had been comparing himself with the rest of men, and pride was springing up in him. Who knows? He might have finished by going gradually back to hate.

The convent stopped him in this descent.

It was the second place of captivity he had seen.

This house, also, was a prison, and bore dismal resemblance to the other from which he had fled, and yet he had never conceived anything like it.

He once more saw gratings, bolts and bars of iron—to shut in whom? Angels.

Those lofty walls which he had seen surrounding tigers, he now saw encircling lambs.

It was a place of expiation, not of punishment; and yet it was still more austere, more somber and more pitiless than the other. These virgins were more harshly bent down than the convicts. A harsh, cold blast, the blast that had frozen his youth, careered across that grated moat and manacled the vultures; but a wind still more biting and more cruel beat upon the dove cage.

And why?

When he thought of these things, all that was in him gave way before this mystery of sublimity. In these meditations, pride vanished. He reverted, again and again, to himself; he felt his own pitiful unworthiness, and often wept. All that had occurred in his existence, for the last six months, led him back toward the holy injunctions of the bishop, Cosette through love, the convent through humility.

Everything around him, this quiet garden, these balmy flowers, these children, shouting with joy, these meek and simple women, this silent cloister, gradually entered into all his being, and, little by little, his soul subsided into silence like this cloister, into fragrance like these flowers, into peace like this garden, into simplicity like these women, into joy like these children. And then he reflected that two houses of God had received him in succession at the two critical moments of his life, the first when every door was closed and human society repelled him; the second, when human society again howled upon his track, and the galleys once more gaped for him; and that, had it not been for the first, he should have fallen back into crime, and had it not been for the second, into punishment.

His whole heart melted in gratitude, and he loved more and more.

Marius

Thomley, 50-55, which is known to the world, the Goddam
Mudbog.

At the period referred to, the material Vol. 50-55, tightly
empty, and terminating to Casanied, with the placed incusts to
the hand, was frequented by several persons who, in
other worlds, were always like men in Paris, had to relax
Stramen? ... hadered ... tittes villes ...

Parvulus

ABOUT eight or nine years after the events narrated in the second part of this story, there was seen, on the Boulevard du Temple, and in the neighborhood of the Château d'Eau, a little boy of eleven or twelve years of age, who would have realized with considerable accuracy the ideal of the gamin of Paris, if, with the laughter of his youth upon his lips, his heart had not been absolutely dark and empty. This child was well muffled up in a man's pair of pantaloons, but he had not got them from his father, and in a woman's chemise, which was not an inheritance from his mother. Strangers had clothed him in these rags out of charity. Still, he had a father and a mother. But his father never thought of him, and his mother did not love him. He was one of those children so deserving of pity from all, who have fathers and mothers, and yet are orphans.

This little boy never felt so happy as when in the street. The pavement was not so hard to him as the heart of his mother.

His parents had thrown him out into life with a kick.

He had quite ingenuously spread his wings and taken flight.

He was a boisterous, pallid, nimble, wide-awake, roguish urchin, with an air at once vivacious and sickly. He went, came, sang, played pitch and toss, scraped the gutters, stole a little, but he did it gaily, like the cats and the sparrows, laughed when people called him an errand boy, and got angry when they called him a ragamuffin. He had no shelter, no food, no fire, no love, but he was lighthearted because he was free.

When these poor creatures are men, the millstone of our social system almost always comes in contact with them, and grinds them, but while they are children they escape because they are little. The smallest hole saves them.

However, deserted as this lad was, it happened sometimes, every two or three months, that he would say to himself: "Come, I'll go and see my mother!" Then he would leave the boulevard, the Cirque, the Porte Saint Martin, go down along the quays, cross the bridges, reach the suburbs, walk as far as the Salpêtrière, and arrive—where? Precisely at that double number, 50-52, which is known to the reader, the Gorbeau building.

At the period referred to, the tenement No. 50-52, usually empty, and permanently decorated with the placard ROOMS TO LET, was, for a wonder, tenanted by several persons who, in all other respects, as is always the case in Paris, had no relation to or connection with each other. They all belonged to that indigent class which begins with the small bourgeois in embarrassed circumstances, and descends, from grade to grade of wretchedness, through the lower strata of society, until it reaches those two beings in whom all the material things of civilization terminate, the scavenger and the ragpicker.

The landlady of the time of Jean Valjean was dead, and had been replaced by another exactly like her. I do not remember what philosopher it was who said: "There is never any lack of old women."

The new old woman was called Madame Burgon, and her life had been remarkable for nothing except a dynasty of three parakeets, which had in succession wielded the scepter of her affections.

Among those who lived in the building, the wretchedest of all were a family of four persons, father, mother, and two daughters nearly grown, all four lodging in the same garret room, one of those cells of which we have already spoken.

This family at first sight presented nothing very peculiar but its extreme destitution; the father, in renting the room, had given his name as Jondrette. Some time after his moving in, which had singularly resembled, to borrow the memorable expression of the landlady, the entrance of "nothing at all," this Jondrette said to the old woman, who, like her predecessor, was, at the same time, portress and swept the stairs: "Mother So-and-so, if anybody should come and ask for a Pole or an Italian or, perhaps, a Spaniard, that is for me."

Now, this family was the family of our sprightly little barefooted urchin. When he came there, he found distress and, what is sadder still, no smile, and a cold hearthstone and cold hearts. When he came in, they would ask: "Where have you come from?" He would answer: "From the street." When he was going away they would ask him: "Where are you going to?" He would answer: "Into the street." His mother would say to him: "What have you come here for?"

The child lived, in this absence of affection, like those pale plants that spring up in cellars. He felt no suffering from this mode of existence, and bore no ill will to anybody. He did not know how a father and mother ought to be.

But yet his mother loved his sisters.

We had forgotten to say that on the Boulevard du Temple this boy went by the name of Little Gavroche. Why was his name Gavroche? Probably because his father's name was Jondrette.

To break all links seems to be the instinct of some wretched families.

The room occupied by the Jondrettes in the Gorbeau tenement was the last at the end of the hall. The adjoining cell was tenanted by a very poor young man who was called Monsieur Marius.

Let us see who and what Monsieur Marius was.

The Grand Bourgeois

IN the rue Boucherat, rue de Normandie, and rue de Saintonge, there still remain a few old inhabitants who preserve a memory of a fine old man named Monsieur Gillenormand, and who like to talk about him.

Monsieur Gillenormand, who was as much alive as any man can be, in 1831, was one of those men who have become curiosities, simply because they have lived a long time, and who are strange, because formerly they were like everybody else, and now they are no longer like anybody else. He was a peculiar old man, and very truly a man of another age—the genuine bourgeois of the eighteenth century, a very perfect specimen, a little haughty, wearing his good old *bourgeoisie* as marquises wear their marquisates. He had passed his ninetieth year, walked erect, spoke in a loud voice, saw clearly, drank hard, ate, slept, and snored. He had every one of his thirty-two teeth. He wore glasses only when reading. He was of an amorous humor, but said that for ten years past he had decidedly and entirely renounced women. He was no longer pleasing, he said; he did not add: "I am too old," but, "I am too poor." He would say: "If I were not ruined, he, he!" His remaining income in fact was only about fifteen thousand livres. When anybody contradicted him he raised his cane; he beat his servants as in the time of Louis XIV. He had an unmarried daughter over fifty years old, whom he belabored severely when he was angry, and whom he would gladly have horsewhipped. She seemed to him about eight years old. He cuffed his domestics vigorously and would say: "Ah! Slut!"

He lived in the Marais, rue des Filles du Calvaire, No. 6. The house was his own. He occupied an ancient and ample apartment on the first story, between the street and the gardens, covered to the ceiling with fine Gobelin and Beauvais tapestry representing pastoral scenes; the subjects of the ceiling and the panels were repeated in miniature upon the armchairs. He surrounded his bed with a large screen with nine leaves varnished with Coromandel lac. Long, full curtains hung at the windows, and made great, magnificent broken folds. The garden, which was immediately beneath his windows, was connected with the angle between them by means of a staircase of twelve or fifteen steps, which the old man ascended and descended very blithely. In his youth, he had been one of those men who are always deceived by their wives and never by their mistresses, because they are at the same time the most disagreeable husbands and the most charming lovers in the world. Monsieur Gillenormand's dress was not in the fashion of Louis XV, nor even in the fashion of Louis XVI; he wore the costume of the *incroyables* of the Directory. He had thought himself quite young until then, and had kept up with the fashions. His coat was of light cloth, with broad facings, a long swallow tail, and large steel buttons. Add to this short breeches and shoe buckles. He always carried his hands in his pockets. He said authoritatively: "The French Revolution is a mess of scamps."

He had taken several prizes in his youth at the college at Moulins, where he was born, and had been crowned by the hands of the Duke de Nivernais, whom he called the Duke de Nevers. Neither the Convention, nor the death of Louis XVI, nor Napoleon, nor the return of the Bourbons had been able to efface the memory of this coronation. The Duke de Nevers was to him the great figure of the century. "What a noble, great lord," said he, "and what a fine air he had with his blue ribbon!" Monsieur Gillenormand worshiped the Bourbons and held 1789 in horror; he was constantly relating how he saved himself during the Reign of Terror, and how, if he had not had a good deal of gaiety and a good deal of wit, his head would have been cut off. If any young man ventured to eulogize the republic in his presence, he turned black in the face, and was angry enough to faint.

He had two domestics, "a male and a female." When a domestic entered his service, Monsieur Gillenormand rebaptized him. He gave to the men the name of their province: Nimois, Comtois, Poitevin, Picard. His last valet was a big, pursy, wheezy man of fifty-five, incapable of running twenty steps, but as he was born at Bayonne, Monsieur Gillenormand called him Basque. As for female servants, they were all called Nicolette in his house. One day a proud cook, with a blue sash, of the lofty race of porters, presented herself. "How much do you want a month?" asked Monsieur Gillenormand.

"Thirty francs."

"What is your name?"

"Olympie."

"You shall have fifty francs, and your name shall be Nicolette."

He had had two wives, by the first a daughter, who had remained unmarried, and by the second another daughter, who died when about thirty years old, and who had married for love, or luck, or otherwise, a soldier of fortune, who had served in the armies of the republic and the empire, had won the cross at Austerlitz, and been made colonel at Waterloo. "This is the disgrace of my family," said the old bourgeois. He took a great deal of snuff, and had a peculiar skill in ruffling his lace frill with the back of his hand. He had very little belief in God.

He was of the eighteenth century, frivolous and great.

In 1814, and in the early years of the Restoration, Monsieur Gillenormand, who was still young—he was only seventy-four—had lived in the Faubourg Saint Germain, rue Servandoni, near Saint Sulpice. He had retired to the Marais only upon retiring from society, after his eighty years were fully accomplished.

As to the two daughters of Monsieur Gillenormand, we have just spoken of them. They were born ten years apart.

The younger had married the man of her dreams, but she was dead. The elder was not married.

At the moment she makes her entry into the story which we are relating, she was an old piece of virtue, an incombustible prude, one of the sharpest noses and one of the most obtuse minds which could be discovered. A characteristic incident. Outside of the immediate family nobody had ever known her first name. She was called Mademoiselle Gillenormand the elder.

She was sad with an obscure sadness of which she had not the secret herself. There was in her whole person the stupor of a life ended but never commenced.

She kept her father's house. Monsieur Gillenormand had his daughter with him as we have seen Monseigneur Bienvenu have his sister with him. These households of an old man and an old maid are not rare, and always have the touching aspect of two feeblenesses leaning upon each other.

There was besides in the house, between this old maid and this old man, a child, a little boy, always trembling and mute before Monsieur Gillenormand. Monsieur Gillenormand never spoke to this child but with stern voice, and sometimes with uplifted cane: "Here! Monsieur—rascal, blackguard, come here! Answer me, rogue! Let me see you, scapegrace!" etc. etc. He idolized him.

It was his grandson. We shall see this child again.

The Grandfather and the Grandson

I

WHOEVER, at that day, had passed through the little city of Vernon, and walked over that beautiful monumental bridge which will be very soon replaced, let us hope, by some horrid wire bridge, would have noticed, as his glance fell from the top of the parapet, a man of about fifty, with a leather casque on his head, dressed in pantaloons and waistcoat of coarse gray cloth, to which something yellow was stitched which had been a red ribbon, shod in wooden shoes, browned by the sun, his face almost black and his hair almost white, a large scar upon his forehead extending down his cheek, bent, bowed down, older than his years, walking nearly every day with a spade and a pruning knife in his hand, in one of those walled compartments, in the vicinity of the bridge, which, like a chain of terraces, border the left bank of the Seine. All these enclosures are bounded by the river on one side and by a house on the other. The man in the waistcoat and wooden shoes of whom we have just spoken lived, about the year 1817, in the smallest of these enclosures and the humblest of these houses. He lived there solitary and alone, in silence and in poverty, with a woman who was neither young nor old, neither beautiful nor ugly, neither peasant nor bourgeois, who waited upon him. The square of earth which he called his garden was celebrated in the town for the beauty of the flowers which he cultivated in it. Flowers were his occupation.

Whoever, at the same time, had read the military memoirs, the biographies, the *Moniteur*, and the bulletins of the Grand Army, would have been struck by a name which appears rather often, the name of George Pontmercy. When quite young, this George Pontmercy was a soldier in the regiment of Saintonge. At Waterloo he led a squadron of cuirassiers in Dubois' brigade. He it was who took the colors from the Lunenburg battalion. He carried the colors to the emperor's feet. He was covered with blood. He had received, in seizing the colors, a saber stroke across his face. The emperor, well pleased, cried to him: "You are a Colonel, you are a Baron, you are an Officer of the Legion of Honor!" Pontmercy answered: "Sire, thank you for my widow." An hour afterward, he fell in the ravine of Ohain. Now who was this George Pontmercy? He was that very brigand of the Loire.

The Restoration put him on half pay, then sent him to a residence, that is to say under surveillance at Vernon. The king, Louis XVIII, ignoring all that had been done in the Hundred Days, recognized neither his position of officer of the Legion of Honor, nor his rank of colonel, nor his title of baron. He, on his part, neglected no opportunity to sign himself COLONEL BARON PONTMERCY. He had only one old blue coat, and he never went out without putting on the rosette of an officer of the Legion of Honor.

He had nothing but his very scanty half pay as chief of squadron. He hired the smallest house he could find in Vernon. He lived there alone; how we have just seen. Under the empire, between two wars, he had found time to marry Mademoiselle Gillenormand. The old bourgeois, who really felt outraged, consented with a sigh, saying: "The greatest families are forced to it." In 1815, Madame Pontmercy, an admirable woman in every respect, noble and rare, and worthy of her husband, died, leaving a child. This child would have been the colonel's joy in his solitude; but the grandfather had imperiously demanded his grandson, declaring that, unless he were given up to him, he would disinherit him. The father yielded for the sake of the little boy, and not being able to have his child he set about loving flowers.

Monsieur Gillenormand had no intercourse with his son-in-law. The colonel was to him "a bandit," and he was to the colonel "a blockhead." Monsieur Gillenormand never spoke of the colonel, unless sometimes to make mocking allusions to "his barony." It was expressly understood that Pontmercy should never endeavor to see his son or speak to him, under pain of the boy being turned away, and disinherited. To the Gillenormands, Pontmercy was pestiferous. They intended to bring up the child to their liking. The colonel did wrong perhaps to accept these conditions, but he submitted to them, thinking that he was doing right, and sacrificing himself alone.

The inheritance from the grandfather Gillenormand was a small affair, but the inheritance from Mademoiselle Gillenormand the elder was considerable. This aunt, who had remained single, was very rich from the maternal side, and the son of her sister was her natural heir. The child, whose name was Marius, knew that he had a father, but nothing more. Nobody spoke a word to him about him. However, in the society into which his grandfather took him, the whisperings, the hints, the winks, enlightened the little boy's mind at length; he finally comprehended something of it, and as he naturally imbibed, by a sort of infiltration and slow penetration, the ideas and opinions which formed, so to say, the air he breathed, he came little by little to think of his father only with shame and with a closed heart.

While he was thus growing up, every two or three months the colonel would escape, come furtively to Paris like a fugitive from justice breaking his ban, and go to Saint Sulpice, at the hour when Aunt Gillenormand took Marius to mass. There, trembling lest the aunt should turn around, concealed behind a pillar, motionless, not daring to breathe, he saw his child. The scarred veteran was afraid of the old maid.

Twice a year, on the 1st of January and on St. George's Day, Marius wrote filial letters to his father, which his aunt dictated, and which, one would have said, were copied from some *Com-*

plete Letter Writer; this was all that Monsieur Gillenormand
allowed; and the father answered with very tender letters,
which the grandfather thrust into his pocket without reading.

II

MARIUS PONTMERCY went, like all children, through various
studies. When he left the hands of Aunt Gillenormand, his
grandfather entrusted him to a worthy professor, of the purest
classic innocence. This young, unfolding soul passed from a
prude to a pedant. Marius had his years at college, then he entered the law school. He was royalist, fanatical, and austere.
He had little love for his grandfather, whose gaiety and cyni-
cism wounded him, and the place of his father was a dark void.

For the rest, he was an ardent but cool lad, noble, generous,
proud, religious, lofty; honorable even to harshness, pure even
to unsociableness.

In 1827, Marius had just attained his eighteenth year. On
coming in one evening, he saw his grandfather with a letter in
his hand.

"Marius," said Monsieur Gillenormand, "you will set out tomorrow for Vernon."

"What for?" said Marius.

"To see your father."

Marius shuddered. He had thought of everything but this,
that a day might come when he would have to see his father.
Nothing could have been more unlooked for, more surprising,
and, we must say, more disagreeable. It was aversion compelled to intimacy. It was not chagrin; no, it was pure drudgery.

Marius, besides his feelings of political antipathy, was convinced that his father, the saberer, as Monsieur Gillenormand
called him in the gentler moments, did not love him; that was
clear, since he had abandoned him and left him to others.
Feeling that he was not loved at all, he had no love. Nothing
more natural, said he to himself.

He was so astounded that he did not question Monsieur
Gillenormand. The grandfather continued:

"It appears that he is sick. He asks for you."

The next day at dusk, Marius arrived at Vernon. Candles
were just beginning to be lighted. He asked the first person he

met for "the house of Monsieur Pontmercy." For in his feelings he agreed with the Restoration, and he, too, recognized his father neither as baron nor as colonel.

The house was pointed out to him. He rang; a woman came and opened the door with a small lamp in her hand.

"Monsieur Pontmercy?" said Marius.

The woman remained motionless.

"Is he here?" asked Marius.

The woman gave an affirmative nod of the head.

"Can I speak with him?"

The woman gave a negative sign.

"But I am his son!" resumed Marius. "He expects me."

"He expects you no longer," said the woman.

Then he perceived that she was in tears.

She pointed to the door of a low room; he entered.

In this room, which was lighted by a tallow candle on the mantel, there were three men, one of them standing, one on his knees, and one stripped to his shirt and lying at full length upon the floor. The one upon the floor was the colonel.

The two others were a physician and a priest who was praying.

The colonel had been three days before attacked with a brain fever. At the beginning of the sickness, having a presentiment of ill, he had written to Monsieur Gillenormand to ask for his son. He had grown worse. On the very evening of Marius' arrival at Vernon, the colonel had had a fit of delirium; he sprang out of his bed in spite of the servant, crying: "My son has not come! I am going to meet him!" Then he had gone out of his room and fallen upon the floor of the hall. He had but just died.

The doctor and the curé had been sent for. The doctor had come too late; the curé had come too late. The son also had come too late.

By the dim light of the candle, they could distinguish upon the cheek of the pale and supine colonel a big tear which had fallen from his death-stricken eye. The eye was glazed, but the tear was not dry. This tear was for his son's delay.

Marius looked upon this man, whom he saw for the first time, and for the last—this venerable and manly face, these open eyes which saw not, this white hair, these robust limbs upon which he distinguished here and there brown lines which were saber cuts, and a species of red stars which were bullet holes. He looked upon that gigantic scar which imprinted heroism upon this face on which God had impressed goodness. He thought that this man was his father and that this man was dead, and he remained unmoved.

The sorrow which he experienced was the sorrow which he would have felt before any other man whom he might have seen stretched out in death.

Mourning, bitter mourning, was in that room. The servant was lamenting by herself in a corner; the curé was praying, and his sobs were heard; the doctor was wiping his eyes; the corpse itself wept.

This doctor, this priest, and this woman, looked at Marius through their affliction without saying a word; it was he who was the stranger. Marius, too little moved, felt ashamed and embarrassed at his attitude; he had his hat in his hand, he let it fall to the floor, to make them believe that grief deprived him of strength to hold it.

At the same time he felt something like remorse, and he despised himself for acting thus. But was it his fault? He did not love his father, indeed!

The colonel left nothing. The sale of his furniture hardly paid for his burial. The servant found a scrap of paper which she handed to Marius. It contained this, in the handwriting of the colonel:

"*For my son.* The emperor made me a baron upon the battlefield of Waterloo. Since the Restoration contests this title which I have bought with my blood, my son will take it and bear it. I need not say that he will be worthy of it." On the back, the colonel had added: "At this same battle of Waterloo, a sergeant saved my life. This man's name is Thénardier. Not long ago, I believe he was keeping a little tavern in a village in the suburbs of Paris, at Chelles or at Montfermeil. If my son meets him, he will do Thénardier all the service he can."

Not from duty toward his father, but on account of that vague respect for death which is always so imperious in the heart of man, Marius took this paper and pressed it.

No trace remained of the colonel. Monsieur Gillenormand had his sword and uniform sold to a secondhand dealer. The neighbors stripped the garden and carried off the rare flowers. The other plants became briery and scraggy, and died.

Marius remained only forty-eight hours at Vernon. After the burial, he returned to Paris and went back to his law, thinking no more of his father than if he had never lived. In two days the colonel had been buried, and in three days forgotten.

Marius wore crepe on his hat. That was all.

III

MARIUS had preserved the religious habits of his childhood. One Sunday he had gone to hear mass at Saint Sulpice, at this same chapel of the Virgin to which his aunt took him when he was a little boy, and being that day more absent-minded and dreamy than usual, he took his place behind a pillar and knelt down, without noticing it, before a Utrecht velvet chair, on the back of which this name was written: MONSIEUR MABEUF, CHURCHWARDEN. The mass had hardly commenced when an old man presented himself and said to Marius:

"Monsieur, this is my place."

Marius moved away readily, and the old man took his chair.

After mass, Marius remained absorbed in thought a few steps distant; the old man approached him and said: "I beg your pardon, monsieur, for having disturbed you a little while ago, and for disturbing you again now; but you have thought me impertinent, and I must explain myself."

"Monsieur," said Marius, "it is unnecessary."

"Yes!" resumed the old man; "I do not wish you to have a bad opinion of me. You see I think a great deal of that place. It seems to me that the mass is better there. Why? I will tell you. To that place I have seen for ten years, regularly, every two or three months, a poor, brave father come, who had no other opportunity and no other way of seeing his child, being prevented through some family arrangements. He came at the hour when he knew his son was brought to mass. The little one never suspected that his father was here. He did not even know, perhaps, that he had a father, the innocent boy! The father, for his part, kept behind a pillar, so that nobody should see him. He looked at his child, and wept. This poor man worshiped this little boy. I saw that. This place has become sanctified, as it were, for me, and I have acquired the habit of coming here to hear mass. I prefer it to the bench, where I have a right to be as a warden. I was even acquainted slightly with this unfortunate gentleman. He had a father-in-law, a rich aunt, relatives, I do not remember exactly, who threatened to disinherit the child if he, the father, should see him. He had sacrificed himself that his son might some day be rich and happy. They were separated by political opinions. Certainly I approve of political opinions, but there are people who do not know where to stop. Bless me! Because a man was at Waterloo he is not a monster; a father is not separated from his child for that. He was one of Bonaparte's colonels. He is dead, I believe. He lived at Vernon, where my brother is curé, and his name is something like Pontmarie, Montpercy. He had a handsome saber cut."

"Pontmercy," said Marius, turning pale.

"Exactly; Pontmercy. Did you know him?"

"Monsieur," said Marius, "he was my father."

The old churchwarden clasped his hands, and exclaimed:

"Ah! You are the child! Yes, that is it; he ought to be a man now. Well! Poor child, you can say that you had a father who loved you well."

Marius offered his arm to the old man, and walked with him to his house. Next day he said to Monsieur Gillenormand:

"We have arranged a hunting party with a few friends. Will you permit me to be absent for three days?"

"Four," answered the grandfather; "go; amuse yourself."

And, with a wink, he whispered to his daughter:

"Some love affair!"

IV

MARIUS went to Vernon and spent several hours at his father's grave, then he returned to Paris, went straight to the library of the law school, and asked for the file of the *Moniteur*.

He read the *Moniteur*; he read all the histories of the republic and the empire, the *Memorial de Sainte-Hélène*, all the memoirs, journals, bulletins, proclamations; he devoured everything. The first time he met his father's name in the bulletins of the Grand Army he had a fever for a whole week. He went to see the generals under whom George Pontmercy had served —among others, Count H. The churchwarden, Mabeuf, whom he had gone to see again, gave him an account of the life at Vernon, the colonel's retreat, his flowers, and his solitude. Marius came to understand fully this rare, sublime, and gentle man, this sort of lion-lamb who was his father.

In the meantime, engrossed in this study, which took up all his time, as well as all his thoughts, he hardly saw the Gillenormands. At the hours of meals he appeared; then when they looked for him, he was gone. The aunt grumbled. The grandfather smiled. "Poh, poh! It is the age for the lasses!" Sometimes the old man added: "The devil! I thought that it was some gallantry. It seems to be a passion."

It was a passion, indeed. Marius was on the way to adoration for his father.

At the same time an extraordinary change took place in his ideas. The phases of this change were numerous and gradual. As this is the history of many minds of our time, we deem it useful to follow these phases step by step, and to indicate them all.

This history on which he had now cast his eyes startled him. The first effect was bewilderment.

The republic, the empire, had been to him, till then, nothing but monstrous words. The republic, a guillotine in a twilight; the empire, a saber in the night. He had looked into them, and there, where he expected to find only a chaos of darkness, he had seen, with a sort of astounding surprise, mingled with fear and joy, stars shining, Mirabeau, Vergniaud, Saint-Just, Robespierre, Camille Desmoulins, Danton, and a sun rising, Napoleon. He knew not where he was. He recoiled blinded by the splendors. Little by little, the astonishment passed away, he accustomed himself to this radiance; he looked upon acts without dizziness, he examined personages without error; the revolution and the empire set themselves in luminous perspective before his straining eyes; he saw each of these two groups of events and men arrange themselves into two enormous facts: the republic into the sovereignty of the civic right restored to the masses, the empire into the sovereignty of the French idea imposed upon Europe; he saw spring out of the revolution the grand figure of the people, and out of the empire the grand figure of France. He declared to himself that all that had been good.

He was full of regret and remorse, and he thought with despair that all he had in his soul he could say now only to a tomb. Oh! If his father were living, if he had had him still, if God in his mercy and in his goodness had permitted that his father might be still alive, how he would have run, how he would have plunged headlong, how he would have cried to his father: "Father! I am here! It is I! My heart is the same as yours! I am your son!" How he would have embraced his white head, wet his hair with tears, gazed upon his scar, pressed his hands, worshiped his garments, kissed his feet! Oh! Why had this father died so soon, before the adolescence, before the justice, before the love of his son! Marius had a continual sob in his heart which said at every moment: "Alas!" At the same time he became more truly serious, more truly grave, surer of his faith and his thought. Gleams of the true came at every instant to complete his reasoning. It was like an interior growth. He felt a sort of natural aggrandizement which these two new things, his father and his country, brought to him.

From the rehabilitation of his father he had naturally passed to the rehabilitation of Napoleon. One night he was alone in his little room next the roof. His candle was lighted; he was reading, leaning on his table by the open window. All manner of reveries came over him from the expanse of space and mingled with his thought. What a spectacle is night! We hear dull sounds, not knowing whence they come; we see Jupiter, twelve hundred times larger than the earth, glistening like an ember; the welkin is black, the stars sparkle, it is terror-inspiring.

He was reading the bulletins of the Grand Army, those heroic strophes written on the battlefield; he saw there at intervals his father's name, the emperor's name everywhere; the whole of the grand empire appeared before him; he felt as if a tide were swelling and rising within him; it seemed to him at moments that his father was passing by him like a breath and whispering in his ear; gradually he grew wandering; he thought he heard the drums, the cannon, the trumpets, the measured tread of the battalions, the dull and distant gallop of the cavalry; from time to time he lifted his eyes to the sky and saw the colossal constellations shining in the limitless abysses, then they fell back upon the book, and saw there other colossal things moving about confusedly. His heart was full. He was transported, trembling, breathless; suddenly, without himself knowing what moved him, or what he was obeying, he arose, stretched his arms out of the window, gazed fixedly into the gloom, the silence, the darkling infinite, the eternal immensity, and cried: *"Vive l'empereur!"*

From that moment it was all over. The emperor had been

to his father only the beloved captain, whom one admires, and for whom one devotes himself; to Marius he was something more. He was the very incarnation of France, conquering Europe by the sword which he held, and the world by the light which he shed. Marius saw in Bonaparte the flashing specter which will always rise upon the frontier, and which will guard the future. Despot, but dictator; despot resulting from a republic and summing up a revolution. Napoleon became to him the people-man as Jesus is the God-man.

All these revolutions were accomplished in him without a suspicion of it in his family.

When, in this mysterious labor, he had entirely cast off his old Bourbon and ultra skin, when he had shed the aristocrat, the Jacobite, and the royalist, when he was fully revolutionary, thoroughly democratic, and almost republican, he went to an engraver on the Quai des Orfèvres, and ordered a hundred cards bearing this name: BARON MARIUS PONTMERCY.

By a natural consequence, in proportion as he drew nearer to his father, his memory, and the things for which the colonel had fought for twenty-five years, he drew off from his grandfather. As we have mentioned, for a long time Monsieur Gillenormand's capriciousness had been disagreeable to him. There was already between them all the distaste of a serious young man for a frivolous old man. So long as the same political opinions and the same ideas had been common to them, Marius had met Monsieur Gillenormand by means of them as if upon a bridge. When this bridge fell, the abyss appeared. And then, above all, Marius felt inexpressibly revolted when he thought that Monsieur Gillenormand, from stupid motives, had pitilessly torn him from the colonel, thus depriving the father of the child, and the child of the father.

Through affection and veneration for his father, Marius had almost reached aversion for his grandfather.

Nothing of this, however, as we have said, was betrayed externally. Only he was more and more frigid; laconic at meals, and scarcely ever in the house. When his aunt scolded him for it, he was very mild, and gave as an excuse his studies, courts, examinations, dissertations, etc. The grandfather did not change his infallible diagnosis: "In love? I understand it."

Marius was absent for a while from time to time.

"Where can he go to?" asked the aunt.

On one of these journeys, which were always very short, he

went to Montfermeil in obedience to the injunction which his father had left him, and sought for the former sergeant of Waterloo, the innkeeper Thénardier. Thénardier had failed, the inn was closed, and nobody knew what had become of him. While making these researches, Marius was away from the house four days.

"Decidedly," said the grandfather, "he is going astray."

They thought they noticed that he wore something, upon his breast and under his shirt, hung from his neck by a black ribbon.

V

IT was to Vernon that Marius had come the first time that he absented himself from Paris. It was here that he returned every time that Monsieur Gillenormand said: "He sleeps out."

One morning Marius, returning from Vernon, was set down at his grandfather's, and, fatigued by the two nights passed in the diligence, feeling the need of making up for his lack of sleep by an hour at the swimming school, ran quickly up to his room, took only time enough to lay off his traveling coat and the black ribbon which he wore about his neck, and went away to the bath.

Monsieur Gillenormand, who had risen early like all old persons who are in good health, had heard him come in, and hastened as fast as he could with his old legs, to climb to the top of the stairs where Marius' room was, that he might embrace him, question him while embracing him, and find out something about where he came from.

But the youth had taken less time to go down than the octogenarian to go up, and when Grandfather Gillenormand entered the garret room, Marius was no longer there.

The bed was not disturbed, and upon the bed were displayed without distrust the coat and the black ribbon.

"I like that better," said Monsieur Gillenormand.

And a moment afterward he entered the parlor where Mademoiselle Gillenormand the elder was already seated, embroidering her cab wheels.

The entrance was triumphal.

Monsieur Gillenormand held in one hand the coat and in the other the neck ribbon, and cried:

"Victory! We are going to penetrate the mystery! We shall know the end of the end, we shall feel of the libertinism of our trickster! Here we are with the romance even. I have the portrait!"

In fact, a black shagreen box, much like to a medallion, was fastened to the ribbon.

The old man took this box and looked at it some time without opening it.

"Let us see, father," said the old maid.

The box opened by pressing a spring. They found nothing in it but a piece of paper carefully folded.

"From the same to the same," said Monsieur Gillenormand, bursting with laughter. "I know what that is. A love letter!"

"Ah! Then let us read it!" said the aunt.

And she put on her spectacles. They unfolded the paper and read this:

"*For my son.* The emperor made me a baron upon the battlefield of Waterloo. Since the Restoration contests this title which I have bought with my blood, my son will take it and bear it. I need not say that he will be worthy of it."

The feelings of the father and daughter cannot be described. They felt chilled as by the breath of a death's head. They did not exchange a word. Monsieur Gillenormand, however, said in a low voice, and as if talking to himself:

"It is the handwriting of that saberer."

The aunt examined the paper, turned it on all sides, then put it back in the box.

Just at that moment, a little oblong package, wrapped in blue paper, fell from a pocket of the coat. Mademoiselle Gillenormand picked it up and unfolded the blue paper. It was Marius' hundred cards. She passed one of them to Monsieur Gillenormand, who read: BARON MARIUS PONTMERCY.

The old man rang. Nicolette came. Monsieur Gillenormand took the ribbon, the box, and the coat, threw them all on the floor in the middle of the parlor, and said:

"Take away those things."

A full hour passed in complete silence. The old man and the old maid sat with their backs turned to one another, and were probably, each on their side, thinking over the same things. At the end of that hour, Aunt Gillenormand said:

"Pretty!"

A few minutes afterward, Marius made his appearance. He

came in. Even before crossing the threshold of the parlor, he perceived his grandfather holding one of his cards in his hand, who, on seeing him, exclaimed with his crushing air of sneering, bourgeois superiority:

"Stop! Stop! Stop! Stop! Stop! You are a baron now. I present you my compliments. What does this mean?"

Marius colored slightly, and answered:

"It means that I am my father's son."

Monsieur Gillenormand checked his laugh, and said harshly: "Your father; I am your father."

"My father," resumed Marius with downcast eyes and stern manner, "was a humble and heroic man, who served the republic and France gloriously, who was great in the greatest history that men have ever made, who lived a quarter of a century in the camp, by day under grape and under balls, by night in the snow, in the mud, and in the rain, who captured colors, who received twenty wounds, who died forgotten and abandoned, and who had but one fault; that was in loving too dearly two ingrates, his country and me."

This was more than Monsieur Gillenormand could listen to. At the word republic, he rose, or rather, sprang to his feet. Every one of the words which Marius had pronounced had produced the effect upon the old royalist's face of a blast from a bellows upon a burning coal. From dark he had become red, from red purple, and from purple glowing.

"Marius!" exclaimed he. "Abominable child! I don't know what your father was! I don't want to know! I know nothing about him and I don't know him! But what I do know is that there was never anything but miserable wretches among all that rabble! That they were all beggars, assassins, redcaps, thieves! I say all! I say all! I know nobody! I say all! Do you hear, Marius? Look you, indeed, you are as much a baron as my slipper! They were all bandits who served Robespierre! All brigands who served B-u-o-naparte! All traitors who betrayed, betrayed, betrayed! Their legitimate king! All cowards who ran from the Prussians and English at Waterloo! That is what I know. If your father is among them I don't know him, I am sorry for it, so much the worse, your servant!"

In his turn, Marius now became the coal, and Monsieur Gillenormand the bellows. Marius shuddered in every limb, he knew not what to do, his head burned. His father had been trodden underfoot and stamped upon in his presence, but by whom? By his grandfather. How should he avenge the one without outraging the other? It was impossible for him to insult his grandfather, and it was equally impossible for him not to avenge his father. On one hand a sacred tomb, on the other white hairs. He was for a few moments dizzy and staggering with all this whirlwind in his head; then he raised his eyes, looked straight at his grandfather, and cried in a thundering voice:

"Down with the Bourbons, and the great hog Louis XVIII!"

Louis XVIII had been dead for four years; but it was all the same to him.

The old man, scarlet as he was, suddenly became whiter than his hair. He turned toward a bust of the Duke de Berry which stood upon the mantel, and bowed to it profoundly with a sort of peculiar majesty. Then he walked twice, slowly and in silence, from the fireplace to the window and from the window to the fireplace, traversing the whole length of the room and making the floor crack as if an image of stone were walking over it. The second time, he bent toward his daughter, who was enduring the shock with the stupor of an aged sheep, and said to her with a smile that was almost calm:

"A baron like monsieur and a bourgeois like me cannot remain under the same roof."

And all at once straightening up, pallid, trembling, terrible, his forehead swelling with the fearful radiance of anger, he stretched his arm toward Marius and cried to him:

"Be off!"

Marius left the house.

The next day, Monsieur Gillenormand said to his daughter: "You will send sixty pistoles every six months to this blood drinker, and never speak of him to me again."

Having an immense residuum of fury to expend, and not knowing what to do with it, he spoke to his daughter with coldness for more than three months.

Marius, for his part, went away without saying where he was going, and without knowing where he was going, with thirty francs, his watch, and a few clothes in a carpetbag. He hired a cabriolet by the hour, jumped in, and drove at random toward the Latin Quarter.

What was Marius to do?

The Friends of the A B C

I

AT that period, apparently indifferent, something of a revolutionary thrill was vaguely felt. Whispers coming from the depths of '89 and of '92 were in the air. Young Paris was, excuse the expression, in the process of molting. People were transformed almost without suspecting it, by the very movement of the time. The hand which moves over the dial moves also among souls. Each one took the step forward which was before him. Royalists became liberals, liberals became democrats.

It was like a rising tide, complicated by a thousand ebbs; the peculiarity of the ebb is to make mixtures; thence very singular combinations of ideas; men worshiped at the same time Napoleon and liberty. We are now writing history. These were the mirages of that day. Opinions pass through phases. Voltairian royalism, a grotesque variety, had a fellow not less strange, Bonapartist liberalism.

Other groups of minds were more serious. They fathomed principle; they attached themselves to right. They longed for the absolute, they caught glimpses of the infinite realizations; the absolute by its very rigidity pushes the mind toward the boundless, and makes it float in the illimitable. There is nothing like dream to create the future. Utopia today, flesh and blood tomorrow.

At that time there were not yet in France any of those underlying organizations like the German Tugenbund and the Italian Carbonari; but here and there obscure excavations were branching out. La Cougourde was assuming form at Aix; there was in Paris, among other affiliations of this kind, the Society of the Friends of the A B C.

Who were the Friends of the A B C? A society having as its aim, in appearance, the education of children; in reality, the elevation of men.

They declared themselves the Friends of the A B C.[1] The

---

[1] *A B C* in French is pronounced ah-bay-say, exactly like the French word, *abaissé.*

abaissé [the abased] were the people. They wished to raise them up.

The Friends of the A B C were not numerous, it was a secret society in the embryonic state; we should almost say a coterie, if coteries produced heroes. They met in Paris, at two places, near the Halles, in a wineshop called *Corinthe*, which will be referred to hereafter, and near the Pantheon, in a little coffeehouse on the Place Saint Michel, called *Le Café Musain*, now torn down; the first of these two places of rendezvous was near the workingmen, the second near the students.

The ordinary conventicles of the Friends of the A B C were held in a back room of the *Café Musain*.

This room, quite distant from the café, with which it communicated by a very long passage, had two windows, and an exit by a private stairway upon the little rue des Grès. They smoked, drank, played, and laughed there. They talked very loud about everything, and in whispers about something else. On the wall was nailed, an indication sufficient to awaken the suspicion of a police officer, an old map of France under the republic.

Most of the Friends of the A B C were students, in thorough understanding with a few workingmen. The names of the principals are as follows. They belong to a certain extent to history: Enjolras, Combeferre, Jean Prouvaire, Feuilly, Courfeyrac, Bahorel, Lesgle or Laigle, Joly, Grantaire.

These young men constituted a sort of family among themselves, by force of friendship. All except Laigle were from the South.

Enjolras, whom we have named first, the reason why will be seen by and by, was an only son and was rich.

Enjolras was a charming young man, who was capable of being terrible. He was angelically beautiful. He was Antinoüs wild. You would have said, to see the thoughtful reflection of his eye, that he had already, in some preceding existence, passed through the revolutionary apocalypse. He had the tradition of it like an eyewitness. He knew all the little details of the grand thing, a pontifical and warrior nature, strange in a youth. He was officiating and militant; from the immediate point of view, a soldier of democracy; above the movement of the time, a priest of the ideal.

Beside Enjolras, who represented the logic of the revolution,

Combeferre represented its philosophy. Between the logic of the revolution and its philosophy, there is this difference—that its logic could conclude with war, while its philosophy could only end in peace. Combeferre completed and corrected Enjolras. He was lower and broader. His desire was to instill into all minds the broad principles of general ideas; he said: "Revolution, but civilization"; and about the steep mountain he spread the vast blue horizon. Hence, in all Combeferre's views, there was something attainable and practicable. Revolution with Combeferre was more respirable than with Enjolras. Enjolras expressed its divine right, and Combeferre its natural right.

Jean Prouvaire was yet a shade more subdued than Combeferre. Jean Prouvaire was addicted to love; he cultivated a pot of flowers, played on the flute, made verses, loved the people, mourned over woman, wept over childhood, confounded the future and God in the same faith, and blamed the revolution for having cut off a royal head, that of André Chénier. All day he pondered over social questions: wages, capital, credit, marriage, religion, liberty of thought, liberty of love, education, punishment, misery, association, property, production and distribution, the lower enigma which covers the human anthill with a shadow; and at night he gazed upon the stars, those enormous beings. Like Enjolras, he was rich, and an only son. He spoke gently, bent his head, cast down his eyes, smiled with embarrassment, dressed badly, had an awkward air, blushed at nothing, was very timid, still intrepid.

Feuilly was a fanmaker, an orphan, who with difficulty earned three francs a day, and who had but one thought: to deliver the world. He had still another desire: to instruct himself, which he also called deliverance. He had taught himself to read and write; all that he knew, he had learned alone. Feuilly was a generous heart. He had an immense embrace. This orphan had adopted the peoples. He nurtured within himself, with the deep divination of the man of the people, what we now call "the idea of nationalities." His specialty was Greece, Poland, Hungary, the Danubian Provinces, and Italy. This poor workingman had made himself a teacher of Justice, and she rewarded him by making him grand.

Enjolras was the chief, Combeferre was the guide, Courfeyrac was the center. The others gave more light, he gave more heat; the truth is, that he had all the qualities of a center, roundness and radiance.

Bahorel was a creature of good humor and bad company, brave, a spendthrift, prodigal almost to generosity, talkative almost to eloquence, bold almost to effrontery; the best possible devil's pie; with foolhardy waistcoats and scarlet opinions; a wholesale blusterer, that is to say, liking nothing so well as a quarrel unless it were *émeute*, and nothing so well as an *émeute* unless it were a revolution; always ready to break a paving stone, then to tear up a street, then to demolish a government, to see the effect of it; a student of the eleventh year.

He served as a bond between the Friends of the A B C and some other groups which were without definite shape, but which were to take form afterward.

In this conclave of young heads there was one bald member, Lesgle or Lègle. The king had given his father the post office at Meaux, either intentionally or inadvertently. He signed his name Lègle (de Meaux). His comrades, for the sake of brevity, called him Bossuet.

Bossuet was a cheery fellow who was unlucky. His specialty was to succeed in nothing. On the other hand, he laughed at everything.

Joly was a young *malade imaginaire*. What he had learned in medicine was rather to be a patient than a physician. At twenty-three, he thought himself a valetudinarian, and passed his time in looking at his tongue in a mirror. Nevertheless, he was the gayest of all. All these incoherences, young, notional, sickly, joyous, got along very well together, and the result was an eccentric and agreeable person.

All these young men, diverse as they were, and of whom, as a whole, we ought only to speak seriously, had the same religion: Progress.

All were legitimate sons of the French Revolution. The lightest became solemn when pronouncing this date: '89. Their fathers, according to the flesh, were, or had been Feuillants, Royalists, Doctrinaires; it mattered little; this hurly-burly which antedated them had nothing to do with them; they were young; the pure blood of principles flowed in their veins. They attached themselves without an intermediate shade to incorruptible right and to absolute duty.

Affiliated and initiated, they secretly sketched out their ideas.

Among all these passionate hearts and all these undoubting minds there was one skeptic. How did he happen to be there? From juxtaposition. The name of this skeptic was Grantaire. All these words: rights of the people, rights of man, social contract, French Revolution, republic, democracy, humanity, civilization, religion, progress, were, to Grantaire, very nearly meaningless. He smiled at them. Skepticism, that cries of the intellect, had not left one entire idea in his mind. He lived in irony.

Still, this skeptic had a fanaticism. This fanaticism was neither an idea, nor a dogma, nor an art, nor a science; it was a man: Enjolras. Grantaire admired, loved, and venerated Enjolras. To whom did this anarchical doubter ally himself in this phalanx of absolute minds? To the most absolute. In what way did Enjolras subjugate him? By ideas? No. By a character. Grantaire, in whom doubt was creeping, loved to see faith soaring in Enjolras.

Enjolras, being a believer, disdained this skeptic, and being sober, scorned this drunkard. He granted him a little haughty pity. Grantaire was an unaccepted Pylades. Always rudely treated by Enjolras, harshly repelled, rejected, yet returning, he said of Enjolras: "What a fine statue!"

II

On a certain afternoon, which had, as we shall see, some coincidence with events before related, Laigle de Meaux was leaning lazily back against the doorway of the *Café Musain*. He had the appearance of a caryatid in vacation; he was supporting nothing but his reverie. He was looking at the Place Saint Michel.

Reverie does not hinder a cabriolet from going by, nor the dreamer from noticing the cabriolet. Laigle de Meaux, whose eyes were wandering in a sort of general stroll, perceived, through all his somnambulism, a two-wheeled vehicle turning into the square, which was moving at a walk, as if undecided. What did this cabriolet want? Why was it moving at a walk? Laigle looked at it. There was inside, beside the driver, a young man, and before the young man, a large carpetbag. The bag exhibited to the passers this name, written in big black letters upon a card sewed to the cloth: MARIUS PONTMERCY.

This name changed Laigle's attitude. He straightened up and addressed this apostrophe to the young man in the cabriolet:

"Monsieur Marius Pontmercy?"

The cabriolet, thus called upon, stopped.

The young man, who also seemed to be profoundly musing, raised his eyes.

"Well?" said he.

"You are Monsieur Marius Pontmercy?"

"Certainly."

"I was looking for you," said Laigle de Meaux.

"How is that?" inquired Marius. "I do not know you."

"You were not at school yesterday."

"It is possible."

"It is certain."

"You are a student?" inquired Marius.

"Yes, monsieur. Like you. The day before yesterday I happened to go into the school. You know, one sometimes has such notions. The professor was about to call the roll. You know that they are very ridiculous just at that time. If you miss the third call, they erase your name. Sixty francs gone."

Marius began to listen. Laigle continued:

"It was Blondeau who was calling the roll. You know Blondeau; he has a very sharp and very malicious nose, and delights in smelling out the absent. The roll went on well, no erasure, the universe was present, Blondeau was sad. I said to myself: Blondeau, my love, you won't do the slightest execution today. Suddenly, Blondeau calls: 'Marius Pontmercy'; nobody answers. Blondeau, full of hope, repeats louder: 'Marius Pontmercy?' And he seizes his pen. Monsieur, I have bowels. I said to myself rapidly: 'Here is a brave fellow who is going to be erased. Attention. Let us save him. Death to Blondeau!' At that moment Blondeau dipped his pen, black with erasures, into the ink, cast his tawny eye over the room, and repeated for the third time: 'Marius Pontmercy!' I answered: 'Present!' In that way you were not erased."

"Monsieur—!" said Marius.

"And I was," added Laigle de Meaux.

"I do not understand you," said Marius.

Laigle resumed:

"Nothing more simple. I was near the chair to answer, and near the door to escape. The professor was looking at me with a certain fixedness. Suddenly, Blondeau leaps to the letter L. L is my letter; I am of Meaux, and my name is Lesgle."

"L'Aigle!" interrupted Marius. "What a fine name."

"Monsieur, the Blondeau re-echoes this fine name and cries: 'Laigle!' I answer: 'Present!' Then Blondeau looks at me with the gentleness of a tiger, smiles, and says: 'If you are Pontmercy, you are not Laigle.' A phrase which is uncomplimentary to you, but which brought me only to grief. So saying, he erases me."

Marius exclaimed:

"Monsieur, I am mortified—"

Laigle burst out laughing.

"And I, in raptures; I was on the brink of being a lawyer. This rupture saves me. I intend to pay you a solemn visit of thanks. Where do you live?"

"In this cabriolet," said Marius.

"A sign of opulence," replied Laigle calmly. "I congratulate you. You have here rent of nine thousand francs a year."

Just then Courfeyrac came out of the café.

Marius smiled sadly.

"I have been paying this rent for two hours, and I hope to get out of it, but, it is the usual story, I do not know where to go."

"Monsieur," said Courfeyrac, "come home with me."

And that same evening, Marius was installed in a room at the Hôtel de la Porte Saint Jacques, side by side with Courfeyrac.

III

In a few days, Marius was the friend of Courfeyrac. Youth is the season of prompt weldings and rapid cicatrizations. Marius, in Courfeyrac's presence, breathed freely, a new thing for him. Courfeyrac asked him no questions. He did not even think of it. At that age, the countenance tells all at once. Speech is useless. There are some young men of whom we might say their physiognomies are talkative. They look at one another, they know one another.

Courfeyrac introduced Marius to the *Café Musain*. Then

he whispered in his ear with a smile: "I must give you your admission into the revolution." And he took him into the room of the Friends of the A B C. He presented him to the other members, saying in an undertone this simple word which Marius did not understand: "A pupil."

Marius had fallen into a mental wasps' nest. Still, although silent and serious, he was not the less winged, nor the less armed.

Marius, up to this time solitary and inclined to soliloquy and privacy by habit and by taste, was a little bewildered at this flock of young men about him. All these different progressives attacked him at once, and perplexed him. The tumultuous sweep and sway of all these minds at liberty and at work set his ideas in a whirl. Sometimes, in the confusion, they went so far from him that he had some difficulty in finding them again. He heard talk of philosophy, of literature, of art, of history, of religion, in a style he had not looked for. He caught glimpses of strange appearances, and, as he did not bring them into perspective, he was not sure that it was not a chaos that he saw. On abandoning his grandfather's opinions for his father's, he had thought himself settled; he now suspected, with anxiety, and without daring to confess it to himself, that he was not. The angle under which he saw all things was beginning to change anew. A certain oscillation shook the whole horizon of his brain. A strange internal moving day. He almost suffered from it.

It seemed that there were to these young men no "sacred things." Marius heard, upon every subject, a singular language annoying to his still timid mind.

None of these young men uttered this word: the emperor. Jean Prouvaire alone sometimes said Napoleon; all the rest said Bonaparte. Enjolras pronounced *Buonaparte*.

Marius became confusedly astonished. Initium sapientiae.

IV

Of the conversations among these young men which Marius frequented and in which he sometimes took part, one shocked him severely.

This was held in the back room of the *Café Musain*. Nearly all the Friends of the A B C were together that evening. The large lamp was ceremoniously lighted. They talked of one thing and another, without passion and with noise.

A stern thought, oddly brought out of a clatter of words, suddenly crossed the tumult of speech in which Grantaire, Bahorel, Prouvaire, Bossuet, Combeferre, and Courfeyrac were confusedly fencing. In the midst of the uproar Bossuet suddenly ended some apostrophe to Combeferre with this date:

"The 18th of June, 1815: Waterloo."

"*Pardieu*," exclaimed Courfeyrac, "that number 18 is strange, and striking to me. It is the fatal number of Bonaparte. Put Louis before and Brumaire behind, you have the whole destiny of the man, with this expressive peculiarity, that the beginning is hard pressed by the end."

Enjolras, till now dumb, broke the silence, and thus addressed Courfeyrac:

"You mean the crime by the expiation."

This word, crime, exceeded the limits of the endurance of Marius, already much excited by the abrupt evocation of Waterloo.

Marius turned toward Enjolras, and his voice rang with a vibration which came from the quivering of his nerves:

"I am a newcomer among you, but I confess that you astound me. Where are we? Who are we? Who are you? I thought you were young men. Where is your enthusiasm then? And what do you do with it? Whom do you admire, if you do not admire the emperor? And what more must you have? If you do not like that great man, what great men would you have? Be just, my friends! To be the empire of such an emperor, what a splendid destiny for a people, when that people is France, and when it adds its genius to the genius of such a man! To be the grand nation and to bring forth the grand army, to send your legions flying over the whole earth as a mountain sends its eagles upon all sides, to vanquish, to rule, to thunderstrike, to be in Europe a kind of gilded people through much glory, to sound through history a titan trumpet call, to conquer the world twice, by conquest and by resplendence; this is sublime, and what can be more grand?"

"To be free," said Combeferre.

Marius in his turn bowed his head; these cold and simple words had pierced his epic effusion like a blade of steel, and he felt it vanish within him. When he raised his eyes, Combeferre was there no longer. Suddenly they heard somebody

singing as he was going downstairs. It was Combeferre, and
what he was singing is this:

> Si César m'avait donné
> La gloire et la guerre,
> Et qu'il me fallût quitter
> L'amour de ma mère,
> Je dirais au grand César:
> Reprends ton sceptre et ton char,
> J'aime mieux ma mère, ô gué!
> J'aime mieux ma mère.[1]

The wild and tender accent with which Combeferre sang,
gave to this stanza a strange grandeur. Marius, thoughtful and
with his eyes directed to the ceiling, repeated almost mechanically: "my mother—"

At this moment, he felt Enjolras' hand on his shoulder.

"Citizen," said Enjolras to him, "my mother is the republic."

V

THAT evening left Marius in a profound agitation, with a
sorrowful darkness in his soul. He was experiencing what perhaps the earth experiences at the moment when it is furrowed
with the share that the grains of wheat may be sown; it feels
the wound alone; the thrill of the germ and the joy of the fruit
do not come until later.

Marius was gloomy. He had but just attained a faith; could
he so soon reject it? He decided within himself that he could
not. He declared to himself that he would not doubt, and he
began to doubt in spite of himself. To be between two
religions, one which you have not yet abandoned, and another
which you have not yet adopted, is insupportable; and
twilight is pleasant only to batlike souls. Marius was an open
eye, and he needed the true light. To him the dusk of doubt
was harmful. Whatever might be his desire to stop where he

---

[1] If Caesar had given me
Glory and war,
And if I must abandon
The love of my mother,
I would say to great Caesar:
Take thy scepter and car,
I prefer my mother, ah me!
I prefer my mother.

was, and to hold fast there, he was irresistibly compelled to continue, to advance, to examine, to think, to go forward. Where was that going to lead him? He feared, after having taken so many steps which had brought him nearer to his father, to take now any steps which should separate them. His dejection increased with every reflection which occurred to him. Steep cliffs rose about him. He was on good terms neither with his grandfather nor with his friends; rash toward the former, backward toward the others; and he felt doubly isolated, from old age, and also from youth. He went no more to the *Café Musain*.

In this trouble in which his mind was plunged he scarcely gave a thought to certain serious phases of existence. The realities of life do not allow themselves to be forgotten. They came and jogged his memory sharply.

One morning, the keeper of the house entered Marius' room, and said to him:

"Monsieur Courfeyrac is responsible for you."

"Yes."

"But I am in need of money."

"Ask Courfeyrac to come and speak with me," said Marius.

Courfeyrac came; the host left them. Marius related to him what he had not thought of telling him before, that he was, so to speak, alone in the world, without any relatives.

"What are you going to become?" said Courfeyrac.

"I have no idea," answered Marius.

Meanwhile Aunt Gillenormand, who was really a kind person on sad occasions, had finally unearthed Marius' lodgings.

One morning when Marius came home from the school, he found a letter from his aunt, and the sixty pistoles, that is to say, six hundred francs in gold, in a sealed box.

Marius sent the thirty louis back to his aunt, with a respectful letter, in which he told her that he had the means of living, and that he could provide henceforth   all his necessities. At that time he had three francs left.

The aunt did not inform the grandfather of this refusal, lest she should exasperate him. Indeed, had he not said: "Let nobody ever speak to me of this blood drinker?"

Marius left the Porte Saint Jacques Hotel, unwilling to contract debt.

The Excellence of Misfortune

I

LIFE became stern to Marius. To eat his coats and his watch was nothing. He chewed that inexpressible thing which is called the cud of bitterness. A horrible thing, which includes days without bread, nights without sleep, evenings without a candle, a hearth without a fire, weeks without labor, a future without hope, a coat out at the elbows, an old hat which makes young girls laugh, the door found shut against you at night because you have not paid your rent, the insolence of the porter and the landlord, the jibes of neighbors, humiliations, self-respect outraged, any drudgery acceptable, disgust, bitterness, prostration—Marius learned how one swallows down all these things, and how they are often the only things that one has to swallow. At that period of existence, when man has need of pride, because he has need of love, he felt that he was mocked at because he was badly dressed, and ridiculed because he was poor. At the age when youth swells the heart with an imperial pride, he more than once dropped his eyes upon his worn-out boots, and experienced the undeserved shame and the poignant blushes of misery. Wonderful and terrible trial, from which the feeble come out infamous, from which the strong come out sublime. Crucible into which Destiny casts a man whenever she desires a scoundrel or a demigod.

For there are many great deeds done in the small struggles of life. There is a determined though unseen bravery, which defends itself foot to foot in the darkness against the fatal invasions of necessity and of baseness. Noble and mysterious triumphs which no eye sees, which no renown rewards, which no flourish of triumph salutes. Life, misfortunes, isolation, abandonment, poverty, are battlefields which have their heroes; obscure heroes, sometimes greater than the illustrious heroes.

Strong and rare natures are thus created; misery, almost

always a stepmother, is sometimes a mother; privation gives birth to power of soul and mind; distress is the nurse of self-respect; misfortune is a good breast for great souls.

There was a period in Marius' life when he swept his own hall, when he bought a pennyworth of Brie cheese at the market woman's, when he waited for nightfall to make his way to the baker's and buy a loaf of bread, which he carried furtively to his garret, as if he had stolen it. Sometimes there was seen to glide into the corner meat market, in the midst of the jeering cooks who elbowed him, an awkward young man, with books under his arm, who had a timid and frightened appearance, and who, as he entered, took off his hat from his forehead, which was dripping with sweat, made a low bow to the astonished butcher, another bow to the butcher's boy, asked for a mutton cutlet, paid six or seven sous for it, wrapped it up in paper, put it under his arm between two books, and went away. It was Marius. On this cutlet, which he cooked himself, he lived three days.

The first day he ate the meat; the second day he ate the fat; the third day he gnawed the bone. On several occasions, Aunt Gillenormand made overtures, and sent him the sixty pistoles. Marius always sent them back, saying that he had no need of anything.

He was still in mourning for his father, when the revolution which we have described was accomplished in his ideas. Since then, he had never left off black clothes. His clothes left him, however. A day came, at last, when he had no coat. His trousers were going also. What was to be done? Courfeyrac, for whom he also had done some good turns, gave him an old coat. For thirty sous, Marius had it turned by some porter or other, and it was a new coat. But this coat was green. Then Marius did not go out till after nightfall. That made his coat black. Desiring always to be in mourning, he clothed himself with night.

Through all this, he procured admission to the bar. He was reputed to occupy Courfeyrac's room, which was decent, and where a certain number of law books, supported and filled out by some odd volumes of novels, made up the library required by the rules.

When Marius had become a lawyer, he informed his grandfather of it, in a letter which was frigid, but full of submission and respect. Monsieur Gillenormand took the letter with trembling hands, read it, and threw it, torn in pieces, into the basket. Two or three days afterward, Mademoiselle Gillenormand overheard her father, who was alone in his room, talking aloud. This was always the case when he was much excited. She listened; the old man said: "If you were not a fool, you would know that a man cannot be a baron and a lawyer at the same time."

II

IT is with misery as with everything else. It gradually becomes endurable. It ends by taking form and becoming fixed. You vegetate, that is to say you develop in some wretched fashion, but sufficient for existence. This is the way in which Marius Pontmercy's life was arranged.

He had got out of the narrowest place; the pass widened a little before him. By dint of hard work, courage, perseverance, and will, he had succeeded in earning by his labor about seven hundred francs a year. He had learned German and English; thanks to Courfeyrac, who introduced him to a publisher, Marius filled, in the literary department of the bookhouse, the useful role of utility. He made out prospectuses, translated from the journals, annotated republications, compiled biographies, etc., net result, year in and year out, seven hundred francs. He lived on this. How? Not badly. We are going to tell.

Marius occupied, at an annual rent of thirty francs, a wretched little room in the Gorbeau tenement, with no fireplace, called a cabinet, in which there was no more furniture than was indispensable. The furniture was his own. He gave three francs a month to the old woman who had charge of the building, for sweeping his room and bringing him every morning a little warm water, a fresh egg, and a penny loaf of bread. On this loaf and this egg he breakfasted. His breakfast varied from two to four sous, as eggs were cheap or dear. At six o'clock in the evening he went down into the rue Saint Jacques, to dine at Rousseau's, opposite Basset's the print dealer's, at the corner of the rue des Mathurins. He ate no soup. He took a sixpenny plate of meat, a threepenny half-plate of vegetables, and a threepenny dessert. For three sous, as much bread as he liked. As for wine, he drank water. On paying at the counter, where Madame Rousseau was seated majestically, still plump and fresh also in those days, he gave a sou to the waiter, and Madame Rousseau gave him a smile. Then he went away. For sixteen sous, he had a smile and a dinner.

Thus, breakfast four sous, dinner sixteen sous, his food cost him twenty sous a day, which was three hundred and sixty-five francs a year. Add the thirty francs for his lodging, and the thirty-six francs to the old woman, and a few other trifling expenses, and for four hundred and fifty francs, Marius was fed, lodged, and waited upon. His clothes cost him a hundred francs, his linen fifty francs, his washing fifty francs; the whole did not exceed six hundred and fifty francs. This left him fifty francs. He was rich. He occasionally lent ten francs to a friend. Courfeyrac borrowed sixty francs of him once. As for fire, having no fireplace, Marius had "simplified" it.

Marius always had two complete suits, one old "for every-day," the other quite new, for special occasions. Both were black. He had but three shirts, one he had on, another in the drawer, the third at the washerwoman's. He renewed them as they wore out. They were usually ragged, so he buttoned his coat to his chin.

For Marius to arrive at this flourishing condition had required years. Hard years, and difficult ones; those to get through, these to climb. Marius had never given up for a single day. He had undergone everything, in the shape of privation; he had done everything, except get into debt. He gave himself this credit, that he had never owed a sou to anybody. For him a debt was the beginning of slavery. He felt even that a creditor is worse than a master; for a master owns only your person, a creditor owns your dignity and can belabor that. Rather than borrow, he did not eat. He had had many days of fasting. Feeling that all extremes meet, and that if we do not take care, abasement of fortune may lead to baseness of soul, he watched jealously over his pride. Such a habit or such a carriage as, in any other condition, would have appeared deferential, seemed humiliating, and he braced himself against it. He risked nothing, not wishing to take a backward step. He had a kind of stern blush upon his face. He was timid even to rudeness.

In all his trials he felt encouraged and sometimes even upborne by a secret force within. The soul helps the body, and at certain moments uplifts it. It is the only bird which sustains its cage.

III

MARIUS was now twenty years old. It was three years since he had left his grandfather. They remained on the same terms on both sides, without attempting a reconciliation, and without seeking to meet. And, indeed, what was the use of meeting? To come in conflict? Which would have had the best of it? Marius was a vase of brass, but Monsieur Gillenormand was an iron pot.

To tell the truth, Marius was mistaken as to his grandfather's heart. He imagined that Monsieur Gillenormand had never loved him, and that this crusty and harsh yet smiling old man, who swore, screamed, stormed, and lifted his cane, felt for him at most only the affection, at once slight and severe, of the old men of comedy. Marius was deceived. There are fathers who do not love their children; there is no grandfather who does not adore his grandson. In reality, we have said, Monsieur Gillenormand worshiped Marius. He worshiped him in his own way, with an accompaniment of cuffs, and even of blows; but, when the child was gone, he felt a dark void in his heart; he ordered that nobody should speak of him again, and regretted that he was so well obeyed. At first he hoped that this Buonapartist, this Jacobin, this terrorist, this Septembrist, would return. But weeks passed away, months passed away, years passed away; to the great despair of Monsieur Gillenormand, the blood drinker did not reappear! "But I could not do anything else than turn him away," said the grandfather, and he asked himself: "If it were to be done again, would I do it?" His pride promptly answered yes, but his old head, which he shook in silence, sadly answered no. He had his hours of dejection. He missed Marius. Old men need affection as they do sunshine. It is warmth. However strong his nature might be, the absence of Marius had changed something in him. For nothing in the world would he have taken a step toward the "little rogue"; but he suffered. He never inquired after him, but he thought of him constantly. He lived, more and more retired, in the Marais. He was still, as formerly, gay and violent, but his gaiety had a convulsive harshness as if it contained grief and anger, and his bursts of violence always terminated in a sort of placid and gloomy exhaustion. He said sometimes: "Oh! If he would come back, what a good box on the ear I would give him."

As for the aunt, she thought too little to love very much; Marius was now nothing to her but a sort of dim, dark outline; and she finally busied herself a good deal less about him than with the cat or the parakeet which she probably had. What increased the secret suffering of Grandfather Gillenormand was that he shut her entirely out, and let her suspect nothing of it. His chagrin was like those newly invented furnaces which consume their own smoke. Sometimes it happened that some blundering, officious body would speak to him of Marius, and ask: "What is your grandson doing, or what has become of him?" The old bourgeois would answer, with a sigh, if he was too sad, or giving his ruffle a tap, if he wished to seem gay: "Monsieur the Baron Pontmercy is pettifogging in some hole."

While the old man was regretting, Marius was rejoicing. Misery, we must insist, had been good to him. Poverty in youth, when it succeeds, is so far magnificent that it turns the whole will toward effort, and the whole soul toward aspiration. Poverty strips the material life entirely bare, and makes it hideous; thence arise inexpressible yearnings toward the ideal life. The rich young man has a hundred brilliant and coarse amusements: racing, hunting, dogs, cigars, gaming, feasting, and the rest, busying the lower portions of the soul at the expense of its higher and delicate portions. The poor young man must work for his bread; he eats; when he has eaten, he has nothing more but reverie. He goes free to the play which God gives; he beholds the sky, space, the stars, the flowers, the children, the humanity in which he suffers, the creation in which he shines. He looks at humanity so much that he sees the soul, he looks at creation so much that he sees God. He dreams, he feels that he is great; he dreams again, and he feels that he is tender. From the egotism of the suffering man, he passes to the compassion of the contemplating man. A wonderful feeling springs up within him, forgetfulness of self, and pity for all. In thinking of the numberless enjoyments which nature offers, gives, and gives lavishly to open souls, and refuses to closed souls, he, a millionaire of intelligence, comes to grieve for the millionaires of money. All hatred goes out of his heart in proportion as all light enters his mind. And then is he unhappy? No. The misery of a young man is never miserable. The first lad you meet, poor as he may be, with his health, his strength, his quick step, his shining eyes, his blood which circulates warmly, his black locks, his fresh cheeks, his rosy lips, his white teeth, his pure breath, will always be envied by an old emperor. And then every morning he sets about earning his bread; and while his hands are earning his living, his backbone is gaining firmness, his brain is gaining ideas. When his work is done, he returns to ineffable ecstasies, to contemplation, to joy; he sees his feet in difficulties, in obstacle, on the pavement, in thorns, sometimes in the mire; his head is in the light. He is firm, serene, gentle, peaceful, attentive, serious, content with little, benevolent; and he blesses God for having given him these two estates which many of the rich are without: labor which makes him free, and thought which makes him noble.

Marius had two friends, one young, Courfeyrac, and one old, Monsieur Mabeuf. He inclined toward the old one. First he was indebted to him for the revolution through which he had gone; he was indebted to him for having known and loved his father. "He operated upon me for the cataract," said he.

Certainly, this churchwarden had been decisive.

Monsieur Mabeuf was not, however, on that occasion anything more than the calm and passive agent of Providence. He had enlightened Marius accidentally and without knowing it, as a candle does which somebody carries; he had been the candle and not the somebody.

As to the interior political revolution in Marius, Monsieur Mabeuf was entirely incapable of comprehending it, desiring it, or directing it.

As we shall meet Monsieur Mabeuf hereafter, a few words will not be useless.

IV

THE day that Monsieur Mabeuf said to Marius: "Certainly, I approve of political opinions," he expressed the real condition of his mind. All political opinions were indifferent to him, and he approved them all without distinction, provided they left him quiet, as the Greeks called the Furies, "the beautiful, the good, the charming," the Eumenides. Monsieur Mabeuf's political opinion was a passionate fondness for plants, and a still greater one for books.

He did not understand how men could busy themselves with hating one another about such bubbles as the charter, democracy, legitimacy, the monarchy, the republic, etc., when there were in this world all sorts of mosses, herbs, and shrubs, which they could look at, and piles of folios and even of 32mos which they could pore over. He took good care not to be useless; having books did not prevent him from reading, being a botanist did not prevent him from being a gardener. He went to mass rather from good feeling than from devotion, and because he loved the faces of men, but hated their noise, and he found them, at church only, gathered together and silent. He lived alone, with an old governess. He was a little gouty, and when he slept, his old fingers, stiffened with rheumatism, were clenched in the folds of the clothes. He had written and published a *Flora of the Environs of Cauteretz* with colored illustrations, a highly esteemed work, the plates of which he owned and which he sold himself. People came two or three times a day and rang his bell, in the rue Mézières, for it. He received fully two thousand francs a year for it; this was nearly all his income. Though poor, he had succeeded in gathering together, by means of patience, self-denial, and time, a valuable collection of rare copies on every subject. The sight of a sword or a gun chilled him. In his whole life, he had never been near a cannon, even at the Invalides. He had a passable stomach, a brother who was a curé, hair entirely white, no teeth left either in his mouth or in his mind, a tremor of the whole body, a Picard accent, a childlike laugh, weak nerves, and the appearance of an old sheep. With all that, no other friend nor any other intimate acquaintance among the living, but an old bookseller of the Porte Saint Jacques named Royol. His mania was the naturalization of indigo in France.

His servant was, also, a peculiar variety of innocence. The poor, good old woman was a maid. None of her dreams went as far as man. She had never got beyond her cat. She had, like him, mustaches. Her glory was in the whiteness of her caps. She spent her time on Sunday after mass in counting her linen in her trunk, and in spreading out upon her bed the dresses in the piece which she had bought and never made up. She could

read. Monsieur Mabeuf had given her the name of Mother
Plutarch.

Toward 1830, his brother the curé died, and almost immediately after, as at the coming on of night, the whole horizon of
Monsieur Mabeuf was darkened. By a failure—of a notary—
he lost ten thousand francs, which was all the money that he
possessed in his brother's name and his own. The revolution of
July brought on a crisis in bookselling. In hard times, the first
thing that does not sell is a *Flora. The Flora of the Environs
of Cauteretz* stopped short. Weeks went by without a pur-
chaser. Sometimes Monsieur Mabeuf would start at the sound
of the bell. "Monsieur," Mother Plutarch would say sadly, "it
is the water porter." In short, Monsieur Mabeuf left the rue
Mézières one day, resigned his place as churchwarden, gave
up Saint Sulpice, sold a part, not of his books, but of his prints
—which he prized the least—and installed himself in a little
house on the Boulevard Montparnasse, where however he remained but one quarter, for two reasons: first, the ground floor
and the garden let for three hundred francs, and he did not
dare to spend more than two hundred francs for his rent; secondly, being near the Fatou shooting gallery, he heard pistol
shots, which was insupportable to him.

He carried off his *Flora,* his plates, his herbariums, his port-
folios, and his books, and established himself near La Salpêtrière in a sort of cottage in the village of Austerlitz, where
at fifty crowns a year he had three rooms, a garden enclosed
with a hedge, and a well. He took advantage of this change to
sell nearly all his furniture. The day of his entrance into this
new dwelling, he was very gay, and drove nails himself on
which to hang the engravings and the herbariums; he dug in
his garden the rest of the day, and in the evening, seeing that
Mother Plutarch had a gloomy and thoughtful air, he tapped
her on the shoulder and said with a smile: "We have the indigo."

Only two visitors, the bookseller of the Porte Saint Jacques
and Marius, were admitted to his cottage at Austerlitz, a
tumultuous name which was, to tell the truth, rather disagreeable to him.

Amid this darkness which was gathering about him, all his
hopes going out one after another, Monsieur Mabeuf had remained serene, somewhat childishly, but very thoroughly. His
habits of mind had the swing of a pendulum. Once wound up

by an illusion, he went a very long time, even when the illusion
had disappeared. A clock does not stop at the very moment
you lose the key.

V

It was Marius' delight to take long walks alone on the outer
boulevards, or in the Champ de Mars, or in the less frequented
walks of the Luxembourg. He sometimes spent half a day in
looking at a vegetable garden, at the beds of salad, the fowls
on the dungheap, and the horse turning the wheel of the
pump. The passers-by looked at him with surprise, and some
thought that he had a suspicious appearance and an ill-omened
manner. He was only a poor young man, dreaming without an
object.

It was in one of these walks that he had discovered the Gorbeau tenement, and its isolation and cheapness being an attraction to him, he had taken a room in it. He was only known
in it by the name of Monsieur Marius.

All passions, except those of the heart, are dissipated by
reverie. Marius' political fevers were over. The revolution of
1830, by satisfying him, and soothing him, had aided in this.
He remained the same, with the exception of his passionate-
ness. He had still the same opinions. But they were softened.
Properly speaking, he held opinions no longer; he had sym-
pathies. Of what party was he? Of the party of humanity. Out
of humanity he chose France; out of the nation he chose the
people; out of the people he chose woman. To her, above all,
his pity went out. He now preferred an idea to a fact, a poet
to a hero, and he admired a book like Job still more than an
event like Marengo. And then, when, after a day of meditation,
he returned at night along the boulevards, and saw through
the branches of the trees the fathomless space, the nameless
lights, the depths, the darkness, the mystery, all that which
is only human seemed to him very pretty.

Toward the middle of this year, 1831, the old woman who
waited upon Marius told him that his neighbors, the wretched
Jondrette family, were to be turned into the street. Marius,
who passed almost all his days outdoors, hardly knew that he
had any neighbors.

"Why are they turned out?" said he.

"Because they do not pay their rent; they owe for two terms."

"How much is that?"

"Twenty francs," said the old woman.

Marius had thirty francs in reserve in a drawer.

"Here," said he to the old woman. "There are twenty-five francs. Pay for these poor people, give them five francs, and do not tell them that it is from me."

The Conjunction of Two Stars

I

MARIUS was now a fine-looking young man, of medium height, with heavy jet black hair, a high, intelligent brow, large and passionate nostrils, a frank and calm expression, and an indescribable something beaming from every feature, which was at once lofty, thoughtful, and innocent. His profile, all the lines of which were rounded, but without loss of strength, possessed that Germanic gentleness which has made its way into French physiognomy through Alsace and Lorraine, and that entire absence of angles which rendered the Sicambri so recognizable among the Romans, and which distinguishes the leonine from the aquiline race. He was at that season of life at which the minds of men who think are made up in nearly equal proportions of depth and simplicity. In a difficult situation he possessed all the essentials of stupidity; another turn of the screw, and he could become sublime. His manners were reserved, cold, polished, far from free. But as his mouth was very pleasant, his lips the reddest and his teeth the whitest in the world, his smile corrected the severity of his physiognomy. At certain moments there was a strange contrast between this chaste brow and this voluptuous smile. His eye was small, his look great.

At the time of his most wretched poverty, he noticed that girls turned when he passed, and with a deathly feeling in his heart he fled or hid himself. He thought they looked at him on account of his old clothes, and that they were laughing at him;

the truth is, that they looked at him because of his graceful appearance, and that they dreamed over it.

There were, however, in all the immensity of creation, two women from whom Marius never fled, and whom he did not at all avoid. Indeed he would have been very much astonished had anybody told him that they were women. One was the old woman with the beard, who swept his room, and who gave Courfeyrac an opportunity to say: "As his servant wears her beard, Marius does not wear his." The other was a little girl whom he saw very often, and whom he never looked at.

For more than a year Marius had noticed in a retired walk of the Luxembourg, the walk which borders the parapet of the Pépinière, a man and a girl quite young, nearly always sitting side by side, on the same seat, at the most retired end of the walk, near the rue de l'Ouest. Whenever that chance which controls the promenades of men whose eye is turned within led Marius to this walk, and it was almost every day, he found this couple there. The man might be sixty years old; he seemed sad and serious; his whole person presented the robust but wearied appearance of a soldier retired from active service. Had he worn a decoration, Marius would have said: "It is an old officer." His expression was kind, but it did not invite approach, and he never returned a look. He wore a blue coat and pantaloons, and a broad-brimmed hat, which always appeared to be new, a black cravat, and Quaker linen, that is to say, brilliantly white, but of coarse texture. A grisette passing near him one day, said: "There is a very nice widower." His hair was perfectly white.

The first time the young girl that accompanied him sat down on the seat which they seemed to have adopted, she looked like a girl of about thirteen or fourteen, puny to the extent of being almost ugly, awkward, insignificant, yet promising, perhaps, to have rather fine eyes. But they were always looking about with a disagreeable assurance. She wore the dress, at once aged and childish, peculiar to the convent schoolgirl, an ill-fitting garment of coarse black merino. They appeared to be father and daughter.

For two or three days Marius scrutinized this old man, who was not yet an aged man, and this little girl, not yet a woman; then he paid no more attention to them. For their part they did not even seem to see him. They talked with each other peacefully, and with indifference to all else. The girl chatted incessantly and gaily. The old man spoke little, and at times looked upon her with an unutterable expression of fatherliness.

Marius had acquired a sort of mechanical habit of promenading on this walk. He always found them there.

It was usually thus:

Marius would generally reach the walk at the end opposite their seat, promenade the whole length of it, passing before them, then return to the end by which he entered, and so on. He performed this turn five or six times in his promenade, and this promenade five or six times a week, but they and he had never come to exchange bows. This man and this young girl, though they appeared, and perhaps because they appeared, to avoid observation, had naturally excited the attention of the five or six students, who, from time to time, took their promenades along the Pépinière; the studious after their lecture, the others after their game of billiards. Courfeyrac, who belonged to the latter, had noticed them at some time or other, but finding the girl homely, had very quickly and carefully avoided them. He had fled like a Parthian, launching a nickname behind him. Struck especially by the dress of the little girl and the hair of the old man, he had named the daughter Mademoiselle Lanoire [Black] and the father Monsieur Leblanc [White]; and so, as nobody knew them otherwise, in the absence of a name, this surname had become fixed. The students said: "Ah! Monsieur Leblanc is at his seat!" And Marius, like the rest, had found it convenient to call this unknown gentleman Monsieur Leblanc.

We shall do as they did, and say Monsieur Leblanc for the convenience of this story.

Marius saw them thus nearly every day at the same hour during the first year. He found the man very much to his liking, but the girl rather disagreeable.

II

THE second year, at the precise point of this history at which the reader has arrived, it so happened that Marius broke off this habit of going to the Luxembourg, without really knowing why himself, and there were nearly six months during which he did not set foot in his walk. At last he went back there again one day; it was a serene summer morning, Marius was as happy as one always is when the weather is fine. It seemed to him as if he had in his heart all the bird songs which he heard, and all the bits of blue sky which he saw through the trees.

He went straight to "his walk," and as soon as he reached it, he saw, still on the same seat, this well-known pair. When he came near them, however, he saw that it was indeed the same man, but it seemed to him that it was no longer the same girl. The woman whom he now saw was a noble, beautiful creature, with all the most bewitching outlines of woman, at the precise moment at which they are yet combined with all the most charming graces of childhood—that pure and fleeting moment which can only be translated by these two words: sweet fifteen. Beautiful chestnut hair, shaded with veins of gold, a brow which seemed chiseled marble, cheeks which seemed made of roses, a pale incarnadine, a flushed whiteness, an exquisite mouth, whence came a smile like a gleam of sunshine, and a voice like music, a head which Raphael would have given to Mary, on a neck which Jean Goujon would have given to Venus. And that nothing might be wanting to this ravishing form, the nose was not beautiful, it was pretty, neither straight nor curved, neither Italian nor Greek; it was the Parisian nose, that is, something sprightly, fine, irregular, and pure, the despair of painters and the charm of poets.

When Marius passed near her, he could not see her eyes, which were always cast down. He saw only her long chestnut lashes, eloquent of mystery and modesty.

But that did not prevent the beautiful girl from smiling as she listened to the white-haired man who was speaking to her, and nothing was so transporting as this maidenly smile with these downcast eyes.

At the first instant Marius thought it was another daughter of the same man, a sister, doubtless, of her whom he had seen before. But when the invariable habit of his promenade led him for the second time near the seat, and he had looked at her attentively, he recognized that she was the same. In six months the little girl had become a young woman; that was all. Nothing is more frequent than this phenomenon. There is a moment when girls bloom out in a twinkling, and become roses all at once. Yesterday we left them children, today we find them dangerous.

She had not only grown; she had become idealized. As three

April days are enough for certain trees to put on a covering of flowers, so six months had been enough for her to put on a mantle of beauty.

And then she was no longer the schoolgirl with her plush hat, her merino dress, her shapeless shoes, and her red hands; taste had come to her with beauty. She was a woman well dressed, with a sort of simple and rich elegance without any particular style. She wore a dress of black damask, a mantle of the same, and a white crepe hat. Her white gloves showed the delicacy of her hand which played with the Chinese ivory handle of her parasol, and her silk boot betrayed the smallness of her foot. When you passed near her, her whole toilet exhaled the penetrating fragrance of youth.

As to the man, he was still the same.

The second time that Marius came near her, the young girl raised her eyes; they were of a deep celestial blue, but in this veiled azure was nothing yet beyond the look of a child. She looked at Marius with indifference, as she would have looked at any little monkey playing under the sycamores, or the marble vase which cast its shadow over the bench; and Marius also continued his promenade thinking of something else.

He passed four or five times more by the seat where the young girl was, without even turning his eyes toward her.

On the following days he came as usual to the Luxembourg; as usual he found "the father and daughter" there, but he paid no attention to them. He thought no more of this girl now that she was handsome than he had thought of her when she was homely. He passed very near the bench on which she sat, because that was his habit.

III

One day the air was mild, the Luxembourg was flooded with sunshine and shadow, the sky was as clear as if the angels had washed it in the morning, the sparrows were twittering in the depths of the chestnut trees. Marius had opened his whole soul to nature, he was thinking of nothing, he was living and breathing, he passed near this seat, the young girl raised her eyes, their glances met.

But what was there now in the glance of the young girl?

Marius could not have told. There was nothing, and there was everything. It was a strange flash.

She cast down her eyes, and he continued on his way.

What he had seen was not the simple, artless eye of a child; it was a mysterious abyss, half-opened, then suddenly closed.

There is a time when every young girl looks thus. Woe to him upon whom she looks!

This first glance of a soul which does not yet know itself is like the dawn in the sky. It is the awakening of something radiant and unknown. Nothing can express the dangerous chasm of this unlooked-for gleam which suddenly suffuses adorable mysteries, and which is made up of all the innocence of the present, and of all the passion of the future. It is a kind of irresolute lovingness which is revealed by chance, and which is waiting. It is a snare which Innocence unconsciously spreads, and in which she catches hearts without intending to, and without knowing it. It is a maiden glancing like a woman.

It is rare that deep reverie is not born of this glance wherever it may fall. All that is pure, and all that is vestal, is concentrated in this celestial and mortal glance, which, more than the most studied ogling of the coquette, has the magic power of suddenly forcing into bloom in the depths of a heart, this flower of the shade full of perfumes and poisons, which is called love.

At night, on returning to his garret, Marius cast a look upon his dress, and for the first time perceived that he had the slovenliness, the indecency, and the unheard-of stupidity, to promenade in the Luxembourg with his "everyday" suit, a hat broken near the band, coarse teamsters' boots, black pantaloons shiny at the knees, and a black coat threadbare at the elbows.

IV

THE next day, at the usual hour, Marius took from his closet his new coat, his new pantaloons, his new hat, and his new boots; he dressed himself in this panoply complete, put on his gloves, prodigious prodigality, and went to the Luxembourg.

On reaching the Luxembourg, Marius took a turn around the fountain and looked at the swans; then he remained for a long time in contemplation before a statue, the head of which was black with moss, and which was minus a hip. Then he took another turn around the fountain. Finally, he went toward "his walk" slowly, and as if with regret. One would have said that he was at once compelled to go and prevented from going. He was unconscious of all this, and thought he was doing as he did every day.

When he entered the walk he saw Monsieur Leblanc and the young girl at the other end "on their seat." He buttoned his coat, stretched it down that there might be no wrinkles, noticed with some complaisance the luster of his pantaloons, and marched upon the seat. There was something of attack in this march, and certainly a desire of conquest. I say, then, he marched upon the seat, as I would say: Hannibal marched upon Rome.

As he drew nearer, his step became slower and slower. At some distance from the seat, long before he had reached the end of the walk, he stopped, and he did not know himself how it happened, but he turned back. He did not even say to himself that he would not go to the end. It was doubtful if the young girl could see him so far off, and notice his fine appearance in his new suit. However, he held himself very straight, so that he might look well, in case anybody who was behind should happen to notice him.

He reached the opposite end and then returned, and this time he approached a little nearer to the seat. He even came to within about three trees of it, but there he felt an indescribable lack of power to go further, and he hesitated. He thought he had seen the young girl's face bent toward him. Still he made a great and manly effort, conquered his hesitation, and continued his advance. In a few seconds, he was passing before the seat, erect and firm, blushing to his ears, without daring to cast a look to the right or the left, and with his hand in his coat like a statesman. At the moment he passed under the guns of the fortress, he felt a frightful palpitation of the heart. She wore, as on the previous day, her damask dress and her crepe hat. He heard the sound of an ineffable voice, which might be "her voice." She was talking quietly. She was very pretty. He felt it, though he made no effort to see her.

He passed the seat, went to the end of the walk, which was quite near, then turned and passed again before the beautiful girl. This time he was very pale. Indeed, he was experiencing nothing that was not very disagreeable. He walked away from the seat and from the young girl, and although his back was turned, he imagined that she was looking at him, and that made him stumble.

He made no effort to approach the seat again, he stopped midway on the walk, and sat down there—a thing which he never did—casting many side glances, and thinking, in the most indistinct depths of his mind, that after all it must be difficult for persons whose white hat and black dress he admired, to be absolutely insensible to his glossy pantaloons and his new coat.

At the end of a quarter of an hour, he rose, as if to recommence his walk toward this seat, which was encircled by a halo. He, however, stood silent and motionless. For the first time in fifteen months, he said to himself, this gentleman, who sat there every day with his daughter, had undoubtedly noticed him, and probably thought his assiduity very strange.

For the first time, also, he felt a certain irreverence in designating this unknown man, even in the silence of his thought, by the nickname of Monsieur Leblanc.

He remained thus for some minutes with his head down, tracing designs on the ground with a little stick which he had in his hand.

Then he turned abruptly away from the seat, away from Monsieur Leblanc and his daughter, and went home.

That day he forgot to go to dinner. At eight o'clock in the evening he discovered it, and as it was too late to go down to the rue Saint Jacques: "No matter," said he, and he ate a piece of bread.

He did not retire until he had carefully brushed and folded his coat.

V

THUS a fortnight rolled away. Marius went to the Luxembourg, no longer to promenade, but to sit down, always in the same place, and without knowing why. Once there he did not stir. Every morning he put on his new suit, not to be conspicuous, and he began again the next morning.

She was indeed of a marvelous beauty. The only remark which could be made, that would resemble a criticism, is that the contradiction between her look, which was sad, and her smile, which was joyous, gave to her countenance something a little wild, which produced this effect, that at certain moments this sweet face became strange without ceasing to be charming.

On one of the last days of the second week, Marius was as usual sitting on his seat, holding in his hand an open book of which he had not turned a leaf for two hours. Suddenly he trembled. A great event was commencing at the end of the walk. Monsieur Leblanc and his daughter had left their seat, the daughter had taken the arm of the father, and they were coming slowly toward the middle of the walk where Marius was. Marius closed his book, then he opened it, then he made an attempt to read. He trembled. The halo was coming straight toward him. "O dear!" thought he. "I shall not have time to take an attitude." However, the man with the white hair and the young girl were advancing. It seemed to him that it would last a century, and that it was only a second. "What are they coming by here for?" he asked himself. "What! Is she going to pass this place? Are her feet to press this ground in this walk, but a step from me?" He was overwhelmed, he would gladly have been very handsome, he would gladly have worn the cross of the Legion of Honor. He heard the gentle and measured sound of their steps approaching. He imagined that Monsieur Leblanc was hurling angry looks upon him. "Is he going to speak to me?" thought he. He bowed his head; when he raised it they were quite near him. The young girl passed, and in passing she looked at him. She looked at him steadily, with a sweet and thoughtful look which made Marius tremble from head to foot. It seemed to him that she reproached him for having been so long without coming to her, and that she said: "It is I who come." Marius was bewildered by these eyes full of flashing light and fathomless abysses.

He felt as though his brain were on fire. She had come to him, what happiness! And then, how she had looked at him! She seemed more beautiful than she had ever seemed before. Beautiful with a beauty which combined all of the woman with all of the angel, a beauty which would have made Petrarch sing and Dante kneel. He felt as though he were swimming in the deep blue sky. At the same time he was horribly disconcerted, because he had a little dust on his boots.

He felt sure that she had seen his boots in this condition.

He followed her with his eyes till she disappeared; then he

began to walk in the Luxembourg like a madman. It is probable that at times he laughed, alone as he was, and spoke aloud. He was so strange and dreamy when near the children's nurse that everyone thought he was in love with her.

VI

A WHOLE month passed during which Marius went every day to the Luxembourg. When the hour came, nothing could keep him away. "He is out at service," said Courfeyrac. Marius lived in transports. It is certain that the young girl looked at him.

He finally grew bolder, and approached nearer to the seat. However he passed before it no more, obeying at once the instinct of timidity and the instinct of prudence, peculiar to lovers. He thought it better not to attract the "attention of the father." He formed his combinations of stations behind trees and the pedestals of statues, with consummate art, so as to be seen as much as possible by the young girl and as little as possible by the old gentleman. Sometimes he would stand for half an hour motionless behind some Leonidas or Spartacus, with a book in his hand, over which his eyes, timidly raised, were looking for the young girl, while she, for her part, was turning her charming profile toward him, suffused with a smile. While yet talking in the most natural and quiet way in the world with the white-haired man, she rested upon Marius all the dreams of a maidenly and passionate eye. Ancient and immemorial art which Eve knew from the first day of the world, and which every woman knows from the first day of her life! Her tongue replied to one and her eyes to the other.

We must, however, suppose that Monsieur Leblanc perceived something of this at last, for often when Marius came, he would rise and begin to promenade. He had left their accustomed place, and had taken the seat at the other end of the walk, near the Gladiator, as if to see whether Marius would follow them. Marius did not understand it, and committed that blunder. The father began to be less punctual and did not bring his daughter every day. Sometimes he came alone. Then Marius did not stay. Another blunder.

He committed a third, a monstrous one. He wanted to know where she lived. He followed her.

She lived in the rue de l'Ouest, in the least frequented part of it, in a new three-story house, of modest appearance.

From that moment Marius added to his happiness in seeing her at the Luxembourg, the happiness of following her home.

One night after he had followed them home, and seen them disappear at the porte-cochère, he entered after them, and said boldly to the porter:

"Is it the gentleman on the first floor who has just come in?"

"No," answered the porter. "It is the gentleman on the third."

Another fact.

Next day Monsieur Leblanc and his daughter made but a short visit to the Luxembourg; they went away while it was yet broad daylight. Marius followed them into the rue de l'Ouest, as was his custom. On reaching the porte-cochère, Monsieur Leblanc passed his daughter in, and then stopped, and before entering himself, turned and looked steadily at Marius. The day after that they did not come to the Luxembourg. Marius waited in vain all day.

At nightfall he went to the rue de l'Ouest, and saw a light in the windows of the third story. He walked beneath these windows until the light was put out.

He passed a week in this way.

On the eighth day when he reached the house, there was no light in the windows. "What!" said he. "The lamp is not yet lighted. But yet it is dark. Or they have gone out?" He waited till ten o'clock. Till midnight. Till one o'clock in the morning. No light appeared in the third-story windows, and nobody entered the house. He went away very gloomy.

On the morrow Marius knocked at the porte-cochère, went in, and said to the porter:

"The gentleman of the third floor?"

"Moved," answered the porter.

Marius tottered, and said feebly:

"Since when?"

"Yesterday."

"Where does he live now?"

"I don't know anything about it."

"He has not left his new address, then?"

"No."

Patron-Minette

I

EVERY human society has what is called in the theaters "a third substage." The social soil is mined everywhere, sometimes for evil. These works are in strata; there are upper mines and lower mines. There is a top and a bottom in this dark subsoil which sometimes sinks beneath civilization, and which our indifference and our carelessness trample underfoot. The Encyclopaedia, in the last century, was a mine almost on the surface. The dark caverns, these gloomy protectors of primitive Christianity, were awaiting only an opportunity to explode beneath the Caesars, and to flood the human race with light. For in these sacred shades there is latent light. Volcanoes are full of a blackness, capable of flashing flames. All lava begins at midnight. The catacombs, where the first mass was said, were not merely the cave of Rome; they were the cavern of the world.

Society has hardly a suspicion of this work of undermining which, without touching its surface, changes its substance. So many subterranean degrees, so many differing labors, so many varying excavations. What comes from all this deep delving? The future.

The deeper we sink, the more mysterious are the workers. To a degree which social philosophy can recognize, the work is good; beyond this degree it is doubtful and mixed; below, it becomes terrible. At a certain depth, the excavations become impenetrable to the soul of civilization, the respirable limit of man is passed; the existence of monsters becomes possible.

Below all these mines which we have pointed out, below all these galleries, below all this immense underground venous system of progress and of utopia, far deeper in the earth, lower than Marat, lower than Babeuf, lower, much lower, and without any connection with the upper galleries, is the last sap. A fear-inspiring place. This is what we have called the third substage. It is the grave of the depths. It is the cave of the blind *inferi*.

This communicates with the gulfs.

There disinterestedness vanishes. The demon is dimly rough-hewn; everyone for himself. The eyeless I howls, searches, gropes, and gnaws. The social Ugolino is in this gulf.

The savage outlines which prowl over this grave, half brute, half phantom, have no thought for universal progress; they ignore ideas and words; they have no care but for individual glut. They are almost unconscious, and there is in them a horrible defacement. They have two mothers, both stepmothers: ignorance and misery. They have one guide: want, and their only form of satisfaction is appetite. They are voracious as beasts, that is to say ferocious, not like the tyrant, but like the tiger. From suffering, these goblins pass to crime; fated filiation, giddy procreation, the logic of darkness. What crawls in the third substage is no longer the stifled demand for the absolute, it is the protest of matter. Man there becomes dragon. Hunger and thirst are the point of departure; Satan is the point of arrival.

II

A QUARTET of bandits, Claquesous, Gueulemer, Babet, and Montparnasse, ruled from 1830 to 1835 over the third substage of Paris.

Gueulemer was a Hercules without a pedestal. His cave was the Arche-Marion sewer. He was six feet high, and had a marble chest, brazen biceps, cavernous lungs, a colossus' body, and a bird's skull. You would think you saw the Farnese Hercules dressed in duck pantaloons and a cotton-velvet waistcoat. Gueulemer, built in this sculptural fashion, could have subdued monsters; he found it easier to become one.

The diaphaneity of Babet contrasted with the meatiness of Gueulemer. Babet was thin and shrewd. He was transparent, but impenetrable. You could see the light through his bones, but nothing through his eye. He professed to be a chemist. He had been barkeeper for Bobèche, and clown for Bobino. He had played vaudeville at Saint-Mihiel. He was an affected man, a great talker, who italicized his smiles and quoted his gestures.

What was Claquesous? He was night. Before showing himself, he waited till the sky was daubed with black. At night he came out of a hole, which he went into again before day. Where was this hole? Nobody knew. In the most perfect obscurity, and to his accomplices, he always turned his back when he spoke. Was his name Claquesous? No. He said: "My name is Nothing-at-all." If a candle was brought he put on a mask. He was a ventriloquist. Babet said: "Claquesous is a night bird with two voices." Claquesous was restless, roving, terrible. It was not certain that he had a name, Claquesous being a nickname; it was not certain that he had a voice, his chest speaking oftener than his mouth; it was not certain that he had a face, nobody having ever seen anything but this mask. He disappeared as if he sank into the ground; he came like an apparition.

A mournful sight was Montparnasse. Montparnasse was a child, less than twenty, with a pretty face, lips like cherries, charming black locks, the glow of spring in his eyes; he had all the vices and aspired to all the crimes. The digestion of what was bad gave him an appetite for what was worse. He was the gamin turned vagabond, and the vagabond become an assassin. He was genteel, effeminate, graceful, robust, weak, and ferocious. At eighteen, he had already left several corpses on his track. More than one traveler lay in the shadow of this wretch, with extended arms and with his face in a pool of blood. Frizzled, pomaded, with slender waist, hips like a woman, the bust of a Prussian officer, a buzz of admiration about him from the girls of the boulevard, an elaborately tied cravat, a slung shot in his pocket, a flower in his buttonhole; such was this charmer of the sepulcher.

These four men were not four men; it was a sort of mysterious robber with four heads preying upon Paris by wholesale; it was the monstrous polyp of evil which inhabits the crypt of society.

By means of their ramifications and the underlying network of their relations, Babet, Gueulemer, Claquesous, and Montparnasse, controlled the general lying-in-wait business of the Department of the Seine. Originators of ideas in this line, men of midnight imagination came to them for the execution. The four villains being furnished with the single draft, they took charge of putting it on the stage. They worked upon scenario. They were always in condition to furnish a company proportioned and suitable to any enterprise which stood in need of aid, and was sufficiently lucrative. A crime being in search of arms, they sublet accomplices to it. They had a company of actors of darkness at the disposition of every cavernous tragedy.

They usually met at nightfall, their waking hour, in the waste grounds near La Salpêtrière. There they conferred. They had the twelve dark hours before them; they allotted their employ.

Patron-Minette, such was the name which was given in subterranean society to the association of these four men. In the old, popular, fantastic language, which now is dying out every day, Patron-Minette means morning, just as *entre chien et loup* [between dog and wolf] means night. This appellation, Patron-Minette, probably came from the hour at which their work ended, the dawn being the moment for the disappearance of phantoms and the separation of bandits. These four were known by this title. When the Chief Judge of the Assizes visited Lacenaire in prison, he questioned him in relation to some crime which Lacenaire denied. "Who did do it?" asked the judge. Lacenaire made this reply, enigmatical to the magistrate, but clear to the police: "Patron-Minette, perhaps."

The Noxious Poor

I

SUMMER passed, then autumn; winter came. Neither Monsieur Leblanc nor the young girl had set foot in the Luxembourg. Marius had now but one thought, to see that sweet, that adorable face again. He searched continually; he searched everywhere; he found nothing. He was no longer Marius the enthusiastic dreamer, the resolute man, ardent yet firm, the bold challenger of destiny, the brain which projected and built future upon future, the young heart full of plans, projects, prides, ideas, and desires; he was a lost dog. He fell into a melancholy. It was all over with him. Work disgusted him, walking fatigued him, solitude wearied him; vast nature, once so full of forms, of illuminations, of voices, of counsels, of perspectives, of horizons, of teachings, was now a void before him. It seemed to him that everything had disappeared.

He still lived in the Gorbeau tenement. He paid no attention to anybody there.

At this time, it is true, there were no occupants remaining in the house but himself and those Jondrettes whose rent he had once paid, without having ever spoken, however, either to the father, or to the mother, or to the daughters. The other tenants had moved away or died, or had been turned out for not paying their rent.

One day, in the course of this winter, he had got up and breakfasted, and was trying to set about his work when there was a gentle rap at his door.

As he owned nothing, he never locked his door, except sometimes, and that very rarely, when he was about some pressing piece of work. And, indeed, even when absent, he left his key in the lock.

There was a second rap, very gentle like the first.

"Come in," said Marius.

The door opened.

"I beg your pardon, Monsieur—"

It was a hollow, cracked, smothered, rasping voice, the voice of an old man, roughened by brandy and by liquors.

Marius turned quickly and saw a young girl.

II

A GIRL who was quite young was standing in the half-opened door. The little round window through which the light found its way into the garret was exactly opposite the door, and lit up this form with a pallid light. It was a pale, puny, meager creature; nothing but a chemise and a skirt covered a shivering and chilly nakedness. A string for a belt, a string for a headdress, sharp shoulders protruding from the chemise, a blond and lymphatic pallor, dirty shoulder blades, red hands, the mouth open and sunken, some teeth gone, the eyes dull, bold, and drooping, the form of an unripe young girl and the look of a corrupted old woman; fifty years joined with fifteen; one of those beings who are both feeble and horrible at once, and who make those shudder whom they do not make weep.

Marius arose and gazed with a kind of astonishment upon this being, so much like the shadowy forms which pass across our dreams.

The most touching thing about it was that this young girl had not come into the world to be ugly. In her early childhood, she must have even been pretty. The grace of her youth was still struggling against the hideous old age brought on by debauchery and poverty. A remnant of beauty was dying out upon this face of sixteen, like the pale sun which is extinguished by frightful clouds at the dawn of a winter's day.

"What do you wish, mademoiselle?" asked he.

The young girl answered with her voice like a drunken galley slave's:

"Here is a letter for you, Monsieur Marius."

She called Marius by his name; he could not doubt that her business was with him. But what was this girl? How did she know his name?

Without waiting for an invitation, she entered. She entered resolutely, looking at the whole room and the unmade bed with a sort of assurance which chilled the heart. She was barefooted. Great holes in her skirt revealed her long limbs and her sharp knees. She was shivering.

She had really in her hand a letter which she presented to Marius.

Marius, in opening this letter, noticed that the enormously large wafer was still wet. The message could not have come far. He read:

My amiable neighbor, young man!

I have lerned your kindness toward me, that you have paid my rent six months ago. I bless you, young man. My eldest daughter will tell you that we have been without a morsel of bread for two days, four persons, and my spouse sick. If I am not desseived by my thoughts, I think I may hope that your generous heart will soften at this exposure and that the desire will subjugate you of being propitious to me by deigning to lavish upon me some light gift.

I am with the distinguished consideration which is due to the benefactors of humanity,

JONDRETTE

P. S. My daughter will await your orders, dear Monsieur Marius.

Meantime, while Marius fixed upon her an astonished and sorrowful look, the young girl was walking to and fro in the room with the boldness of a specter. She bustled about regardless of her nakedness. At times, her chemise, unfastened and torn, fell almost to her waist. She moved the chairs, she disarranged the toilet articles on the bureau, she felt of Marius' clothes, she searched over what there was in the corners.

"Ah," said she, "you have a mirror!"

And she hummed, as if she had been alone, snatches of songs, light refrains which were made dismal by her harsh and guttural voice. Beneath this boldness could be perceived an indescribable constraint, restlessness, and humility. Effrontery is a shame.

Marius was reflecting, and let her go on.

She went to the table.

"Ah!" said she. "Books!"

A light flashed through her glassy eye. She resumed, and her tone expressed that happiness of being able to boast of something, to which no human creature is insensible:

"I can read, I can."

She hastily caught up the book which lay open on the table, and read fluently.

She put down the book, took up a pen, and exclaimed:

"And I can write, too!"

She dipped the pen in the ink, and turning toward Marius:

"Would you like to see? Here, I am going to write a word to show."

And before he had had time to answer, she wrote upon a sheet of blank paper which was on the middle of the table: "The Cognes are here."

Then she looked at Marius, put on a strange manner, and said to him:

"Do you know, Monsieur Marius, that you are a very pretty boy?"

And at the same time the same thought occurred to both of them, which made her smile and made him blush.

She went to him, and laid her hand on his shoulder: "You pay no attention to me, but I know you, Monsieur Marius. I meet you here on the stairs, and then I see you visiting a man named Father Mabeuf, who lives out by Austerlitz, sometimes, when I am walking that way. That becomes you very well, your tangled hair."

Her voice tried to be very soft, but succeeded only in being very low. Some of her words were lost in their passage from the larynx to the lips, as upon a keyboard in which some notes are missing.

Marius had drawn back quietly.

Meanwhile she had unfolded a petition addressed "to the beneficent gentleman of the church Saint Jacques du Haut Pas."

"Here!" said she. "This is for the old fellow who goes to mass. And this too is the hour. I am going to carry it to him. He will give us something perhaps for breakfast."

Then she began to laugh, and added:

"Do you know what it will be if we have breakfast today? It will be that we shall have had our breakfast for day before yesterday, our dinner for day before yesterday, our breakfast for yesterday, our dinner for yesterday, all that at one time this morning. Yes! Zounds! If you're not satisfied, stuff till you burst, dogs!"

This reminded Marius of what the poor girl had come to his room for.

He felt in his waistcoat; he found nothing there.

The young girl continued, seeming to talk as if she were no longer conscious that Marius was there present.

"Sometimes I go away at night. Sometimes I do not come back. Before coming to this place, the other winter, we lived under the arches of the bridges. We hugged close to each other so as not to freeze. My little sister cried: 'How chilly the water is!' When I thought of drowning myself, I said: 'No; it is too cold.' I go all alone when I want to; I sleep in the ditches sometimes. Do you know, at night, when I walk on the boulevards, I see the trees like gibbets, I see all the great black houses like the towers of Notre Dame, I imagine that the white walls are the river, I say to myself: 'Here, there is water there!' The stars are like illumination lamps;

one would say that they smoke, and that the wind blows them out. I am confused, as if I had horses breathing in my ear; though it is night, I hear hand organs and spinning wheels, I don't know what. I think that somebody is throwing stones at me, I run without knowing it; it is all a whirl, all a whirl. When one has not eaten, it is very queer."

And she looked at him with a wandering eye.

After a thorough exploration of his pockets, Marius had at last got together five francs and sixteen sous. This was at the time all that he had in the world. "That is enough for my dinner today," thought he, "tomorrow we will see." He took the sixteen sous, and gave the five francs to the young girl.

She took the piece eagerly.

"Good," said she, "there is some sunshine!"

She drew her chemise up over her shoulders, made a low bow to Marius, then a familiar wave of the hand, and moved toward the door, saying:

"Good morning, monsieur."

On her way she saw on the bureau a dry crust of bread molding there in the dust; she sprang upon it, and bit it, muttering:

"That is good! It is hard! It breaks my teeth!"

Then she went out.

III

For five years Marius had lived in poverty, in privation, in distress even, but he perceived that he had never known real misery. Real misery he had just seen. It was this sprite which had just passed before his eyes. In fact, he who has seen the misery of man only has seen nothing, he must see the misery of woman; he who has seen the misery of woman only has seen nothing, he must see the misery of childhood.

This young girl was to Marius a sort of messenger from the night.

She revealed to him an entire and hideous aspect of the darkness.

Marius almost reproached himself with the fact that he had been so absorbed in his reveries and passion that he had not until now cast a glance upon his neighbors. Paying their rent was a mechanical impulse; everybody would have had that impulse, but he, Marius, should have done better. What! A mere wall separated him from these abandoned beings, who lived by groping in the night without the pale of the living; he came in contact with them, he was in some sort the last link of the human race which they touched, he heard them live or rather breathe beside him, and he took no notice of them! Every day at every moment, he heard them through the wall, walking, going, coming, talking, and he did not lend his ear! And in these words there were groans, and he did not even listen, his thoughts were elsewhere, upon dreams, upon impossible glimmerings, upon loves in the sky, upon infatuations; and all the while human beings, his brothers in Jesus Christ, his brothers in the people, were suffering death agonies beside him! Agonizing uselessly. He even caused a portion of their suffering, and aggravated it. For had they had another neighbor, a less chimerical and more observant neighbor, an ordinary and charitable man, it was clear that their poverty would have been noticed, their signals of distress would have been seen, and long ago perhaps they would have been gathered up and saved! Undoubtedly they seemed very depraved, very corrupt, very vile, very hateful, even, but those are rare who fall without becoming degraded; there is a point, moreover, at which the unfortunate and the infamous are associated and confounded in a single word, a fatal word, *les misérables;* whose fault is it? And then, is it not when the fall is lowest that charity ought to be greatest?

When he thus preached to himself, for there were times when Marius, like all truly honest hearts, was his own monitor, and scolded himself more than he deserved, he looked at the wall which separated him from the Jondrettes, as if he could send his pitying glance through that partition to warn those unfortunate beings. The wall was a thin layer of plaster, upheld by laths and joists, through which, as we have just seen, voices and words could be distinguished perfectly. None but the dreamer, Marius, would not have perceived this before. There was no paper hung on this wall, either on the side of the Jondrettes, or on Marius' side; its coarse construction was bare to the eye. Almost unconsciously, Marius examined this partition; sometimes reverie examines, observes, and scrutinizes, as thought would do. Suddenly he arose; he noticed toward the top, near the ceiling, a triangular hole, where three laths left a space between them. The plaster which should have stopped this hole was gone, and by getting upon the bureau he could see through that hole into the Jondrettes' garret. Pity has and should have its curiosity. This hole was a kind of Judas. It is lawful to look upon misfortune like a betrayer for the sake of relieving it. "Let us see what these people are," thought Marius, "and to what they are reduced."

He climbed upon the bureau, put his eye to the crevice, and looked.

IV

WHAT Marius saw was a hole.

Marius was poor and his room was poorly furnished, but even as his poverty was noble, his garret was clean. The den into which his eyes were at that moment directed was abject, filthy, fetid, infectious, gloomy, unclean. All the furniture were two straw chairs, a rickety table, a few old broken dishes, and in two of the corners two indescribable pallets; all the light came from a dormer window of four panes, curtained with spiders' webs. Just enough light came through that loophole to make a man's face appear like the face of a phantom. The walls had a leprous look, and were covered with seams and scars like a face disfigured by some horrible malady; a putrid moisture oozed from them. Obscene pictures could be discovered upon them coarsely sketched in charcoal.

The room which Marius occupied had a broken brick pavement; this one was neither paved nor floored; the inmates walked immediately upon the old plastering of the ruinous tenement, which had grown black under their feet. Upon this uneven soil where the dust was, as it were, encrusted, and which was virgin soil in respect only of the broom, were grouped at random constellations of socks, old shoes, and hideous rags; however, this room had a fireplace, so it rented for forty francs a year. In the fireplace there was a little of everything, a chafing dish, a kettle, some broken boards, rags hanging on nails, a bird cage, some ashes, and even a little fire. Two embers were smoking sullenly.

By the table, upon which Marius saw a pen, ink, and paper, was seated a man of about sixty, small, thin, livid, haggard, with a keen, cruel, and restless air; a hideous harpy.

Lavater, if he could have studied this face, would have found in it a mixture of vulture and pettifogger; the bird of prey and the man of tricks rendering each other ugly and complete, the man of tricks making the bird of prey ignoble, the bird of prey making the man of tricks horrible.

This man had a long gray beard. He was dressed in a woman's chemise, which showed his shaggy breast and his naked arms bristling with gray hairs. Below this chemise were a pair of muddy pantaloons and boots from which the toes stuck out.

He had a pipe in his mouth, and was smoking. There was no more bread in the den, but there was tobacco.

The man talked aloud, and Marius heard his words:

"To think that there is no equality even when we are dead! Look at Père Lachaise! The great, those who are rich, are in the upper part, in the avenue of the acacias, which is paved. They can go there in a carriage. The low, the poor, the unfortunate, they are put in the lower part, where there is mud up to the knees, in holes, in the wet. They are put there so that they may rot sooner! You cannot go to see them without sinking into the ground."

Here he stopped, struck his fist on the table, and added, gnashing his teeth:

"Oh! I could eat the world!"

A big woman, who might have been forty years old or a hundred, was squatting near the fireplace, upon her bare feet.

She also was dressed only in a chemise and a knit skirt patched with pieces of old cloth. A coarse tow apron covered half the skirt. Although this woman was bent and drawn up into herself, it could be seen that she was very tall. She was a kind of giantess by the side of her husband. She had hideous hair, light red sprinkled with gray, that she pushed back from time to time with her huge shining hands which had flat nails.

Upon one of the pallets Marius could discern a sort of slender little wan girl seated, almost naked, with her feet hanging down, having the appearance neither of listening, nor of seeing, nor of living.

The younger sister, doubtless, of the one who had come to his room.

She appeared to be eleven or twelve years old.

She was of that sickly species which long remains backward, then pushes forward rapidly, and all at once. These sorry human plants are produced by want. These poor creatures have neither childhood nor youth. At fifteen they appear to be twelve; at sixteen they appear to be twenty. Today a little girl, tomorrow a woman. One would say that they leap through life, to have done with it sooner.

This being now had the appearance of a child.

Nothing, moreover, indicated the performance of any labor in this room; not a loom, not a wheel, not a tool. In one corner a few scraps of iron of an equivocal appearance. It was that gloomy idleness which follows despair, and which precedes the death agony.

Marius looked for some time into that funereal interior, more fearful than the interior of a tomb; for here were felt the movements of a human soul, and the palpitation of life.

The man became silent, the woman did not speak, the girl did not seem to breathe.

The man muttered out: "Rabble! Rabble! All is rabble!"

V

MARIUS, with a heavy heart, was about to get down from the sort of observatory which he had extemporized, when a sound attracted his attention, and induced him to remain in his place.

The door of the garret was hastily opened. The eldest daughter appeared upon the threshold. On her feet she had coarse men's shoes, covered with mud, which had been spattered as high as her red ankles, and she was wrapped in a ragged old gown which Marius had not seen upon her an hour before, but which she had probably left at his door that she might inspire the more pity, and which she must have put on upon going out. She came in, pushed the door to behind her, stopped to take breath, for she was quite breathless, then cried with an expression of joy and triumph:

"He is coming!"

The father turned his eyes, the woman turned her head, the younger sister did not stir.

"Who?" asked the father.

"The gentleman!"

"The philanthropist?"

"Yes."

"Of the church of Saint Jacques?"

"Yes."

"There, true, he is coming?"

"He is coming in a fiacre."

"In a fiacre. It is Rothschild?"

The father arose.

"And you are sure then, sure that he is coming? The brute may have forgotten the address! I will bet that the old fool—"

Just then there was a light rap at the door, the man rushed forward and opened it, exclaiming with many low bows and smiles of adoration:

"Come in, monsieur! Deign to come in, my noble benefactor, as well as your charming young lady."

A man of mature age and a young girl appeared at the door of the garret.

Marius had not left his place. What he felt at that moment escapes human language.

It was She.

Whoever has loved knows all the radiant meaning contained in the three letters of this word: She.

It was indeed she. Marius could hardly discern her through the luminous vapor which suddenly spread over his eyes. It was that sweet absent being, that star which had been his light, for six months, it was that eye, that brow, that mouth, that beautiful vanished face which had produced night when it went away. The vision had been in an eclipse; it was reappearing.

She appeared again in this gloom, in this garret, in this shapeless den, in this horror!

Marius shuddered desperately. What! It was she! The beating of his heart disturbed his sight. He felt ready to melt into tears. What! At last he saw her again after having sought for her so long! It seemed to him that he had just lost his soul and that he had just found it again.

She was still the same, a little paler only; her delicate face was set in a violet velvet hat, her form was hidden under a black satin pelisse; below her long dress he caught a glimpse of her little foot squeezed into a silk buskin.

She was still accompanied by Monsieur Leblanc.

She stepped into the room and laid a large package on the table.

The elder Jondrette girl had retreated behind the door and was looking upon that velvet hat, that silk dress, and that charming happy face, with an evil eye.

VI

MONSIEUR LEBLANC approached with his kind and compassionate look, and said to the father:

"Monsieur, you will find in this package some new clothes, some stockings, and some new coverlids."

"Our angelic benefactor overwhelms us," said Jondrette, bowing down to the floor. Then, stooping to his eldest daughter's ear, while the two visitors were examining this lamentable abode, he added rapidly in a whisper:

"Well! What did I tell you? Rags? No money. They are all alike!"

For some moments, Jondrette had been looking at "the philanthropist" in a strange manner. Even while speaking, he seemed to scrutinize him closely, as if he were trying to recall some reminiscence. Suddenly he passed over to his wife who was lying in her bed, appearing to be overwhelmed and stupid, and said to her quickly and in a very low tone:

"Notice that man!"

Then turning toward Monsieur Leblanc, and continuing his lamentation:

"You see, monsieur! My whole dress is nothing but a chemise of my wife's! And that all torn! In the heart of winter. I cannot go out, for lack of a coat. Well, monsieur, my worthy monsieur, do you know what is going to happen tomorrow? Tomorrow is the 4th of February, the fatal day, the last delay that my landlord will give me; if I do not pay him this evening, tomorrow my eldest daughter, myself, my spouse with her fever, my child, we shall all four be turned outdoors, and driven off into the street, upon the boulevard, without shelter, into the rain, upon the snow. You see, monsieur, I owe four quarters, a year! That is sixty francs."

Jondrette lied. Four quarters would have made but forty francs, and he could not have owed for four, since it was not six months since Marius had paid for two.

Monsieur Leblanc took five francs from his pocket and threw them on the table.

Jondrette had time to mutter into the ear of his elder daughter:

"The whelp! What does he think I am going to do with his five francs?"

Meantime, Monsieur Leblanc had taken off a large brown overcoat, which he wore over his blue surtout, and hung it over the back of the chair.

"I will be here at six o'clock," said he, "and I will bring you the sixty francs."

"My benefactor!" cried Jondrette, distractedly.

And he added in an undertone:

"Take a good look at him, wife!"

Just then the overcoat on the chair caught the eye of the elder daughter.

"Monsieur," said she, "you forget your coat."

Jondrette threw a crushing glance at his daughter, accompanied by a terrible shrug of the shoulders.

Monsieur Leblanc turned and answered with a smile:

"I do not forget it, I leave it."

"O my patron," said Jondrette, "my noble benefactor, I am melting into tears! Allow me to conduct you to your carriage."

"If you go out," replied Monsieur Leblanc, "put on this overcoat. It is really very cold."

Jondrette did not make him say it twice. He put on the brown overcoat very quickly.

And they went out all three, Jondrette preceding the two strangers.

Marius had lost nothing of all this scene, and yet in reality he had seen nothing of it. His eyes had remained fixed upon the young girl; his heart had, so to speak, seized upon her and enveloped her entirely, from her first step into the garret. During the whole time she had been there, he had lived that life of ecstasy which suspends material perceptions and precipitates the whole soul upon a single point. He contemplated, not that girl, but that light in a satin pelisse and a velvet hat. Had the star Sirius entered the room he would not have been more dazzled.

When she went out, he had one thought, to follow her, not to give up her track, not to leave her without knowing where she lived, not to lose her again, at least, after having so miraculously found her! He leaped down from the bureau and took his hat. As he was putting his hand on the bolt, and was just going out, he reflected and stopped. The hall was long, the stairs steep, Jondrette a great talker; Monsieur Leblanc doubtless had not yet got into his carriage; if he should turn around in the passage, or on the stairs, or on the doorstep, and perceive him, Marius, in that house, he would certainly be alarmed and would find means to escape him anew, and it would be all over at once. What was to be done? Wait a little? But during the delay the carriage might go. Marius was perplexed. At last he took the risk and went out of his room.

There was nobody in the hall. He ran to the stairs. There was nobody on the stairs. He hurried down, and reached the boulevard in time to see a fiacre turn the corner of the rue du Petit Banquier and return into the city.

VII

MARIUS mounted the stairs of the old tenement with slow steps, went into his room and pushed to his door behind him.

It did not close; he turned and saw a hand holding the door partly open.

"What is it?" he asked. "Who is there?"

It was the Jondrette girl.

"Is it you?" said Marius almost harshly. "You again? What do you want of me?"

She seemed thoughtful and did not look at him. She had lost the assurance which she had had in the morning. She did not come in, but stopped in the dusky hall, where Marius perceived her through the half-open door.

"Come now, will you answer?" said Marius. "What is it you want of me?"

She raised her mournful eyes, in which a sort of confused light seemed to shine dimly, and said to him:

"Monsieur Marius, you look sad. What is the matter with you?"

"With me?"

"Yes, you."

"There is nothing the matter with me."

"Yes!"

"No."

"I tell you there is!"

"Let me be quiet!"

Marius pushed the door anew, she still held it back.

"Stop," said she, "you are wrong. Though you may not be rich, you were good this morning. Be so again now. Can I serve you in anything? Let me. I do not ask your secrets, you need not tell them to me, but yet I may be useful. I can certainly help you, since I help my father. When it is necessary to carry letters, go into houses, inquire from door to door, find out an address, follow somebody, I do it."

An idea came into Marius' mind. What straw do we despise when we feel that we are sinking.

He approached the girl.

"Listen," said he to her kindly.

She interrupted him with a flash of joy in her eyes.

"Oh! Yes, talk softly to me! I like that better."

"Well," resumed he, "you brought this old gentleman here with his daughter."

"Yes."

"Do you know their address?"

"No."

"Find it for me."

The girl's eyes, which had been gloomy, had become joyful; they now became dark.

"Is that what you want?" she asked.

"Yes."

"Do you know them?"

"No."

"That is to say," said she hastily, "you do not know her, but you want to know her."

This "them" which had become "her" had an indescribable significance and bitterness.

"What will you give me?"

"Anything you wish!"

"Anything I wish?"

"Yes."

"You shall have the address."

She looked down, and then with a hasty movement closed the door.

Marius was alone.

He dropped into a chair, with his head and both elbows on the bed, swallowed up in thoughts which he could not grasp, and as if he were in a fit of vertigo.

Suddenly he was violently awakened from his reverie.

He heard the loud, harsh voice of Jondrette pronounce these words for him, full of the strangest interest:

"I tell you that I am sure of it, and that I recognized him!"

Of whom was Jondrette talking? He had recognized whom? Monsieur Leblanc? What! Did Jondrette know him? Was Marius just about to get in this sudden and unexpected way all the information the lack of which made his life obscure to himself? Was he at last to know whom he loved, who that young girl was? Who her father was? Was the thick shadow which enveloped them to be rolled away? Was the veil to be rent? Oh! Heavens!

He sprang, rather than mounted, upon the bureau, and resumed his place near the little aperture in the partition.

He again saw the interior of the Jondrette den.

VIII

NOTHING had changed in the appearance of the family, except that the wife and daughters had opened the package, and put on the woolen stockings and underclothes. Two new coverlids were thrown over the two beds.

Jondrette had evidently just come in. He had not yet recovered his regular breathing. His daughters were sitting on the floor near the fireplace. His wife lay as if exhausted upon the pallet near the fireplace, with an astonished countenance. Jondrette was walking up and down the garret with rapid strides. His eyes had an extraordinary look.

The woman, who seemed timid and stricken with stupor before her husband, ventured to say to him:

"What, really? You are sure?"

"Sure! It was eight years ago! But I recognize him! Ah! I recognize him! I recognized him immediately. What! It did not strike you?"

"No."

"And yet I told you to pay attention. But it is the same

height, the same face, hardly any older; there are some men who do not grow old; I don't know how they do it; it is the same tone of voice. He is better dressed, that is all! Ah! Mysterious old devil, I have got you, all right!"

He checked himself, and said to his daughters:

"You go out! It is queer that it did not strike your eye."

The two girls went out.

Just as they were passing the door, the father caught the elder by the arm, and said with a peculiar tone:

"You will be here at five o'clock precisely. Both of you. I shall need you."

Marius redoubled his attention.

Alone with his wife, Jondrette began to walk the room again, and took two or three turns in silence. Then he spent a few minutes in tucking the bottom of the woman's chemise which he wore into the waist of his trousers.

Suddenly he turned toward the woman, folded his arms, and exclaimed:

"And do you want I should tell you one thing? The young lady—"

"Well, what?" said the woman. "The young lady?"

Marius could doubt no longer, it was indeed of her that they were talking. He listened with an intense anxiety. His whole life was concentrated in his ears.

But Jondrette stooped down, and whispered to his wife. Then he straightened up and finished aloud:

"It is she!"

"That girl?" said the wife.

"That girl!" said the husband.

No words could express what there was in the "that girl" of the mother. It was surprise, rage, hatred, anger, mingled and combined in a monstrous intonation. The few words that had been spoken, some name, doubtless, which her husband had whispered in her ear, had been enough to rouse this huge drowsy woman and to change her repulsiveness to hideousness.

"Impossible!" she exclaimed. "When I think that my daughters go barefoot and have not a dress to put on! What! A satin pelisse, a velvet hat, buskins, and all! More than two hundred francs worth! One would think she was a lady! No, you are mistaken! Why, in the first place she was horrid; this one is not bad! She is really not bad! It cannot be she!"

"I tell you it is she. You will see."

At this absolute affirmation, the woman raised her big red and blond face and looked at the ceiling with a hideous expression. At that moment she appeared to Marius still more terrible than her husband. She was a swine with the look of a tigress.

"What!" she resumed. "This horrible beautiful young lady who looked at my girls with an appearance of pity, can she be that beggar! Oh, I would like to stamp her heart out!"

She sprang off the bed, and remained a moment standing, her hair flying, her nostrils distended, her mouth half open, her fists clenched and drawn back. Then she fell back upon the pallet. The man still walked back and forth, paying no attention to his female.

After a few moments of silence, he approached her and stopped before her, with folded arms, as before.

"And do you want I should tell you one thing?"

"What?" she asked.

He answered in a quick and low voice:

"My fortune is made."

The woman stared at him with that look which means: Has the man who is talking to me gone crazy?

He continued:

"Listen attentively. He is caught, the Croesus! It is all right. It is already done. Everything is arranged. I have seen the men. He will come this evening at six o'clock. To bring his sixty francs, the rascal! Did you see how I got that out, my sixty francs, my landlord, my 4th of February! It is not even a quarter! Was that stupid! He will come then at six o'clock! Our neighbor is gone to dinner then. Mother Burgon is washing dishes in the city. There is nobody in the house. Our neighbor never comes back before eleven o'clock. The girls will stand watch. You shall help us. He will be his own executor."

"And if he should not be his own executor?" asked the wife.

Jondrette made a sinister gesture and said:

"We will execute him."

And he burst into a laugh.

It was the first time that Marius had seen him laugh. This laugh was cold and feeble, and made him shudder.

Jondrette opened a closet near the chimney, took out an old cap and put it on his head after brushing it with his sleeve.

"Now," said he, "I am going out. I have still some men to see. Some good ones. You will see how it is going to work. I shall be back as soon as possible; it is a great hand to play; look out for the house."

Marius heard his steps recede along the hall and go rapidly down the stairs.

Just then the clock of Saint Médard struck one.

IX

On reaching No. 14, rue de Pontoise, Marius went upstairs and asked for the commissary of police.

"The commissary of police is not in," said one of the office boys; "but there is an inspector who answers for him. Would you like to speak to him? Is it urgent?"

"Yes," said Marius.

The office boy introduced him into the commissary's private room. A man of tall stature was standing there, behind a railing, in front of a stove, and holding up with both hands the flaps of a huge overcoat with three capes. He had a square face, a thin and firm mouth, very fierce, bushy, grayish whiskers, and an eye that would turn your pockets inside out. You might have said of this eye, not that it penetrated, but that it ransacked.

This man's appearance was not much less ferocious or formidable than Jondrette's; it is sometimes no less startling to meet the dog than the wolf.

"What do you wish?" said he to Marius, without adding monsieur.

"The commissary of police?"

"He is absent. I answer for him."

"It is a very secret affair."

"Speak, then."

"And very urgent."

"Then speak quickly."

This man, calm and abrupt, was at the same time alarming and reassuring. He inspired fear and confidence. Marius related his adventure. The inspector remained silent a moment, then answered between his teeth, speaking less to Marius than to his cravat:

"There ought to be a dash of Patron-Minette in this."

He relapsed into silence, then resumed:

"Number 50-52. I know the shanty. Impossible to hide ourselves in the interior without the artists perceiving us, then they would leave and break up the play. They are so modest! The public annoys them. None of that, none of that. I want to hear them sing, and make them dance."

Marius interrupted him:

"That is well enough; but what are you going to do?"

The inspector merely answered:

"The lodgers in that house have latchkeys to get in with at night. You must have one?"

"Yes," said Marius.

"Have you it with you?"

"Yes."

"Give it to me," said the inspector.

Marius took his key from his waistcoat, handed it to the inspector, and added:

"If you trust me you will come in force."

The inspector threw a glance upon Marius such as Voltaire would have thrown upon a provincial academician who had proposed a rhyme to him; with a single movement he plunged both his hands, which were enormous, into the two immense pockets of his overcoat, and took out two small steel pistols, of the kind called fisticuffs. He presented them to Marius, saying hastily and abruptly:

"Take these. Go back home. Hide yourself in your room; let them think you have gone out. They are loaded. Each with two balls. You will watch; there is a hole in the wall, as you have told me. The men will come. Let them go on a little. When you deem the affair at a point, and when it is time to stop it, you will fire off a pistol. Not too soon. The rest is my affair. A pistol shot in the air, into the ceiling, no matter where. Above all, not too soon. Wait till the consummation is commenced; you are a lawyer, you know what that is."

Marius took the pistols and put them in the side pocket of his coat. As he placed his hand on the latch of the door to go out, the inspector called to him:

"By the way, if you need me between now and then, come or send here. You will ask for Inspector Javert."

Evening had come; night had almost closed in; there was now but one spot in the horizon or in the whole sky which was lighted by the sun; that was the moon.

She was rising red behind the low dome of La Salpêtrière.

Marius returned to No. 50-52 with rapid strides. The door was still open when he arrived. He ascended the stairs on tiptoe, and glided along the wall of the hall as far as his room. This hall, it will be remembered, was lined on both sides by garrets, which were all at that time empty and to let. Madame Burgon usually left the doors open. As he passed by one of these doors, Marius thought he perceived in the unoccupied cell four motionless heads, which were made dimly visible by a remnant of daylight falling through the little window. Marius, not wishing to be seen, did not endeavor to see. He succeeded in getting into his room without being perceived and without any noise. It was time. A moment afterward he heard Madame Burgon going out and closing the door of the house.

X

Marius sat down on his bed. It might have been half-past five o'clock. A half hour only separated him from what was to come. He heard his arteries beat as one hears the ticking of a watch in the dark. He thought of this double march that was going on that moment in the darkness: crime advancing on the one hand, justice coming on the other. He was not afraid, but he could not think without a sort of shudder of the things which were so soon to take place. To him, as to all those whom some surprising adventure has suddenly befallen, this whole day seemed but a dream; and, to assure himself that he was not the prey of a nightmare, he had to feel the chill of the two steel pistols in his fob pockets.

It was not now snowing; the moon, growing brighter and brighter, was getting clear of the haze, and its light, mingled with the white reflection from the fallen snow, gave the room a twilight appearance.

There was a light in the Jondrette den. Marius saw the hole in the partition shine with a red gleam which appeared to him bloody.

He was sure that this gleam could hardly be produced by a candle. However, there was no movement in their room, nobody was stirring there, nobody spoke, not a breath, the stillness was icy and deep, and save for that light he could have believed that he was beside a sepulcher.

Marius took his boots off softly, and pushed them under his bed.

Some minutes passed. Marius heard the lower door turn on its hinges; a heavy and rapid step ascended the stairs and passed along the corridor, the latch of the garret was noisily lifted; Jondrette came in.

Several voices were heard immediately. The whole family was in the garret. Only they kept silence in the absence of the master, like the cubs in the absence of the wolf.

A moment afterward, Marius heard the sound of the bare feet of the two young girls in the passage, and the voice of Jondrette crying to them.

"Pay attention, now! One toward the barrière, the other at the corner of the rue du Petit Banquier. Don't lose sight of the house door a minute, and if you see the least thing, here immediately! Tumble along! You have a key to come in with."

The elder daughter muttered:

"To stand sentry barefoot in the snow!"

"Tomorrow you shall have boots of beetle-colored silk!" said the father.

They went down the stairs, and, a few seconds afterward, the sound of the lower door shutting announced that they had gone out.

There were now in the house only Marius and the Jondrettes, and probably also the mysterious beings of whom Marius had caught a glimpse in the twilight behind the door of the untenanted garret.

Marius judged that the time had come to resume his place at his observatory. In a twinkling, and with the agility of his age, he was at the hole in the partition.

He looked in.

The interior of the Jondrette apartment presented a singular appearance, and Marius found the explanation of the strange light which he had noticed. A candle was burning in a verdigrised candlestick, but it was not that which really lighted the

room. The entire den was, as it were, illuminated by the
reflection of a large sheet-iron furnace in the fireplace, which
was filled with lighted charcoal. The charcoal was burning and
the furnace was red hot, a blue flame danced over it and
helped to show the form of a chisel which was growing ruddy
among the coals. In a corner near the door, and arranged as if
for anticipated use, were two heaps which appeared to be a
heap of old iron and a heap of ropes. All this would have
made one, who had known nothing of what was going forward, waver between a very sinister idea and a very simple
idea. The room thus lighted up seemed rather a smithy than
a mouth of hell, but Jondrette, in that glare, had rather the
appearance of a demon than of a blacksmith.

The heat of the glowing coals was such that the candle
upon the table melted on the side toward the furnace and was
burning fastest on that side. An old dark copper lantern,
worthy of Diogenes turned Cartouche, stood upon the mantel.

The furnace, which was set into the fireplace, beside the
almost extinguished embers, sent its smoke into the flue of
the chimney and exhaled no odor.

The moon, shining through the four panes of the window,
threw its whiteness into the ruddy and flaming garret; and to
Marius' poetic mind, a dreamer even in the moment of
action, it was like a thought of heaven mingled with the shapeless nightmares of earth.

Jondrette had lighted his pipe, sat down on a chair, and was
smoking. His wife was speaking to him in a low tone.

Suddenly Jondrette raised his voice:

"By the way, now, I think of it. In such weather as this he
will come in a fiacre. Light the lantern, take it, and go down.
You will stay there behind the lower door. The moment you
hear the carriage stop, you will open immediately, he will
come up, you will light him up the stairs and above the hall,
and when he comes in here, you will go down again immediately, pay the driver, and send the fiacre away."

"And the money?" asked the woman.

Jondrette fumbled in his trousers, and handed her five
francs.

"What is that?" she asked.

Jondrette answered with dignity:

"It is the monarch which our neighbor gave this morning.
And here is the lantern. Go down quick."

She hastily obeyed, and Jondrette was left alone.

The fireplace and the table, with two chairs, were exactly opposite Marius. The furnace was hidden; the room was now lighted only by the candle; the least thing upon the table or the mantel made a great shadow. A broken water pitcher masked the half of one wall. There was in the room a calm which was inexpressibly hideous and threatening. The approach of some appalling thing could be felt.

Jondrette had let his pipe go out—a sure sign that he was intensely absorbed—and had come back and sat down. The candle made the savage ends and corners of his face stand out prominently. There were contractions of his brows, and abrupt openings of his right hand, as if he were replying to the last counsels of a dark interior monologue. In one of these obscure replies which he was making to himself, he drew the table drawer out quickly toward him, took out a long carving knife which was hidden there, and tried its edge on his nail. This done, he put the knife back into the drawer, and shut it.

Marius, for his part, grasped the pistol which was in his right fob pocket, took it out, and cocked it.

The pistol in cocking gave a little clear, sharp sound.

Jondrette started, and half rose from his chair.

"Who is there?" cried he.

Marius held his breath; Jondrette listened a moment, then began to laugh, saying:

"What a fool I am! It is the partition cracking."

Marius kept the pistol in his hand.

XI

JUST then the distant and melancholy vibration of a bell shook the windows. Six o'clock struck on Saint Médard.

Jondrette marked each stroke with a nod of his head. At the sixth stroke, he snuffed the candle with his fingers.

Then he began to walk about the room, listened in the hall, walked, listened again. "Provided he comes!" muttered he; then he returned to his chair.

He had hardly sat down when the door opened.

The mother Jondrette had opened it, and stood in the hall

making a horrible, amiable grimace, which was lighted up from beneath by one of the holes of the dark lantern.

"Walk in," said she.

"Walk in, my benefactor," repeated Jondrette, rising precipitately.

Monsieur Leblanc appeared.

He had an air of serenity which made him singularly venerable.

He laid four louis upon the table.

"That is for your rent and your pressing wants. We will see about the rest."

"God reward you, my generous benefactor!" said Jondrette, and rapidly approaching his wife:

"Send away the fiacre!"

She slipped away, while her husband was lavishing bows and offering a chair to Monsieur Leblanc. A moment afterward she came back and whispered in his ear:

"It is done."

The snow which had fallen that morning was so deep that they had not heard the fiacre arrive, and did not hear it go away.

Meanwhile Monsieur Leblanc had taken a seat.

Jondrette had taken possession of the other chair opposite Monsieur Leblanc.

Now, to form an idea of the scene which follows, let the reader call to mind the chilly night, the solitudes of La Salpêtrière covered with snow, and white in the moonlight, like immense shrouds, the flickering light of the streetlamps here and there reddening these tragic boulevards and the long rows of black elms, not a passer perhaps within a mile around, the Gorbeau tenement at its deepest degree of silence, horror, and night, in that tenement, in the midst of these solitudes, in the midst of this darkness, the vast Jondrette garret lighted by a candle, and in this den two men seated at a table, Monsieur Leblanc tranquil, Jondrette smiling and terrible, his wife, the wolf dam, in a corner, and, behind the partition, Marius, invisible, alert, losing no word, losing no movement, his eye on the watch, the pistol in his grasp.

Marius, moreover, was experiencing nothing but an emotion of horror, no fear. He clasped the butt of the pistol, and felt reassured. "I shall stop this wretch when I please," thought he.

He felt that the police were somewhere nearby in ambush, awaiting the signal agreed upon, and all ready to stretch out their arms.

He hoped, moreover, that from this terrible meeting between Jondrette and Monsieur Leblanc some light would be thrown upon all that he was interested to know.

XII

WHILE Jondrette was talking to Monsieur Leblanc, with an apparent disorder which detracted nothing from the crafty and cunning expression of his physiognomy, Marius raised his eyes, and perceived at the back of the room somebody whom he had not before seen. A man had come in so noiselessly that nobody had heard the door turn on its hinges. This man had a knit woolen waistcoat of violet color, old, worn out, stained, cut, and showing gaps at all its folds, full trousers of cotton velvet, socks on his feet, no shirt, his neck bare, his arms bare and tattooed, and his face stained black. He sat down in silence and with folded arms on the nearest bed, and as he kept behind the woman, he was distinguished only with difficulty.

That kind of magnetic instinct which warns the eye made Monsieur Leblanc turn almost at the same time with Marius. He could not help a movement of surprise.

"Who is that man?" said he.

"That man?" said Jondrette. "That is a neighbor. Pay no attention to him."

The neighbor had a singular appearance. However, factories of chemical products abound in Faubourg Saint Marceau. Many machinists might have their faces blacked. The whole person of Monsieur Leblanc, moreover, breathed a candid and intrepid confidence. He resumed:

"Pardon me; what were you saying to me?"

"I was telling you, monsieur and dear patron," replied Jondrette, leaning his elbows on the table, and gazing at Monsieur Leblanc with fixed and tender eyes, similar to the eyes of a boa constrictor, "I was telling you that I had a picture to sell."

A slight noise was made at the door. A second man

entered, and sat down on the bed behind the female Jondrette. He had his arms bare, like the first, and a mask of ink or of soot.

Although this man had, literally, slipped into the room, he could not prevent Monsieur Leblanc from perceiving him.

"Do not mind them," said Jondrette. "They are people of the house. I was telling you, then, that I have a valuable painting left. Here, monsieur, look."

He got up, went to the wall, at the foot of which stood a panel, which he turned round, still leaving it resting against the wall. It was something, in fact, that resembled a picture and which the candle scarcely revealed. Marius could make nothing out of it, Jondrette being between him and the picture; he merely caught a glimpse of a coarse daub, with a sort of principal personage colored in the crude and glaring style of strolling panoramas and paintings upon screens.

"What is that?" asked Monsieur Leblanc.

Jondrette exclaimed:

"A painting by a master; a picture of great price, my benefactor! I cling to it as to my two daughters; it calls up memories to me! But I have told you, and I cannot unsay it, I am so unfortunate that I would part with it."

Whether by chance, or whether there was some beginning of distrust, while examining the picture, Monsieur Leblanc glanced toward the back of the room. There were now four men there, three seated on the bed, one standing near the door casing; all four bare-armed, motionless, and with blackened faces. One of those who were on the bed was leaning against the wall, with his eyes closed, and one would have said he was asleep. This one was old; his white hair over his black face was horrible. The two others appeared young; one was bearded, the other had long hair. None of them had shoes on; those who did not have socks were barefooted.

Jondrette noticed that Monsieur Leblanc's eye was fixed upon these men.

"They are friends. They live nearby," said he. "They are dark because they work in charcoal. They are chimney doctors. Do not occupy your mind with them, my benefactor, but buy my picture. Take pity on my misery. I shall not sell it to you at a high price. How much do you estimate it to be worth?"

"But," said Monsieur Leblanc, looking Jondrette full in the face like a man who puts himself on his guard, "this is some tavern sign, it is worth about three francs."

Jondrette answered calmly:

"Have you your pocketbook here? I will be satisfied with a thousand crowns."

Monsieur Leblanc rose to his feet, placed his back to the wall, and ran his eye rapidly over the room. He had Jondrette at his left on the side toward the window, and Jondrette's wife and the four men at his right on the side toward the door. The four men did not stir, and had not even the appearance of seeing him; Jondrette had begun again to talk in a plaintive key, with his eyes so wild and his tones so mournful that Monsieur Leblanc might have thought that he had before his eyes nothing more nor less than a man gone crazy from misery.

"If you do not buy my picture, dear benefactor," said Jondrette, "I am without resources, I have only to throw myself into the river."

While speaking Jondrette did not look at Monsieur Leblanc, who was watching him. Monsieur Leblanc's eye was fixed upon Jondrette, and Jondrette's eye upon the door; Marius' breathless attention went from one to the other. Monsieur Leblanc appeared to ask himself, "Is this an idiot?" Jondrette repeated two or three times with all sorts of varied inflections in the drawling and begging style: "I can only throw myself into the river! I went down three steps for that the other day by the side of the Bridge of Austerlitz!"

Suddenly his dull eye lighted up with a hideous glare, this little man straightened up and became horrifying, he took a step toward Monsieur Leblanc and cried to him in a voice of thunder:

"But all this is not the question! Do you know me?"

XIII

THE door of the garret had been suddenly flung open, disclosing three men in blue blouses with black paper masks. The first was spare and had a long ironbound cudgel; the second, who was a sort of colossus, held by the middle of the handle, with the axe down, a butcher's poleax. The third, a broad-shouldered man, not so thin as the first, nor so heavy as the second, held in his clenched fist an enormous key stolen from some prison door.

It appeared that it was the arrival of these men for which Jondrette was waiting. A rapid dialogue commenced between him and the man with the cudgel, the spare man.

"Is everything ready?" said Jondrette.

"Yes," answered the spare man.

"Where is Montparnasse then?"

"The young primate stopped to chat with your daughter."

"Which one?"

"The elder."

"Is there a fiacre below?"

"Yes."

"The *maringote* is ready?"

"Ready."

"With two good horses?"

"Excellent."

"It is waiting where I said it should wait?"

"Yes."

"Good," said Jondrette.

Monsieur Leblanc was very pale. He looked over everything in the room about him like a man who understands into what he has fallen, and his head, directed in turn toward all the heads which surrounded him, moved on his neck with an attentive and astonished slowness, but there was nothing in his manner which resembled fear. He had made an extemporized entrenchment of the table; and this man who, the moment before, had the appearance only of a good old man, had suddenly become a sort of athlete, and placed his powerful fist upon the back of his chair with a surprising and formidable gesture.

Three of the men of whom Jondrette had said: "They are chimney doctors," had taken from the heap of old iron a large pair of shears, a steelyard bar, and a hammer, and placed themselves before the door without saying a word. The old man was still on the bed, and had merely opened his eyes. The woman Jondrette was sitting beside him.

Marius thought that in a few seconds more the time would come to interfere, and he raised his right hand toward the ceiling, in the direction of the hall, ready to let off his pistol shot.

Jondrette, after his colloquy with the man who had the cudgel, turned again toward Monsieur Leblanc and repeated his question, accompanying it with that low, smothered, and terrible laugh of his:

"You do not recognize me, then?"

Monsieur Leblanc looked him in the face, and answered:

"No."

Then Jondrette came up to the table. He leaned forward over the candle, folding his arms, and pushing his angular and ferocious jaws up toward the calm face of Monsieur Leblanc, as nearly as he could without forcing him to draw back, and in that posture, like a wild beast just about to bite, he cried:

"My name is not Jondrette, my name is Thénardier! I am the innkeeper of Montfermeil! Do you understand me? Thénardier! Now do you know me?"

An imperceptible flush passed over Monsieur Leblanc's forehead, and he answered without a tremor or elevation of voice, and with his usual placidness:

"No more than before."

Marius did not hear this answer. Could anybody have seen him at that moment in that darkness, he would have seen that he was haggard, astounded, and thunderstruck. When Jondrette had said: "My name is Thénardier," Marius had trembled in every limb, and supported himself against the wall as if he had felt the chill of a sword blade through his heart. Then his right arm, which was just ready to fire the signal shot, dropped slowly down, and at the moment that Jondrette had repeated: "Do you understand me? Thénardier!" Marius' nerveless fingers had almost dropped the pistol. Jondrette, in unveiling who he was, had not moved Monsieur Leblanc, but he had completely unnerved Marius. That name of Thénardier, which Monsieur Leblanc did not seem to know, Marius knew. Remember what that name was to him! That name he had worn on his heart, written in his father's will! He mingled it with the name of his father in his worship. What! Here was Thénardier, here was that Thénardier, here was that innkeeper of Montfermeil, for whom he had so long and so vainly sought! He had found him at last, and how? This savior of his father was a bandit! What a fatality! What a bitter mockery of Fate! He had resolved, if ever he found this Thénardier, to accost him in no other wise than by throwing himself at his feet, and now he found him indeed, but to deliver him to the executioner! What a mockery to have worn so long upon his breast the last wishes of his father, written by his hand, only to act so frightfully contrary to them! But on the other hand, to see him ambuscade and not prevent it! To condemn the victim and spare the assassin, could he be bound to any gratitude toward such a wretch? All the ideas which Marius had had for the last four years were, as it were, pierced through and through by this unexpected blow. He shuddered. He felt that he was mad. His knees gave way beneath him; and he had not even time to deliberate, with such fury was the scene which he had before his eyes rushing forward. It was like a whirlwind, which he had thought himself master of, and which was carrying him away. He was on the point of fainting.

Meanwhile Thénardier, we will call him by no other name henceforth, was walking to and fro before the table in a sort of bewilderment and frenzied triumph.

He clutched the candle and put it on the mantel with such a shock that the flame was almost extinguished and the tallow was spattered upon the wall.

Then he turned toward Monsieur Leblanc, and with a frightful look, spit out this:

"Singed! Smoked! Basted! Spitted!"

And he began to walk again, in full explosion.

"Ha!" cried he. "I have found you again at last, Monsieur Philanthropist! Monsieur Threadbare Millionaire! Monsieur Giver of Dolls! Old Marrowbones! Ha! You do not know me? No, it was not you who came to Montfermeil, to my inn, eight years ago, the night of Christmas, 1823! It was not you who took away Fantine's child from my house! The Lark! It was not you who had a yellow coat! No! And a package of clothes in your hand just as you came here this morning! Say now, wife! It is his mania it appears, to carry packages of woolen stockings into houses! Old Benevolence, get out! Are you a hosier, Monsieur Millionaire? You give the poor your shop sweepings, Holy Man! What a charlatan! Ha! You do not know me? Well, I knew you! I knew you immediately as soon as you stuck your nose in here. Zounds! You made a mock of me once! You are the cause of all my misfortunes!

For fifteen hundred francs you got a girl that I had, and who certainly belonged to rich people, and who had already brought me in a good deal of money, and from whom I ought to have got enough to live on all my life! Say, now! You must have thought me green when you went away with the Lark! Revenge! The trumps are in my hand today. You are skunked, my good man! Oh! But don't I laugh! Indeed, I do! Didn't he fall into the trap? The ridiculous fool! And these four paltry philippes that he brings me! Rascal! He had not even heart enough to go up to a hundred francs! And how he swallowed my platitudes! The fellow amused me. I said to myself: 'Blubberlips! Go on, I have got you, I lick your paws this morning! I will gnaw your heart tonight!'"

Thénardier stopped. He was out of breath. His little narrow chest was blowing like a blacksmith's bellows. His eye was full of the base delight of a feeble, cruel, and cowardly animal, which can finally prostrate that of which it has stood in awe, and insult what it has flattered, the joy of a dwarf putting his heel upon the head of Goliath, the joy of a jackal beginning to tear a sick bull, dead enough not to be able to defend himself, alive enough yet to suffer.

Monsieur Leblanc did not interrupt him, but said when he stopped:

"I do not know what you mean. You are mistaken. I am a very poor man and anything but a millionaire. I do not know you; you mistake me for another."

"Ha!" screamed Thénardier. "Good Mountebank! You stick to that joke yet! You are in the fog, my old boy! Ah! You do not remember! You do not see who I am!"

"Pardon me, monsieur," answered Monsieur Leblanc, with a tone of politeness which, at such a moment, had a peculiarly strange and powerful effect, "I see that you are a bandit."

Who has not noticed it, hateful beings have their tender points; monsters are easily annoyed. At this word bandit, the Thénardiess sprang off the bed. Thénardier seized his chair as if he were going to crush it in his hands: "Don't you stir," cried he to his wife, and turning toward Monsieur Leblanc:

"Bandit! Yes, I know that you call us so, you rich people! Yes! It is true I have failed; I am in concealment; I have no bread; I have not a sou; I am a bandit. Here are three days that I have eaten nothing; I am a bandit! Ah! You warm your feet; you have Sacoski pumps, you have wadded overcoats like archbishops, you live on the first floor in houses with a porter, you eat truffles, you eat forty-franc bunches of asparagús in the month of January, and green peas; you stuff yourselves, and when you want to know if it is cold you look in the newspaper to see at what degree the thermometer of the inventor, Chevalier, stands. But we are our own thermometers! We have no need to go to the quay at the corner of the Tour de l'Horloge, to see how many degrees below zero it is; we feel the blood stiffen in our veins and the ice reach our hearts, and we say: 'There is no God!' And you come into our caverns, yes, into our caverns, and call us bandits. But we will eat you! But we will devour you, poor little things! Monsieur Millionaire! Know this: I have been a man established in business, I have been licensed, I have been an elector; I am a citizen, I am! And you, perhaps, are not one?"

When Thénardier had taken breath he fixed his bloodshot eyes upon Monsieur Leblanc, and said in a low and abrupt tone:

"What have you to say before we begin to dance with you?"

Monsieur Leblanc said nothing. In the midst of this silence a hoarse voice threw in this ghastly sarcasm from the hall:

"If there is any wood to split, I am on hand!"

It was the man with the poleax who was making merry.

At the same time a huge face, bristly and dirty, appeared in the doorway, with a hideous laugh, which showed not teeth, but fangs.

It was the face of the man with the poleax.

"What have you taken off your mask for?" cried Thénardier, furiously.

"To laugh," replied the man.

For some moments, Monsieur Leblanc had seemed to follow and to watch all the movements of Thénardier, who, blinded and bewildered by his own rage, was walking to and fro in the den with the confidence inspired by the feeling that the door was guarded, having armed possession of a disarmed man, and being nine to one, even if the Thénardiess should count but for one man. In his apostrophe to the man with the poleax, he turned his back to Monsieur Leblanc.

Monsieur Leblanc seized this opportunity, pushed the chair away with his foot, the table with his hand; and at one bound, with a marvelous agility, before Thénardier had had time to turn around, he was at the window. To open it, get up and step through it, was the work of a second. He was half outside when six strong hands seized him, and drew him forcibly back into the room. The three "chimney doctors" had thrown themselves upon him. At the same time the Thénardiess had clutched him by the hair.

. At the disturbance which this made, the other bandits ran in from the hall. The old man, who was on the bed, and who seemed overwhelmed with wine, got off the pallet, and came tottering along with a road mender's hammer in his hand.

A herculean struggle had commenced. With one blow full in the chest Monsieur Leblanc had sent the old man sprawling into the middle of the room, then with two back strokes had knocked down two other assailants, whom he held one under each knee; the wretches screamed under the pressure as if they had been under a granite millstone; but the four others had seized the formidable old man by the arms and the back, and held him down over the two prostrate "chimney doctors." Thus, master of the latter and mastered by the former, crushing those below him and suffocating under those above him, vainly endeavoring to shake off all the violence and blows which were heaped upon him, Monsieur Leblanc disappeared under the horrible group of the bandits, like a wild boar under a howling pack of hounds and mastiffs.

They succeeded in throwing him over upon the bed nearest to the window and held him there in awe. The Thénardiess had not let go of his hair.

Two of the "chimney doctors" pushed the drunkard up to the heap of old iron with their feet.

"Babet, what did you bring so many for?" said Thénardier in a low tone to the man with the cudgel. "It was needless."

"What would you have?" replied the man with the cudgel. "They all wanted to be in. The season is bad. There is nothing doing."

The pallet upon which Monsieur Leblanc had been thrown was a sort of hospital bed supported by four big roughly squared wooden posts. Monsieur Leblanc made no resistance. The brigands bound him firmly, standing, with his feet to the floor, by the bedpost furthest from the window and nearest to the chimney.

When the last knot was tied, Thénardier took a chair and came and sat down nearly in front of Monsieur Leblanc.

Thénardier looked no longer like himself; in a few seconds
the expression of his face had passed from unbridled violence
to tranquil and crafty mildness. Marius hardly recognized in
that polite, clerkly smile, the almost beastly mouth which was
foaming a moment before; he looked with astonishment upon
this fantastic and alarming metamorphosis, and he experienced
what a man would feel who should see a tiger change itself
into an attorney.

"Monsieur," said Thénardier.

And with a gesture dismissing the brigands who still had
their hands upon Monsieur Leblanc:

"Move off a little, and let me talk with monsieur."

They all retired toward the door. He resumed:

"Monsieur, you were wrong in trying to jump out the
window. You might have broken your leg. Now, if you please,
we will talk quietly. In the first place I must inform you of a
circumstance I have noticed, which is that you have not yet
made the least outcry. Indeed! You might have cried thief
a little, for I should not have found it inconvenient. Murder!
That is said upon occasion, and, as far as I am concerned, I
should not have taken it in bad part. It is very natural that
one should make a little noise when he finds himself with
persons who do not inspire him with as much confidence as
they might. But, in short, you did not cry out; that was better;
I make you my compliments for it, and I will tell you what
I conclude from it: my dear monsieur, when a man cries out,
who is it that comes? The police. And after the police? Justice.
Well! You did not cry out; because you were no more anxious
than we to see justice and the police come. It is because—I
suspected as much long ago—you have some interest in concealing something. For our part we have the same interest.
Now we can come to an understanding."

Thénardier quietly got up, went to the fireplace, took away
the screen, which he leaned against the nearest pallet, and
thus revealed the furnace full of glowing coals in which the
prisoner could plainly see the chisel at a white heat, spotted
here and there with little scarlet stars.

Then Thénardier came back and sat down by Monsieur
Leblanc.

"I continue," said he. "Now we can come to an understanding. Let us arrange this amicably. I was wrong to fly
into a passion just now. I do not know where my wits were;

I went much too far; I talked extravagantly. For instance, because you are a millionaire, I told you that I wanted money, a good deal of money, an immense deal of money. That would not be reasonable. My God, rich as you may be, you have your expenses; who does not have them? I do not want to ruin you; I am not a catchpole, after all. I am not one of those people who, because they have the advantage in position, use it to be ridiculous. Here, I am willing to go halfway and make some sacrifice on my part. I need only two hundred thousand francs. You will say: but I have not two hundred thousand francs with me. Oh! I am not exacting. I do not require that. I only ask one thing. Have the goodness to write what I shall dictate."

"How do you expect me to write? I am tied."

"That is true, pardon me!" said Thénardier. "You are quite right."

When the prisoner's right hand was free, Thénardier dipped the pen into the ink, and presented it to him.

Monsieur Leblanc took the pen.

Thénardier began to dictate:

"My daughter—"

The prisoner shuddered and lifted his eyes to Thénardier.

"Put 'my dear daughter,'" said Thénardier. Monsieur Leblanc obeyed.

Thénardier continued:

"Come immediately, I have imperative need of you. The person who will give you this note is directed to bring you to me. I am waiting for you. Come with confidence."

Monsieur Leblanc had written the whole. Thénardier added:

"Put on the address."

The prisoner remained thoughtful for a moment, then he took the pen and wrote:

Mademoiselle Fabre, at Monsieur Urbain Fabre's, rue Saint Dominique d'Enfer, No. 17.

Thénardier seized the letter with a sort of feverish convulsive movement.

"Wife!" cried he.

The Thénardiess sprang forward.

"Here is the letter. You know what you have to do. There is a fiacre below. Go right away, and come back ditto."

There were now but five bandits left in the den with Thénardier and the prisoner. A gloomy stillness had succeeded the savage tumult which filled the garret a few moments before.

Marius was waiting in an anxiety which everything increased.

This fearful situation had lasted for more than an hour, when they heard the sound of the door of the stairway, which opened, then closed.

The prisoner made a movement in his bonds.

"Here is the bourgeoise," said Thénardier.

He had hardly said this, when in fact the Thénardiess burst into the room, red, breathless, panting, with glaring eyes, and cried, striking her hands upon her hips both at the same time:

"False address!"

The bandit whom she had taken with her came in behind her and picked up his poleax again.

"False address?" repeated Thénardier.

She continued:

"Nobody! Rue Saint Dominique, Number 17, no Monsieur Urbain Fabre! They do not know who he is!"

She stopped for lack of breath, then continued:

"Monsieur Thénardier! This old fellow has cheated you! You are too good, do you see! I would have cut up the *margoulette* for you in quarters, to begin with! And if he had been ugly, I would have cooked him alive! Then he would have had to talk, and had to tell where the girl is, and had to tell where the rhino is! That is how I would have fixed it! No wonder that they say men are stupider than women!"

While his exasperated wife was vociferating, Thénardier had seated himself on the table; he sat a few seconds without saying a word, swinging his right leg, which was hanging down, and gazing upon the furnace with a look of savage reverie.

At last he said to the prisoner with a slow and singularly ferocious inflection:

"A false address! What did you hope for by that?"

"To gain time!" cried the prisoner with a ringing voice.

And at the same moment he shook off his bonds; they were cut. The prisoner was no longer fastened to the bed save by one leg.

Before the seven men had had time to recover themselves and spring upon him, he had bent over to the fireplace and reached his hand toward the furnace; then he rose up, and now Thénardier, the Thénardiess, and the bandits, thrown by the shock into the back part of the room, beheld him with stupefaction, holding above his head the glowing chisel, from which fell an ominous light, almost free and in a formidable attitude.

At the judicial inquest, to which the ambuscade in the Gorbeau tenement gave rise in the sequel, it appeared that a big sou, cut and worked in a peculiar fashion, was found in the garret, when the police made a descent upon it; this big sou was one of those marvels of labor which the patience of the galleys produces in the darkness and for the darkness, marvels which are nothing else but instruments of escape. These hideous and delicate products of a wonderful art are to jewelry what the metaphors of argot are to poetry. There are Benvenuto Cellinis in the galleys, even as there are Villons in language. The unhappy man who aspires to deliverance finds the means, sometimes without tools, with a folding knife, with an old case knife, to split a sou into two thin plates, to hollow out these two plates without touching the stamp of the mint, and to cut a screw thread upon the edge of the sou, so as to make the plates adhere anew. This screws and unscrews at will; it is a box. In this box, they conceal a watch spring, and this watch spring, well handled, cuts off rings of some size, and bars of iron. The unfortunate convict is supposed to possess only a sou; no, he possesses liberty. A big sou of this kind, on subsequent examination by the police, was found open and in two pieces in the room under the pallet near the window. There was also discovered a little saw of blue steel which could be concealed in the big sou. It is probable that when the bandits were searching the prisoner's pockets, he had this big sou upon him and succeeded in hiding it in his hand; and that afterward, having his right hand free, he unscrewed it and used the saw to cut the ropes by which he was fastened.

Being unable to stoop down for fear of betraying himself, he had not cut the cords on his left leg.

The prisoner now raised his voice:

"You are pitiable, but my life is not worth the trouble of so long a defense. As to your imagining that you could make me speak, that you could make me write what I do not wish to write, that you could make me say what I do not wish to say—"

He pulled up the sleeve of his left arm, and added:

"Here."

At the same time he extended his arm, and laid upon the naked flesh the glowing chisel, which he held in his right hand, by the wooden handle.

They heard the hissing of the burning flesh; the odor peculiar to chambers of torture spread through the den. Marius staggered, lost in horror; the brigands themselves felt a shudder; the face of the wonderful old man hardly contracted, and while the red iron was sinking into the smoking, impassable, and almost august wound, he turned upon Thénardier his fine face, in which there was no hatred, and in which suffering was swallowed up in a serene majesty.

With great and lofty natures the revolt of the flesh and the senses against the assaults of physical pain brings out the soul, and makes it appear on the countenance, in the same way as mutinies of the soldiery force the captain to show himself.

"Wretches," said he, "have no more fear for me than I have of you."

And drawing the chisel out of the wound, he threw it through the window, which was still open; the horrible glowing tool disappeared, whirling into the night, and fell in the distance, and was quenched in the snow.

The prisoner resumed:

"Do with me what you will."

He was disarmed.

"Lay hold of him," said Thénardier.

Two of the brigands laid their hands upon his shoulders, and the masked man with the ventriloquist's voice placed himself in front of him, ready to knock out his brains with a blow of the key, at the least motion.

At the same time Marius heard beneath him, at the foot of the partition, but so near that he could not see those who were talking, this colloquy, exchanged in a low voice:

"There is only one thing more to do."

"To kill him!"

"That is it."

It was the husband and wife who were holding counsel.

Thénardier walked with slow steps toward the table, opened the drawer, and took out the knife.

Marius was tormenting the trigger of his pistol.

Suddenly he started.

At his feet, on the table, a clear ray of the full moon illuminated, and seemed to point out to him, a sheet of paper. Upon that sheet he read this line, written in large letters that very morning, by the elder of the Thénardier girls:

"The Cognes are here."

An idea, a flash crossed Marius' mind; that was the means which he sought; the solution of this dreadful problem which was torturing him: to spare the assassin and to save the victim. He knelt down upon his bureau, reached out his arm, caught up the sheet of paper, quietly detached a bit of plaster from the partition, wrapped it in the paper, and threw the whole through the crevice into the middle of the den.

It was time. Thénardier had conquered his last fears, or his last scruples, and was moving toward the prisoner.

"Something fell!" cried the Thénardiess.

"What is it?" said the husband.

The woman had sprung forward, and picked up the piece of plaster wrapped in the paper. She handed it to her husband.

"How did this come in?" asked Thénardier.

"Egad!" said the woman. "How do you suppose it got in? It came through the window."

Thénardier hurriedly unfolded the paper, and held it up to the candle.

"It is Eponine's writing. The devil!"

He made a sign to his wife, who approached quickly, and he showed her the line written on the sheet of paper; then he added in a hollow voice:

"Quick! The ladder! Leave the meat in the trap, and clear the camp!"

"Without cutting the man's throat?" asked the Thénardiess.

"We have not the time."

The brigands, who were holding the prisoner, let go of him; in the twinkling of an eye, a rope ladder was unrolled out of the window, and firmly fixed to the casing by two iron hooks.

The prisoner paid no attention to what was passing about him. He seemed to be dreaming or praying.

As soon as the ladder was fixed, Thénardier cried:

"Come, bourgeoise!"

And he rushed toward the window.

"No," said one of the bandits, "let us draw lots who shall go out first."

Thénardier exclaimed:

"Are you fools? Are you cracked? You are a mess of *jobards!* Losing time, isn't it? Drawing lots, isn't it? With a wet finger! For the short straw! Write our names! Put them in a cap—!"

"Would you like my hat?" cried a voice from the door.

They all turned round. It was Javert.

He had his hat in his hand, and was holding it out smiling.

XIV

A SQUAD of *sergents de ville* with drawn swords, and officers armed with axes and clubs, rushed in at Javert's call. They bound the bandits. This crowd of men, dimly lighted by a candle, filled the den with shadow.

"Handcuffs on all!" cried Javert.

"Come on, then!" cried a voice which was not a man's voice, but of which nobody could have said: "It is the voice of a woman."

The Thénardiess had entrenched herself in one of the corners of the window, and it was she who had just uttered this roar.

The *sergents de ville* and officers fell back.

She had thrown off her shawl, but kept on her hat; her husband, crouched down behind her, was almost hidden beneath the fallen shawl, and she covered him with her body, holding a paving stone with both hands above her head with the poise of a giantess who is going to hurl a rock.

"Take care!" she cried.

They all crowded back toward the hall. A wide space was left in the middle of the garret.

The Thénardiess cast a glance at the bandits who had

allowed themselves to be tied, and muttered in a harsh and guttural tone:

"The cowards!"

Javert smiled, and advanced into the open space which the Thénardiess was watching with all her eyes.

"Don't come near! Get out," cried she, "or I will crush you!"

"What a grenadier!" said Javert. "Mother, you have a beard like a man, but I have claws like a woman."

And he continued to advance.

The Thénardiess, her hair flying wildly and terrible, braced her legs, bent backward, and threw the paving stone wildly at Javert's head. Javert stooped, the stone passed over him, hit the wall behind, from which it knocked down a large piece of the plastering, and returned, bounding from corner to corner across the room, luckily almost empty, finally stopping at Javert's heels.

At that moment Javert reached the Thénardier couple. One of his huge hands fell upon the shoulder of the woman, and the other upon her husband's head.

"The handcuffs!" cried he.

The police officers returned in a body, and in a few seconds Javert's order was executed.

The Thénardiess, completely crushed, looked at her manacled hands and those of her husband, dropped to the floor and exclaimed, with tears in her eyes:

"My daughters!"

"They are provided for," said Javert.

The six manacled bandits were standing; however, they still retained their spectral appearance, three blackened, three masked.

"Keep on your masks," said Javert.

And, passing them in review with the eye of a Frederic II at parade at Potsdam, he said to the three "chimney doctors":

"Good day, Bigrenaille. Good day, Brujon. Good day, Deux Milliards."

Then, turning toward the three masks, he said to the man of the poleax:

"Good day, Gueulemer."

And to the man of the cudgel:

"Good day, Babet."

And to the ventriloquist:

"Your health, Claquesous."

Just then he perceived the prisoner of the bandits, who, since the entrance of the police, had not uttered a word, and had held his head down.

"Untie monsieur!" said Javert. "And let nobody go out."

This said, he sat down with authority before the table, on which the candle and the writing materials still were, drew a stamped sheet from his pocket, and commenced his *procès-verbal*.

When he had written the first lines, a part of the formula which is always the same, he raised his eyes:

"Bring forward the gentleman whom these gentlemen had bound."

The officers looked about them.

"Well," asked Javert, "where is he now?"

The prisoner of the bandits, Monsieur Leblanc, Monsieur Urban Fabre, had disappeared.

The door was guarded, but the window was not. As soon as he saw that he was unbound, and while Javert was writing, he had taken advantage of the disturbance, the tumult, the confusion, the obscurity, and a moment when their attention was not fixed upon him, to leap out of the window.

An officer ran to the window, and looked out; nobody could be seen outside.

The rope ladder was still trembling.

"The Devil!" said Javert, between his teeth. "That must have been the best one."

XV

THE day following that in which these events took place in the house on the Boulevard de l'Hôpital, a child, who seemed to come from somewhere near the Bridge of Austerlitz, went up by the cross alley on the right in the direction of the Barrière de Fontainebleau. Night had closed in. This child was pale, thin, dressed in rags, with tow trousers in the month of February, and was singing with all his might.

At the corner of the rue du Petit Banquier, an old crone was fumbling in a manure heap by the light of a streetlamp; the child knocked against her as he passed, then drew back, exclaiming:

"Why! I took that for an enormous, enormous dog!"

He pronounced the word enormous the second time with a pompous and sneering voice which capitals would express very well: an enormous, ENORMOUS dog!

The old woman rose up furious.

"Jailbird!" muttered she. "If I had not been stooping over, I know where I would have planted my foot!"

The child was now at a little distance.

"K'sss! K'sss!" said he. "After all, perhaps I was not mistaken."

The old woman, choking with indignation, sprang up immediately, and the red glare of the lantern fully illuminated her livid face, all hollowed out with angles and wrinkles, with crows' feet at the corners of her mouth. Her body was lost in the shadow, and only her head could be seen. One would have said it was the mask of Decrepitude shrivelled by a flash in the night. The child looked at her.

"Madame," said he, "has not the style of beauty that suits me."

He went on his way and began to sing again:

> Le roi Coupdesabot
> S'en allait à la chasse,
> A la chasse aux corbeaux—

At the end of these three lines he stopped. He had reached No. 50-52, and finding the door locked, had begun to batter it with kicks, heroic and re-echoing kicks, that revealed rather the men's shoes which he wore, than the child's feet which he had.

Meantime, this same old woman, whom he had met with at the corner of the rue du Petit Banquier, was running after him with much clamor and many crazy gestures:

"What's the matter? What's the matter? Good God! They are staving the door down! They are breaking into the house!"

The kicks continued.

The old woman exhausted her lungs.

"Is that the way they use houses nowadays?"

Suddenly she stopped. She had recognized the gamin.

"What! It is that Satan!"

"Hullo, it is the old woman," said the child. "Good day, Burgonmuche. I have come to see my ancestors."

The old woman responded, with a composite grimace, an

admirable extemporization of hatred making the most of decay and ugliness, which was unfortunately lost in the obscurity:

"There is nobody there, nosy."

"Pshaw!" said the child. "Where is my father, then?"

"At La Force."

"And my mother?"

"At Saint Lazare."

"Well! And my sisters?"

"At Les Madelonnettes."

The child scratched the back of his ear, looked at Madame Burgon, and said:

"Ah!"

Then he turned on his heel, and a moment afterward, the old woman, who stopped on the doorstep, heard him sing with his clear, fresh voice, as he disappeared under the black elms shivering in the wintry winds:

> Le roi Coupdesabot
> S'en allait à la chasse,
> A la chasse aux corbeaux,
> Monte sur des échasses.
> Quand on passait dessous,
> On lui payait deux sous.

St. Denis

and the Idyl of the Rue Plumet

Eponine

I

MARIUS had seen the unexpected denouement of the ambuscade upon the track of which he had put Javert; but hardly had Javert left the old ruin, carrying away his prisoners in three coaches, when Marius also slipped out of the house. It was only nine o'clock in the evening. Marius went to Courfeyrac's. Courfeyrac was no longer the imperturbable inhabitant of the Latin Quarter; he had gone to live in the rue de la Verrerie "for political reasons"; this quarter was one of those in which the insurrection was fond of installing itself in those days. Marius said to Courfeyrac: "I have come to sleep with you." Courfeyrac drew a mattress from his bed, where there were two, laid it on the floor, and said: "There you are."

The next day, by seven o'clock in the morning, Marius went back to the tenement, paid his rent, and what was due to Madame Burgon, had his books, bed, table, bureau, and his two chairs loaded upon a handcart, and went off without leaving his address.

Javert thought that the young man, whose name he had not retained, had been frightened and had escaped, or, perhaps, had not even returned home at the time of the ambuscade; still he made some effort to find him, but he did not succeed.

Marius, moreover, was in sore affliction. Everything had relapsed into darkness. He no longer saw anything before him; his life was again plunged into that mystery in which he had been blindly groping. He had for a moment seen close at hand in that obscurity, the young girl whom he loved, the old man who seemed her father, these unknown beings who were his only interest and his only hope in this world; and at the moment he had thought to hold them fast, a breath had swept all those shadows away. Not a spark of certainty or truth had escaped even from that most fearful shock. No conjecture was possible. Bitter wretchedness; Marius had a passion in his heart, and night over his eyes. He was pushed, he was drawn, and he could not stir. All had vanished, except love. Even of love, he had lost the instincts and the sudden illuminations. His whole life was now resumed in two words: an absolute uncertainty in an impenetrable mist. To see her again, Her; he aspired to this continually; he hoped for it no longer.

To crown all, want returned. He felt close upon him, behind him, that icy breath. During all these torments, and now for a long time, he had discontinued his work, and nothing is more dangerous than discontinued labor; it is habit lost. A habit easy to abandon, difficult to resume.

Man, in the dreamy state, is naturally prodigal and luxurious; the relaxed mind cannot lead a severe life. There is, in this way of living, some good mingled with the evil, for if the softening be fatal, the generosity is wholesome and good. But the poor man who is generous and noble, and who does not work, is lost. His resources dry up, his necessities mount up.

Fatal slope, down which the firmest and the noblest are drawn, as well as the weakest and the most vicious, and which leads to one of these two pits, suicide or crime. Marius was descending this slope with slow steps, his eyes fixed upon her whom he saw no more.

A single sweet idea remained to him; that she had loved him, that her eyes had told him so, that she did not know his name but that she knew his soul, and that, perhaps, where she was, whatever that mysterious place might be, she loved him still. Who knows but she was dreaming of him as he was dreaming of her. Sometimes in the inexplicable hours, such as every heart has which loves, having reasons for sorrow only, yet feeling nevertheless a vague thrill of joy, he said to himself: "It is her thoughts which come to me!" Then he added: "My thoughts reach her also, perhaps!"

The days passed, however, one after another, and there was nothing new. It seemed to him, merely, that the dreary space which remained for him to run through was contracting with every instant. He thought that he already saw distinctly the brink of the bottomless precipice.

"What!" he repeated to himself. "Shall I never see her again?"

If you go up the rue Saint Jacques, leave the *barrière* at your side, and follow the old interior boulevard to the left for some distance, you come to the rue de la Santé, then La Glacière, and, a little before reaching the small stream of the Gobelins, you find a sort of field, which is, in the long and monotonous circuit of the boulevards of Paris, the only spot where Ruisdael would be tempted to sit down.

That indescribable something from which grace springs is there, a green meadow crossed by tight drawn ropes, on which rags are drying in the wind, an old market-garden farmhouse built in the time of Louis XIII, with its large roof grotesquely pierced with dormer windows; broken palisade fences, a small pond between the poplars, women, laughter, voices; in the horizon the Pantheon, the tree of the Deaf-mutes, the Val de Grâce, black, squat, fantastic, amusing, magnificent, and in the background the severe square summits of the towers of Notre Dame.

As the place is worth seeing, nobody goes there. Hardly a cart or a wagon once in a quarter of an hour.

It happened one day that Marius' solitary walks conducted him to this spot near this pond. That day there was a rarity on the boulevard, a passer. Marius, vaguely struck with the almost sylvan charm of the spot, asked this traveler: "What is the name of this place?"

The traveler answered: "It is the Field of the Lark."

And he added: "It was here that Ulbach killed the shepherdess of Ivry."

But after that word, Lark, Marius had heard nothing more. There are such sudden congelations in the dreamy state, which a word is sufficient to produce. The whole mind condenses abruptly about one idea, and ceases to be capable of any other perception.

"Yes," said he in the kind of unreasoning stupor peculiar to these mysterious asides, "this is her field. I shall learn here where she lives."

This was absurd, but irresistible.

And he came every day to this Field of the Lark.

II

Javert's triumph in the Gorbeau tenement had seemed complete, but it was not so.

In the first place, and this was his principal regret, Javert had not made the prisoner prisoner. The victim who slips away is more suspicious than the assassin; and it was probable that this personage, so precious a capture to the bandits, would be a not less valuable prize to the authorities.

And then, Montparnasse had escaped Javert.

He must await another occasion to lay his hand upon "that devilish dandy." Montparnasse, in fact, having met Eponine, who was standing sentry under the trees of the boulevard, had led her away. Well for him that he did so. He was free. As to Eponine, Javert "nabbed" her; trifling consolation. Eponine had rejoined Azelma at Les Madelonnettes.

Finally, on the trip from the Gorbeau tenement to La Force, one of the principal prisoners, Claquesous, had been lost. Nobody knew how it was done, the officers and sergeants "didn't understand it"; he had changed into vapor, he had got out of the handcuffs, he had slipped through the cracks of the carriage—the fiacre was leaky—and had fled; nothing could be said, save that on reaching the prison there was no Claquesous. There were either fairies or police in the matter. Had Claquesous melted away into the darkness like a snowflake in the water? Was there some secret connivance of the officers? Did this man belong to the double enigma of disorder and of order? There are such two-edged rascals. However it might be, Claquesous was lost, and was not found again. Javert appeared more irritated than astonished at it.

As to Marius, "that dolt of a lawyer," who was "probably frightened," and whose name Javert had forgotten, Javert cared little for him. Besides, he was a lawyer; they are always found again. But was he a lawyer merely?

The trial commenced.

III

Marius now visited nobody, but he sometimes happened to meet Father Mabeuf.

While Marius was slowly descending those dismal steps, which one might call cellar stairs, and which lead into places without light where we hear the happy walking above us, Monsieur Mabeuf also was descending.

The *Flora of Cauteretz* had absolutely no sale more. The experiments upon indigo had not succeeded in the little garden of Austerlitz, which was very much exposed. Monsieur Mabeuf could only cultivate a few rare plants which like moisture and shade. He was not discouraged, however. He had obtained a bit of ground in the Jardin des Plantes, with a good exposure, to carry on, "at his own cost," his experiments upon indigo. For this he had put the plates of his *Flora* into pawn. He had reduced his breakfast to two eggs, and he left one of them for his old servant, whose wages he had not paid for fifteen months. And often his breakfast was his only meal. He laughed no more with his childlike laugh, he had become morose, and he now received no visits. Marius was right in not thinking to come. Sometimes, at the hour when Monsieur Mabeuf went to the Jardin des Plantes, the old man and the young man met on the Boulevard de l'Hôpital. They did not speak, but sadly nodded their heads. It is a bitter thing that there should be a moment when misery unbinds! They had been two friends; they were two passers.

Monsieur Mabeuf now knew only his books, his garden, and his indigo; those were to him the three forms which happiness, pleasure, and hope had taken. This fed his life. He said to himself: "When I have made my blue balls, I shall be rich, I will take my plates out of pawn, I will bring my *Flora* into vogue through charlatanism, by big payments and by announcements in the journals, and I will buy, I well know where, a copy of Pierre de Médine's *Art de Naviguer*, with woodcuts, edition of 1559." In the meantime he worked all day on his indigo bed, and at night returned home to water his garden, and read his books. Monsieur Mabeuf was at this time very nearly eighty years old.

One night he saw a singular apparition.

He had come home while it was still broad day. Mother Plutarch, whose health was poor, was sick and gone to bed. He had dined on a bone on which a little meat was left, and a bit of bread which he had found on the kitchen table, and had sat down on a block of stone, which took the place of a seat in his garden.

Monsieur Mabeuf had begun to look through, reading by the way, with the help of his spectacles, two books which enchanted him, and in which he was even absorbed, a more serious thing at his age. His natural timidity fitted him, to a certain extent, to accept superstitions. The first of these books was the famous treatise of President Delancre, *On the in-*

constancy of Demons, the other was the quarto of Mutor de la Rubaudière, *On the devils of Vauvert and the goblins of La Bièvé.* This last book interested him the more, since his garden was one of the spots formerly haunted by goblins. Twilight was beginning to whiten all above and to blacken all below. As he read, Father Mabeuf was looking over the book which he held in his hand, at his plants, and among others at a magnificent rhododendron which was one of his consolations; there had been four days of drought, wind, and sun, without a drop of rain; the stalks bent over, the buds hung down, the leaves were falling, they all needed to be watered; the rhododendron especially was a sad sight. Father Mabeuf was one of those to whom plants have souls. The old man had worked all day on his indigo bed, he was exhausted with fatigue, he got up nevertheless, put his books upon the bench, and walked, bent over and with tottering steps, to the well, but when he had grasped the chain, he could not even draw it far enough to unhook it. Then he turned and looked with a look of anguish toward the sky which was filling with stars.

The evening had that serenity which buries the sorrows of man under a strangely dreary yet eternal joy. The night promised to be as dry as the day had been.

"Stars everywhere!" thought the old man. "Not the smallest cloud! Not a drop of water."

And his head, which had been raised for a moment, fell back upon his breast.

He raised it again and looked at the sky, murmuring:

"A drop of dew! A little pity!"

He endeavored once more to unhook the well chain, but he could not.

At this moment he heard a voice which said:

"Father Mabeuf, would you like to have me water your garden?"

At the same time he heard a sound like that of a passing deer in the hedge, and he saw springing out of the shrubbery a sort of tall, slender girl, who came and stood before him looking boldly at him. She had less the appearance of a human being than of a form which had just been born of the twilight.

Before Father Mabeuf, who was easily startled, and who was, as we have said, subject to fear, could answer a word, this being, whose motions seemed grotesquely abrupt in the obscurity, had unhooked the chain, plunged in and drawn out the bucket, and filled the watering pot, and the goodman saw this apparition with bare feet and a ragged skirt running along the beds, distributing life about her. The sound of the water upon the leaves filled Father Mabeuf's soul with transport. It seemed to him that now the rhododendron was happy.

When the first bucket was emptied, the girl drew a second, then a third. She watered the whole garden.

Moving thus along the walks, her outline appearing entirely black, shaking her torn shawl over her long angular arms, she seemed something like a bat.

When she had ended, Father Mabeuf approached her with tears in his eyes, and laid his hand upon her forehead.

"God will bless you," said he, "you are an angel, since you care for flowers."

"No," she answered, "I am the devil, but that is all the same to me."

The old man exclaimed, without waiting for and without hearing her answer:

"What a pity that I am so unfortunate and so poor, and that I cannot do anything for you!"

"You can do something," said she.

"What?"

"Tell me where Monsieur Marius lives."

The old man did not understand.

"What Monsieur Marius?"

He raised his glassy eye and appeared to be looking for something that had vanished.

"A young man who used to come here."

Meanwhile Monsieur Mabeuf had fumbled in his memory.

"Ah! Yes——" he exclaimed. "I know what you mean. Listen, now! Monsieur Marius—the Baron Marius Pontmercy, yes! He lives—or rather he does not live there now—ah! Well, I don't know."

While he spoke, he had bent over to tie up a branch of the rhododendron, and he continued:

"Ah! I remember now. He passes up the boulevard very often, and goes toward La Glacière, rue Croulebarbe. The Field of the Lark. Go that way. He isn't hard to find."

When Monsieur Mabeuf rose up, there was nobody there; the girl had disappeared.

He was decidedly a little frightened.

"Really," thought he, "if my garden was not watered, I should think it was a spirit."

An hour later when he had gone to bed, this returned to him, and, as he was falling asleep, at that troubled moment when thought, like that fabulous bird which changes itself into fish to pass through the sea, gradually takes the form of dream to pass through sleep, he said to himself confusedly:

"Indeed, this much resembles what Rubaudière relates of the goblins. Could it be a goblin?"

IV

ONE morning Marius had gone "to take a little walk," hoping that it would enable him to work on his return. It was eternally so. As soon as he rose in the morning, he sat down before a book and a sheet of paper to work upon some translation; he read four lines, tried to write one of them, could not, saw a star between his paper and his eyes, and rose from his chair, saying: "I will go out. That will put me in trim."

And he would go to the Field of the Lark.

That morning, he heard behind and below him, on both banks of the stream, the washerwomen of the Gobelins beating their linen; and over his head, the birds chattering and singing in the elms. On the one hand the sound of liberty, of happy unconcern, of winged leisure; on the other, the sound of labor. A thing which made him muse profoundly, and almost reflect, these two joyous sounds.

All at once, in the midst of his ecstasy of exhaustion, he heard a voice which was known to him say:

"Ah! There he is!"

He raised his eyes and recognized the unfortunate child who had come to his room one morning, the elder of the Thénardier girls, Eponine; he now knew her name. Singular fact, she had become more wretched and more beautiful, two steps which seemed impossible. She had accomplished a double progress toward the light, and toward distress. She was barefooted and in rags, as on the day when she had so resolutely entered his room, only her rags were two months older; the holes were larger, the tatters dirtier. It was the same rough voice, the same forehead tanned and wrinkled by exposure; the same free, wild, and wandering gaze. She had, in addition to her former expression, that mixture of fear and sorrow which the experience of a prison adds to misery.

And with all this, she was beautiful. What a star thou art, O youth!

Meantime, she had stopped before Marius, with an expression of pleasure upon her livid face, and something which resembled a smile.

She stood for a few seconds, as if she could not speak.

"I have found you, then?" said she at last. "Father Mabeuf was right; it was on this boulevard. How I have looked for you! If you only knew! Do you know? I have been in the jug. A fortnight! They have let me out! Seeing that there was nothing against me, and then I was not of the age of discernment. It lacked two months. Oh! How I have looked for you! It is six weeks now. You don't live down there any longer?"

"No," said Marius.

"Where do you live now?"

Marius did not answer.

"Ah!" she continued. "You have a hole in your shirt. I must mend it for you."

She resumed with an expression which gradually grew darker:

"You don't seem to be glad to see me?"

Marius said nothing; she herself was silent for a moment, then exclaimed:

"But if I would, I could easily make you glad!"

"How?" inquired Marius. "What does that mean?"

"Ah! You used to speak more kindly to me!" replied she.

"Well, what is it that you mean?"

She bit her lip; she seemed to hesitate, as if passing through a kind of interior struggle. At last, she appeared to decide upon her course.

"So much the worse, it makes no difference. You look sad, I want you to be glad. But promise me that you will laugh; I want to see you laugh and hear you say: 'Ah, well! That is good.' Poor Monsieur Marius! You know, you promised me that you would give me whatever I should ask—"

"Yes! But tell me!"

She looked into Marius' eyes and said:

"I have the address."

Marius turned pale. All his blood flowed back to his heart.

"What address?"

"The address you asked me for."

She added as if she were making an effort:

"The address—you know well enough!"

"Yes!" stammered Marius.

"Of the young lady!"

Having pronounced this word, she sighed deeply.

Marius sprang up from the bank on which he was sitting, and took her wildly by the hand.

"Oh! Come! Show me the way, tell me! Ask me for whatever you will! Where is it?"

"Come with me," she answered. "I am not sure of the street and the number; it is away on the other side from here, but I know the house very well. I will show you."

She withdrew her hand and added in a tone which would have pierced the heart of an observer, but which did not even touch the intoxicated and transported Marius:

"Oh! How glad you are!"

Marius' brow clouded over. He seized Eponine by the arm.

"Show me the way."

"Right away?"

"Right away."

"Come. Oh! How glad he is!" said she.

After a few steps, she stopped.

"By the way, you know you have promised me something?"

Marius fumbled in his pocket. He had nothing in the world but five francs. He took it, and put it into Eponine's hand.

She opened her fingers and let the piece fall on the ground, and, looking at him with a gloomy look:

"I don't want your money," said she.

The House in the
Rue Plumet

I

TOWARD the middle of the last century, a velvet-capped president of the Parlement of Paris having a mistress and concealing it, for in those days the great lords exhibited their mistresses and the bourgeois concealed theirs, had *une petite maison* built in the Faubourg Saint Germain, in the deserted rue de Blomet, now called the rue Plumet, not far from the spot which then went by the name of the Combat des Animaux.

This was a summerhouse of but two stories; two rooms on the ground floor, two chambers in the second story, a kitchen below, a boudoir above, a garret next the roof, the whole fronted by a garden with a large iron-grated gate opening on the street. This garden contained about an acre. This was all that the passers-by could see; but in the rear of the house there was a small yard, at the further end of which there was a low building, two rooms only and a cellar, a convenience intended to conceal a child and nurse in case of need. This building communicated, from the rear, by a masked door opening secretly, with a long narrow passage, paved, winding, open to the sky, bordered by two high walls, and which, concealed with wonderful art, and, as it were, lost between the enclosures of the gardens and fields, all the corners and turnings of which it followed, came to an end at another door, also concealed, which opened a third of a mile away, almost in another quarter, upon the unbuilt end of the rue de Babylone.

This house and this passage, which have since disappeared, were still in existence fifteen years ago. The house remained, furnished with its old furniture, and always for sale or to let, and the ten or twelve persons who passed through the rue Plumet in the course of a year were notified of this by a yellow and illegible piece of paper which had hung upon the railing of the garden since 1810.

Toward the end of the Restoration, these same passers might have noticed that the paper had disappeared, and that, also, the shutters of the upper story were open. The house was indeed occupied. The windows had "little curtains," a sign that there was a woman there.

In the month of October, 1829, a man of a certain age had appeared and hired the house as it stood, including, of course, the building in the rear, and the passage which ran out to the rue de Babylone. He had the secret openings of the two doors of this passage repaired. The new tenant had ordered a few repairs, and finally came and installed himself with a young girl and an aged servant, without any noise, rather like somebody stealing in than like a man who enters his own house. The neighbors did not gossip about it, for the reason that there were no neighbors.

This tenant, to partial extent, was Jean Valjean; the young girl was Cosette. The servant was a spinster named Toussaint, whom Jean Valjean had saved from the hospital and misery, and who was old, stuttering, and a native of a province, three qualities which had determined Jean Valjean to take her with him. He hired the house under the name of Monsieur Fauchelevent, gentleman. In what has been related hitherto, the reader doubtless recognized Jean Valjean even before Thénardier did.

Why had Jean Valjean left the Convent of the Petit Picpus? What had happened?

Nothing had happened.

As we remember, Jean Valjean was happy in the convent, so happy that his conscience at last began to be troubled. He saw Cosette every day, he felt paternity springing up and developing within him more and more, he brooded this child with his soul, he said to himself that she was his, that nothing could take her from him, that this would be so indefinitely, that certainly she would become a nun, being every day gently led on toward it. In reflecting upon this, he at last began to find difficulties. He questioned himself. He asked himself if all this happiness were really his own, if it were not made up of the happiness of another, of the happiness of this child whom he was appropriating and plundering, he, an old man: if this was not a robbery? He said to himself that this child had a right to know what life was before renouncing it; that to cut her off, in advance, and, in some sort, without consulting her, from all pleasure, under pretense of saving her from all trial, to take advantage of her ignorance and isolation to give her an artificial vocation, was to outrage a human creature and to lie to God. And who knows but, thinking over all this some day, and being a nun with regret, Cosette might come to hate him? A final thought, which was almost selfish and less heroic than the others, but which was insupportable to him. He resolved to leave the convent.

His determination once formed, he awaited an opportunity. It was not slow to present itself. Old Fauchelevent died.

Jean Valjean asked an audience of the reverend prioress, and told her that having received a small inheritance on the death of his brother, which enabled him to live henceforth without labor, he would leave the service of the convent, and take away his daughter; but that, as it was not just that Cosette, not taking her vows, should have been educated gratuitously, he humbly begged the reverend prioress to allow him to offer the community, as indemnity for the five years which Cosette had passed there, the sum of five thousand francs.

On leaving the convent, he took in his own hands, and would not entrust to any assistant, the little box, the key of which he always had about him. This box puzzled Cosette, on account of the odor of embalming which came from it.

Let us say at once, that henceforth this box never left him more. He always had it in his room. It was the first, and sometimes the only thing that he carried away in his changes of abode. Cosette laughed about it, and called this box the Inseparable, saying: "I am jealous of it."

Jean Valjean nevertheless did not appear again in the open city without deep anxiety.

He discovered the house in the rue Plumet, and buried himself in it. He was henceforth in possession of the name of Ultimus Fauchelevent.

At the same time he hired two other lodgings in Paris, very humble, and of a poor appearance, in two quarters widely distant from each other, one in the rue de l'Ouest, the other in the rue de l'Homme Armé.

He went from time to time, now to the rue de l'Homme Armé, and now to the rue de l'Ouest, to spend a month or six weeks, with Cosette, without taking Toussaint. He was waited upon by the porters, and gave himself out for a man of some means of the suburbs, having a foothold in the city. This lofty virtue had three domiciles in Paris in order to escape from the police.

Still, properly speaking, he lived in the rue Plumet, and he had ordered his life there in the following manner:

Cosette with the servant occupied the house; she had the large bedroom with painted piers, the boudoir with gilded moldings, the president's parlor furnished with tapestry and huge armchairs; she had the garden. All winter Cosette's Petite Maison was warmed from top to bottom. For his part, he lived in the sort of porter's lodge in the back yard, with a mattress on a cot bedstead, a white wood table, two straw chairs, an earthen water pitcher, a few books upon a board, his dear box in a corner, never any fire. He dined with Cosette, and there was a black loaf on the table for him.

Cosette had been trained to housekeeping in the convent, and she regulated the expenses, which were very moderate. Every day Jean Valjean took Cosette's arm, and went to walk with her. They went to the least frequented walk of the Luxembourg, and every Sunday to mass, always at Saint Jacques du Haut Pas, because it was quite distant. As that is a very poor quarter, he gave much alms there, and the unfortunate surrounded him in the church. He was fond of taking Cosette to visit the needy and the sick. No stranger came into the house in the rue Plumet. Toussaint brought the provisions, and Jean Valjean himself went after the water to a watering trough which was nearby on the boulevard.

Monsieur Fauchelevent belonged to the National Guard; he had not been able to escape the close meshes of the enrollment of 1831. The municipal investigation made at that time had extended even to the Convent of the Petit Picpus, a sort of impenetrable and holy cloud from which Jean Valjean had come forth venerable in the eyes of his magistracy and, in consequence, worthy of mounting guard.

Three or four times a year, Jean Valjean donned his uniform, and performed his duties; very willingly moreover; it was a good disguise for him, which associated him with everybody else while leaving him solitary. To resemble the crowd who pay their taxes, this was his whole ambition. This man had for his ideal within, the angel—without, the bourgeois.

Neither Jean Valjean, nor Cosette, nor Toussaint, ever came

in or went out except by the gate on the rue de Babylone.
Unless one had seen them through the grated gate of the
garden, it would have been difficult to guess that they lived
in the rue Plumet. This gate always remained closed. Jean
Valjean had left the garden uncultivated, that it might not
attract attention.

II

COSETTE had left the convent, still almost a child; she was a
little more than fourteen years old, and she was "at the ungrateful age"; as we have said, apart from her eyes, she
seemed rather homely than pretty; she had, however, no
ungraceful features, but she was awkward, thin, timid, and
bold at the same time; a big child in short.

Nothing prepares a young girl for passions like the convent.
The convent turns the thoughts in the direction of the unknown. The heart, thrown back upon itself, makes for itself a
channel, being unable to overflow, and deepens, being unable
to expand.

On leaving the convent, Cosette could have found nothing
more grateful and more dangerous than the house on the rue
Plumet. It was the continuation of solitude with the beginning
of liberty; an enclosed garden, but a sharp, rich, voluptuous,
and odorous nature; the same dreams as in the convent, but
with glimpses of young men; a grating, but upon the street.

Still, we repeat, when she came there she was but a child.
She loved her father, that is to say, Jean Valjean, with all
her heart, with a frank filial passion which made the good
man a welcome and very pleasant companion for her. This
simple man was sufficient for Cosette's thought, even as this
wild garden was to her eyes. When she had had a good chase
after the butterflies, she would come up to him breathless
and say: "Oh! How I have run!" He would kiss her forehead.

Cosette had but vague remembrance of her childhood. She
prayed morning and evening for her mother, whom she had
never known. The Thénardiers had remained to her like two
hideous faces of some dream. She remembered that she had
been "one day, at night," sent into a wood after water. She

thought that that was very far from Paris. It seemed to her that she had commenced life in an abyss, and that Jean Valjean had drawn her out of it. Her childhood impressed her as a time when there were only centipedes, spiders, and snakes about her. When she was dozing at night, before going to sleep, as she had no very clear idea of being Jean Valjean's daughter, and that he was her father, she imagined that her mother's soul had passed into this goodman and come to live with her.

While Cosette was a little girl, Jean Valjean had been fond of talking with her about her mother; when she was a young maiden, this was impossible for him. It seemed to him that he no longer dared. Was this on account of Cosette? Was it on account of Fantine? He felt a sort of religious horror at introducing that shade into Cosette's thoughts, and at bringing in the dead as a third sharer of their destiny. The more sacred that shade was to him, the more formidable it seemed to him. He thought of Fantine and felt overwhelmed with silence. He saw dimly in the darkness something which resembled a finger on a mouth. Had all that modesty which had once been Fantine's and which, during her life, had been forced out of her by violence, returned after her death to take its place over her, to watch, indignant, over the peace of the dead woman, and to guard her fiercely in her tomb? Did Jean Valjean, without knowing it, feel its influence? We who believe in death are not of those who would reject this mysterious explanation. Hence the impossibility of pronouncing, even at Cosette's desire, this name: Fantine.

One day Cosette said to him:

"Father, I saw my mother in a dream last night. She had two great wings. My mother must have attained to sanctity in her life."

"Through martyrdom," answered Jean Valjean.

Still, Jean Valjean was happy.

When Cosette went out with him, she leaned upon his arm, proud, happy, in the fullness of her heart. Jean Valjean, at all these marks of a tenderness so exclusive and so fully satisfied with him alone, felt his thought melt into delight. The poor man shuddered, overflowed with an angelic joy; he declared in his transport that this would last through life; he said to himself that he really had not suffered enough to deserve such radiant happiness, and he thanked God, in the depths of his soul, for having permitted that he, a miserable man, should be so loved by this innocent being.

III

ONE day Cosette happened to look in her mirror, and she said to herself: "What!" It seemed to her almost that she was pretty. This threw her into strange anxiety. Up to this moment she had never thought of her face. She had seen herself in her glass, but she had not looked at herself. And then, she had often been told that she was homely; Jean Valjean alone would quietly say: "Why no! Why no!" However that might be, Cosette had always thought herself homely, and had grown up in that idea with the pliant resignation of childhood. And now suddenly her mirror said like Jean Valjean: "Why no!" She had no sleep that night. "If I were pretty!" thought she. "How funny it would be if I should be pretty!" And she called to mind those of her companions whose beauty had made an impression in the convent, and said: "What! I should be like Mademoiselle Such-a-one!"

She was in the garden one day, and heard poor old Toussaint saying: "Monsieur, do you notice how pretty mademoiselle is growing?" Cosette did not hear what her father answered. Toussaint's words threw her into a sort of commotion. She ran out of the garden, went up to her room, hurried to the glass—it was three months since she had looked at herself—and uttered a cry. She was dazzled by herself.

She was beautiful and handsome; she could not help being of Toussaint's and her mirror's opinion. Her form was complete, her skin had become white, her hair had grown lustrous, an unknown splendor was lighted up in her blue eyes. The consciousness of her beauty came to her entire, in a moment, like broad daylight when it bursts upon us; she went down into the garden again, thinking herself a queen, hearing the birds sing—it was in winter—seeing the sky golden, the sunshine in the trees, flowers among the shrubbery, wild, mad, in an inexpressible rapture.

For his part, Jean Valjean felt a deep and undefinable anguish in his heart.

He had in fact, for some time past, been contemplating

with terror that beauty which appeared every day more radiant upon Cosette's sweet face. A dawn, charming to all others, dreary to him.

He said to himself: "How beautiful she is! What will become of me?"

From the morrow of the day on which she had said: "Really, I am handsome!" Cosette gave attention to her dress.

In less than a month little Cosette was, in that Thebaid of the rue de Babylone, not only one of the prettiest women, which is something, but one of "the best dressed" in Paris, which is much more.

The first day that Cosette went out with her dress and mantle of black damask and her white crepe hat she came to take Jean Valjean's arm, gay, radiant, rosy, proud, and brilliant. "Father," said she, "how do you like this?" Jean Valjean answered in a voice which resembled the bitter voice of envy: "Charming!"

From that day, he noticed that Cosette, who previously was always asking to stay in, saying: "Father, I enjoy myself better here with you," was now always asking to go out. Indeed, what is the use of having a pretty face and a delightful dress, if you do not show them?

Cosette, by learning that she was beautiful, lost the grace of not knowing it; an exquisite grace, for beauty heightened by artlessness is ineffable, and nothing is so adorable as dazzling innocence, going on her way, and holding in her hand, all unconscious, the key of a paradise. But what she lost in ingenuous grace, she gained in pensive and serious charm. Her whole person, pervaded by the joys of youth, innocence, and beauty, breathed a splendid melancholy.

It was at this period that Marius, after the lapse of six months, saw her again at the Luxembourg.

IV

Cosette, in her seclusion, like Marius in his, was all ready to take fire. Destiny, with its mysterious and fatal patience, was slowly bringing these two beings near each other, fully charged and all languishing with the stormy electricities of passion—these two souls which held love as two clouds hold lightning, and which were to meet and mingle in a glance like clouds in a flash.

The power of a glance has been so much abused in love stories, that it has come to be disbelieved in. Few people dare now to say that two beings have fallen in love because they have looked at each other. Yet it is in this way that love begins, and in this way only. The rest is only the rest, and comes afterward. Nothing is more real than these great shocks which two souls give each other in exchanging this spark.

At that particular moment when Cosette unconsciously looked with this glance which so affected Marius, Marius had no suspicion that he also had a glance which affected Cosette. She received from him the same harm and the same blessing.

We remember Marius' hesitations, his palpitations, his terrors. He remained at his seat and did not approach, which vexed Cosette. One day she said to Jean Valjean: "Father, let us walk a little this way." Seeing that Marius was not coming to her, she went to him.

That day Cosette's glance made Marius mad, Marius' glance made Cosette tremble. Marius went away confident, and Cosette anxious. From that day onward, they adored each other.

The first thing that Cosette felt was a vague yet deep sadness. It seemed to her that since yesterday her soul had become black. She no longer recognized herself. The whiteness of soul of young girls, which is composed of coldness and gaiety, is like snow. It melts before love, which is its sun.

It proved that the love which presented itself was precisely that which best suited the condition of her soul. It was a sort of far-off worship, a mute contemplation, a deification by an unknown votary. It was the apprehension of adolescence by adolescence, the dream of her nights become a romance and remaining a dream, the wished-for phantom realized at last, and made flesh, but still having neither name, nor wrong, nor stain, nor need, nor defect; in a word, a lover distant and dwelling in the ideal, a chimera having a form. Any closer and more palpable encounter would at this first period have terrified Cosette, still half buried in the magnifying mirage of the cloister. She had all the terrors of children and all the terrors of nuns commingled. The spirit of the convent, with which she had been imbued for five years, was still slowly evaporating from her whole person, and made everything tremulous about her. In this condition, it was not a lover that she needed, it was not even an admirer, it was a vision. She began to adore Marius as something charming, luminous, and impossible.

As extreme artlessness meets extreme coquetry, she smiled upon him, very frankly.

Marius and Cosette were in the dark in regard to each other. They did not speak, they did not bow, they were not acquainted; they saw each other, and, like the stars in the sky separated by millions of leagues, they lived by gazing upon each other.

Thus it was that Cosette gradually became a woman, and beautiful and loving, grew with consciousness of her beauty, and in ignorance of her love. Coquettish withal, through innocence.

V

EVERY condition has its instinct. The old and eternal mother, Nature, silently warned Jean Valjean of the presence of Marius. Jean Valjean shuddered in the darkest of his mind. Jean Valjean saw nothing, knew nothing, but still gazed with persistent fixedness at the darkness which surrounded him, as if he perceived on one side something which was building, and on the other something which was falling down. Marius, also warned, and, according to the deep law of God, by this same mother, Nature, did all that he could to hide himself from the "father." It happened, however, that Jean Valjean sometimes perceived him. Marius' ways were no longer at all natural. He had an equivocal prudence and an awkward boldness. Jean Valjean cordially detested this young man.

He had never opened his mouth to Cosette about the unknown man. One day, however, he could not contain himself, and with that uncertain despair which hastily drops the plummet into its unhappiness, he said to her: "What a pedantic air that young man has!"

Cosette, a year before, an unconcerned little girl, would have answered: "Why no, he is charming." Ten years later, with the love of Marius in her heart, she would have answered: "Pedantic and insupportable to the sight! You are quite right!" At the period of life and of heart in which she then was, she merely answered with supreme calmness: "That young man!"

As if she saw him for the first time in her life.

"How stupid I am!" thought Jean Valjean. "She had not even noticed him. I have shown him to her myself."

O simplicity of the old! Depth of the young!

There was nevertheless a painful tremor in the heart. The moment when Cosette would fall in love might come at any instant. Does not everything begin by indifference?

Jean Valjean had not discontinued the promenades in the Luxembourg, not wishing to do anything singular, and above all dreading to excite any suspicion in Cosette; but during those hours so sweet to the two lovers, while Cosette was sending her smile to the intoxicated Marius, who perceived nothing but that, and now saw nothing in the world save one radiant, adored face, Jean Valjean fixed upon Marius glaring and terrible eyes. He who had come to believe that he was no longer capable of a malevolent feeling had moments in which, when Marius was there, he thought that he was again becoming savage and ferocious, and felt opening and upheaving against this young man those old depths of his soul where there had once been so much wrath. It seemed to him almost as if the unknown craters were forming within him again.

We know the rest. The insanity of Marius continued. One day he followed Cosette to the rue de l'Ouest. A week after, Jean Valjean had moved. He resolved that he would never set his foot again either in the Luxembourg, or in the rue de l'Ouest. He returned to the rue Plumet.

Cosette did not complain, she said nothing, she asked no questions, she did not seek to know any reason; she was already at that point at which one fears discovery and self-betrayal. Jean Valjean had no experience of this misery, the only misery which is charming, and the only misery which he did not know; for this reason, he did not understand the deep significance of Cosette's silence. He noticed only that she had become sad, and he became gloomy.

Sometimes he asked her:

"What is the matter with you?"

She answered:

"Nothing."

And after a silence, as she felt that he was sad also, she continued:

"And you, father, is not something the matter with you?"

"Me? Nothing," said he.

These two beings, who had loved each other so exclusively, and with so touching a love, and who had lived so long for each other, were now suffering by each other, and through each other; without speaking of it, without harsh feeling, and smiling the while.

The End of Which Is
Unlike the Beginning

I

COSETTE's grief, so poignant still, and so acute four or five months before, had, without her knowledge even, entered upon convalescence. Nature, spring, her youth, her love for her father, the gaiety of the birds and the flowers, were filtering little by little, day by day, drop by drop, into this soul so pure and so young, something which almost resembled oblivion. Was the fire dying out entirely, or was it merely becoming a bed of embers? The truth is, that she had scarcely anything left of that sorrowful and consuming feeling.

One day she suddenly thought of Marius: "What!" said she. "I do not think of him now."

This was the very time when Marius was descending gloomily toward agony, and saying: "If I could only see her again before I die!"

Whose fault was it? Nobody's.

Marius was of that temperament which sinks into grief, and remains there; Cosette was of that which plunges in, and comes out again.

A singular incident followed.

In the garden, near the grated gate, on the street, there was a stone seat protected from the gaze of the curious by a hedge, but which, nevertheless, by an effort, the arm of a passer could reach through the grating and the hedge.

One evening in this same month of April, Jean Valjean had

gone out; Cosette, after sunset, had sat down on this seat. The wind was freshening in the trees, Cosette was musing; a vague sadness was coming over her little by little, that invincible sadness which evening gives and which comes perhaps—who knows?—from the mystery of the tomb half-opened at that hour.

Fantine was perhaps in that shadow.

Cosette rose, slowly made the round of the garden, walking in the grass which was wet with dew, and saying to herself through the kind of melancholy somnambulism in which she was envoloped: "One really needs wooden shoes for the garden at this hour. I shall catch cold."

She returned to the seat.

Just as she was sitting down, she noticed in the place she had left a stone of considerable size which evidently was not there the moment before.

Cosette reflected upon this stone, asking herself what it meant. Suddenly, the idea that this stone did not come upon the seat of itself, that somebody had put it there, that an arm had passed through that grating, this idea came to her and made her afraid. There was the stone; no doubt was possible. She did not touch it, fled without daring to look behind her, took refuge in the house, and immediately shut the glass door of the stairs with shutter, bar, and bolt. She asked Toussaint:

"Has my father come in?"

"Not yet, mademoiselle."

Cosette had all the doors and windows carefully closed, made Toussaint go over the whole house from cellar to garret, shut herself up in her room, drew her bolts, looked under her bed, lay down, and slept badly. All night she saw the stone big as a mountain and full of caves.

At sunrise—the peculiarity of sunrise is to make us laugh at all our terrors of the night, and our laugh is always proportioned to the fear we have had—at sunrise Cosette, on waking, looked upon her fright as upon a nightmare, and said to herself: "What have I been dreaming about?"

The sun, which shone through the cracks of her shutters, and made the damask curtains purple, reassured her to such an extent that it all vanished from her thoughts, even the stone.

She dressed herself, went down to the garden, ran to the bench, and felt a cold sweat. The stone was there.

But this was only for a moment. What is fright by night is curiosity by day.

"Pshaw!" said she. "Now let us see."

She raised the stone, which was pretty large. There was something underneath which resembled a letter.

It was a white paper envelope. Cosette seized it; there was no address on the one side, no wafer on the other. Still the envelope, although open, was not empty. Papers could be seen in it.

Cosette examined it. There was no more fright, there was curiosity no more; there was a beginning of anxious interest.

Cosette took out of the envelope what it contained, a quire of paper, each page of which was numbered and contained a few lines written in a rather pretty handwriting, thought Cosette, and very fine.

Cosette looked for a name, there was none; a signature, there was none. To whom was it addressed? To her probably, since a hand had placed the packet upon her seat. From whom did it come? An irresistible fascination took possession of her, she endeavored to turn her eyes away from these leaves which trembled in her hand; she looked at the sky, the street, the acacias all steeped in light, some pigeons which were flying about a neighboring roof; then all at once her eye eagerly sought the manuscript, and she said to herself that she must know what there was in it.

This is what she read:

II

THE reduction of the universe to a single being, the expansion of a single being even to God, this is love.

———

God is behind all things, but all things hide God. Things are black, creatures are opaque. To love a being is to render her transparent.

———

Love partakes of the soul itself. It is of the same nature. Like it, it is a divine spark; like it, it is incorruptible, indivisible, imperishable. It is a point of fire which is within us, which is immortal and infinite, which nothing can limit and which nothing can extinguish. We feel it burn even in the marrow of our bones, and we see it radiate even to the depths of the sky.

O love! Adorations! Light of two minds which comprehend each other, of two hearts which are interchanged, of two glances which interpenetrate! You will come to me, will you not, happiness? Walks together in the solitudes! Days blessed and radiant! I have sometimes dreamed that from time to time hours detached themselves from the life of the angels and came here below to pass through the destiny of men.

God can add nothing to the happiness of those who love one another but to give them unending duration. After a life of love, an eternity of love is an augmentation indeed; but to increase in its intensity the ineffable felicity which love gives to the soul in this world is impossible, even with God. God is the plenitude of heaven; love is the plenitude of man.

You look at a star from two motives: because it is luminous and because it is impenetrable. You have at your side a softer radiance and a greater mystery: woman.

If you are stone, be loadstone; if you are plant, be sensitive; if you are man, be love.

"Does she still come to the Luxembourg?" "No, monsieur." "She hears mass in this church, does she not?" "She comes here no more." "Does she still live in this house?" "She has moved away!" "Whither has she gone to live?" "She did not say!"

What a gloomy thing, not to know the address of one's soul!

You who suffer because you love, love still more. To die of love is to live by it.

What a grand thing, to be loved! What a grander thing still, to love! The heart becomes heroic through passion. It is no longer composed of anything but what is pure; it no longer rests upon anything but what is elevated and great. An unworthy thought can no more spring up in it than a nettle upon a glacier. The soul, lofty and serene, inaccessible to common passions and common emotions, rising above the clouds and the shadows of this world, its follies, its falsehoods, its hates, its vanities, its miseries, inhabits the blue of the skies, and only feels more the deep and subterranean commotions of destiny, as the summit of the mountains feels the quaking of the earth.

———

Were there not someone who loved, the sun would be extinguished.

III

DURING the reading, Cosette entered gradually into reverie. This manuscript, in which she found still more clearness than obscurity, had the effect upon her of a half-opened sanctuary. Each of these mysterious lines was resplendent to her eyes, and flooded her heart with a strange light. The education which she had received had always spoken to her of the soul and never of love, almost like one who should speak of the brand and not of the flame. This manuscript revealed to her suddenly and sweetly the whole of love, the sorrow, the destiny, the life, the eternity, the beginning, the end. It was like a hand which had opened and thrown suddenly upon her a handful of sunbeams. She felt in these few lines a passionate, ardent, generous, honest nature, a consecrated will, an immense sorrow and a boundless hope, an oppressed heart, a glad ecstasy.

Now these pages, from whom could they come? Who could have written them?

Cosette did not hesitate for a moment. One single man.

He!

Day had revived in her mind; all had appeared again. She felt a wonderful joy and deep anguish. It was he! He who wrote to her! He who was there! He whose arm had passed through that grating! While she was forgetting him, he had found her again! But had she forgotten him? No, never! She was mad to have thought so for a moment. She had always loved him, always adored him. The fire had been covered and had smoldered for a time, but she clearly saw it had only sunk in the deeper, and now it burst out anew and fired her whole being. This letter was like a spark dropped from that other soul into hers. She felt the conflagration rekindling. She was penetrated by every word of the manuscript: "Oh, yes!" said she. "How I recognize all this! This is what I had already read in his eyes."

She went back to the house and shut herself up in her room to read over the manuscript again, to learn it by heart, and to muse. When she had read it well, she kissed it, and put it in her bosom.

It was done. Cosette had fallen back into the profound seraphic love. The abyss of Eden had reopened.

All that day Cosette was in a sort of stupefaction. She could hardly think, her ideas were like a tangled skein in her brain. She could really conjecture nothing, she hoped while yet trembling, what? Vague things. She dared to promise herself nothing, and she would refuse herself nothing. Pallors passed over her face and chills over her body. It seemed to her at moments that she was entering the chimerical; she said to herself: "Is it real?" Then she felt of the beloved paper under her dress, she pressed it against her heart, she felt its corners upon her flesh, and if Jean Valjean had seen her at that moment, he would have shuddered before that luminous and unknown joy which flashed from her eyes. "Oh, yes!" thought she. "It is indeed he! This comes from him for me!"

And she said to herself that an intervention of angels, that a celestial chance, had restored him to her.

IV

WHEN evening came, Jean Valjean went out; Cosette dressed herself. She arranged her hair in the manner which best became her, and she put on a dress the neck of which, as it had received one cut of the scissors too much, and as, by this slope, it allowed the turn of the neck to be seen, was, as young girls say, "a little immodest." It was not the least in the world immodest, but it was prettier than otherwise. She did all this without knowing why.

Did she intend to go out? No.

Did she expect a visit? No.

At dusk, she went down to the garden. Toussaint was busy in her kitchen, which looked out upon the back yard.

She began to walk under the branches, putting them aside with her hand from time to time, because there were some that were very low.

She thus reached the seat.

The stone was still there.

She sat down, and laid her soft white hand upon that stone as if she would caress it and thank it.

All at once, she had that indefinable impression which we feel, though we see nothing, when there is somebody standing behind us.

She turned her head and arose.

It was he.

He was bareheaded. He appeared pale and thin. She hardly discerned his black dress. The twilight dimmed his fine forehead, and covered his eyes with darkness. He had, under a veil of incomparable sweetness, something of death and of night. His face was lighted by the light of a dying day, and by the thought of a departing soul.

It seemed as if he was not yet a phantom, and was now no longer a man.

His hat was lying a few steps distant in the shrubbery.

Cosette, ready to faint, did not utter a cry. She drew back slowly, for she felt herself attracted forward. He did not stir. Through the sad and ineffable something which enwrapped him, she felt the look of his eyes, which she did not see.

Cosette, in retreating, encountered a tree, and leaned against it. But for this tree, she would have fallen.

Then she heard his voice, that voice which she had never really heard, hardly rising above the rustling of the leaves, and murmuring:

"Pardon me, I am here. My heart is bursting, I could not live as I was, I have come. Have you read what I placed there on this seat? Do you recognize me at all? Do not be afraid of me. It is a long time now. Do you remember the day when you looked upon me? It was at the Luxembourg, near the Gladiator. And the day when you passed before me? It was the 16th of June and the 2nd of July. It will soon be a year. For a very long time now, I have not seen you at all. At night I come here. Do not be afraid; nobody sees me. I come for a near look at your windows. I walk very softly that you may not hear, for perhaps you would be afraid. Once I heard you sing. I was happy. Does it disturb you that I should hear you sing through the shutter? It can do you no harm. It cannot, can it? See, you are my angel, let me come sometimes; I believe I am going to die. If you but knew! I adore you! Pardon me, I am talking to you, I do not know what I am saying to you, perhaps I annoy you; do I annoy you?"

"O mother!" said she.

And she sank down upon herself as if she were dying.

He caught her, she fell, he caught her in his arms, he grasped her tightly, unconscious of what he was doing. He supported her even while tottering himself. He felt as if his head were enveloped in smoke; flashes of light passed through his eyelids; his ideas vanished; it seemed to him that he was performing a religious act, and that he was committing a profanation. Moreover, he did not feel one passionate emotion for this ravishing woman, whose form he felt against his heart. He was lost in love.

She took his hand and laid it on her heart. He felt the paper there, and stammered:

"You love me, then?"

She answered in a voice so low that it was no more than a breath which could scarcely be heard:

"Hush! You know it!"

And she hid her blushing head in the bosom of the proud and intoxicated young man.

He fell upon the seat, she by his side. There were no more words. The stars were beginning to shine. How was it that their lips met? How is it that the birds sing, that the snow melts, that the rose opens, that May blooms, that the dawn whitens behind the black trees on the shivering summit of the hills?

One kiss, and that was all.

Both trembled, and they looked at each other in the darkness with brilliant eyes.

They felt neither the fresh night, nor the cold stone, nor the damp ground, nor the wet grass, they looked at each other, and their hearts were full of thought. They had clasped hands, without knowing it.

She did not ask him, she did not even think of it, in what way and by what means he had succeeded in penetrating into the garden. It seemed so natural to her that he should be there.

From time to time Marius' knee touched Cosette's knee, which gave them both a thrill.

At intervals, Cosette faltered out a word. Her soul trembled upon her lips like a drop of dew upon a flower.

Gradually they began to talk. Overflow succeeded to silence, which is fullness. The night was serene and splendid above their heads. These two beings, pure as spirits, told each other all their dreams, their frenzies, their ecstasies, their chimeras, their despondencies, how they had adored each other from afar, how they had longed for each other, their despair when they had ceased to see each other. They confided to each other in an intimacy of the ideal, which even now nothing could have increased, all that was most hidden and most mysterious of themselves. These two hearts poured themselves out into each other, so that at the end of an hour it was the young man who had the young girl's soul and the young girl who had the soul of the young man. They interpenetrated, they enchanted, they dazzled each other.

When they had finished, when they had told each other everything, she laid her head upon his shoulder, and asked him:

"What is your name?"

"My name is Marius," said he. "And yours?"

"My name is Cosette."

The Escape

At La Force, an escape had been concerted between Babet, Brujon, Gueulemer, and Thénardier, although Thénardier was in solitary. Babet had done the business for himself during the day: having been transferred to the Conciergerie, he had escaped by turning to the left instead of turning to the right in the vestibule of the Examination hall. Montparnasse was to help them from without.

Brujon, having spent a month in a chamber of punishment, had had time, first, to twist a rope, secondly, to perfect a plan. As he was reputed very dangerous in the Charlemagne Court, he was put into the Bâtiment Neuf. The first thing which he found in the Bâtiment Neuf was Gueulemer; the second was a nail. Gueulemer, that is to say crime; a nail, that is to say liberty.

What rendered the moment peculiarly favorable for an attempt at escape was that some workmen were taking off and re-laying, at that very time, a part of the slating of the prison. The Cour Saint Bernard was not entirely isolated from the Charlemagne Court and the Cour Saint Louis. There were scaffoldings and ladders up aloft; in other words, bridges and stairways leading toward deliverance.

The Bâtiment Neuf contained four dormitories, one above the other, and an attic which was called the Bel Air. A large chimney, probably of some ancient kitchen of the Dukes de La Force, started from the ground floor, passed through the four stories, cutting in two all the dormitories, in which it appeared to be a kind of flattened pillar, and went out through the roof.

Gueulemer and Brujon were in the same dormitory. They had been put into the lower story by precaution. It happened that the heads of their beds rested against the flue of the chimney.

Thénardier was exactly above them in the attic known as the Bel Air.

Nobody has ever discovered how, or by what contrivance, he had succeeded in procuring and hiding a bottle of that wine invented, it is said, by Desrues, with which a narcotic is mixed, and which the band of the *Endormeurs* has rendered celebrated.

There are in many prisons treacherous employees, half jailers and half thieves, who aid in escapes, who sell a faithless service to the police, and who make much more than their salary.

Brujon and Gueulemer, knowing that Babet, who had escaped that very morning, as well as Montparnasse, was waiting for them in the street, got up softly and began to pierce the flue of the chimney which touched their beds, with the nail which Brujon had found. The fragments fell upon Brujon's bed, so that nobody heard them. A hailstorm and thunder shook the doors upon their hinges, and made a frightful and convenient uproar in the prison. Those of the prisoners who awoke made a feint of going to sleep again, and let Gueulemer and Brujon alone. Brujon was adroit; Gueulemer was vigorous. Before any sound had reached the watchman who was lying in the grated cell with a window opening into the sleeping room, the wall was pierced, the chimney scaled, the iron trellis which closed the upper orifice of the flue forced, and the two formidable bandits were upon the roof. The rain and the wind redoubled, the roof was slippery.

"What a good *sorgue* for a *crampe*,"[1] said Brujon.

A gulf of six feet wide and eighty feet deep separated them from the encircling wall. At the bottom of this gulf they saw a sentinel's musket gleaming in the obscurity. They fastened one end of the rope which Brujon had woven in his cell to the stumps of the bars of the chimney which they had just twisted off, threw the other end over the encircling wall, cleared the gulf at a bound, clung to the coping of the wall, bestrode it, let themselves glide one after the other down along the rope to a little roof which adjoined the bathhouse, pulled down their rope, leaped into the bathhouse yard, crossed it, pushed open the porter's slide, near which hung the cord, pulled the cord, opened the porte-cochère, and were in the street.

It was not three-quarters of an hour since they had risen to their feet on their beds in the darkness, their nail in hand, their project in their heads.

A few moments afterward they had rejoined Babet and Montparnasse, who were prowling about the neighborhood.

In drawing down their rope, they had broken it, and there was a piece remaining fastened to the chimney on the roof. They had received no other damage than having pretty thoroughly skinned their hands.

That night Thénardier had received a warning—it never could be ascertained in what manner—and did not go to sleep.

About one o'clock in the morning, the night being very dark, he saw two shadows passing on the roof, in the rain and in the raging wind, before the window opposite his cage. One stopped at the window long enough for a look. It was Brujon. Thénardier recognized him, and understood. That was enough for him. Thénardier, described as an assassin, and detained under the charge of lying in wait by night with force and arms, was kept constantly in sight. A sentinel, who was relieved every two hours, marched with loaded gun before his cage. The Bel Air was lighted by a reflector. The

---

[1] What a good night for an escape.

prisoner had irons on his feet weighing fifty pounds. Every day, at four o'clock in the afternoon, a warden, escorted by two dogs—this was customary at that period—entered his cage, laid down near his bed a two-pound loaf of black bread, a jug of water, and a dish full of very thin soup in which a few beans were swimming, examined his irons, and struck upon the bars. This man, with his dogs, returned twice in the night.

Thénardier had obtained permission to keep a kind of iron spike which he used to nail his bread into a crack in the wall, "in order," said he, "to preserve it from the rats." As Thénardier was constantly in sight, they imagined no danger from this spike. However, it was remembered afterward that a warden had said: "It would be better to let him have nothing but a wooden pike."

At two o'clock in the morning, the sentinel, who was an old soldier, was relieved, and his place was taken by a conscript. A few moments afterward, the man with the dogs made his visit, and went away without noticing anything, except the extreme youth and the "peasant air" of the "greenhorn." Two hours afterward, at four o'clock, when they came to relieve the conscript, they found him asleep, and lying on the ground like a log near Thénardier's cage. As to Thénardier, he was not there. His broken irons were on the floor. There was a hole in the ceiling of his cage, and above, another hole in the roof. A board had been torn from his bed, and doubtless carried away, for it was not found again. There was also seized in the cell a half-empty bottle, containing the rest of the drugged wine with which the soldier had been put to sleep. The soldier's bayonet had disappeared.

At the moment of this discovery, it was supposed that Thénardier was out of all reach. The reality is, that he was no longer in the Bâtiment Neuf, but that he was still in great danger.

Thénardier on reaching the roof of the Bâtiment Neuf, found the remnant of Brujon's cord hanging to the bars of the upper trap of the chimney, but this broken end being much too short, he was unable to escape over the sentry's path as Brujon and Gueulemer had done.

On turning from the rue des Ballets into the rue du Roi de Sicile, on the right you meet almost immediately with a dirty recess. There was a house there in the last century, of which only the rear wall remains, a genuine ruin wall which rises to the height of the third story among the neighboring buildings. This ruin can be recognized by two large square windows which may still be seen.

The void which the demolished house left upon the street is half filled by a palisade fence of rotten boards, supported by five stone posts. Hidden in this enclosure is a little shanty built against that part of the ruin which remains standing. The fence has a gate which a few years ago was fastened only by a latch.

Thénardier was upon the crest of this ruin a little after three o'clock in the morning.

How had he got there? That is what nobody has ever been able to explain or understand. However this may be, dripping with sweat, soaked through by the rain, his clothes in strips, his hands skinned, his elbows bleeding, his knees torn, Thénardier had reached what children, in their figurative language, call the edge of the wall of the ruin; he had stretched himself on it at full length, and there his strength failed him. A steep escarpment, three stories high, separated him from the pavement of the street.

The rope which he had was too short.

He was waiting there, pale, exhausted, having lost all the hope which he had had, still covered by night, but saying to himself that day was just about to dawn, dismayed at the idea of hearing in a few moments the neighboring clock of Saint Paul's strike four, the hour when they would come to relieve the sentinel and would find him asleep under the broken roof, gazing with a kind of stupor through the fearful depth, by the glimmer of the lamps, upon the wet and black pavement, that longed for yet terrible pavement which was death yet which was liberty.

The clock struck four. Thénardier shuddered. A few moments afterward, that wild and confused noise which follows upon the discovery of an escape broke out in the prison. The sounds of doors opening and shutting, the grinding of gratings upon their hinges, the tumult in the guardhouse, the harsh calls of the gatekeepers, the sound of the butts of muskets upon the pavement of the yards reached him. Lights moved up and down in the grated windows of the dormitories, a torch ran along the attic of the Bâtiment Neuf, the firemen of the barracks alongside had been called. Their caps, which the torches lighted up in the rain, were going to and fro along the roofs. At the same time Thénardier saw in the direction of the Bastille a whitish cloud throwing a dismal pallor over the lower part of the sky.

He was on the top of a wall ten inches wide, stretched out beneath the storm, with two precipices, at the right and at the left, unable to stir, giddy at the prospect of falling, and horror-stricken at the certainty of arrest, and his thoughts, like the pendulum of a clock, went from one of these ideas to the other: "Dead if I fall, taken if I stay."

In this anguish, he suddenly saw, the street being still wrapped in obscurity, a man who was gliding along the walls, and who came from the direction of the rue Pavée, stop in the recess above which Thénardier was, as it were, suspended. This man was joined by a second, who was walking with the same precaution, then by a third, then by a fourth. Thénardier, not being able to distinguish their faces, listened to their words with the desperate attention of a wretch who feels that he is lost.

Something which resembled hope passed before Thénardier's eyes; these men spoke argot.

The first said, in a low voice, but distinctly:

"*Décarrons.* What is it we *maquillons icigo?*" [1]

The second answered:

"*Il lansquine* enough to put out the *riffe* of the *rabouin.* And then the *coqueurs* are going by. There is a *grivier* there who carries a *gaffe.* Shall we let them *emballer* us *icicaille?*" [2]

These two words, *icigo* and *icicaille*, which both mean *ici* [here], and which belong, the first to the argot of the Barrières, the second to the argot of the Temple, were revelations to Thénardier. By *icigo* he recognized Brujon, who was a prowler of the Barrières, and by *icicaille* Babet, who, among all his other trades, had been a secondhand dealer at the Temple.

Meanwhile the third put in a word:

"Nothing is urgent yet, let us wait a little. How do we know that he doesn't need our help?"

By this, which was only French, Thénardier recognized

---

[1] Let us go. What are we doing here?

[2] It rains enough to put out the devil's fire. And then the police are going by. There is a soldier there who is standing sentinel. Shall we let them arrest us here?

Montparnasse, whose elegance consisted in understanding all argots and speaking none.

As to the fourth, he was silent, but his huge shoulders betrayed him. Thénardier had no hesitation. It was Gueulemer.

He dared not call them, a cry overheard might destroy all; he had an idea, a final one, a flash of light; he took from his pocket the end of Brujon's rope, which he had detached from the chimney of the Bâtiment Neuf, and threw it into the enclosure.

This rope fell at their feet.

"A widow!"[1] said Babet.

"My *tortouse!*"[2] said Brujon.

"There is the innkeeper," said Montparnasse.

They raised their eyes. Thénardier advanced his head a little.

"Quick!" said Montparnasse. "Have you the other end of the rope, Brujon?"

"Yes."

"Tie the two ends together, we will throw him the rope, he will fasten it to the wall, he will have enough to get down."

Thénardier ventured to speak:

"I am benumbed."

"Only tie the rope to the wall."

"I can't."

"One of us must get up," said Montparnasse.

"Three stories!" said Brujon.

An old plaster flue, which had served for a stove which had formerly been in use in the shanty, crept along the wall, rising almost to the spot at which they saw Thénardier. This flue, then very much cracked and full of seams, has since fallen, but its traces can still be seen. It was very small.

"We could get up by that," said Montparnasse.

"By that flue!" exclaimed Babet. "An *orgue*,[3] never! It would take a *mion*."[4]

"It would take a *môme*,"[5] added Brujon.

"Where can we find a brat?" said Gueulemer.

---

[1] A rope (argot of the Temple).
[2] My rope (argot of the Barrières).
[3] A man.
[4] A child (argot of the Temple).
[5] A child (argot of the Barrières).

"Wait," said Montparnasse, "I have the thing."

He opened the gate of the fence softly, made sure that nobody was passing in the street, went out carefully, shut the gate after him, and started on a run in the direction of the Bastille.

Seven or eight minutes elapsed, eight thousand centuries to Thénardier; Babet, Brujon, and Gueulemer kept their teeth clenched; the gate at last opened again, and Montparnasse appeared, out of breath, with Gavroche. The rain still kept the street entirely empty.

Little Gavroche entered the enclosure and looked upon these bandit forms with a quiet air. The water was dripping from his hair. Gueulemer addressed him:

"Brat, are you a man?"

Gavroche shrugged his shoulders and answered:

"A *môme* like *mézig* is an *orgue*, and *orgues* like *vousailles* are *mômes*." [1]

"How the *mion* plays with the spittoon!" [2] exclaimed Babet.

"The *môme pantinois* isn't *maquillé* of *fertille lansquinée*," [3] added Brujon.

"What is it you want?" said Gavroche.

Montparnasse answered:

"To climb up by this flue."

"With this widow," said Babet.

The gamin examined the rope, the flue, the wall, the windows, and made that inexpressible and disdainful sound with the lips which signifies:

"What's that?"

"There is a man up there whom you will save," replied Montparnasse.

"Will you?" added Brujon.

"Goosy!" answered the child, as if the question appeared to him absurd; and he took off his shoes.

Gueulemer caught up Gavroche with one hand, put him on the roof of the shanty, the worm-eaten boards of which bent beneath the child's weight, and handed him the rope which Brujon had tied together during the absence of Montparnasse. The gamin went toward the flue, which was easy to enter, thanks to a large hole at the roof. Just as he was about to

---

[1] A child like me is a man, and men like you are children.
[2] How well the child's tongue is hung!
[3] The Parisian child isn't made of wet straw.

start, Thénardier, who saw safety and life approaching, bent over the edge of the wall; the first gleam of day lighted up his forehead reeking with sweat, his livid cheeks, his thin and savage nose, his gray bristly beard, and Gavroche recognized him:

"Hold on!" said he. "It is my father! Well, that don't hinder!"

And taking the rope in his teeth, he resolutely commenced the ascent.

He reached the top of the ruin, bestrode the old wall like a horse, and tied the rope firmly to the upper crossbar of the window.

A moment afterward Thénardier was in the street.

Meantime none of these men appeared any longer to see Gavroche, who had seated himself upon one of the stone supports of the fence; he waited a few minutes, perhaps for his father to turn toward him, then he put on his shoes, and said:

"It is over? You have no more use for me? Men! You are out of your trouble. I am going."

And he went away.

The five men went out of the enclosure one after another. When Gavroche had disappeared at the turn of the rue des Ballets, Babet took Thénardier aside.

"Did you notice that *mion*?" he asked him.

"What *mion*?"

"The *mion* who climbed up the wall and brought you the rope."

"Not much."

"Well, I don't know, but it seems to me that it is your son."

"Pshaw!" said Thénardier. "Do you think so?"

Enchantments and Desolations

I

MARIUS, drawn by that force which pushes the iron toward the magnet and the lover toward the stones of which the house of her whom he loves is built, had finally entered Cosette's garden as Romeo did the garden of Juliet. It had even been easier for him than for Romeo; Romeo was obliged to scale a wall, Marius had only to push aside a little one of the bars of the decrepit grating, which was loosened in its rusty socket, like the teeth of old people. Marius was slender, and easily passed through.

As there was never anybody in the street, and as, moreover, Marius entered the garden only at night, he ran no risk of being seen.

From that blessed and holy hour when a kiss affianced these two souls, Marius came every evening.

Through all the month of May of that year 1832, there were there, every night, in that poor, wild garden, under that shrubbery each day more odorous and more dense, two beings composed of every chastity and every innocence, overflowing with all the felicities of Heaven, more nearly archangels than men, pure, noble, intoxicated, radiant, who were resplendent to each other in the darkness.

What passed between these two beings? Nothing. They were adoring each other.

At night, when they were there, this garden seemed a living and sacred place. All the flowers opened about them, and proffered them their incense; they too opened their souls and poured them forth to the flowers; the lusty and vigorous vegetation trembled full of sap and intoxication about these two innocent creatures, and they spoke words of love at which the trees thrilled.

Their existence was vague, bewildered with happiness. They did not perceive the cholera which decimated Paris that very month. They had been as confidential with each other as they could be, but this had not gone very far beyond their names. Marius had told Cosette that he was an orphan, that his name was Marius Pontmercy, that he was a lawyer, that he lived by writing things for publishers, that his father was a colonel, that he was a hero, and that he, Marius, had quarreled with his grandfather who was rich. He had also said something about being a baron, but that had produced no effect upon Cosette. Marius a baron! She did not comprehend. She did not know what that word meant. Marius was Marius. On her part she had confided to him that she had been brought up at the Convent of the Petit Picpus, that her mother was dead as well as his, that her father's name was Monsieur Fauchelevent, that he was very kind, that he gave much to the poor, but that he was poor himself, and that he deprived himself of everything while he deprived her of nothing.

Strange to say, in the kind of symphony in which Marius had been living since he had seen Cosette, the past, even the most recent, had become so confused and distant to him that what Cosette told him satisfied him fully. He did not even think to speak to her of the night adventure at the Gorbeau tenement, the Thénardiers, the burning, and the strange attitude and the singular flight of her father. Marius had temporarily forgotten all that; he did not even know at night what he had done in the morning, nor where he had breakfasted, nor who had spoken to him; he had songs in his ear which rendered him deaf to every other thought; he existed only during the hours in which he saw Cosette. Then, as he was in heaven, it was quite natural that he should forget the earth. They were both supporting with languor the undefinable burden of the immaterial pleasures. Thus live these somnambulists called lovers.

Alas! Who has not experienced all these things? Why comes there an hour when we leave this azure, and why does life continue afterward?

These two beings, then, were living thus, very high, with all the improbability of nature; neither at the nadir nor at the zenith, between man and the seraph, above earth, below the ether, in the cloud; scarcely flesh and bone, soul and ecstasy from head to foot; too sublimated already to walk upon the earth, and yet too much weighed down with humanity to disappear in the sky, in suspension like atoms which are awaiting precipitation; apparently outside of destiny; ignoring that beaten track yesterday, today, tomorrow; astounded, swooping, floating; at times, light enough to soar into the infinity; almost ready for the eternal flight.

They were sleeping awake in this rocking cradle. O splendid lethargy of the real overwhelmed by the ideal!

Sometimes, beautiful as was Cosette, Marius closed his eyes before her. With closed eyes is the best way of looking at the soul.

Marius and Cosette did not ask where this would lead them. They looked upon themselves as arrived. It is a strange demand for men to ask that love should anywhither.

II

JEAN VALJEAN suspected nothing.

Cosette, a little less dreamy than Marius, was cheerful, and that was enough to make Jean Valjean happy. The thoughts of Cosette, her tender preoccupations the image of Marius which filled her soul, detracted nothing from the incomparable purity of her beautiful, chaste, and smiling forehead. She was at the age when the maiden bears her love as the angel bears her lily. And then when two lovers have an understanding they always get along well; any third person who might disturb their love is kept in perfect blindness by a very few precautions, always the same for all lovers. Thus never any objections from Cosette to Jean Valjean. Did he wish to take a walk? "Yes, my dear father." Did he wish to remain at home? "Very well." Would he spend the evening with Cosette? She was in raptures. As he always retired at ten o'clock, at such times Marius would not come to the garden till after that hour, when from the street he would hear Cosette open the glass door leading out onto the steps. We need not say that Marius was never met by day. Jean Valjean no longer even thought that Marius was in existence. Once, only, one morning, he happened to say to Cosette: "Why, you have something white on your back!" The evening before, Marius, in a transport, had pressed Cosette against the wall. Old Toussaint, who went to bed early, thought of nothing but going to sleep, once her work was done, and was ignorant of all, like Jean Valjean.

Never did Marius set foot in the house. When he was with Cosette they hid themselves in a recess near the steps, so that they could neither be seen nor heard from the street, and they sat there, contenting themselves often, by way of conversation, with pressing each other's hands twenty times a minute while looking into the branches of the trees. At such moments, a thunderbolt might have fallen within thirty paces of them, and they would not have suspected it, so deeply was the reverie of the one absorbed and buried in the reverie of the other.

Meanwhile various complications were approaching.

One evening Marius was making his way to the rendezvous by the Boulevard des Invalides; he usually walked with his head bent down; as he was just turning the corner of the rue Plumet, he heard someone saying very near him:

"Good evening, Monsieur Marius."

He looked up, and recognized Eponine.

This produced a singular effect upon him. He had not thought even once of this girl since the day she brought him to the rue Plumet; he had not seen her again, and she had completely gone out of his mind. He had only motives of gratitude toward her; he owed his present happiness to her, and still it was annoying to him to meet her.

It is a mistake to suppose that passion, when it is fortunate and pure, leads man to a state of perfection; it leads him simply, as we have said, to a state of forgetfulness. In this situation man forgets to be bad, but he also forgets to be good. Gratitude, duty, necessary and troublesome memories, vanish.

He answered with some embarrassment:

"What! Is it you, Eponine?"

"Why do you speak to me so sternly? Have I done anything to you?"

"No," answered he.

Certainly, he had nothing against her. Far from it. Only, he felt that he could not do otherwise, now that he had whispered to Cosette, than speak coldly to Eponine.

As he was silent, she exclaimed:

"Tell me now——"

Then she stopped. It seemed as if words failed this creature, once so reckless and so bold. She attempted to smile and could not. She resumed:

"Well—?"

Then she was silent again, and stood with her eyes cast down.

"Good evening, Monsieur Marius," said she all at once abruptly, and she went away.

III

The next day, it was the 3rd of June, the 3rd of June, 1832, a date which must be noted on account of the grave events which were at that time suspended over the horizon of Paris like thunderclouds, Marius, at nightfall, was following the same path as the evening before, with the same rapturous thoughts in his heart, when he perceived, under the trees of the boulevard, Eponine approaching him. Two days in succession, this was too much. He turned hastily, left the boulevard, changed his route, and went to the rue Plumet through the rue Monsieur.

This caused Eponine to follow him to the rue Plumet, a thing which she had not done before. She had been content until then to see him on his way through the boulevard without even seeking to meet him. The evening previous, only, had she tried to speak to him.

Eponine followed him then, without a suspicion on his part. She saw him push aside the bar of the grating, and glide into the garden.

"Why!" said she. "He is going into the house."

She approached the grating, felt of the bars one after another, and easily recognized the one which Marius had displaced.

She murmured in an undertone, with a mournful accent: "None of that, Lisette!"

She sat down upon the surbase of the grating, close beside the bar, as if she were guarding it. It was just at the point at which the grating joined the neighboring wall. There was an obscure corner there, in which Eponine was entirely hidden.

She remained thus for more than an hour, without stirring and without breathing, a prey to her own thoughts.

About ten o'clock in the evening, one of the two or three passers in the rue Plumet, a belated old bourgeois who was hurrying through this deserted and ill-famed place, keeping along the garden grating, on reaching the angle which the grating made with the wall, heard a sullen and threatening voice which said:

"I am not surprised that he comes every evening!"

He cast his eyes about him, saw nobody, dared not look into that dark corner, and was very much frightened. He doubled his pace.

IV

MEANWHILE Marius was with Cosette.

Never had the sky been more studded with stars, or more charming, the trees more tremulous, the odor of the shrubs more penetrating; never had the birds gone to sleep in the leaves with a softer sound; never had all the harmonies of the universal serenity better responded to the interior music of love; never had Marius been more enamored, more happy, more in ecstasy. But he had found Cosette sad. Cosette had been weeping. Her eyes were red.

It was the first cloud in this wonderful dream.

Marius' first words were:

"What is the matter?"

"See."

Then she sat down on the seat near the stairs, and as he took his place all trembling beside her, she continued:

"My father told me this morning to hold myself in readiness, that he had business, and that perhaps we should go away."

Marius shuddered from head to foot.

When we are at the end of life, to die means to go away; when we are at the beginning, to go away means to die.

For six weeks Marius, gradually, slowly, by degrees, had been each day taking possession of Cosette. A possession entirely ideal, but thorough. Marius then possessed Cosette, as minds possess; but he wrapped her in his whole soul, and clasped her jealously with an incredible conviction. To have Cosette, to possess Cosette, this to him was not separable from breathing. Into the midst of this faith, of this intoxication, of this virginal possession, marvelous and absolute, of this sovereignty, these words: "We are going away," fell all at once, and the sharp voice of reality cried to him: "Cosette is not yours!"

Marius awoke. For six weeks Marius had lived, as we have said, outside of life; these words, "going away," brought him roughly back to it.

He could not find a word. She said to him in her turn: "What is the matter?"

He answered so low that Cosette hardly heard him: "I don't understand what you have said."

She resumed:

"This morning my father told me to arrange all my little affairs and to be ready, that he would give me his clothes to pack, that he was obliged to take a journey, that we were going away, that we must have a large trunk for me and a small one for him, to get all that ready within a week from now, and that we should go perhaps to England."

"But it is monstrous!" exclaimed Marius.

He asked in a feeble voice:

"And when would you start?"

"He didn't say when."

"And when should you return?"

"He didn't say when."

Marius arose, and said coldly:

"Cosette, shall you go?"

Cosette took Marius' hand and pressed it without answering.

"Very well," said Marius. "Then I shall go elsewhere."

Cosette felt the meaning of this word still more than she understood it. She turned so pale that her face became white in the darkness. She stammered:

"What do you mean?"

Marius looked at her, then slowly raised his eyes toward heaven and answered:

"Nothing."

When his eyes were lowered, he saw Cosette smiling upon him. The smile of the woman whom we love has a brilliancy which we can see by night.

"How stupid we are! Marius, I have an idea."

"What?"

"Go if we go! I will tell you where! Come and join me where I am!"

Marius was now a man entirely awakened. He had fallen back into reality. He cried to Cosette:

"Go with you? Are you mad? But it takes money, and I have none! Go to England? Ah! I have not the means to pay for a passport!"

He threw himself against a tree which was nearby, standing with his arms above his head, his forehead against the bark, feeling neither the tree which was chafing his skin, nor the fever which was hammering his temples, motionless, and ready to fall, like a statue of Despair.

He was a long time thus. One might remain through eternity in such abysses. At last he turned. He heard behind him a little stifled sound, soft and sad.

It was Cosette sobbing.

She had been weeping more than two hours while Marius had been thinking.

He came to her, fell on his knees, and, prostrating himself slowly, he took the tip of her foot which peeped from under her dress and kissed it.

"Now listen," said he, "do not expect me tomorrow."

"Why not?"

"Do not expect me till the day after tomorrow!"

"Oh! Why not?"

"You will see."

"A day without seeing you! Why, that is impossible."

"Let us sacrifice one day to gain perhaps a whole life."

"You wish it?"

"Yes, Cosette."

She took his head in both her hands, rising on tiptoe to reach his height, and striving to see his hope in his eyes.

Marius continued:

"It occurs to me, you must know my address, something may happen, we don't know; I live with a friend named Courfeyrac, rue de la Verrerie, Number 16."

He put his hand in his pocket, took out a penknife, and wrote with the blade upon the plastering of the wall:

16, *rue de la Verrerie*.

Cosette, meanwhile, began to look into his eyes again.

"Day after tomorrow you will come early; I shall expect you at night, at nine o'clock precisely. I forewarn you. Oh, dear! How sad it is that the days are long! You understand—when the clock strikes nine, I shall be in the garden."

"And I too."

And without saying it, moved by the same thought, drawn on by those electric currents which put two lovers in continual communication, both intoxicated with pleasure even in their grief, they fell into each other's arms, without perceiving that their lips were joined, while their uplifted eyes, overflowing with ecstasy and full of tears, were fixed upon the stars.

V

GRANDFATHER GILLENORMAND had, at this period, fully completed his ninety-first year. He still lived with Mademoiselle Gillenormand, rue des Filles du Calvaire, No. 6, in that old house which belonged to him. He was, as we remember, one of those antique old men who await death still erect, whom age loads without making them stoop, and whom grief itself does not bend.

Still, for some time, his daughter had said: "My father is failing." He no longer beat the servants; he struck his cane with less animation on the landing of the stairs, when Basque was slow in opening the door. The revolution of July had hardly exasperated him for six months. The fact is, that the old man was filled with dejection. He did not bend, he did not yield; that was no more a part of his physical than of his moral nature; but he felt himself interiorly failing. Four years he had been waiting for Marius, with his foot down, that is just the word, in the conviction that that naughty little scapegrace would ring at his door some day or other; now he had come, in certain gloomy hours, to say to himself that even if Marius should delay, but little longer—. It was not death that was insupportable to him; it was the idea that perhaps he should never see Marius again. Never see Marius again—that had not, even for an instant, entered into his thought until this day; now this idea began to appear to him, and it chilled him. Absence, as always happens when feelings are natural and true, had only increased the grandfather's love for his ungrateful child who had gone away like that. It is on December nights, with the thermometer at zero, that we think most of the sun. Monsieur Gillenormand was, or thought himself, in any event, incapable of taking a step, he the grandfather, toward his grandson; "I would die first," said he. He acknowledged no fault on his part; but he thought of Marius only with a deep tenderness and the mute despair of an old goodman who is going away into the darkness.

He was beginning to lose his teeth, which added to his sadness.

Once, as he was sitting, his knees pressed together, and his eyes almost closed, in a posture of dejection, his daughter ventured to say to him:

"Father, are you still so angry with him?"

She stopped, not daring to go further.

"With whom?" asked he.

"With that poor Marius?"

He raised his old head, laid his thin and wrinkled fist upon the table, and cried in his most irritated and quivering tone:

"Poor Marius, you say? That gentleman is a rascal, a worthless knave, a little ungrateful vanity, with no heart, no soul, a proud, a wicked man!"

And he turned away that his daughter might not see the tears he had in his eyes.

Three days later, after a silence which had lasted for four hours, he said to his daughter snappishly:

"I have had the honor to beg Mademoiselle Gillenormand never to speak to me of him."

One evening, it was the 4th of June, which did not prevent Monsieur Gillenormand from having a blazing fire in his fireplace, he had said good night to his daughter who was sewing in the adjoining room. He was alone in his room with the rural scenery, his feet upon the andirons, half enveloped in his vast Coromandel screen with nine folds, leaning upon his table on which two candles were burning under a green shade, buried in his tapestried armchair, a book in his hand, but not reading.

Monsieur Gillenormand thought of Marius lovingly and bitterly; and, as usual, the bitterness predominated. An increase of tenderness always ended by boiling over and turning into indignation. He was at that point where we seek to adopt a course, and to accept what rends us. But his whole nature revolted; his old paternity could not consent to it. "What?" said he. This was his sorrowful refrain: "He will not come back!" His bald head had fallen upon his breast, and

he was vaguely fixing a lamentable and irritated look upon the
embers on his hearth.

In the deepest of this reverie, his old domestic, Basque,
came in and asked:

"Can monsieur receive Monsieur Marius?"

The old man straightened up, pallid and like a corpse which
rises under a galvanic shock. All his blood had flown back
to his heart. He faltered:

"Monsieur Marius what?"

"I don't know," answered Basque, intimidated and thrown
out of countenance by his master's appearance. "I have not
seen him. Nicolette just told me: 'There is a young man here;
say that it is Monsieur Marius.'"

Monsieur Gillenormand stammered out in a whisper:

"Show him in."

And he remained in the same attitude, his head shaking,
his eyes fixed on the door. It opened. A young man entered.
It was Marius.

Marius stopped at the door, as if waiting to be asked to
come in.

His almost wretched dress was not perceived in the
obscurity produced by the green shade. Only his face, calm
and grave, but strangely sad, could be distinguished.

Monsieur Gillenormand, as if congested with astonishment
and joy, sat for some moments without seeing anything but
a light, as when one is in presence of an apparition. He was
almost fainting; he perceived Marius through a blinding haze.
It was indeed he, it was indeed Marius!

At last! After four years! He seized him, so to speak, all
over at a glance. He thought him beautiful, noble, striking,
adult, a complete man, with graceful attitude and pleasing
air. He would gladly have opened his arms, called him, rushed
upon him, his heart melted in rapture, affectionate words
welled and overflowed in his breast; indeed, all his tenderness
started up and came to his lips, and, through the contrast
which was the groundwork of his nature, there came forth a
harsh word. He said abruptly:

"What is it you come here for?"

Marius answered with embarrassment:

"Monsieur—"

Monsieur Gillenormand would have had Marius throw
himself into his arms. He was displeased with Marius and

with himself. He felt that he was rough, and that Marius was cold. It was to the goodman an insupportable and irritating anguish, to feel himself so tender and so much in tears within, while he could only be harsh without. The bitterness returned. He interrupted Marius in a sharp tone:

"Then what do you come for?"

This then signified: "If you don't come to embrace me." Marius looked at his grandfather, whose pallor had changed to marble.

"Monsieur—"

The old man continued, in a stern voice:

"Do you come to ask my pardon? Have you seen your fault?"

He thought to put Marius on the track, and that "the child" was going to bend. Marius shuddered; it was the disavowal of his father which was asked of him; he cast down his eyes and answered:

"No, monsieur."

"And then," exclaimed the old man impetuously, with a grief which was bitter and full of anger, "what do you want with me?"

Marius clasped his hands, took a step, and said in a feeble and trembling voice:

"Monsieur, have pity on me."

This word moved Monsieur Gillenormand; spoken sooner, it would have softened him, but it came too late. The grandfather arose; he supported himself upon his cane with both hands, his lips were white, his forehead quivered, but his tall stature commanded the stooping Marius.

"Pity on you, monsieur! The youth asks pity from the old man of ninety-one! Zounds, Molière forgot this. If that is the way you jest at the Palais, Messieurs Lawyers, I offer you my sincere compliments. You are funny fellows."

And the octogenarian resumed in an angry and stern voice:

"Come now, what do you want of me?"

"Monsieur," said Marius, "I know that my presence is displeasing to you, but I come only to ask one thing of you, and then I will go away immediately."

"You are a fool!" said the old man. "Who tells you to go away?"

"Monsieur," said Marius, with the look of a man who feels

that he is about to fall into an abyss, "I come to ask your permission to marry."

Monsieur Gillenormand rang. Basque half-opened the door. "Send my daughter in."

A second later the door opened again. Mademoiselle Gillenormand did not come in, but showed herself. Marius was standing, mute, his arms hanging down, with the look of a criminal. Monsieur Gillenormand was coming and going up and down the room. He turned toward his daughter and said to her:

"Nothing. It is Monsieur Marius. Bid him good evening. Monsieur wishes to marry. That is all. Go."

The crisp, harsh tones of the old man's voice announced a strange fullness of feeling. The aunt looked at Marius with a bewildered air, appeared hardly to recognize him, allowed neither a motion nor a syllable to escape her, and disappeared at a breath from her father, quicker than a dry leaf before a hurricane.

Meanwhile Grandfather Gillenormand had returned and stood with his back to the fireplace.

"You marry! At twenty-one! You have arranged that! So you want to marry? Whom? Can the question be asked without indiscretion?"

He stopped, and, before Marius had had time to answer, he added violently:

"Come now, you have a business? Your fortune made? How much do you earn at your lawyer's trade?"

"Nothing," said Marius, with a firmness and resolution which were almost savage.

"Nothing? You have nothing to live on but the twelve hundred livres which I send you?"

Marius made no answer. Monsieur Gillenormand continued:

"Then I understand the girl is rich?"

"As I am."

"What! No dowry?"

"No."

"Some expectations?"

"I believe not."

"With nothing to her back! And what is the father?"

"I do not know."

"What is her name?"

"Mademoiselle Fauchelevent."

"Fauchewhat?"

"Fauchelevent."

"Ptttl" said the old man.

"Monsieur!" exclaimed Marius.

Monsieur Gillenormand interrupted him with the tone of a man who is talking to himself.

"That is it, twenty-one, no business, twelve hundred livres a year, Madame the Baroness Pontmercy will go to the market to buy two sous' worth of parsley."

"Monsieur," said Marius, in the desperation of the last vanishing hope, "I supplicate you! I conjure you, in the name of heaven, with clasped hands, monsieur, I throw myself at your feet, allow me to marry her!"

The old man burst into a shrill, dreary laugh, through which he coughed and spoke.

"Ha, ha, ha! You said to yourself: 'The devil! I will go and find that old wig, that silly dolt! I will say to him: "Old idiot, you are too happy to see me, I desire to marry, I desire to espouse Mamselle No-matter-whom, daughter of Monsieur No-matter-what, I have no shoes, she has no chemise, all right; I desire to throw to the dogs my career, my future, my youth, my life; I desire to make a plunge into misery with a wife at my neck; that is my idea, you must consent to it!" And the old fossil will consent.' Go, my boy, as you like, tie your stone to yourself, espouse your Pousselevent, your Couplevent—never, monsieur! Never!"

"Father!"

"Never!"

At the tone in which this "never" was pronounced, Marius lost all hope. He walked the room with slow steps, his head bowed down, tottering, more like a man who is dying than like one who is going away. Monsieur Gillenormand followed him with his eyes, and, at the moment the door opened and Marius was going out, he took four steps with the senile vivacity of impetuous and self-willed old men, seized Marius by the collar, drew him back forcibly into the room, threw him into an armchair, and said to him:

"Tell me about it!"

It was that single word, father, dropped by Marius, which had caused this revolution.

Marius looked at him in bewilderment. The changing

countenance of Monsieur Gillenormand expressed nothing now but a rough and ineffable good nature. The guardian had given place to the grandfather.

"Come, let us see, speak, tell me about your love scrapes, jabber, tell me all! Lord! How foolish these young folks are!"

"Father—" resumed Marius.

The old man's whole face shone with an unspeakable radiance.

"Yes! That *is* it! Call me father, and you shall see!"

There was now something so kind, so sweet, so open, so paternal, in this abruptness, that Marius, in this sudden passage from discouragement to hope, was, as it were, intoxicated, stupefied. He was sitting near the table, the light of the candle made the wretchedness of his dress apparent, and the grandfather gazed at it in astonishment.

"Well, father—" said Marius.

"Come now," interrupted Monsieur Gillenormand, "then you really haven't a sou? You are dressed like a robber."

He fumbled in a drawer and took out a purse, which he laid upon the table:

"Here, there is a hundred louis; buy yourself a hat."

"Father," pursued Marius, "my good father, if you knew. I love her. You don't realize it; the first time that I saw her was at the Luxembourg, she came there; in the beginning I did not pay much attention to her, and then I do not know how it came about, I fell in love with her. Oh! How wretched it has made me! Now at last I see her every day, at her own house, her father does not know it, only think that they are going away, we see each other in the garden in the evening, her father wants to take her to England, then I said to myself: 'I will go and see my grandfather and tell him about it.' I should go crazy in the first place, I should die, I should make myself sick, I should throw myself into the river. I must marry her because I should go crazy. Now, that is the whole truth, I do not believe that I have forgotten anything."

Grandfather Gillenormand, radiant with joy, had sat down by Marius' side. While listening to him and enjoying the sound of his voice, he enjoyed at the same time a long pinch of snuff.

"Marius! I think it is very well for a young man like you to be in love. It belongs to your age. Pretty women are pretty women, the Devil! There is no objection to that. As to the little girl, she receives you unknown to papa. That is all right. I have had adventures like that myself. More than one. Do you know how we do? We don't take the thing ferociously; we don't rush into the tragic; we don't conclude with marriage and with Monsieur the Mayor and his scarf. We are altogether a shrewd fellow. We have good sense. Slip over it, mortals, don't marry. We come and find grandfather who is a goodman at heart, and who almost always has a few rolls of louis in an old drawer; we say to him: 'Grandfather, that's how it is.' And grandfather says: 'That is all natural. Youth must fare and old age must wear. I have been young, you will be old. Go on, my boy, you will repay this to your grandson. There are two hundred pistoles. Amuse yourself, roundly! Nothing better! That is the way the thing should be done. We don't marry, but that doesn't hinder.' You understand me?"

Marius, petrified and unable to articulate a word, shook his head.

The goodman burst into a laugh, winked his old eye, gave him a tap on the knee, looked straight into his eyes with a significant and sparkling expression, and said to him with the most amorous shrug of the shoulders:

"Stupid! Make her your mistress."

Marius turned pale. He had understood nothing of all that his grandfather had been saying. The goodman was wandering. But this wandering had terminated in a word which Marius did understand, and which was a deadly insult to Cosette. That phrase, "make her your mistress," entered the heart of the chaste young man like a sword.

He rose, picked up his hat which was on the floor, and walked toward the door with a firm and assured step. There he turned, bowed profoundly before his grandfather, raised his head again, and said:

"Five years ago you outraged my father; today you have outraged my wife. I ask nothing more of you, monsieur. Adieu."

Grandfather Gillenormand, astounded, opened his mouth, stretched out his arms, attempted to rise, but before he could utter a word, the door closed and Marius had disappeared.

The old man was for a few moments motionless, and, as it were, thunderstruck, unable to speak or breathe, as if a hand were clutching his throat. At last he tore himself from his chair, ran to the door as fast as a man who is ninety-one can run, opened it, and cried:

"Help! Help!"

His daughter appeared, then the servants. He continued with a pitiful rattle in his voice:

"Run after him! Catch him! What have I done to him! He is mad! He is going away! Oh! My God! Oh! My God—this time he will not come back!"

He went to the window which looked upon the street, opened it with his tremulous old hands, hung more than half his body outside, while Basque and Nicolette held him from behind, and cried:

"Marius! Marius! Marius! Marius!"

But Marius was already out of hearing, and was at that very moment turning the corner of the rue Saint Louis.

The octogenarian carried his hands to his temples two or three times with an expression of anguish, drew back tottering, and sank into an armchair, pulseless, voiceless, tearless, shaking his head and moving his lips with a stupid air, having now nothing in his eyes or in his heart but something deep and mournful, which resembled night.

Where Are They Going?

I

THAT very day, toward four o'clock in the afternoon, Jean Valjean was sitting alone upon the reverse of one of the most solitary embankments of the Champ de Mars. He was now calm and happy in regard to Cosette; what had for some time alarmed and disturbed him was dissipated, but within a week or two anxieties of a different nature had come upon him. One day, when walking on the boulevard, he had seen Thénardier. Thénardier there! This was all dangers at once. Moreover, Paris was not quiet: the political troubles had this inconvenience for him who had anything in his life to conceal, that the police had become very active, and very secret, and that in seeking to track out a man like Pépin or Morey, they would be very likely to discover a man like Jean Valjean. Jean Valjean had decided to leave Paris, and even France, and to pass over to England. He had told Cosette. In less than a week he wished to be gone. He was sitting on the embankment in the Champ de Mars, revolving all manner of thoughts in his mind: Thénardier, the police, the journey, and the difficulty of procuring a passport.

On all these points he was anxious.

Finally, an inexplicable circumstance which had just burst upon him, and with which he was still warm, had added to his alarm. On the morning of that very day, being the only one up in the house, and walking in the garden before Cosette's shutters were open, he had suddenly come upon this line scratched upon the wall, probably with a nail:

16, rue de la Verrerie.

It was quite recent; the lines were white in the old black mortar, a tuft of nettles at the foot of the wall was powdered with fresh fine plaster. It had probably been written during the night. What was it? An address? A signal for others? A warning for him? At all events, it was evident that the garden had been violated, and that some persons unknown had penetrated into it.

In the midst of these meditations, he perceived, by a shadow which the sun had projected, that somebody had just stopped upon the crest of the embankment immediately behind him. He was about to turn around, when a folded paper fell upon his knees, as if a hand had dropped it from above his head. He took the paper, unfolded it, and read on it this word, written in large letters with a pencil: REMOVE.

Jean Valjean rose hastily; there was no longer anybody on the embankment; he looked about him, and perceived a species of being larger than a child, smaller than a man, dressed in a gray blouse, and trousers of dirt-colored cotton velvet, which jumped over the parapet and let itself slide into the ditch of the Champ de Mars.

Jean Valjean returned home immediately, full of thought.

II

MARIUS had left Monsieur Gillenormand's desolate. He had entered with a very small hope; he came out with an immense despair.

He began to walk the streets, the resource of those who suffer. He thought of nothing which he could ever remember. At two o'clock in the morning he returned to Courfeyrac's, and threw himself, dressed as he was, upon his mattress. It was broad sunlight when he fell asleep, with that frightful, heavy slumber in which the ideas come and go in the brain. When he awoke, he saw standing in the room, their hats upon their heads, all ready to go out, and very busy, Courfeyrac, Enjolras, Feuilly, and Combeferre.

Courfeyrac said to him:

"Are you going to the funeral of General Lamarque?"

It seemed to him that Courfeyrac was speaking Chinese.

He went out some time after them. He put into his pocket the pistols which Javert had given to him at the time of the adventure of the 3rd of February, and which had remained in his hands. These pistols were still loaded. It would be difficult to say what obscure thought he had in his mind in taking them with him.

He rambled about all day without knowing where; it rained at intervals, he did not perceive it; for his dinner he bought a penny roll at a baker's, put it in his pocket, and forgot it. He waited for night with feverish impatience, he had but one clear idea; that was, that at nine o'clock he should see Cosette. This last happiness was now his whole future; afterward, darkness. At intervals, while walking along the most deserted boulevards, he seemed to hear strange sounds in Paris. He roused himself from his reverie, and said: "Are they fighting?"

At nightfall, at precisely nine o'clock, as he had promised Cosette, he was in the rue Plumet. When he approached the grating he forgot everything else. It was forty-eight hours since he had seen Cosette, he was going to see her again, every other thought faded away, and he felt now only a deep and wonderful joy. Those minutes in which we live centuries always have this sovereign and wonderful peculiarity, that for the moment while they are passing, they entirely fill the heart.

Marius displaced the grating and sprang into the garden. Cosette was not at the place where she usually waited for him. He crossed the thicket and went to the recess near the steps. "She is waiting for me there," said he. Cosette was not there. He raised his eyes and saw that the shutters of the house were closed. He took a turn around the garden, the garden was deserted. Then he returned to the house, and, mad with love, intoxicated, dismayed, exasperated with grief and anxiety, like a master who returns home at an untoward hour, he rapped on the shutters. He rapped, he rapped again, at the risk of seeing the window open and the forbidding face of the father appear and ask him: "What do you want?" This was nothing compared with what he now began to see. When he had rapped, he raised his voice and called Cosette. "Cosette!" cried he. "Cosette!" he repeated imperiously. There was no answer. It was settled. Nobody in the garden; nobody in the house.

Marius fixed his despairing eyes upon that dismal house, as black, as silent, and more empty than a tomb. He looked at the stone seat where he had passed so many adorable hours with Cosette. Then he sat down upon the steps, his heart full of tenderness and resolution; he blessed his love in the depths of his thought, and he said to himself that since Cosette was gone, there was nothing more for him but to die.

Suddenly he heard a voice which appeared to come from the street, and which cried through the trees:

"Monsieur Marius!"

He arose.

"Hey?" said he.

"Monsieur Marius, is it you?"

"Yes."

"Monsieur Marius," added the voice, "your friends are expecting you at the barricade, in the rue de la Chanvrerie."

This voice was not entirely unknown to him. It resembled the harsh and roughened voice of Eponine. Marius ran to the grating, pushed aside the movable bar, passed his head through, and saw somebody who appeared to him to be a young man rapidly disappearing in the twilight.

III

MONSIEUR MABEUF had continued to descend.

The experiments upon indigo had succeeded no better at the Jardin des Plantes than in his garden at Austerlitz. The year before, he owed his housekeeper her wages; now he owed three-quarters of his rent. The pawnbroker, at the expiration of thirteen months, had sold the plates of his *Flora*. Some coppersmith had made saucepans of them. His plates gone, being no longer able even to complete the broken sets of his *Flora* which he still possessed, he had given up engravings and text at a wretched price to a secondhand bookseller, as odd copies. He had now nothing left of the work of his whole life. He began to eat up the money from these copies. When he saw that this slender resource was failing him, he renounced his garden and left it uncultivated. Before this, and for a long time before, he had given up the two eggs and the bit of beef which he used to eat from time to time. He dined on bread and potatoes. He had sold his last furniture, then all his spare bedding and clothing, then his collections of plants and his pictures; but he still had his most precious books, several of which were of great rarity, among others a Diogenes Laërtius, printed at Lyons in 1644, containing the famous variations of the manuscript 411, of the thirteenth century, in the Vatican, and those of the two manuscripts of Venice, 393 and 394, so fruitfully consulted by Henri Estienne, and all the passages in the Doric dialect which are found only in the celebrated manuscript of the twelfth century of the library of Naples. Monsieur Mabeuf never made a fire in his room, and went to bed by daylight so as not to burn a candle. It seemed that he had now no neighbors; he was shunned when he went out; he was aware of it. The misery of a child is interesting to a mother, the misery of a young man is interesting to a young woman, the misery of an old man is interesting to nobody. This is of all miseries the coldest. Still Father Mabeuf had not entirely lost his childlike serenity. His eye regained some vivacity when it was fixed upon his books, and he smiled when he thought of the Diogenes Laërtius, which was a unique copy. His glass bookcase was the only piece of furniture which he had preserved beyond what was indispensable.

One day Mother Plutarch said to him:

"I have nothing to buy the dinner with."

What she called the dinner was a loaf of bread and four or five potatoes.

"On credit?" said Monsieur Mabeuf.

"You know well enough that they refuse me."

Monsieur Mabeuf opened his library, looked long at all his books one after another, as a father compelled to decimate his children would look at them before choosing, then took one of them hastily, put it under his arm, and went out. He returned two hours afterward with nothing under his arm, laid thirty sous on the table, and said:

"You will get some dinner."

From that moment, Mother Plutarch saw settling over the old man's white face a dark veil which was never lifted again.

The next day, the day after, every day, he had to begin again. Monsieur Mabeuf went out with a book and came back with a piece of money. Volume by volume, the whole library passed away. He said at times: "I am eighty years old however," as if he had some lingering hope of reaching the end of his days before reaching the end of his books. His sadness increased. Once, however, he had a pleasure. He went out with a Robert Estienne which he sold for thirty-five sous on the Quai Malaquais and returned with an Aldine which he had bought for forty sous in the rue des Grès. "I owe five sous," said he to Mother Plutarch, glowing with joy.

That day he did not dine.

He had acquired the habit, every evening before going to bed, of reading a few pages in his Diogenes Laërtius. He knew Greek well enough to enjoy the peculiarities of the text which he possessed. He had now no other joy. Some weeks rolled by. Suddenly Mother Plutarch fell sick. There is one thing sadder than having nothing with which to buy bread from the baker; that is, having nothing with which to buy drugs from the apothecary. One night, the doctor had ordered a very dear potion. And then—the sickness was growing worse—a nurse was needed. Monsieur Mabeuf opened his bookcase; there was nothing more there. The last volume had gone. The Diogenes Laërtius alone remained.

He put the unique copy under his arm and went out; it was the 4th of June, 1832; he went to the Porte Saint Jacques and returned with a hundred francs. He laid the pile of five-franc pieces on the old servant's bedroom table and went back to his room without saying a word.

The next day, by dawn, he was seated on the stone post in the garden, and he might have been seen from over the hedge all the morning motionless, his head bowed down, his eyes vaguely fixed upon the withered beds. At intervals he wept; the old man did not seem to perceive it. In the afternoon, extraordinary sounds broke out in Paris. They resembled musket shots, and the clamor of a multitude.

Father Mabeuf raised his head. He saw a gardener going by, and asked:

"What is that?"

The gardener answered, his spade upon his shoulder, and in the most quiet tone:

"It's the *émeutes*."

"What *émeutes*?"

"Yes. They are fighting."

"What are they fighting for?"

"Oh! Lordy!" said the gardener.

"Whereabouts?" continued Monsieur Mabeuf.

"Near the Arsenal."

Father Mabeuf went into the house, took his hat, looked mechanically for a book to put under his arm, did not find any, said: "Ah! It is true!" and went away with a bewildered air.

June 5th, 1832

I

OF what is the *émeute* composed? Of nothing and of everything. Of an electricity gradually evolved, of a flame suddenly leaping forth, of a wandering force, of a passing wind. This wind meets talking tongues, dreaming brains, suffering souls, burning passions, howling miseries, and sweeps them away.

Whither?

At hazard. Across the state, across the laws, across the prosperity and the insolence of others.

Irritated convictions, eager enthusiasms, excited indignations, the repressed instincts of war, exalted young courage, noble impulses; curiosity, the taste for change, the thirst for the unexpected, that sentiment which gives us pleasure in reading the bill of a new play, and which makes the ringing of the prompter's bell at the theater a welcome sound; vague hatreds, spites, disappointments, every vanity which believes that destiny has caused it to fail; discomforts, empty dreams, ambitions shut in by high walls, whoever hopes for an issue from a downfall; finally, at the very bottom, the mob, that mud which takes fire, such are the elements of the *émeute*.

Whatever is greatest and whatever is most infamous; the beings who prowl about outside of everything, awaiting an opportunity, bohemians, people without occupation, loafers about the streetcorners, those who sleep at night in a desert of houses, with no other roof than the cold clouds of the sky, those who ask their bread each day from chance and not from labor, the unknown ones of misery and nothingness, the bare arms, the bare feet, belong to the *émeute*.

Whoever feels in his soul a secret revolt against any act whatever of the state, of life, or of fate, borders on the *émeute*, and, as soon as it appears, begins to shiver, and to feel himself uplifted by the whirlwind.

The *émeute* is a sort of waterspout in the social atmosphere which suddenly takes form in certain conditions of temperature, and which, in its whirling, mounts, runs, thunders, tears up, razes, crushes, demolishes, uproots, dragging with it the grand natures and the paltry, the strong man and the feeble mind, the trunk of the tree and the blade of straw.

Woe to him whom it sweeps away, as well as to him whom it comes to smite! It breaks them one against the other.

In the spring of 1832, although for three months the cholera had chilled all hearts and thrown over their agitation an inexpressibly mournful calm, Paris had for a long time been ready for a commotion. As we have said, the great city resembles a piece of artillery; when it is loaded the falling of a spark is enough, the shot goes off. In June, 1832, the spark was the death of General Lamarque.

Lamarque was a man of renown and of action. He had had successively, under the empire and under the Restoration, the two braveries necessary to the two epochs, the bravery of the battlefield and the bravery of the rostrum. He was eloquent as he had been valiant; men felt a sword in his speech. Like Foy, his predecessor, after having upheld command, he upheld liberty. He sat between the left and the extreme left, loved by the people because he accepted the chances of the future, loved by the masses because he had served the emperor well. He hated Wellington with a direct hatred which pleased the multitude, and for seventeen years, hardly noticing intermediate events, he had majestically preserved the sadness of Waterloo. In his death agony, at his latest hour, he had pressed against his breast a sword which was presented to him by the officers of the Hundred Days. Napoleon died pronouncing the word *armée*, Lamarque pronouncing the word *patrie*.

His death, which had been looked for, was dreaded by the people as a loss and by the government as an opportunity. This death was a mourning. Like everything which is bitter, mourning may turn into revolt. This is what happened.

On the 5th of June then, a day of mingled rain and sunshine, the procession of General Lamarque passed through Paris with the official military pomp, somewhat increased by way of precaution. Two battalions, drums muffled, muskets reversed, ten thousand National Guards, their sabers at their sides, the batteries of artillery of the National Guard, escorted the coffin. The hearse was drawn by young men. The officers of the Invalides followed immediately, bearing branches of laurel. Then came a countless multitude, strange and agitated, the sectionaries of the Friends of the People, the law school, the medical school, refugees from all nations, Spanish, Italian, German, Polish flags, horizontal tricolored flags, every possible banner, children waving green branches, stonecutters and carpenters, who were on a strike at that very moment, printers recognizable by their paper caps, walking two by two, three by three, uttering cries, almost all brandishing clubs, a few swords, without order, and yet with a single soul, now a rout, now a column. Some platoons chose chiefs; a man, armed with a pair of pistols openly worn, seemed to be passing others in review as they filed off before him. On the cross alleys of the boulevards, in the branches of the trees, on the balconies, at the windows, on the roofs, were swarms of heads, men, women, children; their eyes were full of anxiety. An armed multitude was passing by; a terrified multitude was looking on.

The government also was observing. It was observing with its hand upon the hilt of the sword. One might have seen, all ready to march, with full cartridge boxes, guns and musketoons loaded, in the Place Louis XV, four squadrons of carbineers, in the saddle, trumpets at their heads; in the Latin Quarter and at the Jardin des Plantes, the Municipal Guard, *en échelon* from street to street; at the Halle aux Vins a squadron of dragoons; at La Grève one half of the 12th Light, the other half at the Bastille; the 6th dragoons at the Célestins; the Court of the Louvre full of artillery. The rest of the troops were stationed in the barracks, without counting the regiments in the environs of Paris. Anxious authority held suspended over the threatening multitude twenty-four thousand soldiers in the city and thirty thousand in the *banlieue*.

Divers rumors circulated in the cortege. They talked of legitimist intrigues; they talked of the Duke of Reichstadt, whom God was marking for death at that very moment when the populace was designating him for empire. A personage still unknown announced that at the appointed hour two foremen who had been won over would open to the people the doors of a manufactory of arms. The dominant expression on the uncovered foreheads of most of those present was one of subdued enthusiasm. Here and there in this multitude, a prey to so many violent, but noble, emotions, could also be seen some genuine faces of malefactors and ignoble mouths, which said "pillage!" There are certain agitations which stir up the bottom of the marsh, and which make clouds of mud rise in the water. A phenomenon to which "well-regulated" police are not strangers.

The cortege made its way, with a feverish slowness, from the house of death, along the boulevards as far as the Bastille. It rained from time to time; the rain had no effect upon that throng.

The hearse passed the Bastille, followed the canal, crossed the little bridge, and reached the esplanade of the Bridge of Austerlitz. There it stopped. At this moment a bird's-eye view of this multitude would have presented the appearance of a comet, the head of which was at the esplanade, while the tail, spreading over the Quai Bourdon, covered the Bastille, and stretched along the boulevard as far as the Porte Saint Martin. A circle was formed about the hearse. The vast assemblage became silent. Lafayette spoke and bade farewell to Lamarque. It was a touching and august moment, all heads were uncovered, all hearts throbbed. Suddenly a man on horseback, dressed in black, appeared in the midst of the throng with a red flag, others say with a pike surmounted by a red cap. Lafayette turned away his head. Exelmans left the cortege.

This red flag raised a storm and disappeared in it. From the Boulevard Bourdon to the Bridge of Austerlitz one of those shouts which resemble billows moved the multitude. Two prodigious shouts arose: "Lamarque to the Pantheon! Lafayette to the Hôtel de Villel" Some young men, amid the cheers of the throng, harnessed themselves and began to draw Lamarque in the hearse over the Bridge of Austerlitz, and Lafayette in a fiacre along the Quai Morland.

In the crowd which surrounded and cheered Lafayette, was noticed and pointed out a German named Ludwig Snyder, who afterward died a centenarian, who had also been in the war of 1776, and who had fought at Trenton under Washington, and under Lafayette at Brandywine.

Meanwhile, on the left bank, the municipal cavalry was in motion and had just barred the bridge; on the right bank the dragoons left the Célestins and deployed along the Quai Morland. The men who were drawing Lafayette suddenly perceived them at the corner of the quay and cried: "The dragoons!" The dragoons were advancing at a walk, in silence, their pistols in their holsters, their sabers in their sheaths, their musketoons in their rests, with an air of gloomy expectation.

At two hundred paces from the little bridge they halted. The fiacre in which Lafayette was, made its way up to them; they opened their ranks, let it pass, and closed again behind it. At that moment the dragoons and the multitude came together. The women fled in terror.

What took place in that fatal moment? Nobody could tell. It was the dark moment when two clouds mingle. Some say that a trumpet flourish sounding the charge was heard from the direction of the Arsenal, others that a dagger thrust was given by a child to a dragoon. The fact is that three shots were suddenly fired; the first killed the chief of the squadron, Cholet; the second killed an old deaf woman who was closing her window in the rue Contrescarpe; the third singed the epaulet of an officer. A woman cried: "They are beginning too soon!" and all at once there was seen, from the side opposite the Quai Morland, a squadron of dragoons which had remained in the barracks turning out on the gallop, with swords drawn, from the rue Bassompierre and the Boulevard Bourdon, and sweeping all before them.

There are no more words, the tempest breaks loose, stones fall like hail, musketry bursts forth, many rush headlong down the bank and cross the little arm of the Seine now filled up, the yards of the Ile Louviers, that vast ready-made citadel, bristle with combatants; they tear up stakes, they fire pistol

shots, a barricade is planned out; the young men, crowded
back, pass the Bridge of Austerlitz with the hearse at a run
and charge on the Municipal Guard, the carbineers rush up,
the dragoons ply the saber, the mass scatters in every direction; a rumor of war flies to the four corners of Paris, men
cry: "To arms!" They run, they tumble, they fly, they resist.
Wrath sweeps along the *émeute* as the wind sweeps along a
fire.

II

NOTHING is more extraordinary than the first swarming of an
émeute. Everything bursts out everywhere at once. Was it
foreseen? Yes. Was it prepared? No. Whence does it spring?
From the pavements. Whence does it fall? From the clouds.
Here the insurrection has the character of a plot; there of an
improvisation. The first comer takes possession of a current
of the multitude and leads it whither he will. A beginning full
of terror with which is mingled a sort of frightful gaiety. At
first there are clamors, the shops close, the displays of the
merchants disappear; then some isolated shots; people flee;
butts of guns strike against porte-cocheres; you hear the
servant girls laughing in the yards of the houses and saying:
"There is going to be a row!"

A quarter of an hour had not elapsed and here is what
had taken place nearly at the same time at twenty different
points in Paris.

Right bank, left bank, on the quays, on the boulevards,
in the Latin Quarter, in the region of the markets, breathless
men, workingmen, students, sectionaries, read proclamations,
cried: "To arms!" broke the streetlamps, unharnessed wagons,
tore up the pavements, broke in the doors of the houses, uprooted the trees, ransacked the cellars, rolled hogsheads,
heaped up paving stones, pebbles, pieces of furniture, boards,
made barricades.

What had really assumed the direction of the *émeute* was
a sort of unknown impetuosity which was in the atmosphere.
The insurrection, abruptly, had built the barricades with one
hand, and with the other seized nearly all the posts of the
garrison. In less than three hours, like a train of powder
which takes fire, the insurgents had invaded and occupied

on the right bank, the Arsenal, the Mayor's office of the Place Royale, all the Marais, the Popincourt manufactory of arms, the Galiote, the Château d'Eau, all of the streets near the markets; on the left bank, the barracks of the Vétérans, Sainte Pélagie, the Place Maubert, the powder mill of the Deux Moulins, all the *barrières*. At five o'clock in the afternoon they were masters of the Bastille, the Lingerie, the Blancs Manteaux; their scouts touched the Place des Victoires, and threatened the bank, the barracks of the Petits Pères, and the Hôtel des Postes. A third of Paris was in the *émeute*.

At all points the struggle had commenced on a gigantic scale, and from the disarmings, from the domiciliary visits, from the armorers' shops hastily invaded, there was this result, that the combat which was commenced by throwing stones was continued by throwing balls.

About six o'clock in the afternoon, the arcade du Saumon became a field of battle. The *émeute* was at one end, the troops at the end opposite. They fired from one grating to the other. An observer, a dreamer, the author of this book, who had gone to get a near view of the volcano, found himself caught in the arcade between the two fires. He had nothing but the projection of the pilasters which separate the shops to protect him from the balls; he was nearly half an hour in this delicate situation.

Meanwhile the drums beat the long roll, the National Guards dressed and armed themselves in haste, the legions left the *mairies*, the regiments left their barracks.

The insurrection had made the center of Paris a sort of inextricable, tortuous, colossal citadel.

There was the focus; there was evidently the question. All the rest were only skirmishes. What proved that there all would be decided was that they were not yet fighting there.

In some regiments, the soldiers were doubtful, which added to the frightful obscurity of the crisis. They remembered the popular ovation which in July, 1830, had greeted the neutrality of the 53rd of the line. Two intrepid men, who had been proved by the great wars, Marshal de Lobau and General Bugeaud, commanded, Bugeaud under Lobau. Enormous patrols, composed of battalions of the line surrounded by entire companies of the National Guard, and preceded by a commissary of police with his badge, went out reconnoitering the insurgent streets. On their side, the insurgents placed pickets at the corners of the streets and boldly sent patrols outside of the barricades. They kept watch on both sides. The government, with an army in its hand, hesitated; night was coming on, and the tocsin of Saint Merry began to be heard. The Minister of War of the time, Marshal Soult, who had seen Austerlitz, beheld this with gloomy countenance.

These old sailors, accustomed to correct maneuvering, and having no resource or guide save tactics, that compass of battles, are completely lost in the presence of that immense foam which is called the wrath of the people. The wind of revolutions is not tractable.

Solitude reigned at the Tuileries. Louis Philippe was full of serenity.

The Atom Fraternizes
with the Hurricane

I

At the moment the insurrection, springing up at the shock of the people with the troops in front of the Arsenal, determined a backward movement in the multitude which was following the hearse and which, for the whole length of the boulevards, weighed, so to say, upon the head of the procession, there was a frightful reflux. The mass wavered, the ranks broke, all ran, darted, slipped away, some with cries of attack, others with the pallor of flight. The great river which covered the boulevards divided in a twinkling, overflowed on the right and on the left, and poured in torrents into two hundred streets at once with the rushing of an opened mill sluice. At this moment a ragged child who was coming down the rue Ménilmontant, holding in his hand a branch of laburnum in bloom, which he had just gathered on the heights of Belleville, caught sight, before a secondhand dealer's shop, of an old horse pistol. He threw his flowering branch upon the pavement, and cried:

"Mother What's-your-name, I'll borrow your machine."

And he ran off with the pistol.

It was Little Gavroche going to war.

On the boulevard he perceived that the pistol had no hammer.

Gavroche nonetheless continued on his way.

At the Saint Jean market where the guard was already disarmed, he effected his junction with a band led by Enjolras, Courfeyrac, Combeferre, and Feuilly. They were almost armed. Bahorel and Jean Prouvaire had joined them and enlarged the group. Enjolras had a double-barreled fowling piece; Combeferre a National Guard's musket bearing the number of the legion, and at his waist two pistols which could be seen, his coat being unbuttoned; Jean Prouvaire an old cavalry musketoon; Bahorel a carbine; Courfeyrac was brandishing an unsheathed sword cane. Feuilly, a drawn saber in his hand, marched in the van, crying: "Poland forever!"

They came from the Quai Morland cravatless, hatless, breathless, soaked by the rain, lightning in their eyes. Gavroche approached them calmly:

"Where are we going?"

"Come on," said Courfeyrac.

Behind Feuilly marched, or rather bounded, Bahorel, a fish in the water of the *émeute*. A tumultuous cortege accompanied them, students, artists, young men affiliated with the Cougourde d'Aix, workingmen, rivermen, armed with clubs and bayonets; a few, like Combeferre, with pistols thrust into their waistbands. An old man, who appeared very old, was marching with this band. He was not armed, and he was hurrying, that he should not be left behind, although he had a thoughtful expression. Gavroche perceived him:

"Whossat?" said he to Courfeyrac.

"That is an old man."

It was Monsieur Mabeuf.

He advanced almost to the front rank of the column, having at once the motion of a man who is walking and the countenance of a man who is asleep.

"What a desperate goodman!" murmured the students. The rumor ran through the assemblage that he was—an ancient Conventionist—an old regicide. The company had turned into the rue de la Verrerie.

Little Gavroche marched on. They made their way toward Saint Merry.

II

THE band increased at every moment. Toward the rue des Billettes a man of tall stature, who was turning gray, whose rough and bold mien Courfeyrac, Enjolras, and Combeferre noticed, but whom none of them knew, joined them. Gavroche, busy singing, whistling, humming, going forward and rapping on the shutters of the shops with the butt of his hammerless pistol, paid no attention to this man.

It happened that, in the rue de la Verrerie, they passed by Courfeyrac's door.

"That is lucky," said Courfeyrac, "I have forgotten my purse, and I have lost my hat." He left the company and went up to his room, four stairs at a time. He took an old hat and his purse. He took also a large square box, of the size of a big valise, which was hidden among his dirty clothes. As he was running down again, the portress hailed him:

"There is somebody who wishes to speak to you."

At the same time, a sort of young workingman, thin, pale, small, freckled, dressed in a torn blouse and patched pantaloons of ribbed velvet, and who had rather the appearance of a girl in boy's clothes than of a man, came out of the lodge and said to Courfeyrac in a voice which, to be sure, was not the least in the world like a woman's voice:

"Monsieur Marius, if you please?"

"He is not in."

"Will he be in this evening?"

"I don't know anything about it."

And Courfeyrac added: "As for myself, I shall not be in."

The young man looked fixedly at him, and asked him:

"Why so?"

"Because."

"Where are you going then?"

"What is that to you?"

"Do you want me to carry your box?"

"I am going to the barricades."

"Do you want me to go with you?"

"If you like," answered Courfeyrac. "The road is free; the streets belong to everybody."

And he ran off to rejoin his friends. When he had rejoined

them, he gave the box to one of them to carry. It was not until a quarter of an hour afterward that he perceived that the young man had in fact followed them.

A mob does not go precisely where it wishes. We have explained that a gust of wind carries it along. They went beyond Saint Merry and found themselves, without really knowing how, in the rue Saint Denis.

Corinth

I

THE passer who came, thirty years ago, from the rue Saint Denis into the rue de la Chanvrerie saw it gradually narrow away before him as if he had entered an elongated funnel. At the end of the street, which was very short, he found the passage barred on the market side, and he would have thought himself in a cul-de-sac if he had not perceived on the right and on the left two black openings by which he could escape. These were the rue Mondétour, which communicated on the one side with the rue des Prêcheurs, on the other with the rues du Cygne and Petite Truanderie. At the end of this sort of cul-de-sac, at the corner of the opening on the right, might be seen a house lower than the rest, and forming a kind of cape on the street.

In this house, only two stories high, had been festively installed for three hundred years an illustrious wineshop.

In the times of Mathurin Régnier, this wineshop was called the *Pot aux Roses* (Pot of Roses), and as rebuses were in fashion, it had for a sign a post (*poteau*) painted a rose color. In the last century, the worthy Natoire, having got tipsy several times in this wineshop at the same table where Régnier had got drunk, out of gratitude painted a bunch of Corinth grapes upon the rose-colored post. The landlord, from joy, changed his sign and had gilded below the bunch these words: THE GRAPE OF CORINTH. Hence the name Corinth. Corinth gradually dethroned the *Pot aux Roses*. The last landlord of the dynasty, Father Hucheloup, not even knowing the tradition, had the post painted blue.

A basement room in which was the counter, a room on the first floor in which was the billiard table, a spiral wooden staircase piercing the ceiling, wine on the tables, smoke on the walls, candles in broad day, such was the wineshop. A stairway with a trapdoor in the basement room led to the cellar. On the second floor were the rooms of the Hucheloups. You ascended by a stairway, which was rather a ladder than a stairway, the only entrance to which was by a back door in the large room on the first floor. In the attic were two garret rooms with dormer windows, nests for servants. The kitchen divided the ground floor with the counting room.

Hucheloup had always an ill-humored face, seemed to wish to intimidate his customers, grumbled at people who came to his house, and appeared more disposed to pick a quarrel with them than to serve them their soup. And still they were always welcome.

His wife was Mother Hucheloup, a bearded creature, and very ugly.

Toward 1830, Father Hucheloup died. His widow, scarcely consolable, continued the wineshop. But the cuisine degenerated and became execrable; the wine, which had always been bad, became frightful. Courfeyrac and his friends continued to go to Corinth, however—"from pity," said Bossuet.

The room on the first floor, in which was "the restaurant," was a long and wide room, encumbered with stools, crickets, chairs, benches, and tables, and a rickety old billiard table. It was reached by the spiral staircase which terminated at the corner of the room in a square hole like the hatchway of a ship.

Two servants, called Chowder and Fricassee, and for whom nobody had ever known any other names, helped Mother Hucheloup to put upon the tables the pitchers of blue wine and the various broths which were served to the hungry in earthen dishes.

Before entering the restaurant room, you might read upon the door this line written in chalk by Courfeyrac:

Régale si tu peux et mange si tu l'oses.[1]

---

[1] Feast if you can and eat if you dare.

LAIGLE DE MEAUX, we know, lived more with Joly than elsewhere. He had a lodging as the bird has a branch. The two friends lived together, ate together, slept together. On the morning of the 5th of June, they went to breakfast at Corinth.

They went up to the first floor.

Chowder and Fricassee received them. "Oysters, cheese, and ham," said Laigle.

And they sat down at a table.

The wineshop was empty; they two only were there.

Fricassee, recognizing Joly and Laigle, put a bottle of wine on the table.

As they were at their first oysters, a head appeared at the hatchway of the stairs, and a voice said:

"I was passing. I smelled in the street a delicious odor of Brie cheese. I have come in."

It was Grantaire.

Grantaire took a stool and sat down at the table.

Fricassee, seeing Grantaire, put two bottles of wine on the table.

That made three.

The others had begun by eating. Grantaire began by drinking.

He was entering on his second bottle when a new actor emerged from the square hole of the stairway. It was a boy of less than ten years, ragged, very small, yellow, a mug of a face, a keen eye, monstrous long hair, wet to the skin, a complacent look.

The child, choosing without hesitation among the three, although he evidently knew none of them, addressed himself to Laigle de Meaux.

"Are you Monsieur Bossuet?" asked he.

"That is my nickname," answered Laigle. "What do you want of me?"

"This is it. A big light-complexioned fellow on the boulevard said to me: 'Do you know Mother Hucheloup?' I said: 'Yes, rue Chanvrerie, the widow of the old man.' He said to me: 'Go there. You will find Monsieur Bossuet there, and

you will tell him from me: "A—B—C." ' It is a joke that somebody is playing on you, isn't it? He gave me ten sous."

"Joly, lend me ten sous," said Laigle, and turning toward
Grantaire: "Grantaire, lend me ten sous."

This made twenty sous which Laigle gave the child.

"Thank you, monsieur," said the little fellow.

"What is your name?" asked Laigle.

"Navet, Gavroche's friend."

"Stop with us," said Laigle.

"Breakfast with us," said Grantaire.

The child answered:

"I can't, I am with the procession, I am the one to cry:
'Down with Polignac.' "

And giving his foot a long scrape behind him, which is
the most respectful of all possible bows, he went away.

Meanwhile Laigle was meditating; he said in an undertone:

"A—B—C, that is to say: Lamarque's funeral."

"The big light-complexioned man," observed Grantaire, "is
Enjolras, who sent to notify you."

Grantaire, melancholy, was drinking.

"Enjolras despises me," murmured he. "Enjolras said: 'Joly
is sick. Grantaire is drunk.' It was to Bossuet that he sent
Navet. If he had come for me I would have followed him.
So much the worse for Enjolras! I won't go to his funeral."

This resolution taken, Bossuet, Joly, and Grantaire did not
stir from the wineshop. About two o'clock in the afternoon,
the table on which they were leaning was covered with empty
bottles. Two candles were burning, one in a perfectly green
copper candlestick, the other in the neck of a cracked de-
canter.

Grantaire was extravagantly gay, and Bossuet and Joly
kept pace with him. They touched glasses. Grantaire rested
his left wrist upon his knee with dignity, his arms akimbo
and his cravat untied; bestriding a stool, his full glass in his
right hand, he threw out to the fat servant Chowder these
solemn words:

"Let the palace doors be opened! Let everybody belong
to the Académie Française, and have the right of embracing
Madame Hucheloup! Let us drink."

And turning toward Mother Hucheloup he added:

"Antique woman consecrated by use, approach that I may gaze upon thee!"

And Joly, who had a bad cold, exclaimed:

"Chowder add Fricassee, dod't give Gradtaire ady bore to drigk. He spedds his bodey foolishly. He has already devoured sidce this bordigg in desperate prodigality two fragcs didety-five cedtibes."

Bossuet, very drunk, had preserved his calmness.

He sat in the open window, wetting his back with the falling rain, and gazed at his two friends.

Suddenly he heard a tumult behind him, hurried steps and cries. "To arms!" He turned, and saw in the rue Saint Denis, at the end of the rue de la Chanvrerie, Enjolras passing, carbine in hand, and Gavroche with his pistol, Feuilly with his saber, Courfeyrac with his sword, Jean Prouvaire with his musketoon, Combeferre with his musket, Bahorel with his musket, and all the armed and stormy gathering which followed them.

The rue de la Chanvrerie was hardly as long as the range of a carbine. Bossuet improvised a speaking trumpet with his two hands and shouted:

"Courfeyrac! Courfeyrac! Ahoy!"

Courfeyrac heard the call, perceived Bossuet, and came a few steps into the rue de la Chanvrerie, crying a "What do you want?" which was met on the way by a "Where are you going?"

"To make a barricade," answered Courfeyrac.

"Well, here! This is a good place! Make it here!"

"That is true, Eagle," said Courfeyrac.

And at a sign from Courfeyrac, the band rushed into the rue de la Chanvrerie.

III

THE place was indeed admirably chosen, the entrance of the street wide, the further end contracted and like a cul-de-sac, Corinth throttling it, rue Mondétour easy to bar at the right and left, no attack possible except from the rue Saint Denis, that is from the front, and without cover. Bossuet tipsy had the *coup d'œil* of Hannibal fasting.

At the irruption of the mob, dismay seized the whole street, not a passer but had gone into eclipse. In a flash, at the end, on the right, on the left, shops, stalls, alley gates, windows, blinds, dormer windows, shutters of every size, were closed from the ground to the roofs. One frightened old woman had fixed a mattress before her window on two clothes poles, as a shield against the musketry. The wineshop was the only house which remained open; and that for a good reason, because the band had rushed into it. "Oh my God! Oh my God!" sighed Mother Hucheloup.

Meanwhile, in a few minutes, twenty iron bars had been wrested from the grated front of the wineshop, twenty yards of pavement had been torn up; Gavroche and Bahorel had seized on its passage and tipped over the dray of a lime merchant named Anceau; this dray contained three barrels full of lime, which they had placed under the piles of paving stones; Enjolras had opened the trap door of the cellar and all the Widow Hucheloup's empty casks had gone to flank the lime barrels; Feuilly, with his fingers accustomed to coloring the delicate folds of fans, had buttressed the barrels and the dray with two massive heaps of stones. Stones improvised like the rest, and obtained nobody knows where. Some shoring timbers had been pulled down from the front of a neighboring house and laid upon the casks. When Bossuet and Courfeyrac turned around, half the street was already barred by a rampart higher than a man. There is nothing like the popular hand to build whatever can be built by demolishing.

An omnibus with two white horses passed at the end of the street.

Bossuet sprang over the pavement, ran, stopped the driver, made the passengers get down, gave his hand "to the ladies," dismissed the conductor, and came back with the vehicle, leading the horses by the bridle.

"An omnibus," said he, "doesn't pass by Corinth. Non licet omnibus adire Corinthum."

A moment later the horses were unhitched and going off at will through the rue Mondétour, and the omnibus, lying on its side, completed the barring of the street.

Mother Hucheloup, completely upset, had taken refuge in the first story.

Her eyes were wandering, and she looked without seeing, crying in a whisper. Her cries were dismayed and dared not come out of her throat.

"It is the end of the world," she murmured.

Joly deposited a kiss upon Mother Hucheloup's coarse, red, and wrinkled neck, and said to Grantaire: "My dear fellow, I have always considered a woman's neck an infinitely delicate thing."

But Grantaire was attaining the highest regions of dithyramb. Chowder having come up to the first floor, Grantaire seized her by the waist and pulled her toward the window with long bursts of laughter.

"Chowder is ugly!" cried he; "Chowder is the dream of ugliness! Chowder is a chimera. Listen to the secret of her birth: a Gothic Pygmalion who was making cathedral waterspouts fell in love with one of them one fine morning, the most horrible of all. He implored Love to animate her, and that made Chowder. Behold her, citizens! Her hair is the color of chromate of lead, like that of Titian's mistress, and she is a good girl. I warrant you that she will fight well. Every good girl contains a hero. Chowder, embrace me! You are voluptuous and timid! You have cheeks which call for the kiss of a sister, and lips which demand the kiss of a lover."

"Be still, wine cask!" said Courfeyrac.

Grantaire answered:

"I am Capitoul and Master of Floral Games!"

Enjolras, who was standing on the crest of the barricade, musket in hand, raised his fine austere face. Enjolras, we know, had something of the Spartan and of the Puritan. He would have died at Thermopylae with Leonidas, and would have burned Drogheda with Cromwell.

"Grantaire," cried he. "go sleep yourself sober away from here. This is the place for intoxication and not for drunkenness. Do not dishonor the barricade!"

This angry speech produced upon Grantaire a singular effect. One would have said that he had received a glass of cold water in his face. He appeared suddenly sobered. He sat down, leaned upon a table near the window, looked at Enjolras with an inexpressible gentleness, and said to him:

"Let me sleep here."

"Go sleep elsewhere," cried Enjolras.

But Grantaire, keeping his tender and troubled eyes fixed upon him, answered:

"Let me sleep here—until I die here."

Enjolras regarded him with a disdainful eye.

"Grantaire, you are incapable of belief, of thought, of will, of life, and of death."

Grantaire stammered out a few more unintelligible words; then his head fell heavily upon the table, and—a common effect of the second stage of inebriety into which Enjolras had rudely and suddenly pushed him—a moment later he was asleep.

IV

THE rain had ceased. Recruits had arrived. Some workingmen had brought under their blouses a keg of powder, a hamper containing bottles of vitriol, two or three carnival torches, and a basketful of lamps, "relics of the king's fete," which fete was quite recent, having taken place the 1st of May. They broke the only lamp in the rue de la Chanvrerie, the lamp opposite the rue Saint Denis, and all the lamps in the surrounding streets, Mondétour, du Cygne, des Prêcheurs, and de la Grande and de la Petite Truanderie.

Enjolras, Combeferre, and Courfeyrac directed everything. Two barricades were now building at the same time, both resting on the house of Corinth and making a right angle; the larger one closed the rue de la Chanvrerie, the other closed the rue Mondétour in the direction of the rue du Cygne. This last barricade, very narrow, was constructed only of casks and paving stones. There were about fifty laborers there, some thirty armed with muskets, for, on their way, they had effected a wholesale loan from an armorer's shop.

Nothing could be more fantastic and more motley than this band. One had a short-jacket, a cavalry saber, and two horse pistols; another was in shirt sleeves, with a round hat and a powder horn hung at his side; a third had a breast plate of nine sheets of brown paper, and was armed with a saddler's awl. There was one of them who cried: "Let u exterminate to the last man, and die on the point of ou bayonets!" This man had no bayonet. Another displayed ove his coat a crossbelt and cartridge box of the National Guard with the box cover adorned with this inscription in red cloth PUBLIC ORDER. Many muskets bearing the numbers of thei legions, few hats, no cravats, many bare arms, some pike Add to this all ages, all faces, small pale young men, bronze wharfmen. All were hurrying, and, while helping each other, they talked about the possible chances—that they would have help by three o'clock in the morning—that they were sure of one regiment—that Paris would rise. Terrible subjects, with which was mingled a sort of cordial joviality. One would have said they were brothers; they did not know each other's names. Great perils have this beauty, that they bring to light the fraternity of strangers.

A fire had been kindled in the kitchen, and they were melting pitchers, dishes, forks, all the pewterware of the wine-shop into bullets. They drank through it all. Percussion caps and buckshot rolled pell-mell upon the tables with glasses of wine. In the billiard room, Mother Hucheloup, Chowder, and Fricassee, variously modified by terror, one being stupefied, another breathless, the third alert, were tearing up old linen and making lint; three insurgents assisted them, three long-haired, bearded, and mustachioed wags who tore up the cloth with the fingers of linen drapers, and who made them tremble.

The man of tall stature whom Courfeyrac, Combeferre, and Enjolras had noticed, at the moment he joined the company at the corner of the rue des Billettes, was working on the little barricade and making himself useful there. Gavroche worked on the large one. As for the young man who had waited for Courfeyrac at his house, and had asked him for Monsieur Marius, he had disappeared very nearly at the moment the omnibus was overturned.

Gavroche, completely carried away and radiant, had charged himself with making all ready. He went, came, mounted, descended, remounted, bustled, sparkled. He seemed to be there for the encouragement of all. Had he a spur? Yes, certainly, his misery; had he wings? Yes, certainly, his joy. Gavroche was a whirlwind. They saw him incessantly, they heard him constantly. He filled the air, being everywhere at once. He was a kind of stimulating ubiquity; no stop possible with him. The enormous barricade felt him on its back. He vexed the loungers, he excited the idle, he reanimated the weary, he provoked the thoughtful, kept some in cheerfulness, others in breath, others in anger, all in motion, piqued a student, was biting to a workingman; he took position, stopped, started on, flitted above the tumult and the effort, leaped from these to those, murmured, hummed, and stirred up the whole train—the fly on the revolutionary coach.

Still he was furious at his pistol without a hammer. He went from one to another, demanding: "A musket! I want a musket! Why don't you give me a musket?"

"A musket for you?" said Combeferre.

"Well?" replied Gavroche. "Why not? I had one in 1830, in the dispute with Charles X."

Enjolras shrugged his shoulders.

"When there are enough for the men, we will give them to the children."

Gavroche turned fiercely and answered him:

"If you are killed before me, I will take yours."

"Gamin!" said Enjolras.

"Smooth-face?" said Gavroche.

A stray dandy who was lounging at the end of the street made a diversion.

Gavroche cried to him:

"Come with us, young man? Well, this poor old country—you won't do anything for her then?"

The dandy fled.

V

THE journals of the time which said that the barricade of the rue de la Chanvrerie—that "almost inexpugnable construction," as they call it—attained the level of a second story were mistaken. The fact is, that it did not exceed an average height of six or seven feet. It was built in such a manner that the combatants could, at will, either disappear behind the wall, or look over it, or even scale the crest of it by means of a quadruple range of paving stones superposed and arranged like steps on the inner side. The front of the barricade on the outside, composed of piles of paving stones and of barrels bound together by timbers and boards which were interlocked in the wheels of the Anceau cart and the overturned omnibus, had a bristling and inextricable aspect.

An opening sufficient for a man to pass through had been left between the wall of the houses and the extremity of the barricade furthest from the wineshop; so that a sortie was possible. The pole of the omnibus was turned directly up and held with ropes, and a red flag, fixed to this pole, floated over the barricade.

The little Mondétour barricade, hidden behind the wineshop, was not visible. The two barricades united formed a staunch redoubt. Enjolras and Courfeyrac had not thought it proper to barricade the end of the rue Mondétour, which opens a passage to the markets through the rue des Prêcheurs, wishing doubtless to preserve a possible communication with the outside, and having little dread of being attacked from the dangerous and difficult alley des Prêcheurs.

The two barricades finished and the flag run up, a table was dragged out of the wineshop, and Courfeyrac mounted upon the table. Enjolras brought the square box and Courfeyrac opened it. This box was filled with cartridges. When they saw the cartridges, there was a shudder among the bravest and a moment of silence.

Courfeyrac distributed them with a smile.

Each one received thirty cartridges. Many had powder and set about making others with the balls which they were molding. As for the keg of powder, it was on a table by itself near the door, and it was reserved.

The long roll which was running through all Paris was not discontinued, but it had got to be only a monotonous sound with melancholy undulations, to which they paid no more attention.

They all loaded their muskets and their carbines together, without precipitation, with a solemn gravity. Enjolras placed three sentinels outside the barricades, one in the rue de la Chanvrerie, the second in the rue des Prêcheurs, the third at the corner of la Petite Truanderie.

Then, the barricades built, the posts assigned, the muskets loaded, the videttes placed, alone in these fearful streets in which there were now no passers, surrounded by these dumb, and as it were dead houses, which throbbed with no human motion, enwrapped by the deepening shadows of the twilight, which was beginning to fall, in the midst of this obscurity and this silence, through which they felt the advance of something inexpressibly tragical and terrifying, isolated, armed, determined, tranquil, they waited.

VI

In these hours of waiting, what did they do? This we must tell, for this is history.

While the men were making cartridges and the women lint, while a large frying pan, full of melted pewter and lead, destined for the bullet mold, was smoking over a burning furnace, while the videttes were watching the barricades with arms in their hands, while Enjolras, whom nothing could distract, was watching the videttes, Combeferre, Courfeyrac, Jean Prouvaire, Feuilly, Bossuet, Joly, Bahorel, and a few others besides, sought each other and got together, as in the most peaceful days of their student chats, and in a corner of this wineshop changed into a casemate, within two steps of the redoubt which they had thrown up, their carbines primed and loaded resting on the backs of their chairs, these gallant young men, so near their last hour, began to sing love rhymes.

The hour, the place, the few stars which began to shine in the sky, the funereal repose of these deserted streets, the imminence of the inexorable event gave a pathetic charm to these rhymes, murmured in a low tone in the twilight by Jean Prouvaire, who, as we have said, was a sweet poet.

Meanwhile they had lighted a lamp at the little barricade, and at the large one, one of those wax torches which are seen on Mardi Gras in front of the wagons loaded with masks, which are going to the Comtille.

The torch had been placed in a kind of cage, closed in with paving stones on three sides to shelter it from the wind, and disposed in such a manner that all the light fell upon the flag. The street and the barricade remained plunged in obscurity, and nothing could be seen but the red flag, fearfully lighted up, as if by an enormous dark lantern.

This light gave to the scarlet of the flag an indescribably terrible purple.

VII

It was now quite night; nothing came. There were only confused sounds and at intervals volleys of musketry, bu rare, ill-sustained, and distant. This respite, which was thus prolonged, was a sign that the government was taking its time and massing its forces. These fifty men were awaiting sixty thousand.

Enjolras felt himself possessed by that impatience which seizes strong souls on the threshold of formidable events. He went to find Gavroche, who had set himself to making cartridges in the basement room by the doubtful light of two candles.

Gavroche at this moment was very much engaged, not exactly with his cartridges.

The man from the rue des Billettes had just entered the basement room and had taken a seat at the table which was least lighted. An infantry musket of large model had fallen to his lot, and he held it between his knees. Gavroche hitherto, distracted by a hundred "amusing" things, had not even seen this man.

When he came in, Gavroche mechanically followed him with his eyes, admiring his musket, then, suddenly, when the man had sat down, the gamin arose. Had anyone watched this man up to this time, he would have seen him observe everything in the barricade and in the band of insurgents with a singular attention, but since he had come into the room, he had fallen into a kind of meditation and appeared to see nothing more of what was going on. The gamin approached this thoughtful personage, and began to turn about him on the points of his toes as one walks when near somebody whom he fears to awake. At the same time, over his childish face, at once so saucy and so serious, so flighty and so profound, so cheerful and so touching, there passed all those grimaces of the old which signify: "Oh, bah! Impossible! I am befogged! I am dreaming! Can it be? No, it isn't! Why yes! Why no!" etc.

It was in the deepest of this meditation that Enjolras accosted him.

"You are small," said Enjolras, "nobody will see you. Go out of the barricades, glide along by the houses, look about the streets a little, and come and tell me what is going on."

Gavroche straightened himself up.

"Little folks are good for something then! That is very lucky! I will go! Meantime, trust the little folks, distrust the big—" And Gavroche, raising his head and lowering his voice, added, pointing to the man of the rue des Billettes:

"You see that big fellow there?"

"Well?"

"He is a spy."

"You are sure?"

"It isn't a fortnight since he pulled me by the ear off the cornice of the Pont Royal where I was taking the air."

Enjolras hastily left the gamin, and murmured a few words very low to a workingman from the wine docks who was there. The workingman went out of the room and returned almost immediately, accompanied by three others. The four men, four broad-shouldered porters, placed themselves, without doing anything which could attract his attention, behind the table on which the man of the rue des Billettes was leaning. They were evidently ready to throw themselves upon him.

Then Enjolras approached the man and asked him:

"Who are you?"

At this abrupt question, the man gave a start. He looked straight to the bottom of Enjolras' frank eye and appeared to catch his thought. He smiled with a smile which, of all things in the world, was the most disdainful, the most energetic, and the most resolute, and answered with a haughty gravity:

"I see how it is—well, yes!"

"You are a spy?"

"I am an officer of the government."

"Your name is?"

"Javert."

Enjolras made a sign to the four men. In a twinkling, before Javert had had time to turn around, he was collared, thrown down, bound, searched.

The search finished, they raised Javert, tied his arms behind his back, fastened him in the middle of the basement room to that celebrated post which had formerly given its name to the wineshop.

Gavroche, who had witnessed the whole scene and approved the whole by silent nods of his head, approached Javert and said to him:

"The mouse has caught the cat."

All this was executed so rapidly that it was finished as soon as it was perceived about the wineshop. Javert had not uttered a cry. Seeing Javert tied to the post, Courfeyrac, Bossuet, Joly, Combeferre, and the men scattered about the two barricades ran in.

Javert, backed up against the post, and so surrounded with ropes that he could make no movement, held up his head with the intrepid serenity of the man who has never lied.

"It is a spy," said Enjolras.

And turning toward Javert:

"You will be shot ten minutes before the barricade is taken."

Javert replied in his most imperious tone:

"Why not immediately?"

"We are economizing powder."

"Then do it with a knife."

"Spy," said the handsome Enjolras, "we are judges, not assassins."

Then he called Gavroche.

"You! Go about your business! Do what I told you."

"I am going," cried Gavroche.

And stopping just as he was starting:

"By the way, you will give me his musket!" And he added: "I leave you the musician, but I want the clarinet."

The gamin made a military salute, and sprang gaily through the opening in the large barricade.

VIII

THE tragic picture which we have commenced would not be complete, the reader would not see in their exact and real relief these grand moments of social parturition and of revolutionary birth in which there is convulsion mingled with effort, were we to omit, in the outline here sketched, an incident full of epic and savage horror which occurred almost immediately after Gavroche's departure.

Mobs, as we know, are like snowballs and gather a heap of tumultuous men as they roll. These men do not ask one another whence they come. Among the passers who had joined themselves to the company led by Enjolras, Combeferre, and Courfeyrac, there was a person wearing a porter's waistcoat worn out at the shoulders, who gesticulated and vociferated and had the appearance of a sort of savage drunkard. This man, who was named or nicknamed Le Cabuc, and who was moreover entirely unknown to those who attempted to recognize him, very drunk, or feigning to be, was seated with a few others at a table which they had brought outside of the wineshop. This Cabuc, while inciting those to drink who were with him, seemed to gaze with an air of reflection upon the large house at the back of the barricade, the five stories of which overlooked the whole street and faced toward the rue Saint Denis. Suddenly he exclaimed:

"Comrades, do you know? It is from that house that we must fire. If we are at the windows, devil a one can come into the street."

"Yes, but the house is shut up," said one of the drinkers.

"Knock!"

"They won't open."

"Stave the door in!"

Le Cabuc runs to the door, which had a very massive knocker, and raps. The door does not open. He raps a second time. Nobody answers. A third rap. The same silence.

"Is there anybody here?" cries Le Cabuc.

Nothing stirs.

Then he seizes a musket and begins to beat the door with the butt. It was an old alley door, arched, low, narrow, solid, entirely of oak, lined on the inside with sheet iron and with iron braces, a genuine postern of a bastille. The blows made the house tremble, but did not shake the door.

Nevertheless it is probable that the inhabitants were alarmed, for finally a little square window on the third story was seen to light up and open, and there appeared at this window a candle, and the pious and frightened face of a gray-haired goodman who was the porter.

The man who was knocking stopped.

"Messieurs," asked the porter, "what do you wish?"

"Open!" said Le Cabuc.

"Messieurs, that cannot be."

"Open, I tell you!"

"Impossible, messieurs!"

Le Cabuc took his musket and aimed at the porter's head; but as he was below, and it was very dark, the porter did not see him.

"Yes or no, will you open?"

"No, messieurs!"

"You say no?"

"I say no, my good—"

The porter did not finish. The musket went off; the ball entered under his chin and passed out at the back of the neck, passing through the jugular. The old man sank down without a sigh. The candle fell and was extinguished, and nothing could now be seen but an immovable head lying on the edge of the window, and a little whitish smoke floating toward the roof.

"That's it!" said Le Cabuc, letting the butt of his musket drop on the pavement.

Hardly had he uttered these words when he felt a hand pounce upon his shoulder with the weight of an eagle's talons, and heard a voice which said to him:

"On your knees."

The murderer turned and saw before him the cold white face of Enjolras. Enjolras had a pistol in his hand.

At the explosion, he had come up.

He had grasped with his left hand Le Cabuc's collar, blouse, shirt, and suspenders.

"On your knees," he repeated.

And with a majestic movement the slender young man of twenty bent the broad-shouldered and robust porter like a reed and made him kneel in the mud. Le Cabuc tried to resist, but he seemed to have been seized by a superhuman grasp.

Pale, his neck bare, his hair flying, Enjolras, with his woman's face, had at that moment an inexpressible something of the ancient Themis. His distended nostrils, his downcast eyes, gave to his implacable Greek profile that expression of wrath and that expression of chastity which from the point of view of the ancient world belonged to justice.

The whole barricade ran up, then all ranged in a circle at a distance, feeling that it was impossible to utter a word in presence of the act which they were about to witness.

La Cabuc, vanquished, no longer attempted to defend himself, but trembled in every limb. Enjolras let go of him and took out his watch.

"Collect your thoughts," said he. "Pray or think. You have one minute."

"Pardon!" murmured the murderer, then he bowed his head and mumbled some inarticulate oaths.

Enjolras did not take his eyes off his watch; he let the

minute pass, then he put his watch back into his fob. This done, he took Le Cabuc, who was writhing against his knees and howling, by the hair, and placed the muzzle of his pistol at his ear. Many of those intrepid men, who had so tranquilly entered upon the most terrible of enterprises, turned away their heads.

They heard the explosion, the assassin fell face forward on the pavement, and Enjolras straightened up and cast about him his look, determined and severe.

Then he pushed the body away with his foot and said:

"Throw that outside."

Three men lifted the body of the wretch, which was quivering with the last mechanical convulsions of the life that had flown, and threw it over the small barricade into the little rue Mondétour.

Enjolras had remained thoughtful. Shadow, mysterious and grand, was slowly spreading over his fearful serenity. He suddenly raised his voice. There was a silence.

"Citizens," said Enjolras, "what that man did is horrible, and what I have done is terrible. He killed, that is why I killed him. I was forced to do it, for the insurrection must have its discipline. Assassination is a still greater crime here than elsewhere; we are under the eye of the revolution, we are the priests of the republic, we are the sacramental host of duty, and none must be able to calumniate our combat. I therefore judged and condemned that man to death. As for myself, compelled to do what I have done, but abhorring it, I have judged myself also, and you shall soon see to what I have sentenced myself."

Those who heard shuddered.

"We will share your fate," cried Combeferre.

"So be it," added Enjolras. "A word more. In executing that man, I obeyed necessity, but necessity is a monster of the old world, the name of necessity is Fatality. Now the law of progress is that monsters disappear before angels, and that Fatality vanish before Fraternity. This is not a moment to pronounce the word love. No matter, I pronounce it, and I glorify it. Love, thine is the future. Death, I use thee, but I hate thee. Citizens, there shall be in the future neither darkness nor thunderbolts; neither ferocious ignorance nor blood for blood. As Satan shall be no more, so Michael shall be no more. In the future no man shall slay his fellow, the earth shall be radiant, the human race shall love. It will come, citizens, that day when all shall be concord, harmony, light, joy, and life; it will come, and it is that it may come that we are going to die."

Enjolras was silent. His virgin lips closed, and he remained some time standing on the spot where he had spilled blood, in marble immobility. His fixed eye made all about him speak low.

Jean Prouvaire and Combeferre silently grasped hands, and, leaning upon one another in the corner of the barricade, considered, with an admiration not unmingled with compassion, this severe young man, executioner and priest, luminous like the crystal, and rock also.

Let us say right here that later, after the action, when the corpses were carried to the Morgue and searched, there was a police officer's card found on Le Cabuc. The author of this book had in his own hands, in 1848, the special report made on that subject to the prefect of police in 1832.

Let us add that, if we are to believe a police tradition, strange, but probably well founded, Le Cabuc was Claquesous. The fact is, that after the death of La Cabuc, nothing more was heard of Claquesous. Claquesous left no trace on his disappearance; he would seem to have been amalgamated with the invisible. His life had been darkness, his end was night.

The whole insurgent group was still under the emotion of this tragic trial, so quickly instituted and so quickly terminated, when Courfeyrac again saw in the barricade the small young man who in the morning had called at his house for Marius.

This boy, who had a bold and reckless air, had come at night to rejoin the insurgents.

Marius Enters the Shadow

I

THAT voice which through the twilight had called Marius to the barricade of the rue de la Chanvrerie sounded to him like the voice of destiny. He wished to die, the opportunity presented itself; he was knocking at the door of the tomb, a hand in the shadow held out the key. These dreary clefts in the darkness before despair are tempting. Marius pushed aside the bar which had let him pass so many times, came out of the garden, and said: "Let us go!"

Mad with grief, feeling no longer anything fixed or solid in his brain, incapable of accepting anything henceforth from fate, after these two months passed in the intoxications of youth and of love, whelmed at once beneath all the reveries of despair, he had now but one desire: to make an end of it very quick.

He began to walk rapidly. It happened that he was armed, having Javert's pistols with him.

The young man whom he thought he had seen was lost from his eyes in the streets.

Marius, who had left the rue Plumet by the boulevard, crossed the esplanade and the Bridge of the Invalides, the Champs Elysées, the Place Louis XV and entered the rue de Rivoli.

Marius entered through the Delorme arcade into the rue Saint Honoré. As he receded from the Palais Royal, there were fewer lighted windows; the shops were entirely closed, nobody was chatting in the doors, the street grew gloomy, and at the same time the throng grew dense. For the passers now were a throng. Nobody was seen to speak in this throng, and still there came from it a deep and dull hum.

After having crossed the belt of the multitude and passed the fringe of troops, he found himself in the midst of something terrible. Not a passer more, not a soldier, not a light—

nobody. Solitude, silence, night—a mysterious chill which seized upon him. To enter a street was to enter a cellar.

He continued to advance.

He took a few steps. Somebody passed near him running. Was it a man? A woman? Were there several? He could not have told. It had passed and had vanished.

By a circuitous route, he came to a little street which he judged to be the rue de la Poterie. He walked very near the posts and guided himself by the walls of the houses. A little beyond the barricade, he seemed to catch a glimpse of something white in front of him. He approached; it took form. It was two white horses—the omnibus horses unharnessed by Bossuet earlier, which had wandered at chance from street to street all day long, and had finally stopped there, with the exhausted patience of brutes, who no more comprehended the ways of man than man comprehends the ways of Providence.

From that moment he met nothing more.

This whole route resembled a descent down dark stairs.

II

MARIUS had arrived at the markets.

There all was more calm, more obscure, and more motionless still than in the neighboring streets. One would have said that the icy peace of the grave had come forth from the earth and spread over the sky.

A red glare, however, cut out upon this dark background the high roofs of the houses which barred the rue de la Chanvrerie on the side toward Saint Eustache. It was the reflection of the torch which was blazing in the barricade of Corinth. Marius directed his steps toward this glare. He felt that he was very near what he had come to seek, and he walked on tiptoe. He reached in this way the elbow of that short end of the rue Mondétour, which was, as we remember, the only communication preserved by Enjolras with the outside. Around the corner of the last house on his left, cautiously advancing his head, he looked into this end of the rue Mondétour.

A little beyond the black corner of the alley, he perceived a light upon the pavement, a portion of the wineshop, and behind, a lamp twinkling in a kind of shapeless wall, and men crouching down with muskets on their knees. All this was within twenty yards of him. It was the interior of the barricade.

Marius had but one step more to take.

Then the unhappy young man sat down upon a stone, folded his arms, and thought of his father.

He thought of that heroic Colonel Pontmercy who had been so brave a soldier.

He said to himself that his day had come to him also, that his hour had at last struck, that after his father, he also was to be brave, intrepid, bold, to run amid bullets, to bare his breast to the bayonets, to pour out his blood, to seek the enemy, to seek death, that he was to wage war in his turn and to enter upon the field of battle, and that that field of battle upon which he was about to enter was the street, and that war which he was about to wage was civil war!

He saw civil war yawning like an abyss before him, and that in it he was to fall.

Then he shuddered.

And then he began to weep bitterly.

It was horrible. But what could he do? Live without Cosette he could not. Since she had gone away, he must surely die. And then, indeed! To have come so far, and to recoil! To have approached the danger, and to flee! To have come and looked into the barricade, and to slink away!

A prey to the swaying of his thoughts, he bowed his head.

Suddenly he straightened up. A sort of splendid rectification was wrought in his spirit. There was an expansion of thought fitted to the confinity of the tomb; to be near death makes us see the truth. The vision of the act upon which he felt himself perhaps on the point of entering, appeared to him no longer lamentable, but superb. The war of the street was suddenly transfigured by some indescribable interior throe of the soul, before the eye of his mind.

Let us see, why should his father be indignant? Are there not cases when insurrection rises to the dignity of duty? The country laments, so be it, but humanity applauds. Besides is it true that the country mourns? France bleeds, but liberty smiles, and before the smile of liberty, France forgets her wound.

An enormous fortress of prejudices, of privileges, of superstitions, of lies, of exactions, of abuses, of violence, of iniquity, of darkness, is still standing upon the world with its towers of hatred. It must be thrown down. This monstrous pile must be made to fall. To conquer at Austerlitz is grand; to take the Bastille is immense.

Even while thinking thus, overwhelmed but resolute, hesitating, however, and, indeed, shuddering in view of what he was about to do, his gaze wandered into the interior of the barricade. The insurgents were chatting in an undertone, without moving about, and that quasi silence was felt which marks the last phase of delay. Above them, at a third-story window, Marius distinguished a sort of spectator or witness who seemed to him singularly attentive. It was the porter killed by Le Cabuc. From below, by the reflection of the torch hidden among the paving stones, this head was dimly perceptible. Nothing was more strange in that gloomy and uncertain light than that livid, motionless, astonished face with its bristling hair, its staring eyes, and its gaping mouth, leaning over the street in an attitude of curiosity. One would have said that he who was dead was gazing at those who were about to die. A long trail of blood which had flowed from his head descended in ruddy streaks from the window to the height of the first story, where it stopped.

The Grandeurs of Despair

I

Nothing came yet. The clock of Saint Merry had struck ten. Enjolras and Combeferre had sat down, carbine in hand, near the opening of the great barricade. They were not talking; they were listening, seeking to catch even the faintest and most distant sound of a march.

A headlong run startled the empty street; they saw a creature nimbler than a clown climb over the omnibus, and Gavroche bounded into the barricade all breathless, saying:

"My musket! Here they are."

An electric thrill ran through the whole barricade, and a moving of hands feeling for their muskets was heard.

"Do you want my carbine?" said Enjolras to the gamin.

"I want the big musket," answered Gavroche.

And he took Javert's musket.

Forty-three insurgents, among them Enjolras, Combeferre, Courfeyrac, Bossuet, Joly, Bahorel, and Gavroche, were on their knees in the great barricade, their heads even with the crest of the wall, the barrels of their muskets and their carbines pointed over the paving stones as through loopholes, watchful, silent, ready to fire. Six, commanded by Feuilly, were stationed with their muskets at their shoulders, in the windows of the two upper stories of Corinth.

A few moments more elapsed; then a sound of steps, measured, heavy, numerous, was distinctly heard from the direction of Saint Leu. This sound, at first faint, then distinct, then heavy and sonorous, approached slowly, without halt, without interruption, with a tranquil and terrible continuity. Nothing but this could be heard. It was at once the silence and the sound of the statue of the Commander, but this stony tread was so indescribably enormous and so multiplex that it called up at the same time the idea of a throng and of a specter.

There was still a pause, as if on both sides they were awaiting. Suddenly, from the depth of that shadow, a voice, so much the more ominous because nobody could be seen, and because it seemed as if it were the obscurity itself which was speaking, cried:

"Who is there?"

At the same time they heard the click of the leveled muskets.

Enjolras answered in a lofty and ringing tone:

"French Revolution!"

"Fire!" said the voice.

A flash empurpled all the façades on the street, as if the door of a furnace were opened and suddenly closed.

A fearful explosion burst over the barricade. The red flag fell. The volley had been so heavy and so dense that it had cut the staff, that is to say, the very point of the pole of the omnibus. Some balls, which ricocheted from the cornices of the houses, entered the barricade and wounded several men.

The impression produced by this first charge was freezing. The attack was impetuous, and such as to make the boldest ponder. It was evident that they had to do with a whole regiment at least.

"Comrades," cried Courfeyrac, "don't waste the powder. Let us wait to reply till they come into the street."

"And first of all," said Enjolras, "let us hoist the flag again!"

He picked up the flag which had fallen just at his feet.

They heard from without the rattling of the ramrods in the muskets: the troops were reloading.

Enjolras continued:

"Who is there here who has courage? Who replants the flag on the barricade?"

Nobody answered. To mount the barricade at the moment when without doubt it was aimed at anew, was simply death. The bravest hesitates to sentence himself. Enjolras himself felt a shudder. He repeated:

"Nobody volunteers!"

II

SINCE they had arrived at Corinth and had commenced building the barricade, hardly any attention had been paid to Father Mabeuf. Monsieur Mabeuf, however, had not left the company. He had entered the ground floor of the wine-shop and sat down behind the counter. There he had been, so to speak, annihilated in himself. He no longer seemed to look or to think. Courfeyrac and others had accosted him two or three times, warning him of the danger, entreating him to withdraw, but he had not appeared to hear them. When nobody was speaking to him, his lips moved as if he were answering somebody, and as soon as anybody addressed a word to him, his lips became still and his eyes lost all appearance of life. Some hours before the barricade was attacked, he had taken a position which he had not left since, his hands upon his knees and his head bent forward as if he were looking into an abyss. Nothing had been able to draw him out of this attitude; it appeared as if his mind were not in the barricade. When everybody had gone to take his place for the combat, there remained in the basement room only Javert tied to the post, an insurgent with drawn saber watching Javert, and he, Mabeuf. At the moment of the attack, at the discharge, the physical shock reached him, and, as it were, awakened him; he rose suddenly, crossed the room, and at the instant when Enjolras repeated his appeal: "Nobody volunteers!" they saw the old man appear in the doorway of the wineshop.

His presence produced some commotion in the group. A cry arose:

"It is the Voter! It is the Conventionist! It is the Representative of the people!"

It is probable that he did not hear.

He walked straight to Enjolras, the insurgents fell back before him with a religious awe, he snatched the flag from Enjolras, who drew back petrified, and then, nobody daring to stop him or to aid him, this old man of eighty, with shaking head but firm foot, began to climb slowly up the stairway of paving stones built into the barricade. It was so gloomy and so grand that all about him cried: "Hats off!" At each step it was frightful; his white hair, his decrepit face, his large forehead bald and wrinkled, his hollow eyes, his quivering and open mouth, his old arm raising the red banner, surged up out of the shadow and grew grand in the bloody light of the torch, and they seemed to see the ghost of '93 rising out of the earth, the flag of terror in its hand.

When he was on the top of the last step, when this trembling and terrible phantom, standing upon that mound of rubbish before twelve hundred invisible muskets, rose up, in the face of death and as if he were stronger than it, the whole barricade had in the darkness a supernatural and colossal appearance.

There was one of those silences which occur only in presence of prodigies.

In the midst of this silence the old man waved the red flag and cried:

"Vive la révolution! Vive la république! Fraternity! Equality! And death!"

They heard from the barricade a low and rapid muttering like the murmur of a hurried priest dispatching a prayer. It was probably the commissary of police who was making the legal summons at the other end of the street.

Then the same ringing voice which had cried: "Who is there?" cried:

"Disperse!"

Monsieur Mabeuf, pallid, haggard, his eyes illumined by the mournful fires of insanity, raised the flag above his head and repeated:

"Vive la république!"

"Fire!" said the voice.

A second discharge, like a shower of grape, beat against the barricade.

The old man fell upon his knees, then rose up, let the flag drop, and fell backward upon the pavement within, like a log, at full length with his arms crossed.

Streams of blood ran from beneath him. His old face, pale and sad, seemed to behold the sky.

One of those emotions superior to man, which make us forget even to defend ourselves, seized the insurgents, and they approached the corpse with a respectful dismay.

"What men these regicides are!" said Enjolras.

Courfeyrac bent over to Enjolras' ear.

"This is only for you, and I don't wish to diminish the enthusiasm. But he was anything but a regicide. I knew him. His name was Father Mabeuf. I don't know what ailed him today. But he was a brave blockhead. Just look at his head."

"Blockhead and Brutus heart," answered Enjolras.

Then he raised his voice:

"Citizens! This is the example which the old give to the young. We hesitated, he came! We fell back, he advanced! Behold what those who tremble with old age teach those who tremble with fear! This patriarch is august in the sight of the country. He has had a long life and a magnificent death! Now let us protect his corpse, let everyone defend this old man dead as he would defend his father living, and let his presence among us make the barricade impregnable!"

A murmur of gloomy and determined adhesion followed these words.

Enjolras stooped down, raised the old man's head, and timidly kissed him on the forehead; then separating his arms, and handling the dead with a tender care, as if he feared to hurt him, he took off his coat, showed the bleeding holes to all, and said:

"There now is our flag."

THEY threw a long black shawl belonging to the Widow Hucheloup over Father Mabeuf. Six men made a barrow of their muskets, they laid the corpse upon it, and they bore it, bareheaded, with solemn slowness, to the large table in the basement room.

These men, completely absorbed in the grave and sacred thing which they were doing, no longer thought of the perilous situation in which they were.

When the corpse passed near Javert, who was still impassible, Enjolras said to the spy:

"You! Directly."

During this time Little Gavroche, who alone had not left his post and had remained on the watch, thought he saw some men approaching the barricade with a stealthy step. Suddenly he cried:

"Take care!"

Courfeyrac, Enjolras, Jean Prouvaire, Combeferre, Joly, Bahorel, Bossuet all sprang tumultuously from the wineshop. There was hardly a moment to spare. They perceived a sparkling breadth of bayonets undulating above the barricade. Municipal Guards of tall stature were penetrating, some by climbing over the omnibus, others by the opening, pushing before them the gamin, who fell back, but did not fly.

The moment was critical. It was that first fearful instant of the inundation, when the stream rises to the level of the bank and when the water begins to infiltrate through the fissures in the dike. A second more, and the barricade had been taken.

Bahorel sprang upon the first Municipal Guard who entered, and killed him at the very muzzle of his carbine; the second killed Bahorel with his bayonet. Another had already prostrated Courfeyrac, who was crying "Help!" The largest of all, a kind of colossus, marched upon Gavroche with fixed bayonet. The gamin took Javert's enormous musket in his little arms, aimed it resolutely at the giant, and pulled the trigger. Nothing went off. Javert had not loaded his musket. The Municipal Guard burst into a laugh and raised his bayonet over the child.

Before the bayonet touched Gavroche the musket dropped from the soldier's hands; a ball had struck the Municipal Guard in the middle of the forehead, and he fell on his back. A second ball struck the other Guard, who had assailed Courfeyrac, full in the breast, and threw him upon the pavement.

It was Marius who had just entered the barricade.

IV

MARIUS, still hidden in the corner of the rue Mondétour, had watched the first phase of the combat, irresolute and shuddering. However, he was not able long to resist that mysterious and sovereign infatuation which we may call the appeal of the abyss. Before the imminence of the danger, before the death of Monsieur Mabeuf, that fatal enigma, before Bahorel slain, Courfeyrac crying "Help!" that child threatened, his friends to succor or to avenge, all hesitation had vanished, and he had rushed into the conflict, his two pistols in his hands. By the first shot he had saved Gavroche, and by the second delivered Courfeyrac.

At the shots, at the cries of the wounded Guards, the assailants had scaled the entrenchment, upon the summit of which could now be seen thronging Municipal Guards, soldiers of the Line, National Guards of the *banlieue*, musket in hand. They already covered more than two-thirds of the wall, but they did not leap into the enclosure; they seemed to hesitate, fearing some snare. They looked into the obscure barricade as one would look into a den of lions. The light of the torch only lighted up their bayonets, their bearskin caps, and the upper part of their anxious and angry faces.

Marius had now no arms, he had thrown away his discharged pistols, but he had noticed the keg of powder in the basement room near the door.

As he turned half round, looking in that direction, a soldier aimed at him. At the moment the soldier aimed at Marius, a hand was laid upon the muzzle of the musket, and stopped it. It was somebody who had sprung forward, the young workingman with velvet pantaloons. The shot went off, passed through the hand, and perhaps also through the workingman, for he fell, but the ball did not reach Marius. All this in the smoke, rather guessed than seen. Marius, who was entering the basement room, hardly noticed it. Still he had caught a dim glimpse of that musket directed at him, and that hand which had stopped it, and he had heard the shot. But in moments like that the things which we see waver and rush headlong, and we stop for nothing. We feel ourselves vaguely pushed toward still deeper shadow, and all is cloud.

The insurgents, surprised, but not dismayed, had rallied. The most determined, with Enjolras, Courfeyrac, Jean Prouvaire, and Combeferre, had haughtily placed their backs to the houses in the rear, openly facing the ranks of soldiers and guards which crowded the barricade.

Suddenly a thundering voice was heard crying:

"Begone, or I'll blow up the barricade!"

All turned in the direction whence the voice came.

Marius had entered the basement room, and had taken the keg of powder; then he had profited by the smoke and the kind of obscure fog which filled the entrenched enclosure, to glide along the barricade as far as that cage of paving stones in which the torch was fixed. To pull out the torch, to put the keg of powder in its place, to push the pile of paving stones upon the keg, which stove it in, with a sort of terrible self-control—all this had been for Marius the work of stooping down and rising up; and now all, National Guards, Municipal Guards, officers, soldiers, grouped at the other extremity of the barricade, beheld him with horror, his foot upon the stones, the torch in his hand, his stern face lighted by a deadly resolution, bending the flame of the torch toward that formidable pile in which they discerned the broken barrel of powder, and uttering that terrific cry:

"Begone, or I'll blow up the barricade!"

Marius upon this barricade, after the octogenarian, was the vision of the young revolution after the apparition of the old.

"Blow up the barricade!" said a sergeant. "And yourself also!"

Marius answered:

"And myself also."

And he approached the torch to the keg of powder.

But there was no longer anybody on the wall. The assailants, leaving their dead and wounded, fled pell-mell and in dis-

order toward the extremity of the street, and were again lost
in the night. It was rout.

The barricade was redeemed.

V

ALL flocked round Marius. Courfeyrac sprang to his neck.

"You here!"

"How fortunate!" said Combeferre.

"You came in good time!" said Bossuet.

"Without you I should have been dead!" continued Courfeyrac.

"Without you I'd been gobbled!" added Gavroche.

A bitter emotion came to darken their joy over the redeemed
barricade.

They called the roll. One of the insurgents was missing.
And who? One of the dearest. One of the most valiant, Jean
Prouvaire. They sought him among the wounded, he was
not there. They sought him among the dead, he was not
there. He was evidently a prisoner.

Combeferre said to Enjolras:

"They have our friend; we have their officer. Have you
set your heart on the death of this spy?"

"Yes," said Enjolras, "but less than on the life of Jean
Prouvaire."

This passed in the basement room near Javert's post.

"Well," replied Combeferre, "I am going to tie my handkerchief to my cane, and go with a flag of truce to offer to give
them their man for ours."

"Listen," said Enjolras, laying his hand on Combeferre's
arm.

There was a significant clicking of arms at the end of the
street.

They heard a manly voice cry:

"Vive la France! Vive l'avenir!"

They recognized Prouvaire's voice.

There was a flash and an explosion.

Silence reigned again.

"They have killed him!" exclaimed Combeferre.

Enjolras looked at Javert and said to him:

"Your friends have just shot you."

THE whole attention of the insurgents was directed to the great barricade, which was evidently the point still threatened, and where the struggle must infallibly recommence. Marius, however, thought of the little barricade and went to it. It was deserted, and was guarded only by the lamp which flickered between the stones.

As Marius, the inspection made, was retiring, he heard his name faintly pronounced in the obscurity:

"Monsieur Marius!"

He shuddered, for he recognized the voice which had called him two hours before, through the grating in the rue Plumet.

Only this voice now seemed to be but a breath.

He looked about him and saw nobody.

"At your feet," said the voice.

He stooped and saw a form in the shadow, which was dragging itself toward him. It was crawling along the pavement. It was this that had spoken to him.

The lamp enabled him to distinguish a blouse, a pair of torn pantaloons of coarse velvet, bare feet, and something which resembled a pool of blood. Marius caught a glimpse of a pale face which rose toward him and said to him:

"You do not know me?"

"No."

"Eponine."

Marius bent down quickly. It was indeed that unhappy child. She was dressed as a man.

"How came you here? What are you doing there?"

"I am dying," said she.

There are words and incidents which rouse beings who are crushed. Marius exclaimed with a start:

"You are wounded! "

And he tried to pass his arm under her to lift her.

In lifting her he touched her hand.

She uttered a feeble cry.

"Have I hurt you?" asked Marius.

"A little."

"But I have only touched your hand."

She raised her hand into Marius' sight, and Marius saw in the center of that hand a black hole.

"What is the matter with your hand?" said he.

"It is pierced."

"Pierced?"

"Yes."

"By what?"

"By a ball."

"How?"

"Did you see a musket aimed at you?"

"Yes, and a hand which stopped it."

"That was mine."

Marius shuddered.

"What madness! Poor child! But that is not so bad; if that is all, it is nothing, let me carry you to a bed. They will care for you, people don't die from a shot in the hand."

She murmured:

"The ball passed through my hand, but it went out through my back. It is useless to take me from here. I will tell you how you can care for me, better than a surgeon. Sit down by me on that stone."

He obeyed; she laid her head on Marius' knees, and without looking at him, she said:

"Oh! How good it is! How kind he is! That is it! I don't suffer any more!"

She remained a moment in silence, then she turned her head with effort and looked at Marius.

"You thought me ugly, didn't you?"

She continued:

"See, you are lost! Nobody will get out of the barricade, now. It was I who led you into this, it was! You are going to die, I am sure. And still when I saw him aiming at you, I put up my hand upon the muzzle of the musket. How droll it is! But it was because I wanted to die before you. When I got this ball, I dragged myself here, nobody saw me, nobody picked me up. I waited for you, I said: 'He will not come then?' Oh! if you knew, I bit my blouse, I suffered so much! Now I am well. Do you remember the day when I came into your room, and when I looked at myself in your mirror, and the day when I met you on the boulevard near some workwomen? How the birds sang! It was not very long ago. You gave me a hundred sous, and I said to you: 'I don't want your money.'

Did you pick up your piece? You are not rich. I didn't think to tell you to pick it up. The sun shone bright, I was not cold. Do you remember, Monsieur Marius? Oh! I am happy! We are all going to die."

She had a wandering, grave, and touching air. Her torn blouse showed her bare throat. While she was talking she rested her wounded hand upon her breast where there was another hole, from which there came with each pulsation a flow of blood like a jet of wine from an open bunghole.

Marius gazed upon this unfortunate creature with profound compassion.

"Oh!" she exclaimed suddenly. "It is coming back. I am stifling!"

She seized her blouse and bit it, and her legs writhed upon the pavement.

"Oh! Don't go away!" said she. "It will not be long now!"

She was sitting almost upright, but her voice was very low and broken by hiccoughs. At intervals the death rattle interrupted her. She approached her face as near as she could to Marius' face. She added with a strange expression:

"Listen, I don't want to deceive you. I have a letter in my pocket for you. Since yesterday. I was told to put it in the post. I kept it. I didn't want it to reach you. But you would not like it of me perhaps when we meet again so soon. We do meet again, don't we? Take your letter."

She grasped Marius' hand convulsively with her wounded hand, but she seemed no longer to feel the pain. She put Marius' hand into the pocket of her blouse. Marius really felt a paper there.

"Take it," said she.

Marius took the letter.

She made a sign of satisfaction and of consent.

"Now for my pains, promise me—"

And she hesitated.

"What?" asked Marius.

"Promise me!"

"I promise you."

"Promise to kiss me on the forehead when I am dead. I shall feel it."

She let her head fall back upon Marius' knees and her eyelids closed. He thought that poor soul had gone. Eponine lay motionless, but just when Marius supposed her forever asleep, she slowly opened her eyes in which the gloomy deepness of death appeared, and said to him with an accent the sweetness of which already seemed to come from another world:

"And then, do you know, Monsieur Marius, I believe I was a little in love with you."

She essayed to smile again and expired.

VII

MARIUS kept his promise. He kissed that livid forehead from which oozed an icy sweat. This was not infidelity to Cosette; it was a thoughtful and gentle farewell to an unhappy soul.

He had not taken the letter which Eponine had given him without a thrill. He had felt at once the presence of an event. He was impatient to read it. The heart of man is thus made; the unfortunate child had hardly closed her eyes when Marius thought to unfold this paper. He laid her gently upon the ground and went away. Something told him that he could not read that letter in sight of this corpse.

He went to a candle in the basement room. It was a little note, folded and sealed with the elegant care of a woman. The address was in a woman's hand, and ran:

Monsieur Marius Pontmercy, Monsieur Courfeyrac's, rue de la Verrerie, No. 16.

He broke the seal and read:

"My beloved, alas! My father wishes to start immediately. We shall be tonight in the rue de l'Homme Armé, No. 7. In a week we shall be in England. COSETTE. June 4th."

Such was the innocence of this love that Marius did not even know Cosette's handwriting.

He covered Cosette's letter with kisses. She loved him then? He had for a moment the idea that now he need not die. Then he said to himself: "She is going away. Her father takes her to England, and my grandfather refuses to consent to the marriage. Nothing is changed in the fatality." Dreamers, like Marius, have these supreme depressions, and paths hence are chosen in despair. The fatigue of life is insupportable; death is sooner over. Then he thought that there were two duties remaining for him to fulfill: to inform Cosette of his death and to send her a last farewell, and to save from the imminent catastrophe which was approaching, this poor child, Eponine's brother and Thénardier's son.

He had a pocketbook with him; the same that had contained the pages upon which he had written so many thoughts of love for Cosette. He tore out a leaf and wrote with a pencil these few lines:

"Our marriage was impossible. I have asked my grandfather, he has refused; I am without fortune, and you also. I ran to your house, I did not find you. You know the promise that I gave you? I keep it, I die, I love you. When you read this, my soul will be near you, and will smile upon you."

Having nothing to seal this letter with, he merely folded the paper and wrote upon it this address:

Mademoiselle Cosette Fauchelevent, Monsieur Fauchele-vent's, rue de l'Homme Armé, No. 7.

The letter folded, he remained a moment in thought, took his pocketbook again, opened it, and wrote these lines on the first page with the same pencil:

"My name is Marius Pontmercy. Carry my corpse to my grandfather's, Monsieur Gillenormand, rue des Filles du Calvaire, No. 6, in the Marais."

He put the book into his coat pocket, then he called Gavroche. The gamin, at the sound of Marius' voice, ran up with his joyous and devoted face.

"Will you do something for me?" Marius asked.

"Anything," said Gavroche. "God of the good God! Without you I should have been cooked, sure."

"You see this letter?"

"Yes."

"Take it. Go out of the barricade immediately (Gavroche, disturbed, began to scratch his ear), and tomorrow morning you will carry it to its address, to Mademoiselle Cosette, at Monsieur Fauchelevent's, rue de l'Homme Armé No. 7."

The heroic boy answered:

"Ah, well, but in that time they'll take the barricade, and I shan't be here."

"The barricade will not be attacked again before daybreak, according to all appearance, and will not be taken before tomorrow noon."

"All right," said he.

And he started off on a run by the little rue Mondétour.

Gavroche had an idea which decided him, but which he did

not tell, for fear Marius would make some objection to it.

That idea was this:

"It is hardly midnight, the rue de l'Homme Armé is not far, I will carry the letter right away, and I shall get back in time."

The Rue de l'Homme Armé

I

WHAT are the convulsions of a city compared with the *émeutes* of the soul? Man is a still deeper depth than the people. Jean Valjean, at that very moment, was a prey to a frightful uprising. All the gulfs were reopened within him. He also, like Paris, was shuddering on the threshold of a formidable and obscure revolution. A few hours had sufficed. His destiny and his conscience were suddenly covered with shadow. Of him also, as of Paris, we might say: the two principles are face to face. The angel of light and the angel of darkness are to wrestle on the bridge of the abyss. Which of the two shall hurl down the other? Which shall sweep him away?

On the eve of that same day, June 5th, Jean Valjean, accompanied by Cosette and Toussaint, had installed himself in the rue de l'Homme Armé. A sudden turn of fortune awaited him there.

Cosette had not left the rue Plumet without an attempt at resistance. For the first time since they had lived together, Cosette's will and Jean Valjean's will had shown themselves distinct, and had been, if not conflicting, at least contradictory. There was objection on one side and inflexibility on the other. The abrupt advice: "remove," thrown to Jean Valjean by an unknown hand, had so far alarmed him as to render him absolute. He believed himself tracked out and pursued. Cosette had to yield.

In this departure from the rue Plumet, which was almost a flight, Jean Valjean carried nothing but the little embalmed valise christened by Cosette the Inseparable. Full trunks would have required porters, and porters are witnesses. They had a

coach come to the door on the rue Babylone, and they went
away. They arrived in the rue de l'Homme Armé after nightfall.

They went silently to bed.

We are reassured almost as foolishly as we are alarmed;
human nature is so constituted. Hardly was Jean Valjean in
the rue de l'Homme Armé, before his anxiety grew less, and
by degrees was dissipated. By what means could anybody find
him there?

His first care was to place the Inseparable by his side.

He slept well. Night counsels; we may add: night calms.
Next morning he awoke almost cheerful.

As for Cosette, she had Toussaint bring a bowl of soup to
her room, and did not make her appearance till evening.

About five o'clock, Toussaint, who was coming and going,
very busy with this little removal, set a cold fowl on the
dining-room table, which Cosette, out of deference to her
father, consented to look at.

This done, Cosette, upon pretext of a severe headache, said
good night to Jean Valjean, and shut herself in her bedroom.
Jean Valjean ate a chicken's wing with a good appetite, and,
leaning on the table, clearing his brow little by little, was
regaining his sense of security.

While he was making this frugal dinner, he became confusedly aware, on two or three occasions, of the stammering
of Toussaint, who said to him: "Monsieur, there is a row;
they are fighting in Paris." But, absorbed in a multitude of
interior combinations, he paid no attention to it. To tell the
truth, he had not heard.

He arose and began to walk from the window to the door,
and from the door to the window, growing calmer and calmer.

With calmness, Cosette, his single engrossing care, returned
to his thoughts. Cosette sufficed for his happiness; the idea
that perhaps he did not suffice for Cosette's happiness, this
idea, once his fever and his bane, did not even present itself
to his mind. He arranged in his own mind, and with every
possible facility, the departure for England with Cosette,
and he saw his happiness reconstructed, no matter where,
in the perspective of his reverie.

While yet walking up and down, with slow steps, his eye
suddenly met something strange.

He perceived facing him, in the inclined mirror which hung

above the sideboard, and he distinctly read, the lines which follow:

"My beloved, alas! My father wishes to start immediately. We shall be tonight in the rue de l'Homme Armé, No. 7. In a week we shall be in London. COSETTE. June 4th."

Jean Valjean stood aghast.

Cosette, on arriving, had laid her blotter on the sideboard before the mirror, and, wholly absorbed in her sorrowful anguish, had forgotten it there.

The mirror reflected the writing.

There resulted what is called in geometry the symmetrical image, so that the writing reversed on the blotter was corrected by the mirror, and presented its original form, and Jean Valjean had beneath his eyes the letter written in the evening by Cosette to Marius.

It was simple and withering.

Jean Valjean went to the mirror. He read the five lines again, but he did not believe it. They produced upon him the effect of an apparition in a flash of lightning. It was a hallucination. It was impossible. It was not.

Little by little his perception became more precise; he looked at Cosette's blotter, and the consciousness of the real fact returned to him. He took the blotter and said: "It comes from that."

Jean Valjean tottered, let the blotter fall, and sank down into the old armchair by the sideboard, his head drooping, his eyes glassy, bewildered. He said to himself that it was clear, and that the light of the world was forever eclipsed, and that Cosette had written that to somebody. Then he heard his soul, again become terrible, give a sullen roar in the darkness. Go, then, take from the lion the dog which he has in his cage.

Of all the tortures which he had undergone in that inquisition of destiny, this was the most fearful. Never had such pincers seized him. He felt the mysterious quiver of every latent sensibility. He felt the laceration of the unknown fiber. Alas, the supreme ordeal, let us say rather, the only ordeal, is the loss of the beloved being.

Poor old Jean Valjean did not, certainly, love Cosette otherwise than as a father, but, as we have already mentioned, into his paternity the very bereavement of his life had introduced every love. He loved Cosette as his daughter, and he loved her as his mother, and he loved her as his sister, and, as he had never had either sweetheart or wife, as nature is a creditor who accepts no protest, that sentiment, also, the most indestructible of all, was mingled with the others, vague, ignorant, pure with the purity of blindness, unconscious, celestial, angelic, divine—less like a sentiment than like an instinct, less like an instinct than like an attraction, imperceptible and invisible, but real; love, properly speaking, existed in his enormous tenderness for Cosette as does the vein of gold in the mountain, dark and virgin.

So, when he saw that it was positively ended, that she escaped him, that she glided from his hands, that she eluded him, that it was cloud, that it was water; when he had before his eyes this crushing evidence: another is the aim of her heart, another is the desire of her life, there is a beloved, I am only the father, I no longer exist; when he could no more doubt when he said to himself: "She is going away out of me!" the grief which he felt surpassed the possible. To have done all that he had done to come to this! And, what! To be nothing! Then, as we have just said, he felt from head to foot a shudder of revolt. He felt even to the roots of his hair the immense awakening of selfishness, and the Me howled in the abyss of his soul.

His instinct did not hesitate. He put together certain circumstances, certain dates, certain blushes, and certain pallors of Cosette, and he said to himself: "It is he." He perceived distinctly, at the bottom of the implacable evocation of memory, the unknown prowler of the Luxembourg, that wretched seeker of amours, that romantic idler, that imbecile, that coward, for it is cowardice to come and make sweet eyes at girls who are beside their father who loves them.

After he had fully determined that that young man was at the bottom of this state of affairs, and that it all came from him, he, Jean Valjean, the regenerated man, the man who had labored so much upon his soul, the man who had made so many efforts to resolve all life, all misery, and all misfortune into love; he looked within himself, and there he saw a specter, Hatred.

While he was thinking, Toussaint entered. Jean Valjean arose, and asked her:

"In what direction is it? Do you know?"

Toussaint, astonished, could only answer:

"If you please?"

Jean Valjean resumed:

"Didn't you tell me just now that they were fighting?"

"Oh! Yes, monsieur," answered Toussaint. "It is over by Saint Merry."

There are some mechanical impulses which come to us, without our knowledge even, from our deepest thoughts. It was doubtless under the influence of an impulse of this kind, and of which he was hardly conscious, that Jean Valjean five minutes afterward found himself in the street.

He was bareheaded, seated upon the stone block by the door of his house. He seemed to be listening.

The night had come.

II

How much time did he pass thus? What were the ebbs and the flows of that tragic meditation? Did he straighten up? Did he remain bowed? Had he been bent so far as to break? Could he yet straighten himself, and regain a foothold in his conscience upon something solid? He himself probably could not have told.

Suddenly he raised his eyes, somebody was walking in the street, he heard steps near him, he looked, and, by the light of the lamp, in the direction of the Archives, he perceived a livid face, young and radiant.

Gavroche had just arrived in the rue de l'Homme Armé.

Gavroche was looking in the air, and appeared to be searching for something. He saw Jean Valjean perfectly, but he took no notice of him.

Jean Valjean, who, the instant before, in the state of mind in which he was, would not have spoken nor even replied to anybody, felt irresistibly impelled to address a word to this child.

"Small boy," said he, "what is the matter with you?"

"The matter is that I am hungry," answered Gavroche tartly. And he added: "Small yourself."

Jean Valjean felt in his pocket and took out a five-franc piece.

But Gavroche, who was of the wagtail species, and who passed quickly from one action to another, had picked up a stone. He had noticed a lamp.

"Hold on," said he, "you have your lamps here still. You are not regular, my friends. It is disorderly. Break me that."

And he threw the stone into the lamp, the glass from which fell with such a clatter that some bourgeois, hid behind the curtains in the opposite house, cried: "There is '93!"

The lamp swung violently and went out. The street became suddenly dark.

Jean Valjean approached Gavroche.

"Poor creature," said he, in an undertone, and speaking to himself, "he is hungry."

And he put the hundred-sous piece into his hand.

Gavroche felt softened. Besides he had just noticed that the man who was talking to him had no hat, and that inspired him with confidence.

"Really," said he, "it isn't to prevent my breaking the lamps?"

"Break all you like."

"You are a fine fellow," said Gavroche.

And he put the five-franc piece into one of his pockets. His confidence increasing, he added:

"Do you belong in the street?"

"Yes; why?"

"Could you show me Number Seven?"

"What do you want with Number Seven?"

Here the boy stopped; he feared that he had said too much; he plunged his nails vigorously into his hair, and merely answered:

"Ah! That's it."

An idea flashed across Jean Valjean's mind. Anguish has such lucidities. He said to the child:

"Have you brought the letter I am waiting for?"

"You?" said Gavroche. "You are not a woman."

"The letter is for Mademoiselle Cosette, isn't it?"

"Cosette?" muttered Gavroche. "Yes, I believe it is that funny name."

"Well," resumed Jean Valjean, "I am to deliver the letter to her. Give it to me."

"In that case you must know that I am sent from the barricade?"

"Of course," said Jean Valjean.

Gavroche thrust his hand into another of his pockets and drew out a folded paper.

Then he gave a military salute.

"Respect for the dispatch," said he. "It comes from the provisional government."

And he handed the paper to Jean Valjean.

"And hurry yourself, Monsieur What's-your-name, for Mamselle What's-her-name is waiting."

Gavroche was proud of having produced this word.

Jean Valjean asked:

"Is it to Saint Merry that the answer is to be sent?"

"In that case," exclaimed Gavroche, "you would make one of those cakes vulgarly called blunders. That letter comes from the barricade in the rue de la Chanvrerie, and I am going back there. Good night, citizen."

This said, Gavroche went away, or rather, resumed his flight like an escaped bird toward the spot whence he came. He replunged into the obscurity as if he made a hole in it, with the rapidity and precision of a projectile; the little rue de l'Homme Armé again became silent and solitary; in a twinkling, this strange child, who had within him shadow and dream, was buried in the dusk of those rows of black houses, and was lost therein like smoke in the darkness; one might have thought him dissipated and vanished, if, a few minutes after his disappearance, a loud crashing of glass and the splendid *patatras* of a lamp falling upon the pavement had not abruptly reawakened the indignant bourgeois. It was Gavroche passing along the rue du Chaume.

III

JEAN VALJEAN went in with Marius' letter.

He groped his way upstairs, pleased with the darkness like an owl which holds his prey, opened and softly closed the door, listened to see if he heard any sound, decided that, according to all appearances, Cosette and Toussaint were asleep, and plunged three or four matches into the bottle of the Fumade tinderbox before he could raise a spark, his hand trembled so much; there was theft in what he was about to do. At last his candle was lighted, he leaned his elbows on the table, unfolded the paper, and read.

In Marius' note to Cosette, Jean Valjean saw only these words:

". . . I die. . . . When you read this, my soul will be near you. . . ."

Before these two lines, he was horribly dazzled; he sat a moment as if crushed by the change of emotion which was wrought within him, he looked at Marius' note with a sort of drunken astonishment; he had before his eyes that splendor, the death of the hated being.

He uttered a hideous cry of inward joy. So, it was finished. The end came sooner than he had dared to hope. The being who encumbered his destiny was disappearing. He was going away of himself, freely, of his own accord. Without any intervention on his, Jean Valjean's part, without any fault of his, "that man" was about to die. Jean Valjean felt that he was delivered. He would then find himself once more alone with Cosette. Rivalry ceased; the future recommenced. He had only to keep the note in his pocket. Cosette would never know what had become of "that man." "I have only to let things take their course. That man cannot escape. If he is not dead yet, it is certain that he will die. What happiness!"

All this said within himself, he became gloomy.

Then he went down and waked the porter.

About an hour afterward, Jean Valjean went out in the full dress of a National Guard, and armed. The porter had easily found in the neighborhood what was necessary to complete his equipment. He had a loaded musket and a cartridge box full of cartridges. He went in the direction of the markets.

—— *Jean Valjean* ——

a range of bayonet points could be seen. A company of the
line was posted behind this barricade, on the watch. At his

War Between Four Walls

I

THE insurgents, under the eye of Enjolras, for Marius no longer looked to anything, turned the night to advantage. The barricade was not only repaired, but made larger. They raised it two feet. Iron bars planted in the paving stones resembled lances in rest. All sorts of rubbish added, and brought from all sides, increased the exterior intricacy. The redoubt was skillfully made over into a wall within and a thicket without.

They rebuilt the stairway of paving stones, which permitted ascent, as upon a citadel wall.

They put the barricade in order, cleared up the basement room, took the kitchen for a hospital, completed the dressing of the wounds, gathered up the powder scattered over the floor and the tables, cast bullets, made cartridges, scraped lint, distributed the arms of the fallen, cleaned the interior of the redoubt, picked up the fragments, carried away the corpses.

They deposited the dead in a heap in the little rue Mondétour, of which they were still masters. The pavement was red for a long time at that spot. Among the dead were four National Guards of the *banlieue*. Enjolras had their uniforms laid aside.

The three women took advantage of the night's respite to disappear finally, which made the insurgents breathe more freely.

They found refuge in some neighboring house.

Day was beginning to dawn. They had just extinguished the torch which had been replaced in its socket of paving stones. The interior of the barricade, that little court taken in on the street, was drowned in darkness, and seemed, through the dim twilight horror, the deck of a disabled ship. The combatants going back and forth, moved about in it like black forms. Above this frightful nest of shadow, the stories of the mute houses were lividly outlined; at the very top the wan chimneys appeared. The sky had that charming undecided hue, which is perhaps white, and perhaps blue. Some birds were flying with joyful notes. The tall house which formed the rear of the barricade, being toward the east, had a rosy reflection upon its roof. At the window on the third story, the morning breeze played with the gray hairs of the dead man's head.

Enjolras had gone to make a reconnaissance. He went out by the little rue Mondétour, creeping along by the houses.

The insurgents, we must say, were full of hope. With that facility for triumphant prophecy which is a part of the strength of the fighting Frenchman, they divided into three distinct phases the day which was opening: at six o'clock in the morning a regiment, "which had been labored with," would come over; at noon, insurrection of all Paris; at sundown, revolution.

Enjolras reappeared. He returned from his gloomy eagle's walk in the obscurity without. He listened for a moment to all this joy with folded arms, one hand over his mouth. Then, fresh and rosy in the growing whiteness of the morning, he said:

"The whole army of Paris fights. A third of that army is pressing upon the barricade in which you are. You will be attacked in an hour. As for the people, they were boiling yesterday, but this morning they do not stir. Nothing to expect, nothing to hope. No more from a *faubourg* than from a regiment. You are abandoned."

These words fell upon the buzzing of the groups and wrought the effect which the first drops of the tempest produce upon the swarm. All were dumb. There was a moment of inexpressible silence, when you might have heard the flight of death.

This moment was short.

A voice, from the most obscure depths of the groups, cried to Enjolras:

"So be it. Let us make the barricade twenty feet high, and let us all stand by it. Citizens, let us offer the protest of corpses. Let us show that, if the people abandon the republicans, the republicans do not abandon the people."

These words relieved the minds of all from the painful

cloud of personal anxieties. They were greeted by an enthusiastic acclamation.

The name of the man who thus spoke was never known; it was some obscure blouse-wearer, an unknown, a forgotten man, a passing hero, that great anonymous always found in human crises and in social births, who, at the proper instant, speaks the decisive word supremely, and who vanishes into the darkness after having for a moment represented, in the light of a flash, the people and God.

II

AFTER the man of the people, who decreed "the protest of corpses," had spoken and given the formula of the common soul, from all lips arose a strangely satisfied and terrible cry, funereal in meaning and triumphant in tone:

"Long live death! Let us all stay!"

"Why all?" said Enjolras.

"All! All!"

Enjolras resumed:

"The position is good, the barricade is fine. Thirty men are enough. Why sacrifice forty?"

They replied:

"Because nobody wants to go away."

Chief to his finger tips, Enjolras, seeing that they murmured, insisted. He resumed haughtily:

"Let those who fear to be one of but thirty, say so."

The murmurs redoubled.

"Besides," observed a voice from one of the groups, "to go away is easily said. The barricade is hemmed in."

Enjolras, without answering, touched Combeferre's shoulder, and they both went into the basement room.

They came back a moment afterward. Enjolras held out in his hands the four uniforms which he had reserved. Combeferre followed him, bringing the crossbelts and shakos.

"With this uniform," said Enjolras, "you can mingle with the ranks and escape. Here are enough for four."

And he threw the four uniforms upon the unpaved ground.

No wavering in the stoical auditory.

"There are among you some who have families, mothers, sisters, wives, children. Let those leave the ranks."

Then those heroic men began to inform against each other. "That is true," said a young man to a middle-aged man. "You are the father of a family. Go away." "It is you rather," answered the man, "you have two sisters whom you support." And an unparalleled conflict broke out. It was as to which should not allow himself to be laid at the door of the tomb.

"Citizens," continued Enjolras, "this is the republic, and universal suffrage reigns. Designate yourselves those who ought to go."

They obeyed. In a few minutes five were unanimously designated and left the ranks.

"There are five!" exclaimed Marius.

There were only four uniforms.

"Well," resumed the five, "one must stay."

At this moment a fifth uniform dropped, as if from heaven, upon the four others.

The fifth man was saved.

Marius raised his eyes and saw Monsieur Fauchelevent.

Jean Valjean had just entered the barricade.

Whether by information obtained, or by instinct, or by chance, he came by the little rue Mondétour. Thanks to his National Guard dress, he had passed easily.

The commotion was indescribable.

"Who is this man?" asked Bossuet.

"He is," answered Combeferre, "a man who saves others."

Marius added in a grave voice:

"I know him."

This assurance was enough for all.

Enjolras turned toward Jean Valjean:

"Citizen, you are welcome."

And he added:

"You know that we are going to die."

Jean Valjean, without answering, helped the insurgent whom he saved to put on his uniform.

III

THE situation of all, in this hour of death and in this inexorable place, found its resultant and summit in the supreme melancholy of Enjolras.

Enjolras had within himself the plenitude of revolution;

he was incomplete notwithstanding, as much as the absolute can be; he clung too much to Saint-Just, and not enough to Anacharsis Clootz; still his mind, in the Society of the Friends of the A B C, had at last received a certain polarization from the ideas of Combeferre; for some time, he had been leaving little by little the narrow form of dogma, and allowing himself to tread the broad paths of progress, and he had come to accept, as its definitive and magnificent evolution, the transformation of the great French Republic into the immense human republic. As to the immediate means, in a condition of violence, he wished them to be violent, in that he had not varied; he was still of that epic and formidable school which is summed up in this word: '93.

Enjolras was standing on the paving-stone steps, his elbow upon the muzzle of his carbine. He was thinking; he started, as at the passing of a gust; places where death is have such tripodal effects. There came from his eyes, full of the interior sight, a kind of stifled fire. Suddenly he raised his head—his fair hair waved backward like that of the angel upon his somber car of stars; it was the mane of a startled lion flaming with a halo—and exclaimed:

"Citizens, do you picture to yourselves the future? The streets of the cities flooded with light, green branches upon the thresholds, the nations sisters, men just, the old men blessing the children, the past loving the present, thinkers in full liberty, believers in full equality, for religion the heavens, God priest direct, human conscience become the altar, no more hatred, the fraternity of the workshop and the school, for reward and for penalty notoriety, to all, labor, for all, law, over all, peace, no more bloodshed, no more war, mothers happy! To subdue matter is the first step; to realize the ideal is the second. Reflect upon what progress has already done. Once the early human races looked with terror upon the hydra which blew upon the waters, the dragon which vomited fire, the griffin, monster of the air, which flew with the wings of an eagle and the claws of a tiger; fearful animals which were above man. Man, however, has laid his snares, the sacred snares of intelligence, and has at last caught the monsters. We have tamed the hydra, and he is called the steamer; we have tamed the dragon, and he is called the locomotive; we are on the point of taming the griffin, we have him already, and he is called the balloon. The day when this Promethean

work shall be finished, and when man shall have definitely
harnessed to his will the triple chimera of the ancients: the
hydra, the dragon, and the griffin, he will be the master of
the water, the fire, and the air, and he will be to the rest of
the animated creation what the ancient gods were formerly
to him. Courage, and forward! Citizens, whither are we
tending? To science made government, to the force of things,
recognized as the only public force, to the natural law having
its sanction and its penalty in itself and promulgated by its
self-evidence, to a dawn of truth, corresponding with the dawn
of the day. We are tending toward the union of the peoples;
we are tending toward the unity of man. No more fictions; no
more parasites. The real governed by the true, such is the
aim. Civilization will hold its courts on the summit of Europe,
and later at the center of the continents, in a grand parliament
of intelligence. Something like this has been seen already.
The Amphictyons had two sessions a year, one at Delphi, place
of the gods, the other at Thermopylae, place of the heroes.
Europe will have her Amphictyons; the globe will have its
Amphictyons. France bears within her the sublime future. This
is the gestation of the nineteenth century. That which was
sketched by Greece is worth being finished by France. Listen
to me, then, Feuilly, valiant workingman, man of the people,
man of the peoples. I venerate thee. Yes, thou seest clearly
future ages; yes, thou art right. Thou hadst neither father nor
mother, Feuilly; thou hast adopted humanity for thy mother,
and the right for thy father. Thou art going to die here; that
is, to triumph. Citizens, whatever may happen today, through
our defeat as well as through our victory, we are going to
effect a revolution. Just as conflagrations light up the whole
city, revolutions light up the whole human race. And what
revolution shall we effect? I have just said, the revolution of
the True. From the political point of view, there is but one
single principle: the sovereignty of man over himself. This
sovereignty of myself over myself is called Liberty. Where two
or several of these sovereignties associate the state begins.
But in this association there is no abdication. Each sovereignty
gives up a certain portion of itself to form the common right.
That portion is the same for all. This identity of concession
which each makes to all is Equality. The common right is
nothing more or less than the protection of all radiating upon
the right of each. This protection of all over each is called

Fraternity. The point of intersection of all these aggregated sovereignties is called Society. This intersection being a junction, this point is a knot. Hence what is called the social tie. Some day social contract, which is the same thing, the word contract being etymologically formed with the idea of tie. Let us understand each other in regard to equality, for, if liberty is the summit, equality is the base. Equality, citizens, is not all vegetation on a level, a society of big spears of grass and little oaks; a neighborhood of jealousies emasculating each other; it is, civilly, all aptitudes having equal opportunity; politically, all votes having equal weight; religiously, all consciences having equal rights. Equality has an organ: gratuitous and obligatory instruction. The right to the alphabet, we must begin by that. The primary school obligatory upon all, the higher school offered to all, such is the law. From the identical school springs equal society. Yes, instruction! Light! Light! All comes from light, and all returns to it. Citizens, the nineteenth century is grand, but the twentieth century will be happy. Then there will be nothing more like old history. Men will no longer have to fear, as now, a conquest, an invasion, a usurpation, a rivalry of nations with the armed hand, an interruption of civilization depending on a marriage of kings, a birth in the hereditary tyrannies, a partition of the peoples by a Congress, a dismemberment by the downfall of a dynasty, a combat of two religions meeting head to head, like two goats of darkness, upon the bridge of the infinite; they will no longer have to fear famine, speculation, prostitution from distress, misery from lack of work, and the scaffold, and the sword, and the battle, and all the brigandages of chance in the forest of events. We might almost say: there will be no events more. Men will be happy. The human race will fulfill its law as the terrestrial globe fulfills its; harmony will be re-established between the soul and the star; the soul will gravitate about the truth like the star about the light. Friends, the hour in which we live, and in which I speak to you, is a gloomy hour, but of such is the terrible price of the future. A revolution is a tollgate. Oh! The human race shall be delivered, uplifted, and consoled! We affirm it on this barricade. Whence shall arise the shout of love, if it be not from the summit of sacrifice? O my brothers, here is the place of junction between those who think and those who suffer; this barricade is made neither of paving stones, nor of timbers, nor of iron; it is made of two mounds, a mound of ideas and a mound of sorrows. Misery here encounters the ideal. Here day embraces night, and says: I will die with thee and thou shalt be born again with me. From the pressure of all desolations faith gushes forth. Sufferings bring their agony here, and ideas their immortality. This agony and this immortality are to mingle and compose our death. Brothers, he who dies here dies in the radiance of the future, and we are entering a grave illuminated by the dawn."

Enjolras broke off rather than ceased, his lips moved noiselessly, as if he were continuing to speak to himself, and they looked at him with attention, endeavoring still to hear. There was no applause; but they whispered for a long time. Speech being breath, the rustling of intellects resembles the rustling of leaves.

IV

It was growing light rapidly. But not a window was opened, not a door stood ajar; it was the dawn, not the hour of awakening. A mysterious movement was taking place at some distance. It was evident that the critical moment was at hand. As in the evening the sentries were driven in; but this time all.

Enjolras had piled up near the door of the wineshop some thirty paving stones, "torn up uselessly," said Bossuet.

The silence was now so profound on the side from which the attack must come that Enjolras made each man resume his post for combat.

A ration of brandy was distributed to all.

As on the evening before, the attention of all was turned, and we might almost say threw its weight upon the end of the street, now lighted and visible.

They had not long to wait. Activity distinctly recommenced in the direction of Saint Leu, but it did not resemble the movement of the first attack. A rattle of chains, the menacing jolt of a mass, a clicking of brass bounding over the pavement, a sort of solemn uproar, announced that an ominous body of iron was approaching. There was a shudder in the midst of those peaceful old streets, cut through and built up for the fruitful circulation of interests and ideas, and which were not made for the monstrous rumbling of the wheels of war.

The stare of all the combatants upon the extremity of the street became wild.

A piece of artillery appeared.

The gunners pushed forward the piece. The smoke of the burning match was seen.

"Fire!" cried Enjolras.

The whole barricade flashed fire, the explosion was terrible; an avalanche of smoke covered and effaced the gun and the men; in a few seconds the cloud dissipated, and the cannon and the men reappeared; those in charge of the piece placed it in position in front of the barricade, slowly, correctly, and without haste. Not a man had been touched. Then the gunner, bearing his weight on the breech, to elevate the range, began to point the cannon with the gravity of an astronomer adjusting a telescope.

"Bravo for the gunners!" cried Bossuet.

And the whole barricade clapped hands.

"Reload arms," said Enjolras.

How was the facing of the barricade going to behave under fire? Would the shot make a breach? That was the question. While the insurgents were reloading their muskets, the gunners loaded the cannon.

There was intense anxiety in the redoubt.

The gun went off; the detonation burst upon them.

"Present!" cried a cheerful voice.

And at the same time as the ball, Gavroche tumbled into the barricade.

He came by way of the rue du Cygne, and he had nimbly clambered over the minor barricade, which fronted upon the labyrinth of the Petite Truanderie.

Gavroche produced more effect in the barricade than the ball.

The ball lost itself in the jumble of the rubbish. At the very utmost it broke a wheel of the omnibus, and finished the old Anceau cart. Seeing which, the barricade began to laugh.

"Proceed," cried Bossuet to the gunners.

V

GAVROCHE warned his "comrades," as he called them, that the barricade was surrounded. He had had great difficulty in getting through. A battalion of the line, whose muskets were stacked in the Petite Truanderie, were observing the side on the rue du Cygne; on the opposite side the Municipal Guard occupied the rue des Prêcheurs. In front, they had the bulk of the army.

This information given, Gavroche added:

"I authorize you to give them a dose of pills."

Meanwhile Enjolras, on his battlement, was watching, listening with intense attention.

The assailants, dissatisfied doubtless with the effect of their fire, had not repeated it.

A company of infantry of the line had come in and occupied the extremity of the street, in the rear of the gun. The soldiers tore up the pavement, and with the stones constructed a little low wall, a sort of breastwork, which was hardly more than eighteen inches high, and which fronted the barricade. At the corner on the left of this breastwork, they saw the head of the column of a battalion of the *banlieue* massed in the rue Saint Denis.

Enjolras, on the watch, thought he distinguished the peculiar sound which is made when canisters of grape are taken from the caisson, and he saw the gunner change the aim and incline the piece slightly to the left. Then the cannoneers began to load. The gunner seized the linstock himself and brought it near the touchhole.

"Heads down, keep close to the wall!" cried Enjolras. "And all on your knees along the barricade!"

The insurgents, who were scattered in front of the wineshop, and who had left their posts of combat on Gavroche's arrival, rushed pell-mell toward the barricade, but before Enjolras' order was executed, the discharge took place with the fearful rattle of grapeshot. It was so in fact.

The charge was directed at the opening of the redoubt, i' ricocheted upon the wall, and this terrible ricochet killed two men and wounded three.

If that continued, the barricade was no longer tenable. I' was not proof against grape.

There was a sound of consternation.

"Let us prevent the second shot, at any rate," said Enjolras

And, lowering his carbine, he aimed at the gunner, who at that moment, bending over the breech of the gun, was cor recting and finally adjusting the aim.

This gunner was a fine-looking sergeant of artillery, quite young, of fair complexion, with a very mild face, and the intelligent air peculiar to that predestined and formidable arm which, by perfecting itself in horror, must end in killing war.

Combeferre, standing near Enjolras, looked at this young man.

"What a pity!" said Combeferre. "What a hideous thing these butcheries are! Come, when there are no more kings, there will be no more war. Enjolras, you are aiming at that sergeant, you are not looking at him. Just think that he is a charming young man; he is intrepid; you see that he is a thinker; these young artillerymen are well educated; he has a father, a mother, a family; he is in love, probably; he is at most twenty-five years old; he might be your brother."

"He is," said Enjolras.

"Yes," said Combeferre, "and mine also. Well, don't let us kill him."

"Let me alone. We must do what we must."

And a tear rolled slowly down Enjolras' marble cheek.

At the same time he pressed the trigger of his carbine. The flash leaped forth. The artilleryman turned twice around, his arms stretched out before him, and his head raised as if to drink the air; then he fell over on his side upon the gun and lay there motionless. His back could be seen, from the center of which a stream of blood gushed upward. The ball had entered his breast and passed through his body. He was dead.

It was necessary to carry him away and to replace him. It was indeed some minutes gained.

VI

THERE was confusion in the counsel of the barricade. The gun was about to be fired again. They could not hold out a quarter of an hour in that storm of grape. It was absolutely necessary to deaden the blows.

Enjolras threw out his command:

"We must put a mattress there."

"We have none," said Combeferre, "the wounded are on them."

Jean Valjean, seated apart on a block, at the corner of the wineshop, his musket between his knees, had, up to this moment, taken no part in what was going on. He seemed not to hear the combatants about him say: "There is a musket which is doing nothing."

At the order given by Enjolras, he got up.

It will be remembered that on the arrival of the company in the rue de la Chanvrerie, an old woman, foreseeing bullets, had put her mattress before her window. This window, a garret window, was on the roof of a house of six stories standing a little outside of the barricade. The mattress, placed crosswise, rested at the bottom upon two clothes poles, and was sustained above by two ropes which, in the distance, seemed like threads, and which were fastened to nails driven into the window casing. These two ropes could be seen distinctly against the sky like hairs.

"Can somebody lend me a double-barreled carbine?" said Jean Valjean.

Enjolras, who had just reloaded his, handed it to him.

Jean Valjean aimed at the window and fired.

One of the two ropes of the mattress was cut.

The mattress now hung only by one thread.

Jean Valjean fired the second barrel. The second rope struck the glass of the window. The mattress slid down between the two poles and fell into the street.

All cried:

"There is a mattress!"

"Yes," said Combeferre, "but who will go after it?"

Jean Valjean went out at the opening, entered the street, passed through the storm of balls, went to the mattress, picked it up, put it on his back, and returned to the barricade.

He put the mattress into the opening himself. He fixed it against the wall in such a way that the artillerymen did not see it.

This done, they awaited the charge of grape.

They had not long to wait.

The cannon vomited its package of shot with a roar. But there was no ricochet. The grape miscarried upon the mattress. The desired effect was obtained. The barricade was preserved.

"Citizen," said Enjolras to Jean Valjean, "the republic thanks you."

Bossuet admired and laughed. He exclaimed:

"It is immoral that a mattress should have so much power. Triumph of that which yields over that which thunders. But it is all the same; glory to the mattress which nullifies a cannon."

VII

The fire of the assailants continued. The musketry and the grape alternated, without much damage indeed. The top of the façade of the Corinth alone suffered; the window of the first story and the dormer windows on the roof, riddled with shot and ball, were slowly demolished. The combatants who were posted there had to withdraw. Besides, this is the art of attacking barricades; to tease for a long time, in order to exhaust the ammunition of the insurgents, if they commit the blunder of replying. When it is perceived, from the slackening of their fire, that they have no longer either balls or powder, the assault is made. Enjolras did not fall into this snare; the barricade did not reply.

But a new personage had just entered upon the scene. It was a second piece of ordnance.

The artillerymen quickly executed the maneuvers, and placed this second piece in battery near the first.

This suggested the conclusion.

A few moments afterward, the two pieces, rapidly served, opened directly upon the redoubt; the platoon firing of the line and the *banlieue* supported the artillery.

Another cannonade was heard at some distance. At the same time that two cannon were raging against the redoubt in the rue de la Chanvrerie, two other pieces of ordnance, pointed, one on the rue Saint Denis, the other on the rue Aubry le Boucher, were riddling the Barricade Saint Merry. The four cannon made dreary echo to one another.

The bayings of the dismal dogs of war answered each other.

Of the two pieces which were now battering the barricade in the rue de la Chanvrerie, one fired grape, the other ball.

The gun which threw balls was elevated a little, and the range was calculated so that the ball struck the extreme edge of the upper ridge of the barricade, dismantled it, and crumbled the paving stones over the insurgents in showers.

This peculiar aim was intended to drive the combatants from the summit of the redoubt, and to force them to crowd together in the interior; that is, it announced the assault.

"We must at all events diminish the inconvenience of those pieces," said Enjolras. And he cried: "Fire upon the cannoneers!"

All were ready. The barricade, which had been silent for a long time, opened fire desperately; seven or eight discharges succeeded each other with a sort of rage and joy; the street was filled with a blinding smoke, and after a few minutes, through this haze pierced by flame, they could confusedly make out two-thirds of the cannoneers lying under the wheels of the guns. Those who remained standing continued to serve the pieces with rigid composure, but the fire was slackened.

"This goes well," said Bossuet to Enjolras. "Success."

Enjolras shook his head and answered:

"A quarter of an hour more of this success, and there will not be ten cartridges in the barricade."

It would seem that Gavroche heard this remark.

VIII

COURFEYRAC suddenly perceived somebody at the foot of the barricade, outside in the street, under the balls.

Gavroche had taken a basket from the wineshop, had gone out by the opening, and was quietly occupied in emptying into his basket the full cartridge boxes of the National Guards who had been killed on the slope of the redoubt.

"What are you doing there?" said Courfeyrac.

Gavroche cocked up his nose.

"Citizen, I am filling my basket."

"Why, don't you see the grape?"

Gavroche answered:

"Well, it rains. What then?"

Courfeyrac cried:

"Come back!"

"Directly," said Gavroche.

And with a bound, he sprang into the street.

Some twenty dead lay scattered along the whole length of

the street on the pavement. Twenty cartridge boxes for Gavroche, a supply of cartridges for the barricade.

The smoke in the street was like a fog. This obscurity, probably desired and calculated upon by the leaders who were to direct the assault upon the barricade, was of use to Gavroche.

Under the folds of this veil of smoke, and thanks to his small size, he could advance far into the street without being seen. He emptied the first seven or eight cartridge boxes without much danger.

He crawled on his belly, ran on his hands and feet, took his basket in his teeth, twisted, glided, writhed, wormed his way from one body to another, and emptied a cartridge box as a monkey opens a nut.

From the barricade, of which he was still within hearing, they dared not call to him to return, for fear of attracting attention to him.

On one corpse, that of a corporal, he found a powder flask.

"In case of thirst," said he as he put it into his pocket.

By successive advances, he reached a point where the fog from the firing became transparent.

So that the sharpshooters of the line drawn up and on the alert behind their wall of paving stones, and the sharpshooters of the *banlieue* massed at the corner of the street, suddenly discovered something moving in the smoke.

Just as Gavroche was relieving of his cartridges a sergeant who lay near a stone block, a ball struck the body.

"The deuce!" said Gavroche. "So they are killing my dead for me."

A second ball splintered the pavement beside him. A third upset his basket.

Gavroche looked and saw that it came from the *banlieue*.

He rose up straight, on his feet, his hair in the wind, his hands upon his hips, his eye fixed upon the National Guards who were firing, and he sang:

> On est laid à Nanterre,
> C'est la faute à Voltaire,
> Et bête à Palaiseau,
> C'est la faute à Rousseau.

Then he picked up his basket, put into it the cartridges

which had fallen out, without losing a single one, and, advancing toward the fusillade, began to empty another cartridge box. There a fourth ball just missed him again. Gavroche sang:

> Je ne suis pas notaire,
> C'est la faute à Voltaire;
> Je suis petit oiseau,
> C'est la faute à Rousseau.

A fifth ball succeeded only in drawing a third couplet from him:

> Joie est mon caractère,
> C'est la faute à Voltaire;
> Misère est mon trousseau,
> C'est la faute à Rousseau.

This continued thus for some time.

The sight was appalling and fascinating. Gavroche, fired at, mocked the firing. He appeared to be very much amused. It was the sparrow pecking at the hunters. He replied to each discharge by a couplet. They aimed at him incessantly, they always missed him. The National Guards and the soldiers laughed as they aimed at him. He lay down, then rose up, hid himself in a doorway, then sprang out, disappeared, reappeared, escaped, returned, retorted upon the volleys by wry faces, and meanwhile pillaged cartridges, emptied cartridge boxes, and filled his basket. The insurgents, breathless with anxiety, followed him with their eyes. The barricade was trembling; he was singing. It was not a child; it was not a man; it was a strange fairy gamin. One would have said the invulnerable dwarf of the melee. The bullets ran after him; he was more nimble than they. He was playing an indescribably terrible game of hide-and-seek with death; every time the flat-nosed face of the specter approached, the gamin snapped his fingers.

One bullet, however, better aimed or more treacherous than the others, reached the will-o'-the-wisp child. They saw Gavroche totter, then he fell. The whole barricade gave a cry, but there was an Antaeus in this pigmy; for the gamin to touch the pavement is like the giant touching the earth; Gavroche had fallen only to rise again; he sat up, a long stream of blood rolled down his face, he raised both arms in the air, looked in the direction whence the shot came, and began to sing:

> Je suis tombé par terre,
> C'est la faute à Voltaire,
> La nez dans le ruisseau,
> C'est la faute à ——

He did not finish. A second ball from the same marksman cut him short. This time he fell with his face upon the pavement, and did not stir again. That little great soul had taken flight.

IX

MARIUS had sprung out of the barricade. Combeferre had followed him. But it was too late. Gavroche was dead. Combeferre brought back the basket of cartridges; Marius brought back the child.

When Marius re-entered the redoubt with Gavroche in his arms, his face, like the child's, was covered with blood.

Just as he had stooped down to pick up Gavroche, a ball grazed his skull; he did not perceive it.

Courfeyrac took off his cravat and bound up Marius' forehead.

They laid Gavroche on the same table with Mabeuf, and they stretched the black shawl over the two bodies. It was large enough for the old man and the child.

Combeferre distributed the cartridges from the basket which he had brought back.

This gave each man fifteen shots.

Jean Valjean was still at the same place, motionless upon his block. When Combeferre presented him his fifteen cartridges, he shook his head.

"There is a rare eccentric," said Combeferre in a low tone to Enjolras. "He finds means not to fight in this barricade."

"Which does not prevent him from defending it," answered Enjolras.

A notable fact, the fire which was battering the barricade hardly disturbed the interior. Those who have never passed through the whirlwind of this kind of war can have no idea

of the singular moments of tranquillity which are mingled
with these convulsions. Combeferre, with apron at his waist,
was dressing the wounded; Bossuet and Feuilly were making
cartridges with the flask of powder taken by Gavroche from
the dead corporal, and Bossuet said to Feuilly: "We shall
soon take the diligence for another planet"; Courfeyrac, upon
the few paving stones which he had reserved for himself near
Enjolras, was disposing and arranging a whole arsenal—
his sword cane, his musket, two horse pistols, and a pocket
pistol—with the care of a girl who is putting a little workbox
in order. Jean Valjean was looking in silence at the opposite
wall. A workingman was fastening on his head with a string
a large straw hat belonging to Mother Hucheloup; "for fear
of sunstroke," said he. The young men of the Cougourde d'Aix
were chatting gaily with one another, as if they were in a
hurry to talk patois for the last time. Joly, who had taken
down the Widow Hucheloup's mirror, was examining his
tongue in it. A few combatants, having discovered some crusts
of bread, almost moldy, in a drawer, were eating them
greedily. Marius was anxious about what his father would
say to him.

X

WE *must* dwell upon a psychological fact, peculiar to barricades. Nothing which characterizes this surprising war of
the streets should be omitted.

There is an apocalypse in civil war, all the mists of the
unknown are mingled with these savage flames, revolutions
are sphinxes, and he who has passed through a barricade
believes he has passed through a dream.

What is felt in those places, as we have indicated in refer-
ence to Marius, and as we shall see in what follows, is more
and is less than life. Once out of the barricade, a man no
longer knows what he has seen in it. He was terrible; he does
not know it. He was surrounded by combating ideas which
had human faces; he had his head in the light of the future.
There were corpses lying and phantoms standing. The hours
were colossal, and seemed hours of eternity. He lived in death.
Shadows passed by. What were they? He saw hands on which
there was blood; it was an appalling uproar, it was also a

hideous silence; there were open mouths which shouted, and other open mouths which held their peace; he was in the smoke, in the night, perhaps. He thinks he has touched the ominous ooze of the unknown depths; he sees something red in his nails. He remembers nothing more.

Let us return to the rue de la Chanvrerie.

Suddenly between two discharges they heard the distant sound of a clock striking.

"It is noon," said Combeferre.

The twelve strokes had not sounded when Enjolras sprang to his feet, and flung down from the top of the barricade this thundering shout:

"Carry some paving stones into the house. Fortify the windows with them. Half the men to the muskets, the other half to the stones. Not a minute to lose."

A platoon of sappers, their axes on their shoulders, had just appeared in order of battle at the end of the street.

This could only be the head of a column; and of what column? The column of attack, evidently. The sappers, whose duty it is to demolish the barricade, must always precede the soldiers whose duty it is to scale it.

Enjolras' order was executed with the correct haste peculiar to ships and barricades, the only places of combat whence escape is impossible. In less than a minute, two-thirds of the paving stones which Enjolras had had piled up at the door of Corinth were carried up to the first story and to the garret; and before a second minute had elapsed, these stones, artistically laid one upon another, walled up half the height of the window on the first story and the dormer windows of the attic. A few openings, carefully arranged by Feuilly, chief builder, allowed musket barrels to pass through. This armament of the windows could be performed the more easily since the grape had ceased. The two pieces were now firing balls upon the center of the wall, in order to make a hole, and if it were possible, a breach for the assault.

Then they barricaded the basement window, and they held in readiness the iron crosspieces which served to bar the door of the wineshop on the inside at night.

The fortress was complete. The barricade was the rampart, the wineshop was the donjon.

With the paving stones which remained, they closed up the opening beside the barricade.

Enjolras said to Marius: "We are the two chiefs; I will give the last orders within. You stay outside and watch."

Marius posted himself for observation upon the crest of the barricade.

Enjolras had the door of the kitchen, which, we remember, was the hospital, nailed up.

"No spattering on the wounded," said he.

He gave his last instructions in the basement room in a quick, but deep and calm voice; Feuilly listened, and answered in the name of all.

"First story, hold your axes ready to cut the staircase. Have you them?"

"Yes," said Feuilly.

"How many?"

"Two axes and a poleax."

"Very well. There are twenty-six effective men left."

"How many muskets are there?"

"Thirty-four."

"Eight too many. Keep these eight muskets loaded like the rest, and at hand. Swords and pistols in your belts. Twenty men to the barricade. Six in ambush at the dormer windows and at the window on the first story to fire upon the assailants through the loopholes in the paving stones. Let there be no useless laborer here. Immediately, when the drum beats the charge, let the twenty from below rush to the barricade. The first there will get the best places."

These dispositions made, he turned toward Javert and said to him:

"I won't forget you."

And, laying a pistol on the table, he added:

"The last man to leave this room will blow out the spy's brains!"

"Here?" inquired a voice.

"No, do not leave this corpse with ours. You can climb over the little barricade on the rue Mondétour. It is only four feet high. The man is well tied. You will take him there, and execute him there."

There was one man, at that moment, who was more impassible than Enjolras; it was Javert.

Here Jean Valjean appeared.

He was in the throng of insurgents. He stepped forward and said to Enjolras:

"You are the commander?"

"Yes."

"You thanked me just now."

"In the name of the republic. The barricade has two saviors, Marius Pontmercy and you."

"Do you think that I deserve a reward?"

"Certainly."

"Well, I ask one. "

"What?"

"To blow out that man's brains myself."

Javert raised his head, saw Jean Valjean, made an imperceptible movement, and said:

"That is appropriate."

As for Enjolras, he had begun to reload his carbine; he cast his eyes about him:

"No objection."

And turning toward Jean Valjean: "Take the spy."

Jean Valjean, in fact, took possession of Javert by sitting down on the end of the table. He caught up the pistol, and a slight click announced that he had cocked it.

Almost at the same moment, they heard a flourish of trumpets.

"Come on!" cried Marius, from the top of the barricade.

Javert began to laugh with that noiseless laugh which was peculiar to him, and, looking fixedly upon the insurgents, said to them:

"Your health is hardly better than mine."

"All outside?" cried Enjolras.

The insurgents sprang forward in a tumult, and, as they went out, they received in the back, allow us the expression, this speech from Javert:

"Farewell till immediately!"

XI

WHEN Jean Valjean was alone with Javert, he untied the rope that held the prisoner by the middle of the body, and, drawing him after him, went out of the wineshop slowly, for Javert, with his legs fettered, could take only very short steps.

Jean Valjean had the pistol in his hand.

They crossed thus the interior trapezium of the barricade. The insurgents, intent upon the imminent attack, were looking the other way.

Marius, alone, placed toward the left extremity of the wall, saw them pass. This group of the victim and the executioner borrowed a light from the sepulchral gleam which he had in his soul.

Jean Valjean, with some difficulty, bound as Javert was, but without letting go of him for a single instant, made him scale the little entrenchment on the rue Mondétour.

When they had climbed over this wall, they found themselves alone in the little street. Nobody saw them now. The corner of the house hid them from insurgents. The corpses carried out from the barricades made a terrible mound a few steps off.

They distinguished in a heap of dead a livid face, a flowing head of hair, a wounded hand, and a woman's breast half naked. It was Eponine.

Javert looked aside at this dead body, and, perfectly calm, said in an undertone:

"It seems to me that I know that girl."

Then he turned toward Jean Valjean.

Jean Valjean put the pistol under his arm, and fixed upon Javert a look which had no need of words to say: "Javert, it is I."

Javert answered.

"Take your revenge."

Jean Valjean took a knife out of his pocket and opened it.

"A *surin!*" exclaimed Javert. "You are right. That suits you better."

Jean Valjean cut the martingale which Javert had about his neck, then he cut the ropes which he had on his wrists, then, stooping down, he cut the cord which he had on his feet, and, rising, he said to him:

"You are free."

Javert was not easily astonished. Still, complete master as he was of himself, he could not escape an emotion. He stood aghast and motionless.

Jean Valjean continued:

"I don't expect to leave this place. Still, if by chance I

should, I live, under the name of Fauchelevent, in the rue de l'Homme Armé, Number Seven."

Javert had the scowl of a tiger half opening the corner of his mouth, and he muttered between his teeth:

"Take care."

"Go," said Jean Valjean.

Javert resumed:

"You said Fauchelevent, rue de l'Homme Armé?"

"Number Seven."

Javert repeated in an undertone: "Number Seven." He buttoned his coat, restored the military stiffness between his shoulders, turned half around, folded his arms, supporting his chin with one hand, and walked off in the direction of the markets. Jean Valjean followed him with his eyes. After a few steps, Javert turned back and cried to Jean Valjean:

"You annoy me. Kill me rather."

Javert did not notice that his tone was more respectful toward Jean Valjean.

"Go away," said Jean Valjean.

Javert receded with slow steps. A moment afterward, he turned the corner of the rue des Prêcheurs.

When Javert was gone, Jean Valjean fired the pistol in the air.

Then he re-entered the barricade and said: "It is done."

Meanwhile what had taken place is this:

Marius, busy rather with the street than the wineshop, had not until then looked attentively at the spy who was bound in the dusky rear of the basement room.

When he saw him in broad day clambering over the barricade on his way to die, he recognized him. A sudden reminiscence came into his mind. He remembered the inspector of the rue de Pontoise, and the two pistols which he had handed him and which he had used, he, Marius, in this very barricade, and not only did he recollect the face, but he recalled the name.

This reminiscence, however, was misty and indistinct, like all his ideas. It was not an affirmation which he made to himself, it was a question which he put: "Is not this that inspector of police who told me his name was Javert?"

Was there perhaps still time to interfere for this man? But he must first know if it were indeed that Javert.

Marius called to Enjolras, who had just taken his place at the other end of the barricade.

"Enjolras!"

"What?"

"What is that man's name?"

"Who?"

"The police officer. Do you know his name?"

"Of course. He told us."

"What is his name?"

"Javert."

Marius sprang up.

At that moment they heard the pistol shot.

Jean Valjean reappeared and cried: "It is done."

A dreary chill passed through the heart of Marius.

XII

PROGRESS is the mode of man. The general life of the human race is called Progress; the collective advance of the human race is called Progress. Progress marches; it makes the great human and terrestrial journey toward the celestial and the divine; it has its halts where it rallies the belated flock; it has its stations where it meditates, in sight of some splendid Canaan suddenly unveiling its horizon; it has its nights when it sleeps, and it is one of the bitter anxieties of the thinker to see the shadow upon the human soul, and to feel in the darkness progress asleep, without being able to waken it.

He who despairs is wrong. Progress infallibly awakens, and, in short, we might say that it advances even in sleep, for it has grown. When we see it standing again, we find it taller. To be always peaceful belongs to progress no more than to the river; raise no obstruction, cast in no rock; the obstacle makes water foam and humanity seethe. Hence troubles, but after these troubles, we recognize that there has been some ground gained. Until order, which is nothing more nor less than universal peace, be established, until harmony and unity reign, progress will have revolutions for stations.

What then is progress? We have just said. The permanent life of the peoples.

Now, it sometimes happens that the momentary life of individuals offers resistance to the eternal life of the human race. Hence, at certain periods, a deep chill upon the magnanimous vanguard of the human race.

Utopia, moreover, we must admit, departs from its radiant sphere in making war. The truth of tomorrow, she borrows her process, battle, from the lie of yesterday. She, the future, acts like the past. She, the pure idea, becomes an act of force. This reservation made, and made in all severity, it is impossible for us not to admire, whether they succeed or not, the glorious combatants of the future, the professors of Utopia. Even when they fail, they are venerable, and it is perhaps in failure that they have the greater majesty. Victory, when it is according to progress, deserves the applause of the peoples, but a heroic defeat deserves their compassion. One is magnificent, the other is sublime. For ourselves, who prefer martyrdom to success, John Brown is greater than Washington, and Pisacane is greater than Garibaldi.

Surely some must be on the side of the vanquished.

Men are unjust toward these great essayists of the future when they fail.

Even when fallen, especially when fallen, august are they who, upon all points of the world, with eyes fixed on France, struggle for the great work with the inflexible logic of the ideal; they give their life a pure gift for progress; they accomplish the will of Providence; they perform a religious act. At the appointed hour, with as much disinterestedness as an actor who reaches his cue, obedient to the divine scenario, they enter into the tomb. And this hopeless combat, and this stoical disappearance, they accept to lead to its splendid and supreme universal consequences the magnificent movement of man, irresistibly commenced on the 14th of July, 1789; these soldiers are priests. The French Revolution is an act of God.

These passages at arms for progress often fail. The throng is restive under the sway of the paladins. The heavy masses, the multitudes, fragile on account of their very weight, dread uncertainties, and there is uncertainty in the ideal.

Moreover, let it not be forgotten, interests are there, little friendly to the ideal and the emotional. Sometimes the stomach paralyzes the heart.

The grandeur and the beauty of France are that she cares less for the belly than other peoples; she knots the rope about her loins more easily. She is first awake, last asleep. She goes in advance. She is a pioneer.

That is because she is an artist.

The ideal is nothing more nor less than the culminating point of logic, even as the beautiful is nothing more nor less than the summit of the true. The artist people is thus the consistent people. To love beauty is to see light. This is why the torch of Europe, that is to say, civilization, was first borne by Greece, who passed it to Italy, who passed it to France. Divine pioneer peoples! *Vitai lampada tradunt!*

A word more before returning to the conflict.

A battle like this which we are now describing is nothing but a convulsive movement toward the ideal. Enfettered progress is sickly, and it has these tragic epilepsies. This disease of progress, civil war, we have had to encounter upon our passage. It is one of the fatal phases, at once act and interlude, of this drama the pivot of which is a social outcast, and the true title of which is: *Progress*.

Progress!

This cry which we often raise is our whole thought; and at the present point of this drama, the idea that it contains having still more than one ordeal to undergo, it is permitted us perhaps, if not to lift the veil from it, at least to let the light shine clearly through.

The book which the reader has now before his eyes is from one end to the other, in its whole and in its details whatever may be the intermissions, the exceptions, or the defaults, the march from evil to good, from injustice to justice, from the false to the true, from night to day, from appetite to conscience, from rottenness to life, from brutality to duty, from Hell to Heaven, from nothingness to God. Starting point: matter; goal: the soul. Hydra at the beginning, angel at the end.

XIII

SUDDENLY the drum beat the charge.

The attack was a hurricane. A powerful column of infantry of the line, intersected at equal intervals by National Guards and Municipal Guards on foot, and supported by deep masses heard but unseen, turned into the street at a quickstep, drums beating, trumpets sounding, bayonets fixed, sappers at their head, and, unswerving under the projectiles, came straight upon the barricade with the weight of a bronze column upon a wall.

The wall held well.

The insurgents fired impetuously. The barricade scaled was like a mane of flashes. The assault was so sudden that for a moment it was overflowed by assailants; but it shook off the soldiers as the lion does the dogs, and it was covered with besiegers only as a cliff is with foam, to reappear, a moment afterward, steep, black, and formidable.

Enjolras was at one end of the barricade, and Marius at the other. Enjolras, who carried the whole barricade in his head, reserved and sheltered himself; three soldiers fell one after the other under his battlement, without even having perceived him; Marius fought without shelter. He took no aim. He stood with more than half his body above the summit of the redoubt. There is no wilder prodigal than a miser who takes the bit in his teeth; there is no man more fearful in action than a dreamer. Marius was terrible and pensive. He was in the battle as in a dream. One would have said a phantom firing a musket.

There was assault after assault. The horror continued to increase.

Then resounded over this pile of paving stones, in this rue de la Chanvrerie, a struggle worthy of the walls of Troy. These men, wan, tattered, and exhausted, who had not eaten for twenty-four hours, who had not slept, who had but a few more shots to fire, who felt their pockets empty of cartridges, nearly all wounded, their heads or arms bound with smutty and blackened cloths, with holes in their coats whence the blood was flowing, scarcely armed with worthless muskets and with old hacked swords, became titans. The barricade was ten times approached, assaulted, scaled, and never taken.

They fought breast to breast, foot to foot, with pistols, with sabers, with fists, at a distance, close at hand, from above, from below, from everywhere, from the roofs of the house, from the windows of the wineshop, from the gratings of the cellars into which some had slipped. They were one against sixty. The façade of Corinth, half demolished, was hideous. The window, riddled with grape, had lost glass and sash, and was now nothing but a shapeless hole, confusedly blocked with paving stones. Bossuet was killed; Feuilly was killed; Courfeyrac was killed; Joly was killed; Combeferre, pierced by three bayonet thrusts in the breast, just as he was lifting a wounded soldier, had only time to look to heaven, and expired.

Marius, still fighting, was so hacked with wounds, particularly about his head, that the countenance was lost in blood, and you would have said that he had his face covered with a red handkerchief.

Enjolras alone was untouched.

XIV

WHEN there were none of the chiefs alive save Enjolras and Marius, who were at the extremities of the barricade, the center, which Courfeyrac, Joly, Bossuet, Feuilly, and Combeferre had so long sustained, gave way. The artillery, without making a practicable breach, had deeply indented the center of the redoubt; there, the summit of the wall had disappeared under the balls, and had tumbled down, and the rubbish which had fallen, sometimes on the interior, sometimes on the exterior, had finally made, as it was heaped up, on either side of the wall, a kind of talus, both on the inside and on the outside. The exterior talus offered an inclined plane for attack.

A final assault was now attempted, and this assault succeeded. The mass, bristling with bayonets and hurled at a double-quick step, came on irresistible, and the dense battlefront of the attacking column appeared in the smoke at the top of the escarpment. This time, it was finished. The group of insurgents who defended the center fell back pell-mell.

Then grim love of life was roused in some. Covered by the aim of that forest of muskets, several were now unwilling to die. This is a moment when the instinct of self-preservation raises a howl, and the animal reappears in the man. They were pushed back to the high six-story house which formed the rear of the redoubt. This house might be safety. This house was barricaded, and, as it were, walled in from top to bottom. Before the troops of the line would be in the interior of the redoubt, there was time for a door to open and shut, a flash was enough for that, and the door of this house suddenly half-opened and closed again immediately, to these despairing men was life. In the rear of this house, there were streets, possible flight, space. They began to strike this door with the butts of their muskets, and with kicks, calling, shouting, begging, wringing their hands. Nobody opened. From the window on the third story, the death's head looked at them.

Enjolras was now in the little interior court of the redoubt, with his back to the house of Corinth, his sword in one hand, his carbine in the other, keeping the door of the wineshop open while he barred it against the assailants. He cried to the despairing: "There is but one door open. This one." And, covering them with his body, alone facing a battalion, he made them pass in behind him. All rushed in. For an instant it was horrible, the soldiers struggling to get in, the insurgents to close the door. The door was closed with such violence that, in shutting into its frame, it exposed, cut off, and adhered to the casement the thumb and fingers of a soldier who had caught hold of it.

Marius remained without. A ball had broken his shoulder blade; he felt that he was fainting, and that he was falling. At that moment, his eyes already closed, he experienced the shock of a vigorous hand seizing him, and his fainting fit, in which he lost consciousness, left him hardly time for this thought, mingled with the last memory of Cosette: "I am taken prisoner. I shall be shot."

When the door was barricaded, Enjolras said to the rest: "Let us sell ourselves dearly."

The barricade had struggled like a gate of Thebes; the wineshop struggled like a house of Saragossa. Nothing was wanting to the storming of the Hucheloup wineshop: neither the paving stones raining from the window and the roof upon the besiegers, and exasperating the soldiers by their horrible mangling, nor the shots from the cellars and the garret windows, nor fury of attack, nor rage of defense; nor, finally, when the door yielded, the frenzied madness of the extermination. The assailants, on rushing into the wineshop, their feet entangled in the panels of the door, which were beaten in and scattered over the floor, found no combatant there. The spiral stairway, which had been cut down with the axe, lay in the middle of the basement room, a few wounded had just expired, all who were not killed were in the first story, and there, through the hole in the ceiling, which had been the entrance for the stairway, a terrific firing broke out. It was the last of the cartridges. The edge of the hole in the ceiling was very soon surrounded with the heads of the dead, from which flowed long red and reeking lines. The uproar was inexpressible; a stifled and burning smoke made night almost over this combat. Words fail to express horror when it reaches this degree. There were men no longer in this now infernal conflict. They were no longer giants against colossi. It resembled Milton and Dante rather than Homer. Demons attacked, specters resisted.

It was the heroism of monsters.

XV

At last, mounting on each other's shoulders, helping themselves by the skeleton of the staircase, climbing up the walls, hanging from the ceiling, cutting to pieces at the very edge of the hatchway the last to resist, some twenty of the besiegers, soldiers, National Guards, Municipal Guards, pell-mell, most disfigured by wounds in the face in this terrible ascent, blinded with blood, furious, become savages, made an irruption into the room of the first story. There was now but a single man there on his feet, Enjolras. Without cartridges, without a sword, he had now in his hand only the barrel of his carbine, the stock of which he had broken over the heads of those who were entering. He had put the billiard table between the assailants and himself; he had retreated to the corner of the room, and there, with proud eye, haughty head, and that stump of a weapon in his grasp, he was still so formidable that a large space was left about him. A cry arose:

"This is the chief. It is he who killed the artilleryman. As he has put himself there, it is a good place. Let him stay. Let us shoot him on the spot."

"Shoot me," said Enjolras.

And, throwing away the stump of his carbine, and folding his arms, he presented his breast.

Twelve men formed in platoon in the corner opposite Enjolras and made their muskets ready in silence.

Then a sergeant cried: "Take aim!"

Within a few seconds Grantaire had awakened.

Grantaire, it will be remembered, had been asleep since the day previous in the upper room of the wineshop, sitting in a chair, leaning heavily forward on a table.

Noise does not waken a drunkard; silence wakens him. This peculiarity has been observed more than once. The fall of everything about him augmented Grantaire's oblivion; destruction was a lullaby to him. The kind of halt in the tumult before Enjolras was a shock to his heavy sleep. It was the effect of a wagon at a gallop stopping short. The sleepers are roused by it. Grantaire rose up with a start, stretched his arms, rubbed his eyes, looked, gaped, and understood.

Retired as he was in a corner, and, as it were, sheltered behind the billiard table, the soldiers, their eyes fixed upon Enjolras, had not even noticed Grantaire, and the sergeant was preparing to repeat the order: "Take aim!" when suddenly they heard a powerful voice cry out beside them:

"*Vive la République!* I belong to it."

Grantaire had arisen.

The immense glare of the whole combat, which he had missed and in which he had not been, appeared in the flashing eye of the transfigured drunkard.

He repeated: "*Vive la République!*" crossed the room with a firm step, and took his place before the muskets beside Enjolras.

"Two at one shot," said he.

And, turning toward Enjolras gently, he said to him:

"Will you permit it?"

Enjolras grasped his hand with a smile.

The smile was not finished when the report was heard.

Enjolras, pierced by eight balls, remained backed against the wall as if the balls nailed him there. He only bowed his head.

Grantaire, struck down, fell at his feet.

A few moments afterward, the soldiers dislodged the last insurgents who had taken refuge in the top of the house. They fired through a wooden lattice into the garret. They fought in the attics. They threw the bodies out of the windows, some living. Two *voltigeurs*, who were trying to raise the shattered omnibus, were killed by two shots from a carbine fired from the dormer windows. A man in a blouse was pitched out headlong, with a bayonet thrust in his belly, and his death rattle was finished upon the ground. A soldier and an insurgent slipped together on the slope of the tiled roof, and would not let go of each other, and fell, clasped in a wild embrace.

Similar struggle in the cellar. Cries, shots, savage stamping. Then silence. The barricade was taken.

The soldiers commenced the search of the houses round about and the pursuit of the fugitives.

XVI

MARIUS was in fact a prisoner. Prisoner of Jean Valjean.

The hand which had seized him from behind at the moment he was falling, and the grasp of which he had felt in losing consciousness, was the hand of Jean Valjean.

Jean Valjean, in the thick cloud of the combat, did not appear to see Marius; the fact is, that he did not take his eyes from him. When a shot struck down Marius, Jean Valjean bounded with the agility of a tiger, dropped upon him as upon a prey, and carried him away.

The whirlwind of the attack at that instant concentrated so fiercely upon Enjolras and the door of the wineshop that nobody saw Jean Valjean cross the unpaved field of the barricade, holding the senseless Marius in his arms, and disappear behind the corner of the house of Corinth.

It will be remembered that this corner was a sort of cape on the street; it sheltered from balls and grape, and from sight also, a few square feet of ground. Thus, there is sometimes in conflagrations a room which does not burn; and in the most furious seas, beyond a promontory or at the end of a cul-de-sac of shoals, a placid little haven. It was in this recess of the interior trapezium of the barricade that Eponine had died.

There Jean Valjean stopped; he let Marius slide to the ground, set his back to the wall, and cast his eyes about him.

The situation was appalling.

Before him he had that deaf and implacable house of six stories, which seemed inhabited only by the dead man, leaning over his window; on his right he had the low barricade, which closed the Petite Truanderie; to clamber over this obstacle appeared easy, but above the crest of the wall a range of bayonet points could be seen. A company of the line was posted beyond this barricade, on the watch. At his left he had the field of combat. Death was behind the corner of the wall.

What should he do?

A bird alone could have extricated himself from that place. And he must decide upon the spot, find an expedient, adopt his course. They were fighting a few steps from him; by good luck all were fiercely intent upon a single point, the door of the wineshop, but let one soldier, a single one, conceive the idea of turning the house, of attacking it in flank, and all was over.

Jean Valjean looked at the house in front of him, he looked at the barricade by the side of him, then he looked upon the ground, with the violence of the last extremity, in desperation, and as if he would have made a hole in it with his eyes.

Beneath his persistent look, something vaguely tangible in such an agony outlined itself and took form at his feet, as if there were a power in the eye to develop the thing desired. He perceived a few steps from him, at the foot of the little wall, under some fallen paving stones which partly hid it, an iron grating laid flat and level with the ground. This grating, made of strong transverse bars, was about two feet square. The stone frame which held it had been torn up, and it was, as it were, unset. Through the bars a glimpse could be caught of an obscure opening, something like the flue of a chimney or the main of a cistern. Jean Valjean sprang forward. His old science of escape mounted to his brain like a flash. To remove the stones, to lift the grating, to load Marius, who was as inert as a dead body, upon his shoulders, to descend, with that burden upon his back, by the aid of his elbows and knees, into this kind of well, fortunately not very deep, to let fall over his head the heavy iron trap door upon which the stones were shaken back again, to find a foothold upon a flagged surface ten feet below the ground, this was executed like what is done in delirium, with the strength of a giant and the rapidity of an eagle; it required but very few moments.

Jean Valjean found himself, with Marius still senseless, in a sort of long underground passage.

There, deep peace, absolute silence, night.

The impression which he had formerly felt in falling from the street into the convent came back to him. Only what he was now carrying away was not Cosette; it was Marius.

He could now hardly hear above him, like a vague murmur, the fearful tumult of the wineshop taken by assault.

Mire, But Soul

I

It was in the sewer of Paris that Jean Valjean found himself.

Further resemblance of Paris with the sea. As in the ocean, the diver can disappear.

The transition was marvelous. From the very center of the city, Jean Valjean had gone out of the city, and, in the twinkling of an eye, the time of lifting a cover and closing it again, he had passed from broad day to complete obscurity, from noon to midnight, from uproar to silence, from the whirl of the thunder to the stagnation of the tomb, and, by a mutation much more prodigious still than that of the rue Polonceau, from the most extreme peril to the most absolute security.

The spring trap of safety had suddenly opened beneath him. Celestial goodness had in some sort taken him by treachery. Adorable ambuscades of Providence!

Only the wounded man did not stir, and Jean Valjean did not know whether what he was carrying away in this grave was alive or dead.

His first sensation was blindness. Suddenly he saw nothing more. It seemed to him also that in one minute he had become deaf. He heard nothing more. He reached out one hand, then the other, and touched the wall on both sides, and realized that the passage was narrow; he slipped, and realized that the pavement was wet. He advanced one foot with precaution, fearing a hole, a pit, some gulf; he made sure that the flagging continued. A whiff of fetidness informed him where he was.

After a few moments, he ceased to be blind. A little light fell from the air hole through which he had slipped in, and his eye became accustomed to this cave. He had laid Marius upon the ground, he gathered him up, this is again the right word, replaced him upon his shoulders, and began his journey. He resolutely entered that obscurity.

At the end of fifty paces he was obliged to stop. A question presented itself. The passage terminated in another which it met transversely. These two roads were offered. Which should he take? Should he turn to the left or to the right? How guide himself in this black labyrinth? This labyrinth has a clue: its descent. To follow the descent is to go to the river.

Jean Valjean understood this at once.

He said to himself that he was probably in the sewer of the markets; that, if he should choose the left and follow the descent, he would come in less than a quarter of an hour to some mouth upon the Seine between the Pont au Change and the Pont Neuf, that is to say, he would reappear in broad day in the most populous portion of Paris. He would be seized before getting out. It was better to plunge into the labyrinth, to trust to this darkness, and to rely on Providence for the issue.

He chose the right, and went up the ascent.

When he had turned the corner of the gallery, the distant gleam of the air hole disappeared, the curtain of obscurity fell back over him, and he again became blind. He went forward nonetheless, and as rapidly as he could. Marius' arms were passed about his neck, and his feet hung behind him. He held both arms with one hand, and groped for the wall with the other. Marius' cheek touched his and stuck to it, being bloody. He felt a warm stream, which came from Marius, flow over him and penetrate his clothing. Still, a moist warmth at his ear, which touched the wounded man's mouth, indicated respiration, and consequently life. The passage through which Jean Valjean was now moving was not so small as the first. Jean Valjean walked in it with difficulty. The rains of the previous day had not yet run off, and made a little stream in the center of the floor, and he was compelled to hug the wall, to keep his feet out of the water. Thus he went on in midnight. He resembled the creatures of night groping in the invisible, and lost underground in the veins of the darkness.

He went forward, with anxiety, but with calmness, seeing nothing, knowing nothing, plunged into chance, that is to say, swallowed up in Providence.

Suddenly he was surprised. At the most unexpected moment, and without having diverged from a straight line, he discovered that he was no longer rising; the water of the brook struck coming against his heels instead of upon the tops of his feet. The sewer now descended. What? Would he then soon reach the Seine? This danger was great, but the peril of retreat was still greater. He continued to advance.

It was not toward the Seine that he was going. The saddle-back which the topography of Paris forms upon the right bank empties one of its slopes into the Seine and the other into the Grand Sewer. He was making his way toward the belt sewer; he was on the right road. But he knew nothing of it.

At a certain moment he felt that he was getting away from under the Paris which was petrified by the *émeute*, in which the barricades had suppressed the circulation, and that he was coming beneath the Paris which was alive and normal. He heard suddenly above his head a sound like thunder, distant, but continuous. It was the rumbling of the vehicles.

II

In the afternoon of the 6th of June at the brink of the Seine, on the beach of the right bank, a little beyond the Bridge of the Invalides, two men some distance apart seemed to be observing each other, one avoiding the other. The one who was going before was endeavoring to increase the distance, the one who came behind to lessen it.

These two men could not have been easily seen, except from the quay in front, and to him who might have examined them from that distance, the man who was going forward would have appeared like a bristly creature, tattered and skulking, restless and shivering under a ragged blouse, and the other, like a classic and official person, wearing the over-coat of authority buttoned to the chin.

The reader would perhaps recognize these two men if he saw them nearer.

The closely buttoned man, perceiving from the shore a fiacre which was passing on the quay empty, beckoned to the driver; the driver understood, evidently recognized with whom he had to do, turned his horse, and began to follow the two men on the upper part of the quay at a walk. This was not noticed by the equivocal and ragged personage who was in front.

The fiacre rolled along the trees of the Champs Élysées. There could be seen moving above the parapet, the bust of the driver, whip in hand.

While maneuvering, each on his side, with an irreproachable strategy, these two men approached a slope of the quay descending to the beach, which, at that time, allowed the coach drivers coming from Passy to go to the river to water their horses.

It seemed probable that the man in the blouse would go up by this slope in order to attempt escape into the Champs Élysées.

To the great surprise of his observer, the man pursued did not take the slope of the watering place. He continued to advance on the beach along the quay.

His position was visibly becoming critical.

If not to throw himself into the Seine, what was he going to do?

It is true that this end of the beach was masked from sight by a mound of rubbish from six to seven feet high, the product of some demolition. But did this man hope to hide with any effect behind this heap of fragments, which the other had only to turn? The expedient would have been puerile. He certainly did not dream of it. The innocence of robbers does not reach this extent.

The heap of rubbish made a sort of eminence at the edge of the water, which prolonged like a promontory, as far as the wall of the quay.

The man pursued reached this little hill and doubled it, so that he ceased to be seen by the other.

The latter, not seeing, was not seen; he took advantage of this to abandon all dissimulation, and to walk very rapidly. In a few seconds he came to the mound of rubbish, and turned it. There, he stopped in amazement. The man whom he was hunting was gone.

Total eclipse of the man in the blouse.

The beach beyond the mound of rubbish had scarcely a length of thirty yards, then it plunged beneath the water which beat against the wall of the quay.

The fugitive could not have thrown himself into the Seine nor scaled the quay without being seen by him who was following him. What had become of him?

The man in the closely buttoned coat walked to the end of the beach, and stopped there a moment thoughtful, his fists convulsive, his eyes ferreting. Suddenly he slapped his forehead. He had noticed, at the point where the land and the water began, an iron grating broad and low, arched, with a heavy lock and three massive hinges. This grating, a sort of door cut into the bottom of the quay, opened upon the river as much as upon the beach. A blackish stream flowed from beneath it. This stream emptied into the Seine.

Beyond its heavy rusty bars could be distinguished a sort of corridor arched and obscure.

The man folded his arms and looked at the grating reproachfully.

This look not sufficing, he tried to push it; he shook it, it resisted firmly. It was probable that it had just been opened, although no sound had been heard, a singular circumstance with a grating so rusty; but it was certain that it had been closed again. That indicated that he before whom this door had just turned had not a hook but a key.

This evident fact burst immediately upon the mind of the man who was exerting himself to shake the grating, and forced from him this indignant epiphonema:

"This is fine! A government key!"

Then, calming himself immediately, he expressed a whole world of interior ideas by this whiff of monosyllables accented almost ironically:

"Well! Well! Well! Well!"

This said, hoping nobody knows what, either to see the man come out, or to see others go in, he posted himself on the watch behind the heap of rubbish, with the patient rage of a pointer.

For its part, the fiacre, which followed all his movements, had halted above him near the parapet. The few passers over the Pont d'Iéna, before going away, turned their heads to look for a moment at these two motionless features of the landscape, the man on the beach, the fiacre on the quay.

JEAN VALJEAN had resumed his advance, and had not stopped again.

This advance became more and more laborious. Jean Valjean was hungry and thirsty, thirsty especially, and this place, like the sea, is one full of water where you cannot drink. His strength, which was prodigious, and very little diminished by age, thanks to his chaste and sober life, began to give way notwithstanding. Fatigue grew upon him, and as his strength diminished, the weight of his load increased. Marius, dead perhaps, weighed heavily upon him as inert bodies do.

It might have been three o'clock in the afternoon when he arrived at the belt sewer.

He was first astonished at this sudden enlargement. He abruptly found himself in the gallery where his outstretched hands did not reach the two walls, and under an arch which his head did not touch. But there the question returned: to descend, or to ascend? He thought that the condition of affairs was urgent, and that he must, at whatever risk, now reach the Seine. In other words, descend. He turned to the left.

A little beyond an affluent which was probably the branching of the Madeleine, he stopped. He was very tired. A large air hole, probably the vista on the rue d'Anjou, produced an almost vivid light. Jean Valjean, with the gentleness of movement of a brother for his wounded brother, laid Marius upon the side bank of the sewer. Marius' bloody face appeared, under the white gleam from the air hole, as if at the bottom of a tomb. His eyes were closed, his hair adhered to his temples like brushes dried in red paint, his hands dropped down lifeless, his limbs were cold, there was coagulated blood at the corners of his mouth. A clot of blood had gathered in the tie of his cravat; his shirt was bedded in the wounds, the cloth of his coat chafed the gaping gashes in the living flesh. Jean Valjean, removing the garments with the ends of his fingers, laid his hand upon his breast; the heart still beat. Jean Valjean tore up his shirt, bandaged the wounds as well as he could, and stanched the flowing blood; then, bending in the twilight over Marius, who was still unconscious and almost lifeless, he looked at him with an inexpressible hatred.

In opening Marius' clothes, he had found two things in his pockets, the bread which had been forgotten there since the day previous, and Marius' pocketbook. He ate the bread and opened the pocketbook. On the first page he found the four lines written by Marius. They will be remembered.

"My name is Marius Pontmercy. Carry my corpse to my grandfather's, Monsieur Gillenormand, rue des Filles du Calvaire, No. 6, in the Marais."

By the light of the air hole, Jean Valjean read these lines, and stopped a moment as if absorbed in himself, repeating in an undertone: "Rue des Filles du Calvaire, Number Six, Monsieur Gillenormand." He replaced the pocketbook in Marius' pocket. He had eaten, strength had returned to him; he took Marius on his back again, laid his head carefully upon his right shoulder, and began to descend the sewer.

The rumblings of the wagons above his head, from continuous having become intermittent, then having almost ceased, he concluded that he was under central Paris no longer, and that he was approaching some solitary region, in the vicinity of the outer boulevards or the furthest quays. Where there are fewer houses and fewer streets, the sewer has fewer air holes. The darkness thickened about Jean Valjean. He nonetheless continued to advance, groping in the obscurity.

This obscurity suddenly became terrible.

IV

He felt that he was entering the water, and that he had under his feet pavement no longer, but mud.

Jean Valjean felt the pavement slipping away under him. He entered into this slime. It was water on the surface, mire at the bottom. He must surely pass through. To retrace his steps was impossible. Marius was expiring, and Jean Valjean exhausted. Where else could he go? Jean Valjean advanced. Moreover, the quagmire appeared not very deep for a few steps. But in proportion as he advanced, his feet sank in. He very soon had the mire half-knee-deep, and water above his knees. He walked on, holding Marius with both arms as high above the water as he could. The mud now came up to his knees, and the water to his waist. He could not longer turn back. He sank in deeper and deeper. This mire, dense enough for one man's weight, evidently could not bear two. Marius and Jean Valjean would have had a chance of escape separately. Jean Valjean continued to advance, supporting this dying man, who was perhaps a corpse.

The water came up to his armpits; he felt that he was foundering; it was with difficulty that he could move in the depth of mire in which he was. The density, which was the support, was also the obstacle. He still held Marius up, and, with an unparalleled outlay of strength, he advanced; but he sank deeper. He now had only his head out of the water, and his arms supporting Marius. There is, in the old pictures of the deluge, a mother doing thus with her child.

He sank still deeper, he threw his face back to escape the water, and to be able to breathe; he who should have seen him in this obscurity would have thought he saw a mask floating upon the darkness; he dimly perceived Marius' drooping head and livid face above him; he made a desperate effort, and thrust his foot forward; his foot struck something solid; a support. It was time.

He rose and writhed and rooted himself upon this support with a sort of fury. It produced the effect upon him of the first step of a staircase reascending toward life. He ascended this inclined plane, and reached the other side of the quagmire.

On coming out of the water, he struck against a stone, and fell upon his knees. This seemed to him fitting, and he remained thus for some time, his soul lost in unspoken prayer to God.

He rose, shivering, chilled, infected, bending beneath this dying man, whom he was dragging on, all dripping with slime, his soul filled with a strange light.

V

He resumed his route once more.

This supreme effort had exhausted him. His exhaustion was so great, that every three or four steps he was obliged to take breath, and leaned against the wall. Once he had to sit down upon the curb to change Marius' position and he thought he should stay there. But if his vigor was dead his energy was not. He rose again. He walked with desperation, almost with rapidity, for a hundred paces, without raising his head, almost without breathing, and suddenly struck against the wall. He raised his eyes, and at the extremity of the passage, down there before him, far, very far away, he perceived a light.

Jean Valjean saw the outlet.

A condemned soul who, from the midst of the furnace, should suddenly perceive an exit from Gehenna, would feel what Jean Valjean felt. It would fly frantically with the stumps of its burned wings toward the radiant door. Jean Valjean felt exhaustion no more, he felt Marius' weight no longer, he found again his knees of steel, he ran rather than walked.

Jean Valjean reached the outlet.

There he stopped.

It was indeed the outlet, but it did not let him out.

The arch was closed by a strong grating, and the grating which, according to all appearance, rarely turned upon its rusty hinges, was held in its stone frame by a stout lock which, red with rust, seemed an enormous brick. He could see the keyhole, and the strong bolt deeply plunged into the iron staple. The lock was plainly a double lock. It was one of those Bastille locks with which the old Paris was so lavish.

Beyond the grating, the open air, the river, the daylight, the beach, very narrow, but sufficient to get away. The distant quays, Paris, that gulf in which one is so easily lost, the wide horizon, liberty. He distinguished at his right, below him, the Bridge of Iéna, and at his left, above, the Bridge of the Invalides; the spot would have been propitious for awaiting night and escaping. It was one of the most solitary points in Paris; the beach which fronts on the Gros Caillou. The flies came in and went out through the bars of the grating.

It might have been half-past eight o'clock in the evening. The day was declining.

Jean Valjean laid Marius along the wall on the dry part of the floor, then walked to the grating and clenched the bars with both hands; the shaking was frenzied, the shock nothing. The grating did not stir. Jean Valjean seized the bars one after another, hoping to be able to tear out the least solid one and to make a lever of it to lift the door or break the lock. Not a bar yielded. A tiger's teeth are not more solid in their sockets. No lever; no possible purchase. The obstacle was invincible. No means of opening the door. He had only succeeded in escaping into a prison.

It was over. All that Jean Valjean had done was useless. Exhaustion ended in abortion.

They were both caught in the gloomy and immense web of death, and Jean Valjean felt running over those black threads trembling in the darkness, the appalling spider.

He turned his back to the grating, and dropped upon the pavement, rather prostrate than sitting, beside the yet motionless Marius, and his head sank between his knees. No exit. This was the last drop of anguish.

Of whom did he think in this overwhelming dejection? Neither of himself nor of Marius. He thought of Cosette.

VI

In the midst of this annihilation, a hand was laid upon his shoulder, and a voice which spoke low, said to him:

"Go halves."

Somebody in that darkness? Nothing is so like a dream as despair. Jean Valjean thought he was dreaming. He had heard no steps. Was it possible? He raised his eyes.

A man was before him.

This man was dressed in a blouse; he was barefooted; he held his shoes in his left hand; he had evidently taken them off to be able to reach Jean Valjean without being heard.

Jean Valjean had not a moment's hesitation. Unforeseen as was the encounter, this man was known to him. This man was Thénardier.

There was a moment of delay.

Jean Valjean perceived immediately that Thénardier did not recognize him.

They gazed at each other for a moment in this penumbra, as if they were taking each other's measure. Thénardier was first to break the silence.

"How are you going to manage to get out?"

Jean Valjean did not answer.

Thénardier continued:

"Impossible to pick the lock. Still you must get away from here."

"That is true," said Jean Valjean.

"Well, go halves."

"What do you mean?"

"You have killed the man; very well. For my part, I have the key."

Thénardier pointed to Marius. He went on:

"I don't know you, but I would like to help you. You must be a friend."

Jean Valjean began to understand. Thénardier took him for an assassin.

Thénardier resumed:

"Listen, comrade. You haven't killed that man without looking to see what he had in his pockets. Give me my half. I will open the door for you."

And, drawing a big key half out from under his blouse, which was full of holes, he added:

"Would you like to see how the key of the fields is made? There it is."

Jean Valjean "remained stupid"—the expression is the elder Corneille's—so far as to doubt whether what he saw was real. It was Providence appearing in a guise of horror, and the good angel springing out of the ground under the form of Thénardier.

"Now, let us finish the business. Let us divide. You have seen my key, show me your money."

Jean Valjean felt in his pockets. He had only some coins in his waistcoat pocket. He turned out his pocket, all soaked with filth, and displayed upon the curb of the sewer a louis d'or, two five-franc pieces, and five or six big sous.

Thénardier thrust out his underlip with a significant twist of the neck.

"You didn't kill him very dear," said he.

He began to handle, in all familiarity, the pockets of Jean Valjean and Marius. Jean Valjean, principally concerned in keeping his back to the light, did not interfere with him. While he was feeling Marius' coat, Thénardier, with the dexterity of a juggler, found means, without attracting Jean Valjean's attention, of tearing off a strip, which he hid under his blouse, probably thinking that this scrap of cloth might assist him afterward in identifying the assassinated man and the assassin. He found, however, nothing more than the thirty francs.

"It is true," said he, "both together, you have no more than that."

And, forgetting his words, "go halves," he took the whole.

"Now, friend, you must go out. This is like the fair, you pay on going out. You have paid, go out."

And he began to laugh.

Thénardier helped Jean Valjean to replace Marius upon his shoulders; then he went toward the grating upon the points of his bare feet, beckoning to Jean Valjean to follow him; he looked outside, laid his finger on his mouth, and stood a few seconds as if in suspense; the inspection over, he put the key into the lock. The bolt slid and the door turned. There was neither snapping nor grinding. It was done very quietly. It was plain that this grating and its hinges, oiled with care, were opened oftener than would have been guessed. This quiet was ominous; you felt in it the furtive goings and comings, the silent entrances and exits of the men of the night, and the wolflike tread of crime. The sewer was evidently in complicity with some mysterious band. This taciturn grating was a receiver.

Thénardier half-opened the door, left just a passage for Jean Valjean, closed the grating again, turned the key twice in the lock, and plunged back into the obscurity, without making more noise than a breath. He seemed to walk with the velvet paws of a tiger. A moment afterward, this hideous Providence had entered again into the invisible.

Jean Valjean found himself outside.

VII

He let Marius slide down upon the beach.

They were outside!

The miasmas, the obscurity, the horror, were behind him. The balmy air, pure, living, joyful, freely respirable, flowed around him. Everywhere about him silence, but the charming silence of a sunset in a clear sky. Twilight had fallen; night was coming, the great liberatress, the friend of all those who need a mantle of darkness to escape from an anguish. The sky extended on every side like an enormous calm. The river came to his feet with the sound of a kiss. He heard the airy dialogues of the nests bidding each other good night in the elms of the Champs Élysées. A few stars, faintly piercing the pale blue of the zenith, and visible to reverie alone, produced their imperceptible little resplendencies in the immensity. Evening was unfolding over Jean Valjean's head all the caresses of the infinite.

Jean Valjean could not but gaze at that vast clear shadow which was above him; pensive, he took in the majestic silence of the eternal heavens, a bath of ecstasy and prayer. Then, hastily, as if a feeling of duty came back to him, he bent over Marius, and, dipping up some water in the hollow of his hand, he threw a few drops gently into his face. Marius' eyelids did not part; but his half-open mouth breathed.

Jean Valjean was plunging his hand into the river again, when suddenly he felt an indescribable uneasiness, such as we feel when we have somebody behind us, without seeing him.

He turned around.

A man of tall stature, wrapped in a long overcoat, with folded arms, and holding in his right hand a club, the leaden knob of which could be seen, stood erect a few steps in the rear of Jean Valjean, who was stooping over Marius.

It was, with the aid of the shadow, a sort of apparition. A simple man would have been afraid on account of the twilight, and a reflective man on account of the club.

Jean Valjean recognized Javert.

These two encounters, blow on blow, to fall from Thénardier upon Javert—it was hard.

Javert did not recognize Jean Valjean, who, as we have said, no longer resembled himself. He did not unfold his arms, he secured his club in his grasp by an imperceptible movement, and said in a quick and calm voice:

"Who are you?"

"I."

"What you?"

"Jean Valjean."

Javert put the club between his teeth, bent his knees, inclined his body, laid his two powerful hands upon Jean Valjean's shoulders, which they clamped like two vices, examined him, and recognized him. Their faces almost touched. Javert's look was terrible.

Jean Valjean stood inert under the grasp of Javert, like a lion who should submit to the claw of a lynx.

"Inspector Javert," said he, "you have got me. Besides, since this morning, I have considered myself your prisoner. I did not give you my address to try to escape you. Take me. Only grant me one thing. Dispose of me as you please; but help me first to carry this man home."

Javert's face contracted, as happened to him whenever anybody seemed to consider him capable of a concession. Still he did not say no.

He stooped down again, took a handkerchief from his pocket, which he dipped in the water, and wiped Marius' bloodstained forehead.

"This man was in the barricade," said he in an undertone, and as if speaking to himself. "This is he whom they called Marius."

Jean Valjean resumed:

"He lives in the Marais, rue des Filles du Calvaire, at his grandfather's—I forget the name."

Jean Valjean felt in Marius' coat, took out the pocketbook, opened it at the page penciled by Marius, and handed it to Javert.

Javert deciphered the lines written by Marius, and muttered: "Gillenormand, rue des Filles du Calvaire, Number Six."

Then he cried: "Driver?"

The reader will remember the fiacre which was waiting in case of need.

Javert kept Marius' pocketbook.

A moment later, the carriage, descending by the slope of the watering place, was on the beach. Marius was laid upon the back seat, and Javert sat down by the side of Jean Valjean on the front seat.

When the door was shut, the fiacre moved rapidly off, going up the quays in the direction of the Bastille.

They left the quays and entered the streets. The driver, a black silhouette upon his box, whipped up his bony horses. Icy silence in the coach. Marius, motionless, his body braced in the corner of the carriage, his head dropping down upon his breast, his arms hanging, his legs rigid, appeared to await nothing now but a coffin; Jean Valjean seemed made of shadow, and Javert of stone; and in that carriage full of night, the interior of which, whenever it passed before a lamp, appeared to turn lividly pale, as if from an intermittent flash, chance grouped together, and seemed dismally to confront the three tragic immobilities, the corpse, the specter, and the statue.

VIII

At every jolt over the pavement, a drop of blood fell from Marius' hair.

It was after nightfall when the fiacre arrived at No. 6, in the rue des Filles du Calvaire.

Javert first set foot on the ground, and, lifting the heavy wrought-iron knocker, struck a violent blow. The fold of the door partly opened, and Javert pushed it. The porter showed himself, gaping and half awake, a candle in his hand.

Meanwhile Jean Valjean and the driver lifted Marius out of the coach, Jean Valjean supporting him by the armpits, and the coachman by the knees.

Javert called out to the porter in the tone which befits the government, in presence of the porter of a factious man.

"Somebody whose name is Gillenormand?"

"It is here. What do you want with him?"

"His son is brought home."

"His son?" said the porter with amazement.

"He is dead."

Jean Valjean, who came ragged and dirty, behind Javert, and whom the porter beheld with some horror, motioned to him with his head that he was not.

The porter did not appear to understand either Javert's words or Jean Valjean's signs.

Javert continued:

"He has been to the barricade, and here he is."

"To the barricade!" exclaimed the porter.

"He has got himself killed. Go and wake his father."

The porter did not stir.

"Why don't you go?" resumed Javert.

The porter merely woke Basque. Basque woke Nicolette; Nicolette woke Aunt Gillenormand. As to the grandfather, they let him sleep, thinking that he would know it soon enough at all events.

They carried Marius up to the first story, without anybody, moreover, perceiving it in the other portions of the house, and they laid him on an old couch in Monsieur Gillenormand's antechamber. While Basque went for a doctor and Nicolette was opening the linen closets, Jean Valjean felt Javert touch him on the shoulder. He understood, and went downstairs, having behind him Javert's following steps.

The porter saw them depart as he had seen them arrive, with drowsy dismay.

They got into the fiacre again, and the driver mounted upon his box.

"Inspector Javert," said Jean Valjean, "grant me one thing more."

"What?" asked Javert roughly.

"Let me go home a moment. Then you shall do with me what you will."

Javert remained silent for a few seconds, his chin drawn back into the collar of his overcoat; then he let down the window in front.

"Driver," said he, "rue de l'Homme Armé, Number Seven."

IX

They did not open their mouths again for the whole distance.

At the entrance of the rue de l'Homme Armé, the fiacre stopped, this street being too narrow for carriages to enter. Javert and Jean Valjean got out.

Javert dismissed the fiacre.

Jean Valjean thought that Javert's intention was to take him on foot to the post of the Blancs Manteaux or to the post of the Archives, which are quite nearby.

They entered the street. It was, as usual, empty. Javert followed Jean Valjean. They reached No. 7. Jean Valjean rapped. The door opened.

"Very well," said Javert. "Go up."

He added with a strange expression and as if he were making an effort in speaking in such a way:

"I will wait here for you."

Jean Valjean looked at Javert. This manner of proceeding was little in accordance with Javert's habits. Jean Valjean opened the door, went into the house, cried to the porter, who was in bed and who had drawn the cord without getting up: "It is I!" and mounted the stairs.

On reaching the first story, he paused. All painful paths have their halting places. The window on the landing, which was a sliding window, was open.

Jean Valjean, either to take breath or mechanically, looked out of this window. He leaned over the street. It is short, and the lamp lighted it from one end to the other. Jean Valjean was bewildered with amazement; there was nobody there.

Javert was gone.

X

BASQUE and the porter had carried Marius into the parlor, still stretched motionless upon the couch on which he had been first laid. The doctor, who had been sent for, had arrived. Aunt Gillenormand had got up.

Aunt Gillenormand went to and fro, in terror, clasping her hands, and incapable of doing anything but to say: "My God, is it possible?"

On the doctor's order, a cot had been set up near the couch. The doctor examined Marius, and, after having determined that the pulse still beat, that the sufferer had no wound penetrating his breast, and that the blood at the corners of his mouth came from the nasal cavities, he had him laid flat upon the bed, without a pillow, his head on a level with his body, and even a little lower, with his chest bare, in order to facilitate respiration. Mademoiselle Gillenormand, seeing that they were taking off Marius' clothes, withdrew. She began to tell her beads in her room.

The body had not received any interior lesion; a ball, deadened by the pocketbook, had turned aside, and made the tour of the ribs with a hideous gash, but not deep, and consequently not dangerous. The long walk underground had completed the dislocation of the broken shoulder blade, and there were serious difficulties there. There were sword cuts on the arms. No scar disfigured his face; the head, however, was, as it were, covered with hacks; what would be the result of these wounds on the head? Did they stop at the scalp? Did they affect the skull? That could not yet be told. A serious symptom was that they had caused the fainting, and men do not always wake from such faintings. The hemorrhage, moreover, had exhausted the wounded man. From the waist, the lower part of the body had been protected by the barricade.

Basque and Nicolette tore up linen and made bandages; Nicolette sewed them, Basque folded them. There being no lint, the doctor stopped the flow of blood from the wounds temporarily with rolls of wadding. By the side of the bed, three candles were burning on a table upon which the surgical instruments were spread out. The doctor washed Marius' face and hair with cold water. A bucketful was red in a moment. The porter, candle in hand, stood by.

At the moment the doctor was wiping the face and touching the still-closed eyelids lightly with his finger, a door opened at the rear end of the parlor, and a long, pale figure approached.

It was the grandfather.

He was on the threshold, one hand on the knob of the half-opened door, his head bent a little forward and shaking, his body wrapped in a white nightgown, straight and without folds like a shroud; he was astounded; and he had the appearance of a phantom who is looking into a tomb.

He perceived the bed, and on the mattress that bleeding young man, white with a waxy whiteness, his eyes closed, his mouth open, his lips pallid, naked to the waist, gashed everywhere with red wounds, motionless, brightly lighted.

The grandfather had, from head to foot, as much of a shiver as ossified limbs can have; his eyes, the corneas of which had become yellow from his great age, were veiled with a sort of glassy haze; his whole face assumed in an instant the cadaverous angles of a skeleton head, his arms fell pendent as if a spring were broken in them, and his stupefied astonishment was expressed by the separation of the fingers of his aged, tremulous hands; his knees bent forward, showing through the opening of his nightgown his poor naked legs bristling with white hairs, and he murmured:

"Marius!"

"Monsieur," said Basque, "monsieur has just been brought home. He has been to the barricade, and—"

"He is dead!" cried the old man in a terrible voice. "Oh! The brigand."

Then a sort of sepulchral transfiguration made this centenarian as straight as a young man.

"Monsieur," said he, "you are the doctor. Come, tell me one thing. He is dead, isn't he?"

The physician, in the height of anxiety, kept silence.

Monsieur Gillenormand wrung his hands with a terrific burst of laughter.

"He is dead! He is dead! He has got killed at the barricade! In hatred of me! It is against me that he did this! Ah, the blood drinker! This is the way he comes back to me! Misery of my life, he is dead!"

The physician, who began to be anxious on two accounts, left Marius a moment, and went to Monsieur Gillenormand and took his arm. The grandfather turned around, looked at him with eyes which seemed swollen and bloody, and said quietly:

"Monsieur, I thank you. I am calm, I am a man, I saw the death of Louis XVI, I know how to bear up under events. There is one thing which is terrible, to think that it is your newspapers that do all the harm. You will have scribblers, talkers, lawyers, orators, tribunes, discussions, progress, lights, rights of man, freedom of the press, and this is the way they bring home your children for you. Oh! Marius! It is abominable! Killed! Dead before me! That is a child I brought up. I was an old man when he was yet quite small. He played at the Tuileries with his little spade and his little chair, and, so that the keeper should not scold, with my cane I filled up the holes in the ground that he made with his spade. One day he cried: 'Down with Louis XVIII!' and went away. It is not my fault. He was all rosy and fair. It was such a head as you see in pictures. I spoke to him in my gruff voice, I frightened him with my cane, but he knew very well it was for fun. In the morning, when he came into my room, I scolded, but it seemed like sunshine to me. You can't defend yourself against these brats. They take you, they hold onto you, they never let go of you. The truth is, that there was never any amour like that child. Now, what do you say of your Lafayette, your Benjamin Constant, and of your Tirecuir de Corcelles, who kill him for me! It can't go on like this."

He approached Marius, who was still livid and motionless, and to whom the physician had returned, and he began to wring his hands. The old man's white lips moved as if mechanically, and made way for almost indistinct words, like whispers in a death rattle, which could scarcely be heard: "Oh! Heartless! Oh! Clubbist! Oh! Scoundrel! Oh! Septembrist!"

At this moment, Marius slowly raised his lids, and his gaze, still veiled in the astonishment of lethargy, rested upon Monsieur Gillenormand.

"Marius!" cried the old man. "Marius! My darling Marius! My child! My dear son! You are opening your eyes, you are looking at me, you are alive, thanks!"

And he fell fainting.

Javert off the Track

JAVERT made his way with slow steps from the rue de l'Homme Armé.

He walked with his head down, for the first time in his life, and, for the first time in his life as well, with his hands behind his back.

He plunged into the silent streets.

Still he followed one direction.

He took the shortest route toward the Seine, reached the Quai des Ormes, went along the quay, passed the Grève, and stopped, at a little distance from the post of the Place du Châtelet, at the corner of the Pont Notre Dame. The Seine there forms between the Pont Notre Dame and the Pont au Change in one direction, and in the other between the Quai de la Mégisserie and the Quai aux Fleurs, a sort of square lake crossed by a rapid.

Javert leaned both elbows on the parapet, with his chin in his hands, and while his fingers were clenched mechanically in the thickest of his whiskers, he reflected.

There had been a new thing, a revolution, a catastrophe in the depths of his being; and there was matter for self-examination.

Javert was suffering frightfully.

For some hours Javert had ceased to be natural. He was troubled; this brain, so limpid in its blindness, had lost its transparency; there was a cloud in this crystal. Javert felt that duty was growing weaker in his conscience, and he could not hide it from himself. When he had so unexpectedly met Jean Valjean upon the beach of the Seine, there had been in him something of the wolf, which seizes his prey again, and of the dog which again finds his master.

He saw before him two roads, both equally straight, but he saw two, and that terrified him—him, who had never in his life known but one straight line. And, bitter anguish, these two roads were contradictory. One of these two straight lines excluded the other. Which of the two was the true one?

His condition was inexpressible.

One thing had astonished him, that Jean Valjean had spared him, and one thing had petrified him, that he, Javert, had spared Jean Valjean.

Where was he? He sought himself and found himself no longer.

What should he do now? Give up Jean Valjean? That was wrong. Leave Jean Valjean free? That was wrong. In the first case, the man of authority would fall lower than the man of the galley; in the second, a convict rose higher than the law and set his foot upon it. In both cases, dishonor to him, Javert. In every course which was open to him, there was a fall. Destiny has certain extremities precipitous upon the impossible, and beyond which life is no more than an abyss. Javert was at one of these extremities.

One of his causes of anxiety was that he was compelled to think. The very violence of all these contradictory emotions forced him to it. Thought was an unaccustomed thing to him, and singularly painful.

There is always a certain amount of internal rebellion in thought; and he was irritated at having it within him.

Upon what should he resolve? A single resource remained: to return immediately to the rue de l'Homme Armé and have Jean Valjean arrested. It was clear that that was what he must do. He could not.

Something barred the way to him on that side.

Something? What? Is there anything else in the world besides tribunals, sentences, police, and authority? Javert's ideas were overturned.

Javert felt that something horrible was penetrating his soul, admiration for a convict. Respect for a galley slave, can that be possible? He shuddered at it, yet could not shake it off. It was useless to struggle, he was reduced to confess before his own inner tribunal the sublimity of this wretch. That was hateful.

His supreme anguish was the loss of all certainty. He felt that he was uprooted. The code was now but a stump in his hand. He had to do with scruples of an unknown species. There was in him a revelation of feeling entirely distinct from the declarations of the law, his only standard hitherto. To retain his old virtue, that no longer sufficed. An entire order of unexpected facts arose and subjugated him. An entire new world appeared to his soul; favor accepted and returned, devotion, compassion, indulgence, acts of violence committed by pity upon austerity, respect of persons, no more final condemnation, no more damnation, the possibility of a tear in the eye of the law, a mysterious justice according to God going counter to justice according to men. He perceived in the darkness the fearful rising of an unknown moral sun; he was horrified and blinded by it. An owl compelled to an eagle's gaze.

He asked himself: "This convict, this desperate man, whom I have pursued even to persecution, and who has had me beneath his feet, and could have avenged himself, and who ought to have done so, as well as for his revenge as for his security, in granting me life, in sparing me, what has he done? His duty? No. Something more. And I, in sparing him in my turn, what have I done? My duty? No. Something more. There is then something more than duty." Here he was startled; since he had been of the age of a man, and an official, he had put almost all his religion into the police, being, and we employ the words here without the slightest irony and in their most serious acceptation, being, we have said, a spy as men are priests. He had a superior, Monsieur Gisquet; he had scarcely thought, until today, of that other superior, God.

This new chief, God, he felt unawares, and was perplexed thereat.

God, always interior to man, and unyielding, he the true conscience, to the false; a prohibition to the spark to extinguish itself; an order to the ray to remember the sun; an injunction to the soul to recognize the real absolute when it is confronted with the fictitious absolute; humanity imperishable; the human heart inadmissible; that splendid phenomenon, the most beautiful perhaps of our interior wonders—did Javert comprehend it? Did Javert penetrate it? Did Javert form any idea of it? Evidently not. But under the pressure of this incontestable incomprehensible, he felt that his head was bursting.

He was less the transfigured than the victim of this miracle. He bore it, exasperated. He saw in it only an immense difficulty of existence. It seemed to him that henceforth his breathing would be oppressed for ever.

Could that be endurable? No.

Unnatural state, if ever there was one. There were only two ways to get out of it. One, to go resolutely to Jean Valjean, and to return the man of the galleys to the dungeon. The other—

Javert left the parapet, and, his head erect this time, made his way with a firm step toward the post indicated by a lamp at one of the corners of the Place du Châtelet.

On reaching it, he saw a *sergent de ville* through the window, and he entered. Javert gave his name, showed his card to the *sergent*, and sat down at the table of the post, on which a candle was burning. There was a pen on the table, a leaden inkstand, and some paper in readiness for chance reports and the orders of the night patrol.

Javert took the pen and a sheet of paper, and began to write. This is what he wrote:

SOME OBSERVATIONS FOR THE BENEFIT OF THE SERVICE

First: I beg monsieur the prefect to glance at this.

Secondly: the prisoners, on their return from examination, take off their shoes and remain barefooted upon the pavement while they are searched. Many cough on returning to the prison. This involves hospital expenses.

Thirdly: spinning is good, with relays of officers at intervals; but there should be, on important occasions, two officers at least who do not lose sight of each other, so that, if, for any cause whatever, one officer becomes weak in the service, the other is watching him, and supplies his place.

Fourthly: it is difficult to explain why the special regulation of the prison of the Madelonnettes forbids a prisoner having a chair, even on paying for it.

Fifthly: at the Madelonnettes, there are only two bars

to the sutler's window, which enables the sutler to let the prisoners touch her hand.

Sixthly: the prisoners, called barkers, who call the other prisoners to the parlor, make the prisoner pay them two sous for calling his name distinctly. This is a theft.

Seventhly: for a dropped thread, they retain ten sous from the prisoner in the weaving shop; this is an abuse on the part of the contractor, since the cloth is just as good.

Javert wrote these lines in his calmest and most correct handwriting, not omitting a dot, and making the paper squeak resolutely under his pen. Beneath the last line he signed:

> JAVERT,
> Inspector of the 1st class.

At the Post of the Place du Châtelet.
June 7, 1832, about one o'clock in the morning.

Javert dried the fresh ink of the paper, folded it like a letter, sealed it, wrote on the back: "Note for the administration," left it on the table, and went out of the post. The glazed and grated door closed behind him.

He again crossed the Place du Châtelet diagonally, regained the quay, and returned with automatic precision to the very point which he had left a quarter of an hour before; he leaned over there, and found himself again in the same attitude, on the same stone of the parapet. It seemed as if he had not stirred.

The darkness was complete. It was the sepulchral moment which follows midnight. A ceiling of clouds concealed the stars. The sky was only an ominous depth. The houses in the city no longer showed a single light; nobody was passing; all that he could see of the streets and the quays was deserted; Notre Dame and the towers of the Palais de Justice seemed like features of the night. A lamp reddened the curb of the quay. The silhouettes of the bridges were distorted in the mist, one behind the other. The rains had swelled the river.

The place where Javert was leaning was, it will be remembered, situated exactly over the rapids of the Seine, perpendicularly over that formidable whirlpool which knots and unknots itself like an endless screw.

Javert bent his head and looked. All was black. He could distinguish nothing. A fierce breath rose from that abyss. The swollen river guessed at, rather than perceived, the tragical whispering of the flood, the dismal vastness of the arches of the bridge, the imaginable fall into that gloomy void; all that shadow was full of horror.

Javert remained for some minutes motionless, gazing into that opening of darkness; he contemplated the invisible with a fixedness which resembled attention. The water gurgled. Suddenly he took off his hat and laid it on the edge of the quay. A moment afterward, a tall and black form, which from the distance some belated passer might have taken for a phantom, appeared standing on the parapet, bent toward the Seine, then sprang up, and fell straight into the darkness; there was a dull splash; and the shadow alone was in the secret of the convulsions of that obscure form which had disappeared under the water.

The Grandson and the Grandfather

I

SOME time after the events which we have just related, the Sieur Boulatruelle had a vivid emotion.

Boulatruelle, it will perhaps be remembered, was a man occupied with troublous and various things. He broke stones and damaged travelers on the highway. Digger and robber, he had a dream; he believed in treasures buried in the forest of Montfermeil. He hoped one day to find money in the ground at the foot of a tree; in the meantime, he was willing to search for it in the pockets of the passers-by.

One morning a little before the break of day, Boulatruelle, while on the way to his work according to his habit, and upon the watch, perhaps, perceived a man among the branches, whose back only he could see, but whose form, as it seemed to him, through the distance and the twilight, was not altogether unknown to him. Boulatruelle, although a drunkard, had a correct and lucid memory, an indispensable defensive arm to him who is slightly in conflict with legal order.

Boulatruelle thought of the treasure. By dint of digging into his memory he dimly recollected having already had, several years before, a similar surprise in relation to a man who, it struck him, was very possibly the same man.

While he was meditating, he had, under the very weight of his meditation, bowed his head, which was natural, but not very cunning. When he raised it again there was no longer anything there. The man had vanished in the forest and the twilight.

"The deuce," said Boulatruelle, "I will find him again. I will discover the parish of that parishioner. This Patron-Minette prowler has a why, I will find it out. Nobody has a secret in my woods without I have a finger in it."

He took his pickax, which was very sharp.

"Here is something," he muttered, "to pry into the ground or a man with."

And, as one attaches one thread to another thread, limping along at his best in the path which the man must have followed, he took his way through the thicket.

When he had gone a hundred yards, daylight, which began to break, aided him. There was nearby a beech tree of great height, worthy of Tityrus and Boulatruelle. Boulatruelle climbed the beech as high as he could.

The idea was good. In exploring the solitude on the side where the wood was entirely wild and tangled, Boulatruelle suddenly perceived the man.

Hardly had he perceived him when he lost sight of him.

The man entered, or rather glided, into a distant glade, masked by tall trees, but which Boulatruelle knew very well from having noticed there, near a great heap of buhrstone, a wounded chestnut tree bandaged with a plate of zinc nailed upon the bark. This glade is the one which was formerly called the Blaru ground.

Boulatruelle, with the rapidity of joy, let himself fall from the tree rather than descend. The lair was found, the problem was to catch the game. That famous treasure of his dreams was probably there.

Boulatruelle threw himself resolutely into the thickest of the bushes.

He had to deal with hollies, with nettles, with hawthorns,

with sweetbriers, with thistles, with exceedingly irascible brambles. He was very much scratched.

At the bottom of a ravine he found a stream which must be crossed.

He finally reached the Blaru glade, at the end of forty minutes, sweating, soaked, breathless, torn, ferocious.

Nobody in the glade.

Boulatruelle ran to the heap of stones. It was in its place. Nobody had carried it away.

As for the man, he had vanished into the forest. He had escaped. Where? On which side? In what thicket? Impossible to guess.

And, a bitter thing, there was behind the heap of stones, before the tree with the plate of zinc, some fresh earth, a pick, forgotten or abandoned, and a hole.

This hole was empty.

"Robber!" cried Boulatruelle, showing both fists to the horizon.

II

MARIUS was for a long time neither dead nor alive. He had for several weeks a fever accompanied with delirium, and serious cerebral symptoms resulting rather from the concussion produced by the wounds in the head than from the wounds themselves. As long as there was danger, Monsieur Gillenormand, in despair at the bedside of his grandson, was, like Marius, neither dead nor alive.

Every day, and sometimes twice a day, a very well-dressed gentleman with white hair, such was the description given by the porter, came to inquire after the wounded man, and left a large package of lint for the dressings.

At last, on the 7th of September, three months to a day after the sorrowful night when they had brought him home dying to his grandfather, the physician declared him out of danger. Convalescence began.

At each new phase of improvement, which continued to grow more and more visible, the grandfather raved. He did a thousand mirthful things mechanically; he ran up and down stairs without knowing why. A neighbor, a pretty woman withal, was amazed at receiving a large bouquet one morning;

it was Monsieur Gillenormand who sent it to her. The husband made a scene. Monsieur Gillenormand attempted to take Nicolette upon his knees. He called Marius Monsieur the Baron.

He cried, "*Vive la République!*"

As for Marius, while he let them dress his wounds and care for him, he had one fixed idea: Cosette.

To him the idea of life was not distinct from the idea of Cosette; he had decreed in his heart that he would not accept the one without the other; and he was unalterably determined to demand from anybody, no matter whom, who should wish to compel him to live, from his grandfather, from Fate, from Hell, the restitution of his vanished Eden.

He did not hide the obstacles from himself.

Monsieur Gillenormand, without manifesting it in any way, noticed that Marius, since he had been brought home and restored to consciousness, had not once said to him: "father." He did not say "monsieur," it is true; but he found means to say neither the one nor the other, by a certain manner of turning his sentences.

A crisis was evidently approaching.

As it almost aways happens in similar cases, Marius, in order to try himself, skirmished before offering battle. This is called feeling the ground. One morning it happened that Monsieur Gillenormand, over a newspaper which had fallen into his hands, spoke lightly of the Convention and discharged a royalist epiphonema upon Danton, Saint-Just, and Robespierre. "The men of '93 were giants," said Marius, sternly. The old man was silent, and did not whisper for the rest of the day.

III

One day Monsieur Gillenormand, while his daughter was putting in order the vials and the cups upon the marble top of the bureau, bent over Marius and said to him in his most tender tone:

"Do you see, my darling Marius, in your place I would eat meat now rather than fish. A fried sole is excellent to begin a convalescence, but, to put the sick man on his legs, it takes a good cutlet."

Marius, nearly all whose strength had returned, gathered it together, sat up in bed, rested his clenched hands on the sheets, looked his grandfather in the face, assumed a terrible air, and said:

"This leads me to say something to you."

"What is it?"

"It is that I wish to marry."

"Foreseen," said the grandfather. And he burst out laughing.

"How foreseen?"

"Yes, foreseen. You shall have her, your lassie."

Marius, astounded, and overwhelmed by the dazzling burst of happiness, trembled in every limb.

Monsieur Gillenormand continued:

"Yes, you shall have her, your handsome, pretty little girl. She comes every day in the shape of an old gentleman to inquire after you. Since you were wounded, she has passed her time in weeping and making lint. I have made inquiry. She lives in the rue de l'Homme Armé, Number Seven. Ah, we are ready! Ah! You want her! Well, you shall have her. That catches you. Ah! You thought that the old fellow was going to storm, to make a gruff voice, to cry no, and to lift his cane upon all this dawn. Not at all. Cosette, so be it; love, so be it; I ask nothing better. Monsieur, take the trouble to marry. Be happy, my dear child."

This said, the old man burst into sobs.

And he took Marius' head, and he hugged it in both arms against his old breast, and they both began to weep. That is one of the forms of supreme happiness.

"Father!" exclaimed Marius.

"Ah! You love me then!" said the old man.

There was an ineffable moment. They choked and could not speak.

At last the old man stammered:

"Come! The ice is broken. He has called me 'Father.'"

Marius released his head from his grandfather's arms, and said softly:

"But, father, now that I am well, it seems to me that I could see her."

"Foreseen again, you shall see her tomorrow."

"Father!"

"What?"

"Why not today?"

"Well, today. Here goes for today. You have called me 'Father' three times; it is well worth that. I will see to it. She shall be brought to you. Foreseen, I tell you. This has already been put into verse. It is the conclusion of André Chénier's elegy of the *Jeune malade*, André Chénier who was murdered by the scound—, by the giants of '93."

IV

COSETTE and Marius saw each other again.

What the interview was we will not attempt to tell. There are things which we should not undertake to paint; the sun is of the number.

The whole family, including Basque and Nicolette, were assembled in Marius' room when Cosette entered.

She appeared on the threshold; it seemed as if she were in a cloud.

Just at that instant the grandfather was about to blow his nose; he stopped short, holding his nose in his handkerchief, and looking at Cosette above it:

"Adorable!" he exclaimed.

Then he blew his nose with a loud noise.

Cosette was intoxicated, enraptured, startled, in Heaven. She was as frightened as one can be by happiness. She stammered, quite pale, quite red, wishing to throw herself into Marius' arms, and not daring to. Ashamed to show her love before all those people. We are pitiless toward happy lovers; we stay there when they have the strongest desire to be alone. They, however, have no need at all of society.

With Cosette and behind her had entered a man with white hair, grave, smiling nevertheless, but with a vague and poignant smile. This was "Monsieur Fauchelevent"; this was Jean Valjean.

He was very well dressed, as the porter had said, in a new black suit, with a white cravat.

The porter was a thousand miles from recognizing in this correct bourgeois, in this probable notary, the frightful corpse bearer who had landed at his door on the evening of the 6th of June, ragged, muddy, hideous, haggard, his face masked by blood and dirt, supporting the fainting Marius in his arms.

Monsieur Fauchelevent, in Marius' room, stayed near the

door, as if apart. He had under his arm a package similar in appearance to an octavo volume, wrapped in paper. The paper of the envelope was greenish, and seemed moldy.

"Does this gentleman always have books under his arm like that?" asked Mademoiselle Gillenormand, who did not like books, in a low voice of Nicolette.

"Well," answered Monsieur Gillenormand, who had heard her, in the same tone, "he is a scholar. What then? Is it his fault?"

And bowing, he said, in a loud voice:

"Monsieur Tranchelevent—"

Father Gillenormand did not do this on purpose, but in-attention to proper names was an aristocratic way he had.

"Monsieur Tranchelevent, I have the honor of asking of you for my grandson, Monsieur the Baron Marius Pontmercy, the hand of mademoiselle."

Monsieur Tranchelevent bowed.

"It is done," said the grandfather.

And, turning toward Marius and Cosette, with arms extended and blessing, he cried:

"Permission to adore each other."

They did not make him say it twice. It was all the same! The cooing began. They talked low, Marius leaning on his long chair, Cosette standing near him. "Oh, my God!" murmured Cosette. "I see you again! It is you! It is you! For four months I have been dead." "Angel!" said Marius.

Then, as there were spectators, they stopped, and did not say another word, contenting themselves with touching each other's hands very gently.

Aunt Gillenormand witnessed with amazement this irruption of light into her aged interior. This amazement was not at all aggressive; it was not the least in the world the scandalized and envious look of an owl upon two ringdoves; it was the dull eye of a poor innocent girl of fifty-seven; it was incomplete life beholding that triumph, love.

The grandfather sat down near them, made Cosette sit down, and took their four hands in his old wrinkled hands:

"She is exquisite, this darling. She is a masterpiece, this Cosette! She is a very little girl and a very great lady. She will be only a baroness, that is stooping; she was born a mar-chioness. Hasn't she lashes for you? My children, fix it well in your noddles that you are in the right of it. Love one another.

Be foolish about it. Love is the foolishness of men and the wisdom of God. Adore each other. Only," added he, suddenly darkening, "what a misfortune! This is what I am thinking of! More than half of what I have is in annuity; as long as I live, it's all well enough, but after my death, twenty years from now, ah! My poor children, you will not have a sou. Your beautiful white hands, Madame the Baroness, will do the devil the honor to pull him by the tail."

"Mademoiselle Euphrasie Fauchelevent has six hundred thousand francs."

It was Jean Valjean's voice.

He had not yet uttered a word, nobody seemed even to remember that he was there, and he stood erect and motionless behind all these happy people.

"How is Mademoiselle Euphrasie in question?" asked the grandfather, startled.

"That is me," answered Cosette.

"Six hundred thousand francs!" resumed Monsieur Gillenormand.

"Less fourteen or fifteen thousand francs, perhaps," said Jean Valjean.

And he laid on the table the package which Aunt Gillenormand had taken for a book.

Jean Valjean opened the package himself; it was a bundle of bank notes. They ran through them, and they counted them. There were five hundred bills of a thousand francs, and a hundred and sixty-eight of five hundred. In all, five hundred and eighty-four thousand francs.

"That is a good book," said Monsieur Gillenormand.

"Five hundred and eighty-four thousand francs!" murmured the aunt. "Five hundred and eighty-four! You might call it six hundred thousand, indeed!"

As for Marius and Cosette, they were looking at each other during this time; they paid little attention to this incident.

V

ALL the preparations were made for the marriage. The physician being consulted said that it might take place in February. This was in December. Some ravishing weeks of perfect happiness rolled away.

The least happy was not the grandfather. He would remain for a quarter of an hour at a time gazing at Cosette.

Cosette and Marius had passed abruptly from the grave to paradise. There had been but little caution in the transition, and they would have been stunned if they had not been dazzled.

"Do you understand anything about it?" said Marius to Cosette.

"No," answered Cosette, "but it seems to me that the good God is caring for us."

Jean Valjean did all, smoothed all, conciliated all, made all easy. He hastened toward Cosette's happiness with as much eagerness, and apparently as much joy, as Cosette herself.

As he had been a mayor, he knew how to solve a delicate problem, in the secret of which he was alone: Cosette's civil state. To bluntly give her origin, who knows? That might prevent the marriage. He drew Cosette out of all difficulty. He arranged a family of dead people for her, a sure means of incurring no objection. Cosette was what remained of an extinct family; Cosette was not his daughter, but the daughter of another Fauchelevent.

As for the five hundred and eighty-four thousand francs, that was a legacy left to Cosette by a dead person who desired to remain unknown.

Cosette learned that she was not the daughter of that old man whom she had so long called father. He was only a relative; another Fauchelevent was her real father. At any other time, this would have broken her heart. But at this ineffable hour, it was only a little shadow, a darkening, and she had so much joy that this cloud was of short duration. She had Marius. The young man came, the goodman faded away; such is life.

She continued, however, to say "father" to Jean Valjean.

Cosette, in raptures, was enthusiastic about Grandfather Gillenormand. It is true that he loaded her with madrigals and with presents. Every morning, a new offering of finery from the grandfather to Cosette. Every possible furbelow blossomed out splendidly about her.

It was arranged that the couple should live with the grandfather. Monsieur Gillenormand absolutely insisted upon giving them his room, the finest in the house. "It will rejuvenate me," he declared. "It is an old project. I always had the idea of making a wedding in my room." He filled this room with a profusion of gay old furniture.

Monsieur Gillenormand's library became the attorney's office which Marius required; an office being rendered necessary by the rules of the order.

VI

THE lovers saw each other every day. Cosette came with Monsieur Fauchelevent.

Marius, inwardly and in the depth of his thought, surrounded this Monsieur Fauchelevent, who was to him simply benevolent and cold, with all sorts of silent questions. There came to him at intervals doubts about his own recollections. In his memory there was a hole, a black place, an abyss scooped out by four months of agony. Many things were lost in it.

Marius hesitated to believe that the Fauchelevent of the barricade was the same as this Fauchelevent in flesh and blood, so gravely seated near Cosette. The first was probably one of those nightmares coming and going with his hours of delirium. Moreover, their two natures showing a steep front to each other, no question was possible from Marius to Monsieur Fauchelevent. The idea of it did not even occur to him.

Once only, Marius made an attempt. He brought the rue de la Chanvrerie into the conversation, and, turning toward Monsieur Fauchelevent, he said to him:

"You are well acquainted with that street?"

"What street?"

"The rue de la Chanvrerie."

"I have no idea of the name of that street," answered Monsieur Fauchelevent in the most natural tone in the world.

The answer, which bore upon the name of the street, and not upon the street itself, appeared to Marius more conclusive than it was.

"Decidedly," thought he, "I have been dreaming. I have had a hallucination. It was somebody who resembled him. Monsieur Fauchelevent was not there."

The enchantment, great as it was, did not efface other preoccupations from Marius' mind.

During the preparations for the marriage, and while waiting for the time fixed upon, he had some difficult and careful retrospective researches made.

He owed gratitude on several sides, he owed some on his father's account, he owed some on his own.

There was Thénardier; there was the unknown man who had brought him, Marius, to Monsieur Gillenormand's.

Marius persisted in trying to find these two men, not intending to marry, to be happy, and to forget them, and fearing lest these debts of duty unpaid might cast a shadow over his life, so luminous henceforth.

None of the various agents whom Marius employed succeeded in finding Thénardier's track. Effacement seemed complete on that side. The Thénardiess had died in prison pending the examination of the charge. Thénardier and his daughter Azelma, the two who alone remained of that woeful group, had plunged back into the shadow. The gulf of the social Unknown had silently closed over these beings.

As for the other, as for the unknown man who had saved Marius, the researches at first had some result, then stopped short. They succeeded in finding the fiacre which had brought Marius to the rue des Filles du Calvaire on the evening of the 6th of June. The driver declared that on the 6th of June, by order of a police officer, he had been "stationed," from three o'clock in the afternoon until night, on the quay of the Champs Élysées, above the outlet of the Grand Sewer; that, about nine o'clock in the evening, the grating of the sewer, which overlooks the river beach, was opened; that a man came out, carrying another man on his shoulders, who seemed to be dead; that the officer, who was watching at that point, arrested the living man, and seized the dead man; that, on the order of the officer, he, the driver, received "all those people" into the fiacre; that they went first to the rue des Filles du Calvaire; that they left the dead man there; that the dead man was Monsieur Marius, and that he, the driver, recognized him plainly, although he was alive "this time"; that they then got into his carriage again; that he whipped up his horses; that, within a few steps of the door of the Archives, he had been called to stop; that there, in the street, he had been paid and left, and that the officer took away the other man; that he knew nothing more, that the night was very dark.

Marius was lost in conjectures.

He could not doubt his own identity. How did it come about, however, that, falling in the rue de la Chanvrerie, he had been picked up by the police officer on the banks of the Seine, near the Bridge of the Invalides? Somebody had carried him from the quarter of the markets to the Champs Élysées. And how? By the sewer. Unparalleled devotion!

Somebody? Who? What kind of a man was this? How did he look? Nobody could tell. The driver answered: "The night was very dark." Basque and Nicolette, in their amazement, had only looked at their young master covered with blood. The porter, whose candle had lighted the tragic arrival of Marius, alone had noticed the man in question, and this is the description which he gave of him: "This man was horrible."

In the hope of deriving aid in his researches from them, Marius had had preserved the bloody clothes which he wore when he was brought back to his grandfather's. On examining the coat, it was noticed that one skirt was oddly torn. A piece was missing.

One evening Marius spoke, before Cosette and Jean Valjean, of all this singular adventure, of the numberless inquiries which he had made, and of the uselessness of his efforts. The cold countenance of "Monsieur Fauchelevent" made him impatient. He exclaimed with a vivacity which had almost the vibration of anger:

"Yes, that man, whoever he may be, was sublime. Oh! If Cosette's six hundred thousand francs were mine—"

"They are yours," interrupted Jean Valjean.

"Well," resumed Marius, "I would give them to find that man!"

Jean Valjean kept silence.

The White Night

I

THE night of the 16th of February, 1833, was a blessed night. Above its shade the heavens were opened. It was the wedding night of Marius and Cosette.

The day had been adorable.

It rained that day, but there is always a little patch of blue in the sky at the service of happiness, which lovers see, even though the rest of creation be under an umbrella.

On the previous evening, Jean Valjean had handed to Marius, in presence of Monsieur Gillenormand, the five hundred and eighty-four thousand francs.

There was a beautiful room in the Gillenormand house furnished expressly for him, and Cosette had said to him so irresistibly: "Father, I pray you," that she had made him almost promise that he would come and occupy it.

To realize his dream. To whom is that given? There must be elections for that in heaven; we are all unconscious candidates; the angels vote. Cosette and Marius had been elected.

Cosette, at the *mairie* and in the church, was brilliant and touching. Toussaint, aided by Nicolette, had dressed her.

Marius' beautiful hair was perfumed and lustrous; here and there might be discerned, under the thickness of the locks, pallid lines, which were the scars of the barricade.

The grandfather, superb, his head held high, uniting more than ever in his toilet and manner all the elegances of the time of Barras, conducted Cosette.

When, at the completion of all the ceremonies, after having pronounced before the mayor and the priest every possible yes, after having signed the registers at the municipality and at the sacristy, after having exchanged their rings, after having been on their knees elbow to elbow under the canopy of white moire in the smoke of the censer, hand in hand, admired and envied by all, Marius in black, she in white, preceded by the usher in colonel's epaulettes, striking the pavement with his halberd, between two hedges of marveling spectators, they arrived under the portal of the church where the folding doors were both open, ready to get into the carriage again, and all was over, Cosette could not yet believe it. She beheld Marius in a glory; Marius beheld Cosette upon an altar. And upon that altar and in that glory, the two apotheoses mingling, in the background, mysteriously, behind a cloud to Cosette, in flashing flame to Marius, there was the ideal, the real, the rendezvous of the kiss and the dream, the nuptial pillow.

Then they returned to the rue des Filles du Calvaire, to their home. Marius, side by side with Cosette, ascended, triumphant and radiant, that staircase up which he had been carried dying. The poor gathered before the door, and, sharing their purses, they blessed them.

A banquet had been prepared in the dining room.

In the antechamber three violins and a flute played some of Haydn's quartettes in softened strains.

Jean Valjean sat in a chair in the parlor, behind the door, which shut back upon him in such a way as almost to hide him. A few moments before they took their seats at the table, Cosette came, as if from a sudden impulse, and made him a low courtesy, spreading out her bridal dress with both hands, and, with a tenderly frolicsome look, she asked him:

"Father, are you pleased?"

"Yes," said Jean Valjean, "I am pleased."

"Well, then, laugh."

Jean Valjean began to laugh.

A few moments afterward, Basque announced dinner.

The guests, preceded by Monsieur Gillenormand giving his arm to Cosette, entered the dining room, and took their places, according to the appointed order, about the table.

Two large armchairs were placed, on the right and on the left of the bride, the first for Monsieur Gillenormand, the second for Jean Valjean. Monsieur Gillenormand took his seat. The other armchair remained empty.

All eyes sought "Monsieur Fauchelevent."

He was not there.

Monsieur Gillenormand called Basque.

"Do you know where Monsieur Fauchelevent is?"

"Monsieur," answered Basque. "Exactly. Monsieur Fauchelevent told me to say to monsieur that he was suffering a little from his sore hand, and could not dine with Monsieur the Baron and Madame the Baroness. That he begged they would excuse him, that he would come tomorrow morning. He has just gone away."

The empty armchair chilled for a moment the effusion of the nuptial repast. But what is one dark corner in such a deluge of joy? Cosette and Marius were in one of those selfish and blessed moments when we have no faculty save for the perception of happiness. Marius took Jean Valjean's place at Cosette's side; and things arranged themselves in such a way that Cosette, at first saddened by Jean Valjean's absence, was finally satisfied with it. From the moment that Marius was the substitute, Cosette would not have regretted God. She put her soft little foot encased in white satin upon Marius' foot.

The armchair occupied, Monsieur Fauchelevent was effaced; and nothing was missed. And, five minutes later, the whole table was laughing from one end to the other with all the spirit of forgetfulness.

The evening was lively, gay, delightful. The sovereign good humor of the grandfather gave the keynote to the whole festival, and everybody regulated himself by this almost centenarian cordiality. They danced a little, they laughed much; it was a good childlike wedding. They might have invited the goodman Formerly. Indeed, he was there in the person of Grandfather Gillenormand.

There was tumult, then silence.

The bride and groom disappeared.

A little after midnight the Gillenormand house became a temple.

Here we stop. Upon the threshold of wedding nights stands an angel smiling, his finger on his lip.

The soul enters into contemplation before this sanctuary, in which is held the celebration of love.

There must be gleams of light above those houses. The joy which they contain must escape in light through the stones of the walls, and shine dimly into the darkness. It is impossible that this sacred festival of destiny should not send a celestial radiation to the infinite. Love is the sublime crucible in which is consummated the fusion of man and woman; the one being, the triple being, the final being, the human trinity, springs from it. This birth of two souls into one must be an emotion for space. The lover is priest; the rapt maiden is affrighted. Something of this joy goes to God. Where there is really marriage, that is where there is love, the ideal is mingled with it. A nuptial bed makes a halo in the darkness. Were it given to the eye of flesh to perceive the fearful and enchanting sights of the superior life, it is probable that we should see the forms of night, the winged strangers, the blue travelers of the invisible, bending, a throng of shadowy heads, over the luminous house, pleased, blessing, showing to one another the sweetly startled maiden bride, and wearing the reflection of the human felicity upon their divine countenances. If, at that supreme hour, the wedded pair, bewildered with pleasure, and believing themselves alone, were to listen, they would hear in their chamber a rustling of confused wings. Perfect happiness implies the solidarity of the angels. That little obscure alcove has for its ceiling the whole heavens. When two mouths, made sacred by love, draw near each other to create, it is impossible that above that ineffable kiss there should not be a thrill in the immense mystery of the stars.

These are the true felicities. No joy beyond these joys. Love is the only ecstasy, everything else weeps.

To love or to have loved, that is enough. Ask nothing further. There is no other pearl to be found in the dark folds of life. To love is a consummation.

II

WHAT had become of Jean Valjean?

Immediately after having laughed, upon Cosette's playful injunction, nobody observing him, Jean Valjean had left his seat, got up, and, unperceived, had reached the antechamber. It was that same room which he had entered eight months before, black with mire, blood, and powder, bringing the grandson home to the grandfather. The old woodwork was garlanded with leaves and flowers; the musicians were seated on the couch upon which they had placed Marius. Basque, in a black coat, short breeches, white stockings, and white gloves, was arranging crowns of roses about each of the dishes which was to be served up. Jean Valjean had charged him to explain his absence, and gone away.

Jean Valjean returned home. He lighted his candle and went upstairs. The apartment was empty. Toussaint herself was no longer there. Jean Valjean's step made more noise than usual in the rooms. All the closets were open. He went into Cosette's room. There were no sheets on the bed. The pillow, without a pillowcase and without laces, was laid upon the coverlets folded at the foot of the mattress of which the ticking was to be seen and on which nobody should sleep henceforth. All the little feminine objects to which Cosette clung had been carried away; there remained only the heavy furniture and the four walls.

Jean Valjean looked at the walls, shut some closet doors, went and came from one room to the other.

Then he found himself again in his own room, and he put his candle on the table.

He approached his bed, and his eye fell (was it by chance, or with intention?) upon the Inseparable, of which Cosette had been jealous, upon the little trunk which never left him. On the 4th of June, on arriving in the rue de l'Homme Armé, he had placed it upon a candlestand at the head of his bed. He went to this stand with a sort of vivacity, took a key from his pocket, and opened the valise.

He took out slowly the garments in which, ten years before, Cosette had left Montfermeil; first the little dress, then the black scarf, then the great heavy child's shoes which Cosette could have almost put on still, so small a foot she had, then the bodice of very thick fustian, then the knit skirt, then the apron with pockets, then the woolen stockings. Those stockings, on which the shape of a little leg was still gracefully marked, were hardly longer than Jean Valjean's hand. These were all black. He had carried these garments for her to Montfermeil. As he took them out of the valise, he laid them on the bed. He was thinking. He remembered. It was in winter, a very cold December, she shivered half-naked in rags, her poor little feet all red in her wooden shoes. He, Jean Valjean, he had taken her away from those rags to clothe her in this mourning garb. The mother must have been pleased in her tomb to see her daughter wear mourning for her, and especially to see that she was clad, and that she was warm. He thought of that forest of Montfermeil; they had crossed it together, Cosette and he. He arranged the little things upon the bed, the scarf next to the skirt, the stockings beside the shoes, the bodice beside the dress, and he looked at them one after another. She was no higher than that, she had her great doll in her arms, she laughed, they walked holding each other by the hand, she had nobody but him in the world.

Then his venerable white head fell upon the bed, this old stoical heart broke, his face was swallowed up, so to speak, in Cosette's garments, and anybody who had passed along the staircase at that moment would have heard fearful sobs.

THE formidable old struggle, several phases of which we have already seen, recommenced.

Jacob wrestled with the angel but one night. Alas! How many times have we seen Jean Valjean clenched, body to body, in the darkness with his conscience, and wrestling desperately against it.

That night, however, Jean Valjean felt that he was giving his last battle.

A poignant question presented itself.

He had reached the last crossing of good and evil. He had that dark intersection before his eyes. This time again, as it had already happened to him in other sorrowful crises, two roads opened before him; the one tempting, the other terrible. Which should he take?

The one which terrified him was advised by the mysterious indicating finger which we all perceive whenever we fix our eyes upon the shadow.

The question which presented itself was this:

In what manner should Jean Valjean comport himself in regard to the happiness of Cosette and Marius? This happiness, it was he who had willed it, it was he who had made it; he had thrust it into his own heart, and at this hour, looking upon it, he might have the same satisfaction that an armorer would have, who should recognize his own mark upon a blade, on withdrawing it all reeking from his breast.

Cosette had Marius, Marius possessed Cosette. They had everything, even riches. And it was his work.

But this happiness, now that it existed, now that it was here, what was he to do with it, he, Jean Valjean? Should he impose himself upon this happiness? Should he treat it as belonging to him? Should he put in his catastrophe as a companion for their two felicities? Should he continue to keep silence? In a word, should he be, by the side of these two happy beings, the ominous mute of destiny?

We must be accustomed to fatality and its encounter, to dare to raise our eyes when certain questions appear to us in their horrible nakedness. Good or evil are behind this severe interrogation point. "What are you going to do?" demands the sphinx.

This familiarity with trial Jean Valjean had. He looked fixedly upon the sphinx.

He examined the pitiless problem under all its phases.

Cosette, that charming existence, was the raft of this shipwreck. What was he to do? Cling on, or let go his hold?

If he clung to it, he escaped disaster, he rose again into the sunshine, he let the bitter water drip from his garments and his hair, he was saved, he lived.

If he loosed his hold?

Then, the abyss.

The obedience of matter is limited by friction; is there no limit to the obedience of the soul? If perpetual motion is impossible, is perpetual devotion demandable?

The first step is nothing; it is the last which is difficult. What was the Champmathieu affair compared with Cosette's marriage and all that it involved? What is this: to return to the galleys, compared with this: to enter into nothingness?

Oh, first step of descent, how gloomy thou art! Oh, second step, how black thou art!

How should he not turn away his head this time?

Martyrdom is a sublimation, a corrosive sublimation. It is a torture of consecration. You consent to it the first hour; you sit upon the throne of red-hot iron, you put upon your brow the crown of red-hot iron, you receive the globe of red-hot iron, you take the scepter of red-hot iron, but you have yet to put on the mantle of flame, and is no moment when the wretched flesh revolts, and when you abdicate the torture?

At last Jean Valjean entered the calmness of despair.

He weighed, he thought, he considered the alternatives of the mysterious balance of light and shade.

His giddy reverie lasted all night.

He remained there until dawn, in the same attitude, doubled over on the bed, prostrated under the enormity of fate, crushed perhaps, alas! His fists clenched, his arms extended at a right angle, like one taken from the cross and thrown down with his face to the ground. He remained twelve hours, the twelve hours of a long winter night, chilled, without lifting his head, and without uttering a word. He was as motionless as a corpse, while his thought writhed upon the ground and flew away, now like the hydra, now like the eagle. To see him thus without motion, one would have said he was dead; suddenly he thrilled convulsively, and his mouth, fixedly upon Cosette's garments, kissed them; then one saw that he was alive.

What one? Since Jean Valjean was alone, and there was nobody there?

The One who is in the darkness.

The Last Drop in the Chalice

I

THE day after a wedding is solitary. The privacy of the happy is respected. And thus their slumber is a little belated. The tumult of visits and felicitations does not commence until later. It was on the morning of the 17th of February, a little after noon, when Basque, his napkin and duster under his arm, busy "doing his antechamber," heard a light rap at the door. There was no ring, which is considerate on such a day. Basque opened and saw Monsieur Fauchelevent. He introduced him into the parlor, still cumbered and topsy-turvy, and having the appearance of the battlefield of the evening's festivities.

There was a noise at the door. Jean Valjean raised his eyes.

Marius entered, his head erect, his mouth smiling, an indescribable light upon his face, his forehead radiant, his eye triumphant. He also had not slept.

"It is you, father!" exclaimed he on perceiving Jean Valjean. "But you come too early. It is only half an hour after noon yet. Cosette is asleep."

He continued; words overflowed from him, which is characteristic of these divine paroxysms of joy:

"We have both of us talked much about you. Cosette loves you so much! You will not forget that your room is here. We will have no more of the rue de l'Homme Armé. We will have no more of it at all. You will come and install yourself here.

And that today. Or you will have a bone to pick with Cosette. She intends to lead us all by the nose, I warn you. You have seen your room, it is close by ours, it looks upon the gardens. Every spring, in the clump of acacias which is in front of your windows, there comes a nightingale; you will have her in two months. There is, I believe, a little valise which you treasure, I have selected a place of honor for it. You have conquered my grandfather, you suit him. We will live together. We have absolutely decided to be very happy. And you are part of our happiness, do you understand, father? Come now, you breakfast with us today?"

"Monsieur," said Jean Valjean, "I have one thing to tell you. I am an old convict."

The limit of perceptible acute sounds may be passed quite as easily for the mind as for the ear. Those words: "I am an old convict," coming from Monsieur Fauchelevent's mouth and entering Marius' ear, went beyond the possible. Marius did not hear. It seemed to him that something had just been said to him; but he knew not what. He stood aghast.

He then perceived that the man who was talking to him was terrible. Excited as he was, he had not until this moment noticed that frightful pallor.

Marius stammered out:

"What does this mean?"

"It means," answered Jean Valjean, "that I have been in the galleys."

"You drive me mad!" exclaimed Marius in dismay.

"Monsieur Pontmercy," said Jean Valjean, "I was nineteen years in the galleys. For robbery. Then I was sentenced for life. For robbery. For a second offense. At this hour I am in breach of ban."

It was useless for Marius to recoil before the reality, to refuse the fact, to resist the evidence; he was compelled to yield. He began to comprehend, and as always happens in such a case, he comprehended beyond the truth. He felt the shiver of a horrible interior flash; an idea which made him shudder crossed his mind. He caught a glimpse in the future of a hideous destiny for himself.

"Tell all, tell all!" cried he. "You are Cosette's father!"

And he took two steps backward with an expression of unspeakable horror.

Jean Valjean raised his head with such a majesty of attitude that he seemed to rise to the ceiling.

"It is necessary that you believe me in this, monsieur; although the oath of such as I be not received."

Here he made a pause; then, with a sort of sovereign and sepulchral authority, he added, articulating slowly and emphasizing his syllables:

"You will believe me. I, the father of Cosette! Before God, no. Monsieur Baron Pontmercy, I am a peasant of Faverolles. I earned my living by pruning trees. My name is not Fauchelevent, my name is Jean Valjean. I am nothing to Cosette. Compose yourself."

Jean Valjean continued:

"What am I to Cosette? A passer. Ten years ago, I did not know that she existed. I love her, it is true. She was an orphan. Without father or mother. She had need of me. That is why I began to love her. Children are so weak that anybody, even a man like me, may be their protector. I performed that duty with regard to Cosette. Record that mitigating circumstance. Today Cosette leaves my life; our two roads separate. Henceforth I can do nothing more for her. She is Madame Pontmercy. Her protector is changed. And Cosette gains by the change. All is well."

Jean Valjean looked Marius in the face.

And, with a bitter emphasis, he added:

"Monsieur Pontmercy, this is not common sense, but I am an honest man. It is by degrading myself in your eyes that I elevate myself in my own. This has already happened to me once, but it was less grievous then; it was nothing. Yes, an honest man. I should not be one if you had, by my fault, continued to esteem me; now that you despise me, I am one. I have this fatality upon me that, being forever unable to have any but stolen consideration, that consideration humiliates me and depresses me inwardly, and in order that I may respect myself, I must be despised. Then I hold myself erect. I am a galley slave who obeys his conscience. I know well that is improbable. But what would you have me do? It is so. I have assumed engagements toward myself; I keep them. There are accidents which bind us, there are chances which drag us into duties. You see, Monsieur Pontmercy, some things have happened to me in my life?"

Jean Valjean paused again, swallowing his saliva with effort, as if his words had a bitter aftertaste, and resumed:

"To be a false signature in flesh and blood, to be a living false key, to enter the houses of honest people by picking their locks, never to look again, always to squint, to be infamous within myself, no! No! No! No! It is better to suffer, to bleed, to weep, to tear the skin from the flesh with the nails, to pass the nights in writhing, in anguish, to gnaw away body and soul. That is why I come to tell you all this. In mere wantonness, as you say."

He breathed with difficulty, and forced out these final words:

"To live, once I stole a loaf of bread; today, to live, I will not steal a name."

"To live!" interrupted Marius. "You have no need of that name to live!"

"Ah! I understand," answered Jean Valjean, raising and lowering his head several times in succession.

Marius crossed the parlor slowly, and, when he was near Jean Valjean, extended him his hand.

But Marius had to take that hand which did not offer itself; Jean Valjean was passive, and it seemed to Marius that he was grasping a hand of marble.

"Poor Cosette!" murmured he, "when she knows—"

At these words, Jean Valjean trembled in every limb. He fixed upon Marius a bewildered eye.

"Cosette! Oh, yes, it is true, you will tell this to Cosette. That is right. Stop, I had not thought of that. People have the strength for some things, but not for others. Monsieur, I beseech you, I entreat you, monsieur, give me your most sacred word, do not tell her. Is it not enough that you know it yourself?"

"Be calm," said Marius, "I will keep your secret for myself alone."

And, less softened perhaps than he should have been, but obliged for an hour past to familiarize himself with a fearful surprise, seeing by degrees a convict superimposed before his eyes upon Monsieur Fauchelevent, possessed little by little of this dismal reality, and led by the natural tendency of the position to determine the distance which had just been put between this man and himself, Marius added:

"It is impossible that I should not say a word to you of the trust which you have so faithfully and so honestly restored. That is an act of probity. It is just that a recompense should be given you. Fix the sum yourself, it shall be counted out to you. Do not be afraid to fix it very high."

"I thank you, monsieur," answered Jean Valjean gently.

He remained thoughtful a moment, passing the end of his forefinger over his thumbnail mechanically, then he raised his voice:

"It is all nearly finished. There is one thing left—"

"What?"

Jean Valjean had, as it were, a supreme hesitation, and, voiceless, almost breathless, he faltered out rather than said:

"Now that you know, do you think, monsieur, you who are the master, that I ought not to see Cosette again?"

"I think that would be best," answered Marius coldly.

"I shall not see her again," murmured Jean Valjean. And he walked toward the door.

He placed his hand upon the knob, the latch yielded, the door started, Jean Valjean opened it wide enough to enable him to pass out, stopped a second motionless, then shut the door, and turned toward Marius.

He was no longer pale, he was livid. There were no longer tears in his eyes, but a sort of tragical flame. His voice had again become strangely calm.

"But, monsieur," said he, "if you are willing, I will come and see her. I assure you that I desire it very much. If I had not clung to seeing Cosette, I should not have made the avowal which I have made, I should have gone away; but wishing to stay in the place where Cosette is and to continue to see her, I was compelled in honor to tell you all. You follow my reasoning, do you not? That is a thing which explains itself. You see, for nine years past, I have had her near me. I don't know whether you understand me, Monsieur Pontmercy, but from the present time, to see her no more, to speak to her no more, to have nothing more, that would be hard. If you do not think it wrong, I will come from time to time to see Cosette. I should not come often. I would not stay long. You might say I should be received in the little low room. On the ground floor. I would willingly come in by the back door, which is for the servants, but that would excite wonder, perhaps. It is better, I suppose, that I should enter by the usual door. Monsieur, indeed, I would really like to see Cosette a little still. As rarely as you please. Put yourself in my place, it is all that I have. And then, we must take care. If I should not come at all, it would have a bad effect, it would be thought singular. For instance, what I can do, is to come in the evening, at nightfall."

"You will come every evening," said Marius, "and Cosette will expect you."

"You are kind, monsieur," said Jean Valjean.

Marius bowed to Jean Valjean, happiness conducted despair to the door, and these two men separated.

II

MARIUS was completely unhinged.

The kind of repulsion which he had always felt for the man with whom he saw Cosette was now explained. There was something strangely enigmatic in this person, of which his instinct had warned him. This enigma was the most hideous of disgraces, the galleys. This Monsieur Fauchelevent was the convict Jean Valjean.

Was the happiness of Marius and Cosette condemned henceforth to this fellowship? Was that a foregone conclusion? Did the acceptance of this man form a part of the marriage which had been consummated? Was there nothing more to be done?

Had Marius espoused the convict also?

The former repulsion of Marius toward this man, toward this Fauchelevent become Jean Valjean, was now mingled with horror.

In this horror, we must say, there was some pity, and also a certain astonishment.

This robber, this twice-convicted robber, had restored a trust. And what a trust? Six hundred thousand francs. He was alone in the secret of the trust. He might have kept all, he had given up all.

Moreover, he had revealed his condition of his own accord. Nothing obliged him to do so. And from what motive? From conscientious scruples. He had explained it himself with the irresistible accent of reality. In short, whatever this Jean Valjean might be, he had, incontestably, an awakened conscience. There was in him some mysterious regeneration begun. An awakening of conscience is greatness of soul.

In the mysterious account which Marius thoughtfully drew up concerning this Jean Valjean, he verified the credit, he verified the debit, he attempted to arrive at a balance. But it was all, as it were, in a storm. Marius, endeavoring to get a clear idea of this man, and pursuing, so to speak, Jean Valjean in the depth of his thought, lost him and found him again in a fatal mist.

The trust honestly surrendered, the probity of the avowal, that was good. It was like a break in the cloud, but the cloud again became black.

Why had this man come into the barricade? For now Marius saw that reminiscence again distinctly, reappearing in these emotions like sympathetic ink before the fire. This man was in the barricade. He did not fight there. What did he come there for? Before this question a specter arose, and made response. Javert. Marius recalled perfectly to mind at this hour the fatal sight of Jean Valjean dragging Javert bound outside the barricade, and he again heard the frightful pistol shot behind the corner of the little rue Mondétour. There was, probably, hatred between the spy and this galley slave. The one cramped the other. Jean Valjean had gone to the barricade to avenge himself. He had arrived late. He knew probably that Javert was a prisoner there. Jean Valjean had killed Javert. At least, that seemed evident.

Finally, a last question: but to this no answer. This question Marius felt like a sting. How did it happen that Jean Valjean's existence had touched Cosette's so long? What was this gloomy game of Providence which had placed this child in contact with this man? What was this bandit religiously absorbed in the adoration of a virgin, watching over her, bringing her up, guarding her, dignifying her, and enveloping her, himself impure, with purity? What was this cloaca which had venerated this innocence to such an extent as to leave it immaculate? What was this Jean Valjean watching over the education of Cosette? What was this figure of darkness, whose only care was to preserve from all shadow and from all cloud the rising of a star?

In this was the secret of Jean Valjean; in this was also the secret of God.

Before this double secret, Marius recoiled. The one in some

sort reassured him in regard to the other. God was as visible in this as Jean Valjean. God has his instruments. He uses what tool he pleases. Is it the first time that the dunghill has aided the spring to make the rose?

Jean Valjean was a passer. He had said so, himself. Well, he was passing away. Whatever he might be, his part was finished. Henceforth Marius was to perform the functions of Providence for Cosette. Cosette had come forth to find in the azure her mate, her lover, her husband, her celestial male. In taking flight, Cosette, winged and transfigured, left behind her on the ground, empty and hideous, her chrysalis, Jean Valjean.

In whatever circle of ideas Marius turned, he always came back from it to a certain horror of Jean Valjean. Marius, upon penal questions, although a democrat, still adhered to the inexorable system, and he had, in regard to those whom the law smites, all the ideas of the law. He had not yet, let us say, adopted all the ideas of progress. He had not yet come to distinguish between what is written by man and what is written by God, between law and right. He had not examined and weighed the right which man assumes to dispose of the irrevocable and the irreparable. He had not revolted from the word vengeance. He thought it natural that certain infractions of the written law should be followed by eternal penalties, and he accepted social damnation as growing out of civilization. He was still at that point, infallibly to advance in time, his nature being good, and in reality entirely composed of latent progress.

Through the medium of these ideas, Jean Valjean appeared to him deformed and repulsive. He was the outcast. He was the convict. This word was for him like a sound of the last trumpet; and, after having considered Jean Valjean long, his final action was to turn away his head. Vade retro.

In this frame of mind it was a bitter perplexity to Marius to think that this man should have henceforth any contact whatever with Cosette. He thought himself too good, too mild, let us say the word, too weak. This weakness had led him to an imprudent concession. He had allowed himself to be moved. He had done wrong. He should have merely and simply cast off Jean Valjean.

What should be done now? Jean Valjean's visits were very

repugnant to him. Of what use was this man in his house? What should he do?

Marius turned all this assemblage of ideas over in his mind confusedly, passing from one to another, and excited by all. Hence a deep commotion. It was not easy for him to hide this commotion from Cosette, but love is a talent, and Marius succeeded.

Besides, he put without apparent object, some questions to Cosette, who, as candid as a dove is white, suspected nothing; he talked with her of her childhood and her youth, and he convinced himself more and more that all a man can be that is good, paternal, and venerable, this convict had been to Cosette. All that Marius had dimly seen and conjectured was real. This darkly mysterious nettle had loved and protected this lily.

The Twilight Wane

I

THE next day, at nightfall, Jean Valjean knocked at the Monsieur Gillenormand porte-cochere. Basque received him. Basque happened to be in the courtyard very conveniently, and as if he had had orders.

Basque, without waiting for Jean Valjean to come up to him, addressed him as follows:

"Monsieur the Baron told me to ask monsieur whether he desires to go upstairs or to remain below?"

"To remain below," answered Jean Valjean.

Basque, who was moreover absolutely respectful, opened the door of the basement room and said: "I will inform madame."

The room which Jean Valjean entered was an arched and damp basement, used as a cellar when necessary, looking upon the street, paved with red tiles, and dimly lighted by a window with an iron grating. At the end was a wooden mantel, painted black, with a narrow shelf. A fire was kindled, which indicated that somebody had anticipated Jean Valjean's answer: "To remain below."

Two armchairs were placed at the corners of the fireplace. Between the chairs was spread, in guise of a carpet, an old bedside rug, showing more warp than wool.

The room was lighted by the fire in the fireplace and the twilight from the window.

Jean Valjean was fatigued. For some days he had neither eaten nor slept. He let himself fall into one of the armchairs.

Basque returned, set a lighted candle upon the mantel, and retired. Jean Valjean, his head bent down and his chin upon his breast, noticed neither Basque nor the candle.

Suddenly he started up. Cosette was behind him.

He had not seen her come in, but he had felt that she was coming.

He turned. He gazed at her. She was adorably beautiful. But what he looked upon with that deep look was not her beauty but her soul.

"Ah, well!" exclaimed Cosette. "Father, I knew that you were singular, but I should never have thought this. What an idea! Marius tells me that it is you who wish me to receive you here."

"Yes, it is I."

"I expected the answer. Well, I warn you that I am going to make a scene. Let us begin at the beginning. Father, kiss me."

And she offered her cheek.

Jean Valjean remained motionless.

"This is getting serious," said Cosette. "What have I done to you? I declare I am confounded. You owe me amends. You will dine with us."

"I have dined."

"That is not true. Come. Go up to the parlor with me. Immediately."

"Impossible."

Cosette here lost ground a little. She ceased to order and passed to questions.

"But why not? And you choose the ugliest room in the house to see me in. It is horrible here."

"You know, madame, I am peculiar, I have my whims."

Cosette clapped her little hands together.

"Madame! What does this mean?"

Jean Valjean fixed upon her that distressing smile to which he sometimes had recourse:

"You have wished to be madame. You are so."

"Not to you, father."

"Don't call me father any more."

"What?"

"Call me Monsieur Jean. Jean, if you will."

"You are no longer father? I am no longer Cosette? Monsieur Jean? What does this mean? What have you against me? You give me a great deal of trouble. Fie!"

And, growing suddenly serious, she looked fixedly at Jean Valjean, and added:

"So you don't like it that I am happy?"

Artlessness, unconsciously, sometimes penetrates very deep. This question, simple to Cosette, was severe to Jean Valjean. Cosette wished to scratch; she tore.

Jean Valjean grew pale. For a moment he did not answer, then, with an indescribable accent and talking to himself, he murmured:

"Her happiness was the aim of my life. Now, God may beckon me away. Cosette, you are happy; my time is full."

"Ah, you have called me Cosette!" exclaimed she.

And she sprang upon his neck.

Jean Valjean, in desperation, clasped her to his breast wildly. It seemed to him almost as if he were taking her back.

"Thank you, father!" said Cosette to him.

The transport was becoming poignant to Jean Valjean. He gently put away Cosette's arms, and took his hat.

"Well?" said Cosette.

Jean Valjean answered:

"I will leave you, madame; they are waiting for you."

And, from the door, he added:

"I called you Cosette. Tell your husband that that shall not happen again. Pardon me."

Jean Valjean went out, leaving Cosette astounded at that enigmatic farewell.

The following day, at the same hour, Jean Valjean came.

Cosette put no questions to him, was no longer astonished, no longer exclaimed that she was cold, no longer talked of the parlor; she avoided saying either "father" or "Monsieur Jean." She let him speak as he would. She allowed herself to be called madame. Only she betrayed a certain diminution of joy. She would have been sad, if sadness had been possible for her.

It is probable that she had had one of those conversations with Marius, in which the beloved man says what he pleases, explains nothing, and satisfies the beloved woman. The curiosity of lovers does not go very far beyond their love. The grandfather issued this decree: "He is an originall" and all was said.

Several weeks passed thus. Jean Valjean came very day. The disappearance of familiarity, the madame, the Monsieur Jean, all this made him different to Cosette. The care which he had taken to detach her from him succeeded with her. She became more and more cheerful, and less and less affectionate. However, she still loved him very much, and he felt it.

Little by little he got into the habit of making his visits longer. One would have said that he took advantage of the example of the days, which were growing longer: he came earlier and went away later.

One day Cosette inadvertently said to him: "Father." A flash of joy illuminated Jean Valjean's gloomy old face. He replied to her: "Say Jean." "Ah! True," she answered with a burst of laughter, "Monsieur Jean." "That is right," said he, and he turned away that she might not see him wipe his eyes.

II

THAT was the last time. From that last gleam onward, there was complete extinction. No more familiarity, no more "Good day" with a kiss, never again that word so intensely sweet: Father! He was, upon his own demand and through his own complicity, driven in succession from every happiness, and he had this misery, that after having lost Cosette wholly in one day, he had been obliged afterward to lose her again little by little.

The eye at last becomes accustomed to the light of a cellar. In short, to have a vision of Cosette every day sufficed him. His whole life was concentrated in that hour. He sat by her side, he looked at her in silence, or rather he talked to her of the years long gone, of her childhood, of the convent, of her friends of those days.

One afternoon—it was one of the early days of April, already warm, still fresh—Marius said to Cosette: "We have said that we would go to see our garden in the rue Plumet again. Let us go. We must not be ungrateful." And they flew away like two swallows toward the spring. At night, at the usual hour, Jean Valjean came to the rue des Filles du Calvaire. "Madame has gone out with monsieur, and has not returned yet," said Basque to him. He sat down in silence, and waited an hour. Cosette did not return. He bowed his head and went away.

Cosette was so intoxicated with her walk to the "garden," and so happy over having "lived a whole day in her past," that she did not speak of anything else the next day. It did not occur to her that she had not seen Jean Valjean.

Jean Valjean's visits did not grow shorter. Far from it. When the heart is slipping we do not stop on the descent.

One day he stayed longer than usual. The next day, he noticed that there was no fire in the fireplace. "What!" thought he. "No fire." And he made the explanation to himself: "It is a matter of course. We are in April. The cold weather is over."

"Goodness! How cold it is here!" exclaimed Cosette as she came in.

"Why no," said Jean Valjean.

"So it is you who told Basque not to make a fire?"

"Yes. We are close upon May."

The next day there was a fire. But the two armchairs were placed at the other end of the room, near the door. "What does that mean?" thought Jean Valjean.

He went for the armchairs, and put them back in their usual place near the chimney.

This fire being kindled again encouraged him, however. He continued the conversation still longer than usual. As he was getting up to go away, Cosette said to him:

"My husband said a funny thing to me yesterday."

"What was it?"

"He said: 'Cosette, we have an income of thirty thousand francs. Twenty-seven that you have, three that my grandfather allows me.' I answered: 'That makes thirty.' 'Would you have the courage to live on three thousand?' I answered:

'Yes, on nothing. Provided it be with you.' And then I asked: 'Why do you say this?' He answered: 'To know.'"

Jean Valjean did not say a word. Cosette probably expected some explanation from him; he listened to her in a mournful silence. He went back to the rue de l'Homme Armé; he was so deeply absorbed that he mistook the door, and instead of entering his own house, he entered the next one. Not until he had gone up almost to the second story did he perceive his mistake, and go down again.

His mind was racked with conjectures. It was evident that Marius had doubts in regard to the origin of these six hundred thousand francs, that he feared some impure source, who knows? That he had perhaps discovered that this money came from him, Jean Valjean, that he hesitated before this suspicious fortune, and disliked to take it as his own, preferring to remain poor, himself and Cosette, than to be rich with a doubtful wealth.

Besides, vaguely, Jean Valjean began to feel that the door was shown him.

The next day, he received, on entering the basement room, something like a shock. The armchairs had disappeared. There was not even a chair of any kind.

"Ah now," exclaimed Cosette as she came in, "no chairs! Where are the armchairs, then?"

"They are gone," answered Jean Valjean.

"That is a pretty business!"

Jean Valjean stammered:

"I told Basque to take them away."

Cosette shrugged her shoulders.

"To have the chairs carried away! The other day you had the fire put out. How singular you are!"

"Good-by," murmured Jean Valjean.

He did not say: "Good-by, Cosette." But he had not the strength to say: "Good-by, madame."

He went away overwhelmed.

This time he had understood.

The next day he did not come. Cosette did not notice it until night.

"Why," said she, "Monsieur Jean has not come today?"

She felt something like a slight oppression of the heart, but she hardly perceived it, being immediately diverted by a kiss from Marius.

The next day he did not come.

Cosette paid no attention to it, passed the evening and slept as usual, and thought of it only on awaking. She was so happy! She sent Nicolette very quickly to Monsieur Jean's to know if he was sick, and why he had not come the day before. Nicolette brought back Monsieur Jean's answer. He was not sick. He was busy. He would come very soon. As soon as he could. However, he was going to make a little journey. Madame must remember that he was in the habit of making journeys from time to time. Let there be no anxiety. Let them not be troubled about him.

Nicolette, on entering Monsieur Jean's house, had repeated to him the very words of her mistress. That madame sent to know "why Monsieur Jean had not come the day before." "It is two days that I have not been there," said Jean Valjean mildly.

But the remark escaped the notice of Nicolette, who reported nothing of it to Cosette.

III

DURING the last months of the spring and the first months of the summer of 1833, the scattered wayfarers in the Marais, the storekeepers, the idlers upon the doorsteps, noticed an old man neatly dressed in black, every day, about the same hour, at nightfall, come out of the rue de l'Homme Armé, in the direction of the rue Sainte Croix de la Bretonnerie, pass by the Blancs Manteaux, to the rue Culture Sainte Catherine, and, reaching the rue de l'Echarpe, turn to the left, and enter the rue Saint Louis.

There he walked with slow steps, his head bent forward, seeing nothing, hearing nothing, his eye immovably fixed upon one point, always the same, which seemed studded with stars to him, and which was nothing more nor less than the corner of the rue des Filles du Calvaire. As he approached the corner of that street, his face lighted up; a kind of joy illuminated his eye like an interior halo, he had a fascinated and softened expression, his lips moved vaguely, as if he were speaking to someone whom he did not see, he smiled faintly, and he advanced as slowly as he could. You would have said that even while wishing to reach some destination, he dreaded the mo-

ment when he should be near it. When there were but a few
houses left between him and that street which appeared to
attract him, his pace became so slow that at times you might
have supposed he had ceased to move. The vacillation of his
head and the fixedness of his eye reminded you of the needle
seeking the pole. However long he succeeded in deferring it,
he must arrive at last; he reached the rue des Filles du
Calvaire; then he stopped, he trembled, he put his head with
a kind of gloomy timidity beyond the corner of the last house,
and he looked into that street, and there was in that tragical
look something which resembled the bewilderment of the
impossible and the reflection of a forbidden paradise. Then
a tear, which had gradually gathered in the corner of his eye,
grown large enough to fall, glided over his cheek, and sometimes stopped at his mouth. The old man tasted its bitterness. He remained thus a few minutes, as if he had been stone;
then he returned by the same route and at the same pace;
and, in proportion as he receded, that look was extinguished.

Little by little, this old man ceased to go as far as the corner of the rue des Filles du Calvaire; he stopped halfway
down the rue Saint Louis; sometimes a little further, sometimes
a little nearer. One day, he stopped at the corner of the rue
Culture Sainte Catherine, and looked at the rue des Filles du
Calvaire from the distance. Then he silently moved his head
from right to left as if he were refusing himself something
and retraced his steps.

Very soon he no longer came even as far as the rue Saint
Louis. He reached the rue Pavée, shook his head, and went
back; then he no longer went beyond the rue des Trois Pavil-
lons; then he no longer passed the Blancs Manteaux. You
would have said he was a pendulum which has not been
wound up, and the oscillations of which are growing shorter
ere they stop.

Every day, he came out of his house at the same hour, he
commenced the same walk, but he did not finish it, and,
perhaps unconsciously, he continually shortened it. His whole
countenance expressed this single idea: What is the use? The
eye was dull; no more radiance. The tear also was gone;
no longer gathered at the corner of the lids; that thoughtful
eye was dry. The old man's head was still bent forward; his
chin quivered at times; the wrinkles of his thin neck were

painful to behold. Sometimes, when the weather was bad, he carried an umbrella under his arm, which he never opened. The good women of the quarter said: "He is a natural." The children followed him laughing.

Supreme Shadow, Supreme Dawn

I

ONE day Jean Valjean went downstairs, took three steps into the street, sat down upon a stone block, upon that same block where Gavroche, on the night of the 5th of June, had found him musing; he remained there a few minutes, then went upstairs again. This was the last oscillation of the pendulum. The next day, he did not leave his room. The day after, he did not leave his bed.

His portress, who prepared his frugal meal, some cabbage, a few potatoes with a little pork, looked into the brown earthen plate, and exclaimed:

"Why, you didn't eat anything yesterday, poor dear man! To leave me my whole plateful without touching it! My cole slaw, which was so good!"

Jean Valjean took the old woman's hand.

"I promise to eat it," said he to her in his benevolent voice.

"I am not satisfied with you," answered the portress.

Jean Valjean scarcely ever saw any other human being than this good woman. There are streets in Paris in which nobody walks, and houses into which nobody comes. He was in one of those streets, and in one of those houses.

While he still went out, he had bought of a brazier for a few sous a little copper crucifix, which he had hung upon a nail before his bed. The cross is always good to look upon.

A week elapsed, and Jean Valjean had not taken a step in his room. He was still in bed. The portress said to her husband: "The goodman upstairs does not get up any more, he does not eat any more, he won't last long. He has trouble, he has. Nobody can get it out of my head that his daughter has made a bad match."

She saw a physician of the quarter passing at the end of the street; she took it upon herself to beg him to go up.

"It is on the second floor," said she to him. "You will have nothing to do but go in. As the goodman does not stir from his bed now, the key is in the door all the time."

The physician saw Jean Valjean, and spoke with him.

When he came down, the portress questioned him:

"Well, doctor?"

"Your sick man is very sick."

"What is the matter with him?"

"Everything and nothing. He is a man who, to all appearances, has lost some dear friend. People die of that."

"What did he tell you?"

"He told me that he was well."

"Will you come again, doctor?"

"Yes," answered the physician. "But another than I must come again."

II

ONE evening Jean Valjean had difficulty in raising himself upon his elbow; he felt his wrist and found no pulse; his breathing was short, and stopped at intervals; he realized that he w s weaker than he had been before. Then, undoubtedly under the pressure of some supreme desire, he made an effort, sat up in bed, and dressed himself. He was obliged to stop several times while dressing; the mere effort of putting on his waistcoat made the sweat roll down his forehead.

He opened the valise and took out Cosette's suit.

He spread it out upon his bed.

The bishop's candlesticks were in their place, on the mantel. He took two wax tapers from a drawer, and put them into the candlesticks. Then, although it was still broad daylight—it was in summer—he lighted them. We sometimes se torches lighted thus in broad day, in rooms where the dead li

Each step that he took in going from one piece of furnitur to another exhausted him, and he was obliged to sit down It was not ordinary fatigue which spends the strength th: it may be renewed; it was the remnant of possible motion it was exhausted life pressed out drop by drop in overwhelming efforts, never to be made again.

One of the chairs upon which he sank was standing before that mirror, so fatal for him, so providential for Marius, in which he had read Cosette's note, reversed on the blotter. He saw himself in this mirror, and did not recognize himself. He was eighty years old; before Marius' marriage, one would hardly have thought him fifty; this year had counted thirty. What was now upon his forehead was not the wrinkle of age, it was the mysterious mark of death. You perceived on it the impress of the relentless talon. His cheeks were sunken; the skin of his face was of that color which suggests the idea of earth already above it; the corners of his mouth were depressed as in that mask which the ancients sculptured upon tombs, he looked at the hollowness with a look of reproach; you would have said it was one of those grand tragic beings who rise in judgment.

He was in that condition, the last phase of dejection, in which sorrow no longer flows; it is, so to speak, coagulated; the soul is covered as if with a clot of despair.

Night had come. Suddenly he shivered, he felt that the chill was coming.

"Oh!" exclaimed he within himself (pitiful cries, heard by God alone). "It is all over. I shall never see her more. She is a smile which has passed over me. I am going to enter into the night without even seeing her again. Oh! A minute, an instant, to hear her voice, to touch her dress, to look at her, the angel! And then to die! It is nothing to die, but it is dreadful to die without seeing her. She would smile upon me, she would say a word to me. Would that harm anybody? No, it is over, forever. Here I am, all alone. My God! My God! I shall never see her again."

At this moment there was a rap at his door.

III

THAT very day, or rather that very evening, just as Marius had left the table and retired into his office, having a bundle of papers to study over, Basque had handed him a letter, saying: "the person who wrote the letter is in the antechamber."

He broke the seal, and read:

Monsieur Baron—If the Supreme Being had given me the talents for it, I could have been Baron Thénard, member of the Institute (Academy of Ciences), but I am not so. I merely bear the same name that he does, happy if this remembrance commends me to the excellence of your bounties. The benefit with which you honor me will be reciprocal. I am in possession of a secret conserning an individual. This individual conserns you. I hold the secret at your disposition, desiring to have the honor of being yuseful to you. I will give you the simple means of drivving from your honorable family this individual who has no right in it, Madame the Baroness being of high birth. The sanctuary of virtue could not coabit longer with crime without abdicating.

I atend in the entichamber the orders of Monsieur the Baron. With respect.

The letter was signed THÉNARD.

This signature was not a false one. It was only a little abridged.

Besides, the rigmarole and the orthography completed the revelation. The certificate of origin was perfect. There was no doubt possible.

The emotion of Marius was deep. After the feeling of surprise, he had a feeling of happiness. Let him now find the other man whom he sought, the man who had saved him, Marius, and he would have nothing more to wish.

He opened one of his secretary drawers, took out some bank notes, put them in his pockets, closed the secretary, and rang. Basque appeared.

"Show him in," said Marius.

Basque announced:

"Monsieur Thénard."

A man entered.

A new surprise for Marius. The man who came in was perfectly unknown to him.

This man, old withal, had a large nose, his chin in his cravat, green spectacles with double shade of green silk over his eyes, his hair polished and smoothed down, his forehead close to the eyebrows, like the wigs of Englis coachmen in high life. His hair was gray. He was dressed in black from head to foot, in a well-worn but tidy black; a bunch of trinkets, hanging from his fob, suggested a watch. He held an old hat in his hand. He walked with a stoop, and the crook of his back increased the lowliness of his bow.

Marius' disappointment, on seeing another man enter than the one he was expecting, turned into dislike toward the new-comer. He examined him from head to foot, while the person-age bowed without measure, and asked him in a sharp tone:

"What do you want?"

The stranger thrust his hands into his fobs, raised his head without straightening his backbone, but scrutinizing Marius in his turn with the green gaze of his spectacles.

"Monsieur the Baron, I will explain. I have a secret to sell you."

"A secret?"

"A secret."

"Go on."

"Monsieur Baron, you have in your house a robber and an assassin."

Marius shuddered.

"In my house? No," said he.

The stranger, imperturbable, brushed his hat with his sleeve, and continued:

"I am going to tell you his true name. And to tell it to you for nothing."

"I am listening."

"His name is Jean Valjean."

"I know it."

"I am going to tell you, also for nothing, who he is."

"Say on."

"He is an old convict."

"I know it."

"You know it since I have had the honor of telling you."

"No. I knew it before."

The stranger resumed with a smile:

"I do not permit myself to contradict Monsieur the Baron. At all events, you must see that I am informed. Now, what I have to acquaint you with is known to myself alone."

Marius looked at him steadily.

"I know your extraordinary secret; just as I knew Jean Valjean's name; just as I know your name."

"My name?"

"Yes."

"That is not difficult, Monsieur Baron. I have had the honor of writing it to you and telling it to you. Thénard."

"Dier."

"Eh?"

"Thénardier."

"Who is that?"

In danger the porcupine bristles, the beetle feigns death, the Old Guard forms a square; this man began to laugh.

Marius, taking a bank note from his pocket, threw it in his face.

"Thanks! Pardon! Five hundred francs! Monsieur Baron!"

And the man, bewildered, bowing, catching the note, examined it.

"Five hundred francs!" he repeated in astonishment. And he stammered out in an undertone: "A serious *fafiot!*"

Then bluntly:

"Well, so be it," exclaimed he. "Let us make ourselves comfortable."

And, with the agility of a monkey, throwing his hair off backward, pulling off his spectacles, he took off his countenance as one takes off his hat.

His eye kindled; his forehead, uneven, ravined, humped in spots, hideously wrinkled at the top, emerged; his nose became as sharp as a beak; the fierce and cunning profile of the man of prey appeared again.

"Monsieur the Baron is infallible," said he in a clear voice from which all nasality had disappeared, "I am Thénardier."

And he straightened his bent back.

In Thénardier's opinion, the conversation with Marius had not yet commenced. He had been obliged to retreat, to modify his strategy, to abandon a position, to change his base; but nothing essential was yet lost, and he had five hundred francs in his pocket. After saying: "I am Thénardier," he waited.

Marius interrupted the silence.

"Thénardier, I have told you your name. Now your secret, what you came to make known to me, do you want me to tell you that? I too have my means of information. You shall see that I know more about it than you do. Jean Valjean, as you have said, is an assassin and a robber. A robber, because he robbed a rich manufacturer, Monsieur Madeleine, whose ruin he caused. An assassin, because he assassinated the police officer, Javert."

Thénardier cast upon Marius the sovereign glance of a beaten man, who lays hold on victory again, and who has just recovered in one minute all the ground which he had lost. But the smile returned immediately; the inferior before the superior can only have a skulking triumph, and Thénardier merely said to Marius:

"Monsieur Baron, we are on the wrong track."

"What!" replied Marius. "Do you deny that? These are facts."

"They are chimeras. The confidence with which Monsieur the Baron honors me makes it my duty to tell him so. Before all things, truth and justice. I do not like to see people accused unjustly. Monsieur Baron, Jean Valjean never robbed Monsieur Madeleine, and Jean Valjean never killed Javert."

"You speak strongly! How is that?"

"For two reasons."

"What are they? Tell me."

"The first is this: he did not rob Monsieur Madeleine, since it is Jean Valjean himself who was Monsieur Madeleine."

"What is that you are telling me?"

"And the second is this: he did not assassinate Javert, since Javert himself killed Javert."

"What do you mean?"

"That Javert committed suicide."

"Prove it! Prove it!" cried Marius, beside himself.

Thénardier resumed, scanning his phrase in the fashion of an ancient Alexandrine:

"The—police—of — ficer — Ja — vert — was — found — drowned—under—a—boat—by—the—Pont—au—Change."

"But prove it now!"

Thénardier took from his pocket a large envelope of gray paper, which seemed to contain folded sheets of different sizes.

"I have my documents," said he, with calmness. "When I speak I have the proofs. Not manuscript proofs—writing is suspicious, writing is complaisant—but proofs in print."

While speaking, Thénardier took out of the envelope two newspapers, yellow, faded, and strongly saturated with tobacco. One of these two newspapers, broken at all the folds, and falling in square pieces, seemed much older than the other.

"Two facts, two proofs," said Thénardier. And unfolding the two papers, he handed them to Marius.

One, the oldest, a copy of the *Drapeau Blanc*, of the 25th of July, 1823, established the identity of Monsieur Madeleine and Jean Valjean. The other, a *Moniteur* of the 15th of June, 1832, verified the suicide of Javert, adding that it appeared from a verbal report made by Javert to the prefect that, taken prisoner in the barricade of the rue de la Chanvrerie, he had owed his life to the magnanimity of an insurgent who, though he had him at the muzzle of his pistol, instead of blowing out his brains, had fired into the air.

Marius read. There was evidence, certain date, unquestionable proof. Jean Valjean, suddenly growing grand, arose from the cloud. Marius could not restrain a cry of joy:

"Well, then, this unhappy man is a wonderful man! All that fortune was really his own! He is Madeleine, the providence of a whole region! He is Jean Valjean, the savior of Javert! He is a hero! He is a saint!"

"He is not a saint, and he is not a hero," said Thénardier. "He is an assassin and a robber."

And he added with the tone of a man who begins to feel some authority in himself: "Let us be calm."

Robber, assassin; these words, which Marius supposed were gone, yet which came back, fell upon him like a shower of ice.

"Again," said he.

"Monsieur Baron, on the 6th of June, 1832, about a year ago, the day of the *émeute*, a man was in the Grand Sewer of Paris, near where the sewer empties into the Seine, between the Bridge of the Invalides and the Bridge of Iéna."

Marius suddenly drew his chair near Thénardier's. Thénardier noticed this movement, and continued with the deliberation of a speaker who holds his interlocutor fast, and who feels the palpitation of his adversary beneath his words:

"This man, compelled to conceal himself, for reasons foreign to politics, however, had taken the sewer for his dwelling, and had a key to it. It was, I repeat it, the 6th of June; it might have been eight o'clock in the evening. The man heard a noise in the sewer. Very much surprised, he hid himself, and watched. It was a sound of steps, somebody was walking in the darkness; somebody was coming in his direction. Strange to say, there was another man in the sewer beside him. The grating of the outlet of the sewer was not far off. A little light which came from it enabled him to recognize the newcomer, and to see that this man was carrying something on his back. He walked bent over. The man who was walking bent over was an old convict, and what he was carrying upon his shoulders was a corpse. Assassination *in flagrante delicto*, if ever there was such a thing. As for the robbery, it follows of course; nobody kills a man for nothing. This convict was going to throw his corpse into the river."

Marius' chair drew still nearer. Thénardier took advantage of it to draw a long breath. He continued:

"Monsieur Baron, a sewer is not the Champ de Mars. One lacks everything there, even room. When two men are in a sewer, they must meet each other. That is what happened. The resident and the traveler were compelled to say good day to each other, to their mutual regret. The traveler said to the resident: 'You see what I have on my back, I must get out, you have the key, give it to me.' This convict was a man of terrible strength. There was no refusing him. Still he who had the key parleyed, merely to gain time. He examined the dead man, but he could see nothing, except that he was young, well dressed, apparently a rich man, and all disfigured with blood. While he was talking, he found means to cut and tear off from behind, without the assassin perceiving it, a piece of the assassinated man's coat. A piece of evidence, you understand; means of getting trace of the affair, and proving the crime upon the criminal. He put this piece of evidence in his pocket. After which he opened the grating, let the man out with his encumbrance on his back, shut the grating again and escaped, little caring to be mixed up with the remainder of the adventure, and especially desiring not to be present when the assassin should throw the assassinated man into the river. You understand now. He who was carrying the corpse was Jean Valjean; he who had the key is now speaking to you, and the piece of the coat—"

Thénardier finished the phrase by drawing from his pocket and holding up, on a level with his eyes, between his thumbs and his forefingers, a strip of ragged black cloth, covered with dark stains.

Marius had risen, pale, hardly breathing, his eye fixed upon the scrap of black cloth, and, without uttering a word, without losing sight of this rag, he retreated to the wall, and, with his right hand stretched behind him, groped about for a key which was in the lock of a closet near the chimney. He found this key, opened the closet, and thrust his arm into it without looking, and without removing his startled eyes from the fragment that Thénardier held up.

Meanwhile Thénardier continued:

"Monsieur Baron, I have the strongest reasons to believe that the assassinated young man was an opulent stranger drawn into a snare by Jean Valjean, and the bearer of an enormous sum."

"The young man was myself, and there is the coat!" cried Marius, and he threw an old black coat covered with blood upon the carpet.

Then, snatching the fragment from Thénardier's hands, he bent down over the coat, and applied the piece to the cut skirt. The edges fitted exactly, and the strip completed the coat.

Thénardier was petrified. He thought this: "I am floored."

Marius rose up, quivering, desperate, flashing.

He felt in his pocket, and walked, furious, toward Thénardier, offering him and almost pushing into his face his fist full of five hundred and a thousand franc notes.

"You are a wretch! You are a liar, a slanderer, a scoundrel. You came to accuse this man, you have justified him; you wanted to destroy him, you have succeeded only in glorifying him. And it is you who are a robber! And it is you who are an assassin. I saw you, Thénardier, Jondrette, in that den on the Boulevard de l'Hôpital. I know enough about you to send you to the galleys, and further even, if I wished. Here, there are a thousand francs, braggart that you are!"

And he threw a bill for a thousand francs to Thénardier.

"Ah! Jondrette Thénardier, vile knave! Let this be a lesson to you, peddler of secrets, trader in mysteries, fumbler in the dark, wretch! Take these five hundred francs, and leave this place! Go! Out of my sight! Be happy only, that is all I desire. Ah! Monster! There are three thousand francs more. Take them. You will start tomorrow for America. I will see to your departure, bandit, and I will count out to you then twenty thousand francs. Go and get hung elsewhere!"

"Monsieur Baron," answered Thénardier, bowing to the ground, "eternal gratitude."

And Thénardier went out, comprehending nothing, astounded and transported with this sweet crushing under sacks of gold and with this thunderbolt bursting upon his head in bank notes.

Thunderstruck he was, but happy also, and he would have been very sorry to have had a lightning rod against that thunderbolt.

Let us finish with this man at once. Two days after the events which we are now relating, he left, through Marius' care, for America, under a false name, with his daughter Azelma, provided with a draft upon New York for twenty thousand francs. Thénardier, the moral misery of Thénardier, the broken-down bourgeois, was irremediable; he was in America what he had been in Europe. The touch of a wicked man is often enough to corrupt a good deed and to make an evil result spring from it. With Marius' money, Thénardier became a slaver.

As soon as Thénardier was outdoors, Marius ran to the garden where Cosette was walking.

"Cosette! Cosette!" cried he. "Come! Come quick! Let us go. Basque, a fiacre! Cosette, come. Oh! My God! It was he who saved my life! Let us not lose a minute! Put on your shawl."

Cosette thought him mad, and obeyed.

He did not breathe, he put his hand upon his heart to repress its beating. He walked to and fro with rapid strides, he embraced Cosette: "Oh! Cosette! I am an unhappy man!" said he.

Marius was in amaze. He began to see in this Jean Valjean a strangely lofty and saddened form. An unparalleled virtue appeared before him, supreme and mild, humble in its immensity. The convict was transfigured into Christ. Marius was bewildered by this marvel. He did not know exactly what he saw, but it was grand.

In a moment, a fiacre was at the door.

Marius helped Cosette in and sprang in himself.

"Driver," said he, "rue de l'Homme Armé, Number Seven." The fiacre started.

IV

At the knock which he heard at his door, Jean Valjean turned his head.

"Come in," said he feebly.

The door opened. Cosette and Marius appeared.

Cosette rushed into the room.

Marius remained upon the threshold, leaning against the casing of the door.

"Cosette!" said Jean Valjean, and he rose in his chair, his arms stretched out and trembling, haggard, livid, terrible, with immense joy in his eyes.

Cosette, stifled with emotion, fell upon Jean Valjean's breast.

"Father!" said she.

Jean Valjean, beside himself, stammered:

"Cosette! She? You, madame? It is you, Cosette? Oh, my God!" And, clasped in Cosette's arms, he exclaimed:

"It is you, Cosette? You are here? You forgive me then!"

Marius, dropping his eyelids that the tears might not fall, stepped forward and murmured between his lips, which were contracted convulsively to check the sobs:

"Father!"

"And you too, you forgive me!" said Jean Valjean.

Marius could not utter a word, and Jean Valjean added: "Thanks."

Cosette took off her shawl and threw her hat upon the bed.

"They are in my way," said she.

And, seating herself upon the old man's knees, she stroked away his white hair with an adorable grace, and kissed his forehead.

Jean Valjean, bewildered, offered no resistance.

Cosette, who had but a very confused understanding of all this, redoubled her caresses, as if she would pay Marius' debt.

"So you are here, Monsieur Pontmercy, you forgive me!" repeated Jean Valjean.

At these words, which Jean Valjean now said for the second time, all that was swelling in Marius' heart found an outlet, he broke forth:

"Cosette, do you hear? That is the way with him! He begs

my pardon, and do you know what he has done for me, Cosette? He has saved my life. He has done more. He has given you to me. And, after having saved me, and after having given you to me, Cosette, what did he do with himself? He sacrificed himself. There is the man. And, to me the ungrateful, to me the forgetful, to me the pitiless, to me the guilty, he says: 'Thanks!' Cosette, my whole life passed at the feet of this man would be too little. That barricade, that sewer, that furnace, that cloaca, he went through everything for me, for you, Cosette! He bore me through death in every form, which he put aside from me, and which he accepted for himself. All courage, all virtue, all heroism, all sanctity, he has it all, Cosette, that man is an angel!"

"Hush! Hush!" said Jean Valjean in a whisper. "Why tell all that?"

"Oh! My God!" replied Marius. "When I think it was by accident that I learned it all! We are going to carry you back. You are a part of us. You are her father and mine. You shall not spend another day in this horrid house. Do not imagine that you will be here tomorrow."

"Tomorrow," said Jean Valjean, "I shall not be here, but I shall not be at your house."

"What do you mean?" replied Marius. "Ah now, we shall allow no more journeys. You shall never leave us again. You belong to us. We will not let you go."

"This time, it is for good," added Cosette. "We have a carriage below. I am going to carry you off. If necessary, I shall use force."

And laughing, she made as if she would lift the old man in her arms.

"Your room is still in our house," she continued. "If you knew how pretty the garden is now. The azaleas are growing finely. The paths are sanded with river sand: there are some little violet shells. You shall eat some of my strawberries. I water them myself. And no more madame, and no more Monsieur Jean, we are a republic, are we not, Marius?"

Jean Valjean listened to her without hearing her. He heard the music of her voice rather than the meaning of her words; one of those big tears which are the gloomy pearls of the soul gathered slowly in his eye. He murmured:

"The proof that God is good is that she is here."

"Father!" cried Cosette.

Jean Valjean continued:

"It is very true that it would be charming to live together. They have their trees full of birds. I would walk with Cosette. To be with people who live, who bid each other good morning, who call each other into the garden, would be sweet. We would see each other as soon as it was morning. We would each cultivate our little corner. She would have me eat her strawberries. I would have her pick my roses. It would be charming. Only—"

He paused and said mildly:

"It is a pity."

The tear did not fall, it went back, and Jean Valjean replaced it with a smile.

Cosette took both the old man's hands in her own.

"My God!" said she. "Your hands are colder yet. Are you sick? Are you suffering?"

"No," answered Jean Valjean. "I am very well. Only—"

He stopped.

"Only what?"

"I shall die in a few minutes."

Cosette and Marius shuddered.

"Die!" exclaimed Marius.

"Yes, but that is nothing," said Jean Valjean.

Marius, petrified, gazed upon the old man.

Cosette uttered a piercing cry:

"Father! My father! You shall live. You are going to live. I will have you live, do you hear!"

Jean Valjean raised his head toward her with adoration.

"Oh yes, forbid me to die. Who knows? I shall obey perhaps. I was just dying when you came. That stopped me, it seemed to me that I was born again."

"You are full of strength and life," exclaimed Marius. "Do you think people die like that? You have had trouble, you shall have no more. I ask your pardon now, and that on my knees! You shall live, and live with us, and live long. We will take you back. Both of us here will have but one thought henceforth, your happiness!"

"You see," added Cosette in tears, "that Marius says you will not die."

Jean Valjean continued to smile.

"If you should take me back, Monsieur Pontmercy, would that make me different from what I am? No; God thought a you and I did, and he has not changed his mind; it is best that I should go away. Death is a good arrangement. God knows better than we do what we need."

There was a noise at the door. It was the physician coming in.

"Good day and good-by, doctor," said Jean Valjean. "Here are my poor children."

Marius approached the physician. He addressed this single word to him: "Monsieur?" but in the manner of pronouncing it, there was a complete question.

The physician answered the question by an expressive glance.

"Because things are unpleasant," said Jean Valjean, "that is no reason for being unjust toward God."

There was a silence. All hearts were oppressed.

Jean Valjean turned toward Cosette. He began to gaze at her as if he would take a look which should endure through eternity. At the depth of shadow to which he had already descended, ecstasy was still possible to him while beholding Cosette. The reflection of that sweet countenance illumined his pale face. The sepulcher may have its enchantments.

The physician felt his pulse.

"Ah! It was you he needed!" murmured he, looking at Cosette and Marius.

And, bending toward Marius' ear, he added very low: "Too late."

Jean Valjean, almost without ceasing to gaze upon Cosette, turned upon Marius and the physician a look of serenity. They heard these almost inarticulate words come from his lips:

"It is nothing to die; it is frightful not to live."

Suddenly he arose. These returns of strength are sometimes a sign of the death struggle. He walked with a firm step to the wall, put aside Marius and the physician, who offered to assist him, took down from the wall the little copper crucifix which hung there, came back, and sat down with all the freedom of motion of perfect health, and said in a loud voice, laying the crucifix on the table:

"Behold the great martyr."

Then his breast sank in, his head wavered, as if the dizziness of the tomb seized him, and his hands resting upon his knees began to clutch at his pantaloons.

Cosette supported his shoulders, and sobbed, and attempted

to speak to him, but could not. There could be distinguished, among the words mingled with that mournful saliva which accompanies tears, sentences like this: "Father! Do not leave us. Is it possible that we have found you again only to lose you?"

The agony of death may be said to meander. It goes, comes, advances toward the grave, and returns toward life. There is some groping in the act of dying.

The portress had come up, and was looking through the half-open door. The physician motioned her away, but he could not prevent that good, zealous woman from crying to the dying man before she went:

"Do you want a priest?"

"I have one," answered Jean Valjean.

And, with his finger, he seemed to designate a point above his head, where, you would have said, he saw someone.

It is probable that the bishop was indeed a witness of this death agony.

Cosette slipped a pillow under his back gently.

Jean Valjean resumed:

"Monsieur Pontmercy, have no fear, I conjure you. The six hundred thousand francs are really Cosette's. I shall have lost my life if you do not enjoy it! We succeeded very well in making glasswork. We rivaled what is called Berlin jewelry. Indeed, the German black glass cannot be compared with it. A gross, which contains twelve hundred grains very well cut, costs only three francs."

When a being who is dear to us is about to die, we look at him with a look which clings to him, and which would hold him back. Both, dumb with anguish, knowing not what to say to death, despairing and trembling they stood before him, Marius holding Cosette's hand.

From moment to moment, Jean Valjean grew weaker. He was sinking; he was approaching the dark horizon. His breath had become intermittent; it was interrupted by a slight rattle. He had difficulty in moving his wrist, his feet had lost all motion, and, at the same time that the distress of the limbs and the exhaustion of the body increased, all the majesty of the soul rose and displayed itself upon his forehead. The light of the unknown world was already visible in his eye.

His face grew pale, and at the same time smiled. Life was no longer present, there was something else. His breath died away, his look grew grand. It was a corpse on which you felt wings.

He motioned to Cosette to approach, then to Marius; it was evidently the last minute of the last hour, and he began to speak to them in a voice so faint it seemed to come from afar, and you would have said that there was already a wall between them and him.

"Come closer, come closer, both of you. I love you dearly. Oh! It is good to die so! You too, you love me, my Cosette. I knew very well that you still had some affection for your old goodman. How kind you are to put this cushion under my back! You will weep for me a little, will you not? Not too much. I do not wish you to have any deep grief. Cosette, do you see your little dress, there on the bed? Do you recognize it? Yet it was only ten years ago. How time passes! We have been very happy. It is over. My children, do not weep, I am not going very far, I shall see you from there. You will only have to look when it is night, you will see me smile. Cosette, do you remember Montfermeil? You were in the wood, you were very much frightened; do you remember when I took the handle of the water bucket? Those Thénardiers were wicked. We must forgive them. Cosette, the time has come to tell you the name of your mother. Her name was Fantine. Remember that name: Fantine. Fall on your knees whenever you pronounce it. She suffered much. And loved you much. Her measure of unhappiness was as full as yours of happiness. Such are the distributions of God. He is on high, he sees us all, and he knows what he does in the midst of his great stars. So I am going away, my children. Love each other dearly always. There is scarcely anything else in the world but that: to love one another. You will think sometimes of the poor old man who died here. O my Cosette! It is not my fault, indeed, if I have not seen you all this time, it broke my heart; I went as far as the corner of the street, I must have seemed strange to the people who saw me pass, I looked like a crazy man, once I went out with no hat. My children, I do not see very clearly now, I had some more things to say, but it makes no difference. Think of me a little. You are blessed creatures. I do not know what is the matter with me, I see a light. Come nearer. I die happy. Let me put my hands upon your dear beloved heads."

Cosette and Marius fell on their knees, overwhelmed,

choked with tears, each grasping one of Jean Valjean's hands. Those august hands moved no more.

He had fallen backward, the light from the candlesticks fell upon him; his white face looked up toward heaven, he let Cosette and Marius cover his hands with kisses; he was dead.

The night was starless and very dark. Without doubt, in the gloom some mighty angel was standing, with outstretched wings, awaiting the soul.

V

THERE is, in the cemetery of Père Lachaise, in the neighborhood of the potter's field, far from the elegant quarter of that city of sepulchers, far from all those fantastic tombs which display in presence of eternity the hideous fashions of death, in a deserted corner, beside an old wall, beneath a great yew on which the bindweed climbs, among the dog grass and the mosses, a stone. This stone is exempt no more than the rest from the leprosy of time, from the mold, the lichen, and the droppings of the birds. The air turns it black, the water green. It is near no path, and people do not like to go in that direction, because the grass is high, and they would wet their feet. When there is a little sunshine, the lizards come out. There is, all about, a rustling of wild oats. In the spring, the linnets sing in the tree.

This stone is entirely blank. The only thought in cutting it was of the essentials of the grave, and there was no other care than to make this stone long enough and narrow enough to cover a man.

No name can be read there.

Only many years ago, a hand wrote upon it in pencil these four lines which have become gradually illegible under the rain and the dust, and which are probably effaced:

Il dort. Quoique le sort fût pour lui bien étrange,
Il vivait. Il mourut quand il n'eut plus son ange.
La chose simplement d'elle-même arriva,
Comme la nuit se fait lorsque le jour s'en va.